PRAISE FOR RICHARD ZIMLER

The Seventh Gate

'A gripping, heartbreaking and beautiful thriller ... unforgettable, poetic and original.' **Simon Sebag Montefiore**

'*The Seventh Gate* is not only a superb thriller but an intelligent and moving novel about the heartbreaking human condition.' **Alberto Manguel, author of *The Library at Night***

'Mixing profound reflections on Jewish mysticism with scenes of elemental yet always tender sensuality, Zimler captures the Nazi era in the most human of terms, devoid of sentimentality but throbbing with life lived passionately in the midst of horror.' ***Booklist*** **(starred review)**

'Adding a touch of Jewish mysticism to his historical thriller, Zimler ... excellently captures the gamut of tumultuous emotions in his intense and detailed portrait of a city destined for war, and his exceptionally drawn characters struggling to survive in a world gone mad make for an unforgettable story.' ***Library Journal*** **(starred review)**

'Zimler, a seasoned American writer living in Portugal, combines sexy coming-of-age adventures with coming-of-Hitler terrors in this powerfully understated saga.' ***Kirkus Reviews***

'*The Seventh Gate* is unforgettable ... The reader will be haunted by these brave characters and the stirring murder mystery ... *The Seventh Gate* builds frustration and anxiety into a devastating and haunting conclusion ... gripping, consuming, and shocking ... unforgettable.' **New York Journal of Books**

'Zimler ... surpasses himself with this coming-of-age epic set in Berlin at the start of the Nazi era ... the whodunit is captivating enough, but the book's power lies in its stark and unflinching portrayal of the impact of Hitler's eugenic policies on the infirm and disabled.' **Publishers Weekly**

'Zimler [is] a present-day scholar and writer of remarkable erudition and compelling imagination, an American Umberto Eco.' **Francis King, *The Spectator***

'Zimler has this spark of genius, which critics can't explain but readers recognise, and which every novelist desires but few achieve.' **Michael Eaude, *The Independent***

The Incandescent Threads

ONE OF THE *SUNDAY TIMES*' BEST HISTORICAL FICTION BOOKS OF 2022

'A memorable portrait of the search for meaning in the shadow of the Shoah.' **The Sunday Times**

'exceptional ... This is a richly drawn, original portrayal of tenacity and sacrifice.' **Publishers Weekly (starred review)** 'succeeds with its strong emotion, memorable characters, and mosaiclike structure . . . moving and unsettling. A thoughtful and affecting novel about generational trauma.' *Kirkus Reviews*

'emotionally charged [and] moving . . . compelling and powerful . . . a contemporary classic.' *The Jewish Chronicle*

'a fine wide-ranging novel.' *Tikkun*

'a sublime novel . . . An extraordinary premise and exquisitely written.' *Buzz Magazine*

'Deep [and] moving [with] an enormous emotional charge.' *Time Out*

'beautifully written' **Jewish Book Council**

'Readers already familiar with Zimler's exceptional gift for multigenerational storytelling will find this work among his best' *Hadassah Magazine*

Hunting Midnight

'From Midnight's first words . . . the reader is charmed. Zimler's ability to lay bare the horror of injustice, to find universal truths and poetry in everyday existence, and his faith in the human spirit, make reading *Hunting Midnight* an uplifting experience.' *Jerusalem Post*

'Zimler's book is a triumph of modern fiction: an absolutely gripping narrative of love and loss set against a backdrop of fantastic historic drama. Zimler rises to the incredible quality of his bestselling *The Last Kabbalist of Lisbon*. The characters are rich and fully realized, and their conflicts are vital and real. They grow throughout the book, so that by the end you feel a real intimacy with them. I loved this book. Read it at once.' **Andrew Solomon, winner of the National Book Award (USA)**

'An ambitious historical epic from a superbly talented historical novelist, capable of combining fascinating broad-canvas glimpses of history with the most intimate portraits of the human heart in turmoil.' ***Booklist* (USA)**

'A page-turning story of cruelty, conspiracy and escape, plot-driven in a way that makes you read more greedily, eager to get to the end . . . Brave and intriguing . . . A delicate exploration of the ways in which repressed religion and culture shape experience, identity and loss.' **Sarah Dunant, author of *The Birth of Venus***

'I defy anyone to put this book down. It's a wonderful novel: a big, bold-hearted love story that will sweep you up and take you, uncomplaining, on a journey full of heartbreak and light.' **Nicholas Shakespeare, author of *Bruce Chatwin* and *The Dancer Upstairs***

'Zimler is always an exhilaratingly free writer, free of ordinary taboos, and *Hunting Midnight* shows him at the height of his powers.' ***London Magazine***

'An epic drama, spanning three continents and more than twenty-five years, building up to a genuinely moving climax.' ***Literary Review***

'Reading *Hunting Midnight* was like discovering a rare gem. Richard Zimler is a brilliant author with a touch of genius.' ***Rendevous Magazine* (USA)**

'Enthralling . . . *Hunting Midnight* is a shamelessly sprawling historical novel, spanning continents, Napoleonic wars, a secret Jewish family, Kalahari magic and slavery.' ***Sydney Morning Herald***

'Zimler's tale of friendship and revenge [becomes] a search for the unexpected . . . Zimler is an honest, powerful writer.' ***The Guardian***

'Zimler's writing is pacey and accessible without ever patronising the reader – deeply moving' ***The Observer***

Guardian of the Dawn

'The strength of *Guardian of the Dawn* lies in its rich historical setting and in Richard Zimler's creation of an idiomatic language that reflects the religious and cultural diversity of place and period . . . remarkable.' ***Times Literary Supplement***

'A terrific storyteller and a wizard at conveying a long since vanished way of life.' **Francis King, *Literary Review***

'While this novel is a testimonial for the thousands who suffered under the Inquisition in India, it is also a riveting murder mystery [by a] master craftsman.' ***India Today***

'This is the third volume in Zimler's luminously written series about the Zarcos, Sephardic Jews from the Iberian Peninsula. While the beginning reads like a nostalgic coming-of-age story—though in an exotic locale—a more suspenseful tone steps in halfway through. Its last sections deliver a warning on the dangerous sweetness of revenge, and how it can lead to a tragedy of Shakespearean proportions. As haunting and mysterious as India itself can be, this novel delves into the darkest currents of the human mind and heart. Few readers will emerge untouched.' **Historical Novel Society**

'Crime and punishment work their usual spell in this deeply absorbing work.' *Kirkus Reviews*

'Parallels with Shakespeare's *Othello* are not accidental but nothing, to the smallest detail, is accidental with a writer who has fairly been called an American Umberto Eco.' *The Advertiser*

'An exciting adventure story . . . Scrupulously researched . . . Fascinating.' *The Independent*

The Search for Sana

'a bold investigation of the Palestinian-Israeli conflict . . . By obliging readers to see the past, [Zimler] illuminates the sources of injustice today . . . He writes in calm, clear prose adorned by the occasional glistening image like a jewel in a fast-flowing stream.' **Michael Eaude,** *Tikkun*

'beguiling' *The Guardian*

THE SEVENTH GATE

Richard Zimler was born in New York in 1956 and now resides in Porto, Portugal. His twelve novels have been translated into twenty-three languages and have appeared on bestseller lists in twelve different countries, including the United States, the UK, Australia, Brazil, Italy and Portugal. Five of his works have been nominated for the International Dublin Literary Award and he has won several other accolades for his fiction across Europe and North America. *The Incandescent Threads* is the latest in his *Sephardic Cycle*, an acclaimed group of independent works that explore the lives of different branches and generations of a Portuguese-Jewish family, the Zarcos. zimler.com / @RichardZimler

THE
SEVENTH GATE

RICHARD ZIMLER

PARTHIAN

Parthian, Cardigan SA43 1ED
www.parthianbooks.com
First published in Great Britain in 2007 by Constable
This English edition © Richard Zimler 2007, 2023
Paperback ISBN: 978-1-913640-67-5
Ebook ISBN: 978-1-913640-76-7
Cover design by Syncopated Pandemonium
Typeset by Elaine Sharples
Printed by 4edge Ltd, Hockley
Published with the financial support of the Books Council of Wales
British Library Cataloguing in Publication Data
A cataloguing record for this book is available from the British Library.

For my mother, Ruth G. Zimler, and our many relatives who perished in the death camps. Also, for my in-laws, Lucie Tiedtke (a Berliner!) and Aurelio Quintanilha, who had the good sense to get out of Berlin before it was too late.

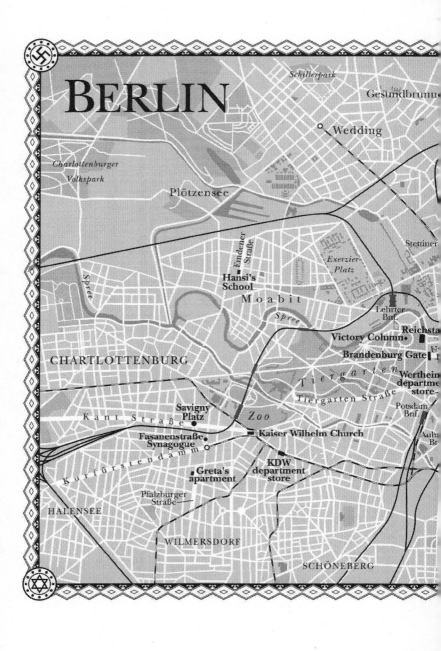

BERLIN

Schillerpark

Gesundbrunnen

○ Wedding

Charlottenburger
Volkspark

Plötzensee

Emdener Straße

Stettiner

**Hansi's
School**

Exerzier-
Platz

M o a b i t

Spree

Lehrter
Bnf.

Spree

Victory Column• ■ **Reichstag**

U

Brandenburg Gate ■

CHARTLOTTENBURG

T i e r g a r t e n

**Wertheim
departme
store**

Tiergarten Straße

Potsdam
Bnf.

K a n t   S t r a ß e

**Savigny
Platz**

Zoo

Kaiser Wilhelm Church

Aubh
Br

Fasanenstraße
Synagogue○

**Greta's
apartment**

**KDW
department
store**

K u r f ü r s t e n d a m m

Pfalzburger
Straße

HALENSEE

WILMERSDORF

SCHÖNEBERG

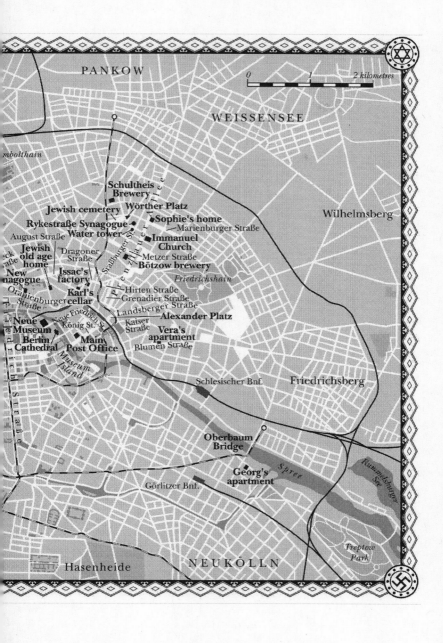

PANKOW

WEISSENSEE

0   1   2 kilometres

Wilhelmsberg

mbolthain

Schultheis
Brewery

Jewish cemetery   Wörther Platz

Rykestraße Synagogue   Sophie's home

August Straße   Water tower   Marienburger Straße

Jewish
old age
home   Dragoner
Straße   Immanuel
Church

New
nagogue   Issac's
factory   Metzer Straße

Oranienburger   Karl's
Straße   cellar   Bötzow brewery

Friedrichshain

Hirten Straße

Grenadier Straße

Landsberger Straße

Neue   Neue Friedrich St   Alexander Platz

Museum   König St.   Kaiser
Straße

Berlin   Main   Vera's
Cathedral   Post Office   apartment

Museum Island   Blumen Straße

Friedrichsberg

Schlesischer Bnf.

Rummelsburger See

Oberbaum
Bridge

Spree

Georg's
apartment

Görlitzer Bnf.

Treptow Park

Hasenheide   NEUKÖLLN

PREFACE

Aunt Sophie is the hollow-cheeked stick figure in the stained hospital gown staring at me from her cot – pink eyes squinting – as if I'm an hallucination. A scarlet woolen scarf is coiled around her neck, and her tiny right hand has vanished inside a gigantic black glove that is cupped on her lap, the leather palm facing up, like a grafted gorilla hand.

Though Sophie will hunt through her sheets and pillows for the missing left glove over the next week, and though she will insist on my demanding its return from every nurse on the floor, it will remain forever lost in the undergrowth of University Hospital.

It's a Friday morning in mid-December in Mineola, New York, eighteen miles due east of Manhattan. Sophie had a heart attack four days ago. Her husband Ben – my mother's older brother – is long dead, and they never had children. Sophie's closest blood relative, a nephew named Hans, lives in Berlin, but I've had no luck reaching him or his wife. So it's pretty much up to me to help out, especially since my mother is in her eighties and no longer driving. I've just flown in from my home in Boston without telling my aunt I was coming. I own a garden center in Lowell and business is slow in the winter; I can stay through Christmas if need be.

"Is that really you?" she asks with disbelief when I reach her doorway.

I rush to her with the urgency of a boy who learned – while

sitting in her lap – that rose blossoms could be picked from behind my ear. Every childhood needs a magician and Sophie was mine.

She doesn't open her arms. Not even a smile. I press my lips to her cool forehead. In the past, even trembling with a fever, she would have held me tight.

"*Ich bin …*" She speaks German.

"English," I tell her.

"Help me drink some orange juice. I'm dying of thirst." She points to the white styrofoam cup on her tray. Her skin is as pleated as crepe paper. She's down to ninety-six pounds, the head nurse told me on the phone. Apparently, she'd stopped eating a week before her heart attack, her appetite taken away by one of her depressions. "Not an ounce of fat on her," the nurse had added, as if she were describing the extra-lean turkey on a deli menu. "If she doesn't eat more …"

What will I do without her? I began thinking then, and I'm still thinking it now.

I hand Sophie the cup. She rocks back and forth to try to sit upright, but she hasn't enough force in her coat-hanger arms to make it. I wedge myself behind her, propping her up. She slurps through the straw. Her back presses into my chest, and it's a relief to have her weight – the history of a woman who has lived through so much – against me. It's like carrying a world. I want to say something heroic that is the measure of my love – *I will hold you up as long as you need me* … Instead, I comb my hands through her frazzled hair, which looks as if the ambulance medics set it on fire.

"You need a shampoo," I tell her.

"I need a lot of things," she replies, in that *oy vey* tone of hers.

I squeeze her bony shoulders and laugh; we've agreed many times before that a sense of humor in the hospital is essential. But amusement is not a rabbit she can pull from her hat right now.

She makes a clucking noise and leans against me – my helpless eighty-nine-year-old child. In a minute, she is asleep and snoring, but with her hazel eyes wide open.

I wriggle gently out from behind her, but she sits up with a start and says harshly, "Why didn't you meet me?"

I ease her head and shoulders back to her pillow. The sun, freed from the low-hanging winter clouds, chooses the gray tile floor, the metal frame of her cot, her feet ... "Meet you where?" I ask.

"I waited all morning at *Karls Keller*. You were supposed to be there."

Karl's Cellar? Her eyes are moist in a strange, unseeing way – as if filled with viscous glue. She's obviously deep inside her childhood in Berlin.

"I'm sorry," I tell her. I know by now – her fourth visit to the hospital in nine months – that her delusions are the result of what the physicians call hospital psychosis. My own theory is that her mind has retreated from a situation she finds unbearable. My best strategy is simply to find a place for myself inside her mad scenarios – to join Alice across the looking glass. But this Alice turns out to be more of a Red Queen.

"You should be ashamed of yourself!" she snaps. "When you didn't come, Isaac left."

"Who's Isaac?"

"He lives there." She points a jutting finger toward the window and the brick building across the parking lot.

"Where's he gone?"

She gives me a puzzled look. "I don't know."

"He'll probably be back in a little while," I say cheerfully.

"Don't bet on it," she retorts in a menacing tone. Then she talks German again.

In June, when Sophie had gastrointestinal bleeding caused by her blood thinner, she informed me she was staying in the White House. The only hitch was that Hillary Clinton had given her a maid's room. Did Sophie add that indignity so she could complain about the uncomfortable bed and bland food? Perhaps our deepest emotional needs are the bricks and mortar of our delusions.

Mom and I visit Sophie the next day. While I'm holding open the hospital door, the harsh fluorescent lighting and the odor of disinfectant tempt us to race back to the car. We promise ourselves a nice lunch if we can stay with Sophie for two hours. The briberies of love.

"Be prepared for cuckoo land again," I tell my mother as we're in the elevator riding up to the Coronary Care Unit.

"Good for Sophie!" she replies, hunting in her bag for her lip balm. Mom's lips get chapped when she's upset. "Who'd want to know they were staying in this dump!"

"It's a nice place," I reply.

"If you want to meet the Angel of Death over a bowl of cottage cheese."

Lack of sleep makes my aunt's psychosis worse over the next few days. She twists and turns on the cot as if she's on a bed of rocks. She claims she never falls asleep at night.

"Not *efen* a *vink*," she informs my mother in a distraught voice.

Sophie and Mom commiserate with flapping hands. My mother is wearing her fuchsia beret and black cardigan. Everybody's cold but me. She takes a blue enamel butterfly from her bag and pins it on Sophie's gown.

"Doesn't your aunt look cute?"

I lower my magazine. The two of them are staring at me expectantly.

"Absolutely."

Satisfied, Mom sits down again and moves on to George W. Bush. I love my mother for her unflagging energy in the face of all obstacles.

"I can't understand how even an idiot could vote for that ignoramus!" she tells Sophie.

"Americans are as asleep as Germans when it comes to politics," my aunt replies.

"They're stupid *bulvans*!" meaning *peasants*, my mother bellows.

"So vat trouble is our Texan *Führer* making now?"

Mom laughs. Sophie doesn't. Later that afternoon, she gives up on English. I decipher what I can and guess the rest. Mom sometimes translates. She assures me that Sophie's Berliner German and her Yiddish are practically the same language, but I have my doubts.

My aunt never closes her eyelids in our presence. She swivels her head around and surveys the world with those gooey eyes like a refugee from a Beckett play.

Two days later, while I'm squatting next to her, untangling her catheter from around her leg, hoping I won't accidentally pull it out – as I had the moist misfortune of doing the day before – she whispers in my ear. "I tried to kill him."

Sophie says that in German, of course, but does me the favor of repeating it in English when I tell her I don't know what she's talking about.

"Who'd you try to kill?" I ask, not taking her seriously.

"Papa."

She nods and holds her finger to her lips like a little girl. "Don't tell anyone."

I want to say, *An Allied bomb dropped on your father*, but I keep my mouth shut and get back to the catheter because bringing up anything to do with the real Führer may only make her retreat further.

"Enough of that," I say, "it's time to take a nap."

I lift her foot, swollen twice its normal size with the fluids that her heart isn't strong enough to pump around her body, and pass it gently through the plastic lasso. Success.

"What are you doing?" she demands.

"Testing your reflexes," I lie as I stand up; informing her she'd been tangled would only start her criticizing the nurses for not paying enough attention to her.

"Will you stay with me if I nap?" she asks.

"Of course."

She looks around as if searching for something she's lost. She holds up her gorilla-grafted hand.

"Have you seen the left glove?" she asks.

"Not that again, please!"

She manages to sit up after several tries, then slides her leg over the side of the bed.

"What are you doing?" I ask.

"I'm going to my bedroom to look for my glove," she replies.

The security belt tied around her waist keeps her from getting to her feet. Stymied, she sits with her shoulders hunched, staring at the white ribbon as if it's from another dimension.

"Take this goddamn belt off of me!" she snarls.

I can feel my frustration as an ever-tightening knot in my chest. By now, it's as big as a billiard ball – the sinister-looking black one.

"I'm not allowed," I reply.

She glares at me. "You're a bastard!"

I'm obviously now part of the plot to keep her here against her will. "Why don't you close your eyes and get some sleep," I tell her.

"Can you … can you take me upstairs?" She tugs on her ear lobe. It's her gesture of terror; I've known it for years.

"There's only more hospital wards upstairs," I say gently.

She gazes down, forlorn. I go to the window. All the oak tree branches are bare and brittle-looking. New York turns into such a frigid wasteland in December. Maybe it's the similarity to Berlin's climate that takes Sophie's thoughts back to her childhood. When I turn around, she throws down her arms, livid with anger. "Vye von't you let me go up to my room?"

"You'll be fine here."

"But I'm not here!" she says despairingly. She scowls at me as if I don't understand her deepest needs and never will.

"If you're not here, then where are you?" I ask.

Stumped, she replies, "I don't know, but I'm not here."

This is the Zen-like declaration I will repeat to a dozen friends over the next few weeks. Now, it takes me a few seconds to think of a reply.

"Well, *wherever you are*," I emphasize, "you need to sleep, so close your eyes and nap."

She starts to speak, then looks at me as if she's forgotten her lines.

"Trust me," I tell her. "I'll keep a watch out for you. They won't get you."

There's no need to say who *they* are; there's only ever been one *they* in my conversations with Sophie about life in Germany in the 1930s.

Four days later, I drive Aunt Sophie to her house in my rental car. She lives in Roslyn, just a few miles from my mom. I've already moved one of the guest beds into the dining room, along with her night table since she won't be able to navigate the stairs for a while. There's no bathroom on the ground floor, so I've also bought a commode. A twenty-nine-year-old Filipino nurse named Maria will spend the first two weeks with my aunt. Then we'll see how much home care she needs.

Maria and my mother help Sophie get from the driveway to the front door. She teeters behind her walker, her stiff, nervous arms holding the metal rim too far from her body to have much balance. Maria is gripping the belt loop of her pants in case she starts to tumble.

"Step up!" my mother keeps prodding, patting the empty fabric where Sophie's rear end used to be.

"I'm stepping, I'm stepping ..."

Sophie's mind returns that afternoon. I know that for sure when she tosses her gorilla glove into the garbage.

"Two points!" I cheer.

I'm in the dining room, eating strawberry ice cream out of the container. High-fat foods help keep me from getting depressed.

When she looks at me the glue is gone from her eyes. "Sit," she says, pounding the bed beside her. As I sink into the mattress, she kisses my cheek and gives me the big hug I've been needing. "You feel good," she says.

"I'm glad you're back," I tell her.

"Thank you for coming." She kisses me again. "And for moving a bed downstairs."

"You're welcome. Where'd you get that glove anyway?"

"It was Ben's."

I give her a spoon of ice cream. She feigns a swoon like a silent-movie actress. "Delicious," she says.

She looks around at her makeshift bedroom: the wooden cabinet where she keeps her china, the dark stain in the ceiling made by the water that leaked last summer from her thirty-year-old, gasping-for-breath air conditioner, a bilingual edition of Rilke's poetry that I've put on her night table, the Otto Dix drawing of a gentlemanly poet with spidery hands on the wall behind her. She ends up focusing on the small mountain of unopened letters on the dining table, probably thinking, *The same pile that would be there if I were dead ...*

She refuses another spoonful of ice cream and leans against me. Making it back across the looking glass only to be exiled from your own bedroom and find two dozen unpaid bills isn't easy, and I hold her while she cries.

"Who's Isaac?" I ask Sophie that evening.

She's got on her big black-rimmed glasses and is trying, unsuccessfully, to thread a needle so she can sew the cuffs on my pants; a few minutes earlier, when I brought her a bowl of raspberry Jello she noticed that the stitching was coming undone.

Only when she's got the needle all ready and is satisfied with her length of thread do I repeat my question. She lowers her hands into her lap.

"I don't know what you mean," she replies.

"You mentioned an Isaac while you were in the hospital."

She shrugs. "What did I say about him?"

"You said he disappeared. You implied that he wasn't coming back any time soon."

She pulls my pants across her lap and huddles over them, daunted by the prospect of the task ahead. She looks like a rabbit planning strategies for a leaf of lettuce too big to fit in its mouth.

"Was he a family friend?" I ask.

"He was *my* friend. A neighbor in Berlin."

"Jewish?"

She nods.

"Do you know what happened to him?"

"More or less, but now isn't the right time to talk about it."

Once my pants are sewn and I've modeled them to Sophie's

satisfaction, she heaves an exhausted sigh and tugs her shawl over her shoulders. "I can't seem to get warm."

"Put your beanie on."

"Then my head itches."

"That's from not shampooing your hair for ten days. I'll give you a shower later today. Put the hat on for now."

It's blue, with a white tassel. My mother dug it out from the nether regions of her closet. It looks like something a high school cheerleader would wear.

Sophie gazes around unhappily. "I must look ridiculous," she says.

"You look fine. You'll just have to forget about your career in high fashion for a while."

"Oh, honey, I'm not long for this world. This is it."

Turning away from emotional meltdown, my mind seizes on a plan: *if I can just fatten her up she'll be fine ...*

"What do you want for dinner?" I ask her.

"What have we got?"

"I bought tuna steaks. And potatoes for baking."

She looks stymied. Maybe she's weighing the advantages and disadvantages of fish. *Protein and useful oils, but also mercury ...*

"I could go buy a barbecue chicken if you like."

At length, she replies, "Tuna with a baked potato would be perfect. Can you stay for dinner?"

"Only if you don't talk about dying again."

"How can I promise that?"

"It's easy," I tell her. "You say, 'I promise to keep my *Schnauze* shut.'"

Sophie giggles. A minor victory.

*

Slumb'ring deep in everything, dreams a song as yet unheard, and the world begins to sing, if you find the magic word ... Aunt Sophie recites this poem to me – translating from German – while I'm giving her a shower. "I learned those verses when I was fourteen," she tells me with an amused smile. Then she asks, "Did you ever see *The Cabinet of Dr Caligari*?"

"No."

"See it sometime. It's about a sleepwalker trained by a circus magician to commit murders. The movie is all shadows climbing up walls and irrational angles, and spaces that don't make sense ... a nightmare come to life. We Germans should have memorized every scene, but we didn't have the courage." She gives me a withering look. "Now, all your American films are comic books. The sleepwalkers have become little children."

My aunt eats like a crocodile over the next few days – zucchini latkes, moussaka, salmon steaks, sweet potatoes, microwave popcorn, coffee yoghurt ... Her mouth opens and the food disappears. Her favorite meal becomes spaghetti with Buitoni tomato sauce, and the moment she licks the last traces of pasta from her plate, she looks up at me, my mother, and Maria with famished, hopeful eyes and asks what's next. She'd make a good Oliver Twist in an old-age-home production. In between meals, she snacks. I joke that she's set Cinnamon Crisp stock soaring on Wall Street.

"Well, I'm hungry," she replies by way of explanation.

"Really? I hadn't noticed."

Maria is patient and cheerful. She makes wonderful *lumpia* – Filipino spring rolls. Maria grew up in Manila and worked for a wealthy banker in Saudi Arabia before moving to New York. She also takes over Jello preparation from me.

One afternoon, while Sophie and I are sipping tea on her bed, she hands me a folded scrap of paper. "Open it," she says.

I find an Istanbul address for her nephew Hans.

"But Hans lives in Berlin," I say. "Don't you remember?"

"No, he lives in Istanbul."

"But you used to go to Berlin every year to see him."

"I would fly to Berlin for a few days and then go on to Turkey. I never told you or your mother. The address and phone you have is for his summer place."

"Why all the secrecy?"

She puts her tea down and breaks off a square of her Ghirardelli chocolate bar. Dark chocolate has become her new obsession – an inheritance from her father, she has told me. "It would take days to explain all the reasons to you, and even then ... You didn't live through the war, you wouldn't understand." She nibbles at her square.

"I might understand if you try to explain. I'm not an idiot."

"That's not what I mean and you know it. The important thing is that if Hans doesn't make it here in time, there are some things I'll want you to tell him."

"In time for what?" I demand, annoyed by her pessimism.

"You know what I mean. If ... if something bad should happen."

"All right, so what does Hans need to know?"

More nibbling. "I'm leaving three-quarters of what I have to him. The other quarter is for you and Ruthie." Ruthie is my mother. "I've named you as the executor, and I want you to make it easy for Hans to collect his inheritance. Also, I've left 1,000 dollars to take care of my brother's grave. It's all in my will – you'll find it upstairs in Ben's file cabinets."

"Your brother? I didn't know you had a brother."

"There's a lot you don't know."

"When did he die?"

"A long time ago. My son was named after him."

"Sophie, I think maybe you're getting confused. You and Ben ... you never had children."

"A great deal happened before the war. Forget it." She twirls her hand in the air as if explaining is useless.

Did Sophie really have a son and did he die during the war? "Talk to me," I plead, an ache opening in my gut. "I'm worried about you."

"I can't – not now," she replies. "Give me time."

Sophie has put on nine pounds by Christmas and has the beginnings of a rear end again, which is good since she no longer has to use a cushion every time she sits down. But her feet are swollen like water balloons. She can hardly hobble around, even with her walker.

Maria coats my aunt's feet with moisturizer at night to keep the reddened skin from tearing. Sophie wears my slippers, size ten and a half.

She has me sit with her one afternoon and asks, "What did I tell you in the hospital about before the war?"

"Mostly gibberish. You told me you tried to kill your father."

"Odd."

"Do you remember what you were thinking?"

"No."

We sit in silence. On her request, I rub her back, which hurts constantly – the result of being permanently arched into a letter C.

"Oh, shit!" she suddenly says.

She's peeing on herself, and not for the first time since she's come home. She can't control her bladder because of the double dose of diuretic she's on – the cardiologist's attempt to shrink the swelling in her feet. I help her hobble over to the commode, then get her pants and underwear down as quick as I can.

"I'm a mess," she says, starting to cry. "I can't take any more of this. This is not a life."

I clean her up with paper towels. Maria helps her change her clothing. When she's under the covers again, her beanie back on, I sit next to her.

"Sophie, you said *you* were friends with that neighbor of yours, Isaac, implying that maybe your parents didn't like him."

"They didn't."

"You haven't ever told me much about your childhood, you know – just a few stories about your mother. I want to hear more."

She rolls over away from me. "No, I think I'd better keep my *Schnauze* shut."

I've coaxed Sophie out of the house for the first time since her return from the hospital and we're sitting around the table in my mom's kitchen, watching *The River of No Return*, a movie we haven't seen in years. I'd forgotten completely that the doe-eyed boy in the film was Tommy Rettig, who later played the kid in the *Lassie* television series. This is the sort of trivial revelation that somehow helps me fight off despair.

Sophie's wearing her shawl around her shoulders and eating her Cinnamon Crisp. After a while, Mom yawns. "I'm beat," she tells us. "I'm going up to nap." To Sophie, she adds, "You can lie down with me if you want – or take a snooze on the sofa."

"Thanks, but I'm not sleepy."

Once we hear Mom close her door, Sophie points the remote at the television and turns off Marilyn Monroe and Robert Mitchum being attacked by Hollywood Indians.

"I'm not Jewish," she announces. "My parents were Christians."

This confession bursts out of her. "Sophie, I think maybe you need to take a nap after all," I reply. "You're over tired."

"Ben and I let your mother and everyone else think I was Jewish. After the war, it was easy to remake my identity. A bit ... a bit like Andre now that I think about it. Though in his case he was able to become himself again once he fled Germany. Not me." She shakes her head bitterly. "I think a part of me died when I left Berlin."

"Who's Andre?" I ask.

"Someone I knew when I was young. And a character in an old silent movie, *The Student from Prague*. It's about a sorcerer who brings a young man's reflection to life."

"You're confusing me."

"Sorry. I really only meant to apologize to you for lying about my father the other day."

"Lying? You hardly said anything about him."

"I said it was odd that I'd told you I tried to kill him, but it wasn't odd at all." She takes off her beanie and heaves it angrily at the television, as if it has been preventing her from thinking. She scratches her head with both hands, raising her hair into a tangled gray crest. "I've got a lot of things I need to tell you before I get any worse. The problem is that there's just too much to say." She leans toward me and knocks her fist on the tabletop between us, as if she's just played her hand at poker and is waiting for my move.

"We can talk anytime you like," I say.

"When do you have to get back home?"

"I should go in another few days."

"Do you have a tape recorder?"

"Upstairs, in my old desk."

"Come over to my house with it tomorrow." She struggles to her feet and takes my hand. "Not a word of this to anyone for now!"

THE FIRST GATE

The First Gate appears as birth, and through its archway all other openings and levels come into view.

One is the point of a pyramid; Noah's ark; the language of paradise; and the horizon line between inside and outside. One is the mystery of the self and the union of Adam and Eve.

One is the first word of every story – including yours ...

The one God is hidden, concealed, and transcendent. He may be known only by unlocking the gates. Gaze far across the Promised Land and you may see Him, waiting for you to take a first step toward yourself.

The First Heaven is Vilon, the veil, which descends at dusk and rises at dawn. It is presided over by Joseph, who had the wisdom to listen to the dreams and men and women, and the courage to enter them.

There was a time when all the world spoke a single language and used the same words – Genesis 11.

Berekiah Zarco, The Book of Birth

CHAPTER ONE

It may take me fifteen minutes to thread a needle, but I have a hunter's vision for the past. So I can see the low sky of that frigid afternoon in February 1932 as if the clouds were within my reach, and I am aware, too, that my mother's troubled face is pressed against our kitchen window, since she is anxious to shout out a warning to me in the courtyard below.

Regret, too, squeezes my heart; there was so much about Mama that I'd been too young to understand.

"It is very difficult to get rid of destiny once it has entered you, and you will need the grace of God to do so," Isaac Zarco once warned me with his hand of blessing resting on my head, and he was right. For the gray clouds of that day have never fully cleared. And my mother has never stopped gazing down at me.

I see Tonio, as well, sprawled on the ground, and Vera turning away from him. Do these images come to me because of their symmetry? After all, Vera and Tonio were destined to pull me in opposite directions.

Cloaked by the darkness of a December night in America, I can feel the rabbit-quick breathing of the eager fourteen-year-old girl that I was, and her depth of belief in herself – just as I can feel the absence of the same confidence inside the woman I would become. I am heading out with my best friend Tonio on another after-school adventure in a childhood built out of curiosity. Tonio, who has just turned fifteen, is small and lithe, with a sweet, thoughtful mouth and large chestnut eyes that often seem to show a suffering way beyond his years. They are an inheritance from his sad-natured Russian mother, and so there is an exotic appeal to him, as well – my chance to voyage far east of Germany.

He and I are stomping over the flagstones of our building's courtyard, talking excitedly, dressed in our heavy woolen coats and boots, vapor clouds puffing out of our mouths. Like most apartment houses in our neighborhood, the courtyard lies between a front building facing the street and a rear one that's hidden. My parents, my brother, and I live in the front. Tonio and his parents live in the back.

We are on our way to Straßburger Straße, where Tonio has heard that a broad linden tree has fallen, crushing a spiffy red American car. Small catastrophes like this etch tiny marks into our childhood, and he and I also extract a sweet, secret joy from making our parents wonder if racing to the scene of fires, burst water mains, and tramway collisions isn't a sign that we aren't quite right in the head. In fact, fear for the safety of her excitable, wayward daughter is why my mother will not turn from the window. I don't wave, of course; I resent her lack of trust the way some kids resent not getting enough attention.

Before Tonio and I reach the door to the front building – intending to walk through the entranceway to the street – it opens and two tiny children step toward us, twins most likely, since they are wearing matching Carnival costumes; most parties and balls in Berlin are scheduled for this evening – Saturday the 6th.

"Hello there," one of them says with an odd, adult-sounding voice.

We don't reply; their beautiful clothes leave us awe-struck – checkerboard jackets and pants in scarlet and black, and floppy yellow hats topped with tiny silver bells. Curiosity overwhelms us. And jealousy too. Why didn't *we* think of putting on our costumes?

Stepping forward in a waddling way, they pass us and walk toward the rear building. When the larger of the two – barely three feet tall – turns around to smile, the diffuse northern light catches his face and we see that he has whiskers on his cheeks.

"Dwarfs," Tonio whispers to me.

They penguin-walk into the apartment house, and we follow them. Starting up the staircase, they talk in hushed voices – about the ill-bred children behind them, most likely. Up three flights they go, laboriously, each step a hurdle that makes them seem to throw their hips out of joint.

We pursue them only to the first-floor landing, our rudeness finding a temporary height limit. "They're *unheimlich*," Tonio says. *Unheimlich*, meaning weirdly sinister, is his favorite word.

Rushing back to the courtyard, we see lights go on in Mr Zarco's sitting room. He lives alone on the third floor. Both his wife and son are long dead.

"Mr Zarco must be having a party," I tell Tonio.

"A *very small* party," he replies, laughing at his wordplay.

I laugh too, but only to keep him company. Tonio is the first boy I've had a crush on, but I've recently had to admit to myself that we do not share the same sense of humor. I've also concluded that I'll have to hide that difference from him if our marriage is to have any chance of success.

"I wish I'd gotten a better look at them," I say, casting my gaze up to my mother's now empty window. I resent that, too – that she nearly always misses out on the adventures that a mother and daughter should share.

The door to the courtyard opens again, and a couple in their twenties step out. The woman, slender, with short blond hair, wears a sequined blue snout over her nose. The man, dressed as a bullfighter, has on a gold brocade vest and tights, and a tri-corn black hat. He is gaunt and pale, and handsome in a desperate way, like a starving student in a romantic novel. They say hello, but their voices are hard to understand; the consonants and vowels seem smudged. We return their greetings this time. The woman smiles at us and makes quick hand signals to the bullfighter. Then they, too, cross the courtyard, enter the rear building, and climb up the staircase to Mr Zarco's apartment.

We're jittery with excitement by now, and we decide to wait to see who'll come next. Tonio lifts his nose and sniffs at the air, which smells of hops because we have a dozen breweries in the neighborhood. "Schultheis," he says, frowning.

He claims to be able to tell which brewery the scent is coming from and prefers the more pungent, stinging odor of Bötzow. I don't drink beer. I prefer wine – just like Greta Garbo, I always tell people.

After a few minutes, a gigantic woman wearing a gargoyle mask enters – a jutting awning of forehead over a big blunt nose, protruding chin, and gaping caveman mouth. "Best costume so far," I whisper to Tonio, thinking that scary creatures may be in style this year.

"She looks just right for the Katakombe," he says. The Katakombe is an avant-garde Berlin cabaret we snuck into a few months earlier.

The woman is well over six feet tall. I look down at her legs expecting to see her standing on stilts. But I can't see her feet; she's cloaked head to toe in black, with a long white scarf around her neck.

Black and white – Vera will never wear any other colors, but I don't know that yet.

"My god!" Tonio suddenly exclaims, gulping for air.

"What's wrong?"

He races off to the side of the courtyard, toward the Munchenbergs' apartment.

"Sophie!" he calls. When I turn, he is waving me over frantically.

By now, the woman is directly in front of me. I wonder what the fuss is; it's comforting to be so small beside her and yet still be the center of my own world.

"What's your name?" she asks me.

It's her distended, lopsided smile – as though her bloated bottom lip might just drop off – that gives the truth away. I do not scream, though I want to. I cover my mouth with my hands. My heart seems to burst out of my chest.

Tonio keeps calling me, but I can't move; the word *hingerissen*, meaning overwhelmed and entranced, gains meaning for me forever after.

"I'm Vera," she tells me. Leaning down, she reaches out her hand with formal grace. Would I have taken it? I'll never know, because Tonio tugs me away.

"Get away from us!" he yells at the woman.

She tosses the end of her scarf over her shoulder and rushes past us, her head down.

"Monster!" Tonio calls after her.

Vera stops. When she turns, her eyes are hooded by rage. She marches back to us, each of her steps too long for a woman.

Vera as she looked to me on the day we met

I can't prevent myself from staring at her; her mask-that-isn't-a-mask is something that should only exist in a nightmare, like blood oozing out of one's pillow. Who could turn away from such an impossibility?

My breathing seems to be deeper than ever before, and I know that I am right where I am meant to be. Years later, I will read the Greek myths and understand this feeling better; it is not often that one encounters a goddess, and even less frequently in the courtyard between two quiet, middle-class apartment houses. It was one of Isaac Zarco's ancestors who said that God appears to us in the form we can most appreciate, and maybe for me that form was Vera.

"You shouldn't talk to anyone so disrespectfully," the giant tells Tonio.

Her voice is gentle; the tone of a woman who has learned how to control herself in front of little creatures that sting.

"You're deformed!" he shrieks.

That may be true, but she is also quick and powerful; her open hand catches my friend on his shoulder, knocking him over. His cap tumbles off. By the time I've picked it up, Vera is entering the back building, tilting forward, as if carrying a leaden locket around her neck.

"Are you all right?" I ask Tonio.

Tears are caught in his lashes. "I'm fine!" he snaps. "Let's get the hell out of here!"

The boy is embarrassed about being knocked over, so we don't talk about it. We go to see the crushed red American luxury car, which turns out to be a small black Peugeot 201 Cabriolet and not nearly as flattened as we'd like.

"What a disappointment," he tells me. "I was really hoping it was a '32 Packard. They've got this hood ornament made of chrome-plated zinc that's called the Goddess of Speed. If the car had been really crushed, I'd have taken it. Imagine having one!"

"What's the ornament look like?"

"It's a winged angel holding up a tire."

A tire? The Goddess of Speed sounds ridiculous to me, but sparks of joy are in Tonio's eyes, so I tell him I'd love to see one. When Tonio is happy, he's irresistible.

A crowd of Berliners gathered around an accident will always include more than enough gaping singularities to please our precocious sense of the grotesque, including double-chinned businessmen with pencil-thin mustaches, my personal favorite, but Tonio doesn't share my delight in faces. He's examining the crushed Peugeot. After a while, silence nestles itself deeply inside me. Suddenly frigid, I watch a group of unemployed men squatting on Metzer Straße by a fire they've made with planks of wood and rags. Behind them, seeming to guard our neighborhood with its protective strength, is my favorite local landmark, the water tower, a cylinder of dark brick rising a hundred feet into the air. I used to imagine a bearded sorcerer living at its pinnacle, and a terrified girl being held captive. Raising my gaze to its highest windows, I think about how much I'd like to talk to the gigantic woman who walloped Tonio, which leads me to consider how little the bent steel of a smashed Peugeot means compared to a face that frightens children.

Darkness falls in an instant during the Berlin winter, and by the time we reach Prenzlauer Allee, we're walking backwards to keep the searing wind off our faces. A tap on my shoulder makes me gasp and nearly tumble over.

"Scared you!"

"Raffi, you idiot! You almost gave me a heart attack!"

Rafael Munchenberg, twenty-four years old, with flappy, elephant ears and the intense eyes of a chess master, faces me, then looks urgently down the street. He lives with his parents on the first floor of our building.

"*Was ist los?*" Tonio asks him. What's up?

"I need your help – both of you. I'm being followed."

"By who?" I ask, a flame of fear in my chest.

"A Nazi."

"Do you owe him some money?" Tonio asks. That question should tell you how little we know about politics.

"Of course, not," Raffi scoffs.

"You're not making this up, are you?" I ask, squinting and shifting my weight to appear insistent; this wouldn't be the first dirty trick he'd played on me.

"Soph, don't make trouble!" he says gruffly, and he snatches my hand. "Come on!"

He runs me down the street into the Immanuel Church, Tonio close on our heels.

Of late, Raffi has tried to change his image by wearing his thick black hair slicked back, so that he looks like a rakish jazz trumpeter. In real life, however, he's a good-as-gold doctoral student in Egyptology and when he can get funding, which isn't all that often given Germany's ruined economy, he goes to Egypt for months at a time. He was my favorite baby-sitter of all time because he'd read the scariest parts of *Emil and the Detective* to me as many times as I liked and even permit me to eat toast on his lap no matter how many crumbs I might spill. We also used to bathe Hansi together and get as soaked as sponges, and even my normally impassive brother would laugh. Tonio and Raffi also play cards every other Friday evening, though I don't join them. I learned the hard way – from Tonio's resentful looks – that boys need some time alone.

We burst into the church. Two sparrowish women are praying in the second pew – knots of blue-gray hair above thick gray coats. Raffi puts his stunning, black felt hat on Tonio's head, takes the boy's ratty cap, and exchanges jackets with him.

"You look like a clown!" I whisper to Tonio after he's got on Raffi's coat, since the sleeves swallow his hands. "Besides, swapping clothes is the oldest trick in the book! I've seen it in a dozen movies." A slight exaggeration, but I think my point is well taken.

Tonio shoos me away. "Shush, Sophie!" The idea of being a decoy is apparently more important than manners.

"Both of you keep quiet," Raffi snaps. He's holding Tonio's jacket, since there's little point in trying to get it on. "It's dark out, Soph, and by the time they notice that Tonio isn't me, I'll be long gone. Besides, we're going out the back exit. Hurry!"

The icy wind swirling through the back alley makes me pull my sweater neck over my mouth and nose, so that the rest of what happens between us has always been accompanied in my memory by the warm smell of wool. Raffi gives me a quick kiss, then shushes up my questions and takes a thick envelope and piece of paper folded into a tight square from his pocket. "Keep these for me," he says. He holds my shoulders tight, telling me with his desperate look that he really is in trouble. "Don't give them to anyone. You hear me?"

"I won't. I swear!"

"Hide them – hurry!"

I slip the envelope and the paper underneath my blouse. They're rough against my skin, and disquieting – like forbidden thoughts.

"I love you, Soph," he says, smiling fleetingly.

Before I can ask him why he's in such a fix, he shakes Tonio's hand with masculine graciousness – a professor and his star pupil. "Tonio, once he sees you aren't me, he'll stop following you. And if he questions you, tell him I've run off to the circus!"

He turns to me. "If I don't come back for what I've given you, then ... then ..." A creaking sound from inside the church makes Raffi jerk his head back. He looks like a thief awaiting a police siren ...

"But Raffi, where are you ..."

Before I can finish my sentence, he's running as fast as he can out of the alley and east down Immanuel-Kirche Straße toward the smokestacks of the Friedrichshain Brewery, his hand on his head to keep Tonio's cap from blowing off. We watch him in silence until he vanishes around the corner. Nobody steps out of the church or dashes past us. Tonio thinks Raffi must have seduced some Nazi's wife, since his mind is never further than one step from sex. Rubbing his frozen hands together, he says in an eager voice, "Good, now let's see what's in that envelope of his."

"We can't!"

"We have to, Sophie. What if he doesn't come back? You heard him."

"Someone might be watching us."

Tonio and I decide to head to Frau Koslowski's grocery. We keep looking behind us, but no one is on our trail. We hide around corners just to make sure, making believe we're secret agents. Tonio presses against me hard as he looks over my shoulder, which I adore.

Frau Koslowski has already closed her shop for the afternoon, so we slip into the Köln Beer Garden, just around the corner, which is frequented by Brewery workers and billiards players. The carpeting of the indoor restaurant stinks like a urinal and the air is filled with enough cigar smoke to choke the Kaiser's army. We rush to the women's bathroom – Tonio's idea – and lock ourselves in a stall.

Tonio, panting with excitement, rips open the envelope. "Wow!" he whispers, and he takes out a stack of English one-pound notes in two different colors, brown and green. The brown ones become my favorites. I call them my Two Georges, because they have a picture of a bearded, serious-looking King George on the right – in profile – and a handsome, bare-chested St George killing a ferocious dragon on the left. We count the bills – fifty-four. "What do you think they're worth?" I ask.

"A fortune!" Tonio spreads them like a fan. "Buckingham Palace here I come!"

"This must be enough money for Raffi to study in Egypt for several months," I say.

"Now hand over the paper," Tonio orders.

"No way." I unfold it myself and find slender rows of tiny, beautifully designed figures – mostly animals like snakes and falcons, but also feathers and scepters. "Hieroglyphics," I whisper.

Tonio's mouth falls open. "Maybe they're magic formulas! We'll be able to make gold out of thin air!"

"Don't be stupid," I reply, more harshly than I intended.

"Stop being mean!"

I explain that I'm worried about Raffi and hand Tonio the sheet of paper to make peace. We count twenty-four lines of writing. The first hieroglyphs in each line are surrounded by a frame, and inside the first frame are a saucer-shape, a staff, two feathers, an eagle, and a triangle.

"This has been the most *unheimlich* afternoon ever!" he says with delight, and he grins as he spreads the notes on his head like a crown. "So what would you like me to buy you? A mink stole ...?"

"Garbo and I prefer ermine," I say coquettishly. "Now give them back."

I put the money and the sheet of writing into the envelope, which I put back beneath my blouse. On the way home, I agree with Tonio that we've had a really strange afternoon – completely unpredictable. Of course, I have no idea that Isaac Zarco's party and

Raffi's escape – and all those intricate little letter-shapes invented 4,000 years ago – are all intimately related.

As soon as I get to my room, I hide Raffi's envelope in my underwear drawer, where I keep my diary. Then I make Mama and myself tea while she prepares supper. I love the way the kettle hisses, and how my feet and hands tingle back to life, as if the warmth is making me a new person from the inside out. When my fingers are supple again, I go to my room, take out my sketchbook, and draw the hieroglyphics one by one, as careful as a spy copying secret war plans, because I suspect that Raffi will lie to me about what's written here and I am determined to know the truth. Then I hide both the original and my copy in my drawer.

The kitchen is now filled with the smell of boiled onions, turnips, cabbage, potatoes, and carrots. Almost all the meals my mother prepares make use of the same five ingredients – or maybe rice and tomatoes if she's feeling adventurous, and *bratwurst* or a slice of pork if we've managed to save for a treat, because meat is too expensive for us to eat regularly. The steam from her cooking can cloud up our windows for hours because – as northern European women have known for centuries – vegetables are done only when they lose all their color and taste, and fall apart on your fork. In fact, most every mother between Danzig and Munich is also coping the best she can on too small an income and too little inventiveness. Not that their economizing stops their thirty million children from praying for something more tasty on their plates, of course.

Once, for my twelfth birthday, Mama made moussaka with two purple eggplants she found at a Levantine grocery on Neue Friedrichstraße. My taste buds were in ecstasy but my little brother Hansi wouldn't go near his plate. And that was when the curtain came down on culinary experimentation in our house.

Mama doesn't ask me about the crushed car. Papa does. We sit together at the kitchen table. Its top is a gorgeous slab of cream-colored travertine marble that was a wedding gift from his parents. Sometimes when I'm alone, I run my hand over its cool, sensual smoothness. Mama is mixing the batter for *Reibekuchen*, fritters. Hansi is with us, too, peeling potatoes, which give off the damp, earthy smell I love. I do not mention our adventure with Raffi, since the story of his escape might get back to his parents and earn him a lecture from his professor father. And I especially don't say anything about Vera. She's a gift I've given myself and might never share with anyone. I haven't decided yet.

I sip my tea through a lumpy sugar crystal, which means that the words of my story tumble out and go off on a sweet-flavored, zigzagging journey. Maybe my father knows I make up a lot of what I say, maybe he doesn't. It doesn't matter because he laughs in the right places, and he's always given me the right to tell him about my life any way I want.

After I finish my story, Papa gives Mama and me presents from Maria Gorman, a secretary at Communist Party headquarters with whom we've gone on picnics: two jars of raspberry jam, one with seeds for me, one without for Mama and Hansi. I'll notice their jar in the garbage that night, and when I rescue it my mother will explain that she tossed it away accidentally while washing the dishes. She's a bit scatterbrained, I think at the time.

My father soon slips away to the sitting room to read the newspaper. I ask Mama if I can go to Uncle Rainer's party as the vampire in *Nosferatu* instead of a Dutch skater. The two of us had shrieked with fright when we'd seen the movie a few months earlier.

"Oh, darling, it's too late," my mother replies. "I'm sorry."

"Please, we could use your face powder to make me look pale

and sickly, and slick my hair down with some black shoe polish.
We could cut me long fingernails out of paper. And ..."

"Shoe polish!"

"I'll get Papa's."

"Don't move! We've got to be at your uncle's in two hours."

Though I know it's useless, or maybe precisely because of that,
I jump up and tell her she's being unfair, which only makes her
glare. My mother is pretty, with silky auburn hair that she's cut
with bangs, just like her favorite actress, Claudette Colbert, and
she has a sweet round face, but her green eyes open as big as murder
when she's irritated.

"Sophie, your skating outfit is beautiful, and I spent hours
sewing it," she warns me, the unspoken finish to her sentence being,
so don't push your luck!

"But I don't want to be beautiful! I want to frighten people. I ...
I want to cause car accidents I'm so ugly. I want terrified men to
chase me out of the Immanuel Church!"

She simply shrugs as though I fell into her life from a remote
galaxy and goes back to whisking the lumps out of her precious
batter. Instead of insisting further, I pounce on what she loves most
in the world, my eight-year-old brother. He hasn't yet finished
peeling a dozen potatoes, although he's been huddling over them
like a worry-sick peahen for half an hour. Maybe it's only because
my parents don't trust him with a sharp knife, but it's also true
that Hansi is a diffident boy who never tells what he's thinking,
and just maybe his slowness is because his brain is too small to
learn how to get to the underside of anything, even something as
simple as a potato from Frau Koslowski's grocery. The two things
he's good at are posing for my sketches and doing jigsaw puzzles.
As far as I can determine, he's taken up permanent residence in
his own hermetic world, which I've named the Hansi Universe.

"Go faster!" I tell him. "We'll eat supper in March at the rate you're going."

"Don't you have anything better to do than annoy your brother!" Mama snaps.

Hansi looks up at me with the great big look of astonishment he inherited from her and says in an earnest voice, "It has to be done right."

"I wish you'd do it wrong just for once."

I'm referring to a lot more than peeling potatoes, of course. If only I could learn what goes on in that mysterious head of his then I suppose I wouldn't resent him being the silent angel of the family.

"It probably just doesn't grow," I tell my mother.

"What doesn't?"

"Hansi's brain!"

"Sophie you are a nightmare!" she shouts.

My goal. Then she banishes me from the kitchen – also an achievement. I embrace my wickedness at such moments as if it's my Oscar award.

Hansi in his own universe, age 8

Exile pleases me because it gives me license to throw some coals on my rage. What really bothers me, however, is that I will have to go to the party at Uncle Rainer's house as a sixteenth-century skater. How could I have been such a dunce? I try to make my feeble choice of costume my mother's fault, but the blame just won't stick to her.

I listen to Bing Crosby and other lovesick American crooners on the radio, sulking, sitting between my father's legs. He's reading the Communist Party's *Rote Fahne* newspaper, as he always does before supper. I try to decipher the words of the songs. It's how I learn English.

After a while I grow bored and put on my Marlene Dietrich records while studying my cigarette cards of movie stars. *Falling in love again* ... I adore the whiskey-soaked gravel in her voice. When someone knocks on our front door, my father asks me to see who it is. To my surprise, I discover Mr Zarco.

He has a gaunt, tender face, with sad blue-gray eyes, and thick and beautiful silver hair springing out in tufts, like the fur of a spooked cat. His large ears have been reddened by the chill. If he were an actor in a play, he'd be the forgetful uncle. Or maybe the fiendish murderer that no one ever suspects because he looks like he lives on warm milk and pumpernickel rolls. I like that dramatic idea, and also the boyish eagerness in the way he gazes down at me, but I only offer him a feeble hello; my mother has warned me about talking to neighbors we don't know very well, and I try not to defy her over small matters so that I can win Papa's support for the bigger ones.

I back away to fetch my father, leaving Mr Zarco standing in the doorway. Not because he's Jewish, I should add. For now, this is still a city where Jews are Germans. As we all now know, they will defy a great many laws of nature by changing into swine and even vermin a bit later. Papa rushes to the door and shakes our guest's hand warmly.

"Come in, come in," he insists, taking our neighbor by the elbow. They stand in the foyer as men in Germany do – not quite sure where to put their hands and feet.

"Please excuse my unexpected visit, but a friend of mine wants to apologize to your daughter, and she's too embarrassed to come down herself," Mr Zarco says nervously.

"Apologize for what?"

Our guest gestures toward me. "Sophie and Tonio ... they were playing in the courtyard and a guest at my party got angry at them and did something she shouldn't have."

"What did she do?" Papa asks.

"She hit Tonio. Apparently, the boy had ridiculed her."

"Tonio is a handful," Papa says with a long, unfavorable sigh, since he's only too aware that I'm in love with an inveterate mischief-maker.

"My friend, Vera ... she can be very excitable. I don't believe she hurt the boy. I'll go see his parents later this evening, when" – here, Mr Zarco gazes up to heaven – "I can summon the courage."

Mama rushes in from the kitchen, a host of worries already scattering in her head. Amplifying troubles is one of her specialties, and the older I get the more I'll suspect it's her compensation for not having any real power.

"What's this about Tonio being injured?" she asks.

"Not injured, hit," Papa tells her. He turns to me. "*Häschen*, you didn't mention any trouble. Tonio *is* all right, isn't he?"

Papa calls me Bunny Rabbit either when he's feeling especially affectionate or when he needs a favor from me. Now, what he wants is honesty. Given my nature that constitutes a favor.

"Tonio is fine," I reply. "Anyway, it was his fault," I add, and with that admission I feel a mix of terror and joy – the previously undreamed of possibility, in fact, of being able to tug my relationship with my friend in a more dangerous direction. He and I will have a quarrel when he finds out I've told on him, but maybe he will finally understand the depth of my love when I break down and sob. With any luck, he'll insist on kissing me to make up.

"What do you mean?" Mama asks.

I begin my explanation. Three adults listening attentively. I'm gratified to be in the witness box without having to testify against myself.

When I get to Tonio calling Vera a monster, Papa gasps. "And what did you say?" he asks me.

"Nothing."

"Sophie ...!" Mama glowers at me, certain I must have behaved even worse than Tonio.

"I didn't say a thing. I was *hingerissen.*"

There's that word again that I now understand in my bones: entranced.

"*Hingerissen?*" my mother questions. "What do you mean?"

"I couldn't move. The woman was ugly. And tall ... like she was standing on stilts."

"Sophie!" Papa snarls. "You mustn't talk like that."

"No, your daughter is right," Mr Zarco says, laughing lightly, then looking at me as if we share an understanding. "Vera is uncommonly ugly."

"Really?" Mama asks, eager curiosity in her voice. She secretly adores gossip.

"Let's just say that she is not a sight easily reconciled with any notions of justice we might wish to have about our world."

Mama wipes her brow with her dishtowel. She sweats a great deal when she panics. "This is all so unexpected and ... and upsetting," she sputters.

"Very," Mr Zarco agrees. He stands very erect – the preamble to a request from a former staff sergeant in the Kaiser's army. "Dr and Mrs Riedesel, would you mind if I escorted your daughter over to my apartment for a few minutes? Vera would like to apologize to Sophie directly. I assure you she is normally harmless."

I like it that Mr Zarco uses the word *escort*. It makes me sound grown up. He calls my father *doktor* because Papa has a degree in chemical engineering.

"*Normally* harmless?" Papa questions.

"When she's not provoked, I mean."

"Sophie would go to your ... apartment and ... and talk to this Vera?" Mama stammers.

Judging from her grimace, she's envisioning headhunters from Borneo hiding under Mr Zarco's bed. *I'm not going to be cooked in a cauldron*, I want to shout. *But if I were, then at least someone would get some supper tonight!*

"I'll take good care of Sophie and have her back to you in fifteen minutes," our elderly neighbor assures her.

"No, it's impossible," Mama announces.

But Papa is raising up onto the balls of his feet, intrigued – the habit of a former gymnast. "I'll go with Sophie," he says eagerly.

CHAPTER TWO

"I must warn you," Mr Zarco says as he trudges up the staircase next to Papa, "Vera is not the only person in my apartment you might find a bit shocking."

"There are two dwarfs," I say, proud to be able to supply this information.

"Yes, Heidi and Rolf."

"And a woman and man who talk with her hands."

"That would be Marianne and Karl-Heinz."

"Are you having a party?" Papa asks.

"Yes, though a bit more than just a party. For me, Carnival is important – as a ritual, I mean, or as a reenactment. All our Jewish holidays are like that – we pretend we are taking part in Biblical events, like the Exodus. Though pretend is too superficial a word."

"Indeed," Papa replies, which is what he says when he's at a loss for words.

"Is Carnival a Jewish holiday?" I ask.

"No, Sophie, but it could be!" Mr Zarco happily replies. "We Jews have a similar holiday when we dress up in costumes. We call it Purim. And though we don't have the jazz bands of a Carnival ball, our celebration can be a lot of fun. We pray and sing, and we give gifts to all our friends."

As we reach the second-floor landing, our neighbor gazes down the stairwell to make sure we're not being overheard and whispers conspiratorially, "During Carnival, we allow what's inside us to come up from the underworld. Even the immortals who rule over us sometimes appear."

"*Ja*," Papa says with a sincere nod, but I can tell he means, *What am I getting myself into …?*

My father is an engineer and a Communist who appreciates a trigonometric equation or a political essay. Poetic interpretations whispered on the staircase of a chilly apartment house are like far-off flares to his literal mind.

Sensing Papa's skepticism, Mr Zarco says, "You'll excuse my metaphorical language." He leads us up one more flight. As we reach his door, he takes Papa's shoulder. "What if there was only one day a year when you felt you had license to leave your home without having to explain yourself?"

Without waiting for my father's reply, he turns the handle.

Twenty faces gaze at us, framed by feathers, sequins, ruffles, and masks. Most of the guests are seated around an old Persian rug of red and gold – with a knotted violet fringe – that's covered with platters of food. A haze of bluish cigar smoke floats in the air, dimming the tightly arranged paintings on the walls and the crammed bookshelves. A woman's scratchy voice is coming from the record player. I spot Marianne seated with her legs crossed, eating with her fingers, and the slender toreador beside her drinking a glass of champagne, and I'm searching for Vera, Heidi and Rolf when a flapping motion from the corner of the room catches my attention. Vera, seated in front of an old wooden secretary, is waving at me. Her fingers are fat and long – like bread dough – and they have knobby joints. She's taken off her cape to reveal a shimmering white-velvet jacket in a military cut, with black pearls sewn at the collar. A slender bare-chested man wearing an animal mask, with a pinecone spiked on each horn, is talking to her.

Aladdin standing before his genie ... That's how big my wonderment is. Papa's hand curls around mine and gives it a protective squeeze.

"Attention everyone!" Mr Zarco says. "This is Dr Friedrich Riedesel and his daughter, Sophie, my dear neighbors."

I feel as if I've just received a letter on which my name has been written in large Gothic letters; once I open it, I'll never be able to return to who I was.

People call out friendly greetings. Vera comes rushing over, her arms hugged around her chest, as if she's chilled, though it's as hot as the tropics in here. Maybe it's the harsh electric lighting, but her face seems more angular than I'd remembered it, and her cavewoman forehead looks as if it must throb. Her clear blue eyes are reassuring, however, and I'm glad to have her towering over me again. Who can explain this love of smallness I've just discovered? And who can say whether it wouldn't be more sensible for a girl in Germany in 1932 to wish she were big?

Marianne in her Carnival costume

"This is Vera," Mr Zarco says to Papa.

She is a head taller than my father. I can see him thinking that there's no scientific theory or series of equations that should add up to her. Even Marx couldn't have predicted her.

"Glad to meet you, Dr Riedesel," she says.

He shakes her outstretched hand, but says nothing. He knows he has been taught, like all good Germans, not to stare, but like the rest of us, targeting his eyes on curiosities happens to be one of the things he does best. In fact, what characterizes my countrymen and women more than our famous admiration for athletes and university professors, far more than our envy of the Italians for their sun and the French their *pâtisserie*, more even than our childlike delight in sentimental operettas, monuments, country lakes, and metronomic marching is our satanic ability to stare.

"Thank you for coming," Vera tells my father.

Papa looks between her and Mr Zarco, at a loss for what to say.

"Sophie, I'm glad to see you again," Vera tells me, covering as best she can the awkwardness between the four of us. "I'm sorry about what happened. I shouldn't have hit your friend." She takes my free hand, so that for a moment I'm stretched like a paper cut-out between her and my father. "Do you accept my apology?" she asks hopefully.

Only when her voice quivers do I realize how apprehensive she is. "Yes, of course," I tell her.

"Would you sit with me and talk for a while?"

I look at Papa for his approval.

"Do you want to?" he asks me, his hand rising to my cheek, which means he'd prefer for me to say no.

"If it's all right with you, Papa."

"They'll be fine," Mr Zarco interjects confidently.

My father gazes down for a moment, then smiles warmly at Vera. "Of course," he says.

I'm proud of him, though I don't think he has much choice; Papa can't subvert his friendly nature for long.

"We have to leave in ten minutes," he warns me, "or your mother will call the police!"

Vera and Mr Zarco laugh, which pleases Papa and me both.

"And don't get lost," he instructs me, wagging his finger in imitation of my mother.

How far afield could I go in a two-bedroom apartment?

Vera leads me to her corner and fetches me a chair with a wicker seat. Papa stands as tall as he can and gazes after me even while he talks with Mr Zarco, which gratifies me. Not all staring is bad, of course.

"Your father loves you a great deal," Vera says.

"Yes, I know."

"Tell me, Sophie, do you like to read?" she asks.

"Sometimes," I reply hesitantly.

"Fiction, poetry ...?"

"Everything."

I can't seem to give any real replies. After all, how am I supposed to converse with a mallet-headed goddess, especially when my mother may somehow find out what I tell her?

"That Portuguese scientist over there" – she points to the young man with the horned mask, now eating a bowl of soup – "just showed me the most wonderful poem in Spanish. I'll read you my favorite part, then translate it into German."

I have never liked adults reading poetry to me because their faces become so deadly serious, and I get drowsy, and the words whiz past me like swallows. If it's one of our German teachers doing the reading, then he's also sure to ask us questions about what the swallows look like, and how fast they fly, and what they *mean*, which irritates me. So my mind curls into a tight defensive ball, and I only catch a few of Vera's words, but years later, Isaac Zarco tracks down the Antonio Machado verse she read to me:

Last night while I lay sleeping,
I dreamt – oh blessed illusion –
that a beehive I was keeping
inside my heart;
And from my bitter, rotting
failures, golden bees
were making
a pure white comb with the sweetest honey.

"If only the poet's dream could come true for us all," Vera says when she's finished. She lays the book on the secretary behind us, next to her black-beaded purse. "Or maybe it's better that dreams stay where they are. Having them come true might confuse us badly. We wouldn't know whether we're awake or asleep." She looks down invitingly at me, asking for my thoughts.

"I'm not sure," I admit, but there will come a time when I believe she has hit upon an important truth.

"Do you ever write poetry?" she asks.

"No."

"That's an excellent sign, Sophie. I used to write poetry when I was your age – all tragic. I knew hundreds of rhymes for *Einsamkeit.*" *Einsamkeit* means loneliness. "The poems were wretched ... I burned them when I was older." Vera grins at me, hoping I'll smile back, but she has overwhelmed me. "I'm glad that you and I are different," she adds.

"Why?"

"Because then if we become friends, our closeness will mean much more."

Something beats below the surface of her that troubles me. It's as if she's made out of different elements from everyone else. And not because she's deformed. Or, at least, not just because of that.

"What I have isn't contagious," she says. "I promise you that. Tell me, would you like to touch my face?"

"I don't know."

"If you touch the parts you find really ugly, you'll be more at ease."

When I agree, Vera moves my fingertips up to her forehead. I want to pull my hand back, but I don't dare. The bony ridge above her eyebrows makes me gasp. "I'm sorry," I tell her.

"Don't apologize. I frighten myself sometimes when I look in the mirror."

Who could breathe properly in my position? Maybe that's why the room seems to grow dim. When we reach her tulip-bulb chin, she says, "What I've got is called gigantism."

I don't like the nervous tingle that our intimacy gives me, and when she releases my hand, I wriggle in my seat, relieved to have borders around myself again.

"That was brave of you," Vera tells me.

"Thank you. Have you always been this way?" I ask.

"No. I started changing when I was about twelve. I'm thirty-one now," she adds, anticipating my question.

"How do you know Spanish?" I ask her.

"My mother was from Madrid. My father is German, from Cologne."

Emboldened now, I say, "Can I feel the pearls on your collar?"

"Of course." She leans toward me, like a tilting tower. Their shiny darkness makes me jealous. It's as if they're made of moonless night. *Think of all the magic that might be hidden inside them ...*

"If we were to crack the pearls open, what do you think we'd find inside?" I ask.

"In all these years, I've never asked myself that," she replies. She gives a little laugh.

"Maybe little demons! It would be nice to have tiny demons

around your neck – curled inside the pearls. They could make your wishes come true."

"That would be good, wouldn't it! What would you ask them, Sophie?"

"I don't know ... to make me a love potion."

"Are you in love?"

"No," I lie, "but a potion might come in very handy some day."

"Smart girl – plan ahead."

"Where'd you get your jacket?" I ask.

"I made it. I make all my clothes. The shops have nothing that fits me."

"My mother sews me clothes sometimes, but I can't imagine her ever making something so beautiful for me."

"Then I'll make you one. I'll just have to measure you."

"When?" I rush to ask, which makes Vera laugh with pleasure.

A man calls her name from across the room. He's slender, with broad shoulders and the erect posture of a dancer. His sinister green eyes are ringed by kohl and a mop of thick brown hair falls over his ears. He wears a scarlet cape, and he looks vaguely familiar – as though he's condensed out of a recent dream. He says something to Vera in German-accented Spanish, then grins.

"Do shut up Georg!" she shouts back, though I can tell she's not really angry.

He lifts his glass to Vera, as though to toast her, then goes back to sipping its cloudy liquid.

"What did he say?"

"That I'm taking too much of your time. Am I?"

"No. Who's he supposed to be?"

"Cesare, the sleepwalker from *The Cabinet of Dr Caligari*."

"That's right!" I exclaim. "His costume is perfect! What's he drinking?"

"Absinthe. He thinks it's romantic." She rolls her eyes as if he's absurd. "Let's get to work now. I'll see if I can get a tape measure. Wait here."

She passes Mr Zarco, who is talking with Papa and a white-haired woman with a peacock feather in her hair, then disappears through a doorway. A powerfully built, blond young man wearing dark glasses and holding a silver cane is now talking with Cesare, who winks at me when he notices me staring. He knows I'm wondering about him – about men who dress up as sleepwalking murderers – but he doesn't seem to mind. After a moment, Rolf waddles up to me. His chest is so squashed that his head seems to sit directly on his legs, a Hieronymus Bosch creature come to life. He's holding his floppy yellow hat in his hand. He has short, graying hair and might be forty or even fifty, but I don't think I can tell the age of a dwarf very well.

"Would you like something to eat?" he asks in his Rhineland accent.

"I don't think I should," I say. "My mother is making supper."

"My wife baked a heavenly chocolate cake," he says, licking his lips. His eyes radiate glee, and I realize I like him. "Come sit with us and have a small slice."

Vera is nowhere to be seen, so I nestle between Rolf and Heidi, who cuts me a piece of her cake. Her fingers are stubby, like those of a doll's. So are Rolf's, but he has tufts of hair on his knuckles. I imagine his compact chest is furry, too, though that seems impossible in someone three feet tall.

"Do you like to bake?" Heidi asks me.

"Sometimes," I reply. "Once, I made a *kugelhopf* with my mother." I take a big bite of the cake. "Delicious," I tell her, and it is.

She whispers, "The secret is to add chopped hazelnuts to the melted chocolate."

THE SEVENTH GATE 47

Her revelation seems to welcome me into a world exclusively for women and girls. "Heidi, would you ever let me go to the movies on a weekday evening with my boyfriend?" I ask.

"You have a boyfriend?" She smiles with delight.

"I think I do, but I'm not sure what he thinks. So would you?"

"If you promised not to be home late. And if I knew exactly where you were."

Fair enough. And a more sensible reply than I'm ever likely to get from my mother.

Heidi introduces me to some of the other guests. Across from us sits a young man with a barrel chest and a small, pear-shaped head, wearing a bright blue shirt and white bow tie. "I want another piece," he says, interrupting our conversation with the imploring voice of a neglected little boy.

"That'll be your third," Heidi replies in a mildly scolding tone, and she looks at the woman next to him for approval. Her billowy pink blouse has a ruffled white collar and she wears golden rings on all her fingers. She's raven-haired, with a slight almond-shape to her eyes – very regal looking.

"Martin can have as much cake as he likes tonight," she says.

While Heidi cuts the young man a slice, he stares at me, afraid to speak.

Rolf whispers to me, "On my last two tours with the circus, Martin and I had an act in which he'd hurl me across the ring. He's very shy, poor boy."

"Hi," I say to him in a little voice, trying to coax him from his hole.

He folds his lips inside his mouth and looks away until Heidi hands him his cake. Then, his deep brown eyes catch fire and he gobbles it down like a wolf.

"I'm Julia," the regal-looking woman tells me. "And this is my son," she adds, taking Martin's shoulder.

Julia and I get to talking about her homeland. She's a Tunshan, which is a tribe that lives near the Caspian Sea. She tells me that she grew up on the Asian steppes. She worked as a fortune-teller in the circus, but now she owns a shop selling herbal cures.

"Everyone here was in the circus?" I whisper to Rolf after Julia turns back to her son.

"Most of us. Even Vera, though now she works for Isaac. Once he discovered she made her own costumes, he gave her a job as a seamstress."

"I thought Mr Zarco worked at Heitinger's department store." That's what I'd heard from Papa.

"He supplies Heitinger's and some of the other fancy shops with women's clothes. He has a small factory on Dragonerstraße. And a warehouse right across the street." Rolf puts his festive yellow hat on my head. "Vera made these for me and Heidi."

The flannel makes me itch, but being able to tinkle when I shake my head is a likeable sensation – like giggling every time I move. With the rim of the hat over my ears, the voices in the room mix together into a buzz if I don't pay close attention. Maybe this is what it would sound like if I could hear the golden bees inside the poet's heart.

Heidi introduces me to Marianne, who removes her snout to exchange kisses with me, and the bullfighter, Karl-Heinz, who smells pleasantly of spicy cologne. I'm jealous of the way he and Marianne talk to each other with their hands – butterflies dancing. While they converse, her emerald eyes glow like a cat's. They kiss all the time. I've never seen people so in love. It makes me feel as if I'm snooping.

Mr Zarco comes over and talks to Karl-Heinz, who rushes off. Rolf tells me that Vera used to sit in a big armchair on a platform while people paid money to gape at her, which makes me shudder. She was called *die Menschenfresserin Maltas* – the Ogre from Malta.

"Is she from Malta?" I ask.

"No, but it sounds a lot more exotic than Cologne," he replies, laughing from his belly. "As long as Vera never spoke, no one could find out she was German, and it was in her contract that she was never to utter a word – even if people called out mean things to her." He gazes down, uncomfortable, maybe thinking he's about to reveal too much to me, but he says it anyway. "She spent nearly a decade on that stage. It was no good for her."

Years later, Vera would show me the famous article on her in the *Morgenpost* from the 3rd of June, 1928, and even a biographical note on her in *German Circus Performers* by Horst Brun, and all I can remember was how much more important she looked than the people around her. How they could not have noticed that remains a mystery to me even today.

"So after all those years of enforced silence, we now have difficulty getting Vera to keep quiet," Heidi tells me, smiling cheekily. She brushes the hair out of my eyes with her doll's hand. Such a delicate person she is. "Anyway, she survived all that humiliation and made a better life for herself – that's the important thing." To me alone, she whispers, "Getting even a little of what you want can be a big accomplishment for people like us."

Karl-Heinz attracts our attention by tapping the box-shaped camera he's brought with him. It stands on a wooden tripod. With precise gestures, he directs Heidi to put her arm over my shoulder and implores Rolf to sit up straight. Marianne kneels behind us and lays her head lightly on Rolf's shoulder, which makes him blush.

"Karl-Heinz has just started taking photographs for *Die Stimme,* a newspaper for the deaf," Heidi tells me, afraid to move an inch lest she provoke his impatience. *Die Stimme* means *The Voice*. "Until a few months ago, he was a police photographer."

He ducks underneath the black curtain at the back of the

camera, fiddles with his plates, then pops back out. "Everyone look at me!" he says in his distorted voice.

My eyes open wide in anticipation, and the flash makes them tear, but it's thrilling to have been photographed by a professional.

When Vera returns, Karl-Heinz gestures for her to drop down next to me.

"I can't!" Vera snaps. "My knee joints are made out of papier-mâché."

Rolf tugs on her leg.

"My goodness," Vera snarls, "it's like being attacked by poodles. I wish you people would just leave me alone."

"You're impossible!" Marianne says.

"You have never said a truer word!" Vera declares, and with her hands on her hips and eyebrows raised, it's clear she's referring to her physical form as much as her temperament.

Martin embraces a black leather armchair in a bear-hug, lifts it up to his shoulder with a grunt, and carries it past those of us sitting down. I hold my breath, imagining all that weight falling onto Heidi or Rolf – or me – and the tragic headline the next morning: *Fourteen-Year-Old Girl Crushed by Circus Strongman – Two Dwarfs Injured.*

I'd be dead but I'd have my own page-one story. Not too unfair an exchange.

With another grunt, Martin places his load on the ground next to Vera and says, "For you."

"Finally, a gentleman!" she exults, and she places a big kiss on his sloping brow. The young man smiles and presses both hands hard against the spot, as though he wants to push her affection deep inside his head.

Vera drops down and fusses in her bag till she comes up with a cigarette. When she looks at Karl-Heinz, he motions for her to lean forward.

"I'm not a trained seal," she tells him testily. "Just take the damned photo."

"Your problem is you're not trained at all," Georg, the man dressed as Cesare, calls from across the room.

"And you just missed another great opportunity to keep your opinion to yourself!" she yells back.

From the delighted way he teases her, I think he might just be in love with Vera.

"What does Georg do?" I ask Heidi.

"He works in an advertising agency, but he used to be a talented trapeze artist. He broke his wrist and hip in a fall last year and is unlikely to perform ever again."

Georg without his Cesare make-up

"And the blond man next to him – with the cane?"

"He's a famous tightrope walker – a main attraction at the Krone Circus in Munich. His name is Roman Bensaude. He's just moved to Berlin."

"But he's blind, isn't he?"

"Yes, he sees the rope with his feet."

So it is that I learn that the first major circus star I've ever been in the same room with is a man with eyes in his toes.

In the photograph, Vera is glowering. You will notice that first, and you will be forgiven if it's all you notice for quite some time. After all, it's hard to turn away from her earthworm lower lip curling down, and those fearsome hooded eyes under her awning of forehead. *Do not cross me!* she is saying.

Perhaps she regards defiance as the only option for a lopsided amazon.

Like me, you might also hear Vera's thoughts coming out to you as you stare at her. *You don't have any right to know anything more about me than my refusal to be acceptable, because whoever you are, I don't want or need your approval.*

In the foreground of the photograph, Heidi is hugging me tight, Rolf is fighting a grin, and Marianne is blowing a kiss at Karl-Heinz, and by extension at the viewer. I'm at the center, doing my best to look angelic, since I see this photograph as a chance to transform a lie into the truth. *If I can't be perfectly sweet in real life, why not in black-and-white?*

Next, Karl-Heinz makes Papa and me pose with several of the guests, then alongside Mr Zarco. Our neighbor pulls on the tip of my hat at the very last moment, so that we're both caught laughing. A serious man who likes to startle people with his playfulness. Attractive to a girl like me.

When the photographer moves on to a portrait of his blue-snouted beloved, Vera gets her chance to take my measurements. She moves my arms and legs as though I'm a puppet.

"How tall *are* you?" I ask her as she measures my arms.

"Six-foot five and a half. And you?"

"Five-foot one. But I'm still growing."

"Me too!"

As we laugh together, Georg comes to talk with her. "Vera, I'm going to the Botanical Gardens on Saturday to look at the flowers in the hothouse. How about coming along?"

"At nine in the morning again?" she asks skeptically.

"That's when the blossoms wake up and are most active."

"But that's when I'm least active. And besides, you know I don't go out during the day."

"Please ... You've got to think like an azalea and open yourself to the sun. Look, I'll come around to your apartment. We'll go for coffee first. If you want, we can have lunch at my place afterward."

"I'll think about it."

Georg turns to me. When he pokes a teasing finger into my shoulder, I notice he's wearing a stunning topaz ring. The stone is the color of the sun. "You want to come, too?" he asks.

"I don't know anything about looking at flowers."

In a Yiddish accent, he says, "What's to know? You see a flower, you look!"

He smiles so eagerly and warmly that I'm charmed. And a bit stunned, too.

"I'll call you," Vera says. "Now leave us alone – I've work to do."

Before he can reply, Papa calls me from across the room. "Sophie, it's time to go. Your mother must be thinking we've been kidnapped by Nazis."

An innocent enough comment, since the Nazi Party is little more than a red and black fringe to the tattered flag of German politics at the moment, but Vera starts at hearing Papa's little jest. Georg reaches for her arm and gives it a reassuring squeeze, whispering, "Don't worry, we'll push them back into their caves."

And with that one gesture, I decide he's a good person.

"Just one more measurement," Vera calls back to Papa, holding up her tape.

After she encircles my wrists and jots down some notes, she embraces me. Her hot breath on my neck raises gooseflesh, but I hug her back. That's when my cheek brushes against hers, chasing a snake up my spine. When we separate, her eyes are moist, maybe because she detected my spasm of terror. Before I can apologize, she says, "You'll have to have a fitting for the jacket. Isaac will let you know when I'm ready."

Then she rushes away, so my apology is never spoken.

Raffi Munchenberg enters the apartment as Karl-Heinz makes Papa and me pose for a last photo. He's got his hat and coat back from Tonio.

"Raffi!" I call out, waving and jumping; he's safe, which means I am too.

"Stop moving!" Karl-Heinz orders, glaring at me, and Papa grabs my hand tight. He and I are standing in front of the crammed bookshelves, beside a bespectacled journalist named Ludwig Renn, an old friend of Mr Zarco's. Communists come in all shapes and sizes, and Papa and the famous writer call each other comrade.

As soon as the flash goes off, I run to Raffi, who's talking now to Mr Zarco. He gives me a big kiss on each cheek.

"So you're all right!" I exclaim.

"Oh, I was just dramatizing," he scoffs.

"I didn't know you knew Mr Zarco."

"Oh, we're old friends. Watch this ..." He wiggles his pink ears. He and Mr Zarco laugh. I don't.

"So I'm not funny anymore?" Raffi asks, pouting comically.

He'd like me to think his escape was just a joke. "You can't fool me," I declare, scowling.

"No, you're too grown up now," he says, grinning like a proud older brother. "So when can I get my things?"

"Papa and I are going now. Come down with us, or I can bring them to you later."

He and I take the stairs two at a time, racing, just as we always have, with Papa patiently bringing up the rear. Raffi kisses my mother effusively at the door, which pleases her and makes her arrange herself in the mirror afterward. Hansi charges into his arms like a long-lost orphan. "Help me with my jigsaw puzzle," he pleads.

"In a couple of days ... maybe Monday. I can't tonight."

"I'll help," I jump in, because I adore the challenge of beating him to the right pieces.

Hansi in his Carnival mask

But his big sister is hardly special and Hansi sulks until Raffi adds, "I'll give you a bath then, too, if your mother and father say it's all right."

"Can he, Mama?"

My mother could never refuse my brother's shining eyes. "As long as you don't leave a flood!" she says, pretending to be severe.

Our guest puts his hand over his heart and promises to keep

the bathroom dry. Hansi imitates him. Raffi and I then go to the room I share with my brother and close the door behind us. I hand him the envelope. "The folded paper is in there too," I explain.

"You've opened it," he says, frowning.

"You know how Tonio is when he gets excited," I reply, and though Raffi does, he still gives me a disappointed look. I defend myself by saying hotly, "If you didn't come back, we had to know what was inside!"

"Fine, but just forget what you saw," he tells me, stern warning in his voice.

I agree to that, but as he reaches for the door-handle I can't stop myself from asking, "What do the hieroglyphics say?"

"It's a shopping list."

"Raffi, be serious!" I stamp on the ground. "You really scared me and now you're lying. I hate you!"

"I promise you I'm telling you the absolute truth. Listen," he continues, calling for peace between us with the tone of his voice, "I'll be leaving for Egypt next week and I'll be gone for two months, so don't be angry with me. Soph, you're still at an age when everything ought to be fun. But this isn't. This is deadly serious. Life is real and people can get hurt."

"Will you use the British pounds in Egypt?" I ask.

"Sophie, don't you understand what I'm saying? Forget what you saw!"

That night, before Hansi and I turn off the lights, I consider destroying my copy of Raffi's hieroglyphics, but I decide to wait; only Tonio knows I have them, and if Raffi *is* hurt, I'll need to show them to someone who can help.

I wake in the early morning disoriented, as if I've fallen from a great height. When I think of my cheek brushing against Vera's, panic – my mother's sweaty, doom-soaked variety – makes me jump out of bed and scurry to the bathroom, where I scrub my face like a surgeon before an operation, sanding away with pumice what I imagine to be microscopic flakes of deformity. Then, tiptoeing to my parents' room, I stand in their open doorway, feeling the silence of the house moving up through my shivering legs and into my hands. When I shake my father awake, he turns over and says, "Sophie, what's wrong?"

"I don't want to turn into a monster," I tell him, bursting into tears.

He throws his legs over the side of the bed, stands up, and puts his hand to my forehead, feeling for a fever. "Let's go to your room so we don't wake Mama," he whispers.

Once I'm seated on my bed, he looks over at Hansi, who is sleeping soundly, and whispers, "Now tell me what this is all about." He looks at me with confident eyes, because he knows that when all else fails his affection can still save me.

I explain about being infected, and he takes me in his arms. "You can't get her disease. Nothing is going to happen to you, *Häschen*."

But my anxieties prove resilient even to his lips pressing to my brow. "When Vera worked in a circus, people paid just to see her," I groan, "and she wasn't allowed to talk, even if they called her bad names. Papa, I don't want people to pay to look at me."

"Sophie, do you think I would have let you sit with her if it was dangerous? Listen, you don't ever have to see her again if you don't want to."

"But she's going to fit me for a jacket she's making for me," I point out. "Mr Zarco is going to tell me when she's ready."

"I'll tell him you're too busy with school."

"He won't believe you. And I don't want to be rude."

"*Häschen*, it's important to protect yourself. You have to learn your limits, especially now that you're becoming a woman ..." He looks away, his profile grave. Maybe this is a conversation he has put off for months, because he tells me, "Sometimes you have to say 'no' and be willing to disappoint other people, even friends – good friends. You have that right. Do you understand?"

His tone makes it clear that he's talking about Tonio, as well as Vera, so I reply that I do.

"Good. In this case, I'm afraid you have to be courageous enough to be rude."

"Don't go just yet, Papa."

He takes my head in his hands and kisses away my fear. "Now hop under the covers," he says eagerly, and he tucks me in.

His hands smoothing the blankets over me make me feel safe, and I cede all my worries to him. The age-old magic between fathers and daughters makes me close my eyes. I hear the click of the light switch and his footsteps fading to silence, and soon I'm sliding into slumber, leaving my waking self behind so very quickly that I don't realize that Papa has made refusing to see Vera into an act of bravery.

CHAPTER THREE

It is Sunday morning, the day after Mr Zarco's Carnival party, and most Berliners are sleeping late, but Tonio and I are slumped on our seats on the underground, sliding and bumping our way to the zoo. This was my idea; I wanted to be sure I wouldn't be home if Vera or Georg came over to ask me to go to the Botanical Gardens. Afterward, we plan to head to the Zeiss Planetarium. Tonio's idea, and an excellent one, since we'll be able to warm our feet and hands, and lean against each other in a darkness lit only by a sparkly, counterfeit Milky Way. Hansi is with us, too – the price we pay for being permitted to shuttle across the city without an adult. Having my little brother along is mostly like having a second shadow, since he generally speaks only when spoken to, and hardly ever makes a fuss, unless it rains, in which case he starts shrieking and flailing, and I have to cover his head to keep him from hurting himself or someone else. A boy who feels drops of rain like pellets of fire. Could there be a good explanation for that? Nobody has been able to give us one. The doctors say that Hansi is likely to grow out of it, but I'm not betting on it.

I feel like a spy sitting next to Tonio – whatever he suspects about my feelings for him, he doesn't know that I've begun to whisper to him after I wake in the morning, waist-deep in moist fantasies. Sometimes, I play my hands over my breasts, too – though he doesn't seem to notice I'm not the little girl I was six months ago.

Tonio got his hair cut yesterday, but he's left a four-inch forelock that he calls a whip at the front. He combs it straight back, which is a style we saw on some *Swing-Jugend,* university-age jazz fans, at the Katakombe, though it looks like a barber's error. I've already told him I think it's daring and wonderful, to which he replied ominously, "Papa ordered me to get rid of it this week."

When Tonio talks about his father, his seductive eyes always grow dark, as though blackened by the punishment he fears. Know this: Tonio is handsome. In life, that makes a difference, especially when it comes to getting away with murder.

I know I'm not supposed to want him so much, since I'm only fourteen, but it's as if everything we do together is a search for treasure. Who could have predicted I'd see Spanish doubloons in a fifteen-year-old boy who has never left Berlin?

Tonio gets to talking to Hansi about a cheetah that he was once allowed to pet, because his father went to high school with the head zookeeper for mammals. "His tongue was like sand paper, and he purred so loud that it was as if there was a drum in his chest."

"You weren't scared?" Hansi asks.

"Of course, I was. If I weren't scared, then having my face licked by him wouldn't have been so exciting."

Good answer, I think. "What's your favorite animal?" I ask Tonio.

"The kangaroo," he shoots back. "I once got it into my head that I wanted one as a pet, but the zookeeper told me that a kangaroo wouldn't be happy in an apartment. He said that maybe I could get one if I had a farm where it could hop around. Kangaroos have to have lots of room to play and forage – and fight with one another for dominance."

"A vampire bat!" I exclaim happily.

"What?" Tonio asks, puzzled.

"That's *my* favorite animal."

I pull back my lips to reveal my blood-sucking fangs and make squeaky noises, then attack Hansi's neck, which makes him laugh and squirm against me. He and I fit together so much better when our parents aren't around. I guess because there's no pressure for one of us to be good and the other evil. And he seems so much more alert, too.

Neither Tonio nor I broach the subject of Vera's having knocked him down, and I say nothing about telling my parents about his having provoked her. He doesn't seem irritated with me, but he could be storing grievances for a major explosion. I plan to save any quarrel we might have until we're off the train, since I'm pretty much like a kangaroo myself and need a lot of room to fight for dominance, especially if I'm going to lose and end up pleading for a reconciliation.

He seems to have forgotten, too, about Raffi's hieroglyphics, but I've a surprise in store about that ...

As we're walking out of the Zoo Station, Tonio takes Hansi's hand. "Which animals do you want to go see first?"

Big-brotherly kindness is not a quality he'd show in front of most people. A troublemaking suitor with a generous spirit – pretty close to ideal, as far as I'm concerned.

"I want to see the birds!" my little brother declares.

"Yes, sir," Tonio replies, saluting.

Suddenly, they're off and running. I call for them to wait for me, but two boys leaving behind a girl aren't about to slow down, let alone stop, and there I am, leaning against the trunk of a tall oak tree. I try not to mind so much, since I'm determined to love all of Tonio and not just his good qualities.

I find them by a big outdoor cage that's home to a solitary white owl – snow turned to feathers. But the two boys aren't watching the snoozing bird. Instead, they're gazing into the scruffy bushes bordering the pathway. Hansi is on all fours. Not a good sign; if he lost his pocket-watch or Grandpa's army compass, my mother will find a way to make his carelessness my fault.

"Did you lose something?" I ask, launching a prayer to God.

My brother doesn't reply. Tonio does. "He saw a squirrel."

"Hansi, there are golden eagles and rainbow lorikeets here, you don't need to search for a filthy rodent."

"It wasn't filthy – it looked thin and hungry," the little boy mumbles to himself, but I hear him plain enough because my parents and I have been trained to pick up even his whispers.

After a minute, I lose my patience. Lifting Hansi up by his arm, as I've been doing since I was eight and he was two, I brush off the dirt from his pants and drag him away from the bushes. "The damn thing probably eats better than we do," I tell him. "Maybe *he* even gets moussaka!"

But my brother has already forgotten Mama's short-lived Hellenic period and is back behind his dim green eyes. In fact, he says nothing over the next hour, not even when we see a peacock with its tail spread in an iridescent fan. He's probably expanded his concern about the well-being of the squirrel to all the rodents in Berlin. And there are a great many of those, particularly in the foul-smelling workers tenements near Schiller Park.

As we set off to visit the African mammals, the wind picks up. Through a mysterious alchemy, my shivering becomes a surge of impatience, and I apologize to Tonio for having denounced him to my parents and Mr Zarco.

"You could have made something up about why Vera hit me," he replies matter-of-factly.

That luke-warm criticism is the extent of his righteous fury? "Yes, I should have," I admit. "It was *terrible* of me to betray you."

The time has come for tears, so I squeeze my eyelids together, but nothing will come.

"Sophie, do you feel sick or something?" Tonio asks.

It must be too early in the morning for high drama. "I felt dizzy for a moment," I reply.

He grips my shoulders to steady me and kisses my cheek. I've been waiting for a gesture like this for weeks, but instead of falling into his arms, I'm *hingerissen* again.

"Come on," he says excitedly, taking my hand and curling his fingers through mine, "let's go see if that cheetah is still around."

The ways of boys are a mystery – letters in a language I can't speak. You put them all together and what do you have but a message that badly needs translating?

To hold hands with Tonio ... My heartbeat races, and my sense of being who I am is hovering somewhere outside me. My feet keep walking, and we continue talking, but time disappears until we are inside a brick building that smells like manure, standing in front of the bars of a huge cage. Hansi, holding his nose, asks Tonio, "Which is the cheetah you petted?"

The biggest of the cats is looking off purposefully toward the other side of the room, standing guard perhaps. Two other cheetahs are behind him, on their bellies. One of them is licking its front paws luxuriously.

Dropping my hand and pointing to the sentinel, Tonio tells Hansi, "That's the one."

With its alert, knowing eyes and high, powerful shoulders, the creature's magnificent compactness seems so different from our loose-limbed angularity. Hansi is scratching his bottom, like he does when he's nervous or awe-struck, which to him are much the same thing. Tonio puts his arm over the boy's shoulder. I don't begrudge my brother Tonio's affection because it seems to me now that all the animals we've seen – and even the day itself, with all its different landscapes and surprises – belong only to me.

It's then that my tears start to come, and Tonio asks what's wrong. Not much intuition, I suppose.

"I looked at the sun while we were outside," I lie.

"Why'd you do that?"

"So I'd remember this moment."

For a few glorious, heart-stopping seconds we stare into each other's eyes, but because of the jumble of emotions that provokes in us we're both cautious for the rest of our visit to the zoo. At the planetarium, we even sit Hansi between us.

Before heading home, I tell Tonio about my surprise destination and we go to the Neue Museum, which houses Germany's ancient Egyptian collection. Raffi gave me a guided tour there years ago. The moment we enter, Hansi starts tugging on my arm and moaning. "The dust makes me sick," he complains.

"If you don't stop pulling my arm out of its socket, I'm going to mummify you and leave you outside for the crows to eat!"

That doesn't deter him at all, and he starts whining, so Tonio takes him outside.

The director of the Egyptian collection isn't in, but a lady at the ticket desk goes off to find an assistant. An hour later – by which time an impatient Tonio has checked on me twice – a bespectacled assistant, bald, with a goat-like tuft of beard, shuffles lazily down the stairs. He tells me his name is Dr Gross, and we shake hands. "Let's see what you have there," he tells me, fighting a grin. He obviously thinks I'm an idiot.

He looks at the paper and, with a puzzled look, summons me over to the entrance doors so he can study it in the sunlight. Showing the sheet to me, he says, "The frames around these pictograms are called cartouches. They signify names. Usually royal names, but in this case, I'd say ..." He studies the page, his finger tapping nervously against his lips. "Listen, come back later this week, say Friday, and I'll have a translation for you."

"You can't do it now? I don't think I can ..."

He gives me a withering look that stops my protest. When I get back to Tonio and explain what happened, he exclaims, "But you let him keep it! What if it has messages Raffi didn't want anyone to know about."

I worry myself sick all weekend that Dr Gross might cause Raffi problems, maybe even get his funding revoked, and I vow to destroy the hieroglyphics as soon as I've got them back. It's only when Raffi leaves for Egypt on Tuesday that I feel my anxious constriction falling away from me.

I desperately want to see Tonio that week, but my parents have refused – as usual – to let me go out with him on weekdays. Nevertheless, I slip away to his apartment on Wednesday evening, but his mother says he's being punished and can't come to the door. She doesn't volunteer the reason why and her cheek has a big blue bruise, which means she's lost a bad quarrel with her husband, so I don't dare ask anything more.

Photographs from Karl-Heinz arrive in the post on Thursday, while I'm at school, and at that precise moment, two astonishing indications of my coming adulthood converge: the correspondence is addressed to me, and Mama leaves the brown envelope on my pillow *unopened* – an instance of self-control worthy of the big kiss I give her in the kitchen.

On the back of each four-by-five-inch image is a white label on which he's typed the date and names of his subjects. That professional touch makes his gift so exciting that I need to make sure I'm not disturbed while I study them, so I lock myself in the bathroom. Sitting on the tile floor and spreading out the pictures like playing cards, I pick up the one with me, Vera, Marianne, Rolf, and Heidi, pleased to see that I look right at home with them.

I examine my face and pose in the four pictures that include me, eager to see if I exude the charisma of a future diva or the pixie charm of a promising starlet, but beside Marianne, whose blond hair glistens like the sun, I look like a drab little afterthought. After I've studied each photograph down to its grainy texture, I read the poem that Karl-Heinz has written at the bottom of his brief note:

Schläft ein Lied in alien Dingen,
Die da träumen fort und fort,
Und die Welt hebt an zu singen,
Triffst du nur das Zauberwort.

Slumb'ring deep in everything
Dreams a song as yet unheard,
And the world begins to sing
If you find the magic word.

The idea of the world changed by one little word gratifies my delight in smallness, and I commit the verses to memory. To this day, I cannot say them to myself without seeing Karl-Heinz's portraits spread on the glassy, olive-green smoothness of the bathroom tiles, and without feeling my own chances for an adventurous life hovering just outside the door.

The photographer signs his friendly note as *K-H*, which is when I start referring to him by his initials.

My mother puts on her big black glasses to examine the photograph that includes Vera. I expect a shriek, or maybe a few tears of sympathy, since this is the first she's seen of her, but Mama merely purses her lips, hands it back to me, and returns to her stew.

"Do you think I look pretty in them?" I ask.

"Of course," she replies, far too easily for my liking.

"Mama, please look at all the photos. You can't judge from just one."

"Sophie, I only have a single picture of Claudette Colbert, but I can assure you it's enough for me to know she's as glamorous as can be. As far as I'm concerned, it's obvious that you're beautiful."

Mama makes my eyes pop open with that nearly perfect answer, and when she grins at me over her shoulder, I realize that I do love her, after all. If only she had more patience for me. An eager tide swayed by too distant and cautious a moon – that's how life is between Sophie Riedesel and her mother Hanna.

Before my father comes home that evening, I discover that the strict order I'd put K-H's pictures in has been disturbed. Mama isn't aware that I collect incriminating details like this. The country girl who grew up to be my mother is too naïve to understand that her every move is being recorded by her Berliner daughter.

I put the picture of Papa and Ludwig Renn on top of the small pile and save the one with Vera and me for last – the grand finale. And Papa *is* impressed. Most of all that he's been forever linked to a famous Communist journalist. I give that one to him as a gift, but he hands it back. "No, I want the picture in which you're sitting on my lap," he tells me. "I'm going to have that one framed and keep it on my desk at work."

A man who knows how to delight his daughter.

On Friday, I sneak out of school early and head back to the Neue Museum. Two hours go by before Dr Gross receives me in his cluttered office. Bits of walnut shell are spread over his desk, and he's clutching a rusted iron nutcracker. He hands me his handwritten translation of the first twelve lines of Raffi's sheet of hieroglyphics. I'll always remember the first line, which reads: *R-S-I-A-K, B: 31–17–11, 10.*

Noticing my puzzlement, he says, "It had me stumped for a while, too." He cracks a nut, which sends shell flying, then comes around to my side of the desk, munching away. "The first word is spelled backwards, you see."

"K-A-I-S-R?" I ask.

"Yes, the hieroglyphic triangle is K, the eagle A, the two feathers I, and so on. In other words, Kaiser without the *e*, presumably because whoever wrote this out decided that particular vowel wasn't necessary." He digs walnut pulp out of its shell with his thumb. "The first words are all names. In the case of common ones, a first initial is usually added, in this case B. Now, are the numbers that I've separated by commas backwards too?" He holds his hands apart and shakes his head to indicate he doesn't know. "I'm afraid you'll have to figure out the rest, young lady. I haven't time."

"What about the last lines – there's no translation at all."

"I didn't bother writing it out – it's just more German names."

"So who are all these people?"

"A good question." He tosses bits of shell onto his desk, wipes the palms of his hands on his pants, and sits down. "Now, before you go, why don't you tell me where you *really* got this?"

I give him the answer I've been practicing. "It's from my father … it's a kind of birthday game. Every year, he gives me a coded message and if I can find out what it means, I get a big present. Last year, I got this watch." I hold out my mother's old wristwatch, which I pilfered from her drawer that morning since it's more impressive than my own.

"Your father knows hieroglyphics?"

"No, but he obviously knows someone who's an expert!"

Does Dr Gross buy my explanation? To be safe, I copy the names and numbers on the inside cover of *Emil and the Detectives*: B. Kaiser, H. Günther, A. Brueggen ... Then I burn my copy of Raffi's hieroglyphics and take a hot bath to calm myself.

Sitting on my bed, I try to work out what *31–17–11, 10* might mean in relation to a Herr or Frau B. Kaiser: thirty-one might be his or her age, of course; or it might signify last year, in which case 17–11 would probably be the month and day backwards. Did someone named Kaiser do something special on the 17th of November, 1931? In that case, ten might be the time of day.

It's while I'm helping Mama with supper that I consider that maybe a man or woman named Kaiser received a shipment of ten somethings on the 17th of November. *Or made a payment of ten British pounds* ...

And just like that, I foolishly believe I've put the last puzzle piece in place.

Tonio comes up to our apartment early on Saturday, while I'm writing my thank you note to K-H. His stylish forelock has been cut off. But his thick skullcap of short black hair is so handsome that I secretly prefer it. I'd baby-sit for Hansi for a whole month just for the chance to run my hands over those soft needles.

I want desperately to tell him what I've learned about Raffi's hieroglyphics, but as soon as we're safely seated on my bed behind my closed door, he pounds his fist into my pillow and says glumly, "It's so unfair. Look at me."

His eyes are glassy, which brings me close to tears myself. "What exactly happened?" I ask.

"When I refused to go to the barber, my father held me down and ordered my mother to cut it. He even tied my hands behind my back with a belt when I got free. I fought, but he's stronger than me, and anyway he's my father, so I couldn't hit him."

"You ought to punch him right in the face sometime, you know. Or your mother should."

He shakes his head as if I don't understand, and he's undoubtedly right – after all, I don't have a father who'd tie me up. Though it's true that Mama once told me that she occasionally wanted to have me arrested. Before I know what I'm doing, and while he's not looking, I kiss Tonio's cheek, which makes me feel as if I've robbed something vital from him. Maybe he feels the loss of whatever it is I've taken, because he frowns.

"I'm sorry," I say.

"It's not your fault. I just wish I had your parents. Sophie, I think I'm going to be mean to you today."

"I don't mind," I reply. "I got some photographs in the post," I add, to cheer us both up and get him ready for my big announcement. "The ones from the party in Mr Zarco's apartment."

Tonio makes no reply and goes to the window, so I bring them to him. He doesn't laugh at Heidi and Rolf, which is a relief, but then he asks, "Which of them are Jews?"

"How should I know?" I reply, disappointed; I want him to be impressed by my having posed with such amazing people.

"How could you not know?" he demands, and he walks across the room to stand by the foot of my bed, obviously intent on distancing himself from me.

"Tonio, in that picture there are a dwarf and his wife from the circus, a giant with a deformed face, and probably the most gorgeous deaf woman in Berlin. So why would I care which of them goes to a synagogue?"

"Because a Christian dwarf is just a dwarf, but a Jewish one is ... is from a different race. They don't belong in Germany."

It suddenly doesn't seem such a good idea to tell him what I've discovered about Raffi's shopping list. "So where do you want the Jews to go?" I ask instead, and to lighten the mood, I say, "To Mars or Venus, maybe? Did you learn something at the planetarium I didn't?"

"Sophie, this is serious," he tells me, adopting a know-it-all tone that makes me grind my teeth. "Jews take jobs away from Christians. They betrayed us in the Great War and will betray us again if we give them the chance."

"Mr Zarco served in the army. He was given a medal for bravery."

I invent the medal because I'm not above inflating the facts in a good cause.

"The exception that proves the rule," he says pompously. "Everyone knows about the Jews." He makes a beak with his hand and holds it to his face.

"Mr Zarco doesn't have a hooked nose. And neither," I add in a menacing tone, "do Rini or Raffi, so be careful what you say."

Irene Bloch, whom I call Rini, is my best friend; we've been inseparable since we first met in a school playground and took turns pushing each other as high as we could on the squeaky old swings.

"Someone in their families must – it's genetics," he replies triumphantly.

I know there are people who dislike Jews, but I've never actually met one – just as I've never come across anyone who would think any less of me for daydreaming about moussaka or wanting to be a vampire bat or having a little brother who can barely peel potatoes. So I look at Tonio hard, wondering why he's voicing opinions that he can't really have. And that he must have acquired out of nowhere. Unless *nowhere* is really his father.

"What's wrong?" he asks, his voice heavy, as if I'm a burden to him.

Sadness washes over me; I don't want a lout for a boyfriend. "Mr Zarco has lived in Berlin since he was born," I tell Tonio. "And he *gives* jobs to people. He gave a job to Vera – the giant we saw the other day in our courtyard."

"He gives jobs only to Jews probably, and that monster must be one of them. He puts on that Berlin accent, too, so we think he's a Christian."

"Tonio, the Comedian Harmonists are Jewish," I say, referring to our favorite singing group. "Do you want them to go to another planet too?"

"Only three of them are Jewish," he declares.

He's obviously been doing research. *Unheimlich* ...

"The other three would have to be at least part Jewish," I add slyly.

"Why?" he asks, falling into my trap.

"Because they're so talented!" As my coup de grace, I add, "Even Lillian Harvey is Jewish." She's Tonio's favorite movie star.

"She's not!"

"Her real name is Sarah Rabinowitz!" I declare, with enough oomph to make it sound like the truth.

Tonio's eyes light up with rage. I'm determined to stand up to him, however – though not for the benefit of Mr Zarco, Rini, Raffi, the Comedian Harmonists, or Lillian Harvey-Rabinowitz. After all, it's only the beginning of 1932 and our Jewish friends, neighbors, and movie stars are not yet in real danger, and even if they were, they would hardly need the likes of me to fight their battles. No, I hold firm simply because I don't want Tonio to become the kind of selfish young man who doesn't appreciate astonishing photographs of his girlfriend.

And why are we arguing politics in the first place, when we should be watching *Grand Hotel* at the Alhambra Theater on the Kurfürstendamm, sitting in those plush velvet seats like two pashas? Going to the movies was what I planned to propose to Tonio before we began this absurd quarrel.

"You don't know anything!" he says snidely. "And your father is a Communist," he adds with a dismissive wave of his hand. "My father says that they're Germany's enemy, too."

So this *is* all about what god-awful Dr Hessel believes!

Tears of frustration cloud my vision, because Tonio has gone too far; I could never allow a boy who thought Papa was a traitor to come any further into my life. Everything between us has gone wrong before we've even had the chance to become a real couple.

I don't ever want to see you again!

I say that line in my head to see how it will sound when I shout it, but Tonio comes to my rescue. "I told you I was going to be mean to you," he says gently. "I'm sorry." He reaches for my shoulder and kisses my brow. "Let's not talk about the Jews or my father."

And so I learn that certain subjects will become taboo between us.

But one question remains: has he given up his right to think for himself in order to avoid having his hands tied behind his back the next time he mounts a minor rebellion? Maybe I've fallen in love with a coward.

"Hey, did you find out anything about Raffi's hieroglyphics?" he asks excitedly.

"No, nothing," I reply, giving him a good shrug of disappointment. "The man at the museum said it was all nonsense. I've given up trying to figure it out."

Lying to him feels terrible. Still, when I lift my gaze, we look hard at each other, and there's that intimacy again, like a blanket of silence that we can hide in whenever we want. I lean into him and he presses his lips to mine, and because of our quarrel it's as if we're making a vow not just to love each other but also to respect each other's beliefs no matter how difficult that may be. Which ought to be a beautiful vow for two young people to make.

On the street outside our school on Monday, I ask Rini what she makes of all the names I've scribbled on the inside cover of *Emil and the Detectives*. For now, I don't mention any hieroglyphics, though I do tell her that a Nazi was after Raffi. As she takes a good look, she twirls her hair by her ear. Handing my book back, she says, "No Jews at all."

Rini has a sultry, world-weary manner of speaking and a sensual way of playing with her thick auburn hair that I adore. And a slouchy posture that defeats my sketches every time. She wears a necklace of stunning tourmaline beads given to her by her mother when she wants to look more adult, which is most of the time, and she steals cigarettes from her father. She even inhales the smoke, to my great envy. I'm nearly a year older than Rini, because I was sick for three months with whooping cough when I was six and lost a year of school. Yet she looks more adult than I do, especially in profile; I'd guess that Marlene Dietrich looked and sounded like Rini when she was fourteen. I have great plans for her and am counting on her to become the biggest cabaret star in Berlin by the second reel of our life stories. She won't even have to learn how to carry a tune, since Dietrich has proved that a voice like a submarine engine can be captivating.

"What do you mean, no Jews?" I ask.

"No Jewish names, though one or two *could* be Jewish, you can never know for sure."

The dramatic way she speaks – as if this particular insight means some of the people might have double identities or secret ancestry – heightens my sense of having stumbled on something important.

"We should start with the two most unusual names," she adds.

"Why?"

"Because there are probably a hundred H. Günthers in Berlin, for instance." She gestures for me to hand her the list, then scans it quickly. "I'd start with von Schirach and ... this is a perfect one – Cnyrim. There can't be too many Cnyrims. It ought to be possible to find out what links him to von Schirach. Ask your father about them, and I'll ask Papa."

"You think your father will help?"

"Of course, silly. Papa knows hundreds of people and he loves untangling things – especially for me."

Rini's father is a political journalist at the *Tageblatt*. And he truly is mad about his only daughter. Just like my father, I'd have said at the time.

"Please don't tell him this comes from Raffi," I tell her.

"What am I, an idiot!" She lights her cigarette professionally, then hooks her arm in mine and pulls me close, which makes me feel as if this will be an adventure we'll one day be able to tell our children about. "We'll only give our fathers a few names. We won't tell anyone about the full list!" she exults.

That evening, in response to my question, Papa says he may have gone to high school with a von Schill whose father was a carpenter. "Or was he a plumber?" He holds up his newspaper between us to block out further enquiry. Mama is also of no use. And in the Berlin phone book, there are seventeen von Schirachs and nine Cnyrims. Am I supposed to call them one by one to ask if they know each other? And would they tell me the truth?

*

I've been drawing Hansi since he was in kindergarten, which has shown me that you do not need to understand people to love them– good practice for Tonio, as I've just discovered. A few days after Rini decides to ask her father for help, I'm doing a sketch of my brother chopping carrots when Papa comes home from work and informs me that he's just told Mr Zarco that I will not be able to accept the coat that Vera was going to make for me.

"Was he very disappointed?" I ask, cringing at my betrayal.

"He'll recover," my father replies matter-of-factly.

"And what exactly did you tell him?"

"The truth." He sits down in his armchair and lifts up his paper. Sometimes I think I spent half my childhood questioning a man hidden behind typeset wings. My father, the newsprint butterfly.

"Couldn't you have made something up?" I press him.

"Sophie, you think too much – just like your mother. I'm sure Vera is used to rejection."

"That only makes it worse!" I groan.

Rini calls me on Friday evening. "Listen to this," she says excitedly, "Papa's found out some interesting things about two von Schirachs!" To heighten the suspense, she pauses.

"Rini, tell me!" I demand, jumping up from my chair.

"Carl von Schirach was a theater manager in Weimar and an early supporter of Hitler, and he married an American woman and they named their son – wait till you hear this! – Baldur, and little Baldur grew up to become a world-class anti-Semite. He's head of the Nazis' youth program."

"And Cnyrim?"

"Nothing yet. But listen, I noticed an H. Günther on your list. When I mentioned it yesterday to Papa, he remembered a Hans Günther who is chair of the Department of Racial Anthropology in Freiburg. He believes in Nordic superiority. He thinks Roman Navarro, Rudolf Valentino, and Louis Armstrong are chimpanzees. Though Günther is a common name, of course, so I don't know how we can be sure it's him."

"Could they all be National Socialists – the people on the list?" I ask.

"I've no idea. But if they are, the question is, why would Raffi be in touch with them?"

"Keep this to yourself, but I think that maybe he's getting support for his research in Egypt from these people."

During the next week, a young officer in the *Sturmabteilung* – a brownshirt – flirts with me while I'm trying to coax Hansi out of some undergrowth in the Tiergarten where a rabbit has vanished. He tells me I can find back issues of *Der Stürmer* at a pub on Landsberger Straße frequented by the party faithful. *Der Stürmer* is the Nazi newspaper that caricatures Jews as big-nosed, thick-lipped traitors on every front page. So I go there one day after school to try to find names from my list in its articles. After an hour, I've found a National Socialist named Stuckart who's a bigwig in the Health Department and a Viktor Brack who is good friends with Hitler.

Reading that horrible newspaper, I realize I'll have to confront Raffi when he returns from Egypt. But if I discover he's taken money from the Nazis, how will we ever continue to be friends?

Having chickened out on my gift from Vera, I slip thief-like around corners and into shadows whenever I spot Mr Zarco, but one sunny Saturday morning in early April, while I'm sitting on my haunches in our courtyard, potting violet-colored pelargoniums in our window boxes, he appears above me without warning.

"How's my little Sophele?" Mr Zarco asks in an exuberant voice, using a Yiddish nickname for me that implies affection and which he pronounces *Spheluh*.

His eyes are inquisitive and amused. He's clearly a man whose delight in young people devours his grievances.

"I'm fine," I say. Standing up and raising my soiled hands – two slick brown mittens – I add, "It's good to get my fingers in some dirt." I want him to know I'm not the kind of girl who thinks she's made of porcelain.

His pipe, set in his jaw, bobs up and down comically. The same boyish energy makes Papa rise up onto his toes. The two of them could be extras in a Charlie Chaplin movie.

"What exactly are you doing, *meine Liebe*?" he asks. He combs a hand back over his tufts of silver hair. His wife, who died when I was little, must have been armed every morning with a wet hairbrush.

"The flowers in our pots died over the winter, and I can't stand looking at them any more."

"I understand. Are they geraniums?"

"Pelargoniums."

"Pel-ar-gon-ium," he says, spreading his right arm in a luxurious arc, as if he's a ballet dancer. "Sounds like a Latin poet." Holding his belly, he adds, "Or maybe a rare stomach disease."

We laugh together, and somewhere inside that sound is the trust I feel for him. His teeth are brown-edged from his pipe smoking, and crooked too, but I once overheard a prostitute on the underground saying to her colleague that a man needs some defects to make him really handsome, and now that I'm in love with a boy who claims to believe that Communists and Jews are no good, I understand what she means.

"Give me the honor of smelling your fingers," he says. He unfurls his hand toward me – another gesture from the stage.

"You'll get dirty," I protest.

He shrugs away my concern. Sniffing rabbit-like at my fingers, he says, "Similar tangy odor to geraniums ... not all that pleasant." His touch draws away my strength. I must not be a normal person around men anymore – even elderly ones with mussed hair. I'd like to simply faint away and float into the sky.

"Are you all right, Sophele?" he asks, releasing his hold on me.

"I'd like to be weightless sometimes. I wish I could just rise up toward the sun."

"And be led away by Hermes to the top of Mount Olympus."

"By who?"

"The messenger of the Greek gods is Hermes. He appears as sunlight in our world." In an enticing voice, he adds, "He might even be telling you something."

"What?"

"That we may not be earth-bound after all!" he declares.

"You think we might be able to fly?" I ask eagerly.

"If God is a bird, then why not?"

"But God's not a bird!" I retort. How sure I was of matters I knew nothing about!

"Someone has given you *meshuge* information, Sophele. I can assure you that for me, the Lord often appears to me as the sacred ibis of Egypt. He is white, with a black head and silver eyes. In fact, some very courageous ibises once guided Moses across an Ethiopian swamp riddled with hungry snakes. That was God protecting a prophet."

"I don't understand."

"To my wife, the Lord was present in those big, shaggy snowflakes that fall in silence. 'The still whiteness of gravity,' she wrote once. A nice thing to say, no? My wife, Marthe, was the poet in our family. My mother was the watercolorist. And if you look closely at her work, you can see God taking form in the sunset over the village near Dresden where her grandparents lived. I'll show you sometime." He gestures toward my flowers. "Who knows, the Lord might even appear to a girl named Sophie as pelargoniums listening in to her conversation with an *alter kacker* neighbor."

"A what?"

"An old shitter," he explains. "A fossil who complains a lot." To my puzzled look, he adds in a thoughtful tone, "I'm speaking like a village idiot. Sorry. All I mean to say is that we each find different things beautiful and symbolic of something greater." He points the stem of his pipe at me. "What touches you most is what God chooses as His hand."

I think about that for a time. "So He has a different hand for each person?" I ask.

"Of course."

"And God's eyes, what are they?"

"His eyes are yours." He raises his thick, caterpillar eyebrows like a trickster. "So when you get a glimpse of the Lord, Sophele, you are also seeing yourself."

I'm more confused than ever, and I let my head drop comically, as though I'm a marionette whose strings have been cut.

Laughing again, he says, "I'm envious of you, you know. I'd like to have pelargoniums at home, but I'd always worry about them when I was away. A plant dying of thirst is not something I'd want on my conscience." Mr Zarco turns out the fraying pockets of his tweed coat, finding keys and an old museum ticket in one, and a silver lighter and a handful of cracker crumbs in the other – the keepsakes of a widower. "Travel light," my papa always told me. "Things just weigh you down."

"But all the books on your shelves! And your paintings."

"I know," he moans. "Unfortunately, my father also told me

that a two-legged donkey is a German who doesn't read books."
He holds up a finger. "Which reminds me of a Yiddish joke. What
do you do if one man calls you a donkey?"

"I've no idea."

"You ignore him – he's just provoking you. And if two people
call you a donkey?" He spreads his hands to call for my reply, and
when I say I still don't know, he replies, "You consider what it
might mean about your character. After all, you're a thoughtful
person, no? And if *three* people call you a donkey?"

"I give up."

"You buy a saddle!"

I laugh, but mostly because he does. And because the melody
of his Yiddish is like German twisted by a thousand years of
conversations on village street corners.

"Tell me, Sophele, do you think a book could get as thirsty as
a pelargonium?" he asks.

With such questions, I come to learn that he is different from
anyone I've ever met.

"Maybe if it weren't ever taken down from its shelf," I reply.
"If nobody ever read it."

"Exactly – I worry about that all the time," he confesses.

This is the first time I consider that he may be deranged. And
maybe it's the first time that he conceives of a plan for how I can
help him in his struggle.

"I could water any plants you decided to get," I say. "When
you're away from home, I mean."

That's an offer made by a girl desperate to scrub off the ink stain
left by her betrayal, of course.

"No, that would be asking too much."

We both know why he says that, and it's now that I should
apologize for my cowardice, or at least try to explain it, but before

I can speak he rubs the residue of my dirt from his hands right onto the seat of his woolen trousers and says, "I'm off to synagogue. And then a funeral." He gazes at me sadly.

"Someone died?"

"A friend. I think you met him at my Carnival party – Georg Hirsch. He was dressed as Cesare from *The Cabinet of Dr Caligari*."

My heart does a somersault. "Georg! Oh my God. What happened to him?"

"He was murdered at his apartment."

I feel as if the ground has shifted beneath me. I can't think of what to say. And I can feel tears rising into my eyes from out of my shock.

"I'm sorry I had to give you bad news," Mr Zarco says gently.

"Did they ... did they catch who did it?"

As he shakes his head, a shudder ripples through me. "Why ... why would someone want to murder him?" I ask.

"Sophele, with the Nazis around, we all have enemies," he replies. "They tried to shoot Georg once in Savigny Platz but missed. We should have gotten him out of Germany."

"Vera said he was involved in politics."

"He'd become the head of a group called The Ring that I founded about twenty years ago. We help circus performers like Rolf and Vera find good work after they stop performing. We've decided to fight for better conditions for brewery workers of late. We try to help wherever we can. Maybe some big Nazi didn't like that and ordered Georg killed. They ... they painted swastikas on his face ... blue swastikas on his cheeks and forehead. And on his hands, too."

"Why blue?"

"I haven't a clue."

"Did you know Georg for a long time?"

"Since he was a boy. We're cousins. I was fifteen years older than him and used to take him all over the city with me when he was a boy." Mr Zarco's smile is made of memories. "You never saw a child so quick. My wife used to say he was a copper wire – all that electricity! His parents were lovely people, too."

"Did you used to take him to the Botanical Gardens?"

"Yes, he loved them, but how did you know that?"

"That's where Georg wanted to go when I met him." Seeing Mr Zarco's puzzled look, I add, "At your party, he asked Vera if she wanted to go there, and he ended up asking me, too."

"It was Georg's personal mission to bring Vera out of her cocoon." He re-lights his pipe, puffing hard, his cheeks hollowing with the effort.

"Would you mind telling me how ... how he was murdered?" I ask hesitantly. It's a question that just pops out, maybe because I've read *Emil and the Detectives* too many times. I'm also aware that I want to help Mr Zarco find the killer – and that any reasonable person would regard it as presumptuous of me to believe I can.

He gives me a hard look from behind a cloud of smoke. He looks like a sorcerer getting ready to cast a spell of silence.

"I sorry if I offended you," I tell him, grimacing. "I'm just ... just curious. My mind has been distorted by reading novels and by watching Hollywood movies – at least, that's what Mama says."

"I see," he says, amused. His expression becomes grave. "The police said he was strangled. Apparently, his windpipe was broken."

"Did they tell you anything else?"

"Not much. They were mainly interested in threatening me."

"Threatening you?"

"They seemed to think that all Jews are liars. And they insisted that I ought to know more than I do about Georg's whereabouts prior to his death."

"Did the Nazis beat him up first?"

"No, there was no evidence of that."

"No bruises on his face or body ... maybe on his arms?"

"Nothing. But Sophele, I'm not sure I should be discussing this with you. It's all so terrible."

"It's just ... don't you think that if Nazis killed Georg they'd have hurt him first, Mr Zarco?"

"I don't know." He looks down and swirls his foot along the ground, as if to lead his mind toward an answer. I can tell he's only now started to consider Georg's death as a mystery that needs solving. Maybe older people don't think like detectives.

"You don't watch many movies, do you?" I ask.

"No, but I get the feeling I should," he replies, amused by me again. He gazes at me keenly, eager now to hear what I have to say.

"Do you know if the lock on his door was broken or ... or a window smashed?"

He funnels his smoke above him. "No, I've been to his apartment. Nothing was broken."

"So there was no struggle, which means he knew the person who killed him."

"But that would mean a friend or acquaintance of his would have to be a secret Nazi," he says, a tone a questioning in his voice.

"Yes, though even if his attacker had been a friend, Georg must have fought back ... and fought back hard. Which would mean he might have been restrained and gagged. But you say there were no marks made on his face or arms. So something doesn't add up." A chain of meaning locks around me. Hoping Mr Zarco will say *no*, I ask, "Is Raffi Munchenberg a member of the group that Georg headed, by any chance?"

"Yes. How did you know?"

"A hunch." So maybe Georg had learned that Raffi was accepting money from Nazis and needed to be silenced. And maybe the color blue has a special meaning to an Egyptologist.

"What's wrong, Sophele?" Mr Zarco asks.

"Nothing," I lie. "Did the police say whether they found any blood on Georg?"

"No, he looked ..." Mr Zarco's eyes moisten. He tries to speak, but fails. Finally, he says, "Sorry, it's just that I had to identify his body. His parents are dead and his sister lives in Hamburg."

"Was anything stolen?"

"His sister told me that when she came to collect his things, his make-up kit was gone." To my puzzled look, he says, "Georg walked the high-wire. Circus people use make-up." He rubs his cheek as if he's afraid to ask me something, and I keep quiet so as not to scare him off. "I'd like you to come with me to synagogue sometime," he finally tells me.

"All right, though I won't know what to do."

"What to do? You just sit with me," he says good-naturedly. "We'll pick a day soon. Sophele, I've got to be off. Happy potting!"

He starts away. Thinking of Papa and suddenly worried for his safety, I call after him, "Was Georg a Communist?"

He turns back. "No, why do you ask?"

"My papa is a Communist," I whisper.

"Your father is going to be fine," he says definitively, understanding my fears. "Georg was Jewish. That's probably what they hated."

"Mr Zarco, do you think a Jew would ever accept money from a Nazi?"

"Some of us own shops where anyone can purchase things."

"No, I mean funding for a project ... a special project."

"I suppose if the money could be put to good use."

"And another thing. Do the Jews have the same God as Christians?" I ask.

"Naturally."

"The sacred ibis?"

"With two silver eyes," he says, dotting each one with the end of his pipe, "and a long beak to scare away snakes." He lifts one of his feet. "And yellow toes."

Mr Zarco is the first adult I've ever met who has ever said anything interesting about God. *He is giving me an invitation*, I think. *And not just to synagogue. I can either ask him to tell me more about the way he thinks or lose this chance forever.*

It's Saturday afternoon, and Tonio and I have just reached our courtyard after visiting a tire factory in Neukölln whose roof caved in the night before. We've also kissed in public for the first time – while sitting on a bench in Treptower Park. And I let him feel my breasts, too, but only for a few shameless and thrilling seconds. Right now we're as sopped as dishrags from the heavy rains that fell as we hurried to the underground for the trip home. Wanting to know what God looks like to Tonio, I ask, "What's the most beautiful thing you've ever seen? Or the thing that touched you the most?"

"I need to think about that," he replies.

Once we're inside, we dry our hair with a towel and drag two armchairs up to the radiator. Tonio's mother throws an eiderdown over us and lectures us in a mixture of German and Russian for having taken along only a single umbrella. She gesticulates wildly. Maybe everyone from Novograd – "the oldest city in Russia," she always tells us proudly – emphasizes their words by making all sorts of waving motions in the air, but to us she's one of a kind.

"You two will end up with pneumonia one day," she concludes.

She and Tonio have decided that hot chocolate is what we need, but there's not a drop of milk in the house. On her way out to Frau Koslowski's grocery, she makes two fists and says in Russian, "Winter holds back springtime in this city with both its hands." Tonio translates. She gives him a big, confirming nod, kisses the top of his head, then mine, and rushes out the door.

Maybe we can blame the blood returning to our youthful hands and feet. Or the eiderdown, which gives our growing warmth the weighty blessing of German family tradition. Or even the possibility of his mother coming back early and shrieking hysterically at us. Whatever the case, Tonio chooses this moment to duck under our covering and begin pawing at my ankles, huffing at my feet, and barking. I'm laughing and squirming, and telling him to quit tickling me, since a protest is a must for any girl in my position, so that later she can testify, *But I told him to stop!*

Gentle now, he cups my knees in his hands. I give a little jump. "What are you doing?" I whisper.

He doesn't answer. I turn back for the front door, imagining steps. The rain batting against the windows means that we cannot be seen or heard. What is developing between us is taking place outside of time. Although maybe that's just a convenient illusion favored by all girls about to fall from grace.

He pushes my legs apart. Moaning, I resist, but he begins to growl.

If I were to draw my feelings, they'd be a luminous river cascading around me, washing the evidence of my desires away, because I'm not yet supposed to feel this way.

A girl cedes herself to a boy because she wants to believe their love will make her a new person. *Anything that won't change me forever does not deserve to be called love.* That's what I decide afterward, trying to remain calm and justify myself.

Now, however, I have no thoughts, only Tonio's velvety hair between my fingers, and his slow licking. The whiskers on his cheeks burn the inside of my thighs, marking all of me as his territory. I tighten my legs around him so that neither of us can escape our fate. We will fall together.

The only thing I whisper the whole time he's at me is, "God help me," because I know that goodness will have to change its meaning if I am ever to explain this to my parents. I'm a girl without a signpost, groping ahead toward herself. Later, I will recall the cheetah Tonio petted and what he told me: "If I weren't scared, then having my face licked by him wouldn't have been so exciting."

I am part of him now, I think afterward, just as Mrs Hessel is turning the key in the door.

"Warmer now?" she asks, and she feels Tonio's brow. "You're burning up!" she shouts.

"I'm fine," he says.

She feels my forehead, too. "You poor children, you both have fevers."

"The hot chocolate ...?" Tonio reminds her.

"Linden tea would be better. With a little honey and pepper. And a thimbleful of vodka." A recipe from Russia that's been curing Tonio's ancestors for centuries.

"Whatever you say, Mama," Tonio agrees, since vodka is an adult treat.

Concealed under our covering, his hardness grows in my hand, and while his mother is busy in the kitchen the next of us to duck below the eiderdown is me.

CHAPTER FOUR

The following week I go again to the pub on Landsberger Straße to hunt through *Der Stürmer* and find several more corresponding names. Disturbing. But maybe Raffi accepted money from Nazis only so he could undermine their work. He wouldn't be capable of doing anything terrible, and I could never believe he was involved in a murder.

I glimpse Vera, Rolf, and Heidi only once more that year, on the evening of the 19th of April, though I spot Mr Zarco coming and going with some regularity, of course. I'm making Hansi pose as a reader at the kitchen table – his hands under his chin and eyes gazing purposefully down at my copy of *The Magic Mountain* – when a harsh and familiar voice coming from outside makes me bolt upright. I rush to the window and find Vera in the courtyard, her hands on her hips, irritated about something. Heidi and Rolf come through the door to the front building a few moments later. He's chomping on a cigar and Heidi, blue lace at the collar of a pretty white dress, is carrying a pink cake box. Vera calls them forward, her hands in a frenzied whirl, and Rolf gives Heidi a peck on the cheek as if to say, *Bear with her ...*

My first urge is to call out. My second is to lean back out of sight, which is what I do. Our window is open, so I can hear them clearly.

"Stop that!" Vera snaps at her friends. "It's enough that you two walk like tree stumps, you don't have to compound the problem with unnecessary affection."

"Define unnecessary," Rolf replies, laughing.

"*All* affection between married couples. It's an affront to all we hold dear in Germany."

"Vera, you make my bones ache!" he tells her, but Heidi, gently, suggests that Vera go on up the stairs and they will catch up.

Impatient with everyone and everything. The modus operandi of a goddess who spent years on view to gaping circus-goers.

Heidi and Rolf penguin-walk behind her into the rear building.

"What is it?" Hansi asks, still posing perfectly. An amazing child. He deserves a medal from the Artists Guild.

"And that's that," I whisper with resentful finality, sensing I'll never get to know such special people. I sit back down and grab my pencil.

"That's what?" my brother asks.

I aim the pencil point at him threateningly. If he were normal, this is where he'd scream at me to stop being such a bully or call my mother for help. But Hansi is who he is; he simply rests his head on the table and vanishes into his cloud of thoughts.

Papa enters the kitchen a short time later and, sensing something is wrong, says, "Show me your drawing, *Häschen*."

A kind man, but sweetness in parents can be irritating – like too soft a pillow. I stifle my urge to scream and hand him my sketchbook. Papa studies my previous drawing – Hansi in profile, his tongue poking between his lips and eyes focused on a distant surprise. "No doubt about it – you've got talent," he says proudly.

"It's all wrong," I say, because some dark part of me wants to spoil our easy intimacy.

"It's not – I'd know that handsome boy anywhere." He rests a gentle hand atop Hansi's head, as he does when he knows his son is lost to us. We both do that a lot. Returning my sketchbook to me, Papa says, "You're more of an artist than you know."

"Thanks," I reply, and it is a lovely thing to say, but I'm really thinking, *Why are my family and Tonio not enough for me?*

Vera, Heidi, and Rolf must have been invited to Mr Zarco's for Passover dinner. If I'd kept the curtains open, I'd probably have spotted K-H and Marianne, too.

That night before bed, Papa discovers that an envelope with my name on it has been pushed under the door. Alone in the room I share with Hansi, I rip it open and find a photo of a woman's swollen belly – as smooth and bright as marble in the moonlight – and a neatly printed note: "Our child and me – first portrait. World premiere four months away! Love, Marianne and K-H."

Raffi comes home in mid-May, his skin as dark as cinnamon and his black hair falling down to his shoulders, the picture of a Biblical acolyte. We talk in our courtyard, and I try to be interested in his descriptions of Egyptian life 3,300 years ago, but the Nazi names we don't mention lie like cadavers between us. A week later, unable to bear the chill I feel whenever I pass his apartment, I knock on his door one evening after supper. His parents are out, and he and I sit in his room, me on his neatly made bed, him at his desk chair, which he has turned around so he can lean forward over the cane-work back.

"I can't tell you much because other people would be in danger," he says even before I have a chance to explain why I've come. "But what I told you was the truth – it was a shopping list."

"Have you been getting money from the Nazis on your list to support your fieldwork?"

He laughs in a single burst. "That's a good one!"

"Then why the British money? Didn't you intend to use it in Egypt?"

"Soph, you've got far too vivid an imagination for your own

good." In a low voice, he tells me, "I was bribing Nazi politicians. And others with similar ideas. They prefer British pounds because it's a more solid currency than the mark. Every time I made a bribe, I wrote down a name and a date."

So I was partially right. "Bribing them why?" I question.

"To get their support on certain issues. To ease up on their hateful rhetoric."

For the first time in weeks, I feel as if the ground is solid beneath me. "And where did you get the money?"

"Isaac told me you know now about The Ring. The members pay dues according to how much they can afford. I used some of our ... our funds to purchase pounds on the black market."

Relief sweeps through me. "Thank God. I thought ..." I shake my head at my silliness.

"You thought I'd switched teams, didn't you?" Only now realizing that I probably copied down his list, he jumps up. "You took down my hieroglyphics and ... and then had them translated somehow," he says, horrified.

"Yes, Dr Gross, at the ..."

"So Dr Gross knows what you found out?"

"No, I never mentioned your name. And he has no idea what links all the names on the list. Or what the numbers mean. He thinks they're part of a game." I explain what I told Dr Gross.

"We can't be sure he's forgotten what he saw."

Raffi looks off into his thoughts. I see fear in the clenching of his jaw.

"I did something really dumb, didn't I?" I observe.

He smiles generously. "No, it's going to be all right. Don't worry."

"I'm sorry, but I was really worried about you."

"Forget about it." He sits with me and tells me to turn so he can braid my hair – a vestige of his baby-sitting duties.

I can see from his face that he's pondering how to rectify the situation. "Raffi, I'm sorry," I say.

"Everything is okay. In any case, I'm out of the bribery business. So none of this matters anymore."

"Can you tell me who was chasing you that day Tonio and I helped you?"

"Soph, I can't make braids if you keep turning around! It was someone who wanted to learn who I'd been bribing."

I love the pull and tug of his hands. "But what if the police interrogate you? Or Nazi thugs?"

"All I could tell them would be old news at this point," he assures me, his voice now secure. "The only people who could get in trouble besides me would be the Nazis themselves. Because I would never reveal the names of the people in The Ring."

Bravado or the truth?

"Did Georg Hirsch plan the bribery campaign? I mean, he was head of The Ring, wasn't he? Was that why he was killed?"

Raffi leans past my shoulder and looks at me darkly. "I told you these were serious, adult matters."

"Does Mr Zarco know why Georg was killed?"

He grips both my shoulders and says threateningly, "Soph, either you shush or we won't be able to be friends anymore."

Georg was killed by a Nazi assassin because he threatened to go public with the names of National Socialists being bribed by The Ring. After all, accepting hush money from a group filled with Jews would discredit them completely – and look very bad for the party in general. That's what I soon conclude, but I don't share my thoughts with anyone, not even Rini. I tell her that Raffi's list consisted of the names of Nazis about whom he'd written letters to the Chancellor, denouncing their anti-Semitic beliefs. She's disappointed, since it's hardly a discovery worthy of the sleuthing we've done, but it's safer for Raffi this way. And maybe for Rini, too.

Over that spring and summer, Mr Zarco and I are friendly whenever we bump into each other, but I can tell from the deliberateness in his speech and hand gestures that he's waiting for me to make the first move to renew our friendship. "Reserved" is how Mama describes him. "Secretly exuberant" seems more accurate, though Papa says that makes no sense. He has the appreciation for poetry of a shoehorn.

Rini suggests that the stunning Nazi victory in the July elections may be responsible for Mr Zarco's reticence. After all, I'm a Christian and he's a Jew, and Hitler now presides over what has become the most powerful party in Germany, with 230 seats in the Reichstag. And it's a fact that everyone I know is more tense than usual. Even Papa, who explodes at me for my faulty dishwashing one warm August evening, sending me to my room in tears. Mama, sitting at the foot of my bed, confides that the election results have left him plagued by insomnia. So maybe sleeplessness is a curse I inherited from him.

Seeing Hitler's speeches in newsreels, we grow familiar with his spasmodic, epileptic rants, as well as his Viennese suburban accent and vocabulary.

"The personality of a village rat-catcher," Papa tells me. "Mark my words, he'll be sent back to his garret in Bavaria in less than a year."

Like most Berliners, Papa pronounces *Bayern*, Bavaria, as if it's a land of toothless troglodytes. That must hurt Mama, who loves her homeland as if it's a magic kingdom in a fairy tale, but I'm too young – and maybe too resentful of her – to direct any words of sympathy her way.

Papa's opinion of Hitler is the popular consensus, but my art teacher, Frau Mittelmann, disagrees. She's the person who first interested me in sketching. No one can draw a daisy, carob pod, or stuffed walrus head like her, except maybe Albrecht Dürer, whose work she always shows us as inspiration. Frau Mittelmann has the pointy face of a fox, with a range of smiles from devilish to beatific that would be the envy of any actress, and she always darts around class as though she has just drunk an entire pot of coffee. She has short brown hair that she combs straight back like a man – very stylish, and she wears antique clothing in bright colors, like one of the Gypsy dancers I once saw on the KuDamm. To begin a drawing session, she always reads a quote from a famous painter. The one that makes me tingle is from Cézanne: "Fruits like having their portrait painted. They seem to sit and ask your forgiveness for fading. Their thoughts are given off with their perfumes. They come with all their scents, they speak of the fields they have left behind, the rain which has nourished them, the daybreaks they have seen."

When I mention Papa's opinion of Hitler before class one day, Frau Mittelmann smooths down the front of her floral-print smock with tense hands. "Your father should never forget that the Pied Piper was a rat-catcher, too," she says menacingly. A few minutes later, while we're sketching two proud yellow apples and the sadly withered pomegranate that doubles as her paperweight, she kneels down beside my desk. "Hitler has vowed to free us from our shame over our defeat in the Great War," she whispers. "But we'll have to give him our children in exchange." Then she stands up, her knobby knees creaking, and says with uncharacteristic coarseness, "I must be mad to discuss these things with you. Get back to your drawing, Sophie."

Is she afraid that I will report her to Dr Hildebrandt, the school principal? We've all heard the rumors that he attended a Nazi rally in Nuremberg last year.

Over lunch that day, I complain about Frau Mittelmann's brusqueness to Rini.

"You just don't understand, Soficka," she tells me. "You can't imagine the pressure we Jews are under."

Rini often calls me Soficka, the *cka* suffix borrowed from my horrid middle name, Ludowicka.

"So explain it to me," I say, digging my fork into my boiled potatoes.

"That would be pointless." She lands with all her certainty on her last word, and I feel the thud deep in my chest. "You are either a Jew or you aren't, and all the goodwill in the world can't change that."

She sounds as if she's glad that a Semitic wall has grown up between us, which makes me so mad I could clock her right over the head with my history book, but Rini is in one of her squinty-eyed black moods, so I ask her instead why she thinks Hitler has had such success of late.

"Once you pass the outskirts of Berlin, my dear, you are back in the Middle Ages as far as the Jews are concerned," she tells me, saying *my dear* in English because it's her latest affectation. "Three steps past Neuenhagen Süd, our country becomes an anti-Semitic wasteland. The people *out there*" – Rini tosses away a dismissive wave in the general direction of Silesia – "still think we have tails and horns, and that we boil Christian children like you and Hansi in cauldrons for our Passover dinner."

"I don't think I've enough meat on me even as an appetizer," I say, making Rini laugh, "and Hansi would taste *really* bland, like over-boiled rice."

Our German teacher, Dr Fabig, gathers Rini, me, and a handful of other students around him a few days later, having overheard our political conversations. He speaks in a hushed voice while stuffing papers in his briefcase – dark leather, with a brass handle – then stands it on his desk. He takes off his wire-rim glasses, which he does only when he's upset. "The *Volk* despise our great writers. They think Goethe is far too effeminate. And Schiller, my God" – here, Dr Fabig shakes his head morosely – "my poor dear Schiller puts them in a catatonic state. And now that the Jews are considered un-German, I'm afraid Heine is done for." He stands up and grabs the handle of his briefcase, making ready to go. "As for Rilke, they could never take the time away from counting their spare change or milking their cows to understand what he writes. They cheer for Hitler because he despises our great men. He prefers reading a weapons catalogue to Novalis. It's as simple as that."

Frau Koslowski, from the neighborhood grocery store, says that posters of Hitler and the Nazi Party are everywhere because we have no icons in our churches. The way her milky eyes focus on me, as if I'm to blame, makes me take a step back. "If you Germans had saints around you, listening to your every heartbeat, then you would not need a leader to speak to you of the glories of this world."

Raffi tells me in a scornful voice, "A gangster is what the rabble want – a man who will barge into the homes of his enemies with both hands swinging and a grenade in his pocket, and send all the crystal crashing to the ground, then blow up the evidence behind him."

Even Hansi has an opinion about Hitler, which he mostly expresses by covering his ears every time our Chancellor rants on the radio. "He shouts too much!" my brother observes.

So it is that we begin referring to Hitler as the little man who shouts.

"He's the only politician with *vision*," Tonio's father, Dr Hessel, tells me.

I'm in his sitting room, waiting for Tonio to dress, studying the framed picture of the Nazi leader that's joined the photograph of Czar Peter on the wall behind the couch. Hitler is giving his stiff-armed salute to a cheering crowd.

"He sees what we could become if we aspire to greatness – to heaven on earth," Dr Hessel continues, speaking to an audience that isn't there, like a man who has confused Wagner's operas for real life.

Tonio himself is convinced you have to shut your eyes to understand the man's charisma. "Sophie, I admit that Hitler is physically repulsive," he says, "so don't look at him. Then you'll hear that his passion is real – more real than anything you've ever heard before."

I close my eyes tight while we're watching a newsreel of a rally in Munich, but all I can hear is his painful, frantic urgency and provincial pronunciation. *A passionate rat-catcher that could only ever appeal to the willfully blind.* That's what I think.

And who would lose to Tarzan in any battle of wits, I add to my description a few minutes after the newsreel ends, because Tonio has dragged me to see *Tarzan, the Ape Man,* and as soon as we're transported to that wondrous black-and-white Hollywood jungle it becomes clear to me – and likely every woman and girl in the Ufa-Palast Theater – that a bare-chested Johnny Weismuller is someone we'd prefer to vote for. But Tonio and I have kissed in that inhabited darkness – floating between the screen and our seats, between California and Berlin – and I don't want to upset him. Though it turns out he has an answer all ready for me ...

"Weismuller is an Aryan name," he says as we step outside in the warm summer evening, "which just proves what Hitler has been saying about the superiority of our race."

Our race? Doesn't one of us have a Slavic mother?

Uncharacteristically, Mama swears she has the definitive answer to all my questions about Hitler: he owes his success to too few calories in German bellies. "Five million people practically starving, and twenty million more who are afraid to join them, are going to make the wrong decision every time. Hunger goes to the brain."

The certainty in her voice ... It occurs to me then that she must have gone without food as a girl. Tender feelings well up inside me. "Did you and your sisters often go hungry?" I ask.

"Of course not," she tells me, and her deadly frown makes me feel foolish for caring about the girl she once was.

While chopping leeks for the potato soup, I gaze down to hide my speculations about what wrong decisions Mama made because of her own hunger. My fear – so bottomless it leaves me in a cold sweat – is that giving birth to a certain badly behaved girl was one of them. Maybe my name is right at the top of her list of errors.

I remember what Mr Zarco told me about how God appears to each of us differently, and I decide to ask Mama what she thinks Hitler finds most beautiful about the world.

She looks up from the mop she's pushing across the floor. "I bet it would be the sound of his own voice. But in that, Sophie," she adds, fixing me with a disgusted look, "he's hardly alone."

Contempt for her fellow human beings? Worth nurturing, so I ask her to elucidate, but she says that she was just babbling and that I better hurry up with the leeks, which makes me roll my eyes since Hansi is only just starting to peel his second potato.

Rini is more forthcoming. "Hitler would love pulling off the wings of a live bird," she declares. Then she flips her hair casually off her forehead and breaks off another square of her chocolate bar. "Want some, my dear?" she asks, not a trace of horror on her face.

Sometimes that girl scares me.

*

The 19th of September is my fifteenth birthday. Tonio gives me a gift wrapped impeccably in blue- and white-striped paper, which means his mother did it for him. The card says, "For Sophie, who'll make us all proud."

I hug him hard, because his words mean he understands – and supports – my desire to excel. I find a sketchbook inside – fifty sheets of smooth, heavy paper, the best I've ever had.

"It's perfect!" I beam. "Thank you." I want to say more but I also don't want to frighten *him* off – my leitmotif with men.

No turning back: that's what our continuing embrace means. At least to me. Who knows what a hug might signify to a sixteen-year-old boy who can't wrap a present by himself?

At supper, after I blow out the candles on my birthday cake, my parents give me a set of twenty-four colored pencils made in Czechoslovakia by Koh-I-Noor. Which means that they and Tonio conspired together to buy complementary gifts. A very encouraging sign!

On Sunday, the 2nd of October, I learn some more about what The Ring has been planning, and I get my first glimpse of the road we are all about to take into our future. It's the day after Rosh Hashanah, the Jewish New Year, and Mr Zarco, eager to celebrate in style, takes scissors to a swastika flag and hangs the tattered fabric out his window facing Prenzlauer Allee. He does an excellent job. I find out later that other members of his group are shredding flags all over Berlin and its suburbs.

When Papa and I return from the bakery with fresh bread, we see how Mr Zarco's handiwork has turned the black, red, and white banner into spaghetti.

"Good for him!" Papa exults.

Mama disagrees hotly. "To make a public spectacle ... it's embarrassing."

"Why?" I ask, pausing as I munch my toast. I give her an innocent look, though I'm well aware I'm playing havoc with her emotions.

Papa and I both stare expectantly at her. Even Hansi is gazing at her above his oatmeal, though maybe he's only trying to communicate telepathically with her that he wants more milk.

"Because it happens to be beneath him," she tells me, escaping to the sink to wash her hands.

"Why is it beneath him?"

"Sophie!" Mama snaps, turning back to me with vengeful eyes. "I hope for the sake of your future husband that you one day learn some restraint."

Papa holds his finger to his lips when I glance at him for support, so I stomp into the sitting room. Mama's testiness gives me the perfect excuse for slipping out of the apartment, and I ease the front door open and dash down the stairs, across the courtyard, and up the back staircase. I'll pay for my rashness later, but for now I feel only a wind of joy blowing through me.

Tonio has been waiting for me and we race to the street. On turning the corner past our building, we spot Mr Zarco's protest and Tonio's lips twist disdainfully. "That sort of affront makes you wonder if the Jews even want to be part of the new Germany we're building," he says.

This is the first time Tonio has used *we* when referring to the Nazis. I'm upset, but overlooking such a major flaw also makes me feel magnanimous.

"I have a special present for you," he adds as we head off, "but it's in the Neue Museum."

"What is it?" I ask, thrilled by his surprise.

"Patience!" he commands, and he grins in that wily way that makes my breathing deepen.

*

We make our way across Berlin, which at the moment is a journey into a myth about a boy and a girl walking beside a river of dark glass – the Spree. On Königstraße, across from the main post office, I decide to play hide and seek, and I duck in through the open doorway of an out-of-business restaurant with fake palms painted on the windows. In richer cities like Paris and New York, do the doors to ruined lives stay boarded up? Here, our homeless and unemployed knock padlocks off doors with old shoes and set their bruised suitcases down inside abandoned shops, their mop-haired kids in tow. We have an entire second city built by the wretched inside the bankrupt, and if you are willing to take a risk, you can look down into this underworld any time you like.

Six filthy mattresses smelling of mildew are spread on the floor, an equal number of old blankets piled neatly on top of one of them. In the far corner spreads a mess of dog-food cans and old newspapers. Behind a smashed-up table and under a copy of the *Morgenpost* from July, I find a black violin case. Inside is a letter addressed to Heinz from Greta and underlined copies of Erich Maria Remarque's two novels: *All Quiet on the Western Front* and *The Road Back*.

"Take a look at this," I tell Tonio eagerly, feeling kinship for Heinz. "Maybe he's performing in Alexanderplatz, playing Beethoven and Brahms for his supper."

After only a cursory look, Tonio sneers. "Remarque is an enemy of the people," he declares.

I don't even try to answer that.

A broken window at the back spreads a sheet of light across the floor and onto a wooden counter where the owners must have set out *Sachertorten* and other cakes in better times. Tonio doesn't fight me as I lead him there, and we don't say another word, because I've slipped my hand through his zipper. As I push him back against the counter, his eyes flutter close. I drop to my knees, eager to have his hands pressing down on my shoulders. The silence, dark and fragile, is ours. Even the clutter belongs to us, because it's proof that our need for each other can resist the vagaries of time and place.

I love the color of his penis – milky brown, but pinkish near its tip – and the silly way it hangs down when it's not yet fully hard. His balls contract like magic when I cup them, and he moans as if he's being flailed. Why didn't anyone ever tell me how easy it was to subdue a boy? I take the pearl of fluid at his slit onto my fingertip and bring it to the tip of my tongue. A small gesture, but it makes him look at me so hard that I know he's my prisoner.

"Am I to be a part of the new Germany?" I ask Tonio.

A swooning young man – his head arched back and neck straining, his fingers digging into my shoulders – who can still laugh. What more could any girl want?

"Please, Sophie ... You're breaking me in half."

I love the thick, pungent taste of his need for me. And the size of his power.

After I've taken all he's got for me and he's shriveled back into a wrinkled acorn, I lick him clean, because I can't get enough of my new sense of adulthood, and because we both need to see what we might lose if we're not careful.

Sex as our detour around *the little man who shouts*, Tonio's contempt for Erich Maria Remarque, Georg's death and all the other things that might separate us. An unusual escape route, I think at the time.

Arm in arm, we amble up the long staircase of the New Museum to the second floor and head into the Engraving Rooms, where

Tonio stands me – hands again on my shoulders, but this time gentle – in front of a Dürer drawing of his mother.

"You need to see a real live Dürer if you are going to keep improving," he says by way of explanation, in an adult voice that's very impressive.

He takes a step back so I can look at it alone. This discretion is new to him. Maybe our devotion to each other is tugging him toward manhood.

According to the indication beside the sketch, it has been 418 years since Mrs Dürer posed for her son, and yet she is still peeking out at the world from beneath her headscarf – captured forever in a moment of wary anticipation. I step closer, into the field of silence and nervous emotion that her face creates in me. Can she be wondering something so unimportant as who is about to come in her front door? Will her husband demand his lunch and a stein of beer? Maybe her son is the one whose footsteps she hears, and he is about to show her his latest canvas. More exciting for her, of course, but at times it must seem that the rivalry between son and father for her attention will never end. I see that tug in different directions in her tightly sealed lips and straining eyes, and maybe it's why her son has drawn her midway between anger and laughter. *My Mother's Two Roads*, he might have called this sketch.

Strength appears in her gaze, as well – a glint of power, a dominance over herself and her home, and her son; though it's 1514 and Albrecht is already famous, she is aware she holds his heart in her hands. That's the womanly power she has, and that I am beginning to acquire over Tonio.

"I'll never be that good," I tell him when he steps beside me.

"You'll go as far as you can."

He holds my arm and kisses my neck. In his touch, I feel why

I've made only tentative attempts to draw him. I can't give form to Tonio yet – he's still too much a mystery to me, and too essential to my well-being to risk fixing on paper. A poor likeness – or even a good one – might be the magic that breaks our spell. No, I won't try to draw Tonio, not even after we're married. And what I *don't* sketch will remain sacred.

We walk back home in the early afternoon. By now, residents from all over the neighborhood have come to see the ruined flag – our first tourist attraction. I begin to believe that having Hitler around might finally put our dull little street on the map!

Tonio kisses me goodbye below Mr Zarco's window because he and his parents are visiting his aunt and cousins that afternoon. I soon strike up a conversation with a Jewish family from Dahlem, a neighborhood ten miles across the city. They were on their way to relatives when they spotted the flag. Their burgundy Ford is parked across the street and has drawn a crowd of screeching kids because the family's bearded old wolfhound, Pfeffer – sitting tall in the driver's seat – is happily licking the hands of anyone reaching inside the window.

"Sophele!" Mr Zarco suddenly calls down. "What a nice surprise!"

I shout up that I want his autograph, which makes him laugh with such pleasure that I'm proud of myself for the rest of that day.

"A good idea I had, no?" he calls down to me enthusiastically.

As I shout up my agreement, a skinny, spectacled photographer wearing a nametag saying that he works for *Der Stürmer* begins to snap away at our neighbor with a tiny black camera. Emboldened by the tourists around me, I step up to him. "Excuse me," I say, "but I don't recall Mr Zarco giving you permission to photograph him."

He gives me a look of violent disdain and goes back to his

work. My pulse races when I think of swatting the camera out of his hands, but I don't have the courage.

In such seemingly insignificant ways did I slip away from myself, I now realize. If only Rini had been with me; she'd have grabbed his damn camera and hurled it against a wall, then casually offered me a square of chocolate.

"Forget the mischief-maker," Mr Zarco calls down, flapping his hand. "He's harmless."

So it was that he, too, let his guard down.

As I would later be told by Mr Zarco and the Munchenbergs, sometime after midnight, three men throw bricks through Mr Zarco's window. Raffi and his parents hear the breaking glass and peer out their kitchen window in time to see them praising each other's aim. Raffi is sure they're wearing the brown shirts and flaring trousers of the S.A., the Nazis' private army.

Mr Zarco bursts out of sleep, terrified, then rushes to his window and sees the men laughing, then running away. He sits on the end of his bed, puts his head in his hands, and sobs as he hasn't since his wife's death, nine years earlier. After sweeping up the broken glass, he throws a towel over any tiny shards that might still be there and lays the bricks one on top of the other on his night table, next to his Yiddish copy of *A Midsummer Night's Dream.* He's shivering from the chilly wind rushing in through the shattered window, but he takes off his nightshirt, wanting the cold to wrap around his naked body, to feel the discomfort of a city – *his* city – becoming a castle under siege. When he slips back under his eiderdown, he imagines that he is snuggling with his wife and making a home for himself in her. From experience, he knows it is the only way he will be able to sleep.

He wakes three times during the night, and each time he is pleased that he has provoked a reaction from the Nazis. The brisk autumn wind now seems to confirm that he has acted bravely. Sitting up during his last bout of sleeplessness, he stares at a linden across Prenzlauer Allee as if its leaves and branches contain the answer to where all of Germany's political turmoil is leading. And he prays, his lips moving over the syllables as quickly as he can, as if to outrace destiny.

To my solemn disappointment, I sleep through all the excitement. Tonio does too.

Two policemen come the next morning to interview Raffi Munchenberg and his parents, and Mr Zarco. They take away the bricks as evidence of the crime. They also order our neighbor to remove his flag, alleging that he is creating a public nuisance.

He cedes to their wishes, but puts it back up on Tuesday morning. An emergency assembly of tenants reluctantly votes that evening to ask Mr Zarco to refrain from any overt displays of political opinions.

"I'm sorry, but the flag stays," he tells their delegation.

That's when Dr Lessing, who lives in the apartment opposite the old tailor's, says, "Until Germany resolves the Jewish question once and for all, it's best for you and your people to make no more trouble than you already have."

"Oh, is that right? Rest assured, Dr Lessing, I haven't even started making trouble yet!" Mr Zarco replies menacingly. "And I would advise you to keep out of my way." He then invites his guests to leave.

Papa was a member of the delegation and tells me all this before tucking me in. Now, he's not so sure that our old neighbor is acting sensibly. "Except in an emergency, individuals ought not to work alone or even in small groups," he says, speaking in that artificial voice that means he's quoting Marx or one of his other heroes. "Party leadership should determine the timing and manner of all protests."

"Maybe for Mr Zarco this *is* an emergency," I reply.

"It's my curse to have so quick-witted a daughter," he says, batting me playfully on the nose like a cat.

The police are back on Wednesday. In raised voices, they threaten to arrest Mr Zarco. And history repeats itself; he takes in his flag only to put it back out at sunrise.

Later that morning, as he walks to his small factory on Dragonerstraße, someone bumps into him from behind. Annoyed, the tailor turns around, and a man – slender, wearing a stylish woolen coat – whacks him in the gut with a plank of wood, breaking two ribs.

Mr Zarco falls to his knees, gasping. A second thug – overweight, with a double-chin and mustache – hisses that he is a parasite. He grabs our old neighbor's hair and tugs him face-down onto the sidewalk, so hard that his chin meets the pavement with a thud. For a time, Mr Zarco is unsure as to where he is. The last thing he recalls is the word *Jew* whispered in his ear as if it were composed of heavy sand. Is he awake or dreaming?

At the Augusta Hospital, doctors in the emergency room bandage Mr Zarco's broken ribs. A nurse stitches up the deep gash on his chin. Feeling the tug of the string, he decides it's delightful being helpless in a woman's hands again.

The next afternoon, while Mr Zarco is snoozing, a cleaning woman lifts his tweed coat off the chair it has been resting on, and page two of the current issue of *Der Stürmer* tumbles out of the pocket. It's folded in four, and when she opens it up, she discovers a photograph of him has been printed near the bottom. She puts it on his night table for safekeeping. Stirring from the sound of her footsteps a few moments later, Mr Zarco reaches for his water glass, and his hand brushes against the newsprint. Sitting up, he sees himself leaning out his window next to the ruined swastika and reads the caption: *A Jewish parasite on Prenzlauer Allee in Berlin desecrates our glorious flag.*

The thugs must have identified him from this clipping and stuffed it in his pocket to be certain he understood that they were avenging his affront. But at least a dozen flags were shredded all over the city, so why did *Der Stürmer* print only Mr Zarco's picture?

A few days later, when I see the photograph, a tremor shakes me, because I'm thinking: *No matter what else he does in his life, Mr Zarco will always be on page two of issue Number 42 of that wretched newspaper and the Nazis will always know where he lives.*

K-H, Mr Zarco's photographer friend, knocks on our door that evening and reassures us that our upstairs neighbor is recovering well. My mother brings him a cup of the coffee she's just made. K-H wears red suspenders and a white bow tie. Very classy. And today, his cologne smells of violets.

"Isaac is already complaining about the *chazerai* that the hospital calls food," K-H tells us, laughing in the relieved way of people who've been crying. "You understand?"

"No," my mother says, because she isn't used to his deaf-person's voice or his Yiddish, so I translate *chazerai*, pig-food, into German; it's a word Rini uses all the time.

Gazing at me over his steaming cup, he says in a somber voice, "Sophie, Isaac wanted me to tell you that you'll have to water his plants until he comes home."

"His plants?"

"He said you agreed to help – to water his pelargoniums whenever he was away."

Tears of gratitude flood my eyes. Worse, I can't assemble a voice to explain myself.

"Didn't you hear? Mr Zarco is going to be fine," says Papa, pressing reassuring lips to my cheek. Mama sits beside me and combs my hair with her fingers.

When I've calmed down, I lead K-H to Mr Zarco's apartment. The photographer asks me about my favorite subjects at school. He speaks in short sentences to better manage all those words he cannot hear. I talk about Frau Mittelmann, but my words float over the image of Mr Zarco lying face down in his own blood.

"Sophie ...?" K-H is holding the front door open for me. Empty of guests, the sitting room is a landscape of books. The Persian rug is gone, too, revealing a dark parquet floor. I feel like a child in a fairy-tale forest, facing the unknown alone. I'd like to knock every last volume off the shelves. Destruction as a way to prove that nothing now can ever be the same.

And Tonio sympathizes with these hooligans ...

My face must give away my despondency, and K-H pours a little schnapps into a shot glass for me. "Drink this, sweetheart," he says as if it's an order, and as the burning descends into my belly, he adds cheerfully, "Isaac won't be stopped by broken ribs. Now, I'm going to leave you for a minute. I have to pack a bag for him in there." He points to the bedroom. "Isaac needs something to read. And he needs more tobacco. So you just water the plants and stop worrying." He plucks his suspenders and smiles handsomely.

Am I evil for wondering about what his penis looks like? "I'm all right, just do what you need to do," I assure him.

Four pink and white pelargoniums huddle under the windows in the sitting room, as quietly exuberant as Mr Zarco himself. They've been planted in canary yellow ceramic pots and arranged on a slate platform. I squat down by them and pull off the wilted flowers, wanting the plants to be perfect for his return. I find a rusted iron watering can under the sink in the kitchen.

When the flowers have soaked up all they can, I pass by the guestroom on my way to Mr Zarco's bedroom. My first look at Wonderland. Twenty blue and green glass fish – each the size of my hand – are dangling from the ceiling, spreading colored shadows around the room, which is a treasury of paintings and drawings. A watercolor of a city of domes and minarets catches my eye first. It's painted in browns and grays under a blue-blue sky, as if even bright sunlight cannot lift the gloom from the city. Istanbul, Mr Zarco will later tell me.

Just above it is a drawing of a bride and groom soaring through the air. Behind the love-struck couple is a cockeyed village centered by a garlic-bulb Orthodox church. My first Chagall. I will study it many times over the coming years, and what never ceases to amaze me is the sense that the artist has reproduced an entire world in a five-by-seven sketch. It's one of the works that changes my life.

Near the window is the drawing that becomes my favorite, however. It's an Otto Dix portrait of a slender, kindly-looking gentleman standing by an open window and wearing an elegant but threadbare coat. The man, in his sixties, is aware he is being sketched, and his lips are pursed in gentle amusement. His long, spidery hands are beautiful – the hands of a father who writes weekly letters to his faraway children with an antique pen, I fantasize. It's his goodness that the artist has sought to capture – I'm sure of it. And I place his name in a special spot in my memory when Mr Zarco tells it to me a few days later: Iwar von Lücken, a German poet and friend of Mr Dix.

As I step into the doorway of Mr Zarco's bedroom, K-H

waves me in. Only one painting is on the walls – a watercolor of a shimmering topaz-colored forest under the purple sky of dusk. The trees seem to be made of fire. Like a premonition of destruction – or rebirth.

Below the painting is a mahogany desk covered by a blotter of faded green felt. On it are three notebooks of black-and-white checked oilcloth, like those used by schoolchildren.

"Sophele," K-H says gently, coming up to me, "I wanted to say something to you before. This country of ours is going through a difficult period, but everything will be all right in the end." He kisses my brow. "You're too young to worry. Live your life."

What good luck I've had to meet such a considerate man, I think, but he seems to have forgotten that I'm at an age where nearly every experience can grow thorns.

"Now the disagreeable part," he says, wrinkling his nose. "The flag has to come down."

"No, please. If you remove it, then Mr Zarco's protest didn't mean anything."

He tilts his head as if weighing his options. "No, next time they might throw firebombs. Or murder him, like they did Georg. We can't take the chance."

"Did you know Georg well?" I ask, and when he nods, I add, "Did you like him?"

"Yes, though he wanted to use violence against the Nazis. I wasn't so sure."

"Is Mr Zarco against violence?"

"He's not sure either."

"And Vera?"

K-H laughs, then crosses himself as though warding off evil. "I'd never presume to speak for Vera." He brings his fist down on his head like Buster Keaton. "She'd clobber me."

So maybe Georg was murdered by the Nazis because he wanted to start using violent tactics against them. "Do you really think Georg was strangled?" I ask. "I mean, there were no signs of a fight."

He shrugs. "Maybe I'll show you the pictures when you're a bit older – if your parents give me permission, that is. Then, you can make up your own mind."

"What pictures?" I question.

"Vera was the one who found Georg dead. She had me take photos, because she wasn't convinced the police would investigate properly. She wanted proof of those swastikas drawn on him. She was very upset, as you can imagine."

"And where are the photos now?"

"Isaac has them."

"Do you know where he keeps them?"

"Yes," he grins, eyeing me suspiciously, "but I'm not going to tell you. We probably shouldn't even be talking about these things."

"K-H, I'm fifteen years old," I declare. "And ... and I knew Georg. So I think I have a right to see the pictures, especially because I'm worried about Mr Zarco and what's going to happen to him and ... and all the Jews." Seeing that he's still going to turn me down, I add, "My parents let me see my father's mother in her casket when I was only twelve. I didn't get the least bit upset." That's a lie, since I spiraled down into nightmares for days afterward, but it's in a good cause.

"Are you sure?"

When I nod, he heaves a sigh of resignation. Men can be such pushovers.

Mr Zarco keeps the photos in an envelope in his desk drawer. The first is of Georg's pale and slender face. His cheeks show a dusting of whiskers, and I'm struck by his high, flaring eyebrows, which seem too bushy for so thin a man. A swastika reaches its evil arms across each cheek, like a grasping spider. A smaller one sits at the center of his forehead. There are no marks on his neck.

I catch Hansi wondering about his reflection

Georg looks older than I remember him, but he was in makeup then, dressed as Cesare.

The second picture is of his hands, a rushed, uneven swastika in each palm. I'd bet the killer made these ones last – as an afterthought, while fearing being caught. So maybe the murder wasn't planned.

"Was it creepy taking pictures of a dead man?" I ask K-H.

"No, I'm used to it. I was a police photographer for several years."

As he goes to the window to take down the spaghetti flag, I rush to him and reach out for his shoulder so he'll turn to me. "K-H, even if the rest of Germany is stuck in the Middle Ages, this is Berlin. Mr Zarco should be able to do what he wants to here."

He shakes his head. "That's the point, Sophie – he can't. Not anymore."

CHAPTER FIVE

I go to bed early that night, my thoughts tangled in my speculations about Georg's murder until Mr Mannheim begins playing his cello in the apartment house directly across the street. I toss off my eiderdown and go to the window. His yellow curtains are drawn tight. The cautiousness of a musician who lives in a country where people are no longer safe in their own homes.

Hansi is still asleep, so I ease the window open and pull up my chair so that I can lean on the sill; I need the reassurance of music. If Tonio were here with me, we'd have our eyes closed and be holding hands, floating together in the darkness.

Mr Mannheim's devotion to Mozart and Telemann unites all of us in our neighborhood, and a good many people I know are likely to be listening to him at this very moment, because every night at nine, and earlier on weekends, this man whose face none of us has ever knowingly spotted picks up his bow and sets to putting the universe in order again. Whether he is aware of it or not, Mr Mannheim's message is this: the world has chords that obey physical laws, and scales that cannot be altered no matter what Hitler says, and ways of modulating between keys that are so gloriously unpredictable that maybe – just maybe – life will get better and not worse: Tonio may come to his senses; my mother will discover she needs to be kinder to me; Hansi will learn to peel potatoes efficiently; Georg's murderer will be caught; and Mr Zarco's ribs will heal perfectly. And I'll get all the moussaka I can eat.

Clouds glide past the moon, as radiant as those in a dream or myth. It is as if I am seated at the center of a city that is showing me its innermost workings, as well, because I can see for the first time that my neighbor is not working alone. Alongside him is the long-haired violinist who plays excerpts from the Brandenburg Concertos outside the Villa Klogge and the blind accordionist who sits on a bench in Kurfürsten Platz every Sunday morning, bellowing out *chansons d'amour*, his hands in fingerless leather gloves. Despair is not our only choice, they tell us, and beauty is a simple thing.

"They looked like Laurel and Hardy," Mr Zarco tells me.

I'm sitting by his bedside in the hospital. Deep pouches sag under his eyes and his lips are cracked, but he swears he hasn't felt this good since he fainted at a spa in Baden-Baden from the scalding water and sulfur fumes.

He's wearing blue flannel pajamas, frayed at the collar and with holes at the elbows. The doctors are keeping him under observation until tomorrow. I've just asked him to describe his assailants. I'm armed with my sketchbook, which sits on my lap, and my box of Czech pencils. My plan is simple: once the police have my drawing, they'll be able to identify the men who attacked him and track them down. I'll be a hero.

"Be serious," I tell him. "What did they really look like?"

"I *am* serious," he assures me. "Imagine Laurel and Hardy as grimy pickpockets." He holds up his hand as if he's swearing before a judge.

"I'm fifteen," I say, as if that's impressive. "You can tell me the truth."

"*Mazel tov*," he says, scratching the gray whiskers on his chin. "Sophele, don't you have to *be* somewhere?"

"Like where?"

"Like school!" he bursts out.

"Cancelled for the day," I lie. In point of fact, I bribed Rini with two strings of licorice into telling Dr Hildebrandt that I had to leave early because Mama was ill. I'll bring the principal a forged note from my father tomorrow.

"Why would school be cancelled?" Suspiciousness reduces Mr Zarco's eyes to slits.

"How should I know?"

He frowns but doesn't insist I leave. A benefit of his not being related to me.

"Laurel hit me first," he begins. "Then Hardy knocked my head against the pavement. What they did after that, I can't tell you." He sighs with gratitude. "I was in dreamland, *Gottze dank*," he says in Yiddish, meaning thank God.

I ask him to describe what they were wearing. He's better on clothing than faces. He even remembers the wooden buttons on Laurel's coat.

"I have a tailor's memory," he explains.

A nurse brings lunch. While Mr Zarco is munching away, I make good use of my pencils. Every time I look up at him, amusement blooms in his eyes. But he's got a big surprise in store because Papa took Hansi and me to see Laurel and Hardy in *The Music Box* not too long ago.

"Some Linzer torte?" he asks me when he's finished his schnitzel. He takes the tart out of its box with infinite care, as if it's a diamond tiara, and eases it onto his tray.

"No, thanks. I'm sketching Laurel's coat. Then I'll be done."

"Heidi is Berlin's number one baker," he adds seductively. "Her *crème pâtissière* is ..."

"Can't you see I'm working?" I interrupt. And doesn't he realize I'm trying to make up for refusing to accept the coat that he and Vera planned to give me? Even intelligent people can be so thickheaded.

Seeing it's best to ignore me for the moment, he gobbles down his piece of torte, licking the raspberry compote off his fingers like Hansi. I wait until he's lit his pipe and leaned back against his pillow with his hands behind his head, the picture of masculine satisfaction, then hold the sketchbook up for him.

"So, you're going to be an artist!" he says triumphantly, as though he's just spotted my destiny. "Let me see that."

He studies the drawing keenly, holding it away from his face at different distances, which pleases me. Then he hands the sketchbook back to me and wipes the crumbs from his blanket onto the floor. If a cleaning lady didn't sweep his room every morning, it would look like a parrot's cage.

"Laurel was more of a *shlemiel*," he says, and seeing I'm stumped, he adds, "A man who trips over his own feet. Or who gets shat on by pigeons. This *shlemiel* looked like he didn't bathe. And the lapels of his coat were wider than the ones you've drawn."

I refine my portraits according to Mr Zarco's observations, though he is very hazy on Hardy. After another half hour, my likenesses are as good as they're going to get.

"Not bad," he says, adding with mock seriousness, "I guess it takes a girl with a criminal mind to be able to draw hoodlums."

I sidestep that criticism with an important question. "Were you the one who thought of shredding swastikas and putting them out all over the city?"

"Yes."

"Who knew about your plans?"

"Only the members of The Ring."

"You're sure?"

"Yes, why?"

"No reason," I lie, because I've just concluded that the editors of *Der Stürmer* must have known that Mr Zarco conceived of the protest or they would have photographed someone else. Which means that there must be a traitor in The Ring who gave them that information. "Mr Zarco, will you show my portraits to the police?" I ask.

"Absolutely."

"What do you think they'll do with Laurel and Hardy if they catch them?"

"Give them a medal. Maybe a monument, too."

"This isn't funny!" I tell him, infuriated by his refusal to treat me like an adult.

"Stop criticizing me and help me sit up. I keep sliding back down and it's bad for the digestion."

I tug on his arm. That's doesn't work, so I get behind him and push. It's like trying to move a sack of potatoes.

When he's finally seated comfortably with his legs over the side of the bed, he rests his pipe on the side table. "Sophele, I know it isn't funny," he says morosely. "But the men who hurt me will not be caught. They're beyond the law."

"Just like whoever murdered Georg?" I ask.

"Perhaps. He reaches for his pipe again and inspects the bowl to keep emotion at bay. "It was wrong of me to let you waste your time with the drawing, but it was reassuring to have you sketching beside me. Please forgive me."

"I don't mind," I tell him.

His eyes look bruised and his hands sit defeated in his lap. At length, he says, "I'm feeling a little fragile now, and I need to think, so maybe you should go home."

But I won't give in to cowardice again. "No," I declare. "I'm staying with you." After he gives me a little smile of thanks, I say, "Mr Zarco, now that Georg is dead, will The Ring still have regular meetings?"

"Yes, we just need to re-structure a bit."

"Can I come to one? Not to join necessarily, just to watch."

"Absolutely not!" he declares. "A fifteen-year-old girl ... You must think I'm crazy."

Even when he is frowning, I can see how much he likes me, and how much life he has. "Don't move," I say, and I turn to the next page in my sketchbook and start to design the grid in which I'm going to draw his face.

"No you don't!" he exclaims, guessing what I'm up to. He throws his hand out as if to stop an onrushing tram. "I look like the Frankenstein monster. And in these pajamas ..."

"Just sit still."

He reaches up to shield his face again, peeking out through his fingers, and this time I allow myself to smile.

"Stop being such an *alter kacker*!" I tell him.

Laughing freely, he sits up straight and combs his hair back with his hands. And there it is again: the youthful radiance in his eyes that I want to try to draw.

The next day after school, Mama sits me down in the kitchen as if I'm in big trouble.

"I didn't do anything wrong," I rush to assure her. "I came straight home."

"I don't want you to visit Mr Zarco," she says.

"Is he back from the hospital?"

"Yes, but you're not to go near him. He's not right in the head." She pokes her forefinger into her forehead as if I'm in need of visual clues like Hansi.

"No, probably not," I agree. "I'll stay away from him, I promise."

Lying is so neat and clean. I love it.

I slip away to Mr Zarco's apartment early the next morning, on my way to school. He comes to his door in his flannel pajamas, his feet bare. He's carrying his coffee in an olive green cup that's badly chipped at its rim. His *Mesopotamian crockery* as he calls it.

"Sophele!" He hugs me gingerly, since his ribs are sore. It's reassuring to be folded inside the sleep-scents of his body and the faint odor of tobacco. It's like laying my head back on my father's pillow while he dresses.

"Thank you for watering my pelargoniums," he says with a big, welcoming smile.

"My pleasure."

"Do you have a few minutes?"

"Yeah, but then I have to go to school."

"So you've started going again!" he says in an astonished voice, as if my evil knows no bounds.

"I go when I'm in the mood," I reply, playing along.

We sit in his kitchen. His round table is covered with a stained pink tablecloth and several big leather-bound volumes, one of them open to a page of Hebrew writing held down with another Mesopotamian cup.

"What's that book about?" I ask.

"God's secrets. Do you drink coffee yet?"

"Of course." Another untruth, but lying has become my Promised Land. *Sophie Discovers the Joys of Subterfuge* would be my preferred subtitle for this section of my film.

"Milk?" he asks as he pours me a cup.

"Yes, please. What secrets does God have?"

He hands me the bottle of milk, then jumps up. "A great many. Be back in a moment."

As I hear books being moved, I sip my coffee, which tastes as bitter as aspirin. I'm wondering whether adults have damaged taste buds when a loud thud makes me gasp.

Mr Zarco comes back into the kitchen with a dusty black portfolio, his face a bit red. "Sit, sit ... Sorry about the racket."

Inside are watercolors. He lifts the first two away – portraits of a boy – and moves them carefully to the side of the table. "This is the one I wanted!" he exults, lifting up the third.

"Are those you?" I ask, pointing to the ones he's put aside.

"Yes, back in Biblical times." He hands me one of a tiny boy with red ears and spiky black hair, his eyes like silver marbles. He's hunched over a sewing machine, wary, his lips pressed together. An earnest, hardworking elf, but one who discovered some truths about the world too young.

"My mother painted me in my father's workshop. I was ten or eleven."

"You look small for your age."

"I shot up when I was thirteen. Mama started calling me *Grashupfer*." Grasshopper.

"Were you happy working for your father?"

"Yes, I was earning my keep. That was very important."

"You didn't like school?"

"I loved school, but the family ... Enough of ancient times, this is the one I wanted you to see."

A man who never complains about sacrifices. A truth about him I ought to write down in my diary.

He places the watercolor before me: a hushed village of stone houses nestled in a valley of golden fields and two strange windmill figures in the distance. The sky is washed pink and violet, with a fire-colored sun at the center, about to melt over a blanket of hazy hills. The sun has tender, almond-shaped eyes, as if it is sad to slip below the rim of the horizon.

"My mother felt watched at her grandparents' house – protected," Mr Zarco explains.

"Even at night?"

"Sophele, even in the coldest night of winter, *even in a blizzard*, we know the sun still exists. We know it's curling around the earth to come back to us."

"You think God is like that, too, don't you?" He grins appreciatively, so I add, "And that a blizzard is coming."

The next morning, I drop in on Mr Zarco again. His hair is mussed and he hasn't shaved. "The Lord receded into Himself so that there would be space for our world to come into being," he says urgently, then tugs me inside.

I write down that opening line on my palm a little while later, so I can remember it word for word. "What exactly does that mean?" I ask at the time.

"I wanted to tell you that the creative act requires withdrawal. Not just for God, but for us as well. And when we go inside ourselves, a poem might become a watercolor, or a feeling of dread might change into a frightening melody ..." He sees I'm puzzled and claps his hands together as if to break a spell. "Sorry," he says. "I tend to get lost sometimes. How about some coffee?" His eyes open wide, as though to entice me. I realize there must be times when he dives down to the bottom of himself and loses all view of the real world.

"Just half a cup," I reply. To make believe I'm an adult, I'll suffer the taste.

I use my thumbnail to pry free some crust on his pink tablecloth while he rinses out a cup for me. Dishes are stacked in the sink.

"Are you feeling all right?" I ask him.

"Why? Do I look that bad?"

"No, it's just ... When does your cleaning lady come?"

"Every Sunday." Looking at me over his shoulder, he adds, "Though sometimes there's hardly a thing for her to do, poor woman."

I raise my eyebrows skeptically.

"That was a joke!" he hollers. Dropping down on his chair, he pours us coffee, then stares at me over the rim of his cup, smiling, his eyes moist.

"Something special *has* happened, hasn't it?" I ask.

"I'm just happy. You see, I've been up all night praying. And now you're here. Sitting before me – an angel who has called me back from the Seventh Gate."

"What's the Seventh Gate?"

"Forget my *meshugene* talk. I get a bit *perdido*, lost, when I pray all night."

He rushes away to his sitting room and comes back with a large, slender volume. "Have you heard of Giotto di Bondone?" he asks. "He was a Florentine painter who lived in the fourteenth century." Not waiting for my answer, he adds, "These are reproductions of his frescoes in Florence and Assisi." He hands the book to me but stills my hand when I open the cover. "No, don't look at them now, Sophele. Keep this book as long as you want. Inside, you'll find a little gift."

"A gift? What for?"

"Do I need a reason to give a friend a present? All I ask in return is that you show me your drawings from time to time. I'm especially eager to see the one of me."

"It's not finished yet."

"No rush. When it's ready ..."

We talk of my schoolwork for a while and then my parents. I

admit for the first time to any adult that Mama drives me crazy. He doesn't try to give me advice, which is a relief.

"Did you get along with your son?" I ask him.

"Joshua?" He puts his pipe down. "Yes, though we had a bad quarrel when he wanted to go to war. And I was stupid enough to let him go. He died in Belgium. We never got his body back. He's still there."

"I'm sorry. Have you ever been to Belgium to see where ...?"

"No, I won't go," he interrupts. He tries to smile, and it's his effort that cuts through my spirit and leaves a trace of blood behind. "My wife went. So that she could forgive him."

"Forgive him?"

"For dying. When a child is killed in a war, and you know he shouldn't have gone, the anger ... it's like having a deep, cold ocean inside you. I turned to stone for seven years – just so I could live without feeling those depths ... those frigid depths pulling me down. My wife did too. Two granite people."

"But you came back to yourself."

"More or less. You're never the same. One day, you realize you're a person again, and you can see above the surface of the ocean where your son has died, and you swim to shore. You stand on land. You don't forget the ocean. But you walk on. Does that make any sense?"

"Yes." We sit in silence. He props his chin on his hands and stares off into his thoughts.

"Mr Zarco, my mother doesn't think it's a good idea for me to come here."

"Maybe you shouldn't," he says.

"But if I listened to her I'd never do *anything*!" I exclaim.

"Sophele, I won't forbid you from talking with me, but I think you should speak to your mother honestly about what you want."

"I will," I say, but I know I won't.

Outside his closed doorway, I sit on the stairs and discover he's slipped his mother's watercolor of a watchful sun and sleeping village under the cover of his book on Giotto. And on the back, he has written in pencil, "For Sophele, who knocked on my door and called me back home from a dangerous place ... and just in time!"

That evening, I study the reproductions of Giotto's frescoes in my bedroom alone, unwilling to show the book to my parents or even Hansi till I've made it all mine. Given my conversation about God with Mr Zarco, the image that catches my eye is of St Francis receiving the stigmata from Jesus, who is depicted as having wings. Four of them, in fact. At least that's what I think until I realize that Giotto has painted Jesus at two different moments in time, one pair of wings superimposed over the other. It never occurred to me that an artist could do that.

A few days later, I slip away again to Mr Zarco's apartment before school. When I tell him what I've discovered about Jesus in the fresco, he replies merrily, "Yes, in his own way, *Signore* Giotto was also a big fan of moving pictures!"

I then hand him the portrait I've done of him. His nose and mouth aren't quite right, but I've captured the depth in his eyes and their radiance. The hollow curves of his cheeks are also good.

He studies the sketch for a long time, squinting through his pipe smoke. "My God, do I really look so ancient?" he asks worriedly. Seeing the quandary he's put me in, he adds, "You don't have to answer that," then looks back at the drawing. "Excellent!" he finally declares. "Can I keep it?" he questions, grimacing like a little boy who's asked for something too expensive, and when I agree he kisses me on both cheeks. We sit at his kitchen table and he pours me coffee with the expression of a pleased host. "How long have you been doing sketches?" he asks.

"Ever since I was ten or eleven."

"Never landscapes or still lifes?"

"Only in class. I prefer faces. I find out about other people when I draw them."

"So what did you find out about me?" he asks eagerly.

"I don't know. Maybe that you're not as playful as you like people to think." Who would have ever thought I could talk like this to an adult?

"No, maybe not." He looks beyond me, seeing recollections of his son, perhaps.

Regret about my speaking so freely inhabits the silence between us. At length, I say, "I hope I didn't offend you."

"No, not at all." He smiles reassuringly at me.

"Mr Zarco, I'd ... I'd like you to tell me more about God," I say.

He pokes his tongue out with surprise. "Where'd that request come from?"

"No one talks to me about certain things that I think about. I've wanted to ask you ever since you told me that you thought the Lord was an ibis."

"Listen, Sophele, all you really need to know for now is that God is in every line you make. And even some of the lines you don't make."

"I don't understand."

"A good artist often alludes to what can't be said, to what exists only in silence."

I think of my vow never to draw Tonio. Maybe I'm alluding to him in every portrait I make – to my hope that a boy and a girl can love each other without reserve.

"Mr Zarco, is it true the Jews never make images of God?" I ask.

"Call me Isaac, please. We're permitted to depict God's hands, but never his face." He searches for the right words. "Our religion forbids the making of idols. In part, because the true God can never be known. We call this unknowable God *Ein Sof.* All we can see of Him are His emanations in our world, his attributes, which our artists have occasionally symbolized as his hands." Mr Zarco holds his coffee cup an inch over the table, casting a shadow below. "Imagine that you are as tiny as an ant and living in the tablecloth, right under my cup, and that you can't see anything outside the fabric. What would you think has just happened?"

"That a circle of darkness had descended over me."

"Exactly. The cup itself would be beyond your vision, so you would make the best interpretation you could. And any drawing you made of the circle of darkness would be accurate in terms of your own perceptions, but it would really be just a representation of the cup's capacity to make a shadow. Now, Sophele," he says, his enthusiasm making him point the stem of his pipe at me, "what's interesting is that people with great imagination might be able to envisage such an object, and the world it comes from, just from the size and shape of the darkness that has descended over them. They might even be able to deduce the presence of my hand holding the cup, from the shadow that it, too, is making. Exploring hidden worlds is one of the great joys of being an artist."

"I think I'm confused," I tell him.

He grins as if that's been part of his purpose. "All I mean is that you can journey as far as you want and make reference to the mysterious things you see along the way – to what isn't easily perceived in a face, for instance." He looks at my drawing of him as if it puzzles him. "Sophele, can I ask you to do something for me?"

"Anything," I reply, hoping to make up further for my betrayal of him and Vera.

"When you're sketching, try to imagine that the face in front of you is like the shadow of my cup."

"I don't understand."

"The human face may have quite a different shape and texture in another, higher world. Even another purpose. Just keep that possibility in the back of your head when you draw a portrait. Because I'd like to know more about the human form and what it means. You can be a kind of sentinel for me. My emissary in the territory of portraiture. And now, *meine Liebe*," he says, drawing in deeply on his pipe, "I've said way too many foolish things and kept you long enough."

"Wait, what else is in this higher world – besides faces, I mean?"

"Everything we can imagine and a great many things we can't." He turns his cup over and some drops of coffee drip to the cloth, creating a spreading stain. "The higher world is filled with receptacles ... with vessels containing things that spill over into our world. They hold all the hidden life that belongs to God – to God and to all of us."

"Does the Seventh Gate have to do with this?" I ask.

He raises his eyebrows questioningly.

"You said I called you back from the Seventh Gate," I explain.

He smiles at me, impressed by my memory, then stands up. "You, young lady, have to get to school. And I need a lot of sleep if I'm going to talk about such matters."

The next day, Wednesday, there's no answer to my knock on Mr Zarco's door. After school, my mother hands me a sealed letter addressed to me.

"You're getting a lot of private correspondence these days," she tells me suspiciously.

Inside my bedroom, I rip open the envelope and find a key and a note from Mr Zarco: *Sophele, I have to be away for three days. The pelargoniums have asked for your help. They want only you. I thank you on their behalf. Love, Isaac.*

Four days and two waterings later, Mr Zarco bicycles right past me on Prenzlauer Allee. This is during the strike of transportation workers that has halted all buses and trams, as well as the underground. His bicycle is old and rusty, and he is way too tall for it. Borrowed. Or rescued from a dump.

I call out, which makes him swerve into the curb and almost fall.

"Sophele!"

I run to him and we kiss cheeks. "Sorry for making you crash," I say.

"It's my fault. I haven't ridden a bicycle since the fifteenth century. It was a crazy idea."

"When did you get home?"

"Late last night. Thank you for watering the pelargoniums."

"Where were you?"

"It's better you don't know." Seeing that doesn't satisfy me, he adds, "At a friend's in Potsdam. Planning things."

"What things?"

"Strategies for ... for shredding more of Nazi ideology, so to speak," he replies.

"Where are you going now?"

"To work. Listen, this transportation strike has made me late. I have to get to my factory."

"On a Sunday?"

"I've a lot of paperwork to catch up on. Come by tomorrow morning if you can."

I agree to that, then watch him go on his wobbling way.

That afternoon, Rini and I accompany my father to a march of striking workers and their supporters. Mama has forced me to leave behind my red Communist Party scarf and made Papa swear to remain on the sidelines; now that German politics have changed, my mother fears that he'll lose his job if he remains politically active.

It's Sunday the 6th of November, and today the Communists are marching side by side with the Nazis, making a show of the first alliance they've ever formed. Papa told me the night before that we had to trust the Communist Party leadership's decision to form a united front with Hitler during the strike – proof that an atheist can still be a man of faith.

He rises up on the balls of his feet as the marchers file past us, waving to an occasional friend, radiating optimism. So young and eager Papa was – only thirty-four. "It's a wonderful thing to see so many Germans coming together for better working conditions," he tells me.

Rini looks at Papa skeptically and says, "But the march ought to be divided in two."

"Just this once it can't do any harm," Papa remarks, and he goes on to quote Marx on proper tactics for change, which may – under certain circumstances – even involve strategic deals with the enemy.

Or the devil, I can see Rini thinking. The way she makes my father defend himself – and reveal the bloody fangs hiding behind all his lovely Marxist theory – embarrasses me. *Can't she stop being a Jew for even a minute,* I think. Another small slide ...

Papa bumps in to acquaintances from high school and university whenever we're in a crowd and today is no exception. At such times, Berlin gives the impression of being the world's largest village. The second old friend he greets that afternoon makes my father so excited that he jiggles his hands as though he needs to pee.

"Sophie, this is Alfred Weidt!" he says gleefully. To my

uncomprehending stare at the corpulent little man's bespectacled face, he adds, "Our star gymnast!"

"Of course!" I exclaim, but I learn that my love for my father has not prevented me from forgetting Alfred.

Rini and I shake the former star's hand. His mountainous belly is padded with all the bratwurst and potatoes he's eaten since graduation and he's wearing a swastika armband. Rini and I look at each other out of the corner of our eyes.

"Alfred was the only one of us who could do an Iron Cross on the rings," Papa informs us, his voice deepened by pride.

I'd like to see him try now! I think nastily, but Rini gushes, "How wonderful!"

No matter how she over-dramatizes, she always remains believable. A natural gift.

"What are you doing with yourself these days?" Papa asks Mr Weidt.

"I took over my father's construction firm. And I'm organizing for the Nazi Party."

One piece of information too many, but Papa vaults over it expertly. "Are you married?" he asks.

"Yes, with two boys, Otto and Ludwig. Would you like to see their photographs?"

Without waiting for Papa's reply, which would be positive in any case, Mr Weidt reaches into his coat pocket for his wallet. It's black leather and monogrammed with his initials in gold Gothic lettering. Otto and Ludwig are handsome, of course, and Papa says so. Does he see a sumptuous dinner with his old friend in the palm court of the Adlon Hotel in his future? Maybe he hears my mother saying, *Pass the caviar, Freddi. And give me a little more French champagne* ...

Rini says the two brats look decidedly intelligent, too. "Like little Einsteins," she adds, to irritate Mr Weidt, since our most famous scientist is Jewish.

The former standout gymnast does some vaulting of his own, smiling sweetly at Rini, and then engages Papa in talk of old classmates.

Whispering in my ear, Rini says, "Soficka, if I ever show you my kids' photos, promise me you'll take scissors to them."

Many times in years since, I've remembered the feel of my best friend leaning against me, her hand squeezing my shoulder. It's as if she were trying to tell me – in between her words – to not give up on her no matter what, because we are soul mates.

Before rushing off to what he calls "pressing matters," Mr Weidt offers us swastika armbands from his leather case.

"Go ahead!" Papa says, as if I'm being rude for hesitating.

Rini and I take our gifts, and we thank Mr Weidt. Once he's gone, I ask my father what we should do with the armbands, and he replies, "We'll throw them out on the way home."

"I'm burning mine and dumping the ashes in the Spree," Rini tells us, dangling hers in the air as if it's a big insect.

"Why did we accept them?" I ask Papa.

"Alfred is an important man. His father's firm is huge. And besides, he's a good friend."

When I spot Rini's disappointment for Papa calling him a good friend, I feel a tingle in my gut that means the Semitic wall between us has now added several more rows of bricks.

That night, I draw Hansi while Papa reads to him in bed, and as I'm shading my brother's mouth, I see how constricted it is with silence. *It's been sealed in some higher world*, I think, but by whom – and how – I haven't a clue. Papa leaves the light on after he kisses us goodnight so that I can continue to draw my brother.

The boy doesn't mind. He just shuts his eyes and slips silently into his dreams, which are never very far away.

Sometime later, I place my sketchbook under my pillow and ease down on his bed behind him, and I watch the rise and fall of his breathing as if it's symbolic of time passing between us, of all we have experienced together, and he seems so much a part of me that I know I'll never be able to live without him. When I comb my brother's short blond hair he doesn't stir. He knows I'm watching over him. A big sister as a tender-eyed sun, high in the sky over the Hansi Universe. That must be why he puts up with me when I'm so mean.

And then a revelation: maybe wanting to help my little brother to speak freely about his inner world is the reason I first picked up a pencil and started to make sketches all those years ago. Perhaps it was my way of creating an intimacy between us that would convince him to trust me.

The next morning, I tell Mr Zarco about the distance coming between Rini and me.

"First, you're supposed to call me Isaac," he reminds me, his finger wagging. "Second, now that the Jews are under threat, she is going to test you from time to time, and you're going to have to be patient with her. And fierce as a dragon in her defense!"

"Why does everything have to be so complicated?" I ask.

"Because you are alive, *meine Liebe*."

What a stupid reply! I think, and I must give away my feelings, because he says, "Sip your coffee, and if you stop thinking I'm a *Dummkopf*, I might tell you about the Seven Gates ..." Sitting up straight, he clasps his hands together. "Have you ever wondered where you were before you were born? According to Jewish tradition, you were far away, in the most distant of the Seven

Heavens. This world is called Araboth in Hebrew, and it is where our souls reside before our birth and after death."

"What's it like there?" I ask, intrigued.

"I've never managed to sneak inside. Two powerful archons guard the gate and have always blocked my way."

"Who are the archons?"

"Angelic gatekeepers. Professional *nudniks*, nuisances, and not at all friendly to tailors from Berlin." He raises a fist over his head as if he's the hero in a Schiller play. "They will fight to the death to prevent any of us from entering their territory. To convince them to allow us inside, we have to speak a magic formula of sorts. And each of the Seven Heavens requires a different one."

"How do you get to Araboth in the first place?"

He leans across and presses his index finger to the center of my forehead. "You fly there inside your prayers." Sitting back, he adds, "The other day, when you came over, I'd been praying all night. And I managed to get through the first six gates, but the archons stopped me at the Seventh Gate because I didn't have the right formula. It's a good thing you came, because they might have subdued me. You stirred me from my prayers just in time." He gives me an admiring look. "You have good timing, Sophele, and that's a real gift."

"But why did you want to pass through the gate if it's so dangerous?"

"Araboth is also the heaven of prophecy. Anyone who ascends into it may see the future and even ask for a wish from the Lord. And He will grant it." Understanding my unspoken request, he grins. "So, you want to know my wish? I'll let you know it if you never reveal it to anyone."

"I promise."

He moves his chair around the table so that we're close

together and whispers into my ear, "I'd like the Lord to repair what has been broken here in our world – especially in Germany." Leaning back and speaking in his natural voice, he adds, "Imagine a stained-glass window that grows larger and more beautiful with each passing year. And that the window has living figures in it – us! Everything alive is inside in the glass, including you and me, and all the animals and trees. And everything glows ruby-red, blue, and green with the light that creates life and keeps us from death – God's light. But the window has recently become damaged. I can see many cracks. They need to be repaired before it starts to shatter."

"So where will you find the magic formula to get into Araboth?"

"Excellent question, Sophele. I've been looking in mystical books written by an ancestor of mine named Berekiah Zarco. I pray very hard and I read, and I look for the right incantation."

I recite for him the poem that K-H had sent me with his photographs from the Carnival Party: *Slumb'ring deep in everything, Dreams a song as yet unheard, And the world begins to sing, If you find the magic word.*

"Where did you learn that?" Mr Zarco asks, surprised and pleased.

"Karl-Heinz the photographer sent it to me."

"Good for him! And anyone can see you've already begun to hear a different sort of music – one that isn't for children."

"How do you know?"

"You're becoming a woman, which means your body is listening to a very powerful song. Sophele, even in Araboth, there is a music of a sort that you may someday be able to hear if you are quiet enough – and when you are a bit older."

"How much older?"

"Why be in such a rush? A lifetime of good things awaits you!"

"If you don't make it to Araboth in your prayers, is there any other way you can have your wish granted by God?"

"Yes, there may be one other way."

"By ... by dying, and having your soul ask after you're dead?" I question, chilled by the image.

"Sophele, this is not about *dybbuks* or *lezim*."

"What are they?"

"Ghosts and poltergeists."

"But you said Araboth is the place of the dead."

"It's the place for our souls, which do not die!"

He shuffles off to his sitting room, comes back with an old leather-bound book, and pages through it until he finds what he wants. The writing is Hebrew. I stand up to get a better look. Pointing to the top of the page, he reads, "'We consecrated the gate in Paris on the fifteenth day of the month of Shevat, just before the eating of the fruit.'"

"What's it mean?" I ask.

"A powerful kabbalist named Simon of Troyes consecrated a gate in Paris in 1342, during the holiday of Tu Bisvat, when Jews celebrate the Tree of Life. Down here," he says, pointing to the bottom of the page, "it's written that the gate in question is the left entrance to Notre Dame, where Adam and Eve are sculpted. The creation of the first man and woman is appropriate for the First Gate, after all. Now, if a righteous person walks through this entranceway during Tu Bisvat, with his or her heart and mind focused on the Lord, that individual will ascend immediately to the First Heaven. He need not speak any magic formula to the archons. Though he must be prepared with study for many weeks." Isaac closes his book and looks up at me cagily.

"But does it work?" I enquire.

"Absolutely!" he declares.

"How do you know?"

"I've walked through the gate."

"The one in Notre Dame in Paris?"

"*Oui, ma chérie*," he says, overdoing a French accent for the comic effect.

"*Quand?*"

"Sophele, it's getting late, and I think we've just used up all our French." He stands up and stretches his arms over his head. "I'll tell you about my travels some other time."

"But I want to hear about them now! You can't just stop in the middle."

"I think God will forgive me – *just this once* – for disappointing you. Now, before you go, tell me if you've been able to find out anything about how our faces might look in a higher world."

I describe my feelings while sketching Hansi the night before. He reaches for his pipe, plainly intrigued. While inspecting the bowl he asks, "So you think his mouth may have been sealed?"

"Why else would he have so much trouble talking to us?"

Fetching a pipe cleaner from a drawer, he asks, "And you think that your sketching his portrait on occasion may be helping ... helping to free him?"

"I hope so."

"Now that's something I need to think about. Alone," he adds, holding up his hand.

At the door, fear quickens my pulse. "Be very careful next time you reach the Seventh Gate," I say. "After all, my timing may not always be so good."

He agrees, obviously gratified by my concern.

I speak as if it's a real place. Maybe I'm losing my mind, too.

THE SECOND GATE

Two is the seer and the seen, the speaker and the listener, the troubadour and the song.

The second gate is selfhood and the instant of separation. Beyond its threshold lies Rakia, the Second Heaven, the temple of the stars, sun, and moon.

Two are good and evil, inside and outside, grief and joy, Mordechai and Esther. Two is the story spoken and heard.

But if they are not convinced even by these two signs and will not accept what you say, then fetch some water from the Nile and pour it upon the dry land; and the water that you take from the river shall turn to blood – Exodus 4.

Berekiah Zarco, The Book of Selfhood

CHAPTER SIX

Over the next weeks, I learn about Jewish tradition and lore during my early morning talks with Isaac. He speaks to me of fire-hurling archons, angelic scribes, and disembodied souls wandering the earth in misery – beings who seem to have been slumbering inside my imagination for years, ready for someone to nudge them awake.

When I tell him that, he says, "All the myths ever written are inside you – Adam and Eve, Noah and his Ark ... If they weren't, then all those ancient tales would simply shed their meaning, dry up and turn to dust."

On a day when I'm overwhelmed by all his crazy notions, he tells me that when I get confused I should remember that all important lessons are written on glass. Especially those in the Torah. "You have to look below the surface for the deeper meanings that are inscribed on a lower level, sometimes in the faintest ink."

"But why doesn't the Torah make the deeper meanings easier to read?"

"Would you want to give up your secrets easily? No, you'd give them up only to people you trusted."

"So who does the Torah trust?"

"Those who want to understand, Sophele, and who work at it – those who look in a mirror and who want to understand the mystery reflected back at them." Munching on some leftover challah bread, he adds, "And another secret I'll tell you is that the whole world around us is just like the Torah. We interpret everything we do and see. It's how we make sense of the world. And the greater your experience and more sensitive your mind, the more truthful and wondrous your interpretations will be."

Isaac and I always talk at his kitchen table, accompanied by the hissing of his old ivory-colored porcelain stove and its well-appreciated heat. One morning, after he's given me my first lessons in the Hebrew alphabet, he takes away our coffee cups to prevent spills and puts down an old leather case in front of me. "Open it," he says.

I find vellum manuscripts bound together with fraying string, the topmost illustrated with a proud peacock whose magnificent blue and green tail is falling luxuriously over a Hebrew title scripted in brilliant gold.

Undoing the bow, he hands it to me with a generous smile. The manuscript feels as though it's pulsing with life, probably because I'm so nervous. And its gold letters are so large and polished that I can see myself in them.

"The author wanted each reader to see himself in this book," Isaac explains. "To be a part of it, in a way."

"Is it a book of magic?"

"No, it's the story of a young man and his family. His name was Berekiah Zarco. He was an ancestor of mine and he wrote this in the sixteenth century. He was a kabbalist from Lisbon. The last one, as it turned out."

"What happened to him?"

"He moved to Istanbul after surviving a pogrom in Lisbon in 1506."

"So your ancestors are from Portugal and Turkey?"

"On my father's side. On my mother's, they're Germans."

"Can you speak Portuguese?"

"Claro, mas falo melhor uma forma medieval que se chama judeo-português ou ladino."

It's the first time I hear the gnashing of Portuguese. "What's that mean?" I ask.

"I said, 'Of course, but I speak a medieval form called Judeo-Portuguese or Ladino better.' In exile, the Portuguese my ancestors spoke got mixed with medieval Spanish of other Jews. It became a *tsimmis*, a big jumble."

"Say something I'll always remember ... written below the surface of the glass."

He touches his pipe stem to his cheek, pensive, then sits up straight and closes his eyes. *Isaac is a sorcerer posing as a tailor*, I think, and not for the last time.

"Abençoados sejam os que são um auto-retrato de Deus," he replies.

"So what's that mean?" I ask.

"It's the very last line in the manuscript you're holding. 'Blessed are all of God's self-portraits.'"

"God painted Himself?"

He laughs contentedly. "In a way of speaking, though the Torah says it differently. It says we were all created in God's image – all self-portraits. And the animals and plants, too. The same laws of creation that determine how you walk and talk also determine the color of a pelargonium blossom, even the spiral arms of the Milky Way. And I'll tell you something only a few people know ..." he whispers. "The only way we can get any idea of what the Lord is like is by looking at ourselves and all the things around us. By listening, touching ... by experiencing the world. You know what my papa used to tell me? 'The only eyes and ears God has are our own!'"

That notion seems to halt all my thoughts, and we don't speak for a while. He offers me some challah bread. A discovery – we can sit together without having to fill up the silence.

"Why is there a peacock on the cover?" I finally ask.

"Berekiah saw God most clearly in birds – in those creatures of light and air."

"And what's the title?"

"It's called *The Bleeding Mirror.** It's about the pogrom in Lisbon. Berekiah gives his interpretation of what it means on the very last page. Two thousand Jews were murdered, you know."

"So what did it mean?"

"Berekiah believed it was a warning for the Jews to leave Europe. Because the kings and bishops here would never let us live in peace ... which is why he and his family moved to Istanbul."

"But one of your ancestors must have come back to Europe."

"Papa. While he was traveling through Germany, he met my mother. They fell in love, got married, and ..." Isaac taps his chest, "a certain someone then came along. Though I can't help thinking at times that there must be some greater significance to Papa's returning to Europe."

I put down *The Bleeding Mirror* gently and pick up the second manuscript, which has a flower designed with black ink on the cover – six petals within a wheel.

"Why is there no title on this one?" I ask.

"Look more closely, Sophele. All the contours of the flower are made with tiny Hebrew letters – a technique called micrography. A different petal spells out the title for each of the six manuscripts that make up what Berekiah calls his *Six Books of Preparation.*" Isaac points to the topmost petal, which is more darkly inked than the others. "This one here says *The Book of Birth.*"

"Why birth?"

---

* Published in English as *The Last Kabbalist of Lisbon*

"Birth is our first gate." He opens his hand. "We enter the world. The Seven Gates of the universe are at work inside our bodies, of course."

"And our second gate?"

He lifts up the second manuscript and points to the petal to the right of the one whose letters he's just deciphered. "When a young girl like you first recognizes herself in a mirror, she passes through the Second Gate. She knows she is alive. So this manuscript is called *The Book of Selfhood*."

"And the third?"

"That's the gate you're walking through at the moment. The Gate of Union. You are becoming a woman and you want to join together with another person."

"What gate have you reached?"

"Me?" He laughs as though surprised and gratified by my question. "I've passed the sixth and am hurtling on my way toward the seventh like a comet."

"So each of these manuscripts is about one of the Seven Gates?"

"Only the first Six."

"What about the Seventh?"

"When I inherited the manuscripts, there was no text about the Seventh Gate. And my father didn't remember there ever being one. Maybe it was lost, though lately I've begun to suspect that Berekiah didn't write one – and for a very good reason."

"Which is?"

"That any intelligent young girl like you who had access to the manuscript and who followed Berekiah's instructions for reaching the Seventh Gate might be able to rise into Araboth. She could see what's in store for the world and have a wish granted by the Lord. That could prove disastrous – even for God. I think that's why Berekiah makes just two direct references to the Seventh

Gate. Both of them are in his difficult-to-decipher code – deep under the surface of the words written under the glass. Though he may have written other things so far down that I haven't been able to find them yet."

"What's he say about it?"

Isaac turns to the second-to-last page of *The Book of Memory*, which is about the Sixth Gate. "Here's the clearest reference Berekiah gives the reader ... 'The Seventh Gate opens like wings as we begin our conversation. It speaks with a million bleeding voices and yet just one. Only he who hears the voices with the eyes of Moses may enter Araboth.'"

"It sounds a bit like a riddle."

"It is in a way – the most important riddle in the world. And on the last page, there's a bit more. Listen ... 'On the arch of the Seventh Gate you shall write my final words, and you shall hold on tight to the silver winds of *mesirat nefesh*, and as you do the winds shall cease to cause your hands to tremble. The music you hear will be the souls speaking in Araboth, readying to greet you. Fear not the shadows that come to pursue you, because these shadows are light. And fear not how you shall be cast into the earth, because that fall is the ascent you have so long been seeking. Welcome the fires around you because they mean life for those who come after you."

Isaac's voice is like none I've ever heard – deep and sure. As though every word he speaks might have the power to create life or destroy it. When he talks to me like this, it often even seems that the words between us have shed their usual veils and become as tangible and generous as the gleam in his eyes when I've understood him. When I think back to those days it seems as if the light coming in his kitchen window from the city that we both loved were telling us: *Remember this time and this place, for you may never have this sense of discovery again.*

And so sadness, too, filled our conversations on occasion – the sadness of knowing that our hours together would someday be only a distant memory.

"What's *mesirat nefesh*?" I ask.

"Hebrew for the willingness to sacrifice oneself." Isaac reaches for *The Bleeding Mirror* and opens it to the Preface. "Berekiah mentions it here. 'The occult power of *mesirat nefesh* rests in the tradition among kabbalists to risk even a journey to hell for a goal that will not only help to heal our ailing world but also effect reparations in God's Upper Realms.'" He lays the book down. "You see, Sophele, whoever desires to pass through the Seventh Gate must be willing to sacrifice himself."

"Do Berekiah's manuscripts tell you where the first Six Gates are?"

"Yes. He researched for years in the writings of other kabbalists in order to find them. The First Gate is in Paris, as I've told you. In the façade of Notre Dame."

"But a cathedral isn't for Jews."

"All the gates were consecrated on the façades of churches." He gives me a cagey look. "Putting them on synagogues might seem more natural, but that would have been short-sighted, because our temples have been destroyed so often by Christian kings. So they were consecrated where no one would guess, but where they'd be easy to find for anyone who knew where to look, and safe from destruction."

"And the other ones?"

"The Second is at the Cathedral in Barcelona, the Third at the Cathedral in Worms, the Fourth at the Ambrosian Basilica in Milan, the Fifth at the Prague Cathedral, and the Sixth at the Church of Mary Magdalene in Lisbon. One must walk through each of these gates before trying to go through the Seventh. Unless ... unless the aspirant is a sage, in which case he needs no geographical or physical help."

"Have you gone through all the geographical gates?"

"Yes."

"And the Seventh ... don't you have any idea where it is?"

"Berekiah gives a veiled clue that it was somewhere in southern Europe, perhaps Spain, but that it was destroyed and never re-consecrated. He could be wrong, however. Maybe it's in London or Budapest, Rhodes, Dubrovnik ..." He opens his hands as though presenting me with a gift. "Or perhaps even here in Berlin! In any case, one thing is certain – until it's found, my only hope of passing into Araboth is in my own head."

On a Friday afternoon when we're not in the mood for Jewish studies, Isaac tells me more about the guests at his Carnival party, including Rolf, Heidi, Vera, K-H, Marianne, and Roman, the blind tightrope walker. It turns out that Julia – the Tunshan woman – is an expert on herbal medications, and she has her own shop next to the New Synagogue.

Nearly all of the friends he invited to the party were members of The Ring. By now, I'm convinced that one of them informed the editors of *Der Stürmer* that he was behind the shredding of swastika flags across Berlin. And told the Nazis that Georg was ready not only to take up arms but also to make public the names of party members who'd accepted Raffi's bribes.

Isaac may suspect this, too, so I'm listening for doubt or mistrust in his voice as he talks of his party guests, but I hear none.

On my request, we go to visit Georg's apartment on Schlesische Straße, a block south of the Spree and the brick, medieval turrets of the Oberbaum Bridge. "He could see both sides of the river from his bedroom window," Isaac tells me, pointing to a fourth-floor, corner apartment. "He loved the view."

As I gaze up, I see Georg dressed in Cesare's scarlet cape, his eyes ringed by kohl. Was his murderer's costume a conscious reference to his decision to start using violence against the Nazis?

"How many people are in The Ring?" I ask.

"About thirty."

Too many to interrogate individually. Maybe I should begin by talking to Georg's neighbors.

"I want to know more about how you're planning to fight the Nazis," I say.

I'm hoping that Isaac hears in my voice – and sees in the determined way that I don't turn away from his questioning eyes – that I'm not simply curious. *We're friends now, and friends need to protect each other* ... That's what I want him to understand in a way beyond words.

Glancing down at his watch, he mumbles to himself, "Almost time to go." Looking at me in a beseeching manner, he says, "Sophele, would you mind coming with me to an appointment I have? I'd like to talk with you along the way."

Amidst the sliding and shifting of the underground, Isaac talks to me about The Ring as if I'm his equal. And from now on that becomes his way with me – to speak to me as if I'm adult enough to understand his full range of emotions and thoughts when we're alone and to be more elusive when we're in the presence of Vera and his other friends.

I learn right away that destroying Nazi flags, though symbolically important, was just a sidelight to The Ring's more pressing work.

"Our efforts have to do with the military build-up Hitler has called for," Isaac whispers to me as we pull out of the Alexanderplatz Station. "He's going to need vital minerals and metals from overseas, and know-how, too."

"So you think he'll become Chancellor."

"The signs are pointing in that direction."

We talk in hushed tones, because the carriage is filled, though that doesn't stop some of the riders around us from trying to eavesdrop – this is, after all, the busybody capital of the world.

"So we're preparing the ground to ask key foreign governments to deny Hitler the raw materials he'll need," Isaac explains to me.

"An embargo?"

"Yes. We've recently started presenting our point of view at various embassies, though it hasn't been easy. Very few ambassadors will see us. Even those who should know better ... the British and French, for instance. They think that Hitler is not the threat we know him to be. They're certain he'll be restrained by the other political parties."

Do words whispered far under the surface of a city take on special meaning? I soon begin to see what he meant about the shattering of our world. "So you think Hitler isn't going to be gone in a few months? And that there'll be a war?"

"Unless a great many of us act now to prevent it."

Twenty minutes later, Isaac hooks his arm around mine as we pass through the chilly shadows cast by the linden trees in Savigny Platz. I feel privileged to be walking beside him. To the west, the sun peeks through some clouds just above the roof of a handsome brick building under a curtain of thick ivy. It is still only early December – not even winter – yet Berlin is already making its descent into an unforgiving darkness.

Our destination is the Portuguese Embassy at Kurfürstendamm, 178. Isaac has told me that each member of The Ring has been assigned at least one embassy. The Portuguese and Turkish ones were the obvious choices for him, since he's fluent in both languages. Roman has been given Italy, and Vera, who grew up speaking Spanish with her mother, chose Spain. Rolf and Heidi have taken Holland. Before he died, Georg had made visits to the English,

French, Polish, and Czech embassies, since he was conversant in all those languages. He had been given some friendly – but off-the-record – responses, particularly by the English cultural attaché.

Might he have been murdered because the Nazis learned he was having some success?

"What will Hitler need from Portugal?" I ask Isaac as he purchases tobacco at a kiosk on Kantstraße. He points up to the S-Bahn tracks, which are above ground here. "To make steel for train tracks and weapons Hitler will need wolframite ore. Portugal is where Germany already gets it, and he'll need as much as they're willing to sell him. If war breaks out, he may also try to use Lisbon and Porto as bases for his operations in the Atlantic."

"And the Portuguese Ambassador ... has he been friendly to you?"

Isaac makes an irritated puffing sound. "So far, I've spoken only with his assistant for trade. I'm meeting with him again today. *He* thinks the Nazis have some fine ideas but that they go too far when it comes to the Jews, and *I'm* supposed to be grateful for that concession. You see the ignorance I'm up against? So I'm trying to educate him about the consequences of Hitler's policies. At the same time, I'm working on his Turkish and English counterparts."

"So you've taken over England from Georg?"

"Yes, though my English is an embarrassment." He gazes up as if asking forgiveness from God. "Every time I go to the embassy, I sweat buckets because I'm petrified I'll make some terrible gaffe. But I've no choice. We need to set the stage for an embargo."

"Maybe you should invite the Portuguese cultural attaché to a meeting of The Ring, so he can see how strongly all of you feel about the Nazis ..."

Isaac nods appreciatively at me. "I thought of that, Sophele, but I think that Vera and some of the others might just scare him off."

A couple blocks before our destination, Isaac stops talking. His eyes grow worried, as if he's reached an impasse within himself. On the sidewalk in front of the Portuguese Embassy, he takes my head in his hands and kisses my cheeks. "Thank you for coming with me. You won't have trouble getting home by yourself, I hope."

"I could find my way home blindfolded. But are you all right?"

"I confess, Sophele, there are many things I may not be capable of doing. If Georg were still here, this would all be easier."

As Isaac starts away, he looks so tired and lost that I realize what ought to have been obvious to me – even confident adults can sometimes be the most fragile of creatures.

The next day I return to Georg's apartment house. My knocking on every door soon pays off; a tiny, elderly Lebanese man named Habbaki tells me that although he heard no quarrel during the days prior to the murder, on the evening before the body was found, a truck was parked outside. Mr Habbaki, who lives below Georg's apartment, invites me in and pours me a cup of mint tea from a tall silver pot. Clutching a red silk pillow over his lap, as if for protection, he says, "Georg and a couple of his friends carried a round table up the stairs and into his apartment. They came in and out a few more times, but I didn't look to see what else they had with them."

"Could you see the faces of his friends?" I enquire.

"No, it was already dark. But there was a gigantic man wearing a black headscarf and cloak. My goodness, he must have been nearly seven feet tall."

It's not hard to figure out who that must have been. But was it just a coincidence that Georg received new furniture the day before he was murdered?

Early that evening, I visit Isaac, who has already changed into his fraying pajamas. When I tell him about the giant who helped

Georg move his furniture, he narrows his eyes to suspicious slits. "How do you know all this?" he asks.

"I talked to Mr Habbaki, Georg's neighbor."

"Sophele, the Nazis do not like snoops whose fathers are Communists. You better stick to portraits. Much safer."

"The Nazis have much more dangerous Berliners to spy on than me – as you well know. So were you one of the people taking furniture into Georg's apartment?"

He crosses his arms over his chest as if he's not going to tell me anything. He seems to have reconsidered his trust in me. I'm hurt, which is why I speak more harshly than I intend when I say, "So you and Vera helped Georg. Anyone else?"

"Sophele, I know you're annoyed, but I worry about you."

"Everybody is always worried about me. You, Mama, Papa ... The only one who lets me get on with my life is Hansi."

"So what makes you think there's a connection between Georg's furniture and his death?"

"Nothing. For now, it's just a curious fact."

"Good, then you can stop snooping."

"I can't."

"You can and you will!" he bellows like a tyrant.

He has never raised his voice to me before. I'm awe-struck. And near tears.

"Sorry, Sophele," he says, gazing down glumly. "But now is not the time ..." His voice cracks. He rubs his pipe stem across his lips – a gesture of distress.

Someone else is dead, I think, terrified it may be Vera. "What's happened?" I ask desperately.

"Sit with me and we'll talk."

He leads me into his kitchen. Once we're seated at his table, he says, "I've had some bad news."

The words tumble out of him: Heidi has had a miscarriage and was rushed to the hospital, where she became gravely ill. She had to have an operation a few days ago because her hemorrhaging might have caused her to bleed to death.

"But she's okay now?" I ask hopefully.

"Yes."

He tries to smile and reaches for my hand. I love the warmth of him, and his ease with me. And I realize that being with a pajama-clad, pipe-smoking Jewish sorcerer and talking with him about adult matters is my refuge from my life. Even Georg's murder serves – in some perverse way – to take my mind from Tonio's delight in Hitler, my mother's disappointment in me, and all I'd like to change. Though now I have another, much more substantial, reason to want to find the murderer – protecting the most unusual person I've ever met.

Over the next weeks, however, my difficulties keep adding up and tugging me away from Georg's death. Worst of all, as we enter into the new year of 1933, Rini and I have a rancorous quarrel, breaking months of giggling solidarity during which we've managed to keep politics at a distance.

Our troubles begin when we read in the *Morgenpost* about Albert Einstein and Erich Maria Remarque fleeing Germany, which prompts me to tell Rini – in a voice of supreme authority – that the two men might have acted hastily. Standing together in our schoolyard, I tell her, "I think they should have stayed and fought."

"Who do you think you are to judge them?" she snaps.

I immediately know she's right and already regret my words, but I play dumb and ask, "What do you mean?"

"If Remarque thinks that Nazi threats against the Jews and Communists are real, and that staying here would only get him

arrested, then who are you to disagree with him? Maybe you ought
to pay more attention to what the Nazis aim to do to people like
him."

"I do pay attention. I have since I first heard Hitler on the
radio!"

"Though you no longer seem to mind him so much. Maybe you
and Tonio both think the Jews are only pretending to be scared
of the Nazis because we secretly run the world from a New York
command post." She raises her hand above her head and jiggles
invisible strings. "I'm an evil puppetmaster controlling all you do
and say, right? Me and the Rothschilds!"

I reply harshly to her, in part because she seems to want to
misunderstand what I'm saying. And her mentioning Tonio has
brought up my dread that I'll have to choose between him and her
someday. Also, I hate her implying that Papa – as a Communist
– could be in imminent danger, and that he might have to flee
Germany. I'd decided by then that never voicing my fears about
my father will help to keep him safe.

Back and forth our quarrel goes, and we're both too hotheaded
to consider that we're inflicting permanent wounds. "I'm sick of you
being a Jew!" I conclude, which isn't true; if anything, I'm jealous
of her for having already learned some of what Isaac is teaching me.

"Coward!" she screams.

Right again, but she gives me a contemptuous look and runs
off before I can either apologize or curse her, leaving me alone with
my guilt, which quickly becomes a vow never to talk to her again
unless she apologizes. The alchemy of dishonesty.

Right afterward, Greta Ullrich – who has made it well known
that her dentist father has decided to no longer fix Jewish cavities
as his contribution to the Fatherland – comes marching up
to me. Her hair is always braided in perfect plaits, as though

she were a milkmaid who gets inspected every morning by the Bavarian Braiding Union. I've never forgiven her for once telling Dr Hildebrandt, the headmaster, that she'd seen Rini smoking on school grounds. Instead of Greta Ullrich, Rini and I call her *Gurka Greulich* – meaning *repugnant snitch; gurka* means pickle but is slang for tattletale.

"Good for you, Sophie!" she tells me, smiling brightly. "We'll show those Jews their place."

"Gurka, if you don't shut your damned mouth, I swear I'll cut off those braids of yours and stuff them up your Bavarian behind!"

Gasping, she runs back to her group of gawking idiots, all of them with that wholesome, empty look of girls bred for a proper marriage, and they start whispering about me as if I'm scandalous. Which compared to them, anyone who looks as if she's from Berlin must be.

Tonio soon adds to my worries, since he insists on bringing up my virginity every time we're alone, pestering me like a hungry fly. Cede to his wishes or lose him – those seem to be my only options. And when he pleads in the softest voice a boy could ever have, clutching my hands in his lap as if he understands how difficult my choice is, I begin to doubt that I can resist much longer. And question why I should.

Once, while we're kissing in my room, he whispers, "When I'm inside you for the first time, we'll be pledged to each other *forever*."

I know a boy will say just about anything to get between a girl's legs, but that *forever* is the word I've been waiting for. And that *we* is clever, too; it implies we're on the same side.

"You're driving me crazy," I tell him, rolling my eyes.

"Sophie, you don't know what it's like for a boy. We have needs that you don't."

He puts my hand over the bulge that's rising down the leg of his trousers. "See, I'm always ready and you're not." He presses himself into my hip and moans. "I ache all over when I'm like this."

I push him off and after he stops pouting, we start reading car magazines side by side on my bed. Much safer. And he's recently figured out a way to include my adoration of Dietrich and Garbo into his automotive reveries ...

Holding up a photo of a big blood-red car, he says, "Sophie, do you think Greta would prefer a 1932 Deusenberg Brunn Torpedo Phaeton or ..." Here, he picks up a glossy picture of a sleek convertible. "... a 1929 Hispano Suiza H6B?"

The car names mean nothing to me, of course, but I can tell in an instant that Garbo would go for the Phaeton – much classier. I point to that one.

"How about Marlene?" he enquires, his face so earnest that I have to suppress a giggle.

Tonio and I go on like this – our feet playing together on the end of the bed – until we've decided on cars for Mary Pickford, Douglas Fairbanks, Norma Shearer, Willy Fritsch, Max Schreck, and creepy but captivating Gloria Swanson, who, in *Tonight or Never*, wore the most gorgeous gowns I ever saw.

Tom Mix and his horse Tony are the hardest to match, but we end up choosing a 1932 Ford Tudor with a trailer at the back. Lon Chaney has been in his grave for two years but Tonio and I still pick out a pink and yellow roadster for him.

Tonio also lets me speculate on what Jewish stars like Groucho Marx would want their chauffeurs to drive. And yet there are signs his kinship with the Nazis is growing deeper ... The worst is that he gives me Hitler's autobiography, *Mein Kampf*, to read when I refuse yet one more time to give up my virginity. My boyfriend is so enraptured by his prophet that he really believes that Hitler's sacred words will convince me to open my legs. In short, he thinks I'll fuck him for the Fatherland! (Little do I know that this is not so crazy as it sounds. Millions of girls will be pressured to do just that over the coming years. Even the lucky ones who aren't forced to slog their way through *Mein Kampf*. After all, Germany's soldiers need their rations.)

While I'm walking the tightrope between my choices, President Hindenberg – who has been doing his own balancing act between political parties for several months – closes his eyes, prays for kind treatment in future history books, and names Herr Hitler as Chancellor, then disappears back into his hole. After the initial sense of panic both Papa and I feel, the announcement on the 30th of January comes as a relief, in the way of all political catastrophes that are expected; after weeks of nervous anticipation, the worst has finally happened, and now at least we will be able to see how disastrous – or prosperous – life will become. "We can now clear away the dust and rubble and start over, with the workers leading us forward!" Papa says confidently, certain that the little man who shouts will soon vanish, though he's pushed back the date of his demise until the beginning of 1934 – a year away.

Isaac sees things differently. "Hitler won't want to lose the element of surprise, so we're in for some fast changes. As for your father's beloved workers, our Chancellor will be only too happy to send them to the front as cannon fodder when he's ready."

Hitler has sworn an oath to uphold the constitution, however, and only two Nazis are in his cabinet, so it's just possible that Isaac's worries will prove unfounded and life will go on much as it has over the last decade.

I never admit it to anyone, but a shadowy part of me is also a bit glad to see threatening changes in our government, since I want Rini to pay for abandoning me. That I regard Hitler's opinions about the Jews as nothing but slanderous lies makes my betrayal of her even easier in a way, since I don't feel tainted by his viciousness. Not that I truly want anything bad to happen to Rini and her family or any other Jewish people, of course. Oh, no, I'm one of the good Germans.

As part of the nation's celebrations, deaf storm-troopers march through the Brandenburg Gate alongside their hearing comrades, carrying upraised torches past our new Führer. They are unable to hear the tens of thousands cheering around them, of course, but they are grateful for the chance to feel united with such a massive, exuberant crowd. Seizing a chance for inclusion – at any price – is a powerful temptation to someone born deaf. At least, that is what Marianne assures me the next time I see her.

Inside that warm sea around the storm-troopers are many who only a few months earlier had referred to Hitler as nothing but a house painter wearing his brush on his upper lip. Now, they're bright shiny new Nazis dreaming of glory – seemingly overnight, our Führer has adopted millions of them. And Tonio is among them. In fact, when he comes home after the celebrations, he rushes up to our apartment like a child who has discovered Roman coins while digging in his yard and tells me in my room, "The giant black Mercedes the Führer was riding in – it was magnificent!" He's so electric with glee that he jumps up to touch the ceiling. "Sophie, a while back you asked me what the most beautiful thing I ever saw was. It was Hitler in that car!"

So God is an ambitious Austrian thug in a Mercedes. Who could have guessed?

K-H attends the same Berlin rally, but with his own weapon of choice, snapping dozens of pictures of deaf friends who have apparently changed into fervent Nazis. He's imagining his exhibition: *The Day the Deaf Lost Their Sight*. Each time his shutter snaps, he feels as though he's vibrating with the power that keeps us all alive – what we feel when we know we are accomplishing an important task beyond the scope of anyone else. This sense of being useful is also a powerful emotion, especially to a man made to feel during his childhood as if his deafness was shameful.

It's a storm-trooper with a German Shepherd on a leash who tells him to stop taking pictures. Reading the man's lips, Karl-Heinz replies, "I'm a photographer – it's my job."

Does the Nazi take exception to the deaf man's mispronounced vowels? Or maybe he suspects that this photographer beginning to focus on the crowd again – without authorization! – is really a Jew only *pretending* to be deaf.

"Karl-Heinz is missing," Isaac tells me the next morning when I come to his apartment.

Marianne is sitting on the sofa at the back of the room, breastfeeding little Werner, now six months old – a red-cheeked pasha. "Sophie!" she calls out, her face brightening, and she reaches out a straining hand to me.

I rush to her, grateful she hasn't forgotten me, and kneel down so we can embrace. Her scent of terror is overpowering. Her trembling seems to enter into me.

Werner is dressed in green flannel pajamas with blue sleeves, and a fire-colored collar.

"A gift from Vera," Marianne tells me. "I think she may want Werner to grow up believing he's a tropical bird."

"He's cute as can be," I tell her, enunciating carefully so she can read my lips. Werner has soft tufts of blond hair and light brown, glowing eyes. And he's wearing a satisfied expression, as if he's an emperor who has just finished a banquet. He's an infant who'll be photographed a thousand times by his papa. And pampered by the tallest aunt in Germany.

"That child is always eager for milk!" Isaac exclaims. "He's going to have a big Prussian belly."

"Shush!" Marianne says, waving off his good-natured laughter. She's wearing a giant silk robe – black, with red stripes – that tumbles to the ground in luscious folds.

While Werner is feeding, Isaac tells me about K-H not coming home the night before. For her sake, the old tailor speaks cheerfully, but we're all thinking about how opponents of Hitler have disappeared over the past year and never been found. Others, like Georg, have been murdered. His is the name we are all thinking of but dare not say.

Isaac brews a fresh pot of coffee. The cold winter light slanting through the windows seems drawn to Marianne, leaving me in shadow. The miracle is that I don't resent her for being so beautiful.

Isaac is of the opinion that a Christian ought to go with her to report Karl-Heinz missing or the police might treat her badly. And someone who can hear, in case she needs to make a phone call. But who can they ask to accompany her at seven-thirty on a winter morning?

I volunteer my father, and as we're discussing alternatives a knock comes on the door. Answering it, I'm caught completely unprepared for Vera. Gasping, I instinctively lift Werner between us – my protection against being clobbered for having failed to accept her gift of a jacket. It might be funny in other circumstances, but she's not laughing.

CHAPTER SEVEN

Vera's eyes, opening wide under her jutting forehead, look at me as if I'm a malignant apparition – a *dybbuk* from last year's Carnival party. Regaining her composure, she snaps, "Who gave you Werner?"

"Marianne, of course."

"Don't drop him!" She strides past me as if I've been discarded.

"Vera ..." I say, not sure how to begin to apologize.

She turns around. *I've no time for you*, her earthworm lips, twisted into a frown, tell me.

"I'm sorry," I continue. "I did everything wrong. You must ... you must hate me."

"I don't hate you." She closes her eyes to consider what to say. "You hurt me ... hurt me badly." She reaches for my arm, gives it a squeeze as if she's saying farewell, and strides into the kitchen with her forward-tilting walk.

I feel like never moving again until I can think of how to make peace with Vera, but instead I comb Werner's hair and shuffle into the kitchen, my mind made up to head off to school. But Marianne has other ideas. As soon as she's got Werner securely in her arms, she says, "Sit next to me," and she tugs me down without waiting for my reply. My back is to Vera, which is just as well. Marianne gives me a conspiratorial look, then faces the angry giant. Vera is lighting a cigarette. She wears a white woolen scarf and a huge black sweater that falls to her knees. The largest pullover ever knitted. A fishing net with a collar.

"Sophie will go with me to the police!" Marianne declares. To Isaac's puzzled look, she says, "She's a Christian and can hear. What else do I need?" She smiles at me enticingly. "Will you come with me?"

"Of course."

"I forbid her to go!" Isaac bellows, flushed with anger.

I'm aware of myself in that prickly way adolescents are when they're being fought over by adults. I manage to say, "Isaac, you can't forbid me to do anything."

"I very well can!" he snaps back.

"Let her go!" Vera tells him, and she waves him away when he glares at her.

"You know, Vera, you're the biggest *nudnik* I've ever met!" Isaac declares.

"I don't speak Yiddish, so save your slanders for your fellow parasites," she tells him, and when she turns to me I see from her look of complicity that we've already agreed that this is how I can earn her forgiveness. I'm grateful.

"Vera," Isaac says after a long, self-pitying sigh, "you are forgetting that this young lady has school to attend. And *you*," he says, pointing an angry finger at me, "are already late."

"I think God will forgive me – just this once – for disappointing you," I reply.

He tries hard not to smile but ends up laughing. Then he says in a tone of warning, "Sophele, my darling, cleverness is not always such a good thing. So try to be a little bit stupid now and again – *ein bisl stumpfsinnig.*"

Werner watching his mother

As we ride a tram to the police station in Alexanderplatz, I snuggle with Werner, who – to my great delight – kicks his legs, waves his hands, and giggles every time I kiss his ears or blow on them. Still, I'm glad that Mama and Papa never gave me another younger brother or sister – one silken-haired albatross around my neck is more than enough.

Marianne smiles her gratitude at me, but that emotion brings others, and the tears that have been waiting inside her are soon sliding down her cheeks. "Sorry, it's just that K-H and I haven't spent a night apart in four years," she explains to me, blowing her nose into her handkerchief.

After we get off at our stop, Werner starts to fuss and holler, so we duck into a café where Marianne can feed him. We sit in the corner, around a wooden table with an empty amber-colored glass vase in the middle; flowers are the first to go in an economic crisis. Marianne unbuttons her blouse and gives the infant her breast. His eyes are entranced. He's lost in a Seventh Heaven whose gate is the soft feel of Mama.

"Werner is the luckiest baby on earth," I tell Marianne.

"That's very sweet of you, Sophie. But he *is* deaf, you know."

"That doesn't seem to matter – not with you two together like that."

I notice now that Marianne smells of mint. "My cousins in England have addicted me to Pascalls Crème de Menthe," she explains.

I accept the candy she offers me, and with all of us happily sucking away, I ask, "Was Georg Hirsch in love with Vera?"

She considers my words. "I *did* always sense a clash of emotions between them. But you never can tell with people."

"Do you know the name of the advertising agency where he worked? And where it was?"

"Bellevue Advertising, on Königstraße ... a new building on the last block before the river."

"Did you ever meet any of his work friends?"

"I don't think so, but I met his boss once – Joseph Brenner."

"Nice?"

"He seemed so. We didn't talk long."

The waiter – a double-chinned gargoyle with his greasy hair combed straight back – glares at us when he takes our order for tea and cake, and he tells Marianne gruffly that she ought to go to the women's room to feed her baby.

"Let's get out of here," she whispers as soon as he's gone.

"But Werner is still hungry. And our order ..."

She's trying unsuccessfully to button her blouse with one hand and doesn't notice me speaking. The moment I take Werner from her he starts to cry again, and as we sneak out, I realize that he'll never hear his own sobbing. The sound enters a realm beyond his senses, and yet that doesn't silence him. So he must know that making noises when he is hungry is useful, that a world exists where his voice can be perceived, because there are beings who *do* hear him – who live in this realm he cannot detect and who will come to his aid.

And I am one of those beings. I live with one foot in his world and the other in a place he'll never know. What higher worlds exist that none of us can detect with our usual senses? And who makes their home there?

"I know a place we can go," Marianne says, and we rush to Kaiserstraße. Inside the squat, brick synagogue where we find refuge, a large chandelier hangs from a cupola patterned in gold and blue, like a crown in a dome of sky. A tiny man in a hat, wearing a white shawl with dangling fringes at its corners, comes shuffling up to us.

"I need a place to feed my baby, rabbi," Marianne tells him. "Is it all right?"

"Cantor," he corrects her, smiling. "Yes, come with me. Sit in the front where it's warmer."

As Werner begins to suckle, he keeps one hand over his right eye, as if he enjoys peeking, the other at Marianne's breast – just to be sure that heaven is not going anywhere.

"My husband, Karl-Heinz Rosenman, went to this synagogue when he was a boy," Marianne tells the cantor. "He lived just around the corner."

"I remember him well, though he was never much of a *schul*goer. Tell him Cantor Kretschmer sends his best regards." He touches his fingertip delicately to Werner's nose and speaks in baby talk, then, smiling again, says, "I'll give you and your sister some privacy now."

Sister? So it is that Marianne, Werner, and I become forever linked.

The stocky officer with a working-class Berlin accent who's sitting at the reception desk at Police Headquarters informs us that he can't take a statement from Marianne because her husband has been missing only for twelve hours. After she pleads with him, however, he agrees to writes down K-H's name in case he hears anything. He leers at her as we leave and even winks when we turn around by the door. If he were any more of a cartoon character, his tongue would be hanging out.

Marianne gets no news about K-H that afternoon or evening. Insomnia for most of those who know him and the start of my own long battle to the death against sleeplessness.

Mr Mannheim's melodies cease to inhabit the darkness near midnight, so I slip into the kitchen to make some camomile tea. Mama hears me stirring, and though I assure her I'm fine, she sits behind me and brushes my hair. The motion of her hands – quick and sure – is the feel of my childhood, and the way she smells faintly of rose perfume brings me back to when we'd go for picnics along the Spree. She's caressing me into the girl I used to be.

"You're getting more lovely every day," she tells me, which would be gratifying to hear but I know every pitch in my mother's voice and can tell she'll soon be asking me serious questions – probably about Tonio – and that this is a compliment meant to loosen my tongue. I also sense that *lovely* is code for *adult*, and that she's not entirely pleased about my maturity.

When she's done brushing, she grips my shoulders to make sure I don't jump up and asks me about my schoolwork. I tell her my studies are going *wonderfully*. A lie, but one that puts me ahead in our little tennis match, fifteen–love. To her further questions, I assure her that Rini and Frau Mittelmann are in good form. Forty–love, as far as I'm concerned.

As I stand up to escape back to bed – game, set, and match – she takes my arm. "Do you want to talk about Tonio?" she asks.

"He's fine, Mama," I say, though we both know that she's not asking how he is.

"*Häschen*," she says, caressing my cheek, "why can't you sleep?"

"It's Papa," I say, thinking that's a safe lie, but as I turn to her, the shock in her face – fear drawing back her pretty lips – opens an ache in my gut. It's a reminder, too, of how alike we are.

"Hitler says that Communists are traitors and Russian agents, and they will die at the end of Nazi knives," I tell her in a rush, and before I can stop there are tears at my eyes – for K-H, as well as Papa.

She kneels next to me and puts her hand gently over my mouth. "Listen, Sophie," she says in a determined voice, "you let me and your father worry about Herr Hitler. Can you do that – can you let me worry for you?"

Evidence of hidden strength in her? I nod my agreement.

"I'm taking my hand away," she says, "and with it I'm taking all your cares."

Trapping my jumble of worries in her fist, including, I hope, my nagging indecision about whether I should give myself to Tonio, she tosses them behind her back, then presses her lips to my brow. "Just give Mama and Papa some time to work things out."

She means well, but panic seizes me because her unusual show of strength gives me the notion she's hiding a decision that's already been made. Maybe we're going to flee Berlin in the middle of the night.

"I couldn't stand leaving home," I tell her. "All my friends are here. Tonio and Rini and ..." I almost add *Mr Zarco* but stop myself just in time.

"Sophie, I've no intention of leaving." Her voice grows harsh – probably because she's frustrated that her magic hasn't calmed me. "Now go back to bed. And please, don't breathe a word of what we've talked about to Hansi." Transforming again, her eyes flash with anger and her coming words remind me of why I can never fully confide in her. "I'm warning you. Don't you dare scare your little brother!"

At one-thirty in the morning, while I'm still tossing and turning, Isaac hears pounding on his front door. According to what he will tell me the next morning, he opens it warily – just a crack – and sees Karl-Heinz kneeling on the landing, shivering like a lost child. His arms are laced behind his back as if he's been handcuffed.

"Thank God!" Isaac exclaims, taking the photographer's elbow and lifting him up. "You must be half-frozen, poor boy."

"Don't be frightened," K-H tells him as he hobbles inside. "I've had a minor accident." He holds out his hands. Several fingers are crusted with blood and his right thumb has been bent at an impossible angle.

"*Mein Gott!*" Isaac gasps. He walks K-H over to the sofa, his arm tight around the young man's waist to keep him from falling. Did the traitor in The Ring tell the Nazis that K-H would be taking photographs at the election celebrations? "Sit here, my boy," he adds, easing K-H down. "I'll get Marianne and we'll go to the hospital."

By the time Marianne rushes into the sitting room, her husband has fallen unconscious. Isaac recognizes – from his days in the army – that K-H has gone into shock. The old man covers him with woolen blankets and calls an ambulance. Marianne sits on the floor, holding her husband's limp hand to her cheek. Though she's in despair, she thanks God that her worst fear – one that has plagued her since she was old enough to know she was deaf – has not been realized: K-H has not had his eyes put out.

*

When I stop by Isaac's apartment before school, his face is so drawn – with pouches of distress under his eyes – that my heart dives toward panic.

"No, K-H isn't dead," Isaac tells me, anticipating my question. "He was beaten badly, but he'll recover. He's in the hospital. Marianne and Werner are asleep in my guestroom. As for me," he adds, letting his body deflate, "I haven't slept a wink."

"Me neither."

Joined by insomnia, we walk to the kitchen. His hand wrapped around mine is a wall separating me from all the bad things that could happen.

"I almost nodded off while Benjamin Mannheim was playing his cello," he tells me, "but then Werner started screaming his head off. I walked the *mieskeit* round and round for half an hour, cooing like a *meshugene* pigeon, and he still didn't shut up!"

"What's a *mieskeit*?"

"A little ugly monster, but one that you can't help but love."

"Mr Mannheim's name is Benjamin?"

Isaac nods, then drops down on a chair and closes his eyes. I make him coffee and oatmeal, then steal his pipe so he's forced to eat. In a hoarse voice, he explains all that happened the night before. "I'm too old for crying children," he confesses. "I passed that gate forty years ago and if I look back I'll turn into a pillar of shit."

"You sound like Vera," I say.

"No, anything but that!" he replies in mock horror, and a clump of oatmeal falls from his spoon to the table. "Please God, send me no *goyishe* amazons this morning." He swipes the fallen cereal with his fingertip and gobbles it down.

He tells me then that brownshirts took a hammer to K-H's hands after interrogating him about his work. "They told him he'd never take another *Jewish* photograph." He pauses with his spoon in the air. "Sophele, what do you think a Jewish photograph is?"

"I don't know, but if the Nazis don't like them then they must be a very good thing."

"Well put, my dear. Every time Mr Hitler raises his arm he points 180 degrees from beauty. He's the perfect opposite-compass."

So it was that we began using Opposite-Compass as our private name for Hitler.

"After they hurt K-H what happened?" I ask.

He sips his coffee. "They drove him to the Tiergarten and pushed him out of their car."

"What kind of car was it?" A question that probably means I've spent too much time with Tonio.

Isaac raises his eyebrows. "Maybe you also want to know what cologne the louts were wearing?" He taps his finger to his temple as if I've lost my mind.

Even with his *cocoons* – as Isaac refers to K-H's bandaged hands – the photographer is able to contribute to his album of baby pictures within a few days. My first favorite: Vera pressing her distended lips to Werner's nose and the baby reaching for her ear. Everything in the picture is sharp except the blur of his teeny hand, which looks like a bird taking wing. And my second: Isaac holding the sleeping Werner and offering the naked boy to the camera as if he's the most gorgeous present in the world. A baby as an entire universe.

Karl-Heinz makes me copies of these two and I add them to what I now call my K-H Collection.

*

On the 5th of February, Hitler closes down all Communist Party buildings and enterprises, and his police begin making arrests. Two labor leaders who went to university with Papa hide out in our apartment.

The younger of the two, Ernst, plays dominoes with me after supper, then helps me and Hansi with a jigsaw puzzle of the Eiffel Tower. He's blond and blue eyed – the Opposite-Compass' ideal. After we've got all the pieces in the Tower, I run off for my collection of photographs of Garbo and Dietrich. Most of the ones I have are cigarette cards given away in the tins of Haus Bergmann cigarettes, which Papa and Ernst both smoke. He laughs at one in which Dietrich's long, arabesque eyebrows are obviously painted on, then argues merrily with me about what he calls my "bourgeois" preferences in actresses. Mama watches us with her eyes like targets, her lips reduced to a resentful slit. She thinks Papa has betrayed us by putting us at risk and that I've committed treason by keeping our guest entertained. I'm ashamed of her.

The other man, Alex, is wiry, with long, oily hair. He chats with Papa in the kitchen. Their voices are hushed, and when I go in to fetch the sugar crystals for Mama's tea, hoping to prove I'm on her side, they stop speaking.

Ernst and Alex sleep on the floor in our sitting room that night and slip away before dawn. Afterward, Papa and Mama have a long, muffled quarrel behind the closed door to their bedroom. "If you don't stop with these accusations, then I swear I'll leave you!" I hear Papa threaten at one point.

Did Mama accuse him of putting us all in danger? I think so at the time, but now I'd be willing to bet my guess was way off the mark.

Over the next week, the tense, clinging silence created by my parents' ongoing feud becomes a living thing lumbering through the house. The caustic winter light doesn't help any; it's too sparse to give us any real hope in a change of fortune. Berlin in February – with that slow ballet of death playing out in every bare tree branch and patch of black ice – makes us all feel as if our spirits are besieged.

Papa reads to Hansi every night before bed as a way, I think, of trying to end the day with something simple and good that we can share together. Our reward for surviving another dark turn of the earth. I often gaze at myself in our mirror after my brother falls asleep, by the light of a single candle I hold in my fist. Sometimes I touch my fingertips to the shadows on my face and wonder where the girl I was has gone.

I often draw Hansi, but my hands seem to have developed their own ideas of how his portrait ought to look. Once, I sketch him with his lips sewn together, like a shrunken head, and it frightens me, not because of what it means about his quiet nature, but because I don't know who I am if I could create such a thing. Did Dürer ever wonder if he'd moved too far from himself?

On occasion, I also try to draw Georg as Cesare, but I'm not good enough to pull his face out of my memory. I visit his advertising agency one afternoon when Mama is on the warpath. It's on the fifth floor of a concrete building with big glass windows on Königstraße, just west of the main post office. I walk all the way up, since I once got stuck in an elevator at Wertheim's department store and fainted dead away into Mama's arms. After a long wait, Georg's former boss, Joseph Brenner, admits me into his wood-paneled office, which has a splendid view of the cathedral's spires poking into the ominous leaden sky. Herr Brenner is dressed in the old style, with his collar up, and he invites me to sit by his desk. He's bald and severe-looking, and quite formal, and as soon as I see him my spirits sink; I realize that he'll never tell a fifteen-year-old girl anything important about his former employee. Nevertheless, after he asks me how he can be of help, I explain about my having met Georg at Isaac's party, and of my being friends with Marianne and K-H. I decide to rely on the truth for a change and tell him that my worry for Isaac and the others prompted me to see where Georg worked. "I'm so sorry to waste your time," I finish. "I've been very silly."

"It's all right, Miss Riedesel," he replies with surprising kindness. "These are violent times we live in. All of us get upset on occasion and do silly things."

"His death must have been a terrible shock to everyone here."

"Very much so," he admits, and he reaches for a cigar.

"Would you just tell me one thing?" I ask.

"If I can." He clips off the tip of his cigar and sticks it in his mouth.

"Do you think he had any idea this might happen?"

He makes me wait while he lights up, puffing mightily. "Georg seemed quite relaxed," he finally replies, leaning back luxuriously in his chair. "We went out to lunch a week or so before he died and he was in great form – joking with me and the others." Taking a satisfied puff, as if glad to confound me, he looks me right in the eye and adds, "But Georg was a born performer, of course, so I don't think we'll ever know what was really in his head."

I see Isaac only infrequently in February because he's so busy with his factory and with his activities for The Ring. Occasionally, we sip coffee together from his cracked, Mesopotamian cups, and discuss his progress at the Portuguese and British embassies, which is too slow for his liking; he hasn't even met with the ambassadors yet.

As usual, Tonio and I often go to the movies on weekends, our intimacy blessed by the flickering darkness. For the moment, he has stopped pestering me to sleep with him, but I can see in the determined way he stares at me – when he thinks I'm too absorbed by Garbo to notice – that he's biding his time. Perhaps he plans on jumping on me and getting it over with. And maybe that's the only way I'll actually ever give in to him.

One day late that month, I return from school to find our kitchen clouded with thick smoke. Mama has been tearing up all of Papa's political books, then burning them in the oven, but in her mad haste she has overloaded it with paper. Her handkerchief is pressed to her mouth, and tears are streaming down her face because she can hardly breathe. The window is open only a crack.

I cup my hand over my nose as she tells me what she's doing. When she's finished, she says, "Now go away and close the door behind you. The smoke is escaping."

"Why didn't you just throw the books out?" I ask.

"Neighbors might find them!" she snarls. "Do you want Papa to be arrested?"

"Stop blaming me!"

"Sophie, I've no time for one of your quarrels right now."

My quarrels? Displaying a new maturity, I decide to overlook that provocation. "At least open the window a bit more," I say. "You're going to suffocate." When she doesn't move, I walk past her to do it myself.

"No!" she says, pushing me hard, so that I crash against the cabinets. "The neighbors will spot the smoke and call the police. Sophie, get out of here and take Hansi with you."

*

Papa doesn't come home that night. Mama suspects he's fled the
city, or maybe even the country. Which, as far as I'm concerned,
gives her the right to shriek, pull out her hair, or even push me
into the kitchen cabinets, but not to steal my property; just before
supper, I discover that a dozen of my books have vanished, including
some that I'd slept with under my pillow for weeks, like Vicki
Baum's *Grand Hotel*, Thomas Mann's *The Magic Mountain*, and
Alfred Döblin's *Berlin Alexanderplatz*, as well as my beloved copy
of *Emil and the Detectives* and a glorious poetry anthology of Rilke's
that Dr Fabig, my German teacher, gave me as a Christmas present
and inscribed in the most beautiful Gothic lettering I'd ever seen.
So my list of Raffi's names is also gone forever.

I race into the kitchen and find her staring out the window,
the ash from her cigarette curling and about to fall. A bad sign;
Mama smokes only when she's been drinking.

"What did you do with my books?" I demand.

"I burned them. They could have gotten us into trouble."

"You could have at least asked me. You had no right!"

Mama turns back to the window as if whatever ghosts she sees
there are more essential to her life than me. I dash away before she
sees me sobbing.

My only relief is that my mother didn't find my K-H Collection
in my underwear drawer. I forgo supper that night as a protest.
Not that Mama notices; the apologetic words whispered through
my bedroom door – the ones I write for her in my head over and
over again – never come. One more grievance to add to my pile.

Papa manages to phone her the next afternoon, just after I return
from school; having learned from an old schoolmate that he was
about to be arrested, he's now in hiding, but he can't let us know
where – the police may be listening to our call. After Mama hangs
up, she repeats to me what he told her – her shock and disbelief

transformed into a frail monotone – then sits on her bed, her hands joined on her lap, her bottom lip folded inside her mouth. She looks as though she's facing a tower of regrets that she will never, now, be able to scale. Maybe she's recalling the moment when she realized that she was not going to live the life she'd wanted. My strangling fear is that it was when she got a first good look at me in the hospital.

I almost ask her if my guess is right, but I couldn't bear to hear I'd stolen her happiness. Is that the real reason she took my books? Her small theft to make up for mine, which was far greater …

She makes no reply to my offer to prepare supper. Are women all across Germany going on strike for a different future at that very minute? I bring her a cup of hot milk on her favorite tray – Japanese black enamel, ornamented with gold flowers – but she won't even take a sip. Later, she snaps the curtains closed and sits by the radio with a glass of brandy in her hand, listening to reports of arrested Communists and street battles between workers and Nazis. When I assure her I'll quit school and work as a waitress if Papa is imprisoned, I'd like her to thank me and tell me that we're a long way yet from having to make such sacrifices, but she gives me a murderous look and orders me not to use the word *eingekerkert*, imprisoned, ever again. "Sophie, you will promise me right now!" she tells me when I hesitate, the foul scent of too much brandy on her breath. She tucks her chin hen-like into her neck, preparing for battle.

"Whatever you want," I tell her, letting her win; she obviously needs a victory more than me.

Sitting alone again in my room, I feel as if our house has hidden staircases I've never dreamed of before, and that Mama climbs up them at night, when we're all asleep. A mother who goes places her daughter can't even imagine. And vice-versa, of course. Each of us summoned by voices the other can't hear.

I consider visiting Tonio, but if he brought up my virginity or even just pressed himself into me I might wallop him. If only I could go visit Rini. Instead, I tug Hansi to Isaac's apartment, promising that if he doesn't fight me I'll make him onion soup with bits of garlic bread floating on top – his third favorite thing, after jigsaw puzzles and squirrels.

We slurp our soup and eat some cheese on matzo. Hansi's lap becomes a blanket of crumbs that Isaac whisks onto the floor with the back of his hand before I can stop him.

Our host sits next to my brother and cuts pieces of cheese for him with scissors, a technique that summons crazy laughter from me – smoke-induced hysteria, I'd guess.

He gives me half a glass of wine to try to calm my nerves. Hansi agrees in his silent, stone-faced way that the scissors method is perfectly reasonable. My brother hasn't uttered a word since Papa's colleagues stayed the night. And why should he? The Hansi Universe has got to be a lot better than our home right now. Every now and then I wave at him just so he knows I'm here.

Heidi and Rolf knock on the door while we're listening to Lotte Lenya on the phonograph. They waddle inside with presents – one of Heidi's chocolate cakes and some incense they bought from a Gypsy family at a flea market. So we have a sweet-scented party – complete with kosher wine.

Heidi's cut her hair short and given herself bangs – a style that nicely frames her face. When we kiss, I detect the faint odor of fading flowers – just what Joachim's cousin in *The Magic Mountain* was said to have smelled like. I can't stop thinking about that book now that Mama has turned it to ash.

Heidi is wearing a beautiful dress – lavender satin, with delicate black lacework at the neck. "Vera designed it for me," she tells me when I offer my compliments.

Heidi, Berlin's best baker

"Does she make all her friends' clothing?" I ask.

"Just the people who are hard to fit," she replies. "Like me and Rolfie," she adds, leaning over to tug on his ear, so that he gives a happy yelp.

"We'd be lost without Vera," Rolf assures me. "Heidi and I used to have to go to children's clothing shops." He raises his upper lip like an irritated donkey.

Rolf is in a giddy mood because he's just found a well-paying job as an accountant at a firm that exports pectin. He does some card tricks for us while we eat our cake, and he's a real wizard. He even makes the ace of spades vanish into thin air, then pulls it out from Hansi's elbow. My brother's eyes sparkle when he sees that miracle.

Heidi and Rolf don't ask me to explain Hansi's silence to them, which is good, because I'm never sure what to say when people come up to me on the street and ask, *What's wrong with your brother?* Based on years of experience, I know that *How the fuck should I know?* is not the answer they want from an older sister.

"Any luck with the Dutch Ambassador?" I ask Rolf.

He starts, then looks questioningly at Isaac.

"I told her we're trying to convince Germany's neighbors to prepare for an embargo," he says.

"So far I've met only with an assistant for commerce," Rolf tells me disappointedly. "He's all of twenty-three years old and seems to think only about wearing stylish clothes."

Isaac keeps topping up my wine glass, and I get tipsy for the first time in my life. Underneath our conversation about the Nazis' plans for a military build-up, I hear my own wheezing breath, and I grow silent so I can listen to it. I must be hearing what my fear for my father's safety sounds like because I'm imagining a hounded fugitive on an evening train to Amsterdam. Watching him sitting alone in a dark compartment, the glow of his cigarette reflecting off the window, I feel as if something important – something made of the night – wants to make itself known to me. But all these voices ... I wish I had the courage to beg Isaac, Rolf, and Heidi to keep quiet. Lifting the silver cake-cutter, I imagine slicing the blade across my arm to get their attention, doing damage that could never be repaired. *Maybe that would be enough to please her*, I think. *Her* is my mother, of course.

But no dark epiphany comes to me – unless it's simply that Mama would end up burning everything in our apartment if Papa went to prison. Then she could leave behind the life she never wanted, marry someone else, and try her best to have two normal children.

How long will it take for Isaac, Heidi, and Rolf to notice that I'm no longer talking? I start counting as if each number is a hammer blow – the mathematics of a girl who has drunk too much. I must be making an odd face because after another minute or so, Isaac says worriedly, "Sophele, what's the matter? You haven't said a word, and the way you look ..."

"I think she's a little drunk," Rolf interjects.

"I'm not!" I exclaim defiantly, which only makes the two men smile conspiratorially and Heidi rest her hand on mine.

Accurately forecasting disaster on the horizon, Isaac tries to take my wine glass away. While jerking it away from his hand, I spill some down my white blouse. Heidi to the rescue. She dabs it with water and then milk to keep the stain from setting, but it's too late. Accompanying my feeling of dread is an image of Georg in K-H's photographs, maybe because I'm only now coming to understand that his death can never be undone.

Kissing my cheek, Isaac says, "No one is making fun of you. We all love you." He grips my hand tightly under the table, which improves my mood.

At length, Heidi tells him, "Isaac, we need your help."

"If it's money again, then stop worrying. I'm sure we can ..."

"No, we're all right for now," Rolf says. Turning to his wife and placing his hand on hers, he adds, "Maybe we shouldn't talk about this now, *Haselnuss*, the children are here." Rolf calls his wife all sorts of names, and I record them in my diary: Hazelnut, Parikeet, Strudel, and my all-time favorite, Gingerbread, *Pfefferkuchen* ...

"I'll take my brother into the sitting room and look at books," I tell them.

"You're an angel, Sophie," Isaac says, smiling gratefully and giving my hand a squeeze.

This is the first time in history I've beaten Hansi to that description, but what Isaac doesn't know is that my eavesdropping powers are first class. I sit my brother down on the sofa. As I'm looking for a picture book he might like, Heidi says, "Can you ask Julia to give me something to ... to enhance my chances of getting pregnant again?"

"So you've had no luck?" Isaac asks his guests.

"None," Rolf replies morosely. "And we haven't missed a night," he adds in a whisper.

I hear a chair slide back, then cabinets opening. "Try this," Isaac says. "Make it into a tea twice a day – once in the morning, and once an hour before ... before ..."

"We understand," Rolf assures him.

"It has herbs that will thin your fluids and give Rolf's sperm a little ... little help in reaching your egg."

Heidi laughs. "Isaac, you make it all sound so biological," she observes.

"You'd prefer I use plumbing metaphors?"

"No, let's leave those to Dr Stangl."

"Have you seen him lately?"

"Him? I'm staying away from him as long as I can," Heidi announces indignantly.

While they're talking, I lug *Ducks of the World* over to Hansi. It's nearly the same size as him and sounds promising. "Look at this," I command. Having decided he's the one to blame for our being banished, I drop it on his lap from high up, which makes him grunt. Good, at least that's some reaction.

I creep beside the door to the kitchen, where I can hear more clearly. Walking on tiptoe fills me with delight. Mephistopheles must have had a great time, despite what Goethe and Dr Fabig might think.

"... And then, before I left the hospital," Heidi says, "he informed me, in that authoritative voice of his, that it was just as well that I lost the baby. According to him, our child would have hurt Germany's development." Resentment coarsens her voice.

Hansi is staring at me. I shake my fist at him, and though I've never once punched him hard enough to do any real damage, he gets my point and opens the book.

"Dr Stangl said that the traits we'd give to our kids would be inferior," Heidi continues.

"We're too small for the new Germany," Rolf adds. "And inferior." Rolf uses the word *minderwertig* for inferior – part of the new Nazi vocabulary we're all being forced to learn.

"The worst part was that before I left the hospital," Heidi continues, "he brought a colleague from the Kaiser Wilhelm Institute to see me – from the Eugenics section."

"Was his name Fischer, by any chance?"

"Yes, Eugen Fischer," she replies, surprised. "Do you know him?"

"I read one of his books. He thinks dwarfs and deaf people are ballast. And he fired a great many Jewish professors when he was head of the University of Berlin."

"Ballast?" Rolf asks.

"That's how he and his physician friends describe people like you and Vera and K-H. Ballast to be tossed overboard at the first opportunity."

He adds something in a whisper I can't make out. But I *do* hear "Hansi" said as a question by Heidi, and then her sharp intake of breath.

Did Isaac whisper that Fischer would regard my brother as ballast too?

I can feel the powerful beating of my worry for my brother underneath the silence. I look at the boy, but he seems perfectly like himself to me – normal, because he's who he is.

"At first, Dr Fischer was friendly enough," Heidi says ominously.

"He said he wanted to give a lecture to his students about dwarf anatomy," Rolf adds, "and that Heidi could be very helpful as an example."

"He asked if I would please consider coming to his lecture hall, so they could see … see my body, and my peculiarities. He said it would be an honor to have me participate. I said I'd need to think it over. But then Dr Stangl told me he'd permit me to get pregnant only if I agreed to help Dr Fischer."

"Permit you!" Isaac shouts. "What business is it of his?"

"I don't really know," Heidi replies sadly, her voice trembling. I picture her husband taking her hand because she says gently to him, "I'm all right, Rolfie."

"I can't believe you let yourself be fooled by those bastards."

Rolf says adamantly, "We weren't fooled, we were threatened! Dr Stangl implied that he could order Heidi to have an abortion the next time she got pregnant. He showed us a letter from the Ministry of Health recommending abortions for people with ... with deformities."

"He must have written that letter himself to convince you. The Nazis haven't yet had time to ..."

"It looked pretty official," Rolf interrupts.

"So what happened when you got there?"

"It started out all right," Heidi replies. "But I began to suspect something bad might happen when they wouldn't let Rolf come into the lecture hall. I went inside by myself, and about a hundred students were in the audience, and a young woman ... a nurse, I guess ... she helped me take off my gown. Dr Fischer had me stand naked in front of everyone. He held a pointer, and he indicated places on my body with it, which made me shiver. I don't recall much after that. My mind ... I couldn't think. I seem to recall him telling his students that my deformities meant I mustn't have children, but I don't know for sure. I don't even know how long I was in there."

"Nearly an hour, *Pfefferkuchen*," Rolf says.

"By the time he was done, my heart ... I felt as if it had stopped."

"That son of a bitch!" Isaac exclaims.

"You're the first person we've told," Rolf says. "The amazing thing is that no one apologized to Heidi afterward. All Dr Stangl said was that if we still insisted on having children after all that Dr Fischer had said, he would live up to his bargain and sell us fertility drugs, though he warned us they were very expensive."

"Have you used anything he's given you?" Isaac demands.

"We haven't gotten the money together yet," Heidi replies nervously.

"Good, just drink the tea I gave you, and for the love of God don't take anything Sebastian Stangl gives you. Shit! To think how excited he used to be to have circus performers as his patients. How people change!"

Silence. After a while, I think they're going to call me and Hansi back inside, but then Isaac says, "When I was a boy, I read of a rooming house that had just been knocked down in Paris. Below the foundations, workmen found about twenty skeletons in a mass grave. They were very tiny skeletons – too small even for babies. So maybe they were from animals – the valuable bones of some ancient deer or extinct rodents. A great find for the Natural History Museum! But forensic specialists ended up concluding that the skeletons belonged to dwarfs and midgets who'd been killed, some just after birth, others when they were a year or two old. They dated the bones back to the eighteenth century. The tiny children had been suffocated or drowned, because there were no signs of bodily injury on any of them. I've never forgotten those skeletons. And not just because they made me realize that dwarfs have been systematically killed for centuries, with full impunity, but also because the Parisian officials were disappointed that they hadn't found rodent bones." Isaac's voice grows enraged. "Rats would have been better than people like you, and they simply discarded those tiny skeletons as if they were garbage. So if you believe Dr

Stangl is right, if you really think you're both just garbage, then use his drugs, because I'm betting they're poison!"

The silence afterward is so deep that I step into the doorway. Rolf has his arm around Heidi, who is crying silently. Looking at the misery in her eyes, I shiver, and I think: *there must be mass graves for* Minderwertige *in Germany, too.*

Papa stays in hiding through one more day of stormy relations between me and my mother, then returns the following evening, his face gaunt and cheeks unshaven, a ghostly double of himself. His eyes glisten as he holds me away – "I want to look at you," he says in a hoarse whisper. His clothes are crumpled and soiled, and he smells of the earth. Our first greetings are weepy, and comic in their awkwardness, like a badly translated Italian opera. After Mama throws her arms around him, she wets a hand towel with hot water and wipes his face, blessing him for returning in a voice choked by emotion. I take his coat off and bring him his favorite plum brandy. I sit close to him, my hand around his leg to keep him from escaping. His graying stubble burns my cheeks pleasantly when we embrace again. Hansi wants to be held, so Papa sits him on his lap.

"Everything is going to be fine," Papa then tells us, giving Hansi kisses on the top of his head and one on his ear, which makes him wriggle happily. "Better than ever, in fact."

My brother still won't say a word, but after a while I can tell from his down-turned glance that he's petrified our father will leave again without warning.

"Freddi, how could everything be better than ever?" Mama questions, more harshly than she probably intends, since the last cinders of her resentment – at his having put us through this torment – must still be burning. Fires go out slowly inside my mother's mind.

"First, you have to agree to never repeat what I'm going to say," he tells us. "After today, there's a great many things we'll need to forget."

My mother and I promise, but then she says, "Freddi, maybe we should talk alone."

The possibility of being excluded again from an adult conversation makes me grip my father's leg in a stranglehold.

"No, let Sophie and Hansi hear," he tells Mama to my relief. "I'll need their help."

He sits my brother beside him, then leans back with a sigh of exhaustion into the cushions of our sofa. "I must look like a mess," he says. He makes believe he's looking at himself in a hand mirror and gives us a comic grimace.

My love for him grows wider at that moment. Maybe I can even talk to him about Tonio pressuring me and confess to him that I've become friends with Isaac. Everything could still work out.

Papa says that he'd received a phone call at his office telling him that he would be arrested the next morning. "So I left work early and went to see Alfred Weidt. You remember him, Sophie?"

"The star gymnast who could do an iron cross."

"Absolutely. And I knew he'd help me – he always had that sort of strength and loyalty." Papa gives me a crazy smile – a fixed, jack-in-the-box grin. I've never seen it before, and it makes me uneasy. "After all," he continues, "we trained for two years on the same team. But when I talked with Alfred, he said he could do nothing for me."

From Papa's odd smile, I infer he's hiding something. And I have a good idea it might be rage.

"Alfred's wife, Greta ... we were friends in high school, too. As she walked me to the door, she pushed a scrap of paper in my hand. She'd written the name and address of an old friend of her family who could help me – a legal magistrate, a *Referendar*."

"So what did you do?" I ask.

"I took the underground across town to his apartment in the evening. I found him at home, and he let me in. A tall man ... very distinguished. And do you know what he wore while he spoke to me, Sophie?" he asks enticingly, putting his arm over my shoulder. "A monocle!"

Papa adds that detail because he knows I find men with monocles hilarious. I can see from the glint in his eyes that he's hoping I'll giggle appreciatively, and I do, but when he does his jack-in-the-box grin again, I feel like asking who he is and where my *real* father has gone. "What happened next?" I ask instead.

"He escorted me into his office and sat behind his desk. I was petrified, and when he asked me to explain why Greta had given me his address, I told him about the phone call informing me I was about to be arrested, and that I could not risk prison because I had a family to support, and though I'd been a Communist I only ever wanted what was best for Germany. I rambled on terribly because I was so tired and overwrought. All he asked me afterward was whether I was prepared to renounce my past political affiliations."

"Did you agree to that?" Mama asks, and her quivering lips move over an *Ave Maria*. An inheritance from her Catholic mother.

"Yes, I had no choice."

Mama's eyes gush with tears. What a scene – my mother weeping as if someone has died, Papa embracing her and reassuring her that all is well, and Hansi – his eyes dull and head angled down – as mirthless as a boiled potato. As for me, my legs have gone all stiff, as if I may need to dash off to save my own skin.

"The *Referendar* told me he would have an answer for me in the morning," Papa continues after Mama calms down. "I was to return at eight. I spent the night in a cheap boarding house, though I couldn't sleep and went walking through the Grünewald, in that clearing where we used to go for picnics when you were little, Sophie. You remember?"

"I think so," I say, because he needs my support, but I don't.

"I returned to the magistrate's home in the morning, but I was told that he could not yet tell me if I could avoid arrest. The person he needed to speak to had been unavailable and would be away from his office all that day and the next one too. So I was to come back only two days later."

"You must have been beside yourself with worry!" Mama observes. She's enjoying her preoccupation now – and making a show of it – because Papa has already indicated that this story has a happy ending. She's like a small child in that way; she loves being scared as long as she's sure that peace and contentment will triumph in the final act.

"No, after a short while a great calm came over me as I walked through the city. I felt as if I could look at my life from a distance. I went to see the Victory Column, and looking up at that winged angel blessing Berlin and all of Germany, I saw that I could be a different man – and still do a great many things I'd no longer considered possible. Doors were opening to me. It was a liberating feeling – like getting a reprieve from a death sentence."

Has my rationally minded engineer father had a religious epiphany? At the time, I think so. It occurs to me only years later that Papa may have invented it. After all, implying angelic intervention would have been the best way to win my religiously inclined mother's support for any difficult decisions he might later have to make – even a move overseas.

And what is this about a *death sentence*? Is that how he has regarded his life with Mama, me, and Hansi up until now?

"When you saw the *Referendar* again, what did he say?" Mama prompts.

"He introduced me to two men. The older of the two, maybe sixty, was a history professor. The younger one was a chemical engineer, just like me. The three of us spent hours talking. About Marxist theory, at first. It was astonishing. I don't know how I could have been so blind, but Professor Furst ... that was the older man's name, though you mustn't tell anyone, you understand? Sophie ...?"

"I understand, Papa."

He caresses my cheek and says, "Good girl," then looks frantically between my mother and me, leaning forward, needing us to understand. "He demonstrated to me ... no, he *proved* to me, using Marx's own words, that our new Chancellor represents the next step in Germany's destiny – that he will bring about the dictatorship of the *Volk*, the common man, that we have all been so ... so eagerly awaiting." Looking at Mama tenderly, he adds, "And that some of us, Hanna, those who live with God in their daily lives, and who often understand the world better than their husbands, have been praying for."

So much rekindled love for Mama fills Papa's eyes that I lean away from him, unwilling to intrude. It has been many years since I've seen tears of adoration for her in his eyes.

"You must be exhausted, Freddi," Mama says, her voice soft. "I'll make you some tea."

The intimacy between them is too overwhelming for her and she wants to escape to the kitchen. But Papa takes her hand and raises it to his lips. "Let me finish my story, Hanna, then you can make us all a snack. Right, Sophie?"

He hugs me again, wanting to reassure himself that I love him no matter what he's renounced, just like Mama, and I do, but the musty scent of him and dirt on his clothes make me wonder where he's really been. I'm certain that my father is lying to us, and maybe for the first time in his life over something important. It's at that

moment that I decide that his clownish smile must mean that he's
making up a story to cover the truth. But what that story is, I have
the distressing feeling I'll never find out ...

"Yes, Papa, a snack would be nice," I tell him.

Hearing the doubt in my voice, he misinterprets it as fear.

"Don't worry, *Häschen*, I'm all right," he says sweetly. He lifts
his tin of Haus Bergmann cigarettes from the coffee table and taps
one out. It's a gesture I've seen 10,000 times, and it's reassuring.
"I just haven't slept and I've been living on chocolate and coffee.
But it's good to finally see the truth and to have a chance to start
over. Who would've thought it would be possible at my age!" He
gives a quick laugh at himself, then lights his cigarette, inhaling
urgently, as if his strength comes from the smoke. But after only
one more puff, he stubs it out angrily in the blue ceramic ashtray
that I made him at school years ago.

"The Führer doesn't smoke," he tells us by way of explanation.

No, but you do, I want to say but just nod instead.

"Professor Furst ... he didn't say a single harsh word to me in
three hours. Imagine his patience! And he was so generous when
he accepted my apologies. He assured me that many a German
patriot had come to the same conclusion as I had, and that my
past was nothing to be ashamed of. 'All roads that lead to Hitler
are the right ones,' he told me."

Papa's voice breaks and he covers his face with his hands as
he starts to cry. Grief for the self he has buried alive ...? And are
Mama's tears for the loss of the man she married?

I will remember my father's bent back and trembling hands
all my life, and always with a sharp sense of guilt; if I'd found the
courage to speak honestly then, I might have convinced Papa to
keep resisting – and thereby saved many lives. I could have even
sacrificed my own desires and told him we should leave right away

for France or Switzerland, where he could still believe in his ideals. But I was too confused – and maybe selfish – to say what I thought.

Maybe Hansi has also realized that the journey we've been on together has reached a dead end. He curls into a ball as soon as Papa starts to cry. Does he think it might be dangerous to come back to a home where our parents are not who we thought they were? After all, maybe our father will decide that his son is also part of a past he must now give up.

While I hold Hansi, Mama kneels next to Papa and pulls his hands away so she can kiss his eyes, as though he's her child.

Hansi gets word that Papa has switched sides

Her maternal fussing irritates me. "What did the second man tell you, Papa?" I interrupt.

He wipes his eyes. "He gave me more good news," he replies, helping Mama back into her chair. Remaining standing, he gazes down at me excitedly and says, "Bernhard ... that was the chemical engineer's name ... he said that our new Chancellor has been looking for men with my qualifications – and who think like him. He and I talked about chemistry for a while. He was testing my knowledge." Papa snaps his fingers and gives me a bright look of triumph.

"But your father proved to him he knows organic and inorganic chemistry inside out. He ended up making me a proposition. If I was ready to follow the Führer wherever his struggle for justice and glory might lead us, then the National Socialist Party was ready to make use of my talents."

"Freddi, they can't expect you to join the army – not at your age!" Mama gasps.

"No, no, they don't need me to carry a gun, just to use my head. And, I must say, it feels good to be wanted so badly. Sophie," he says, rubbing his hands together nervously, "I hope you'll be pleased to hear I promised Bernhard that you would help, too. Because he told me that our young people represent Hitler's secret reserve of strength. And what could be more beautiful than a father and daughter working together for their country?"

When he looks at me questioningly, I give him the required reply, "Nothing could be more beautiful, Papa." I'd like to go to my room and lock the door and cry a while, but I've always been attracted to the scene of a terrible accident – the more anguish the better – so I stay.

"Did they say whether you'll be changing jobs?" Mama asks.

"Yes, but not right away – probably only in a few months. And my salary will be ..."

"Will we have to leave Berlin?" I interrupt in a flash.

"You'll be happy to hear, Sophie, that the answer is no."

Relief makes me shudder; I'll still be able to count on Berlin. Though maybe the city will renounce its past, as well, and sink into the medieval hatred of the rest of the country, just as Rini feared.

"Although," Papa says loudly to get my attention, continuing in the humorously pompous voice he usually reserves for mocking Hindenberg and other ancient politicians, "we may have to find a larger apartment more commensurate with my new position and salary."

"That's wonderful!" Mama exclaims, laughing appreciatively. I do, too, thinking it's my safest option.

So we will leave behind the apartment I've always lived in. And I will have to start hating Isaac, Rini, and Vera.

My fears for my own identity are a clear indication that I've failed completely to understand the ingenious simplicity of Papa's conversion – and the ease with which millions of others have been reinventing themselves since the election. My father has been assured he'll be able to go right on campaigning for a prosperous paradise of workers who sing and dance as they plow, weld, hammer, and type. Indeed, as Professor Furst has told him, the Führer expects nothing less than dreams of glory from his little helpers. My father can go on loving Hansi and me, his wife, gymnastics, chocolate, chemistry (both organic and inorganic!), and the Victory Monument. Little need change. All he really has to do is slip dear old Marx into the magician's hat of Professor Furst's political theory, whisper an incantation from *Mein Kampf*, and presto ... Out will come a black dove named Hitler. Oh, and one more thing: he will have to swear to help destroy those who jeer as the dove spreads his wings over Germany. And who warn foreign ambassadors about the danger the Nazis pose. The Jews in particular. And maybe he will have to stop smoking, too. That will undoubtedly prove much harder than hating the Jews, who were only pretending to be good Germans all along, as we all now know.

An even easier conversion lies in store for me; I won't even have to give up smoking!

"A bigger apartment!" Mama whispers to herself, gazing around, raising her hands to her mouth, which she only does on those rare occasions when reality corresponds to the dreams she had as a girl. Is she envisioning a garden in Dahlem where she can reproduce the apple orchard she had on her childhood farm? Now that she's had a few moments to adjust, she's plainly thrilled by her husband's change of direction, just like a million other wives who've been coping too long with shrinking bank accounts. Why not the farmer's daughter with the willful daughter and mute son, stuck in the dreary life that she can no longer bear?

Still, this sudden plot deviation doesn't seem believable to me; I'm still too young to know that people need only be frightened for their lives to swear that night is day. And that they can believe it's really true.

"Sophie, I don't want you ever mentioning anything about the rallies and meetings I used to take you to," Papa tells me as we sit down to supper that evening, ending any last hopes I had that our lives will get back to normal. "And you're not to visit Rini anymore."

So he's forgotten my fight with her. "Of course, not," I agree, holding my plate out for the potatoes Mama is serving.

"Forget everything that came before now," he adds, not realizing how silly that sounds.

"I'll do my best," I promise.

As I take back my plate, Mama raises her hand threateningly toward me, since my answer isn't assurance enough for her. "This is serious, Sophie," she warns me.

"I know that!" I snarl.

She shoots me a contemptuous glance as she lifts up Hansi's plate, which means she's not done with me yet.

Sure enough, as I'm getting undressed for bed that night, she barges into my room and takes one more book from my shelves, just to spite me – an edition of Goethe's *Faust* that I've never read. It was a gift from Rini's parents for my fourteenth birthday.

"Has Goethe made your blacklist, too?" I ask. "I didn't realize he was a Communist."

"He's far too complex for a girl like you," she tells me in a haughty voice. A literary critic who never reads. Par for Germany.

I realize that she's going to take advantage of Papa's new beliefs to try to tighten her control on me. Obedient mothers and fathers using Hitler's regulations to take revenge on their renegade children ... Has that been written into the script, too?

"Goethe may be too dense to burn well," I observe in a mock-helpful tone. "But if you shred the pages, we can eat the pieces in our soup. Who knows, his poetic words might even improve the taste of your potatoes!"

I grin to provoke her. I can be a jack-in-the-box, too, if I need to be.

"Sophie, that's not in the least bit funny!" she snaps, scowling.

"I'm sure Goethe would find us eating his words hilarious. You know, Mama, if you're very quiet," I add in a conspiratorial whisper, "I think you can even hear him laughing at you right now."

Which brings tears to her eyes. One small and bitter victory for the children of Germany. And for our writers.

But then Papa comes in to scold me for being rude and notes I'm not too old for a beating – unexpected, since he's never even laid a hand on me before. He's got his leather belt stretched tautly between his hands, and his eyes fill with the disdain he used to reserve for Capitalist factory owners as he tells me how he will expect more from me from now on. His words are razor-sharp, meant to wound me permanently – just like he's been hurt – and I'll always remember him sneering, "You think you're a little Kurt Tucholsky, with that nasty Jewish sense of humor, but you're really just an insolent, ungrateful child."

I end up sobbing, since even if I hate myself how can I stop being who I am and knowing that my father has betrayed me?

The dilemmas of a girl who doesn't understand how easy it is to become someone new.

After I've stopped crying, I gain the courage to ask the one question I still need to – so I'll know exactly what's required of me. Papa is seated now on the end of my bed, rubbing my feet, behaving sweetly now that he's been successful at making me feel worthless.

"Have you joined the Nazi Party?" I ask.

"Not yet, but I will, if all goes well."

"Good, I'm glad," I reply. Maybe he'll receive an autographed copy of *Mein Kampf* in the bargain. *To my dearest Friedrich ... All the best, Adolf ...* "Can you bring us home some armbands?" I continue with false eagerness, testing him further.

He's feeding his belt back through his pants loops. "You really want one?" he asks, surprised.

I'd like to make a gushing, absurd reply: *I could never live without one!* That way, he'd be certain that I'm aware this is a farce. And maybe if I shouted that Hitler was nothing but an Austrian ratcatcher, and kept shouting it, I could convince him to tell me in a whisper what really happened to him, and we could plan an escape.

But threatening me must mean he's terrified by what I could do or say. The Opposite-Compass has now made parents across Germany afraid of their children.

"Of course I want an armband," I assure him. "I want to help you – you and Mama. And bring two – you don't want to make Hansi jealous of me," I add with a benevolent smile, as though I'm a good big sister, but I'm really thinking that my brother shouldn't get off easy.

That night, I awake in a cold sweat, convinced that Mama will burn all my German movie magazines unless I make them Jew-free, so I sit on the floor and rip out the pictures of Al Jolson, Paul Muni, Edward G. Robinson, and the Marx Brothers. I eliminate Charlie

Chaplin, too, because most Germans *think* he's Jewish, though he's not. Marlene Dietrich goes, as well, since she's fled Germany for Hollywood, and I even rip away a romantic shot of Carole Lombard dancing with Clark Gable, since I recall something about her having changed her name, and a close-up of James Cagney, because Rini once told me that he grew up in a Jewish neighborhood in New York and can speak Yiddish fluently. An Irish-American who speaks like a Jew – now there's someone to give the Führer shivers!

Then, summoning a kind of frenzied courage, I tear up all my cigarette cards of stars except for Garbo and Dietrich. My K-H Collection proves more troublesome. I consider turning in the photographs to Papa in the morning to win more of his trust. After all, he won't want anyone to know he's had his picture taken – clowning and smiling – with degenerates and Jews. But giving them up would be admitting total defeat. So instead, I take down the framed photograph of Garbo hanging over my bed and slit open its brown paper backing with a knife. The envelope containing K-H's photos fits neatly behind the portrait, and when I hang it back on the wall Greta is still smiling enigmatically, her hair slicked back like a man's, the most gorgeous woman in the world.

The wonderful thing is that no Nazi would dare to suspect Greta Garbo of hiding Jews. Not even my father.

The next day I give Isaac back his book on Giotto, convinced that Italian artists might end up on my mother's blacklist, too.

"But I meant for you to keep it," he says, puzzled. We're standing in his doorway.

"I'm finished looking at it," I tell him, and I use the excuse of being late for school for refusing his invitation for coffee. As I dash away, he calls after me, "We're having our Carnival party this Saturday and I hope you can come."

I was expecting this invitation, since most parties will be held in Berlin this Saturday, four days before Ash Wednesday, which is the 1st of March. But I still don't know how to reply. "I'll try," is all I call back, but it's not likely I'll go, unless – like Papa – I can find an impostor to substitute me at home.

Self-portrait: where is my real father?

The next evening, my father takes me aside to show me a copy of the letter Professor Furst has written in support of his admission to the Nazi Party. He lifts up on the balls of his feet as if the letter is the gymnastics medal he has been waiting for all his life. Party membership as the praise he never received.

To please him, I pretend to read it carefully, then say, "Papa, if you want, I could come with you to a Nazi rally sometime. We could go watch the Chancellor speak."

My real father would spare me this, of course.

He hugs me for a long time, and everything about him is as it always was, except his scent, since he hasn't smoked a cigarette for nearly twenty-four hours. What began as a lie has become truth. In only a few days, the Opposite-Compass has already accomplished that miracle for him. So maybe I'll wake up tomorrow wearing pigtails, and when I run to the mirror I'll see I'm Gurka Greulich.

THE THIRD GATE

Three are the parts of the soul; the blasts of the holy shofar on Rosh Hashana; the periods of Jacob's life; and the pillars of the *sephirot*, the supernal lights of the Lord.

Shehakin, the Third Heaven, is the orchard of holiness, where you shall receive sustenance for your continuing journey. The Third Gate corresponds to the desire of all beings, both great and small, for union with one another and the Lord.

When you enter the land and plant any kind of tree for food, you shall treat it as bearing forbidden fruit. For three years its fruit shall neither be harvested nor eaten – Leviticus 19.

Berekiah Zarco, The Book of Union

CHAPTER EIGHT

On the day of Isaac's Carnival party, I jump out of bed early and dress quickly; I've awakened with a revelation about why the murderer might have chosen blue paint for the swastikas he painted on Georg's cheeks.

Hansi tags along with me as I fly out the door. I've told Mama we're headed to the Tiergarten but we're really going to Wertheim's Book Department. By the time we reach Leipziger Platz the clouds have swollen and darkened with rain. When the heavens open, my brother hollers about being burned even though I've got him covered with our umbrella. So we duck into a café and nurse our hot chocolates for an hour, until it's safe to go out again. Two tall men in sequined dresses, high-heels, and blond wigs – already dressed for a Carnival ball and reeking of beer – hand my brother and me big blue balloons as we reach the street. They bend down and kiss our cheeks too. Hansi wipes the kiss off and signals that he wants my balloon, so I give it to him. Anything to distract him from the puffy gray clouds, which look like they might have more mischief in mind.

Inside Wertheim's, a clerk who looks like Harold Lloyd finds the book I need, which is entitled *A Layman's Guide to Forensic Medicine*, by Siegfried Klein.

I page through it at the counter, saying, "I'll need ten minutes to make sure it's the text I want," which makes Harold Lloyd frown,

so I work as fast as I can. Just as I suspected, a bluish tint to the
skin can be caused by strangulation. Apparently, the body discolors
from lack of oxygen. Which means that blue swastikas might have
been painted on Georg's face to try to prevent policemen from
realizing the cause of death.

Maybe the murderer used Georg's make-up kit and then took
it to prevent his fingerprints from being spotted. And yet that
explanation doesn't make all that much sense: any experienced cop
– and certainly any coroner – would check for skin discolorations.
Abrasions would also have been visible on Georg's neck, but there
were none.

Using the index, I locate a reference to Raynaud's phenomenon,
which I learn is a discoloration of the fingers and soles of the feet
caused by extreme cold. Could Georg have been killed outside,
on a frigid day, then dragged into his apartment? But it was April
when he was murdered.

Later that afternoon, Tonio and I go to two movies. First we see my
choice, a revival of Garbo in *Anna Christie*, but her melodramatic
facial expressions only irritate me now. How could I have never
noticed before that she's just no good? Still, she's beautiful and
maybe that's all that counts. Then we go see *The Mummy*.

Since I can't confide in Tonio about my father's conversion
or my confusion about Georg's murder, we talk mostly about
cars and Hollywood. Then, after the first film, I grow silent as
we walk to the Ufa-Palast Theater, struggling against despair. A
Dixieland jazz band dressed in furry animal costumes – with
trombones, clarinets, and trumpets sticking out of their snouts
– is playing outside the Zoo Station, and my boyfriend does a
goofy little jig to their snappy tune to try to cheer me up, but I
just look at him glumly. When he asks me what's wrong, I tell

him I'm considering sleeping with him, since it's the only answer he really wants to hear.

Give the people what they want. My new motto.

He throws his arms around me and kisses me right in front of a magazine kiosk, so that the gnarled, yellow-skinned owner takes the cigarette from his mouth and whistles, then gives me a happy wink. Thank God for Berliners – there's hope for our country yet.

Further down the street, I realize I intend to give myself to Tonio as a way of punishing myself. And my parents, too, since they would be ashamed of me.

"Tonio, if I needed to die … if that was my only choice not to become someone I didn't want to be, would you put a pillow over my head as I was sleeping and suffocate me?"

"What are you talking about?"

"Never mind. It's not important."

Seeing my mood isn't improving, Tonio kisses me sweetly on the cheek, and after *The Mummy* comes on, he puts his arm over my shoulder. We sit together as friends, and I pretend the musty theater is our own Hansi Universe, with no other world outside. But this turns out to be the wrong film; Boris Karloff as an ancient Egyptian mummy who returns to life – and stalks a woman he mistakes for his long-lost love – is so calculatingly evil that he becomes all I am up against, even my own Jewish sense of humor. Wanting to crawl out of my skin, I go to the bathroom to wash my face, then rush out of the theater. Tonio catches up with me on the street a few minutes later. "What happened?" he asks.

"Nothing."

"What can I do?"

"You can make me into someone new – a woman," I whisper, and I think, *All roads that lead to Hitler are the right ones, so why not the one that goes right through my heart?*

"You mean ...?" Tonio sticks his tongue in the corner of his mouth – his puppy face. When I nod, he takes a key from his pocket. "I've been preparing for a long time," he grins. "I've got a place we can go – where my father takes his women friends."

I dislike him for his eager grin, but it's even better that I do; I already feel wounded by him in a way that I'll never forget.

Tonio rushes me to a dingy, top-floor apartment at 18 Tieckstraße; he stole his father's key and had a copy made. Over the tile roof of the closed ceramics factory across the street is the tall, copper-green steeple of the Sophien Kirche, pointing toward a heaven it will never reach. Through a transformation of the heart, *my* heart, that steeple becomes the needle on which my future turns, and as I balance on its point, with Tonio undressing behind me and chattering on about cars, I see clearly that I don't have to do this. I will often deny to myself that I knew what I was doing in the months to come, but I knew full well.

Dr Hessel keeps only a metal cot and a cheap dresser in the bedroom. No radio, no night table, no rug. But a rectangular mirror has been plastered to the ceiling and seeing myself naked makes me shiver. It's Tonio's body that saves me from panicking. He has beautiful shoulders, and I love how his sleek arms hang down, and the way he scratches his pubic hair. He's a boy verging on manhood – at a threshold we are both about to pass. His penis is already hanging heavily, its tip purplish and shiny – and peeking out of his foreskin. Vulnerable and silly. And all mine.

"Your cock is beautiful," I say. He laughs, so I add, "I'm being serious. It's one of your best qualities. Your somber eyes, your enthusiasm, and that beautiful penis ... And that you can speak some Russian, which is *unheimlichr.*" I'm feeling light-headed, and I hear myself laugh as if from far away. It must be because I'm standing on top of that high needle and trying not to fall off.

"Remember when *unheimlich*, odd, was your favorite word?" I continue. "That wasn't so long ago, though now we seem so much older. You need to shave almost every day now, and me ..."

I stop talking because he's not interested in our changes.

"Come here," he tells me.

He stands by the bed and lifts up his cock. I close the last crack in the curtains as if they're a door that can never again be opened.

His penis responds immediately to my affection. My refuge. After I've got him panting, I ask what's been on my mind since we stepped on the tram to get here. "And your mother? Does she suspect that your father cheats on her?"

"I don't think so. Sophie, for God's sake, don't stop!"

"Don't you think she has the right to know?"

"If she doesn't know by now, then she doesn't want to."

I guess what I said about Tonio not having much intuition was wrong. It's probably just me he doesn't understand.

I lead Tonio onto the bed, and we kiss side by side, and he caresses my hair and shoulders, which is his way of saying that he will be gentle with me. When he takes my hand and squeezes it tight, I realize I *do* want him inside me, after all. And it's then that a first tremor of desire for him shakes me. Whispering a prayer to the God that Isaac worships, the one who watches over us, I lie on my back.

After I insert Tonio's cock inside me, I raise my hands to squeeze his broad shoulders to reassure myself. But panic makes my breathing shallow and insufficient, warning me of present danger and future regrets. I no longer seem to know who I am, and I squirm under him and tell him to get off.

"Now?" he asks in disbelief.

"Tonio!"

"Just give me a minute to finish. I'll go as fast as I can."

He thrusts hard into me, his breath hot on my neck, and his mad burrowing makes me want to push him away as hard as I can. The sheer relentlessness of him, as if I'm a high wall he's got to scale in order to reach manhood – makes me realize I wasn't prepared for this.

It's my own damn fault, I tell myself, squeezing my eyes shut, and within the warm, moist darkness of myself, I repeat over and over that the man hurting me and grunting on top of me is only Tonio. We've been friends for years and I can trust him. This will make us closer. We'll be married someday.

And I tell myself, too, that the burning deep inside me doesn't mean I'm being ripped to shreds. I grab onto him, my fingers digging into his back, as if he's the only one who can help me now. Saved by the same man who is hurting me.

Is this the painful irony that all girls lying under a man for the first time encounter?

"Sophie, if I'm hurting you, I'll stop." The words I've been waiting for. But it's too late now.

"No, don't. Just pull out before you're ready. And go as fast as you can."

"I'll do whatever you want."

True to his word, he does his business quickly and shoots all over my belly. I laugh freely, tears sliding down my cheeks, because of the ridiculousness of his spurts, and because I'm so relieved he's out of me.

Tonio lies close against me. He presses his lips to my cheek, and when I turn to him, his eyes are moist. "I'm sorry I hurt you. I didn't mean to."

Only then do I remember that I love him. And that I was supposed to feel excited.

When I take a streak of his semen on my fingertip and put it in my mouth, I taste the salt of my blood, too. With a shiver, I look up at the bodies in the mirror on the ceiling. Two strangers exiled from the people they were.

When I come home late that afternoon, I make believe I'm sick, so I don't have to go to my Uncle Rainer's annual party.

"What's wrong?" Mama asks skeptically.

"My belly is sore." Which is true enough. I limp past her toward the bathroom, overdoing my frailty.

"*The Mummy* ... what kind of movie is that for a girl to see?"

"You're right. It was awful. I made Tonio leave before it was over."

My agreement pleases her. In a sweeter tone, she asks, "If you stay home, what will you eat for supper?"

"I'll make myself some soup. That's all I could get down, anyway. Now, let me take a bath and get into bed. I need to wash that horrible Boris Karloff off me."

Papa tiptoes into my room just before they leave for Uncle Rainer's house in Westend. Hoping to make me laugh, he's got on his cowboy hat. But I'm under my covers and half-asleep, doing my best to become the girl I was only a few hours before. He kneels next to me and whispers, "I'm sorry you're not feeling well, *Häschen*."

I cling to his voice, to the adoration of my father, but soon Mama comes up behind him, an indignant twist to her lips. She's wearing a long violet-colored skirt and a black shawl. Is she supposed to be a Gypsy? I won't give her the pleasure of asking. In any case, I must be a real dummy about some things, because for the first time in my life I realize she's jealous of my closeness to Papa. "Sophie, I don't want you leaving this apartment!" she tells me in a tone of warning.

"Hanna, please. Let the poor girl sleep."

Catching my glance, Papa rolls his eyes as if Mama is a silly creature. A mistake. In a vague way, I'm beginning to understand that he's worked hard over the last few years for her to become the policeman in our family. That way, he's been free to be sweet to me. And yet there's always been another man inside him – one who holds a stretched belt between his hands. So who is the calculating villain in our movie, after all?

I don't sleep. I get in bed and think about murder – my own, as reflected in a ceiling mirror. Closing my eyes, I picture my limp body being photographed by K-H, but my face isn't mine, it's Georg's. A broken windpipe and no abrasions ... I must not be much of a detective, because I don't understand how that could be. I begin to test possibilities in my mind – to look below the glass – but nothing makes sense.

When I get hungry, I shuffle into the kitchen. I'm stirring my carrot soup when there's a knock at the door.

"Vera!" She's wearing a black cape and scarf. A giant made of shadows ...

We kiss cheeks. My heart jumps at being so close to her.

"Isaac says he saw your parents go out with Hansi," she tells me. "Are you alone?"

"Yes, thank God. You want some soup?"

"Not now. Maybe in a little while."

I lead her into the kitchen. Sniffing, she asks, "Did you have a fire in here?"

"Mama was burning the evidence against my father that he was a Communist."

"So he's joined the National Socialists?"

"Yes. I'm sorry."

"Don't apologize! It's a good strategy. The Nazis might close the doors to new members soon and where would he be then?" Vera sits at the table and leans back, undoing her scarf. She kicks off her shoes and they fly into the oven. She's wearing yellow socks.

"I thought you only wear black and white," I say.

"I allow some hidden color just for myself and my admirers," she replies, grinning mischievously. "So, Cinderella, what's a pretty young thing like you doing home all alone on the night of the ball?"

I go back to my stirring and explain about not wanting to be stuck at my uncle's house. She lights a cigarette. Summoning my courage, I ask if I can have one.

"You smoke now?"

"Hitler says women shouldn't," I say defiantly.

She gives me one and lights it for me. The cigarette tastes awful and feels as creepy as a furry caterpillar between my fingers. I pretend I'm Marlene Dietrich, but I'd cough out a lung if I breathed in all the smoke the way she does.

"Come over to our Carnival party," Vera tells me. Putting on a snobbish accent, she adds, "Everyone who's anyone is going to be there."

I turn back to my soup, afraid to see her disappointed face. "My father would kill me."

After I add a pinch of salt, I practice smoking, but all I can think about is what smelly clouds we're making. I'll have to open all the windows as soon as Vera leaves.

"So how are you and Tonio doing?" she asks.

"We ... we slept together."

I expect her to lurch or shriek. Instead, she lifts an eyebrow and says, "And ..."

"And I'm not sure I should have done it."

"Because your parents would object?"

"Not just that." How to put my feeling of having been betrayed into words? And not by Tonio, but by myself.

"Because you didn't enjoy it?" Vera speculates. "Listen, Sophele, no one ever does – not the first time."

"You didn't?"

"Me? All the time the man was on top of me, I just kept wondering what all the fuss was about. He was two feet shorter than me. It was like being fucked by a ferret." To my laugh, she says, "When he was done, I was really puzzled. I thought, 'This goddamned pounding is what provoked the Trojan War and the *Iliad* and then 2,000 years of literary criticism?'" She shakes her head. "In any case, it certainly wasn't worth paying for."

"You paid a man to sleep with you?"

"How the hell else was I going to get him in my bed?"

"Who was he?"

"A bricklayer from Romania."

"Why him?"

"He was on sale." In a concerned voice, she adds, "I hope you took precautions to keep from getting pregnant."

"Yes."

"So," she grins, "how do you feel now that you're an experienced woman like me?" She bats her eyelashes – the world's most absurd femme fatale.

"You want the truth? It terrified me. I panicked. And I bled ..."

"My first time, I thought I'd made the biggest mistake of my life. And that I'd been fatally wounded."

"So I'm not an idiot?"

"Not entirely. Listen, nobody feels comfortable about sex at first. Not even men. Though they would never admit it."

I take out a soup bowl from the cabinet above the oven. "You're sure you don't want some?" I ask. When she shakes her head, I add, "Have you ever loved anyone?"

"Once, but it didn't last."

"Who was he?"

"That's classified information."

"Was it Georg?"

She makes that lurch I expected before. "How did ... how did you know?"

"The way he teased you at last year's party. I could tell he liked you."

"I liked him, too. But every time we got together we just ended up fighting."

She stubs out her cigarette, which gives me permission to do the same. Then I open the window, fill my bowl, and carry it to the table.

"What was he like?"

She leans back. "Georg? Intelligent and kind, and a born circus star, but ... but not very brave."

"Why do you say that?"

"Well, brave is probably the wrong word. He just didn't like taking risks. Not after falling from the high wire. He wanted everything to be safe and secure. The accident changed him. It made him more reticent with people, more ..." She bites her earthworm lip while looking for the word.

"Untrusting?" I'm thinking of my father, of course.

"No, he was trusting. Just withdrawn. And bitter about not being able to perform. And then the trouble he had in Savigny Platz ... getting shot at, it made him even more withdrawn."

So maybe the joking mood he evidenced at his final lunch with his boss was to cover up a life that was more and more bounded by fear and regret.

I take a first spoonful of soup. The carrots are still crunchy, like I prefer it, but Mama would be horrified. "Do you know if the police are still investigating the murder?" I ask.

"Yes, they called me in a few weeks ago to question me. That was the second time. What's irritating is that they could have spent the time they wasted with me hunting down the killer."

"Did Georg have enemies you knew about? Someone who might want us to think the Nazis murdered him?"

Vera leans forward, eager to hear more. "What do you mean?"

"Painting swastikas on his face would be a good way to shift the blame."

"You've seen too many movies."

"Or whoever killed him saw too many. And why blue swastikas? Have you thought about that?" I stand up to get a slice of pumpernickel bread.

"Of course, I have – Georg was a good friend of mine for fifteen years!" she snarls.

"Sorry, I didn't mean to imply anything bad. It's just ... I consulted a medical text book and I found out that when people don't get enough oxygen their face turns bluish. Maybe the killer was surprised by that strange tint on his cheeks, so he rummaged around and found some face paint. Isaac told me that Georg's make-up kit went missing. But the thing is, Vera, even though his windpipe was broken, I don't think Georg was strangled. I saw the photos K-H took of him and there are no marks on his neck."

As she thinks about that, I tear my bread into tiny pieces, drop them in the soup, and swirl them around. When I finally look up at her, she says dejectedly, "In that case, I don't understand what happened."

"Me neither. But if we ever *are* going to understand anything, we have to figure out how Georg turned blue and had his windpipe broken *without* being strangled."

I feel a strange exhaustion after speaking to Vera about my theories, as though I'm climbing uphill through my own life.

Vera leans forward toward me as I eat my soup. "I can't think of anyone who disliked Georg enough to want to hurt him," she says, "though ..." She pauses, giving me a worried look. "Though maybe the police lied about his windpipe being broken. Maybe they were involved. They wanted to cover up something they'd done to Georg ..."

"I didn't think of that," I admit, "but if they're covering things up, we're unlikely to ever ..."

I don't finish my sentence because tears are caught in her lashes. She wipes them away harshly. I put down my spoon. "I'm sorry to make you talk about these things," I tell her.

"It's not your fault. It's that I hate this time we're living in," she tells me. "And sometimes I can't believe Georg is gone. I dream of him all the time, and I wake up thinking I can just pick up the phone and call him. You know, Sophele, Germany makes you doubt everyone and everything. And the only way to be completely safe is to be already dead!"

A truth I should have paid more attention to ... "Vera, tell me something. I found out that you carried furniture to Georg's apartment the evening before his murder."

"Yes, Isaac told me you'd been talking to his neighbors. Georg had decided to re-do his place a bit."

"But remaining in his apartment and buying new furniture probably means that he had no idea at all that he was in big danger. Yet he'd been shot at. Didn't he ever consider moving or changing jobs? Something in his behavior doesn't quite add up."

"For a while, he *did* change his routines to be less predictable.

But then, after a few months, he decided that he couldn't let the Nazis determine how he lived ... or force him to stop making plans. So when he saw a table he wanted, he bought it, and also an antique carpet he'd had his eye on for a while. It was an act of defiance. Not that he took silly chances. He mostly stayed in at night. And he bought a pistol. He carried it whenever he went out."

"Do you know where the pistol is now?"

"Where it is?" she repeats in a surprised voice, which seems odd. "The police have it, of course."

"So it was in his apartment when you found his body?"

"Yes, he kept it in his night table drawer when he was at home. I handed it over to the cops."

"You're sure?"

"Of course, I'm sure!" she exclaims, banging her fist on the table.

"It's just you seemed surprised by my question. And now you seem angry."

"I am angry! Because the police didn't like it that Georg had a gun ... maybe because he was Jewish. And you don't seem to think he had the right to protect himself either!"

"That's not what I meant at all!" I snap back, since I have the feeling by now that Vera pushes until she meets some resistance. In a softer voice, I say, "But listen, things are getting really odd. The murderer could either have been a stranger or someone Georg knew, right? Imagine he was a stranger. Wouldn't Georg have retrieved his gun before opening his door? Which means he'd probably have gotten off at least one shot before being overcome. But anyone who was a friend of Georg's might have known that he owned a gun. In that case, wouldn't the murderer have brought one with him – to even his odds in a fight? Maybe he'd have shot Georg instead of breaking his windpipe."

"No, a shot would have been heard and the killer obviously wanted to avoid detection."

"Did everyone in The Ring know that Georg owned a gun?" I ask.

"I'm not sure. He didn't announce it at any meeting that I can recall, but after he was shot at most of us assumed he'd arm himself. I know he told me and Isaac about the gun. As for the others ..." She stands up and goes to the doorway. Turning around, she shrugs as if we'll never know.

I eat some more soup and sopping bread, trying to see below the glass. "Maybe the killer wasn't Georg's friend, but merely an acquaintance – a peripheral member of The Ring," I say.

Vera sits with me again but says nothing. She stares beyond me, maybe at Georg. I eat my soup. Then I decide to return to the motive. "Do you know if Georg ever said that he might go public with the names of Nazis being bribed by Raffi?"

"I never heard anything like that."

"And the table and carpet ... was there anything unusual about them? Were they very valuable?"

"You mean was his murder a botched robbery?"

"Yes."

"The carpet was kind of ratty, to tell you the truth. And the table was nice but nothing special. Besides, there was nothing but the make-up kit missing from his place."

"Do you know where the rug and table are now?" I ask. I'd like to get a look at them, though I don't know why.

"I've no idea. All I inherited were a few photographs of Georg performing on the high-wire. I don't know where his other things ended up."

"Do you mind my asking why you and he broke up?"

She rubs a tense hand back through her hair. "We were never

really together. We liked each other, but the way I look posed an obstacle to him. And if I'm going to be honest, I don't think I'm the kind of woman who can be half of a couple. The only reason for me to have sex now is so I can have a baby."

"You want a child?" I ask, stunned.

"As long as it doesn't come out looking like me. That's why I want the handsomest father I can find. I want a man who looks like Rudolf Valentino!"

"But how can you be sure the baby will look like the father?"

"I can't. And that, Sophele, is my biggest problem." She lights another cigarette, but her hands are hesitant now. Leaning back in her chair, she smokes thoughtfully. "It's not that the baby's face would matter so much. I know I'd love my child no matter what. But its future prospects would be so ... so dismal if it came out looking like me."

"Has your life turned out that unhappily?"

"No, but my childhood wasn't easy. As I grew more deformed I lost all my friends." She looks at me as if she has needed to tell me of her past for some time. "My parents hid me away. It was as if I was ... I don't know what ..." She looks inside herself for a word that is sufficiently damning.

"Garbage?" I interject, thinking of Isaac's story about the skeletons of dwarfs that workmen found in Paris.

"That's right. And then when I was old enough to leave, I had to earn a living, but no one would hire me, even just to scrub floors. I was the Ogre from Malta until Isaac found me. He was the first person who figured out that my talents with needle and thread could win me my independence. It had never occurred to me. It proves that the most obvious solutions are sometimes the hardest to find. But you know, I still won't go out during the day – too many people staring."

"Then how do you get to Isaac's factory?" I ask, spooning up the last of the soup.

"I leave before dawn and come home after sundown. In the winter, it's not so inconvenient because the days are so short. The long days of summer are tougher. I go in to work only three days a week then. I sew a lot at home. Isaac is patient with me. He's a Jewish saint." She shows me a wily grin. "But don't tell him I told you so."

"No, of course not," I say, smiling too. "But going out only during the night must limit what you can do at the Spanish Embassy."

"Oh, you mean our future embargo," she says skeptically. "I went only once. They couldn't get over my face. I don't think they heard a word I said."

"Vera, you can make sure your child doesn't suffer like you did," I say pressingly, wanting to reassure her. "I'm sure all your friends would help. I know I would."

She gives me a solemn nod. "Will you come with me if I find a good candidate? To help me evaluate him, I mean."

"A good candidate?"

"I've put ads in newspapers. For a man to father my baby. I've got K-H and Marianne looking for me, too. But the prospective fathers I've met so far weren't right."

"Ferrets?"

She laughs in a wild burst, which I adore.

"No, they were handsome enough, but ..." She holds a hand up then lets it fall slowly to the table, making the hissing sound of a leaky balloon. "Men tend to deflate in front of me. So ... so will you come to meet prospective fathers?"

"If I can get away from my parents. They're sure I go around with all the wrong people."

"Tonio?"

"He's just the tip of the iceberg."

"Oh, I see, like me!"

Vera convinces me to risk my parents' wrath and sneak over to Isaac's party by telling me that Julia might know how Georg's skin turned blue even if he wasn't strangled. At the door, Martin greets us wearing a gold-painted papier-mâché crown. "I'm King Ludwig of Bavaria," he tells us, jumping up out of excitement.

"Glad to meet you, your Highness," I reply.

After I kiss his cheek and gaze around at the crowded room, a man's hands blindfold my eyes from behind. "Guess who?" my assailant asks merrily.

I'd know that voice anywhere. "Raffi!"

When I turn around, my old baby-sitter shows me a face of such delight that I figure I ought to get married to him instead of Tonio. "I brought these back from the Nile," he tells me, holding out a box of luscious dried dates, the first I've ever seen.

Raffi's dates are each the size of a plum, and to me they taste like a mixture of honey and marzipan. As I gobble down a second one, he tells me he's narrowed his research down to the ancient sculptural techniques used by an artist named Thutmose, who worked for the Pharaoh Akenhaten. After we talk about his work, I tell him I hated *The Mummy*.

"But I thought it was funny," he says.

"Funny! Boris Karloff was creepy as can be!"

"You used to like scary stories," he tells me. "I guess you're not that little girl anymore." He shakes his head in disbelief, as if my getting older was unpredictable.

"Raffi," I then whisper, "I need to talk to you for a minute about something serious," and after I've dragged him off to the corner of the room, I ask him if Georg ever said he might go public with the names of the Nazis being bribed.

"He never mentioned anything like that to me," Raffi whispers back. "And don't ask me anything more," he adds gruffly.

"All right, so much for that idea," I say, and since he's still looking at me as if I'm dangerous, I kiss his cheek. He asks me about Frau Mittelmann and my latest sketches, which is his way of apologizing for speaking to me harshly. I gobble down four more dates as we talk, since they're delicious and probably the closest I'll ever get to the Nile. Isaac comes over, wearing a feathered headdress – "I'm an Iroquois chief!" he tells me joyfully. Then he warns me against eating so many dates, which I pay no attention to, of course. So when he reads my palm later that evening, he predicts two weeks of diarrhea followed by an unstoppable urge to see the camels at the Berlin zoo.

Other guests have also brought foods that are scarce – and I get tiny slices of a red banana, a section of a Tuscan tangerine, and a sliver of proscuitto from Parma. No moussaka, but I do see my first avocado. All the way from Greece. Isaac drops a slice in my hand and I let it sit on my tongue, imagining that oily green slipperiness about to enter me.

While Lotte Lenya sings of pirates and sinners on the phonograph, Heidi and Rolf dance a miniature waltz. Marianne lets me hold Werner, who – to my joy – still giggles when I blow on his ears. K-H shows me how the boy loves to hold a ping-pong ball in his hand and then won't let go. A future catcher in a trapeze act? After Werner reaches for my nose, which he pulls to his mouth and drools on, he gives me a giant toothless grin.

"A smile that could make *kreplach* sing," Isaac exults, *kreplach* being dumplings. He entertains the boy by making his pipe bob up and down in his mouth.

Then it's Vera's turn to dote on Werner. She takes him from me, kisses him all over, and tosses him the air, up by the ceiling. Werner looks stunned, then wets his diaper, which is Marianne's cue to take him back. When he's grown up, will he remember the gigantic aunt who always made him pee?

Heidi and Rolf join me after their dance. Tugging me down, she whispers sadly about her continued failure to conceive. "I feel so ... so barren. Like there's a desert inside me."

Vera lifting up Werner

"But it could be Rolf," I say, an awkward attempt to be encouraging.

"No, it's me," she declares glumly. "A woman knows these things."

Julia comes around with a tray, offering me a pink, hibiscus-blossom tea in one of Isaac's Mesopotamian cups. She's wearing a conical headdress of violet silk, a long pink gown, and a quiver of arrows on her back. "I'm a fairy godmother!" she announces when I fail to guess.

"With arrows?"

"Wouldn't you want your fairy godmother armed these days?" she asks, and when she grins, the skin around her eyes wrinkles handsomely. Her eyes are clear and black – as though made of hard obsidian. She tells me her people, the Tunshan, are Buddhists, and she is certain we will reincarnate, which gets us talking about our hopes for a future life. "Whatever I come back as," she tells me, "I want to see the wildflowers that blossom every spring on the Asian steppes. All those yellow petals pushing through snow, as though reaching for our hands ..."

That evening, I'll write down her words in my diary. Getting up my courage, I ask her now what drugs might cause a man's face to turn blue, which flusters her. "Why ... why do you want to know?" she sputters.

Is her reticence suspicious or only natural? In either case, my fertile imagination takes off, and the road I take ahead becomes based on her momentary loss of balance. Though maybe that's how we always grope ahead into our future.

When I explain what I've discovered about Georg's murder, which is frustratingly little, she says in a careful, measured voice, "Sophie, I don't want to risk giving you incorrect information, so I'll ask an apothecary friend of mine and then get back to you."

After we talk about school, which seems just about everyone's favorite tactic for having me talk about safe matters, she excuses herself and goes off to find Martin. Vera summons me into the kitchen with a shout that could splinter wood. Once we're together, she hands me a box wrapped in black paper with a big white ribbon.

"Open it before I have a heart attack!" she pleads with me.

I jiggle it. "It's my jacket!"

Her eyes, full of fondness, confirm the truth.

"Oh, Vera, I'm sorry I was mean to you before." I rush into her arms. Then I sit down and tear off the wrapping paper.

The jacket is black silk with cobalt-blue pockets, pink pearls sewn exquisitely into the collar, and white, mother-of-pearl buttons. The same military cut as Vera's.

"It's perfect!" I exclaim, feeling as if I'm back now on the path I was meant to take.

"Try it on," she says. Designing a curve in the air, she adds, "I've altered it to allow for your ... your maturity, but I'm not sure it's going to fit."

She helps me slip it on. It's tight, but if I breathe in hard ...

"Don't worry. I left ample fabric at the seams. I'll let it out an inch or two this week. Let me get a good look at what I need to do."

She steps around me in a circle, leaning down, chewing on her thumbnail as she concentrates.

"Vera, you're the most talented person I know," I tell her.

"Which only means you know too few people. You can take it off now. I'll get it back to you next weekend."

"No, first I've got to look at myself in a mirror! Let's go to Isaac's bedroom."

We tap on the door and, when there's no answer, steal inside like children on a mission. A big chipped mirror – its glass yellowed from pipe smoke – sits on his dresser.

The pearls look like a floating necklace against the shimmering black silk. I pull my hair back. My cheekbones aren't bad, though my eyes are still too close together. I'd look much more alluring if I were sun-darkened like Raffi.

"Look at that!" Vera says excitedly, and when I turn to her, I see she's pointing to my portrait of Isaac, which hangs next to his mother's watercolor of a forest of fire-colored trees. It's in a stunning, gilded-wood frame. It's as if I've joined Dürer and Rembrandt. I'm a professional artist!

As I'm studying the portrait, Vera exclaims, "Don't move ... we need a photo!"

She drags K-H back to me. His *cocoons* have been removed from his hands and all his fingers work reasonably well, except for his right thumb, which is now just a nub. He's got a tiny black camera with him.

He hops around Vera and me, figuring out the shot he wants, bending and kneeling, framing the picture with his fingers. Am I perverse for wondering again what he'd look like naked? Maybe it's lack of experience that makes me so curious. After all, except for my brother's thimble-sized *putz* – which doesn't count – I've seen only Tonio's.

K-H takes three photos. In my favorite, Vera is turning her head to look at Isaac, who has just entered the room. She's smiling like Werner when he's found something delightful within reach. We all are. Proof that happiness was still possible in Germany in 1933.

After Vera died, I kept that photo by my bedside for years, to commemorate the day we became close friends – and to give me the strength to take my second chance.

CHAPTER NINE

Two days after Isaac's party, our parliament building, the Reichstag, goes up in flames, sabotaged – the radio announcer says – by a Dutch left-wing radical named Marinus van der Lubbe who hoped to start a left-wing coup. The next morning, three policemen come to arrest Raffi. He tries to escape through the courtyard window and is shot in the foot. I was stuck at school during all this excitement, but Mama heard the shot and tells me what happened in an angry voice. I presume that her outrage is directed at the trigger-happy policeman until she suggests that Raffi might have been a member of the plot to topple our government.

"Not unless van der Lubbe is interested in sculptures of the Pharaoh Akenhaten," I tell her.

It's careless of me to reveal that I still talk to Raffi, of course. Scenting my small treason, Mama glares at me. "How do you know so much about Rafael?"

"I can't help who I accidentally bump into, Mama."

"I forbid you to talk to him or his family. He could even be a secret agent."

"A spy for Akenhaten?" I ask, happy to play the innocent.

"No, for Russia! Or France! Why are you pretending you don't understand?"

"I'm not pretending. But he wouldn't do anything like that."

Or would he? And if he worked for a foreign government trying to undermine Hitler wouldn't that be the highest form of patriotism?

"With a name like Rafael, who knows what we should expect!" Mama snarls.

I decide not to dignify that even with sarcasm, since I don't want to be accused again of having a sense of humor. But how can she speak like this about someone she used to love? I want desperately to speak to Raffi's parents about him, but if Mama found out ...

Papa doesn't come home until late that evening because he's being "educated" in National Socialist ideology, which is Mama's way of saying that he's having what's left of his mind replaced. Mama, Hansi, and I listen to the radio while we wait for him, which is how we learn that Raffi was just one of several thousand enemies of Germany arrested in nationwide sweeps. The Nazis have used the Reichstag fire as an excuse to eliminate their opponents. And to abolish freedom of speech, as well as all political parties of the left. When we hear that Papa's old friend Maria Gorman and others at Communist Party headquarters have been arrested, Mama jumps up.

"Sophie, hurry," she bursts out, "bring me any letters from your grandparents you've saved!"

"My grandparents?"

"They might have mentioned your father's ... past affiliations."

"Mama, they never write to me."

"Then get anything Rini gave you. And anything that seems Jewish."

"Seems Jewish?"

"Sophie, don't be difficult! Just bring me anything that might get us in trouble."

I take advantage of my time alone to hide my sketchbooks and diary under my mattress, though I'm going to have to get rid of my drawings of Rini, Isaac, and Vera.

History has a way of repeating itself, and Mama feeds all our letters into the oven. After all, an aunt or cousin may have inadvertently mentioned Papa's Communist past. I hand her my stack of birthday cards from Rini.

How are Jewish gifts like Jews themselves? The start to a joke circulating around Berlin that Paula Noske, one of my girlfriends, will ask me the next day, which must mean thousands of mothers are up to the same frenzied tricks as mine.

You can warm your hands over them when you stick them in the oven, Paula tells me, and she laughs like a donkey.

Of course, the joke isn't funny at all, but it's not really meant to be, since humor is part of the Semitic and Bolshevist plot to detour Germany from its glorious future.

After today, our kitchen walls never lose the charred scent of Mama's panic, and the only phoenix I can see rising out of the ash is her clawing mistrust of everyone except Hansi. If I were to say that suspiciousness stalked all the words she addressed to me for the rest of her life, I would not be exaggerating. Though perhaps if she'd have lived longer ...

When I ask Mama if there's something we can do for Maria Gorman, she says impatiently, "Don't be silly, Sophie. That woman can handle herself just fine."

Papa comes home late and when he slips into my room to say goodnight, I tell him about Maria and say, "I hope she'll be all right." Implied in my tone is, *Can you do something to help her?*

"Don't worry, the worst that will happen is they'll kick her out of Germany. She'll go to Russia. Or maybe to London. She has a sister there." Glaring at me, possibly because I've implied that he has a responsibility toward her, he says, "Forget about Maria."

So it is I learn that enemies of the Fatherland are not even permitted to enter my thoughts.

Rini greets me at the school gate the next morning and summons me out to the street. We haven't shared anything but resentful glances over the last months. Best friends who can't find their way home.

"I just want to make sure your father hasn't been taken by the police," she whispers.

"He's safe," I reply. "He switched teams just in time."

She smiles with such relief that the tide of emotions I've been holding back washes over me, leaving behind deep regret and shame. "Oh, Rini," I say, "I miss being with you."

She tugs at her ear – a sign of anxiety she's been making since we were little kids and that I've come to copy. "Don't say anything more or I'll break down like ... like ..." Resorting to humor to change our mood, she clasps her hands by her cheek and gives me a pathetic, agonized look.

"June, my darling, I'd know you anywhere!" I gush with melodramatic passion, since it's her June Marlowe imitation.

Our friendship renewed by our delight in imitating bad actresses, we watch a tall young man washing the windows in a house across the street, intrigued because he's wearing a black beret.

"Good enough to eat for dessert!" Rini whispers.

Apparently, we've both grown up when it comes to men, and all we haven't said over the past year – especially about boyfriends – sits on our shoulders

"Is everything okay with you and your parents?" I ask.

"No. Mama's brother was arrested and Papa will probably lose his job. Jews can't switch teams, but we've contracted a good Aryan lawyer." She casts a look back at the school and scowls.

"Gurka is watching us," she tells me out of the side of her mouth.

I turn. Five neatly dressed girls – three with perfect pigtails – are staring at us as if they'd like to drive stakes into our hearts. Murdered by Bavarian milkmaids – what a fate!

"One day, I'm going to make that blond-haired toad pay!" I announce.

"It's not her fault," Rini says.

"I don't care!"

She grins at my evil nature. "Give my regards to your parents and give Hansi a kiss," she tells me, and she starts away until I grab her arm.

I have no idea what I want to say. I only want to make her stay with me.

"We'll laugh about this in a few years," she tells me, trying to make her voice sound sure. "Oh, I almost forgot ..." She reaches into her schoolbag and hunts down a cigarette card: Garbo as Mata Hari, a jeweled collar around her neck.

I kiss her when I've got it in my hands; I've been wanting this picture for years. Then the school bell rings. While the other girls file inside, Rini takes out a chocolate bar and breaks off a piece, then bites it in two and gives me half.

Two infantry soldiers sharing a last cigarette in a Remarque novel. We're part of a generation of girls who will never need such a scene explained to them.

If Rini and I were to meet now as two old women, I'd ask her if chocolate ever tasted the same to her after that morning. And I bet her answer would be the same as mine: it became the taste of our forced separation.

As she leaves me, I think about never going to class again, and how gratifying it would be to be expelled, but I shuffle in after all the others. Madame Navarre has moved back to Nantes and our new French teacher, Dr Braun, greets us with "Heil Hitler" and a stiff-armed salute. While we're conjugating verbs, Gurka and her friends throw spitballs at Rini's head, and at the two other Jewish girls in our class, Ruth and Martina. I'm sure Professor Braun sees, but he does nothing, and all I can do is make another one of my seething promises to get revenge.

That afternoon, I stop by the Munchenbergs' apartment to ask if there's any news about Raffi but no one is home. Sitting on my bed after school, I read in the *Berliner Tageblatt* that Ludwig Renn has been arrested. Garbo gives me a look of complicity from the wall, asking me to promise I won't denounce her if Papa demands the photograph of Mr Renn and him from my K-H Collection.

After supper, Papa asks where his newspaper is.

"I'm not ... I'm not sure," I lie.

"You were reading it before, Sophie," Mama observes, setting down her needle and thread. She's sewing up a ripped seam in one of Hansi's shirts.

"But I can't remember where I put it."

"How many places could it be?" my father asks.

"I suppose it might be in my room."

"Then I *suppose* you should get it," Mama says sarcastically.

I beg Papa to do a jigsaw puzzle with Hansi and me instead. I hang on to his arm like a leech, which used to win me easy laughter.

"I'm too tired," he says, shaking me off. "And you're too big for this sort of begging."

I sulk, but as he sits down he says roughly, "Get the paper *now*, Sophie."

After I hand it to him, he spreads his newsprint wings, a gesture that was always a strange comfort before, an assurance that he was an adult with ties of duty to the world outside our home. But no longer. I turn on the radio, loud, but he snaps at me to lower the volume.

"Can't a girl want to do something with her father in the evening?" I demand.

As if it's a civilized answer, he spreads his wings again. I sit behind him, by the radio, so I can keep an eye on his progress through the *Tageblatt*. My brother is lying on his belly beside me, looking at pictures of fancy roadsters in one of Tonio's magazines. If only Papa needed reading glasses, I could accidentally misplace them in the basement garbage. Or trick Mama into stepping on them, which would be even better.

As he reaches the article that could lead me to betray the Jews and dissidents whom Garbo is protecting, I whack Hansi over the head, which makes him burst into tears.

"He hit me first!" I explain. "I swear!"

That's about as likely as Marius van der Lubbe setting the Reichstag fire, and Papa, fuming, stands up and orders me to my room. I leave my door open a crack. After Mama has quieted my brother with kisses and cooing, she and Papa talk in the kitchen.

"It's Tonio," Mama says. "That boy makes her lose her mind."

True enough. But my sex life really isn't the point, is it?

"And she's still obsessed with Garbo and Dietrich," Mama adds indignantly.

"She's bound to grow out of this movie phase of hers," Papa replies calmly.

"Grow out of it? Freddi, Tonio even took her to one of those wretched Westerns a few weeks back."

So it is that I learn Tom Mix and his horse Tony are to blame for my rebelliousness. Good to know in case the Gestapo interrogate me.

Later in their conversation, Mama cites the possibility that I don't eat enough vegetables or get sufficient sleep. Papa thinks I may be jealous of my brother, but can he seriously believe I want to be Mama's favorite any more? They're parents who consider everything but the obvious; I'm not very good at leading a double life. At least, not as good as them.

That night a piece of luck finally squeezes its way into my puzzle; Papa never reads about Mr Renn's arrest.

When I kiss Hansi goodnight, I apologize. "You can hit me back if you like," I tell him. "As hard as you want."

But he doesn't even make a fist, which is disappointing; I'd like there to be justice in the world even if it means a sore arm.

"Say something!" I whisper-scream, because he hasn't made a peep in so long. He shakes his head. "If you come back," I add seductively, poking his belly to make him grab my hand, "then I'll take you to the Tiergarten and buy you nuts to feed the squirrels."

He drops our united touch, closes his eyes, and rolls away from me.

"I've slept with Tonio," I whisper in his ear, and I give his droopy little lobe a pull, which makes him wriggle his shoulders. "But don't tell anyone or I'll be quartered and pickled."

Now, I'm no longer the sole owner of that particular secret, but sharing it with my brother doesn't make me feel much better. A mute nine-year-old must not count as a confidant.

I sketch him going to sleep. And for the first time, I think it will be a good thing if he keeps as far away from our world as he can – at least one person will be blameless when this is all over.

I offer to buy eggs for my mother at Frau Koslowski's grocery the next evening so that afterward I can make a quick detour to the Munchenbergs'. Behind the counter of the crowded little shop, over the candy shelf, hangs a picture of Hitler, his arm upraised in a salute. Frau Koslowski sees me eyeing it and tells me, "The Germans have finally found their Saint George." I expect her to say more, but she just shrugs morosely, meaning, *What can I do but make believe they're right?*

I nod my understanding and pick out my eggs. A whole country nodding and shrugging its way into the sewers.

Mrs Munchenberg opens the door to my knocks. She's a darting, sparrow of a woman, quick-tongued and no-nonsense. Isaac says it's impossible to know exactly what she looks like because she never stays still long enough to be sure. She works as a legal secretary for an important Berlin lawyer. In her hands is an old linen napkin – white with a pink border – that she's been worrying to shreds. Her eyes have a lost look and her mascara, normally precise, has become blue-black smudges.

She invites me in, but I lift up my egg basket and tell her I can't stay.

"Any news from Raffi?" I ask.

"News? Those goddamn bastards won't even tell us where he's being held."

Mrs Munchenberg swears like a coal delivery man when she's enraged. She stares at me hard, and we share a moment of silent union.

"Thank Raffi again for the Egyptian dates when you see him," I tell her, wishing there was something more I could do to help her. "They were delicious."

"Will you have one more, Sophie?" she asks yearningly, as if it's important to her. "I saved a few for good friends."

Have I become a good friend now that we've experienced despairing silence together? Maybe it's because she knows I'll always adore her son.

When she returns from the kitchen with a basket, each date wrapped in a pink ribbon, I lift one out and put it on top of my eggs. Professor Munchenberg suddenly comes up behind her and smiles warmly at me, his hand on his wife's shoulder. His shirt tail is hanging out in back and his unshaven cheeks are creased with sleep. "Sophie, how nice to see you," he says, and I can see in his eyes he means it. "Take three more for your parents and Hansi."

"Yes, do!" Mrs Munchenberg agrees, smiling as best she can.

My parents don't deserve them, I'd like to confess. *Besides, they wouldn't accept them from you now.* Instead, I say, "No, save them for Raffi. He'll want to remember that the Nile is waiting for him when he gets out."

That night I awake to shots coming from the direction of Friedrichshain Park. There's no news in the papers about a gunfight the next morning, but my friend Marthe Salter tells me and a few other girls that workers fought with Nazis in Answalder Platz. She lives with her parents and brothers on the southern side of the square and adds that she saw a young man wearing a dark apron who was wounded and maybe killed. He fell right in front of the Kuntz Dress Shop and blood – much darker than she'd expected – seeped from his head.

He'd been rescued by friends and carried into the back seat of a car, then driven off.

Gurka, excited by talk of the wounded worker, tells everyone that German spies are in Switzerland, France, and America getting ready to assassinate famous Germans who've fled. "Marlene Dietrich included!" she announces to me, happy as a princess who gets to order a rival's execution.

"Who told you that?" I ask.

"My father fixes Robert Ley's cavities and he told us yesterday they'd all be killed within a week." Seeing my puzzlement, she adds with pride, "Herr Ley is the Nazi Party head of organization."

I'm too upset to think of an adequate reply and slink away. All day, I find myself praying that Marlene has fearsome bodyguards. I only really believe Gurka doesn't know what she's talking about when I cross off the seventh day on my calendar. My worry for Marlene is another thing that blond cow will have to pay for.

In mid-March, on one of my furtive, pre-school visits to Isaac's apartment, he hands me the photos of Vera and me that K-H took at his Carnival party. I conceal them in my schoolbag and slip them behind Garbo that evening.

My favorite: an eager girl leaning toward the lens, her thumb lifting up her pearl collar, so electric with excitement that she seems to be giving off light.

Vera always said I looked like no one else in that photograph, which was her greatest compliment. Maybe she wanted a love of uniqueness to serve as the cure to Germany's worship of conformity.

Isaac also gives me my jacket, and now that the seams have been let out, it fits perfectly. But where will I wear it? My parents would never believe that I could afford to buy such a beautiful coat at a shop, and if they knew that Vera had made it for me ... A treasure I'll have to give up until life grows simpler.

Isaac agrees to keep my coat for me, and also to hide my drawings of him, Vera, and Rini in his bookshelves, in between the volume on Giotto that he'd lent me and another on Cimabue. Seeing my work there makes me feel welcome – I'm making room for myself inside Isaac's home and the medieval Italian art that reminds him of God and man and all the levels of heaven in between.

He hands me a note from Julia in which she's written the names of plants and drugs that cause the skin to turn blue: sorghum leaves, black henbane, climbing nightshade, oil of mirbane, antimony, and cyanide. "I know what your next question is," she writes, "and I do indeed sell henbane, but I haven't sold any in quantities that would cause anyone's death. Cyanide and antimony might also, I think, be relatively easy to purchase, though not from me."

When I read the note to Isaac and tell him about my theories, he says, "So how do you think no marks were made on Georg's neck?"

"I think I'm stumped," I admit.

"Tell me, Sophele, is it possible to speak without a voice?"

"No."

"Then how do K-H and Marianne communicate?" He smiles encouragingly. "You and I will keep looking below the glass and I'm sure one of us will find an answer. Though I don't want you taking chances. You can do all the investigating you want in your head and in libraries, but you are not to talk to anyone but me and Vera about any of this! Do you hear me?"

Playing by Isaac's rules for the moment, I go to the National Library and read all I can about strangulation over the next couple of weeks, but I don't find myself any closer to an answer. Then, a shock ... On the 23rd of March, Hitler consolidates his power. Our legislature – cowed into submission by Nazi propaganda and armed brownshirts in the hallways – gives him the right to implement his own laws, control the budget, set foreign policy, and try political opponents in military-style courts where they have no right to legal counsel.

Late that afternoon, while I'm returning from an errand in Alexanderplatz, wondering what this virtual coup will mean for me and my friends, I finally get some news about Raffi ... Mrs Munchenberg is already aboard the Prenzlauer Allee tram when I hop aboard. She's carrying a new shirt for her husband – powder blue. He's to wear it at their nephew's bar-mitzvah in a week.

When I consider that Thursday afternoon now, it seems criminal to me that we continued shopping, riding trams, and pointing happily to the yellow crocuses peeping through the hard soil in the city's parks, but I suppose all of us craved the details of daily life as false reassurance that becoming a dictatorship would change nothing.

After I admire Mrs Munchenberg's purchase, I ask, "Any news about Raffi yet?"

"We just got a letter saying he's being held in Dachau."

Imagine a time when a German girl has to ask where Dachau is!

"Near Munich," she tells me, and she makes the sour face of a Berliner imagining the hinterland. "They say it's a concentration camp."

It's the first time I hear the word *Konzentrationslager*, which is to become an important word in our new vocabulary.

"It's a big sprawling prison in the middle of nowhere," she explains, "and I've been told it's surrounded by barbed-wire fences. The men and women live in barracks, and families are not allowed to visit. No one sees what happens inside." She looks down to keep her emotions from flooding her. "The guards could be doing anything to those poor men and women ... to my Raffi."

"What are they holding him for?" I ask.

"Who the hell knows? The letter hardly said anything."

I give her hand a squeeze, which makes Mrs Munchenberg close her eyes to keep from crying. We ride without talking, though she gives me a little smile from time to time, as if to say, *It's not a betrayal of me for you to go on with your life.* But maybe it is.

It's while I'm watching the endless rush of buildings flying past us that I realize – with a feeling of descent into myself – that the traitor in The Ring may be responsible for Raffi's arrest. Which means I'll have to work harder than I have to learn his identity – and not give up, no matter what the risk. Because these concentration camps are going to fill up with opponents of Hitler, and Isaac and Vera could also be denounced at any time.

A stylish chestnut-haired woman with a fox stole around her

neck is standing next to me. She must have overheard what Mrs Munchenberg and I have been conversing about, because she tells her young daughter that she doesn't think Jews should still be allowed on public transportation. She speaks loudly enough for everyone around us to hear. Twenty eager eyes turn to Mrs Munchenberg and me, expecting a confrontation.

When I frown at the offensive woman, she says with false sweetness, "I just don't think you belong in Germany, dear."

I'll never forget that *dear*. And her twisted little grin, as if she's being clever.

"I don't happen to be Jewish," I reply. *Ich bin aber gar keine Jüdin.* My denial makes me feel as if I've swallowed dirt. I wish immediately I could take it back. But before I can make amends by declaring that I'm a loyal Communist, Mrs Munchenberg whispers to me, "I'm getting off, Sophie." And she stands up.

"But this isn't our stop," I tell her, so desperately ashamed of myself that I add, "Please, Mrs Munchenberg, don't get off."

"You stay on, honey." She touches my arm, then draws her hand back quickly.

I step off behind her. We walk together to our apartment house, in separate silences, because she won't look at me. I want to apologize – even for the blue sky – but say nothing. At her door, we face each other as neighbors who can move toward greater friendship or turn away into distinct worlds, and I can feel her longing as a soft pressure against my heart. But I've enough to conceal from my parents already.

Sensing my dilemma, she smiles as people do when they find the courage to forge on despite the long, hopeless days facing them. Taking two anise drops out of her bag, she hands them to me. "One for you and one for Hansi," she says. "And give him a kiss, if ... if that's all right."

Her *if that's all right* makes my chest ache, and I'm about to apologize, but she puts her finger to her lips. "Sophie, there's no need to say anything more."

But there is. Why don't I reassure her that her being Jewish means nothing to me?

Because it does, I can hear Vera telling me, refusing to let me get away with anything.

I sometimes wonder what would have happened had I gone in and made Mrs Munchenberg a cup of tea, and if we'd sat together talking about Raffi. Or if I'd pushed the rude woman off the tram. Or if I'd started screaming and refused to stop. Maybe I'd have helped to shatter the stained glass of our world sooner, on that day we lost our democracy, before the Nazis had time to make their plans.

Astonishingly to me, prospects for The Ring become dismal right away; Hitler's total command of our government has frightened our European neighbors, who now fear doing anything to provoke him. Isaac is no longer even welcome at the Portuguese Embassy.

"They don't understand that acting now is the only way to stop him," he tells me angrily.

"Maybe you ought to try something less ambitious," I say; the possibility of his being sent to Dachau is a heavy shroud of dread over all my nights of late.

"No, no, no," he declares. "I'm making some slow progress at the Turkish Embassy, and *slow* is at least better than nothing."

Tonio and I use his father's apartment twice more that month, when we have promised to be at the movies. Sex or Hollywood. It appears I cannot have both. No matter; the second time does the trick, and a window opens in my heart. Men and boys are not all ferrets, and I am beginning to understand the Trojan War, Homer, and romantic poetry. All of them are contained in a young man with a beautiful penis that never tires of me, and who carries me out to sea atop his affection, and who talks in soft tones about cars afterwards, as if they are as intimate as the warm cinnamon of our breath when we are nearly asleep and facing each other.

A young man's large, dark eyes as the key to existence – and my refuge. Would our chances for a life together have been better or worse in another, more tranquil, country?

Later, as we're dressing, he brings up the boycott of Jewish shops planned for the 1st of April – the first public display of Hitler's anti-Jewish policies since he was named Chancellor. A test to see if the *Volk* – with all their innate *völkischen* wisdom – are behind him.

"Will you come with me to Ziegelstraße?" Tonio asks. "There's a large kosher butcher there. My Nazi Youth troop will be guarding it."

Guarding it? "I have to help my mother on Saturday," I tell him. "She's going with Papa to the rally where Hitler is going to speak, and she wants me home to take care of Hansi."

The truth for once is good enough. Papa wants Mama to be seen with him in public at a Nazi celebration. He'd take us along, but he's worried that Hansi will be an *embarrassment*, though he uses that word only when he's alone with my mother.

Not that I really plan on staying home; Vera and Isaac have convinced me to be part of a protest that The Ring has organized against the boycott.

"You can bring Hansi along," Tonio says enticingly. "He'll love seeing me in uniform."

"My brother likes onion soup and rodents, though not necessarily in that order."

"He likes me. And I'll be there."

Tonio clearly regards Hansi as the younger brother he never had. I'm moved, but I still decline. "Look," I say gently, "you know my parents would feed me to the pigs if they found out I'd brought him along. And anyway, a boycott of Jewish shops seems pretty silly to me."

"Dr Goebbels doesn't think so."

No, a Minister of Propaganda wouldn't, would he? "Tonio," I say carefully, "let's not talk about Jews. We'll only quarrel."

"What am I going to do with you?" he replies, as if I'm a lovable but difficult child. With a mind of her own he'd prefer I didn't have.

At 9:30 on the morning of the 1st of April, precisely half an hour after my parents leave for a breakfast with Papa's co-workers and then the rally, I lead Hansi out of our apartment and walk to Frau Koslowski's grocery, where I've scheduled a rendezvous with Vera. I've told my brother we're off on a shopping expedition, which is true in a way, since Jewish businessmen have donated funds for those of us participating in the protest to break the boycott by purchasing merchandise.

As soon as Vera arrives, we head into the historic center of the city, to Weinmeisterstraße, because we're to meet Isaac at a restaurant called Karl's Cellar. Vera, who is venturing outside during the day for the first time in years, is cloaked from head to toe in dark gray mohair. "As soft as a whisper," she says without irony. Vera never jokes about clothing.

She's lifted the wing of the cloak over her lips and nose, which makes her look like an Arabian bride. There's little she can do to hide her mallet-like forehead, however, and I learn more about expressions of horror that day than during my previous fifteen years. As we rush down Hirtenstraße, a portly businessman in a derby hat gasps. Further down the block, waifs playing marbles gawk and point, and one of them follows us, squeezing her hands between her legs, gaping like a gargoyle, unable to decide if she should pee in her knickers or dribble over her chin.

Vera walks as fast as she can, which means Hansi and I have to run to stay even, which also means we've less time to avoid the obstacle course on the sidewalk. *Dog Shit Is Berlin's True Pavement*. It's not the title of an Expressionist art exhibit at the famous Der Sturm Gallery, but it could be. As we dodge a gutted armchair left outside a broken-down rooming house, my brother squashes a big one, which really isn't his fault since it's Saturday morning, the time when even the most crippled Berliners get out their silver-tipped canes and hobble down the street behind their eager, nose-to-the-ground mutts, who are themselves bloated with boiled potatoes and liverwurst leftovers from the night before. I scrape Hansi's shoe on the sidewalk while he hops around, and then tie the foul-smelling thing back on him. By the time we're finished, Vera is a hundred of her giant paces ahead. The Alfa Romeo Spider of former circus performers – zero to 120 in only six seconds ...

She waits for us just inside the door to Karl's Cellar. Once we reach her, she sheds her cloak, hands it to me as though I've become her butler, and sits on the carpeted stairs leading down to the dining room. She sighs like she's been through hell.

"It could have been worse," I observe. "If this were ancient Israel, they might have stoned us to death."

"Very reassuring," she replies, eyeing me with hostility. When she reaches out her hand to me, I help her stand, remembering that her knee joints are made out of papier-mâché.

We sit at a table at the back of the dining room. Vera smokes, and I join her, though I dare to inhale only once. Most of the dozen customers are still sleeping off what must have been a night of carousing, though one couple – a raven-haired prostitute and her pale, sickly looking pimp – are having an animated conversation about Czech bonds. Could she make enough in bed to consider foreign investments?

All the table lamps have orange paper thrown over them to keep the glare from waking customers. Given the diffuse lighting, it feels like we're stuck in a fish tank – a gaudy, reddish one, since the wallpaper features gold urns on a scarlet background. A peroxide blond with a stained white blouse takes our order for coffee and a hot chocolate for Hansi.

She must know Vera because she doesn't even blink.

I've brought along an Italian jigsaw puzzle of Michelangelo's *David* for Hansi, and when I take the box from my schoolbag, the boy grabs it and gets to work. Mama has drawn a big black circle over David's you-know-what because she worries that if he handles even cardboard testicles my brother might turn into a *women's shoe salesman*, as she calls men who sleep with other men.

Vera helps Hansi find puzzle pieces and, to my great astonishment, my brother doesn't push her away or caw like a crow, which must mean he has accepted her into his circle of certified assistants, which is composed of me, Papa, Mama, Tonio and Raffi.

My coffee, served in chipped white china, tastes like licorice. "Yuccch!" I groan.

Vera takes a sip. "A kitchen worker must have been drinking absinthe," she explains.

"Don't they bother washing the cups?" I ask, sliding it far away.

"Consider yourself lucky – absinthe is the perfect disinfectant."

She trades coffees with me, but hers tastes faintly of smoked fish.

Isaac arrives just as I'm finishing Hansi's hot chocolate. He's wearing a fawn-colored tweed coat, black pants, white spats, and a floral tie – red roses. His silver hair is combed back and forms dashing wings over his ears. A handsome sorcerer who might take off and fly. Attractive, maybe even sexy, but he smells of mothballs.

"I was busy with final plans," he says excitedly, out of breath, rubbing his hands together. He's humming a tune I don't recognize, then breaks out into full operatic voice. *Ombra mai fu* ... He continues down a sequence of bright, mercurial notes, ending with a smile at me. And I'd expected a baritone made rusty by all that pipe smoking.

Isaac gives us all popping kisses, including Hansi, and then sits next to me and finishes my coffee without remarking on its fishiness. Taste buds ruined by tobacco may also be my fate, because my second cigarette of the morning doesn't make me want to puke like the first one did. Martin and his mother Julia join us shortly. The pear-headed young man is so excited by our outing that he gets up to pee as soon as he sits down. "Strong as a bull but with a bladder the size of an almond," his mother confides in me, and she looks at him so affectionately as he shuffles off that I can't help admiring her. Though I also remain wary, since she could be the person who sent Georg to his death and Raffi to Dachau.

Then an elegantly dressed couple in their thirties arrives. The woman is pushing the wheelchair of a young man whose body is as twisted as a bonsai pine. On his lap is a bearded little mutt with wiry brown fur.

"Minnie!" Isaac exults, standing up and clapping his hands. "Get up here!"

Isaac holds out his arms. The dog hops to the ground and leaps into the man's affectionate embrace with a yelp. She licks at Isaac's face as if his skin is made of sugar crystals, wriggling with excitement. Around her neck is a small sign that reads: "Aryan, Jew, or Dachshund? Guess my race and win a kiss!"

In German, race and breed are the same word – *Rasse*.

The dog's name is Minnie, after the Disney mouse, and she's part dachshund, part Berlin trash hound. She bounces when she walks, with her ears flopping and rump jiggling. For Hansi, it's love at first sight. I order him to stay put but that's simply not going to happen now that he's seen the reception Isaac has gotten; my brother crawls under the table and squats on his haunches next to Minnie when she's lowered to the ground by Isaac. Hansi throws his arms around her neck and gives her kisses on the snout, which are returned with luxurious, full-tongued licking. I'll have to wash the musty smell of dog breath off of him when I get him home or my parents will guess we snuck out.

Minnie's owners are Molly and Klaus Schneider – trapeze flyers at Althof's Circus. They walk like Carmen Miranda balancing bananas on her head, with their feet turned out as if they're always indicating 10:10 on a clock. "We were ballet dancers in a previous incarnation," Klaus explains.

The young man with the twisted body is Arnold Muller. A German-American from St Louis. He was born with a spine disease.

"Arnold is famous!" Vera tells me. "You didn't see the article on him in the *Morgenpost* a year ago? He was left for dead by his parents in a closet – no food and no water, yet ..."

"Vera, I'd prefer not to hear the story again," he tells her in his heavily accented German. "I don't actually like being famous for nearly dying."

Arnold works as a typist at Isaac's factory. "I'm a demon on a keyboard," he tells me, jiggling his fingers in the air.

As we leave, Isaac explains that in order to prevent the Nazis learning our whereabouts, he's informed everyone participating in our small conspiracy of their destination only at the last minute. Twelve groups that he and Vera have organized will be breaking the boycott. He's just been on the phone with the last of them.

In an eager whisper, he informs us that we are to head to Weissman's Fabric Shop on Hirtenstraße, where we will meet K-H, Marianne, and Roman.

Isaac's sense of dangerous intrigue would have thrilled me in the past, but now it only makes me jittery. "Do you think all this precaution really necessary?" I ask him.

"You never know how good the stuffing of a cabbage is until you cut it open."

"Which means what exactly?"

"These days, it's impossible to know who's wearing a mask."

CHAPTER TEN

Although it's only a hundred paces from Alexanderplatz, Grenadierstraße might be Warsaw or Prague at the turn of the century:

Horse carts with dusty, bent-backed peasants at the reins. The smell of burning coal, pickled herring, cheap beer, and sweat coming out from the tenements. Street-corner philosophers in fur hats whose tattered coats sweep the streets, with time-ravaged faces Rembrandt would have loved to draw. Older sisters searching their younger brothers' hair for nits. Feral cats slinking around like spies and racing between the wheels of pushcarts brimming with pickles. And Germany's ever-present war cripples sitting on the sidewalks, hands out, their stubbly cheeks hollowed out by hunger.

"What's the use of a government who leaves them to rot," Vera observes, shaking her head.

In front of us, a cross-eyed loner – pale as bone, with needles of hair standing straight up – tries to blow a tin trumpet but produces only one shrill note. By the Rosenzweig Beer Garden, *alter kackern* are discussing something that has them making furious, whirling hand movements. Their wives ...? Hemorrhoids ...? Next to them is the neighborhood Methuselah, sitting on a green velveteen sofa, tugging thoughtfully on his foot-long red beard, which must have started growing in the 1890s. A young man wearing a wide-brimmed hat is reading to him from Stephan Zweig's biography of Marie

Antoinette, which has been in the windows of all the bookshops over the last year.

"The old lecher still hankers after pretty young princesses with powder on their breasts!" Vera whispers to me.

A rubber ball suddenly bumps into Methuselah's sofa, a tawny-colored hound just behind it. The dog barks at the rubber plaything when it stops rolling, outraged by its failure to move.

The whole neighborhood would clearly benefit from a week at the seaside, where the salt breeze would blow away the dust and grime, and maybe even help that unidentified hacking cough that half the residents seem to have.

"Why are they all here?" I ask Isaac.

"Pogroms and paupery, Sophele."

"But they're poor as dirt here."

"Yes, but maybe their children will be rich!"

I've been to Grenadierstraße before, but never with a Jewish guide, and Isaac explains some of the neighborhood's mysteries to me as we walk along. His deep, sure voice serves to calm me.

"What's he doing?" I ask. I'm pointing to a man mumbling to himself, rocking back and forth in front of the brick wall of a bookshop.

"Praying," Isaac says. *"Davening.* And facing the Wailing Wall. Remember, Sophele, Jerusalem is right in here." He pokes his index finger into my forehead as he does when he wants me to remember that the Torah speaks of worlds inside ourselves.

"And what are they doing?" A man and woman are seated at an outdoor cafe under the tangle of a bare-limbed rose arbor, and though he's wearing a fancy, pin-striped suit, his glasses are held together with black tape. She looks like a giant tropical fish, with puffed-out pink lips and circles of rouge on her cheeks. They seem to be quarreling while he jots down notes in a tiny black book.

"They're buying and selling," Isaac tells me. He summons us closer and we eavesdrop. "Currencies. She's trying to sell him Romanian leu for a price he's not willing to pay."

"He works for a trading house?"

"He *is* a trading house! Moshe Cohen, the Walking Stock Exchange. *Di Geyendike Berzhe*," Isaac translates exultantly into Yiddish.

"And who's she?"

"Eve Gutkind. A matchmaker. It's said she could wed oil to vinegar and their kids would come out as salad dressing." He repeats the saying in Yiddish: "*Zi ken khasene hobn mit naft biz esik, di kinder veln aroyskumen salat sos.*"

"Hey Moshe!" Isaac calls out. "How about buying my friend here fifty acres on Mars!" He indicates my brother with a wave.

Moshe points his pencil at Hansi. "Any special place on Mars, son?"

But Hansi doesn't reply. His love affair with Minnie, whose leash he is now holding, is far more interesting.

"Maybe you'd like a canal, Hansele?" Isaac asks my brother gently.

Hansi covers his ears with his hands. Most people would be offended, but Isaac laughs good-naturedly.

"Somewhere there's lots of squirrels," I yell to Moshe.

"Got it!" he replies, and he notes the transaction in his book.

Further down the street, a young man in a red and green bellhop costume is eating what looks like finely ground oatmeal.

"What's he doing here?"

"Some of the children of immigrants have found jobs with the Gentiles – even in fancy hotels. He must be getting some hot food in his belly before his shift."

"And what's he eating?"

"Kasha. My wife made the best in Berlin! Her kasha will be served on the Mount of Olives after the dead are resurrected and we ..."

While Isaac is finishing his homage to Mrs Zarco, I notice that the shops on this end of the street are closed. And all the apartments have their curtains drawn. No children are playing. Near the corner, the Logirhaus Centrum boarding house has planks nailed over its front door. Standing in front, like wizened guardians, are three old men wearing black hats and prayer shawls, one of whom calls out to us. "You'd better not go any further, Isaac," he says. "*Tsuris* ahead ..."

"We'll be all right, rabbi," Isaac replies.

"What's *tsuris*?" I ask Vera.

"Troubles."

Isaac shakes the rabbi's hand and assures him all will be well, since we are acting as God's hands and feet on earth. But when we turn the corner onto Hirtenstraße, I go all cold: twenty SA storm-troopers – brownshirts – are standing in a stiff line in front of Weissman's, which is only fifty paces away, close enough for one of them to shoot one of God's servants. Me, for instance. Even my brother senses something is wrong, and he looks up at me as if to ask, *What do we do now?*

A good question, but I'm too stunned to conceive of a reply. Isaac faces us, smiling his encouragement. "We're just going to walk into the shop and buy some fabric and then come back out and get on our way."

He makes it sound so simple. Naïveté or stupidity? Possibly both.

He takes Vera's arm and adds, "Please, don't let yourself be provoked. I'm counting on you to hold on tight to Sophele and Hansi."

As Vera grips my shoulder, I pray I haven't made the worst error of my life. An unpleasant realization: if something bad were to happen to my brother, I could never forgive myself. I take Minnie's leash from the boy and give it to Klaus, then order Hansi to give me his hand. He looks as though he might burst into tears, so I say, "When we're all done, you can play with Minnie some more. And don't you dare cry or I will, too. And then I'll have to clobber you!"

"Here come K-H, Marianne, and Roman," Vera says, waving.

They're a hundred yards away, but K-H is already snapping photographs with his camera, so excited that he doesn't wave back, but his wife does. Marianne is wearing men's black trousers, a yellow scarf, and a stylish blue hat pulled low over her ears. She's walking arm in arm with Roman, who's got on a stunning scarlet coat with wide, flaring lapels. Two tropical birds compared to the rest of us.

I look up at Vera and whisper, "Did you make Roman's coat?"

"Who else would pick such a color?" she replies.

Roman walks with a bounce, not unlike Minnie. The happy certitude of a star who senses all of Berlin in his feet. And who is gloriously unable to see any Nazis nearby.

"Now listen everyone, just stay behind me," Isaac says. "We're going to head toward the entrance now."

Vera, Hansi, and I walk forward, hand in hand – a lopsided trio. Each step feels as if it's a descent, and I'm sweating so hard that my blouse clings to my skin.

Vera whispers to me, "I won't let anything happen to you or Hansi. I promise."

Her voice is secure, and I'd give her odds in any fair fight, but *fair* has been eliminated from the German language to make room for more useful and modern expressions such as *lebensunwertes Leben*, life unworthy of life. A language must evolve, after all ...

We pass the storm-troopers one by one. They give us silent looks of hatred, and I don't dare look them in the eyes, since my mouth is as dry as dust, which means tears are closing in on me. I'm aware, too, of the sexual risk between me and the men. *Women can be raped:* now that I've slept with Tonio, my body understands that bad news.

Out of the corner of my eye, I see JUDE written in large white letters on each of the shop windows. A printed banner on the roof catches my attention: *Helft mit an der Befreiung Deutschlands vom jüdischen Kapital. Kauft nicht in jüdischen Geschäften.* Help liberate Germany from Jewish capital. Don't buy at Jewish shops.

"Look at that deformed one!" one of the brownshirts says.

Is that a reference to Vera, Arnold, or Martin? I feel as if I'm part of a circus act myself. *The Girl Who Can't Stop Trembling and Her Brother with the Sealed Lips.*

An epidemic of fear has closed the city. What else but a plague of cowardice could empty a shopping street in a city of two million on a Saturday morning? All the window shutters are closed and the curtains drawn tight. And what I hear is the silence of my own panic pulsing in my ears – a timepiece counting down the seconds it will take for this ordeal to be over.

Minnie begins sniffing at something enticing on the pavement, but the sign around her neck no longer seems funny, because the well-behaved officers standing at attention – all with swastika armbands – know exactly what race needs to leave Germany, and it happens to be Isaac's.

Marianne and Roman greet everyone in our tight cluster with kisses, but no one says more than a few whispered words. Even the Nazis must feel the menace centered here – the frontline of a border conflict between two contrasting views of life and humanity.

Marianne's worried eyes never leave K-H, who is photographing the brownshirts one by one. *Portraits of Men Who Have Sold Their Minds.* The title of another exhibition he has planned.

The uniformed men are not happy about being targeted by him, but they keep their displeasure to themselves. Disciplined, I'll give them that. Until K-H reaches the brute standing in front of the door. He's got pendulous jowls like a bulldog, a thin mustache, and a condescending glint in his eye. As the photographer focuses on the Nazi, he takes his gun from its holster. Isaac, his pipe clamped in his mouth, rushes between the two men.

After all these years, I see one image more clearly than any other: Isaac reaching out to grab the snout of the storm-trooper's gun.

"No violence," Isaac says. A command, not a plea.

The bulldog takes a step back and pulls his gun free, then faces sideways and points it at Isaac's head. The pose of a fencing enthusiast.

"Take a step back, Jew. And you," he shouts at K-H, "get that camera away or I'll shoot you both!"

He has a Swabian accent. *Just what we need*, I think, *a hillbilly with a loaded gun ...*

Isaac – God knows how – glares at the man. "We have come here because we are certain that what you are doing is illegal and immoral," he says in a high German so beautiful that it could make Hugo von Hofmannsthal sit up in his grave in Vienna. "We shall be making some purchases, so if you will just step aside ..."

"Get your ass out of here!" the bulldog snaps back.

"As soon as we're finished shopping."

Does Isaac want to get shot so he can make all the newspapers? By now, he must know that one dead Jew will only merit a sentence or two after the unseasonably warm weather in the Alps.

"Follow me," he says to us, and maybe we really would file behind him directly into the shop and a history book or two, but before he can lead us any further, Mr Weissman – a neatly dressed little man with thinning gray hair – shuffles out of the shop. A tall young Nazi stands behind him, his gun drawn, smirking like a kid who has successfully stolen licorice from a candy shop. In short, a delinquent. For me, it's another threshold passed; he's the first thug I've ever seen who clearly enjoys humiliating another person.

Around the old shopkeeper's neck is a sign that reads: *Kauft nicht bei Juden, kauft in deutschen Geschäften! Don't buy from Jews, shop in German businesses*. Herr Weissman's face is bright red. He's holding his glasses, which I now see are badly cracked – stepped on by the happy delinquent, most likely.

"Look up!" the bulldog orders. "And tell your friend what to do!"

Weissman obeys. His forehead is ribbed and sweaty. "You can't go in, Isaac," he says in an apologetic voice. "You have to leave. The Nazis have been expecting you, and there's a brownshirt inside who'll shoot you when you go in. He'll say you were armed and started a fight."

So the Nazis were warned we'd be here.

Isaac faces me and gives me a grave look in which I see danger for all our futures. "Will you and Hansi go in, Sophele?" he asks. "No one would ever believe you and your brother were armed. You don't have to, of course, but it's important."

In years to come, when I tell this story, Ben and others will be appalled that Isaac took such a risk with our lives, but we didn't have the benefit of hindsight then, and we didn't know that the Nazis were capable of killing children. His request seemed reasonable to me at the time.

I look at Hansi, whose eyes are fixed on Minnie sniffing the pavement, her tail thumping. Every second of my brother's future is in my hesitant breathing. My heartbeat has gone haywire.

Vera squeezes my hand and says, "Don't go in." Then, to Isaac, she adds, "I think we should just go home like Mr Weissman said. We can try later to …"

"No, I'll go in alone," I interrupt. I unpeel Hansi's fingers from around my hand and entrust the boy to Vera.

"Don't move an inch!" I instruct him. "I'll be back in a minute."

He looks at me with a compressed face, confused. I lean down to give him a quick kiss and surprise myself by whispering to myself one of the prayers Isaac taught me: *Baruch ata Adonai Eloheynu Melech ha'olam shehehiyanu ve'kiymanu ve'higianu la'zman ha'zeh.* Blessed are You, O Lord our God, King of the universe, Who has kept us in life and preserved us …

As I walk forward, I feel as if I always knew I would be tested in this way. And as if my death – if that's what happens – will be my revenge against my parents. For exactly what I cannot even now put into words.

Music starts playing loudly down the street: the Comedian Harmonists singing the folksong, *Ach, wie ist's möglich denn? Ah, How Is It Possible?*

Isaac's choice? After all, *How is it possible?* is the perfect question for a boycott of Jewish shops. Later, he will confirm to me that he arranged for the music with some friends.

The Nazis turn in unison to face the Harmonists' angelic voices as though they're synchronized swimmers in an Esther Williams movie. Laughable in better times.

It's time for me to make my move. But the bulldog grabs my arm as I stride past him. Hard enough to cause a mark I'll notice that evening.

Our symmetry has stayed in my mind – lodged in black fear – for seventy years: the Nazi's got me and I've got the door-handle. Who will give in first?

I stare into the face of a man who should be home in Swabia, scaring his children with the Brothers Grimm, like ten generations of good German sadists before him.

"I want to buy some fabric," I tell him matter-of-factly.

"You can't go in," he replies equally calmly.

"I'm from Berlin," I say, since he's not, and we both know I mean that he can't tell me what to do in my city. The courage of place. It shouldn't be discounted at such decisive moments.

"So what?" he sneers.

"So I was born here. I'll shop anywhere I want. And I'll shop at Weissman's long after you go home to Ulm."

Not the answer he wants. He raises his gun and presses the barrel into my cheek. And he smiles. A sexual taunt in addition to a threat.

With death against my tingling skin, I go all stiff and close my eyes. The silence of my own terror squeezes me. And all I can think of is Hansi bursting into tears when I'm dead.

"Sophele, come here ... come back to me," Isaac says pleadingly.

A warm moistness slithers down my legs; I'm peeing on myself. The Nazi lowers his pistol and laughs. Which is when I open the door and step inside.

The most courageous moment of my life. And it happens without any conscious decision. I'm no more aware of why I do it than a dog chasing after a rubber ball on Grenadierstraße.

When I was fifteen. A child in so many ways. And yet if I was able to go on with my life after the war, it was because of that one moment.

The shop is divided into aisles of shelving holding bolts of fabric. A youthful brownshirt is kneeling over a floral print he has spread on the floor. Maybe he is deciding whether he'll steal a few yards for curtains. Hilde Weissman sits behind the counter.

A slender-necked woman wearing a pearl necklace. That's all I'll ever remember about the way she looked.

She has been resting with her head on the cash register, and when she looks up, she thrusts out her hand as if to say, *Wait there, don't move!* And she jumps up.

Her hair is wet. Later, Isaac will tell me the Nazis dunked her head in the toilet.

At the same time, the brownshirt rushes to me with his gun pointing at the center of my chest, but he never reaches me. A shot from outside draws him to the door.

"Hansi!" I yell.

I race onto the street. Minnie is lying on the ground, dead, a flower of blood blooming across her soft pink belly. My brother is seated next to her, reaching for the blossom, but when I try to lift him up, his eyes go dull and he is unable to stand.

The blond delinquent is being yelled at by the bulldog.

"It's just a dead Jewish mutt!" the young man shouts back.

Tears flood me, not out of desperation for Minnie, though blood-spattered memories of her will pursue me for weeks afterwards. All I feel now is relief that Hansi, Isaac, Vera and everyone else are safe.

Later, I find out that the Nazi in charge ordered Molly and Klaus to take the sign off Minnie. Molly refused, saying she'd never obey a Nazi order as long as she lived and that was when the delinquent pulled the trigger.

Vera grabs my arm as if she'll never let me go, while Arnold tries to draw my brother's attention from the dachshund by talking to him gently. Molly is now kneeling over Minnie, sobbing, both her hands pressing at the blood, as though she's trying to keep more petals from forming.

Isaac carries Hansi to the tram; the boy is gone from the world.

"I'm so sorry," the old tailor keeps telling me over and over. "I never expected ..."

"It's not your fault," I reply, and I mean it.

He thinks I blame the Nazis. But I don't; I blame myself.

At home, Isaac eases my brother into his bed. When we're alone in the sitting room, both pale with worry, I say what I've wanted to since I first saw the line of brownshirts waiting for us on Hirtenstraße: "A traitor in your group must have told the Nazis to be ready for us at Weissman's – maybe the same person who killed Georg. It's possible he informed on Raffi, too, though I suppose some other German hero might have done that."

Death comes to Hirtenstraße

"Yes, I've long suspected we were being betrayed."

"Why didn't you tell me?"

"I was hoping, I suppose, that it wasn't true. And I didn't want you to get any more involved than you already were. When you told me you were stumped by Georg not having any bruises on his neck ... I've been hoping you'd get so frustrated that you'd give up playing detective. What's happening in Germany has made me very irresponsible – with you and Hansi most of all. I'm sorry." He rubs a weary hand over his face. "I'm no good at these public protests. I can see now that I'm just going to get the people I love killed."

As we sit inside the morose silence, a revelation comes to me. "Georg found out who was betraying you, and that's why he was murdered!"

"I suppose it's possible."

"And Raffi, too," I whisper to myself, believing I understand things clearly now.

"What did you say?"

"Isaac, I know that Raffi was bribing Nazis with money that your group raised, but maybe that wasn't why he was arrested. Maybe he, too, learned who the traitor was. The Gestapo took him away because he could reveal the man's identity. After all, now he can't tell anyone anything." I then launch a probe. "You think that's right, don't you ... that every time someone gets too close to the truth, he's eliminated?"

"Yes, I've thought of that," he admits, distraught, "but now ... Sophele, it's all too much for me. I'll just have to stop my public activities and concentrate on the Turkish Embassy. In the meantime," he adds, "we can both pray that nothing more happens to anyone we love."

After Isaac leaves, I collapse in the armchair in the sitting room. Hansi stirs from his nap an hour later and taps my head to awaken me.

"What's up?" I ask, relieved that he can walk again. And that he doesn't hate me.

He points to his stomach.

I don't dare mention Minnie or anything else that's happened as I make him lunch. My brother and I will never discuss that day. A secret with deadly thorns.

I've heard many an expert on German history say that forgetfulness became a way of life after the war, but Hansi and I learned to put our memories in a locked *Giftschrank* – a cabinet for poisons, as the Germans say – *long* before our army fought any battles.

I make us potato soup with sliced cheese on toast, and we sit on opposite sides of the kitchen table, munching away while working on his Michelangelo jigsaw puzzle. After a while, we play at stealing what's left of each other's cheese. I have a fit of giggles, till tears are sliding into my mouth. How good it is to be alive and alone with my brother! That afternoon, we listen to Marlene Dietrich on the phonograph, gratitude in every look between us.

In the evening I bathe him and coax him under the covers by promising to read him a story, but I fall asleep before I even open *Treasure Island*, his favorite book at the moment. My parents come in at ten in the evening. I wake up in the chair next to Hansi's bed, and over my legs is a woolen blanket that I didn't put there. My brother the brownie.

I'm overjoyed to hear Mama and Papa's voices – the sound of all the protection I needed this morning. As though they've been away for weeks, I race into the sitting room. I try to give my father a kiss right away, but he grabs my wrist, gives me a shake, and says angrily, "We know what you've been up to!" His face is outraged.

"You do?" I ask. As I pull my hand out of his grip, I notice the dark mark that's already formed on my arm where the Nazi grabbed me.

"Frau von Schilling told us."

"Who's Frau von Schilling?"

Papa begins to slip out of his overcoat. Mama helps him.

"Vicki von Schilling's mother, of course," he replies.

When I give him a puzzled look, Mama shouts, "She goes to school with you!" She tosses Papa's coat onto the sofa, and I can see from her eyes – squinting with animosity – that whatever she learned about me from Frau von Schilling ruined her entire evening.

"What exactly did Vicki's mother tell you?" I ask.

"She said that you've been talking to Rini again," Papa snarls. "And you accepted some chocolate from her!"

He spits out his words as if the government has uncovered proof that Jews own all the cocoa plantations in Africa.

"That's all?" I ask.

"Isn't that enough?" he growls.

Relief sweeps through me like that sea breeze I wanted for the residents of Grenadierstraße. "I suppose it is," I say. "After all, she's a Jew and I'm an Aryan. Or maybe just a dachshund."

"What are you saying, Sophie?" Mama asks.

"It's just a small joke that isn't funny and now ..." I want to add that the joke is now dead, but that wouldn't make sense to anyone who wasn't with me this morning.

I hold out my arms, ready for handcuffs. "Guilty as charged. You may lead me to my cell." I feel another fit of mad giggles approaching, and I'm about to add, *I'll go willingly to the gallows in the morning but now let me get a good night's sleep*, but Papa grabs me and slaps me across the face.

I'm so stunned that I cannot cry. Or catch my breath. I bend over, fighting for air.

Papa shakes me hard again and orders me to my room. Mama leads Hansi away while he takes his belt off. *I'll have to bury all that I like about myself to keep from losing my mind*, I think. A paradox, but it makes perfect sense to me at the time.

Each whack of leather is a shovelful of earth over the girl I want to be.

Papa leaves early the next morning for work. Mama confiscates what's left of my cigarette card collection, including Garbo as Mata Hari. "Your father and I have agreed that you will be spending all your weekends at home for the next three months," she informs me. "No Tonio, no movies – nothing!"

"Can I still draw in my sketchbook?"

"No!" She gives me a contemptuous look and hisses, "I hope you're satisfied now!"

"That depends on your exact definition of satisfied," I reply, defiant. "Though if you're referring to the welts on my backside, no I'm not happy about them."

She's decided to take me to the Immanuel Church this morning. *Mein Kampf* has failed to save me, and she's convinced that the New Testament is my only hope. But wouldn't Jesus have had a Jewish sense of humor, too?

On Monday, I wake up with a sore throat, and my bones ache. My neck feels rusted. Mama takes my temperature. When she discovers I've got a low fever, she snickers.

"You see what your rebelliousness brings you?" she says.

I'm too weak to assure her that she's already more than convinced me how much she despises me and that she can move on to another subject.

"I've got food shopping to do today," she continues, "and now what am I supposed to do with you ill?" She stares at me in challenge.

"I can stay home alone. Don't worry about me."

"Who's worried about you?" she says, and her eyebrows arch

up to emphasize the point. "I'm only concerned you'll give your cold to Hansi."

Possibly the meanest thing she has ever said to me. But I haven't the strength to protest, and she knows it. Mama's philosophy: kick 'em while they're down. Maybe that's to be found in the New Testament if you look at it with her Bavarian eyes.

That afternoon, Dr Nohel comes to visit. Hansi and I have always thought he looks like a horse – giant brown teeth, big ears, a long slender face, and thinning hair slicked back with shoe polish into a creepy black mane. We even once found the brand he uses in his doctor's bag – *Lion Noir*. French and sour-smelling.

After putting on his monocle, he crushes my tongue with one of his satanic wooden sticks and looks down my throat. He smells like limburger cheese. It must have been in his feed-bag at lunch.

Maybe he spots a diagnosis written in tiny letters on my uvula, because he adjusts his monocle for a closer look, and when he finally lifts up his muzzle for a little air he announces I've got the flu. "It's going around," he assures us.

Sure enough, my fever rises that evening. While Mama makes me potato soup, Papa sits with me. We don't mention the beating he gave me. Another memory swept below the surface of our family history. He reads to me from the newspaper as if we're best friends. Among other highlights, I learn that Jews have been arrested for spreading "lies" to the foreign press about violent tactics used by brownshirts during the boycott and that the swastika will become our official flag on the 22nd of April. Our red and black dye-makers must be ecstatic. Hitler's biggest supporters.

"Which reminds me ..." Papa says with an eager smile, and he dashes boyishly out of the room. When he returns, he's holding out an armband for me. "A present I've owed you for some time," he says, grinning. "Show me how it looks."

The proud father at his daughter's National Socialist christening. If only he'd just hit a bottle of champagne over my head instead and knock me out for a few years.

I slip the armband over the sleeve of my nightgown. It clashes badly with the pink.

"Very nice," he beams. "You like it?"

His face is so hopeful that it would be a sin to disappoint him. "I love it," I say. "Thank you. Did you get one for Hansi, too?"

"Absolutely."

So it is I discover that the idea of burying yourself is far more terrifying than the act itself. It's really just like sleeping, which is all I want to do at the moment anyway. I don't care about Nazis, Communists, Georg's murder, Isaac, or even myself.

Papa leans toward me from his chair, takes my hand and presses his lips to my palm. "I hated having to hurt you," he whispers.

He's not the least bit convincing, but until recently I never minded Garbo's wretched acting, so why should I hold this poor performance against him?

"I know you did," I assure him.

"But I have to be strict now. There's too much at stake. *Häschen*, I promise you I'll never hit you again as long as you do what I ask. You have my word."

I smile gratefully, but what's his word worth, given that he was a Communist until three months ago?

As though in reply to my cynicism, he spends most of the night on a chair in my room so he can care for me. I'm burning with fever by now, so he holds a cold compress to my brow, and when I tremble with chills he makes me tea, holding the cup to my mouth while I take mouse sips.

In the morning, my breathing is all stuffed, so he mixes mint leaves into a bowl of boiling water, holds a towel over my head and makes me inhale. A baby bird under a bower. When I look in his eyes, I realize he may not be the man I always knew, but he's close enough – and that I still love him. In a sense, it's only fair that he's changed, since I'm no longer the girl I was either. We are very alike, after all. A father and daughter surviving on secrets.

I wear my swastika armband for the first time on the 1st of May, for the May Day celebrations. Mama, Papa, Hansi, and I watch row after row of storm-troopers goose-stepping down Unter den Linden. A monsoon of patriotism so dense that we're unable to see beyond them, which is the whole point, I'd guess.

"It's like Germany is being born again," Mama tells Papa, awestruck. We all are.

Our women and girls come marching behind the men, which is when Papa turns to us and exclaims, "I can hardly wait to start my new job and be part of this!"

"What exactly will you be doing?" I ask.

"I can't tell you yet."

No, after all, I might still be the enemy.

Mama and I have pinned swastika corsages to the collars of our blouses. And who can deny the simple cleverness of a mother who fastens two carnations to a brass badge to make the prettiest propaganda you ever saw? And what those tiny pink flowers mean – to anyone who wants to think below the surface – is that all the gardens of Europe will one day belong to our Opposite-Compass. Every hedge, flowerbed, and potted plant. Every weed along the Rhine, Danube, Seine, and Ebro. Even Isaac's pelargoniums, which must be spying on him even now.

My brother has been given the duty of holding up a tiny flag, but he keeps letting it fall.

"Higher!" my father barks at him, and Mama lifts the boy's

arm. Papa's emotions are out of control of late, largely because of his troublesome daughter, of course, but also for any number of other good reasons, not the least of which is that he's still trying – and failing – to stop smoking. Hansi, the poor boy, is more interested in scratching his bottom than patriotic gestures, which makes Papa ready to burst. The astonishing thing is that our father has forgotten that his son must see little more than meaningless bent lines in the swastika – a symbol nearly as incomprehensible as a dachshund soaked in blood who won't get up no matter how much you kiss her furry face.

Behind us in the crowd is an old grandfather with pouches of ruffled skin under his eyes and war medals on his chest. He grins with pride and salutes me when I turn to him. Not a single person is complaining about hunger or joblessness. A miracle of unity. Germany as a dead forest bursting into life all at once – just like Mama said.

After the rallies across Germany on May Day, the Semitic wall finds its permanent and natural home in the vision center of everyone's brain. Jews and Aryans as separate species.

Rini and I walk past each other at school without even glancing. And I stay away from Isaac's apartment as if it's the head office of the world Jewish conspiracy we hear so much about on the radio. All of us have been told to imagine a roomful of big-nosed, hairy-eared racketeers playing poker to see who will take Germany's riches. Filled with pipe smoke and Yiddish blasphemies against Hitler, Aryan Superiority, and the German spirit. Our new Trinity.

Secretly, however, I've pledged to myself that it will take more than armbands and beatings from my father to keep me from Isaac, Vera, and my other new friends. And from investigating Georg's murder. Though I will have to bide my time ... And I pray that when this is all over Rini and I will transform back to the people we were, and that Papa and Mama will become themselves, too. All of which means that my hope is dependent on a magic act. Is everyone in Germany counting on a return to normal or am I the only one who still believes the black dove named Hitler can flutter back into the hat? Frau Mittelmann is Jewish and my favorite teacher, so I take a chance with her one day after class and ask when all the other students have gone.

"Sophie, I don't even recognize this damn country anymore!" she replies bad-temperedly, as though my question were an attack, then, seeing she's hurt me, adds quickly, "I'm sorry. I'm under a lot of pressure at the moment." She holds a finger to her lips, closes the door to the classroom, and turns around, her hands behind her back. Her face is grave. "I'm leaving Germany. My husband and I ... we've just arranged a visa for France."

"When will you go?"

"In two weeks. I've handed in my resignation to Dr Hilde-brandt."

"Where will you be living?"

"Outside a town called Libourne. It's not far from Bordeaux. My husband's brother has a house there. He's in the wine business."

"Isn't Bordeaux where Goya was exiled?"

She smiles warmly. "What a wonderful memory you have, Sophie!"

"I could never forget the things you told us about Goya."

My implication that she's had a vital role in my life makes her wipe her hand nervously through her hair. She walks back to her desk and starts putting the sketches we've made today in her big black portfolio. Efficiency as her antidote to despair.

"What ... what will you do in France?" I ask hesitantly.

"Learn French, for one thing," she replies with a bitter laugh. "And give drawing lessons to anyone who wants them."

Every sketch she slips into her portfolio steals one more of my fantasies about becoming a great artist. Soon, she'll carry them all across our border.

"And what about our classes here?" I question.

"I'm sure the substitute will be very competent."

"I don't want someone competent!"

"Sophie, you've got talent, and you're an intelligent girl. And you're an Aryan. Just keep working hard." Echoing our favorite quote from Cézanne, she says, "Make the faces you draw speak of the fields they have left behind, the rain which has nourished them, the daybreaks they have seen."

She ties the portfolio's laces in a tight bow and slips into her bulky old coat, then throws the gray silk scarf around her neck that she's worn since I first met her. Her antique clothing used to seem so Bohemian. Our local Picasso. But now she's just a middle-aged teacher who will have to start her life over a thousand miles away. If I were writing the dialogue between us, she would begin to talk to me now about Dürer. One last time.

From her point of view, of course, I'm a pupil who has worn a Nazi armband to school and who no longer even looks at her Jewish best friend.

I'm still me and I still love Dürer! I want to shout, but why should she believe that?

"Is there something more?" she asks me.

"Can I have your new address?"

Across the space of almost seventy years, I can see her taking out from her coat pocket a tiny red address book – only a bit bigger than a cigarette lighter – and tearing out a page from the back. Is it so small so that she can hide it in her shoe if the Nazis catch her drawing some vicious caricature of Hitler?

Le Grand Moulin, Libourne. The Big Mill. She hands me the

paper and I read her address out loud, in my best French accent, so I can never forget it.

"If you're ever in the neighborhood, come look me up," she says cheerfully.

Frau Mittelmann doesn't add, *you can stay with me* or *I'm really going to miss you.* A conversation that's given depth by what's omitted. Especially no final kiss.

On the way home from school, more confused than I know at the time, I rip up her address and toss it into the garbage in Frau Koslowski's grocery. A heavy drinker getting rid of her last bottle of gin. Or one last shovelful of earth on my grave. Either way it doesn't matter; the Jews are running away, and why should I fight their battles for them?

CHAPTER ELEVEN

Twenty thousand books are burned by university students in Berlin's Opernplatz on the 10th of May. Sigmund Freud, Max Brod, Alfred Döblin, Klaus Mann, Peter Altenberg, Oscar Blumenthal, Richard Beer-Hoffmann ... If you don't know all their names, then the Nazis succeeded in turning more of our culture to ash than you may want to admit.

Tonio leaves a red rose for me on our doormat every Saturday morning, together with a note, which he always signs, *Faithfully yours*. My father and mother are impressed by his loyalty, and they let me see him again long before my three months sentence has elapsed.

I drag Tonio to see Marlene Dietrich in *Blond Venus* in early June, and as revenge, he makes me come with him to see *King Kong*. We take Hansi with us, since I don't see why I should suffer alone.

"The era of Jewish intellectualism is now at an end," says Dr Goebbels in the newsreel before the film. "The future German won't just be a man of books, but a man of character."

Our Propaganda Minister is addressing a throng of students exalted by this chance to destroy a thousand years of poetry and prose they never wanted to read in the first place. Or could it be that Dr Goebbels is talking directly to that pile of ash in the center of the screen – the smoldering jumble that was Germany's culture until three months ago? It's hard to tell from the camera angle and no one would put it past that madman to have a conversation with cinders. As Isaac once told me, "Goebbels' mind is urine."

"Absolutely wonderful!" Tonio whispers to me as the minister reaches his final cadence, which means I'm in love with a young man who likes the scent of piss.

My patriotic boyfriend then moves my left hand over the expanding bulge in his pants, confirming a little-known fact that no one will ever write about, not even after the war: Dr Goebbels knows how to arouse the men of Germany better than the most experienced Neapolitan prostitute on the Kurfürstendamm. That's his most intimate secret, and ours.

Then *King Kong* comes on and Fay Wray is pretty in a mousy way, and the towering gorilla is terrifyingly realistic – almost as realistic as that other wind-up toy, Dr Goebbels – and Tonio, Hansi, and I, and everyone else in a thousand theaters across the country can be scared of something that will end in less than two hours, and forget about the importance of books for a while. Or forever, depending on whether we are men and women of character.

One afternoon after school, Tonio meets me so that we can hunt for old car and movie magazines in the backroom of an overstuffed junk shop on Karlstraße that we sometimes explore when I can bear the dust. Afterward, since we're only a minute from Julia's shop, we go there, and I explain to Tonio that I met her and her son at Isaac's Carnival party, though I'm careful to call him Mr Zarco. We stand across the street, under the awning of a cafe.

"What are you up to?" he asks me suspiciously.

"Nothing. I just want to watch for a while."

Julia helps a man in a derby hat choose tea for whatever problem has made him touch his elbow twice. She's wearing a brown woolen skirt and black blouse, and her dark hair is bound tightly on top of her head. Unless the traitor in The Ring slips up, I realize, we'll never find out who he or she is. So I will have to start things in motion ...

I begin to track Julia's movements over the next weeks, always in the afternoon, but only irregularly because of commitments at home. She eats lunch in her apartment, which is directly above her shop. An assistant – a pale, petite young woman – substitutes her at this time but stays for only an hour and a half. At six in the afternoon, Julia closes up and fetches Martin. Often pausing for coffee at Wolff's Café on Lothringstraße, she walks to a whitewashed, five-story apartment house behind the Bötzow Brewery on Saarbrücker Straße, where the stink of hops and malt is so intense that it brings tears to my eyes. A friend there must tutor the young man during the day, or simply watch over him. The mother and son then walk home leisurely, occasionally arm in arm, though Martin sometimes pauses at shop windows, his hands flat against the glass. They talk as they walk and Julia's laughter is frequent and free. She seems to be a woman who has gotten what she wanted out of life. She usually buys Martin a treat at the Hengstmann Bakery, just next door to Wolff's Café. He adores creampuffs, and she keeps a white handkerchief in her leather bag to wipe his face afterward, though he sometimes insists on doing it himself and shakes his hands as if they're on fire when he doesn't get his way. Anyone can see she is devoted to her son. Sometimes she watches him as he runs ahead of her, his arms flailing, and her eyes aren't worried, like my mother's used to be. They're radiant with an emotion I'd never have expected – admiration.

I try to remember that a contented woman who adores her son might still commit a murder – could even be conspiring with the Nazis. After all, we all have a double life in Germany. And yet, I soon begin to doubt she had anything to do with Georg's death.

Julia's days are confined by a small area of Berlin. Only once does she make a deviation. In early June she fails to fetch Martin at the usual hour and instead walks east down Oranienburger Straße, glancing up briefly at the shimmering golden dome of the New Synagogue. She threads her way through the confusion of shoppers in the Hackescher Market and strides up Rosenthaler Straße like a woman on a mission. As I navigate past the pushcarts, apologizing to the people I bump into, I realize – with an electric jolt – where she's headed and what might be about to take place. So I slip into a beer garden before I'm spotted. After all, if my hunch is correct, then Isaac or Vera could be right behind me.

I force myself to drink a glass of wine so that I'm not tempted to jump up too soon. My legs are tense with the need to catch up to Julia. But being caught now would ruin my plans.

I find Karl's Cellar as dingy and dimly lit as ever, which is a bit of luck since it reduces my chances of being spotted. I'm standing just inside the front door, which is separated from the dining area by an American-style bar. Far at the back, submerged in the watery light from the table lamps, are the people I'm after. They seem elongated, almost dreamlike, as though they're trapped in a canvas of red and reflective black, and a kind of liquid gold that burnishes their skin. They're seated round a long rectangular table, and I hold my hand above my eyes as I count them so no one can see my face. Twenty-two members have arrived. Vera is easy to spot, a head taller than everyone else. Next I notice Isaac, and seated on his right, chatting with their hands, are K-H and Marianne. Heidi doesn't seem to be there, but Rolf is seated across from Vera, who's whispering something to Roman. Julia is there, too, of course.

A big-bellied waiter comes up to me right away and tells me that the restaurant is closed until seven-thirty, which is an hour away. I tell him in a beseeching tone that I've agreed to meet a friend here, but he replies coarsely that I'll have to wait outside. It's plain from his tone that he is protecting The Ring.

"Please, I have a bad head cold," I tell him. "Just let me wait here a few minutes."

"I'm sorry – Karl makes the rules and I can't break them."

"Then can I speak to Karl?"

"You *are* speaking to him," he shoots back – unfortunately, without humor. He raises his arm to prevent me from entering. "Please, Fräulein," he says forcefully, "just wait outside."

The last thing I see before leaving is a black hat being passed around the table, brim up, and K-H placing his hand into its hollow.

On the way home, I realize they must have been drawing lots of some sort, which means I'll have to defy my parents and visit Isaac to find out why. Late the next afternoon, I spill a full bottle of milk down the sink when Mama isn't looking and tell her I'm off to Frau Koslowski's grocery since we've none left. Rushing like a madwoman, I slip off to Isaac's apartment, but he isn't in. Over the next few days, he never answers my knocks. I worry that he has been arrested, but Mrs Munchenberg tells me that he asked her to take in his mail for a few weeks, so he must be on a trip.

I hope Vera or some other friend will come to our apartment house to water Isaac's pelargoniums so I can ask after him. But I never spot anyone.

Two more weeks pass without any word from Isaac. Meanwhile, in late June, Hansi's headmaster gives us the news I've long been fearing, that the boy will not be admitted back to school after the summer vacation. "If he doesn't speak or even react to what is happening in class, what are we supposed to do with him?" Dr Meier tells us.

We have no answer, and Papa tells Hansi – kneeling down to his height to soften the blow – that he'll be spending his days at home now. Does my brother care? I can't tell from his hollow stare. I'm sure, however, that he's fading from us. Still, Mama tells him cheerfully, "Don't worry, you're far better off here with me."

Probably just what the witch told Hansel and Gretl, I think.

Once Papa gives me permission to open my sketchbook again, I get Hansi to pose for me all the time. Among other benefits, it helps me count off the days while Isaac is gone without growing frantic.

Monet had the water-lilies of Giverny and Van Gogh had the sunflowers of Arles, and a moderately talented girl living on Marienburger Straße has a mute little boy with long ear lobes and silken hair. For hours at a time I draw his face and hands, and his elfin feet, which look like they were made for jumping down rabbit holes after his own never-to-be-revealed ideas and opinions. Sometimes in the early morning, I try to draw him inside the spangled dust swirling around us. Fairy powder making us the only two people on earth. If only I could grab hold of my brother as he dives into his own world – his own personal Araboth. So many answers might be waiting for me there: how to get Raffi home and keep him and Isaac safe, and maybe most important of all, how to make my real father return.

I sit by his bed when I have insomnia, which is almost all the time. Hundreds of sketches of a boy with arms and legs at spider angles, or curled into a ball, his covers on or off, snoring, snuffling ... Once, he even talks in his sleep, and though his words are too muffled to understand, I think I hear the word *Finland*.

I sometimes put my hand on Hansi's head while he is in dreamland. I feel the fragile softness of his breathing entering into me. Maybe his very presence – his innocence – is protecting me, keeping me sane. Is that what I'd see if I looked below our surface?

*

After school ends for the year, Mama orders me to join the Bund Deutscher Mädel, the Young German Maidens, so starting in July, two afternoons a week, I train my public double for her place in the Fatherland. Our uniform consists of a knee-length, dark blue woolen skirt with a double pleat in the center, a white blouse with two breast pockets, and a black neckerchief. In it, I could be Gurka. No, let's be honest, I *am* Gurka! Rini may be Jewish and therefore a bloodsucking insect, but at least she doesn't have to suffer the indignity of looking like she's training to become a Prussian prison guard.

Thankfully, we Maidens have to wear our outfits to school only on Hitler's birthday and other such happy occasions, so most of the time I can dress as though I were still living in the twentieth century. As I might have predicted, Tonio and my mother both adore me in my uniform. When Mama sees it on me for the first time, she clasps her hands together and tells me I've never looked more charming. A statement meant to divert me from understanding that what's truly beautiful to her is my being forced to wear such wretched things, but what would she think if she knew that my boyfriend asks me to dress in my uniform at his father's private apartment? A Young Maiden on her knees for Germany ... That's the heroic sculpture Tonio makes with his bowed back and racing heart every time we close his father's adulterous door behind us. I don't mind in the least; that handsome young man's polishing of my desires may be the only thing saving my mind. And the joy he thrusts inside me when I've got my eyes closed and am pleading with him to open me as wide and deep as possible cannot yet be used as evidence against me in any of the Führer's courts.

More than anything else, I love the power I feel when he is in my mouth, that dirt-pure sense of being a girl worshipping an altar older and far more meaningful than Hitler, Göring, and all the other lesser divinities who've created this world where I have to wear a swastika armband to school, and make believe Rini doesn't exist, and stand outside Isaac's door without daring to knock because someone with a mind fit for a latrine has decided that culture is bad for the German soul. I adore the patina of Berlin grime in our dimly lit, one-room shack in the fairy-tale forest we make with our own bodies, with its spider webs in every corner and its gray fungus-muck on the shower curtain, and the lavender-scented foot powder left by Tonio's father's secretary on the chipped red bathroom tiles. In this grotesque refuge from proper behavior that's not on any map in my parents' possession, I'm using every forbidden trick I've got – and I'm discovering I've got plenty! – to please a young man, one who may or may not be worthy of me, as it turns out. Maybe that determination ought to matter to me a great deal, but it doesn't, because he's as breathless and exalted as God was when he first spurted the universe into existence, and I'm doing what's been done by women since Adam and Eve first were exiled for coiling like snakes around the knowledge of good and evil, and giving myself in ways that every father in the Fatherland would despise.

Each stain on my Young Maiden blouse and skirt is *my* victory not just over my mother and father but over my country. You think that's crazy? Then consider yourself very fortunate, because you didn't live in Berlin in 1933.

Sex may be the only hope in a dictatorship like ours. Not that the Maidens know anything about such subjects. We sew and sing, bake cakes, learn how to keep our fingernails clean, and practice the proper Hitler salute. All essential for the German homemaker. We also read about ourselves in *Das Deutsche Mädel* magazine. Each issue is full of lively news of girls scaling the Alps, for instance, but what they do when they finally make it to the top of Mount Wendelstein is anybody's guess. Surely one or two of the more fame-hungry girls might at least stumble from exhaustion over a cliff to give the readers something captivating to read about, but no such luck.

When Maria Borgwaldt, our group leader, inspects me and the other new girls after our first week of training, she strongly advises me to wear my hair in plaits. "Good-looking and practical," she tells me, tugging on the ends of hers like two bell-ropes, which may be her way of either remaining alert or of reminding herself not to say what she really thinks.

Maria speaks in a voice so sincere that it is a miracle God doesn't appear to her and order her to stop talking for Him.

"I'll think seriously about braids," I tell her, but we both know I mean *no*.

The next week, as I'm waiting my turn to shimmy up a rope in the school gymnasium, she pulls me aside to give me private advice. We stand arm in arm, which is a privilege for me, since she is renowned for having mastered all of the more difficult techniques in our Young Maiden Cookbook. Our Lady of Soufflés, is what I call her. Because Maria's personal *soufflé* is never going to fall, of course.

"Sophie," she tells me, "you wouldn't want your hair to slow you down or get caught on something. That could be dangerous. You really must braid it."

Daring to reveal a crack of light from behind the Semitic Wall, I reply, "Do you really believe that letting my hair stay loose is keeping me from setting a world record in the long jump?"

No smile. "That's not the point, Sophie," she says, as if I ever thought it was. "Even if you only jump one centimeter further, that could make all the difference."

"To whom?" I ask. Now that I've started talking like myself, I can't seem to stop.

"To the Führer."

I look around. "He seems to have stepped out for a smoke."

"I don't think he smokes."

"Cigarettes and cigars, maybe not, but he loves smoking books."

"What are you talking about?"

Maria looks like a deer paralyzed by car headlights. A dangerous sight; those blue eyes of hers are so empty and pretty that I might just fall in and never find my way out.

"Forget it," I tell her.

If Maria were to lose her virginity would she gain a sense of humor? A question worth asking of Martin Heidegger and all the other philosophers who are sleeping now in Hitler's bed.

In our studies, I learn that we will be expected to have hordes of happy children and obey our husbands. Aryan rabbits with our legs open. Wearing invisible collars around our necks and chains on our ankles – the Maiden uniform that no one sees or even imagines. Except maybe Tonio: perhaps it's the clanging of my fetters and metal scent that gets him panting like a dog. If so, good for him!

We learn that Maidens may not spit, curse, or get a tattoo. Maria tells us that such debauched habits brought down the Roman Empire. As did frolicking in bed before marriage apparently, because she also implies – using terms so vague that a few of the girls ask me later what I think she may have meant – that it is strictly *verboten* to take our boyfriends in our mouths, let alone allow them inside our baby-making apparatus.

Obviously, any girls trying to model themselves on Marlene Dietrich aren't going to make it in the Maidens. But I am, despite my wry contempt. Within a few weeks, I've forged friendships with two of the more cynical girls – twins living on Senefelder Platz named Betina and Barbara. I've also earned a merit badge – a bass eagle – for embroidering swastikas onto men's woolen hats. I considered making the messiest ones in the history of the Reich, but Papa – who watched me sewing them at home – told me that since the hats were going to be distributed to Berlin's poor, they had to be perfect. He's obviously still on the side of the proletariat, who are now called the *Volk*.

I also win a third-place medal for running the hundred-meter dash faster than everyone except Ursula Krabbe, who has such long legs that she is obviously reincarnated from a stork, and Maria herself, who has her hair braided *and* fastened in a tight knot, and who therefore had an unfair advantage against the rest of us.

I'm also not as bad at javelin throwing as I thought. My best: twelve meters. Excellent news for our defense forces should we be attacked by short-sighted Finns escaping from Hansi's dreams. Or should the Jews rise up against us, as Maria warns.

I begin to feel reasonably comfortable with the other Maidens until a physician named Herbert Linden gives us a lecture on Racial Hygiene, complete with slides of the kind of men we must not marry if we are to keep the Aryan race pure. The Jew is, of course, Number One on our list of *verboten* suitors, and we see a mug shot of a fat-faced specimen in profile so we can better see his monumentally hooked nose. Number Two is a swarthy, smirking Gypsy whom we see head-on so that we can remark his greasy halo of shoulder-length hair. Last but not least of these inferiors is a bare-chested Negro sitting on a stool while a man in a white coat uses calipers to measure his thick lips. Three and a half centimeters of proof that he is beneath our contempt. The girls groan each time another beastly candidate for our German maidenhood comes up, and nervous laughter breaks out when we see dwarfs and hare-lipped men. But nothing compares to the hoots of horror and giggles when a hump-shouldered giant with a cruel, caveman face appears against a background with a grid measuring his height – two meters seven. I'm as silent as death because he could be Vera's brother.

Later in the slideshow we hear about the dangers of marrying men who look normal but who are anything but – idiots, epileptics, syphilitics, the congenitally deaf and blind. And those who live in their own universe, whom Dr Linden calls schizophrenics. One of the types he describes is Hansi, which makes my legs quiver as if I need to run and never stop.

Isaac returns during the third week of July. He's been gone for over a month. "Thank God, you're safe," I say when he opens his door to me.

I'd like to fall into his arms and cede all my worries to him, but he's frowning. "Sophele, it's a risk for you to come here. Your parents ... And the neighbors ..."

"I don't care about them," I tell him, but he doesn't invite me in. "Where have you been?" I ask.

"Istanbul – visiting my relatives."

"You could have told me you were going."

"Maybe, but I wanted to keep my plans something of a secret."

"Are your relatives all right?"

"Just fine." He wants to tell me more – I can tell by the indecision in his eyes and then his quick look away – but at length he says, "You'd better go home. I don't want to get you in trouble." Since I've already started to cry, he says, "Sophele, please, this is hard for me, too. You may never know how hard. Forgive me."

And just like that, he closes his door on me. I sit on his stairs because Mama will only ask me inconvenient questions if she sees me sobbing. And I stay there a long time, because I feel as if I've been discarded by the only man who might help me stop from turning into a Young Maiden.

*

That same week, Papa tells us he has been authorized to tell us about his new job. He's become a Senior Technician in the Health Ministry's Research and Development Department. "In the future," he says, beaming, "we'll be able to cure tuberculosis and other diseases with pills we synthesize in the laboratory. And we shall keep the price of these life-saving medicines down within the reach of even the poorest German."

I try to believe that this isn't a line he's memorized, but I just can't do it. And I try not to think about the other people I'd rather be with. I've decided that I ought to abide by my parents' rules for a while – to make believe I'm the girl they want me to be.

Papa asks me to invite Tonio to go out with us to the Cafe Bauer to celebrate, and my boyfriend wears his Nazi Youth uniform for the occasion. He looks more and more like a young Cary Grant. I play with his feet under the table. He keeps pushing them away. The embarrassed son-in-law.

I eat duck dripping with a sauce of *Preiselbeeren,* tart little berries. It's so good that I fake swooning and end up making even Hansi laugh. After a waiter takes away our plates, all the lights go dark and the tuxedoed maitre d' brings a giant chocolate cake to our table topped with lighted candles. When it reaches us, I see Hansi's name in whipped cream. My brother will be ten on the 16th of August, which is tomorrow, and we sing a rousing happy birthday. I know he wouldn't want his big sister helping him blow out the candles in front of all these people, so I lean back in my chair, but my boyfriend helps him. Then Tonio shows me a grateful smile, and I realize he understands that I withheld my assistance out of respect for the world of men. I could kiss him for that. Being understood by him now seems lifesaving.

*

Over the next months, whenever I see Isaac in the courtyard or walking on the street, I slink away, but his eyes often follow me in my thoughts. A constant, watchful presence – a third eye in my head. I don't dare to break the silence between us, however, though both of us slowly learn that it's safe to smile at each other. That small gesture is our life raft. And what's left of my resistance to our dictatorship.

Despite my pledge, I've let Georg's murder slip away from me completely. Like so much else.

Late that summer, I realize why men like my father have been able to get more rewarding work of late; all the Jews are fired from their government jobs, including our teachers. Dr Fabig, among others, doesn't return for the start of the new school year. According to the rumors, he turned out to be one-quarter Jewish, like his beloved Rainer Maria Rilke, and resigned before getting his letter of dismissal, although maybe a twenty-five percent Jew could have hung on to his job for a while longer.

Rini and the other Jewish girls also fail to return for the start of the new term. It's rumored that she's now attending an Orthodox school on Schützenstraße.

The best friendship of my life, and I allowed it to be buried along with so much else.

And so it is that my sixteenth birthday comes and goes on the 19th of September without much happiness. On top of everything else, this year's theme for presents seems to be hideous clothing: Tonio gives me a cotton skirt in a floral pattern fit for my Bavarian grandmother; Mama buys me a plain white cotton blouse two sizes too large in order to conceal my breasts; and Papa gets me a fringed brown shawl with swastikas at its corners, perfect for a Gypsy Nazi with really bad taste, if such a person exists.

Does the girl they want me to be try on these monstrosities together, as they intend? You bet, and I even tell them that they go together splendidly.

One day in November, I spot Mrs Munchenberg while Mama and I are shopping at Wertheim's. She must have lost her law job because she's a saleswoman at the perfume counter. She holds a finger to her lips, then whips around so Mama won't see her, humiliation in her bowed back.

When she dares to turn to me again, I slip away from my mother, who is busy shopping for soaps. "Any news on Raffi?" I whisper.

Mrs Munchenberg brings my hand to her cheek, then kisses it, as if I'm the confidante she's been waiting for. "Oh, Sophie, not a thing. It's been terrible. All we know is that he's still in Dachau." Her hands are frozen. "Maybe you could ask your father to write to the Justice Ministry for us ...?"

"I'm sorry, but I don't think he'd do that."

"Why? What risk would he run?"

"Please, Mrs Munchenberg, I have to go."

"No, Sophie, you can't. I need ..."

I have to pry her hand off me to get back to my mother, and when I turn to check that Mrs Munchenberg is all right, she's sitting right on the floor, her head in her hands, and another saleswoman is trying to help her up.

Tonio is relieved that Jewish physicians have been forced to leave their posts at state hospitals. Even those in private practice are prohibited from having Aryan patients.

"Imagine a Jew cutting you open," he tells me one afternoon just before Christmas, shuddering for dramatic effect, just as we've reached his father's hideout.

I say nothing, and with a sneer he tells me, "You're always silent when I mention Jews."

"Because I can't think of anything nice to say about your opinions," I reply, which makes him throw up his hands as if I'm hopeless.

For the first time ever, his penis doesn't get hard when I lick it. The cause or the result of his sour mood? After he manages an erection, he thrusts inside me angrily. I roll over onto my belly afterward, because I feel as though he's sliced me open. By the time I look at him again, he's nearly dressed. I reach out to him, but he thrusts my arm away. "You know, you really disgust me," he says contemptuously. I'm too shocked to utter a word, which gives him time to glower at me and add, "I don't even think you're very pretty. If you want the truth, I never did."

He walks into the hallway and I trail after him, naked. He reaches for his coat from the hook, then grabs the door-handle.

"What happened? Where are you going?" I ask, reaching behind me for a wall that's not there; I feel as if I've been clubbed on the head.

"Home," he snarls.

The door opens and closes; just like that, he has walked out on me. And I'm dumb enough not to guess how it's possible for him to hurt me so easily. I sit on the floor, like Mrs Munchenberg, unsure of how to escape the sense of pre-ordained disaster around me. And I stay there a long time, aware of myself in that way we are when we have reached a crossroads. Each of my breaths becomes the admonishment, *You thought you were safe here, but you were wrong.*

After I'm dressed, I lock the apartment with the key Tonio has given me, sensing I've lost my power not just over my boyfriend but also over my own life.

*

Tonio doesn't leave any roses or notes for me over the next week, and I don't dare knock at his apartment or wait for him in the courtyard. Too much humiliation waits for me down that road. I'm shipwrecked on Sophie Island. *A clean break* is what the hundreds of miles of ocean around me are usually called, but the sands of my grief spill over into everything I see and touch. What is it that went wrong? I ache with bewilderment and grief all the time.

Once afternoon during this terrible period, I have the frenzied urge to visit Georg's apartment house. Staring up at his windows, I wonder who's living there, and the feeling that he and I share something important makes me run away. Could it be a life that didn't turn out anything like we wanted?

Mama asks me about my gloomy face one day while I'm cleaning the oven, but I tell her that it's that time of the month. She sits me down and brushes my hair. We talk about Hansi. She's sure he'll start talking again one day soon, and then we'll enroll him in school.

Not if we don't get him some help, I think.

Papa suspects there's more to my sadness than my period and tells me in a concerned voice that he'll call Dr Nohel for an appointment the next day. He turns to leave my room, but then stops. "And where's our Tonio been lately?"

Our Tonio ...? So my father, too, had dreams of seeing us married.

"He goes hiking every weekend with his Nazi Youth colleagues," I reply.

"I'm sorry. That must be hard. Maybe you can start seeing him on weekday evenings. You're old enough now. I'll ask your mother."

It's not fair of Papa to show such kindness to me, because now I can't stop the tears.

"What's wrong?" he asks, sitting with me again.

"I'm just grateful to you."

He wipes my eyes with his thumbs and gazes at me lovingly. "Just leave it to me. I'm sure I can get your mother's permission."

Sure enough, Papa wins agreement from my mother for me to see Tonio on Wednesday evenings. I let them think I'm delighted and grateful. For my first date I tell my parents that he and I will be going to the movies on the KuDamm, but instead I walk to Grenadierstraße. I hide from my life in a smoky café, under a signed photograph of Benjamin Disraeli hanging on the grimy wall. Six young men and two young women – about my age – are seated next to me, which gives me a chance to eavesdrop. They're planning a visit to Palestine. While I sip my hot chocolate, they argue about how best to realize their dreams of a Jewish state. We watch the wooden horse carts passing by and listen to the *clop-clop-clop* of hooves. A pickle-seller pokes his head in, but no one's interested. *I wish I were a Jew*, I think. Not a rational desire these days, but a Mediterranean sun, olive trees, donkey rides, and a warm sea would be waiting to welcome me if I were. Just the antidote to the winds of the Berlin winter. And Tonio.

And if I were a Jew, then I could see Isaac and Vera any time I wanted.

After the youthful Zionists go their separate ways, I head to the Tiergarten. The crazy jiggling of the tram sends me back to my childhood, and the shimmering, fawn-colored wood paneling feels like the surface of my grief. The landscape of Berlin rushing by – all those sooty buildings, train tracks into the provinces, and garish advertising signs for Holstina dyes, Schmeltzer's pumpernickel, and Sonne briquettes – makes my pain more acute by that uncommonly unfair law of the human heart that twins joy with sadness.

From time to time, I used to see someone crying in public,

and I'd stare at the person's reddened, fluttering eyes without much understanding. Now, while passing the dome of St Hedwig's Church, a fearsome-looking black-haired worker sitting near me brushes away tears, and I realize that despair has taught me I'm no different from him or anyone else. All of us hanging on by a thread.

Crying is as infectious as yawning, so I get off by the Finance Ministry on Dorotheenstraße and walk the rest of the way to the park. And I scratch myself under my panties when no one's looking; I've had an itch there for the last few days and it's getting worse. A rash? I can't find anything but a little redness. Maybe it's the pernicious effect of sorrow.

The last thing I want is Dr Nohel putting his hairy muzzle between my legs, so at my check-up on Friday afternoon I refrain from mentioning my itching. He prescribes luminal for my sleeplessness. When I take a first pill that evening, I learn why so many Berliners are trudging around with dull, moonlike faces. Over the next week, I feel as if I'm living inside warm molasses. I wake, trudge through the day, and pass out on my bed, still in my clothes. What people say to me eases through my head like a trail of smoke not worth following. God bless luminal; it allows me to sleep even in class.

"Sophie!" Dr Richter, our math teacher, yells in my ear one morning.

Startled awake, I have no idea where I am until he says, "Are your dreams more interesting than my lesson?"

The other students laugh. I apologize, though even Dr Richter must suspect that *yes* would be the right answer. Or why ask the question in the first place?

The percentage of Berliners under sedation: a statistic that never appears in the papers.

*

I see Tonio from afar one afternoon just before the end of the year, while Hansi and I are making our way home from a trip to Weissee Lake, where we can go skating and watch the little black ducks. There's half a foot of snow on the ground, which means we're both exhausted from our walk.

Tonio is standing at the entrance to our building with two boys I've never met, rubbing their hands together and stepping around to stay warm. New friends laughing – about girls, most likely. I stare at him from down the street. And give a small gasp when he spots me. Hansi tugs on me, wanting to run ahead to Tonio, but I jerk back on his arm.

"Don't you move or I'll bury you in the snow!" I tell him.

He looks up at me as if I've lost my mind. That's what comes of threatening him but never really throttling him.

Tonio asks one of the boys for a cigarette and turns his back to me. I drag Hansi to Frau Koslowski's grocery and we sit with her behind her counter. Her hunched shoulders and heart-wrenching stories about growing up poor suit me, and Hansi is happy to eat candy.

Through Frau Koslowski, I learn that I've just entered the club of spurned young women. Her first boyfriend was Piotr. "Tall and clever and beautiful, but *ein Schwein*," she says. A pig. Sixty years have passed and she still can't forgive him. A good role model.

When I next peer out, Tonio and his friends have gone, and Hansi and I clomp home.

Our Young Maiden troop starts a chorus in the new year, and I've been chosen for the soprano section. Our teacher is Fräulein Schumann. "Sadly, I'm not related to the composer," she tells us that first afternoon. She's slender and graceful, and no more than twenty-five. She plays a pitch pipe to start us on the right key. "Sing it!" she exclaims, and we match the sound as best we can. She says my vibrato needs training, but that I've got potential. She uses a lot of Italian terms: *rubato, sostenuto, scherzo* ... She says *legato* is the most important thing for me to learn – to keep the notes strung together and leave no spaces between them. "No room for even the point of a needle!"

Fräulein Schumann and her lessons are my first indication there is life after Tonio.

On the first Tuesday in early January, I hear a familiar voice calling after me as I'm rushing through the chilly morning to school – Isaac. And before I've realized what I'm doing I'm talking once again to our local Elder of Zion.

"Sophele," he says urgently, out of breath, since he's run a little ways after me. "Please come to my apartment after school today."

"I don't think I can," I tell him. "My father would kill me. And I've got choral practice." *And you owe me an apology*, I'd like to add.

If he hadn't reached out for me with his warm hand in the midst of a frigid morning, I'd have turned away. That scares me even today – how life can take an important turn at any moment.

"It's about Vera," he says.

Fear bursts in my chest. "Is she ill?"

"No, but she needs your help."

Isaac greets me at his apartment late that afternoon. He gives me a bone-crunching hug, then holds my face in his hands and gives me such an adoring smile that I could almost believe that my life is only about being doted on.

"I've missed you, Sophele," he says. "Please forgive me. I was very rude to you. But I was being watched by the police. I noticed the same little twit following me twice to work. An incompetent *schlemiel*. Though maybe he wanted me to spot him – to scare me."

"Why do you think he was following you in the first place?"

"Who knows? Maybe it has to do with Georg's murder. Or maybe Raffi told the Nazis something about me in Dachau."

"He wouldn't do that!"

"I know ... but if he's being beaten ... Anyway," he adds, seeing that he's upset me, "all the excitement is over now. I haven't seen the *schlemiel* in weeks."

"I'm sorry I didn't try coming to see you again, but my parents ..."

He puts his finger to my lips, then to his own. "Sssshhh ... I know."

His delight in me makes me tingle. When we're together, it's as if seeing myself in those radiant eyes of his is magic – as if I've whispered the word that makes the world sing without even knowing it.

"Have you discovered anything about who might be the traitor in The Ring?" I ask.

"Nothing. But we've stopped meeting ... it's just too risky. So each of us is working on his own. I'm doing what I can and so are the others." Isaac points to his shelves, which have been emptied of at least half of their books, but before we can talk about what that has to do with his new tactics, Vera comes out of the kitchen in bare feet, her hair sopping wet, dripping all over the fraying rug.

"You *are* sick!" I say.

"No, I needed to wet my head or I'd have caught on fire. I'm like an overheated engine."

"Why?"

"I'm in a panic."

"Vera, for God's sake," Isaac interrupts, "dry your hair." He points to the moat forming around her feet and then the continuing drip, drip, drip. "You'll turn the rug moldy."

"Isaac, it's just an old *shmata*." She spreads her legs apart and bends down like a giraffe so we can kiss cheeks.

"*Mein Gott*, Vera, can you ever simply do what I say?" He puts his palms together and whispers a Hebrew prayer.

"No need to call on supernatural help!" With a bow, she strides away to the bathroom.

"What's a *shmata*?" I ask Isaac, who tells me it means *rag*.

We hear a cabinet door banging, and the sink turned on and off. Isaac rolls his eyes and begins packing tobacco into the bulb of his pipe.

"When Vera's around you really know it," I observe.

"She does have a certain irrepressible presence." He's got his lighter poised in one hand, the bowl of the pipe in the other, and he's staring at me with happy eyes. Yet there is a certain curiosity in them that makes me uncomfortable, as if he wants my secrets.

"Do you have the jacket Vera made me?" I ask.

"Yes, it's in my wardrobe. You want it?" He raises his eyebrows as if we've just hatched a plot.

After he gets his pipe going, we sneak together to his bedroom. His blankets are in a nest on the floor and dozens of old books are jumbled on the mattress.

"Do you sleep with your books?" I ask.

"*Nu*, doesn't everyone?"

While I'm silently condemning the mess, he slips my jacket over my shoulders. The black silk shimmers as if it's alive, and I'd almost forgotten the blue pockets – the color of Giotto's frescoes. When I look in Isaac's mirror, I reach up to the pink necklace of pearls around the collar, needing to touch their beauty.

"You look like a troubadour," he tells me.

Vera comes in wearing a towel as a turban. She looks like an Arabian giant.

"Stunning piece of work, even if I do say so myself," she tells me, hands on hips, tapping her foot and waiting for a compliment.

"You're a genius," I say, and I embrace her, and the fierce way she hugs me back makes me understand she's been waiting for me. A woman who always needs to be reassured, though no one would ever guess.

The three of us sit in the kitchen over glasses of wine. Vera tells us that people with her overheated metabolism sometimes spontaneously combust. She read recently about a woman in Rouen flaring up and setting her couch on fire. Her husband, seeing her turn into a torch, smothered her in a blanket and saved her life, but the house burned down.

Isaac scoffs.

"I'm serious!" Vera says, lighting a cigarette.

"Then maybe you shouldn't smoke," I suggest.

"I said *spontaneous*! It happens without a fire source." She squints at me vengefully.

"Vera, your story sounds fishy," Isaac says.

"The article was in *Marie-Claire*!" she declares, as if that settles the matter.

"Oy, talk about a *shmata*!"

"I wouldn't expect an *alter kacker* who can't even understand French to understand." She draws in so deeply on her cigarette that it's a wonder she doesn't fall over dead. It's her sign of triumph. I stare in admiration.

"So stop sitting there like a pimple on pickle," she tells me, "and tell us how you are. And don't leave out any hideous details. Your misfortunes will make us feel better."

I talk about the Young Maidens, and she and Isaac adore my stories about Our Lady of the Soufflés and *Das Deutsche Mädel* magazine, which Isaac refers to as *Der Deutsche Madig*, the *Worm-Eaten German*. I end up with the giggles. And as I tell more stories, I feel as if I'm made of fireworks. I'm alert for the first time in weeks. Then I drink some tea to dilute the wine that Isaac says is setting off too many sparks in my head.

"So when are you going to be on the cover of the *Worm-Eaten German*?" he asks me.

"I'd have to do something special to merit that."

"Maybe you could drown an old rabbi," Vera suggests.

"Vera, Sophele has no choice," Isaac notes.

"Is that true?" she asks me, unraveling her towel and shaking her clumped hair down to her shoulders.

"My mother would boil me with her potatoes if I quit. Anyway," I chirp, trying to make the best of it, "what we do isn't always idiotic."

Vera gazes down at me skeptically, her eyebrows lifting under the awning of her forehead. Not a good look for her. I want to find something positive to say about the Young Maidens, so I talk about Fräulein Schumann and our chorus.

"Learning how to sing is like being able to do something I never thought I could," I tell them.

"Like a blessing," Isaac says.

"Exactly."

"Has Hansi resumed talking?" he asks.

"No, not a word."

"And have your parents found a school for him?"

"No, he's home all the time. They're ... they're embarrassed by him now."

Vera snorts. "Soon they'll lock him in a wardrobe!"

"You're not getting along very well with your Mama and Papa, are you?" Isaac asks.

"No, but things have been better since I joined the Young Maidens and ... and started to pretend I'm a good daughter." To defend them, I add, "I just think they're caught up in things beyond their control and don't know what to do."

"Good try, Sophele," Vera says, "but Hansi is *not* beyond their control. Helping him lead his life is, in fact, their *responsibility*."

She lets me get away with nothing. I love her for that, though she doesn't also have to give me such a look of outrage.

"I need my notebook," Isaac says, and he goes off to his bedroom.

I ask Vera for a cigarette and try to copy her style of smoking. Isaac returns and writes a name and phone number on a sheet of paper, then tears it off for me. "Tell your father to call this man, Philip Hassgall. He studied with Rudolf Steiner, the Austrian philosopher and educator. Philip sometimes brings kids like Hansi back to us. Not all the way, but they are able to lead independent lives." Anticipating my question, he adds, "He's an Aryan, so you don't have to worry."

"Where will I say I got his name?"

"In an article in the newspaper. There was one a few months back. I can get a copy of it if you need it." He pours more tea into my cup. "Are you sketching your brother?"

"Sometimes."

"Good. That's important for both of you. Wherever he's gone, he must always know you are there for him." He sips his wine and gives me an inviting smile meant to get me talking again, but I don't make a peep. "What's wrong?" he asks.

"I've mostly stopped drawing. I only draw Hansi ... and only infrequently."

"Why?"

"Frau Mittelmann left for France and ..."

That's when the news of my break-up with Tonio tumbles out of me. Complete with sniffles, tears, and even a nosebleed because I blow too hard into Isaac's handkerchief.

Vera leans forward and catches my blood on her fingertips to prevent my troubadour jacket from getting stained. "Men!" she snarls, as if that's all one needs to say on the subject. She's holding Isaac's handkerchief to my nose. A cigarette dangles from her lips, and the curling smoke forces her to shut one eye. "Tilt further back or it'll never stop."

"If I tilt any further my neck will snap off!"

"Are you still in love with him?" Isaac asks.

"I think so," I reply in my muffled voice.

"Then you might as well just keep bleeding," Vera declares, yanking the handkerchief away.

"Vera!"

"Okay, okay ..." She starts blotting again.

"Sophele, try talking to him about what's bothering you about your parents and the way our country is going," Isaac tells me. "He could be waiting for you to be honest with him. He's caught up in things beyond his control, too."

Vera makes a skeptical *tsk* noise. "Oh, please, Tonio is what ... sixteen, seventeen?"

"Seventeen," I tell her.

"At that age, no one respects anyone else's opinions. I didn't. And I'm quite sure you didn't either, Isaac."

"I respect Tonio's opinion – at least sometimes," I point out.

My nose has stopped bleeding. Vera leans away from me and says, "You respect what the little delinquent says because you've got a *soufflé* that can be bruised, *meine Liebe*. And because his affection seems more important than being right or wrong. That errant belief is what has always doomed us." She shakes her head as if all women are a lost cause. One of the many themes to Vera's life.

"Anyway, I can't go to him," I announce. "He has to come to me."

"Take him a present as an excuse for visiting him," Isaac says excitedly. "How about a drawing of Hansi." Seeing my frown, he says, "Or a book – one of mine. I'm getting rid of them anyway."

"You're not throwing them out?"

"Good God, no! But when there's a war on, books are some of the first casualties, so I'm sending them away. It's part of a new campaign I've just started in this war."

"Is there a war on?"

Vera points a make-believe pistol right between my eyes. "You're the enemy ... you and me and Isaac." She pulls the trigger and makes a popping sound.

"And Hansi too," Isaac adds gravely.

I feel as if I'm backed up against a wall made of my own fear. *I have to fight too*, I think, fiddling with the pearls on my collar. "So where are you sending your books?" I ask.

"To my relatives in Turkey. I'm keeping only the ones I need for my studies."

"Oy!" Vera says, snorting. "You're not still trying to wriggle your way into Araboth?"

"How else will I beat Sophele to the cover of *Worm-Eaten German* magazine?"

"Is that why you went to Istanbul?" I ask. "To prepare your relatives to receive your books."

"No, not really. I went because we've decided to take the war overseas."

"I don't understand."

"We were going around to the embassies, as you know. But we weren't getting very far, so I had another idea," he says excitedly, his hands pushed boyishly between his legs. "Why not start working with journalists in Paris and London, Rome and Budapest? Why not convince them to write about what the Nazis have in store for the world – long, intelligent articles. So I went to Istanbul to present our cause to some reporters there. A few good pieces have already been published. The plan is to build up popular feeling against the Nazis and then, when the time is right, start planting the idea in people's heads for an embargo. While I was in Istanbul, others in The Ring went elsewhere. We're going to work individually from now on. As I told you, no more meetings. It's too dangerous now that the Nazis have so much power. So each person has a country. And we've agreed not to talk about the progress we're making. Even if our telephones are tapped, the Nazis won't learn anything."

"But if they do find out, they'll say you're committing treason! You could be executed."

"I am committing treason – at least from their point of view!" Sticking his pipe stem in his mouth and grinning, he adds, "And I've never felt better."

"Isaac," I say, looking down to prepare for a confession that may irritate him, "back in early June I followed Julia ... to Karl's Cellar."

"Big surprise!" he exclaims, scoffing. Then, with merriment in his eyes, he says, "I'm the one who sent Karl to chase you out."

"How did you spot me?"

"It was K-H," Vera says. "He notices every girl between the age of sixteen and thirty within half a mile. He's got a kind of lecherous radar."

"You drew lots out of a hat," I say.

"For those of us without language skills or preferences, we decided country assignments that way."

"I had to go to Madrid," Vera says glumly.

"It didn't work out?" I ask.

"Sophele, I can assure you that being jeered at in Spanish is even worse than in German. The street kids ... malignant little pests ... and with a satanic ability to spot me even in the dark. As for the journalists, they're doing an excellent job on Hitler, but Spain has its own problems. There might be a civil war."

Checking Vera's watch for the time, I jump up in horror. "Yipes! I've got to get going."

"But I haven't even asked you my question," she whines.

"I'm listening."

"Sit down first."

After I'm seated, she announces, "I've found someone who wants to be the father of my baby." She makes a grimace as if I might condemn her.

"That's wonderful!" I exclaim, though I won't deny thinking she might give birth to the *mieskeit* of the century. "Who's the lucky man?"

"A Polish mason. Very handsome. And get this ... he's seen a photograph of me and my face didn't dissuade him. K-H found him for me while photographing a construction site." She looks up to the sky and mouths, *Thank you, Jesus, Mary, and Karl-Heinz Rosenman* ... "The point is, I'm meeting him in two days to discuss when we'll start to ... to ... you know ..." Vera tilts her head to the side and gives me a girlish smile.

"It's incredible, you haven't even met the Rudolf Valentino of Poznan yet and you're already turning into a blushing bride!" Isaac observes. Pointing his pipe at me, he adds, "What she means is, she has to talk to him about when they'll start *schtuping*."

"Fucking," Vera translates, a furrow in her brow, concerned, perhaps, about how she'll perform after so many years of hiding backstage. "And I can't be alone when I meet him, Sophele. I'll burst into flame and set what's left of the Reichstag and the rest of Berlin on fire. So I want you to come with me."

Before I leave, Isaac gives me a monograph on the German painter Caspar David Friedrich for Tonio, though I know I'll never address so much as a single word to him unless he apologizes to me first. Childish or wise, I know it with the certainty of the small death in my gut.

The following Thursday morning, I tell my mother we're having a special Young Maidens supper and meet Vera at her apartment on Blumenstraße in the late afternoon. It's a top-floor garret in a soot-darkened building with a mildewed wooden staircase that creaks under my feet as if it's been practicing for a film set in a haunted house. On her door she's tacked a photograph of Minnie bleeding onto the street. At the bottom she has written, "If you approve, vote for Hitler."

After I knock, she peers at me through a slowly opening crack, then pulls me in as if I've arrived late. "I don't like my neighbors knowing who comes and goes," she explains.

Her living room is a tobacco-scented hothouse crammed with rickety bookshelves, a small round dining table – wooden with a metal rim, of the kind used in outdoor cafés – and two old chairs that she's upholstered with black and white striped fabric.

"My place is *gemütlich,* cozy, isn't it?" she says cheerfully.

"Absolutely," I enthuse, though suffocatingly cramped would better describe it. Worst of all, the ceiling is badly cracked and sags down half a foot, as if it's filled with rainwater. She reaches up and palms a big fissure. "I can hold it up in an emergency, so don't worry."

"Who's worried?" I say, practicing my acting skills. "Can I see the rest of the apartment?" I want to find the bathroom in case I have the courage to ask her my favor.

"For an Aryan you're pretty nosey, aren't you?"

"If I'm going to inform on you, I need to case the joint."

Her bedroom is just big enough for her cot, which is so long that it looks like a barge. "My mattress was special-ordered from Heitinger's," she tells me. "Isaac got me a discount."

Black curtains frame two small windows. For the first time I realize that Vera is poor.

"Is Isaac's business doing all right?" I ask her.

"It was going well until a few months ago when he started losing his Aryan customers." She feigns polishing a crystal ball and gazing into its depths. "I see hard times ahead for Isaac Zarco and his friends, including ... what's this? I see a girl ... a very pretty but evil girl with a gorgeous, pearl-collared jacket ..."

"You never cease to amaze me," I tell her, laughing.

"Amazing is my only option," she replies, grinning.

"Not true," I tell her. "I don't know what I'd do without you and Isaac."

Vera caresses a hand through my hair, plainly touched, then gives me a tour. The bathroom is covered in mildewed brown tile, and two red-tinted bulbs stick out like clown noses above the mirror. *It'll have to do*, I think. "I need your help before we go find Prince Charming," I tell her.

"With what?"

"I have an itch that won't go away. Down below," I say, pointing. "But I can't find anything. Would you take a look?"

She closes the shutters and goes to her bedroom for a reading lamp and chair. After I take off my skirt and slip, she has me sit on the bathtub rim. Pulling up her chair, she shines the lamp between my legs. It's hot. "Hmmnnn," she says darkly, peering at my personal parts.

"Please say it's nothing serious!" I plead.

"Sophele, I'm afraid you've got *Filzläuse*."

In German, that means felt-lice, and I've never heard of them before. "What are you talking about?" I ask skeptically.

"*Filzläuse*, my dear – you're crawling with them." Vera stands up with a grunt and explains the miniature parasitic nature of crab lice to me. To show me how they're biting into my tender skin, she opens her mouth and bares her teeth – nicotine-stained daggers.

"How many do I have?" I'm expecting she'll say ten, or at the most twenty. I am, at the time, a *total* idiot.

"I don't know, maybe a thousand!"

"Oh, my God!"

A chill shoots up through my body and out the very top of my head. A rocket of dread. The next thing I see is Vera leaning dangerously close to me. For some reason, the ceiling is behind her. She's holding her hand to my forehead, and when I reach up to brush her cheek to make sure she's real, she says, "Welcome back to planet Earth."

She has me sit up and drink a cup of linden tea, everyone's favorite remedy. "You passed out for a few seconds," she tells me. "You'll be fine now."

We put on my slip and skirt. I cradle the teacup in both my hands like a tiny girl. My arms feel as weak and pliant as a rag doll's.

"How long have you let this go on?" she questions, washing her hands at the sink.

"A couple of weeks. Vera, where did they come from?"

"Take a guess," she replies, grinning like a rogue.

"I've been in some pretty run-down movie theaters. And the bathrooms there ..."

"What in God's name do those Young Maidens teach you?" she hollers, scandalized.

"Oh, Vera, tell me how I got them," I moan. "I'm not in the mood for guessing games."

She dries her hands with a dishtowel. "They're a parting gift from Tonio. The only way you can get crab lice is from someone you've slept with."

"Oy," I say.

"Oy is right."

"Which means ..."

I decide not to end that troubling sentence, but Vera does: "... that he must have slept with a girl who was infested."

Now I know how he could leave me so easily! He's found someone else. Or a great many someone elses.

We purchase dusting powder for my lice and I sprinkle it on myself in the bathroom of Karl's Cellar, creating toxic puffs in the air that sting my eyes. I then rub the insecticide around per Vera's instructions, furious at myself for being such an innocent. After I wash my hands raw to get off the stink of powder, I slip back into the restaurant, picturing the busy city of lice feeding off me. My own *Metropolis* right between my legs.

Vera waiting nervously for the Polish Rudolf Valentino

Vera is sipping ouzo – her preferred drink – when I join her. Looking around, I discover the restaurant is filled today with women's shoe salesmen, as my mother would say, some of whom are holding hands and even kissing.

"Are there lots of places in Berlin for men who like other men?" I whisper to Vera.

"Dozens," she says. "And thank God for that or where would I be able to go?"

Our Polish worker enters after ten minutes. Even in the dim, moist lighting of this red-tinted fish-tank, he's gorgeous, though he's more of a middle-aged Randolph Scott than Rudolf Valentino. His thick gray hair is pleasantly mussed, and deep, masculine wrinkles frame his blue-gray eyes. His walk is solid, too, and has a bit of a lilt to it, as though a jig – or more likely, a polka – is playing in his head. I have a vision of him as a rough-talking cowboy in an American Western.

"Oh, my God!" Vera whispers to me, her megalithic jaw dropping open. "Get a look at him! My baby will be gorgeous."

Fearing he'll walk out without noticing us at the back, she waves to him, arms high, as though she's a semaphore specialist helping a battleship into berth. He rushes to us purposefully and shakes her hand and mine in his work-toughened paw, then drops down next to her with the sigh of a heavy laborer and gives us a sweet and eminently seductive smile. His nails are crescented with dirt and his fingers are enormous – as big as cigars.

As we converse, I notice that whenever he really gets a good look at Vera, his eyes tear. Cristophe, the sensitive cowboy from Poznan!

After the introductions and a few pleasantries about the wretched weather, a popular subject of conversation for Berliners at least ten months a year, Vera asks how he likes living here, but his German is no more than rudimentary. "Very big," he says, opening his arms wide. Then he puts his hands over his ears. "And too much noise."

He lights her cigarette, then one for me and finally himself. The touch of his hand makes either my lice or my soufflé itch, though I'm pretty sure I know which.

Vera and Cristophe talk in ever tightening circles around the subject at hand and finally agree to begin meeting at her apartment in two weeks. She hands him a first payment in an envelope and tells him her address is inside. Then she squeezes his arm. "God bless you, Cristophe," she says as if he's saved her life, then races off to the woman's room because she hasn't drunk enough ouzo yet to numb her emotions.

Instead of going directly home, I head to Georg's apartment after saying good-bye to Vera, and I knock again on Mr Habbaki's door; I've thought of some questions I should have asked him the first time around.

My tiny Lebanese host serves me almond cookies and cherry juice, overjoyed to have a visitor, and after he's vented his irritation about his apartment's faulty heating, we get down to business. Unfortunately, he doesn't recall much of anything about Georg's last weeks.

"Was he sick before he was killed?" I ask, thinking he might have been poisoned slowly.

"I don't think so."

"Did he get any unusual guests ... other than the people who moved his furniture? Did he complain of being followed or watched? Did he change the time he left his apartment in the morning?"

Mr Habbaki can't recall anything.

He soon runs out of cookies and I run out of questions. Fortunately, a retired nurse who lives upstairs and who was out the first time I visited remembers more. Mrs Brill and I sit on her black velvet sofa together. After I've complimented her on the beige bedspread she's just crocheted for her son, and the white ceramic water dish she purchased yesterday for her cross-eyed toy poodle, Max – named by her late husband after the German boxer, Max Schmelling – I interrupt her rambling and ask about Georg. Max sits on her lap, pants, and licks his scrotum and paws as we talk. After about ten minutes, she finally says something worth my while. "I do remember one unusual thing," she says, placing her hand in mine, as if we've known each other for ages, "because Georg had such beautiful hair. I saw him one day in the street, just before ... before he died, and all of it was cut off." She makes a slicing motion to emphasize her point. "I told him, it's such a shame that you've cut off all your beautiful hair. And do you know what he told me ...?" I give a big nod, since she's slightly deaf and maybe a bit batty too, and she says, "'It's my new look for the spring, Mrs Brill.'"

Did Georg want to appear less recognizable to his enemies? Maybe he found a new job that required short hair – one that he told no one about, not even Vera.

"Georg was always changing the way he looked," Isaac tells me dismissively when I inform him about the haircut. "He didn't like being ... being trapped by other people's expectations."

"So you don't think he'd taken a new job that he told no one about?"

"Definitely not. We spoke nearly every day on the phone and he'd have at least given me his new number."

On my insistence, Isaac fetches K-H's photographs of the dead man, and as he hovers over me, I confirm that Georg's hair was closely cropped. And a bit ragged around his ears. I'd missed that before, having concentrated solely on the swastikas.

"If you ask me, he got a bad haircut," I tell Isaac, who shrugs as if it's of no interest.

He lets me keep the photos on the condition that I never mention them to anyone, and I slip them in behind Garbo in my K-H Collection.

Over the next few mornings, before anyone else is up, I take them down and study them under the hot circle of light made by my reading lamp. Once, Hansi wakes up and joins me, leaning against my back and pressing his snoozy face over my shoulder. I flip them over right away, but then – figuring Hansi can't do any harm – show them to him and tell him that they're puzzle pieces that don't quite fit. I'm hoping that he'll spot something that's invisible to me, but after a half-hearted look, he just yawns and goes back to bed.

I follow Julia twice more over the next week, but she never deviates from her usual routine. One woman's simple, contented life is another's dead end.

At the end of January, on the appointed day and hour for Vera's rendezvous with Cristophe, an envelope is slid under her door; she rips it open to find a two-word note: "I'm sorry."

"No further explanation," she tells me when we meet at Karl's Cellar later that week. "I guess that once he got a good look at me in the flesh, he decided ..." Her voice breaks and she covers her head with her cloak. A leper whose last hopes have been dashed.

As we sit together, I realize that the only answer is for the prospective father *not* to get a look at her face or body, which means she'll have to wear a mask. Or he'll have to be ...

"Roman Bensaude!" I whisper to her excitedly, but Vera won't come out of her mohair hiding place to hear my new idea, so I tug it off her. "I bet Roman would have a baby with you," I tell her. "I don't know why I didn't think of him before."

"He's blind as the *Bodenschicht* of hell – the bottom layer of hell."

"Exactly. He won't see you. It'll be perfect."

"Sophie, my child could be born blind! *And* deformed! Why are you trying to make me feel worse? Does seeing me distraught give you some sort of perverse pleasure?"

"Look, I thought you were willing to take risks. And you're fond of Roman, right? Be an optimist for a change."

"Optimism is a word without meaning for me."

I quote her one of Isaac's jokes: "What's the difference between an optimist, a pessimist, and a kabbalist?"

"I don't want to know," she groans.

"An optimist sees a fly and thinks it might be an eagle, a pessimist sees an eagle and thinks it's probably just a fly, and a kabbalist sees an eagle and a fly and thinks they're both aspects of God!"

She gives me a dirty look.

"Sorry," I tell her. "All I mean is that with Roman as the father, your child will be talented and handsome. And I'd bet he'll be a very good father."

"Roman is a Jew!" she growls.

"So much the better. You'd make one more enemy for the Nazis in your womb." I risk taking her tulip bulb chin in my hand and say, "It's a war, remember?"

CHAPTER TWELVE

Roman has vowed never to spend another winter north of the Alps and is touring with the Circo Cardinali in Italy. "He's useless to me!" Vera tells me angrily. "It has to be now. I can't wait."

"Why?"

She refuses to give me any explanation, which is odd and infuriating. Nevertheless, I convince her to compose a letter to Roman, and we have it translated into braille by a blind worker at a brush factory run by Otto Weidt, an old friend of Isaac's. We send it care of Gianfranco Cardinali at his office in Rome. Vera's heart is carried overseas in a patterned series of dots …

Also at the end of January 1934, Papa telephones Isaac's schoolmaster friend Philip Hassgall to talk about the possibility of enrolling Hansi in his special program for children who are … He's at a loss for how to put Hansi's difference but soon comes up with *slow*. Accurate, I suppose. Two nights later, I overhear my parents quarreling about whether we can afford to send my brother to a private school. Papa says we will make sacrifices; if we can't get the bigger apartment we'd hoped for, so be it. Mama retorts that a private education for Hansi is beyond our means and that she'd prefer he remain with her.

I don't take my luminal that night so I can think out our family's dilemma, and I realize in the early morning that Mama will do all she can to keep Hansi with her forever. *This will be our last chance to set him free,* I think, and I get into his bed behind him, where his warmth is all the assurance I need that fighting for him is what I was born to do.

Dr Hassgall agrees to come to our apartment the next week to evaluate my brother. On the appointed afternoon, I bathe the boy and dress him in his best white shirt. I try to get one of Papa's ties on him, but he bats my hands away. Sometimes I'd like to bite him hard.

Dr Hassgall is about fifty and very dapper. He's dressed in a dark gray, antique-looking woolen coat and red silk tie. He has thick, closely cropped gray hair, and he makes precise gestures with his hands, as though he's an orchestra leader. His blue eyes light up with eagerness when he spots Hansi sitting on the sofa. In a melodious voice, he asks my parents about when they first noticed he was different, and what happened at his last school. After their explanations, which are incomplete and scattered, our guest asks them why they think the boy stopped talking, which is when Papa and Mama look at each other as though they're two defendants needing to collaborate on a lie. "We really don't know," Mama tells our guest.

"He just stopped," Papa agrees, shrugging away further reflection on the matter.

Dr Hassgall asks if they will permit him to talk with Hansi alone in our bedroom. "I'd like to make my evaluation without anyone else around who might distract him," he says, and seeing he's about to be refused, he holds up both hands and adds, "Please, be patient with me. With children like Hansi, patience is often what we need most."

"Very well," Papa answers, but his voice is deep with warning. *If you hurt a hair on my son's head ...*

Mama glances at Papa as if she's been betrayed, but before she can ruin our hopes, I rush to Hansi and lay my hand on top of his head, which usually calms him. "Listen up," I say cheerfully. "We're going to go into our room and Dr Hassgall is going to come with us, and he only wants to talk with you. Everything will be fine, I promise."

He doesn't answer of course, but I can tell from the way he's tilted his head that he is scared enough to burst into tears at any moment.

"I promise I'll never abandon you," I tell him, pressing down on him. Then, I say something surprising. "If you do this, I'll ask Mama and Papa to get you a dog. As cute as Minnie!"

Where does that little bit of inspiration come from?

He folds his top lip over his bottom – interest piqued. Maybe he's even dancing inside the Hansi Universe.

I lead the boy into his room and summon Dr Hassgall. I close the door behind us, which my parents may find unforgivable, but I haven't any choice.

"Thank you, Sophie," he tells me when I've got Hansi seated on his bed. "You can go now. And Sophie," he says, smiling, "I'm very impressed with you. Isaac was right."

The generous way he looks at me makes me shiver, but from that moment on, I feel a great solidarity with him because I know we are fighting for the same person.

"My brother stopped talking when he got scared," I whisper, and I grimace so that he knows this is top-secret.

He leans toward me, a co-conspirator now. "Scared how?"

"Friends of my father's stayed with us one night – Communists in hiding. Mama panicked, and then Papa decided to change ... to become a Nazi. He feared arrest and he renounced his past, which includes us, too ... me and my brother. You see, Papa is scared of what we might say about him. I think Hansi stopped knowing who our father was. And ..."

Dr Hassgall pats my shoulder. "I understand, Sophie. You needn't continue."

"Just one more thing," I say. "Hansi likes jigsaw puzzles. If you can get him to let you help him with one, you'll be part of the way inside his universe."

Dr Hassgall laughs sweetly. "I understand. We'll work on that first."

I leave the two of them alone.

"Why did you close the door?" Mama demands as soon as I step into our sitting room. She's standing with her hands crossed over her chest.

"Dr Hassgall asked me to close it. I didn't want to be rude and refuse him."

"The nerve of that man!" Mama whisper-screams to Papa, and I can tell she won't be satisfied until she's punished someone – meaning me. "And Sophie, what's this about a dog?" she demands.

"I got ahead of myself there," I say, trying to wriggle free of her attack. "I guess it was a stupid idea, but I couldn't think of anything else."

"*Very* stupid. How could we have a dog in this tiny apartment?"

"You're absolutely right," I say.

I turn to my father and ask for permission to go to the kitchen, which he gives me. I sit there munching on a raw carrot. Waiting and wondering as if caught in a fishing net. After I hear footsteps, I count to ten and then rejoin the others. My brother has given Dr Hassgall his hand. They stand before my parents, supplicants, forming a united front.

Not bad, Dr Hassgall, I think.

"Dr and Mrs Riedesel, I work with what I call *distant children*, and I believe that Hansi is one of them. He could benefit from classes at my school, and I promise you my teachers and I will do our best to help him."

"You're sure he *can* be helped?" Papa asks.

"I believe ... I believe he is behind a kind of wall. I will try to open a window so he can see us clearly, and so we can see him. So he can tell us what he needs."

"But our physician said that he was ..."

Dr Hassgall waves off my father's comments. "Dr Riedesel, would you please consider excusing Hansi from hearing medical matters?"

My father agrees, so I take the boy to our bedroom. To my astonishment, Dr Hassgall waits for me to return before continuing. "Now that we're all here," he says, nodding at me, "German physicians know nothing about Hansi's condition. And I assure you that he is neither feebleminded nor schizophrenic. Please, unless he becomes gravely ill, refrain from taking him to any more doctors. They will only put his health at risk."

That seemed a strange comment at the time.

"Will he ever be ... be normal?" my mother asks.

"I don't believe so, but he can be happy and productive. I have more than ten children similar to Hansi, and if you visit my school, you will see how they play and learn. To tell you the truth, I don't even know what normal means anymore. When you work with children like Hansi, you come to understand that such determinations are not important and even dangerous. I have several former students who now live on their own and hold down good jobs. Some others have found partners for life who love them. That's what's important."

Finally, a speech from a German worth hearing!

"Do you know why ... why he is the way he is?" Mama asks

anxiously. A question she's been storing for eight or nine years, I'd guess.

"No one knows, but I don't believe you did anything to cause his condition."

Mama gasps and raises her hands to her mouth. Embarrassment that he has guessed her feelings of guilt? Or relief that she can now release them? I cannot tell.

"This just happens sometimes, Mrs Riedesel," our guest continues. "But Hansi will need schooling if he's to have a good life. And that's what we all want, isn't it?"

"But your school is so far across the city," Mama points out.

She wants to start one of her tennis matches, but the words *far across the city* are my cue to rush onto the court. "I'll take Hansi to school and pick him up every day except when I have the Young Maidens on Tuesdays and Thursdays," I say. I've been practicing my offer but it still comes out in a desperate rush.

I expect Mama's fury. Instead, she looks at me sadly and says, "If you're willing to do that, Sophie, then ... then ..."

She can't finish her sentence and says nothing more while our guest is with us. Her silent gloom puzzles me until later when I realize it was only when I spoke that she understood she'd lost this battle and would have to give up her innocent little boy to the world. I felt only cruel resentment toward her then, but now I know how hard it is to let go of someone we want to protect. And how much life-affirming courage it took for her to do it.

After Dr Hassgall leaves, Papa picks up Hansi in his arms and kisses him all over his face. God bless him for that. Then he tells Mama firmly that the boy will be enrolling at school as soon as possible.

Mama, stunned, runs to her bedroom. She prepares no dinner that night. Papa and I do not mention what's happened. I make onion soup for Hansi, Papa, and me, and we eat cheese on pumpernickel bread afterward.

When Mama finally emerges near bedtime, her eyes are rimmed red. She avoids Papa, who reads his paper without glancing up. Their distance seems to sit on my shoulders, making all my movements labored. I heat up some soup for her, but she eats it with faraway eyes, as though she's a condemned prisoner – defeated again by the life she never wanted.

When I pick up her empty bowl, she takes my hand and brings it to her cheek, then kisses my palm as if I'm her last hope.

"You'll see, Mama, Hansi will love you even more when he's better," I tell her.

She looks up at me, and I see a fragile woman who's unsure of her place in the world – not so different from me. She was only thirty-six. That seemed so old at the time. And over a distance of seventy years, I hear Isaac tell me, "People generally become bitter for lack of three things – love, attention, and justice." He was talking about Vera then, but it goes for my mother too.

I could almost trust Mama at that moment and confess to her what's happened between Tonio and me. In another time and place, she'd put her arms around me and tell me something soothing and sweet. But not in the Germany I've inherited.

The King David School is a large yellow house on Emdener Straße, a block from St Paul's Church. My mother drops Hansi there for the first time at the end of January and I fetch him that afternoon – early, so I can make sure he's all right.

Dr Hassgall lets me peek into my brother's classroom, which is painted deep blue – the color of the sky in Giotto's frescoes. Something else seems odd, but I can't identify what.

"Children are very sensitive to color," Dr Hassgall tells me, "and blue tends to keep them calmer and more comfortable with themselves than white."

Eccentricity or full-blown lunacy? As long as Dr Hassgall helps my brother, he can paint the whole street blue with pink stripes, I don't care.

Dozens of kids' drawings – jagged landscapes and mop-haired stick figures – are taped on one of the walls. On the other side of the room is a gigantic map of the world. Framing the map are two windows that give out on a garden of bare-limbed trees rising up behind a slide and see-saw.

My brother and eight other students sit at desks pushed together to form a wooden island in the middle of the room. Three girls, five boys, all of them wearing light blue smocks.

The teacher is a young woman, maybe thirty, with copper-colored hair cut very short. She wears trousers and looks like an athletic young man. I bet she'd beat Maria in the hundred-meter dash. Enough reason to like her.

We smile as strangers do who want the same thing – in this case, for my brother to thrive. I wonder if she'll ever lose patience with Hansi, like I do. I hope so.

No swastika flag flies above her head. And she's not wearing an armband. *That's* what's odd.

When she comes to us, she introduces herself as Else König. She explains that Hansi is working on subtraction problems in his notebook.

Dr Hassgall tells me, "We teach subtraction before addition because it's best if children learn that there exists a whole from which we may take things away before they get the erroneous idea that everything is separate."

Could that be true? In any case, his reply is so unexpected that I give a little laugh, which is when Hansi spots me. I wave, but he puts his nose back in his notebook right away. And it's then I understand more of what my mother feels.

Roman's reply to Vera's letter arrives in early March. He writes that he has wanted a child for many years. "I'll be back in Berlin around mid-May and then we can get started on baby-making!"

"I hope I can hold out till then," Vera says ominously.

"You've waited this long, and it's only another ten weeks," I point out.

Mr Cardinali has written the letter for Roman, and his handwriting is so neat and compact that it seems a sign that nothing will go wrong this time, but Vera refuses to accept her good luck. "When he's inside me I'll believe he's kept his word, and not a minute sooner."

Unable to come up with any other rational course of action in my investigation of Georg's murder, I decide to follow other members of The Ring. I start with Molly and Klaus Schneider, the trapeze flyers at Althof's Circus who participated in our protest at Weissman's. The bad news is that they live all the way across town in Wilmersdorf. With all my commitments, I manage to get there only twice at the beginning of the month, risking frostbite while waiting down the street from their apartment, and only once do they come home. They go in at just after five p.m. and don't go out again. My feet are so numb by seven that I trip and have a bad tumble while walking to the underground. I can't see how I'm going to reconcile being a schoolgirl and Young Maiden with my detective work. And with Berlin's winter.

The 9th of March, 1934 – the day I join the war effort. And diminish any chance I had of furthering my investigations. My particular mission is Isaac's idea.

He says he's been buying books by Jewish writers and banned Aryan authors to keep them from being tossed into bonfires. "But as soon as the secondhand bookshop owners see me coming they double their prices," he tells me. "*Goniffs, ladrões*, thieves, gangsters are what they are! You've got to save me – I'm going broke."

So every Wednesday, when I am supposedly out with Tonio, Isaac gives me a list of what he's hunting for and I bargain with the booksellers. After I've made my rounds, I sneak across the courtyard behind our building and eat supper in his apartment. Then we return to our lessons in Judaism.

"Each text you buy for me is another angel who will live to fight another day," Isaac assures me, explaining that Berekiah Zarco used to refer to books as angels given earthly form.

Vera, Heidi, Rolf, K-H, Marianne, and other friends sometimes join us in the evening, though we never talk about mysticism in their presence. "They already think I'm daft," Isaac confides in me, "and I wouldn't want them to know my condition is even worse than they imagine."

I love the secrecy of our time together – and that Isaac is all mine. His youthful happiness of late has lulled me into believing that he is perfectly safe. Maybe we both want to believe that, in fact. No one, after all, wants to spend one's days cramped by fear, even when that would be the logical way to live.

Whenever I ask about his work with Turkish journalists, he says it's going well. He doesn't know how the other members of The Ring are faring in their efforts because they've agreed never to talk about such matters. "The less we can tell the Nazis if we're arrested the better. And this makes it much harder for the traitor in our group to do any damage."

Between dropping off and fetching Hansi, my own studies, Young Maiden meetings, choral practice, and hunting for Isaac's books, I'm generally too exhausted to think about The Ring or Georg's murder, or the Opposite-Compass' rantings, or anything else the world might consider noteworthy. In consequence – and with help from my nightly lullaby from luminal – I sleep like a brick. Though Tonio occasionally steals into my mind as if he's intent on hurting me further ...

On my first list of books are two works by Adolph Jellinek that, according to Isaac, are indispensable for the study of Jewish mysticism: *Philosophie und Kabbala* and *Beiträge zur Geschichte der Kabbala*; and two books by the Jewish story-collector and philosopher, Martin Buber, *The Tales of Rabbi Nachman* and *The Legend of the Baal-Shem*.

I save the list inside my diary because those books seem to mark the beginning of my real life – the one I wanted and chose. I keep my diary in Isaac's wardrobe.

The Jewish booksellers I visit are mostly grouped around the New Synagogue on Oranienburger Straße and on Neue Friedrichstraße. The smell of leather and dust comes to gratify me and put me at ease with myself, since it's the scent of my covert contribution to our cause. I become friends with Mr Poppelauer at Number 59 Neue Friedrichstraße and Mr Henrikkson at Number 61.

I tell all the bookshop owners and clerks that I'm making purchases for my own studies. I'm sure they don't believe me, but nobody asks questions of strangers anymore. I keep my sweater unbuttoned to let my Young Maiden uniform show through when I visit a Christian-owned bookshop, and I button my collar for the Jews.

Isaac calls me his *kyra*, which is what the residents of Istanbul used to call the Greek women who brought merchandise to orthodox Moslem homes so that the wives and daughters cloistered there could purchase what they needed. Every time I put a rare book in his hands, he whispers a Hebrew blessing over my head and tells me, "Another angel saved, my *kyra*."

One Wednesday in early March, Isaac presents me with a book printed in New York called *Four Weeks in the Hands of Hitler's Hell-Hounds: The Nazi Murder Camp of Dachau*. He tells me that the book documents how SS guards are treating political prisoners like slaves. Dozens have been hanged for refusing to follow orders and many others shot for trying to escape. The Jews and Communists amongst the prisoners are being slowly starved to death. The book has been written by a former member of the Reichstag, Hans Beimlar, who managed to escape from Dachau in May 1933.

"Have you told the Munchenbergs about the book?" I ask Isaac.

"Professor and Mrs Munchenberg read it two nights ago, and they left yesterday afternoon for Dachau. Right after going to the bank."

"The bank?"

"They're going to offer the SS a ransom. Apparently that works sometimes. They've taken every Reichsmark they've got."

"You better hide the book somewhere really safe," I tell him.

"No, this angel needs to speak. I'm giving it to K-H and Marianne next."

Two days later, Isaac calls to me from his window as I head out with Hansi for his school, and he drops an envelope into my hands, then slips back inside and shuts his window before anyone can spot him talking to me. He writes, "The bribes worked, but not as the Munchenbergs hoped. They paid a small fortune only to be told that Raffi has been killed. Shot for insubordination. After six hours of standing at attention in the rain, he apparently sat down. They managed to bribe enough Nazis to get his body. The funeral is today. I will make apologies for you for not attending. They are killing our best young people first, so be careful. Maybe you should stop buying books. Come talk to me. I'm worried. Sorry, sorry, sorry to give you this terrible news. Be strong. Love, Isaac."

When I was tiny, Raffi would sling me over his shoulder and carry me laughing to my room and sit with me as I fell asleep, reading to me softly, and I loved his voice, and the feel of the mattress sagging in his direction and the heat on my cheeks made by the candles that he would light and put on my bedside table. Raffi was the gravity of affection. Maybe he was the first person outside my family whom I loved.

So when I read that he is dead, I squat on the pavement, hollowed by disbelief. And then I run to Frau Koslowski's grocery and go to the back where no one can see me and sob over all that will never be. Because now I know that Raffi will never see the Nile again, or bring us home dried dates, or go with me to visit Hansi at his new school. And he will never baby-sit my children, which is a fantasy I didn't even know I had until now. Strange how we only know our deepest hopes too late to do any good.

And I realize, too, that one day in the not-so-distant future I'll be older than Raffi; when I reach thirty and then forty and fifty, he will still be twenty-five and buried in our neighborhood cemetery, a bullet hole in his skull.

I take a luminal to get through the day, but even so tears come to my eyes when Dr Richter greets us with a Heil Hitler that morning. Hate burns in my chest like a sulfurous flame, and I can't get my breath when he asks me what's wrong. I finally stammer, "A friend ... friend of mine died and I need to go to the funeral. I want to be excused."

"Do you have a note from your parents?"

"No."

"Then I'm afraid you'll have to stay."

It was a mistake to reveal my grief, because Gurka – with the intuition that comes to the truly wicked – has guessed that it's a Jewish friend of mine who has died and draws her hand across her neck like a throat being slit whenever she sees me.

What books would Raffi have written on Egyptian sculpture that will never now be read?

And the point is, he would want me at his funeral, and disappointing the dead makes me feel as if I'll be haunted forever by his contempt and my own cowardice. My only comfort is knowing that Raffi would approve of my way to fight this war, so when Isaac returns from the cemetery, I tell him that I'll never stop saving books while Hitler rules Germany. Brave words, but maybe they're just my excuse for not doing more.

The next Saturday, I wake to hear my name being called from the street below my window. Tonio is waving at me to come down. It's too late to make believe I don't see him. And turning away would only sentence me to a life of what-might-have-been, so I hold up my hand, meaning *wait*. I feel as though I'm mesmerized by my own confusion.

Tonio greets me cheerfully. He takes a step forward, so I take one back.

"Do you want to go to a movie with me this afternoon?" he asks. He pokes his tongue out at the corner of his mouth to give me his puppy face, eager for us to embark on mischief, as if we were our younger selves.

"You gave me crabs," I say, dead-voiced. I feel like a shadow stalking my own mind.

"Sophie ..." He gazes down, thinking of what to say. He needs help, but I'm not going to give him any. I feel dry and impoverished. And gray – the color of my thoughts.

An elderly couple passes us, the man in a black suit that's way to big for him and his wife wearing bright red silk flowers in her hat. Down the street, a group of kids are playing tag.

At length, he looks up and says, "Can we go somewhere where we can be alone?"

"If you don't have the courage to talk with me here, then what good are you?"

He looks down again, ashamed. "I was upset," he tells me. "I was feeling pressured. We'd been friends for so long that I ... that I *thought* I wanted something else. And ..."

"And you *got* something else. *Filzläuse.* From someone else. Or more likely, from many someone elses."

He grimaces. "I'm sorry. That was rotten of me. And it was only one other girl."

I don't believe that, but I'm not going to humiliate myself by asking for names, ages, and addresses.

"I only realized I had them when it was ... was too late to warn you," he adds.

Across the street, the wrinkled old grandmother who lives on the top floor of Mr Mannheim's building starts shaking a white rug out her window, making clouds of dust. We've never talked, but I give her a big wave, and she waves back. That's my way of making sure that Tonio knows that my life goes beyond him.

He turns around momentarily to see who it is, not to be left out.

"So will you come with me to the movies?" he asks in a supplicating tone. The sound of real regret or the role he needs to play to win me back?

"You said something terrible to me," I point out.

He kicks the pavement once, then a second time, which means our conversation is not going as he expected. "I'm sorry about that, too," he says. "I lied about you not being pretty. I was angry at you. I felt you were making me decide whether I wanted to be with you forever, and I wasn't sure I was ready." He looks at me firmly. "You may not like what I'm saying, Sophie, but I'm being honest with you. That's what you want, isn't it?"

I keep my lips sealed because I don't know how to answer. As we stare at each other, I feel our intimacy growing around us, blocking out the buildings and the sky, and the rumbling of the tram, and I sense a latch opening inside me. Freeing me to desire a future together. Even though he has betrayed me.

"Please don't hate me," he says, his voice breaking.

"I don't hate you, but you hurt me badly," I reply, my voice about to vanish as well.

"Sophie, I'd never known any girl but you before I ... I ... If only I could take back my betrayal, I would."

His big black eyes – which I've known for so long – are asking for my forgiveness. He plays his trump card: "Sophie, I've got to go into the army in two months. I don't know how often I'll be back in Berlin, and I don't want to go without making up with you."

His eyes are moistening. He wipes them roughly, but I let my tears fall, wanting to taste the salt of my own vulnerability – to make it as real as possible before I let it go.

At length, he says, "How's Hansi?"

"He's started school again."

"Oh, Sophie, that's wonderful!"

"Yes, I'm happy about it."

"I bet it was hard getting your mother to agree."

"Nearly impossible," I admit, and I feel a second click deep in my chest, because I hadn't expected Tonio to understand my family so well. "I had to promise to drop my brother at the school and pick him up three days a week."

"Where's the school located?" he asks, eager to steer our conversation along a safe route.

"Near St Paul's."

"I'll come with you sometimes," he announces.

Showing his solidarity is a good strategy, I'll give him that. "You don't have to," I reply. "I'm sure you're very busy."

"I want to! I've missed Hansi."

"A friend of Mr Zarco's is the headmaster," I say, and as I speak I see what I need to tell Tonio before we can go any further on the road to our union. "Mr Zarco even arranged for my parents to meet with him," I begin.

"That was kind of him," Tonio replies.

A good answer, but not enough. "Yes, *very* kind," I say. "Mr Zarco is a wonderful man and I do not want to see him ever hurt ever again by Nazis. And Rini was my best friend ever. I don't want to see her hurt either."

I speak as if Tonio could protect them against all the men with guns, which I know he can't, but I have to make my point.

"I know you loved Rini," Tonio says, "but times have changed. Maybe later, when things calm down, you two can be friends again."

I don't give that an answer because I've been such a coward. "And another thing," I say instead, "Raffi was shot for insubordination. I will never forgive the Nazis for his death. I want you to know that … and remember it. And I'm worried about Hansi, too."

"Why?"

"He deserves the best life he can have, even if the Nazi Youth would never accept him because he isn't racially hygienic. I'll never leave him behind, wherever I go."

I say these things one after the other in order to draw a magic circle around the people I most love – one that Tonio should not cross. And I close the circle tight around Raffi and Hansi with a trembling voice of warning.

"I love your brother," he assures me. "You know that. But the world is the way it is. And I have my place in it."

That's Tonio drawing *his* circle – and it's around only himself. If someone with more experience were watching us he might notice that our circles don't overlap.

"I don't want you to change," I tell him. "I just want you to understand me."

He looks convinced, but the truth is that I'd prefer us to be real companions, not just lovers, and save all the Yiddish books in Berlin.

"Tonio ..." I'm considering how to put a last request, but when I look up, he comes to me and embraces me, and I can feel our bodies easing into each other, as though into the same waking dream. He kisses my eyes because he knows that makes me feel protected, and I press into him, feeling our potential for a life of kindness and passion, and then he says, "I've thought you're beautiful ever since we met. That's what makes things difficult for me."

"I don't understand."

"Everyone says I should want to be with lots of girls at my age, but I don't want to be. I discovered that the hard way."

"Who's everyone?"

"My Nazi Youth friends. And ... and even my father."

The last thing I wanted to tell him was that we had to be perfectly honest with each other. But now, in his arms, I don't think either of us really wants that. In fact, we have drawn our magic circles to make it clear that our separate lives will continue as before.

Later, after I've asked permission from my parents, we go to the movies – *Dawn*, a heroic film about submarine combat in the Great War – and we take Hansi along. As we ease down in our seats, I realize I've forgotten something essential. "If ever my parents ask," I whisper to Tonio, "we've been going out every Wednesday for the last few months."

"I know." Seeing my shock, he grins. "I've been going out every Wednesday evening so no one would find out about your lie." He puts his arm over my shoulder. "Mostly I play billiards at the Köln Beer Garden. I've gotten pretty good."

"But how did you know that was the deal I had with my parents?"

"Your father came to talk with my father before our first Wednesday together. He wanted to make sure that it was all right with my parents for us to go out on a weekday. So when Papa talked with me, I was confused at first, but I kept dancing till I figured out the steps."

After the movie, we go for a walk, and we end up on Museum Island because a band is performing hymns in front of the Cathedral. We're just five minutes from Oranienburger Straße, so I steer us to Julia's shop, maybe because I miss watching her. Or maybe an idea is already forming inside me ...

We stand across the street, in front of Goldman's Bakery, and the glorious scent of bread is so strong that Tonio makes believe he's dizzy and wobbles around on the sidewalk, making Hansi giggle.

Julia is standing behind her cash register, her hair up, a white scarf around her neck. And just like that, I realize that the time has come for me to start poking answers out of their hiding places.

I've thought a great deal about why I chose Julia in years since, and I think it comes down to this: I suspected that she knew much more about poisons than she'd told me and believed she possessed the fierceness of will to kill anyone who might have threatened her good life. For better or worse, that was enough for me to take a stupid risk.

"Wait here," I tell Tonio, "I'll be back in a minute." I don't want him to overhear what I have to say, of course; he is soon to be a soldier in Hitler's army, after all.

"But what are ..."

I wave away his question. Julia is standing behind her counter reading a thin book when I enter. "Sophie, hi!" she exults, her obsidian eyes opening wide with surprise.

"I was in the neighborhood and thought I'd say hello. How's Martin doing?"

"Oh, he's fine. He's even found a job! He does pick-ups and deliveries for a cleaning company. He goes around with a man in a truck. He loves the truck." Her eyes glow with fondness and humor.

"I ... I want to ask a favor." I lean across her counter and whisper. "A friend of my father's has just arrived secretly in Berlin – back from exile." There's no point in being subtle when setting a trap, so I add, "He's a Communist and a labor leader."

Julia gazes down, considering what to do, then whispers, "Wait, don't say any more."

She gets up to lock the door and turn around the *closed* sign in the window, then leads me into her storage room. We're surrounded by wooden shelves holding hundreds of white porcelain jars with blue Latin lettering. It smells musty, and a bit like ginger.

"So what does your father's friend need?" she asks, her hands playing nervously together.

"He'd like some something for his asthma. If you want some time to make a mixture, you could have it delivered." Clicking the latch on my trap, I say, "He'll be at Number 18 Tieckstraße from five to six this afternoon."

"No, I can give you what he'll need right now."

Inside her shop, she scoops up colt's foot, camomile, and two other herbs I've never heard of into a bowl, then swirls around the mixture with a wooden spoon and funnels it into a pink bag. "He'll have to prepare this as an infusion," she tells me as she folds the top closed. She raises a teacherly finger: "Three times a day. You understand?"

"Thank you," I reply, taking the bag from her. "What do I owe you?"

"Nothing," she says, putting her hands together into a position of prayer. "Just be careful. And please don't tell anyone you were here."

"What did you get?" Tonio asks me as I meet him across the street.

He reaches for my bag but I hold it away from him. "Some medicine for Hansi."

"What's he got?"

"Pinworms."

"Hansi, you've got pinworms?" he asks the boy.

The little lizard shakes his vacant head, which makes Tonio look at me and frown.

"It's to help me sleep," I tell him in a confessional voice.

He buys my explanation, and we go home. But after I've kissed him goodbye and dropped Hansi at home, I dash back to the street. I reach Tieckstraße at ten to five according to my watch. I wait down the block from the apartment where Tonio and I have our trysts, trying to calm my frenzied breathing. But by 5:15 I begin to believe I've misjudged Julia, and when 5:30 goes by, I consider leaving. It's so cold that my teeth are chattering, and my nervous excitement is completely gone.

A few minutes later, however, a black Mercedes drives by and stops in front of Number 18. Two Gestapo officers step out, one with his gun already drawn. Another man – hard to see what he looks like – stays behind in the back seat of the car.

"The traitor in your group is Julia, I'm sure of it!" I tell Isaac as soon as he lets me in his apartment. I'm panting from the thrill of catching a murderess, and because I think I've just saved him and Vera, though I won't deny that I can also hear a whisper from the part of my mind formed by Hollywood saying, *This was too easy* ... "Though I bet she'll deny it," I add. "She'll say the police already knew where he was hiding. She'll ..."

"Sophele, slow down," he pleads. He leads me into his kitchen and points to a chair. I sit down and so does he.

"Isaac, listen to me!" I tell him, and I go on to explain then how I trapped Julia, the words flying out of me like arrows.

He questions me for a time, then stands up and goes to the window. He lights his pipe. I try to speak, but he holds up his hand. "I need to think," he tells me.

When he returns to me, he kneels by my chair. "Now listen, you have to let me handle this. You have to promise me you won't do any more ... you won't go to see Julia."

"Isaac," I say desperately, "how can I promise that? I loved Raffi, and she might be responsible for his death. Who knows what she told the Gestapo about him? And what about Georg? She has to be punished!" *And you're not even grateful!* I want to add, but instead I say in a hesitant voice, "You ... you don't even seem pleased I found out who was betraying you."

"Because Julia is one of my oldest and dearest friends. Though I thank you for finding out about her. Now listen," he adds, standing up, "you are to keep away from her. She might make trouble for you – and even Hansi."

Does he add my brother's name because he knows I won't dare put him in danger again, not after the terror we went through at Weissman's?

Isaac worried for my safety

I agree to let Isaac deal with Julia. And I promise, too, that I will refrain from buying books for at least a month. *No Risks for Sophie* is the title of this new movie, and I am to rejoin my quiet life far from the front lines. Though I am happy to report there are other battles to be won ...

"No, and don't ask again!" Mama says when I beg her for a small dog for Hansi for the third or fourth time, adding, "I don't want to hear of this ever again! The last thing Hansi needs is a mutt leaving his ... his *deposits* all over the house."

I'm nearly seventeen and she still can't say *shit* in front of me.

But Dr Hassgall surprises me by telling me that Mama is perfectly right and that a fish tank would be better for the boy. "Distant children need lots of visual stimulation," he says conclusively. "But nothing too ... exciting. I'd say fish are perfect."

So we buy one orange and one white goldfish at Tannenbaum's Pet Shop on Prenzlauer Allee. They're as fat-bellied as George

Grosz bankers. Still, out of affection, I call them Fred and Ginger, but the names my parents give them are the Germanically dull, Willi and Tilli.

"Be glad they're not Adolf 1 and Adolf 2," Isaac tells me to cheer me up.

Hansi follows the two gulping, marble-eyed fish with a rapt gaze. As for those poor creatures themselves, they're now confined to a two-foot-wide, green-tinted tank that sits on a wooden stand near our radio. Do they prefer Lotte Lenya to Al Jolson? They're not saying. I've planted two daffy-looking, bright green wooden palm trees with yellow coconuts in the white gravel floor of the tank – my homage to *Flying Down to Rio*. My brother can sit there for hours, entranced. Maybe he sees the key to the universe in Fred's air bubbles or in how Ginger swims up to snare the food pellets we shake in.

Dr Hassgall also tells us that Hansi would benefit from a fixed routine. So after school, he watches the goldfish for an hour, then works on a jigsaw puzzle till dinner preparations, when he peels potatoes or carrots as if each one is a block of Garrera marble.

"You're the Michelangelo of potato peeling," I tell him with my best Italian accent.

He smiles up at me, which earns him a kiss, and returns to sculpting. He's more alert since he started school, and happier, but his voice is still on an extended holiday.

After supper, he and I work on his jigsaw puzzle, then Mama puts him to bed. Every Friday and Monday I bathe him. I love knowing the ins and outs of his little body. I draw him whenever I can't sleep.

My own after-school routine becomes Young Maidens on Tuesday, Tonio on Wednesday, and choral practice on Thursday. When I resume book-buying, I make my rounds only when my schedule permits. I've lulled my parents into thinking I'm as loyal as the Rhine, so they've stopped checking up on me. On Saturdays, I generally go to the movies or stroll through the Tiergarten with Tonio and Hansi, and on Sunday, after church, I visit Vera or Isaac on the sly. Sometimes, if we're not in the mood to continue my Jewish studies, he and I go to the Jewish Old Age Home on Große Hamburger Straße, where he has a ninety-year-old friend – Mrs Kaufmann – who adores the poppy-seed cakes we take her. Mrs Kaufmann usually thinks I'm her granddaughter Else and gives me photographs of herself as a girl in Heidelberg that she keeps in a box under her cot.

I find comfort in having a set pattern, too, which may mean I'm more like Hansi than I'd like to believe.

I do not go near Julia's shop. I'm afraid of what I'd say to her, and of getting Isaac in trouble. All he tells me is that she'll never hurt anyone again in a voice darkened by anger. I suspect he's threatened her, and I sense – just as she must have – that he'd be capable of murder to protect the friends he loves.

Near the end of March, Tonio is inducted into the army. He's handsome and commanding in his uniform, and I'd get on my knees before him any time he likes. And he knows it.

He's stationed at a training camp near Potsdam, and he is permitted to leave only one weekend a month, which is good because I enjoy him more in small doses. We never even come close to quarreling, which may mean he likes me better only two days a month, as well. In any case, he adores soldiering. He can talk for hours about rifles and guns, and the gang of boys training with him. We often *do* complain about being apart, but that's just to prove we're committed to each other. Is he sleeping with other girls on occasion? All I know for sure is that no more crabs try to build *Metropolis* in my pubic hair.

Just as leaves sprout on the branches of the linden trees on Prenzlauer Allee, Roman returns, tanned and relaxed. He and Vera get down to the business of baby-making at the end of May. I visit them with Isaac sometimes on Sunday. They've become playful together, like kids who've embarked on a grand adventure, and Vera is so exultant that she's taken to singing as she sews, as off-key as a seal. She's also stopped smoking in her apartment, since Roman hates it. I'd never have guessed she was capable of such a concession.

Vera has worked out a circus act with Roman that makes her laugh as if it's the funniest thing in the world. "How many fingers am I holding up?" she asks him, sticking up three of her massive breadsticks, for instance. But he's as blind as the bottom layer of hell, as she once told me, and what chance is there that he'll spot her fingers from way down there?

"Three," he says. And he's always right, whether she's holding up one or four or none.

She must give him the answer with a particular inflection in her voice, or some coded pattern of words, but she denies it. "I'm not telling how we do it!" she declares, and that's when she collapses giggling and snorting in the nest of overstuffed pillows on her battered couch. I'm guessing it's the effect of several weeks of sex after a decade of chastity.

Not even Roman will let me in on their technique, but I give him a bear hug meant to squeeze the truth out of him, which is really just an excuse for me to touch him; he's all muscle and lithe elegance. If life were a Schiller play, he'd be the good prince who brings peace to his dominion, which worries me sometimes, because wouldn't a good prince only make most people jealous in the real world?

I occasionally accompany Roman home on Sunday evenings, and alongside such a man, I feel as if we're walking across a magic carpet. Of course, this is Berlin and not a Persian rug, so when I'm off in the clouds and not steering him properly, he occasionally puts a foot atop a squashed *bratwurst* or in some other unidentifiable muck, but he doesn't get angry. He's yet to invite me in for drinks. I think he suspects I might jump on him. *I* suspect he's right.

Proof of Vera's love ... Roman performs one Sunday on Grenadierstraße for the benefit of the Jewish Old Age Home and she comes out of hiding during the day to see him. Not only that, she buries her head in her hands as he rides a unicycle across a wire stretched between the roofs on opposite sides of the street, fifty feet over the death waiting for him on all those grimy cobbles. He's bare-chested and wearing shimmering white tights. Every sleek contour is visible, including the one I'm most interested in, which does not disappoint ...

We have blue skies and an unusually warm breeze from the west, so everyone is out in their shirtsleeves. The old folks gaze up from their walkers and wheelchairs, mouths agape, dentures in their hands. Even Mrs Kaufmann watches him with her gooey gray eyes open wide for the first time in ages. Mistaking me for her granddaughter again, she whispers to me, "My God, Else, he's like a Greek statue of Antinous come to life. If I were twenty again ..."

Mrs Kaufmann might occasionally try to water the roses printed on her pillow cases, but she knows the right man to bring her snoozing soufflé to life when she sees him.

A scalding summer day in mid-August brings out an irrepressible sense of curiosity and freedom in me, and I go to Julia's shop. The petite salesgirl I've seen before is helping two customers. After they leave, I go in and explain I'm a friend of Julia's.

"I'm afraid she's no longer here," the young woman tells me. "She decided to stop working."

"But she's still living here – in Berlin, I mean?"

"I don't think so, but I'm not sure where she's gone." She smiles, embarrassed not to know more.

"And Martin?"

"I'm assuming he's with her."

When I tell Isaac that Julia has probably left town, he says, "Then that's that."

"That's what?"

"Sophie, you must learn to let go when you have to. And to move on. Or else you'll find yourself stuck in glue so thick you'll never get out."

Good advice for some people, no doubt, but not for me.

Isaac drops another note to me from his window at the end of August: "Good news: the *mieskeit* is pregnant!"

Vera dances me around her apartment that Sunday, while flapping an ostrich-feather fan she's taken out of mothballs for the occasion.

"Are you absolutely sure you're pregnant?" I ask her.

"Yes, I visited my doctor twice. A little Roman is tightrope walking inside my womb!"

She drops down on her sofa and puts a pillow over her head, then fans herself some more because she claims the pregnancy makes her hot. She sticks her tongue out at me because I'm staring. Vera has the long, pointy tongue of a demon. And it's fuzzy from all her smoking.

"Do you want a boy or a girl?" I ask.

She starts, then gazes down, afraid to speak.

"What's wrong?" I ask, coming to her.

"Oh, Sophele" she says, grabbing my hand, "I don't care if the baby is a boy or a girl, as long as it isn't deformed!" She looks up to heaven then and whispers, "Are you listening, *mein Lieber*, or are you as deaf as death?"

I understand more about Vera's urgency to get pregnant three weeks later, when she receives a letter from Reich Health Department telling her that she is to appear before an *Erbgesundheitsgericht*, one of those new words we're all learning. This one means Hereditary Health Court, and it will decide whether she's to be sterilized or not. Isaac gives me this news as I enter his apartment with an old book I've just bought from Mr Poppelauer. I do not recall its title, or the author, but I'll never forget its dead weight in my hand because it was as I gave it to him that I first heard that brutal German word, *Erbkranke* – meaning people with a hereditary disease.

"Vera falls into one of the categories covered by the *Gesetz zur Verhütung erbkranken Nachwuchses*," Isaac tells me. "So she'll be sterilized."

"I have no idea what you're talking about," I say.

"The Law for the Prevention of Offspring with Hereditary Diseases," he repeats. "The Nazis passed it in July of last year. At the very same time they signed a concordat with the Vatican and declared themselves the only legal political party in Germany, which should tell you something if you look below the glass. Where were you when all this was happening?" Isaac glares at me as if I've torn a page out of his Torah.

"I guess ... guess I missed it."

"I guess you've been asleep!" he shouts.

I rush into his kitchen, but he stalks me there, and since he's about to shout again, I say, "I didn't do anything wrong."

"You should know what's going on in your country. It's that goddamned luminal you're taking! Half the country is asleep and the other half has a mind like urine. And close the curtains!" He stomps past me and snaps them closed to frustrate snooping eyes.

"If I were aware of everything that was happening," I shout back, "then I wouldn't risk buying you books! I could end in Dachau, just like Raffi."

Isaac turns pale. "Oh God, don't even say such a thing, Sophele! Forgive me."

Now it's my turn to glare.

"A schnapps ... I need a schnapps to calm my nerves. And so do you. Please, let me get you one. You're old enough now."

He pours me a glass and kisses the top of my head. "Do you forgive me?" he whispers.

"Yes, but no more yelling." After he agrees to that, I ask, "Does Vera have to go to this hearing?"

"Yes, or she'll be arrested. Her physician must have reported her to the authorities. She should never have had a doctor examine her. That must be why she got the letter now."

He lights his pipe with quick movements. Even when upset, he's agile. Sixty years of sewing seams.

"What did he report her for?" I ask.

"For being deformed."

"Is that a punishable offense?"

He snorts. "Of course." Imitating Hitler's accent and savage delivery, he adds, "And the punishment is we turn your ovaries into a *Wiener Schnitzel*."

"But Vera is pregnant!"

"Yes, she's outwitted them for now. And we can thank God that Roman has avoided this trap so far."

"Why would Roman be sterilized?"

"Sophele, he's congenitally blind!"

"But he's so handsome and ..."

"Sophie, do you think it's fine to sterilize people who are ugly? Or deaf? Or with epilepsy or anything else?"

"I only meant that Roman being so ... so ..."

Isaac laughs from his belly.

"What?" I demand, irritated.

"Nothing. Let's just say that desire is a good thing for a young girl to feel." Seeing that his amusement irritates me, he quickly adds, "I don't mean anything bad. Half the people I know would like to sleep with Roman."

"Would you?"

"Me?" He gazes off into his thoughts. "If he were to ask me, I wouldn't refuse. But I'm afraid I have other preferences." He raises his eyebrows and points the stem of his pipe at me, in that way that makes me feel special. "Do I shock you?"

"Yes and no," I reply. His trust in me makes me understand that I'll continue to take risks for him whenever he wants.

"So is Vera safe now?" I ask.

"Yes, the authorities will have to let her have the baby, and only then will they sterilize her." He downs his schnapps in a gulp, licks his lips like a cat, and refills his glass. "You don't mind if I get so drunk I can't think, do you?"

"Not at all. So there's no way out for her?"

"She can argue her case in court. Some judges resent the government usurping their authority. But in the end," he says, "the laws of Germany will not bend ... at least not for dachshunds, *mieskeits,* and Jews. I know several people who have been sterilized this year. Martin was sterilized three months ago."

I'd never say so, but maybe taking away Martin's ability to make a child isn't a bad thing. Though even thinking that makes me feel disloyal. "I'm ashamed I'm so ignorant," I tell Isaac.

"Don't feel so bad. The Nazis keep their sterilization

program mostly out of the newspapers. Though if you read *Der Stürmer* ..."

"You read that *schmatte*?"

"All the time. Who doesn't want to know their enemy?" Isaac gives me a serious look. "Sophele, I wanted to protect you, and so did Vera, but I think now we were wrong."

"Protect me from what? I don't understand."

"It's Hansi, he's in danger."

I look down to keep the pressure in my chest from making me cry, because I've always known something bad would come of his difference. Isaac moves his chair near mine.

"Do the authorities consider feeblemindedness reason enough for sterilization?" I ask.

"I'm afraid so, my dear."

"So Hansi ... he may ..."

"Yes, but maybe there's still a way to fight." He pats my leg, then leans back in his chair. "Now tell me, has your brother seen any doctors lately?" he asks in a voice of strategizing.

Hansi bathed in my protection

"I don't think so."

"Good, because the doctors are the ones who ..."

"But he's seen Dr Nohel at least a half a dozen times over the last few years," I interrupt, and I understand now why Dr Hassgall asked us to keep Hansi away from physicians.

"If Hansi has already been reported as feebleminded or schizophrenic, then we're out of luck. Unless your father can use his influence to prevent him from being operated."

I ought to rush to Papa, but I feel only a heavy hopelessness. That puzzles me until I realize that my father might believe it would be better if Hansi didn't have children. And he might want to show his superiors that he's willing to sacrifice his own son and grandchildren for his Nazi ideals.

I'll have to talk to Mama alone. And she will have to work on Papa. Our only chance.

THE FOURTH GATE

Four are the letters of God's name, the prayer services on the Sabbath, the cardinal directions, the elements, and the number of times the Torah commands us to tell the story of Exodus. Four are the levels of interpretation.

Beyond the Fourth Gate are the flowers of the field where our union blooms. Known as Machonen, this level of heaven is our spiritual Jerusalem. It is presided over by the Archangel Michael.

And it came to pass in the fourth year of king Darius, that the word of the Lord came unto Zechariah – Zechariah 7.

Berekiah Zarco, The Book of Flowering

CHAPTER THIRTEEN

Vera's doctor testifies at her hearing that she's pregnant, so she's safe for the moment, but she is ordered to report to Wittenau State Hospital so that physicians can make a full evaluation of her deformity and its implications to the Fatherland.

What possible implications could her face have for the nation? would be the obvious objection of her lawyer in any country where people lived on solid ground, but we are knee-deep in the muck of Germany's sewers already and he doesn't challenge the judge's order.

Vera fails to go to Wittenau on the day she's been assigned, convinced that physicians there will try to harm her baby. That same evening, after nightfall, she moves into Isaac's apartment. She takes one suitcase neatly packed with clothes and another holding her sewing machine and supplies. "I'm not going to even step outside until the baby is born!" she explains to me the next day, with a ferocity in her eyes that's not to be doubted.

Over the next few days, I shuttle between Vera's apartment and Isaac's to bring her fabrics she needs for her work. Roman comes over in the evenings to keep her company.

None of Vera's other friends visit, and when I ask her about that she replies, "I have my baby and Roman, and you and Isaac. That's enough for one ugly giant."

"But it's weird they don't come by to congratulate you ... or even just to show their solidarity."

"Maybe some of them aren't so thrilled about me being pregnant."

"You mean Heidi and Rolf – because they've failed so far to have a baby?"

She shrugs, which obviously means *yes*.

Later that week, Isaac's factory is broken into by the Gestapo. A neighbor saw a young Nazi smash in the lock while an older officer looked on. Nothing is stolen but the company files are left in a mess. "They must have wanted to discover who is still buying garments from me," Isaac speculates. "It's no big deal. All the clients I still have know I'm a risk. Most of them are Jewish anyway."

"Did they break in to your warehouse too?" I ask.

"No, they apparently figured there was nothing there for them."

It's while I'm cleaning the kitchen cabinets and Mama is washing the floor that I find the courage to speak to her about the Law for the Prevention of Offspring with Hereditary Diseases. Despite my urgent tone, she waves off my worries. In an offended voice, she says, "I hope you aren't trying to imply that something hereditary is wrong with me or your father?"

"No, I'm only saying there's something wrong with Hansi. He must fall under the new law for *Erbkranke*."

She pushes her mop hard into the leg of the table, probably imagining it's my head. "Sophie, I'll thank you not to use that word to describe your brother. You heard Dr Hassgall, your brother is perfectly normal."

"No, that's not what Dr Hassgall said."

I start to give her my best paraphrase of his words, but Mama interrupts me. "Sophie, make your point quickly. I have work to do." She sighs with exasperation. "And if you're not going to clean the cabinets properly, then leave them to me."

"My point is that one day soon we're going to get a letter saying that Hansi has to go to a Hereditary Health Court. And three old Prussian know-it-alls in long robes are going to decide that he has the brains of a goldfish, just like Fred and Ginger. They aren't going to care that he loves squirrels or that he peels potatoes like they're made of Carrera marble. And they aren't going to think it's a positive thing that he poses for me with more patience than a street sign. They are going to rule that he's not normal and sterilize him."

Mama manages a laugh. Was she acting or was she already so deep in sewer waters that she couldn't see out? "Oh, Sophie, where do you hear these rumors?"

"They aren't rumors!"

"Then show me a newspaper article that says that boys like Hansi are being sterilized."

"The newspapers are run by the National Socialist Party."

"As well they should be."

"Mama, please listen to me," I plead. "If we don't ..."

"Look, Sophie, I know you're worried," she interrupts, "but this could never happen to Hansi because your father is a party member."

"But if we get a letter anyway, what'll you do?"

"Any letter that comes would have to be some sort of mistake and I would speak to your father and he would have the mistake corrected."

"You promise?"

"Sophie, what else would I do?"

*

Vera has a dinner party to celebrate her pregnancy on Sunday, the 28th of October, 1934, and I manage to attend by telling my parents I'm off to a band concert with Tonio, who was in for the weekend but who had to leave for his base at five in the afternoon. To my surprise, she's the only person at home when I arrive.

"Isaac has gone to fetch Heidi and Rolf," she tells me, leaning down so we can kiss cheeks. "The others will be here soon. You can help make the stuffing for the peppers. I need to sit for a while and relieve the pressure in my knees."

Vera supervises how I chop onions and mix them into the meat as though I'm dealing with explosives. "You're driving me crazy!" I warn her.

"Sorry, it's the blind little deformed creature in my belly," she explains.

"Vera!"

"If I talk about the worst that can happen, then it won't happen."

So it is that I learn that she believes in magic. She's opened a bottle of cheap Italian red wine, and I pour her a glass. "Now relax and stop bothering me," I tell her.

Roman, K-H., Marianne, and little Werner, who is now two years old and walking, drive over in K-H's battered old Clyno Tourer, arriving just as Vera's finishing her wine. Marianne has made roast chicken to follow the stuffed peppers.

While K-H is setting the table and telling us about his photography studio, the dwarfs waddle in behind Isaac. Kisses, hugs, and shrieks all around.

"Vera, if you'd have given us some advance notice, I'd have baked something special," Heidi tells her in a scolding tone. "All I had was half a cake I made yesterday."

"Forgive me," Vera replies, "the party was a last-minute decision."

I know that's not true, since she told me two days before, and I give Vera a questioning look, but she just sticks out her tongue.

As I serve the peppers, Vera flies around the table pouring wine, prattling on about maternity dresses she is making for herself. She's boring for the first time in history, but I suppose that's to be expected.

The peppers and chicken are so good that I eat too much. Wine, chicken, and sex on the same day – things are either looking up for me or I'm dreaming.

Before it gets too late, we put Werner to sleep in the guestroom. Marianne lets me tuck him in and kiss him goodnight. I adore the sleepy smell of him. He signals goodnight by waving his little hand beneath his chin, and I signal back. I feel as if we're emissaries from different worlds.

After supper, Isaac grins like a devil in an Italian fresco as he picks apart the poor bird's carcass, sucking the marrow from its bones. Such enjoyment the man gets from making a mess, just like a little boy, and he adores having Heidi clean each of his fingers with a towel.

Rolf tells jokes and smokes a cigar. His face gets all wrinkly and compressed when he smokes, and Heidi whispers to me, quite rightly, that he looks like a turtle.

As Vera and I are putting the dirty dishes in the sink, I whisper, "Apparently, Heidi and Rolf have gotten over their resentment."

"Yes, I'm relieved – it's like putting my heart back in place."

For dessert, we have Heidi's day-old *Frankfurter Kranz*, which has the most delicious meringue anyone has ever eaten. She always adds a special, secret ingredient to her cakes. Pulling me down to her, she whispers, "Grated lemon peel!" as if that's the password that will win me entrance to Araboth.

Heidi's secret is not the only one I learn that night. After coffee,

Vera corners me in the kitchen and says urgently, "I'm leaving tonight for a hiding place. Only you, Isaac, and Roman know I'm going. Don't tell anyone. I'll get word to you when I can, though it may be a few months from now. I can't take any more chances with my baby." She waves off my further questions. "I'm sorry, Sophele, there's no time."

"Be careful," I tell her.

"You, too. And thank you for all your help." She looks at me as if she'll need to remember my face for a long time, which scares me. I start to speak, but she puts her hand over my mouth. "Ssshhh, everything's going to be fine."

K-H and Marianne drive the dwarfs home. I walk Roman back to his apartment, our thoughts inside separate silences. Sensing I'm upset, he puts his arm over my shoulder.

"When do you think we'll see Vera again?" I ask him.

"Only after the baby is born."

From what I later learn, Isaac waits until Roman and I have had time to turn onto Prenzlauer Allee, then slips his coat on and gives Vera a quick hug. "How many fingers am I holding up?" he asks as a joke, holding up five.

"Three," Vera answers to be difficult.

"Exactly, I'll be back in three minutes. Sit tight."

Isaac is borrowing a neighborhood friend's Opel for the occasion but needs to fetch it. He will be taking Vera to a converted boathouse on the Havel River that was built by his grandfather. A retired seamstress from the nearby town of Gatow who worked in Isaac's factory for thirty years will bring Vera supplies. Her name is Olga Hagen.

As he is coming back down Marienburger Straße past Frau Koslowski's grocery, three Gestapo officers get out of a Mercedes parked across the street from our apartment house. They slam their doors, which must mean they want to be heard by Isaac, or that being observed by a Jewish man is beneath their caring.

One of the Gestapo officers is wearing gloves, and he is carrying an axe – a detail forever lodged in terror inside Isaac's memory. The old man's dread is so strong that he feels as if he might faint dead away. Has all his careful planning counted for nothing? But maybe these men are headed to another address ...

I can easily picture the Nazis pushing open the door to our apartment house and striding through the hallway as though they are our unassailable masters. I also see the lead man draw his pistol as he enters our courtyard, though maybe he's the one wearing black leather gloves and carrying the axe. If I spoke to Mrs Munchenberg, maybe I'd know for sure, but I'm too ashamed of having skipped Raffi's funeral and of abandoning her at Wertheim's.

Isaac begins to rush. In the courtyard, he hears our visitors stomping up the back staircase. Praying for strength, he runs ahead and hears one of them call out for Vera to give herself up.

He finds the men standing on the third-floor landing, in front of his door. Panting for breath, he asks what they want.

"Shut your filthy mouth!" the oldest of the Nazis shouts. He has a pinched face, and his thinning gray hair is visible beneath the rim of his cap.

"And back off," says a tall officer with a Hamburg accent.

The youngest man – a handsome boy, Isaac will later tell me – shouts through his door for Vera to open the lock.

She makes for the kitchen window, wondering if she would survive the thirty-foot drop – and be able to hobble off into hiding. Feeling faint, she leans on the sill, crushed by remorse for having dragged Isaac into this mess. Outside her door, Isaac begs the young man to leave them in peace.

"Shut up!" the Nazi orders. Turning around, he shouts, "Open the goddamned door!"

"Vera, don't come out!" Isaac hollers. "Use the phone to call for help!"

He grabs the boy's arm and tugs it as if to pull him down the stairs, falling backwards onto the floor of the landing and taking the Nazi with him.

Another man's fist catches Isaac on his head, by his ear, which makes him grip the boy's arm as tightly as he can. He told me later, "All I knew was that I could never let go."

But he does release the boy's arm when he's hit over the head with a revolver. Moaning, Isaac reaches to his forehead and sees blood. As he looks up, a boot is placed on his chest.

All he remembers next is crashing down the stairs to the landing below.

Vera hears him fall. Her mind shrinks back, as it does when we sense we have been caught by a fate we've long feared. She sees clearly that she has only herself to blame for being caught, though I won't learn why for nearly another six years.

When the axe blade slices through the wood of the door, Vera screams and backs up against the wall, hard, as though trying to push through to another world. A gaping hole by the doorhandle opens, and a gloved hand clicks open the lock.

She meets the intruders with her sewing scissors in her hand. The men are stunned for a moment by her frightening face, which gives her time enough to lunge forward and slash the arm of the gray-haired officer. The two other Gestapo thugs tackle her and push her face against the floor. One of them breaks her right wrist as he snaps on handcuffs. On purpose, I would imagine. Then they drag her away. The officer who has been wounded taunts her as he staunches the blood with his handkerchief.

"You fucking freak!" he spits at her. "Even if we took the axe to your head right here, you couldn't be any uglier."

The men step over Isaac's body, which is lying limp on the landing. Do they kick him? It's impossible to say from the pattern of bruises on his body.

The Gestapo officer in charge shouts that she's a Jew-loving freak while they drag her through the courtyard. Everyone in the building must hear, including my mother. But no one comes to her rescue.

When she tells me what she saw, Mama will say, "It gives me shivers just thinking about that wretched woman. And to think, I let you go to the same party as her two years ago!"

How did the Nazis learn where Vera was hiding? One of our neighbors – or maybe even my mother – might have reported the presence of a giant with a cavewoman's face living in Isaac's flat, but more likely, he and I think, a traitor is still at work.

Miraculously, the old tailor only suffers a badly sprained ankle and some cuts and bruises. To repair the gash on his brow just below his hairline, Dr Manny Löwenstein – a friend since high school – sews him up with five stitches.

Dr Löwenstein also nails a plank of wood over the hole in the door. "No extra charge," he tells Isaac, adding, "no more headlong dives into the stairwell for you. It's not a pool and you, my friend, are no Yiddishe Johnny Weismuller."

How long will the Jewish sense of humor be able to persevere in this country?

I manage to get Dr Löwenstein alone for a minute and ask him to solve an old puzzle for me. "Imagine someone's windpipe has been broken, as if he's been strangled, but there are no bruises on his neck. How could that happen?"

"Are we talking about anyone I know?" he asks.

"I don't think so."

"Let me think about that and then get back to you."

With K-H's help, Isaac hobbles over to Columbia-House, the Gestapo's headquarters on Prinz Albrecht Straße, where Vera has probably been taken, but no one will give him any information. Still, we know exactly what happens to her, because she tells us as soon as we next see her.

The day after her arrest, in the late afternoon, her broken wrist is finally set in plaster. Two days later, at dawn, she is dressed in a hospital gown and taken to a doctor's office in the same brick building where she has been staying. Has a sedative been put in her morning tea? She feels heavy and dull-witted, and she is unable to fight the men who guide her up the stairs. A physician dressed in white greets her in a room with large windows. We will never know his name, but she says he has a beard and tiny brown eyes. She is forced onto an operating table. Her arms are positioned by her side and her legs spread – and fastened with leather straps. She smells ammonia and something else – "A sour scent, like acid," she will tell me. She fears she is about to die. She pulls in vain at her restraints. Fear lodges in her throat like pebbles, and she cannot stop her legs from trembling. After the physician sits on a stool between her legs, he bends down and probes inside her with something metallic and cold, but she can't see what. Then he hurts her badly. Whatever he uses feels like rusted hedge clippers, and she imagines he is about to cut tissues deep inside her. She screams and doesn't stop screaming until she feels a needle prick on her arm and looks to the side to see a nurse gazing down at her contemptuously.

When she awakens, she is on a cot, her bare feet sticking out past the end of the gray bedspread. Her belly feels as though it has been scraped with scissors, and she is weak and cold. A nurse puts another blanket on her and helps her sit up to sip some water. She tries to eat but even bread only sharpens the pain.

A little while later, the doctor who performed the operation comes to see her. He has a bright, cheerful face.

"How are you feeling?" he asks, smiling benevolently.

"What did you cut out of me?" she demands.

"Shush," he says, patting her arm. "You need to rest. There's nothing to worry about. Everything is over now."

Including my baby? she wants to ask, but she fears his reply and wouldn't trust it anyway.

None of the nurses answers her questions about what's been done to her, or about what happened to Isaac, so she keeps silent. She will wait. Sooner or later, they'll have to release her.

She spends the rest of that day crawling inside intricate fantasies of vengeance. The next morning, Thursday, just after breakfast, she is dressed by a friendly young nurse and put in the back seat of a car that smells like new leather, and then taken to the address she gives the driver – Isaac's factory.

Vera throws her arms around Isaac when she sees he is alive, because at least one terrible thing has not come to pass. *I am not responsible for his death, only the baby's ...*

She sits with Isaac in his office and tells him what happened to her, but she's too disoriented to make much sense. He calls a taxi and takes her to his apartment, coaxes her into bed and then sits with her. The words spill out of her as though from a great height. When she's done with her story, she asks, "Do you think they cut the baby out of me?"

"I don't know, but we're going to find out. Just rest."

She starts to run a fever that evening.

"A very bad sign – it could be an infection from her operation," Isaac tells me when I come over.

We give Vera aspirin and make her drink strong, hot tea with lemon. After I leave, K-H comes over with Roman, Rolf, and Heidi.

Late that night, Dr Löwenstein examines her. His medical evaluation is against the law, since he is a Jew and she is an Aryan, but Vera's womb itself has become illegal, so what do the bespectacled eyes of a seventy-year-old Jewish physician matter by comparison?

He discovers incision marks on her belly.

"I've seen those a lot lately," he tells her. "The surgeons tied your ovarian tubes."

"So ... so I'm no longer pregnant?" Vera asks timidly, shivering. She has had the chills for the last hour. "And I'm barren?"

"Yes, I'm sorry, Vera," he tells her, covering her with her blankets again.

She turns her face to the wall, as though away from life, and begins to wail. Heidi climbs up onto the bed, sits beside her, and rubs her back, whispering encouragement. Roman squats in the corner of the room, leaning his head into the wall, while Rolf tries to comfort him.

"What legal authority do the Nazis have to do this?" K-H asks the doctor, but neither he nor anyone else can provide an answer. Besides, back in August, thirty-eight million German voters – ninety percent of our electorate – voted to confirm Hitler's absolute dictatorship, so legal authority, if any is needed, is his.

Isaac covers all his mirrors that night with dark fabric. He's in such a fury that I dare not talk with him. He says he and Vera must sit *shiva* for the baby for a week.

What does she feel and think? Her tears are our only clue. She will not even reply to Roman, though he reminds her in an angry voice that he has also lost a child. Maybe she is thinking, *But you can have others ...*

Dr Löwenstein pulls me aside just before he leaves. "I've got an answer to your question now. If the murdered man was already dead when he was strangled, then the blood in his capillaries and veins would not burst. There'd be no bruises."

"Are you sure?" I ask, gripped by a feeling of truth discovered.

"Positive."

So Julia poisoned Georg, then put her hands on his neck and squeezed as hard as she could, breaking his windpipe. To make sure he was dead, perhaps. Or to confuse the police, just as she confused me.

I feel as if I've reached the end of a long trail, but now that our Führer can order a baby killed anytime he likes, and Hansi may be sterilized, does solving a single murder mean so very much?

Vera's fever goes up to thirty-nine degrees near three in the morning. Isaac nurses her all night, putting cold compresses on her forehead, forcing her to drink as much chicken broth as she can hold down, and when she finally finds sleep near dawn he prays for her to remain on the near bank of the River Sambation and not cross over to the Other Side.

Vera learns what the doctors have stolen from her

Before school the next morning, Friday, I tell my parents I'm beginning private singing lessons with Fräulein Schumann that afternoon. I phone her from Isaac's apartment after school and, on my third try, find her in. I beg her to confirm my lie about lessons if my parents call.

"But what's happened, Sophie?" she asks in a concerned voice.

"Someone I know has been wounded badly by the Nazis," I reply. "But don't tell anyone."

Have I risked telling her the truth because I'm so disoriented by what's happened?

"Be careful," Fräulein Schumann says, and as if she can read my mind, she adds, "I'll be very angry at you if you ever decide to leave the chorus."

After I hang up, I realize for the first time that Vera and Isaac will end up murdered if they stay in Germany; a final confrontation is inevitable.

Isaac is praying silently with his eyes closed when I go back to his bedroom, tilting from side to side like a tower about to come crashing down. His lips sculpt his Hebrew words. His shirt is dripping with sweat. I order him to take a bath and go to sleep in the guestroom, but he replies in a stubborn voice, "No, I must keep praying."

"I'll take over for you," I tell him.

"But you don't know the right prayers!"

"Then teach me."

He writes out Hebrew prayers for me in transliterated German. I repeat them for him, and when he's satisfied that my pronunciation won't oblige the Lord to cover his ears in horror, he raises his hand as if to say something important, then simply rubs his eyes. "I can't remember what I wanted to tell you," he says, sighing.

"That's God's way of letting you know you need to take a

bath and go to bed." When he starts to protest, I raise my hand threateningly. "You don't want to make the Lord angry!"

A surprise: he likes being given orders by a girl, at least when he's exhausted. He stands up and shuffles off as if his legs are bound together by fetters. He knows I'm watching, because he turns around, flaps both hands at me, and says, "Go to Vera!"

I find the giant asleep, breathing fitfully. I wipe her sweaty face with a cool towel. And I pray. When I look in on Isaac in the bathroom, he's not there. And his laundered shirts and socks are still hanging like frayed bats over the shower rod. I find him sitting on the end of the bed in his guestroom, his eyes closed, his lips moving silently over ancient Hebrew words.

I take his shoes off, which makes him yawn, but he still doesn't open his eyes.

"Unbuckle your belt and undo the buttons on your pants," I say, and he does so.

I pull them off, spilling some Pfennige along the way. I lay the trousers and his coins on the purple velvet chair in the corner of the room that he calls the Pope's Throne.

"Now the shirt."

I take his shirt from him and drape it across the back of the Pope's Throne. His chest is a swirl of gray hairs, and he stands up with a bowed back. His posture of fragility and the tender blue bruises on his shoulders and hips make me want to hug him.

His body sags from age, but that's just as it should be for a man who has journeyed to far off worlds inside his head for the last sixty years.

"Sophele, turn the other way while I take off my underwear. Or better still, go back to Vera."

"I'm not a kid anymore. I've seen what you have before."

"I realize that, but a little privacy would be nice."

After I turn around, his underwear flies past me and lands on the parquet, two feet short of the Pope's Throne.

"No aim," he says disgustedly.

I face him as he's crawling into bed. Just in time; his penis hangs down nicely out of a nest of soft gray hair. Darker and more slender than Tonio's. With a purplish head free of foreskin. *My first Jewish penis*, I think. I find it curious and handsome, and just the right shape for a hand ...

With a moan, he lies down, then heaves a sigh of gratitude and pulls the sheet up his waist. I go to him.

"Sophele, I wouldn't know what to do without you," he says in a hoarse voice, reaching out with a grateful, straining hand, which I take. His face is so trusting of me, his eyes so dark and serious, that I wish I had my sketchbook. He kisses my fingers, one by one, then lets my hand fall on his chest. His heartbeat makes me feel as if there are emotions in him yet to be discovered. And as if our intimacy has changed into something far beyond words.

He closes his eyes as though he finally intends to sleep, which means he should release me. Instead, he turns his cheek to me and asks for a kiss in a whisper.

But I know what I want for us now and press my lips to his. He starts and opens his eyes, which are windows on a worried soul unsure of what is happening to him.

His breathing on my face is warm, and the stillness of the room seems a reflection of my thoughts. For once, I am free of expectations. A gate is opening, and we can either walk through it or forever remain outside.

I reach down under the sheet for his penis, which is warm and growing. He stills my hand and looks at me as if studying my mind. We stare at each other for a long time, and I don't turn away because I am not frightened, and he is, and I want him to know he can trust me. And that I trust him with my life.

I play with him gently. He holds my head in his hands, presses his lips to mine, and moves his tongue deep inside me, as though searching for what I have never told him. I love the taste of tobacco and wine in his mouth, and the scratching of his whiskers, because it means he is a man of experience and can open me up and show me more of who I am.

We explore each other in the darkness behind our closed eyes, and his chest hairs might be leaves or flowers for how natural their soft tangle feels to my fingers. I compare the warm, world-tested strength of Isaac, and the easy patience in his touch, to Tonio's urgency and youth. Not better or worse. Different.

Isaac's nipples stand out as though straining to feel my lips and tongue, and I do not disappoint him. He caresses my hair and moans, which is gratifying, but I have other needs. Sensing I am making a decisive break with the past, I slide down and take him in my mouth. His cock is warm and hard, and he trembles as though he has waited far too long.

I feel the transcendence of darkness and light inside me, both of them mine.

He gasps, and his eyes open wide, which pleases me, because it gives me a chance to reassure him with kisses. *You had no idea I would do this for you, did you?* That is what I say with my eyes.

"You shouldn't," he whispers. "Please ..." He grips my arm. "Please, no ..."

His protest only makes me swallow him until I am as full of a man as I ever hope to be, and there is no space left for him to argue with me.

His back bows and he grunts. I am breaking down the walls of a palace that has been locked for a decade, all its rooms musty and dark.

I see in his gaze that he knows I am destroying his widowhood. And he doesn't stop me.

There is so much hope in sex. No one in Germany speaks about that, but I think that's why the intimacy of touching is so important during a war.

Isaac asks me to lie next to him. We kiss gently, exploring each other's desire. Then he helps me out of my skirt and blouse as if it's very serious work. Likely he's convinced that we're being watched by God. Tugging me to the end of the bed, he kneels down and laps at me as if the password to Araboth that he has long wanted is in the taste between my legs, and I am moaning from so deep inside me that I don't know where my voice is coming from. Then, with the insistence of his large warm hands, he turns me over, and I press down on the bed, which seems to have always been waiting to receive me, and I feel myself spreading out like a landscape neither of us has ever seen before.

Is it enough to say I am changed forever as he enters me, and that our trust deepens until it becomes the scents and scope of our bodies? I learn his shadows and hesitancies, and how his voice sounds when he whispers forbidden words in German, words of the earth, *von der Erde*, as later tells me. And he learns that my fragility and strength have not been destroyed by the Semitic Wall, which is only one of the things I mean to tell him when I climb on top of and insert him as deep as he can go.

I am sure now that we will never be able to hide from each other again. But he is a Jew and I am an Aryan, and I am not aware yet of all that means.

Afterward, he combs his fingers through my hair and breathes in what he calls the scent of my youth, then kisses my neck, curls into me and goes to sleep like a baby. I stay awake, staring at the ceiling as if it's as soft as the sky above my beloved city, and at the blue-glass fish hanging from a thin cord as though they're toys for the child I was, and at the Chagall village and all the other paintings welcoming me to my new home. And all the while, I imagine that Isaac and I are on a boat that's drifting, its sails made of our bodies.

We look for our desires in all we do, and yet it takes so long to understand what we really want. Meaning is like a delayed echo, and we begin to hear it only many years after we ask our questions.

As Isaac sleeps, I sit with Vera, wearing Isaac's dressing gown, wanting her to know I have been changed, and that there is still hope for us. I comb her hair with my fingers as if she is my child. And I pray again, but this time for the three of us.

Isaac wakes an hour later and comes into his bedroom, where Vera and I are now having tea. He's wearing his ragged pajamas. She's sitting up, underneath a mountain of tissues. She feels a little better. "The gonging in my head is gone," she tells Isaac.

He feels her forehead with the back of his hand. "Your fever has gone down, too."

He stands behind me as she talks about her continued symptoms. The only indication of what we've done is his hand resting on my shoulder. Once, I look up, and I feel as if I've known him since we were both little.

When he and I are alone in his kitchen, boiling water for more tea, I expect him to apologize to me in a timid voice, and to tell me this can never happen again, but instead he holds my cheeks and kisses me hard. When he backs me up against the wall, I spread my legs as far as I can, picturing wings.

Isaac thrusts so relentlessly and brutally that he knocks the breath out of me, and I laugh at the absurdity and goodness of being fucked by an old satyr in his kitchen, with dirty dishes in this sink. He laughs, too. But he doesn't stop fucking, thank goodness.

Lovers who see the humor in themselves. A good sign.

When we're done, he eases out of me, and I slump down to the floor like a child, and he joins me, panting and smiling, and I wonder if I am going to survive this fall into the depths of myself.

Back in my own soft bed that night, comforted by my old gray woolen blanket, I listen to the slow, ecstatic singing of Mr Mannheim's cello. Through such nights I slowly come to learn that I need my independence from men as much as I need their attention.

Late the next morning, Saturday, Papa takes Hansi to the barbershop for a haircut. The rituals of a father and son. And of a mother and daughter, too; Mama wants to take me shopping for a new winter coat at the KaDeWe department store. We agree to go that afternoon because I tell her I'm meeting friends that morning for roller skating.

Isaac has given me his key, and I let myself in. He's alone in the kitchen having coffee in his pajamas, reading a handwritten letter. Vera is asleep in his bedroom.

"Hello, Sophele," he says to me, smiling sweetly. He lifts up a newspaper clipping from the table and says, "Some good news for a change."

Isaac's cousin Abraham has sent him a Turkish article ferociously criticizing the Nazis. He translates the first few paragraphs for me, then, rubbing his hands together gleefully, adds, "Abraham has heard that the German Ambassador is furious and has complained directly to Ataturk. Do you understand? We've got them worried!"

It's good to see him so happy. I drop down next to him, steal a sip from his cup, and play with him under the table, which makes his eyes flutter closed. Sighing as if he's in pain, he lifts my hand away. "I'd be exhausted all day, and Vera needs my help." He gives me a pecking kiss.

I make potato and carrot soup for Isaac and Vera's lunch. She trudges in to see me. Her face is the color of cigar ash, and her sunken eyes are red from crying. She whines to me that Isaac won't let her go back to her apartment as though trying to get a bullying older brother in trouble. He's seated at the table, reading one of his manuscripts by Berekiah Zarco.

"Maybe he's right and you shouldn't be alone at the moment," I tell her.

She frowns at me as if I'm a stain on the floor and shuffles back to bed.

Isaac pats my arm. "She confessed last night that she thinks of killing herself," he whispers. He picks up his pipe, then lets it fall, helpless.

I try to get Vera to talk to me, but she turns away whenever she hears my footsteps. As I'm making ready to go, Roman brings over stewed tomatoes he's just made. She won't talk to him either. That's when I have an idea and shoo away the two men.

I ease down onto her bed. "Vera, I don't know how, but I think Julia and someone she was working with turned you in to the Gestapo. We've got to do something. We've got to find out who. So you've got to get better as soon as you can."

"You don't know anything," she moans, as if I've been plaguing her for weeks with silly theories. She folds the crook of her arm over her eyes. "Go away," she says roughly.

I don't leave, and she decides to sits up. As I help her, she grabs my wrist as if to keep me from falling. "I want you to stay far away from all this cloak and dagger work," she tells me gravely.

"But I'm already involved. And besides, detective work takes my mind off other matters."

"Heidi and Rolf will do all the investigating necessary."

"Why them?"

"Because they're adults," she says, as if that's obvious. "And they know all the people in The Ring. That's important, because whoever turned me in wasn't Julia. She's been in Istanbul for weeks."

"Istanbul?"

"Isaac sent her there – to his relatives. Just before I was arrested and ..."

"Why didn't he tell me?" I ask angrily.

"Listen, Sophele, there are some things you need to know or you'll never understand Isaac or me, or what's really going on."

"What do you mean?"

"Isaac was worried about you taking too many risks, so we didn't tell you the whole truth. Georg wasn't an innocent victim. He was betraying us. And that's why something had to be done about him."

"I don't understand. You said that Georg was head of The Ring."

"Yes, but we ended up realizing he got himself elected so he could betray us more completely. He was clever ... and he was undermining our work every chance he got. We didn't suspect until it was too late. He even staged his shooting in Savigny Platz."

"So that was how he managed to stay so calm. But ... but why would he become a Nazi?" I ask.

"For the same reason as your father."

"And what about Julia?"

"You were right about her. Do you remember when Isaac went to Potsdam ... that time he had you water his pelargoniums? Some of us, including Julia, were meeting to decide what to do about Georg. You see, we'd learned that he was the one who'd gotten Raffi in trouble for bribing Nazis." She shakes her head sadly. "We warned Raffi against coming back from Egypt, but he thought the National Socialists would regard him as insignificant after their stunning success in the elections. Besides, he'd stopped making bribes. And once he'd destroyed those silly hieroglyphics he kept, there was no proof against him." She slams her arm down against the mattress. "What idiots we were! We didn't realize that no proof was necessary to send a man to a concentration camp."

A burst of fury makes me jump up. "You had me working under the wrong impression for so long! All the times I sneaked out so I could try to help ...!"

"At first, we didn't know if we could trust you. Then your father switched sides and it seemed unwise to tell you the truth, especially after Georg was murdered and Raffi arrested. Sophele," she says gently, reaching up for my hand, "I can't talk with you if you're standing."

"You'd better, because I'm not sitting with you!" To punish her for lying, I want to withhold my love; proof, I suppose, that I've still much growing up to do ...

Vera nods her understanding. "You think that because you're a good person and are on our side that you have a right to know everything that goes on with us – with me and Isaac and the people you love. Under normal circumstances, that might be true. We could always be honest with each other." She spreads her fingers in front of her face. "But Germany has become Carnival all year long ... a time of masks," she whispers, "when we have to keep ourselves hidden. You can't know everything about me or Isaac. Do you understand?"

"No," I reply like a hurt little girl.

Vera sits further up and fixes a pillow behind her head. "Listen, Georg's death ... it was a total shock to us because we hadn't reached any consensus about killing him. And he'd been a good friend. At least, we thought he was. Julia decided to poison him on her own. When I discovered his body, I was sure that brownshirts had killed him. We figured that Georg had tried to defy whoever was paying him ... that they'd asked him to provide incriminating evidence against me or Isaac, and he'd refused. I don't believe he'd have betrayed the two of us." She shrugs sadly. "Though ... though maybe I only *want* to believe that. One other thing ... Before Raffi's last trip to Egypt, he made Isaac and me promise to leave you out of our plans." Vera gives an odd little laugh, charmed and saddened, I'd guess, by a memory of him. "Raffi was devoted to you. And when he died ... Let's just say that we didn't want to break our word to a dead man unless we had to."

Her respect for Raffi calms me. "Vera, if Julia was on your side the whole time, and if she's still your friend, then she'd never have told the police to go to 18 Tieckstraße to find the labor leader I invented. But the Gestapo *were* there! She must have told them."

"No, you were being followed."

"By whom?"

"Georg was not working alone to undermine our projects. Someone was helping him. And whoever it was, you must have raised his suspicions by buying books for Isaac. My guess is that you've been followed on and off for months. And you were trailed from Julia's shop to your home, then to Tieckstraße." She takes a long sip of water. "Except there's a problem ... We still can't figure out how whoever was following you knew it was Number 18, since you told Isaac you didn't go into the apartment or even stand in front of the building."

"I know how," I confess. "I'd been going there for months. To be with Tonio. It's an apartment his father uses. So when I walked to Tieckstraße, whoever was helping Georg must have known immediately that what I'd told Julia had to do with Number 18. He must have called the Gestapo. What I don't get is how would he have known that I'd told her something that the Gestapo would find worth their while?"

She looks away for a time, then eyes me as if she's had a sinister revelation. "You know, it's just possible that it wasn't someone who worked with Georg who followed you. Tonio might have tracked you to Tieckstraße, then called the police. That would also explain how they knew it was Number 18."

"But he didn't hear a word I said to Julia! I'm sure of it."

"He knew you were up to something sneaky, and he knows where your sympathies lie."

"But he wouldn't betray me," I announce, which makes Vera cringe; after all, we both know he has already betrayed me once, so why not again? "I'll have to confront him," I tell her.

"No! We don't want him to know that we suspect him. It's safer and more useful to us if he thinks you still trust him. That could work to our advantage later."

"If you say so," I reply, but my mind is already working out a way to trap him.

Vera knows me by now and says pleadingly, "Just for once, Sophele, do as I say!"

"All right, but I'm still confused about something. If Julia wasn't the traitor in your group, then why did Isaac send her away?"

"Whoever followed you to Tieckstraße saw you talking with her in her shop. He must have told the Gestapo that Julia was willing to help you do something suspect. Not a good thing. And if you were able to figure out that she'd killed Georg, then sooner or later the Gestapo would, too. Before she got her one-way ticket to Dachau, we thought it best for her to go."

"So the Gestapo must know now I'm working against them, too."

"Absolutely! Which is why you have to be more careful than you've ever been before. They could come for you or Isaac or me at any moment if we slip up. So you won't be buying books for a while. You will be a perfect Young Maiden." She tugs on the end of my hair. "You can start by making some goddamn braids!"

We laugh a little too freely – the fear of being sent to a camp is playing havoc with our emotions. And guilt soon creeps up on me. "It's my fault Julia had to leave," I observe.

"Listen closely," Vera says solemnly. "The Nazis are to blame for all these complications. And she isn't angry at you. Isaac's cousins in Istanbul will treat her and Martin well. She'll find good work. And it's *much* safer for Martin there. Both of them will come back when they can."

"Safer?"

"One day soon, the Nazis are going to toss people like Martin and me overboard."

"Vera, you're breaking your word to Raffi by telling me all this. Why are you doing it?"

"Because I need you to let Rolf and Heidi try to find out who was Georg's accomplice by themselves."

"But dwarfs are ... are conspicuous. What can they ..."

"They just need to ask the right questions," she interrupts impatiently. "Nothing more than that. And I refuse to spend my days worrying about you." She slides back down under the covers and gives me a reassuring smile. "And now let me die here alone of whatever I've caught. Pass the tissues. I need to blow my nose."

"You're hardly dying," I say, handing her the packet.

"Sophele, people like me, with gigantism ... I want you to keep what I'm going to tell you to yourself. We grow too big for our hearts. They end up bursting and we drown in our own blood." She honks into her tissue, then studies the gook that's come out as if it's fascinating.

My mouth has gone dry, and I sense I've just started down a pathway that can only end in grief, but she doesn't seem to notice.

"You know," she continues, "I think my lungs are coming out, which given all my smoking may be for the best. In any case, this illness … it's woken me up to what can happen at any time. Now," she says, slapping my hand, "if you tell anyone I told you this I'll knock you senseless! The last thing I want is sympathy from an *alter kacker*, two dwarfs, and a blind women's shoe salesman."

"Vera, please," I moan. "Stop trying to be funny. You're scaring me."

"Anyway, maybe I'll defy the odds and outlive you all." She makes paddling motions with her arms. "I'll swim to the other shore of this dark ocean."

I gaze off, trying to imagine her death, but I can't visualize a world without her. "You need to eat something," I tell her gently. "I've got soup on the stove."

I start to stand, but she says pleadingly, "Don't go. The sadness … it comes in waves." We sit in silence, staring at each other. I don't know what she sees, but I see the most courageous woman I've ever met, a glorious being trapped behind a face that's been twisted and crushed by bad luck, with no way to break out except through her dreams.

"It was wrong, wasn't it?" she asks in a little girl's voice, full of doubt. When she looks up, her eyes are so pained that I reach for her hand. "What they did to me – cutting my baby out and making sure I'd never have another. That was wrong. Even if I'm ugly. Even if I'm someone *erbkrank*?"

"Of course, it was." When I embrace her, she tucks her head below my arm and starts to cry. Then, by a dark alchemy of the heart that I hope to never experience, her tears become dry howls – as though from an animal whose baby is dying. My bones go cold, my hair stands on end; it's a sound that could only come out of a person in hell. If our world were a place of justice, her wails would rescue her unborn child from the underworld, but the world is hardly that, and Vera will always now be barren and deformed. That truth, hitting her with the force of the ocean she would like to cross into old age, makes her begin to tremble.

"I'm here with you," I tell her. "And I won't go no matter what."

Isaac and Roman rush in. Is the terror in their faces a reflection of my own?

I hold Vera as tight as I can, just as Isaac wanted to hold the arm of the Nazi boy who'd come to take her away. And I think, *The truth is, we're losing this war.*

It's not until Monday morning that I have a chance to see Isaac and Vera again, but when I knock at his door, no one answers. From what I find out later, Isaac left for his factory at dawn. Vera assured him she would stay in his apartment and that she could cope alone.

But early that afternoon, she leaves. Isaac panics when he comes home. Vera has vanished, and although she's taken both her suitcases, she has left her sewing machine behind, which must mean that not even her talent means anything to her any more. He takes a taxi to her apartment but she won't let him in and shouts at him to go away.

He tells me all of this when I visit him on Tuesday afternoon, adding, "With Vera, *tsuris schläff nie.*" Trouble never sleeps.

He's worried that she will take her own life, and so am I. We talk for a long time about her – chains of words linked by desperation. Maybe in consequence we make love as though we are trying to burrow so far down into each other that we'll never have to come back up. Afterward, he says sadly, "You're going to ruin everything, Sophele."

"I don't understand."

"Your gravity is strong. I may not ever be able to break free from you. Even in prayer."

At the time, I presume that his tears mean that he has just discovered that he has fallen in love with me – and fears that I will break his heart. "If you're trapped," I say, kissing his cheek, "then so am I." I tell him I love him for the first time, which makes me tense, as if I should not have admitted it aloud. Our spell might break …

Later, he sits at his desk, naked, his legs crossed and shoulders hunched, and reads, looking harder than ever for an entrance to the Seventh Gate in Berekiah Zarco's writings. When I interrupt him to bring him some tea, he talks to me of his search as though it's a race against time. When I ask him why, he replies, "The stained-glass window of our world has just began to break apart. And I now believe the damage may spread faster than I ever thought possible."

I call Vera that evening from Isaac's flat, and early the next morning, too, but she won't pick up the phone. I picture her lying in a pool of blood; I somehow know that if she were to end her life, she'd stick a gun up to her jutting forehead and pull the trigger.

I visit Isaac again on Wednesday, in the late afternoon. He looks as if he hasn't slept, and the musty scent of distress on him is overpowering.

Filled with dread, I ask, "Is it Vera? Is she dead?"

"No. But Heidi hasn't come home."

"What do you mean?"

"Rolf says she hasn't been home for the last two days. He hasn't seen her since Monday morning, when he left for work."

"Did he know her plans for that day?"

"She was going to do some food shopping, and then make a special meal for Vera's lunch – to try to coax her to join the world again." He rubs his eyes, saying, "Oh God, this is too much," then walks into the kitchen without waiting for me.

"And did Heidi visit Vera before she disappeared?" I ask, following him.

He turns on the tap in his sink and splashes his face. When I hand him a dishtowel, he dries himself and replies, "Vera told Rolf that she turned Heidi away from my apartment without opening the door. She has no idea where Heidi went after that."

"Vera asked her and Rolf to do some investigating for her, you know."

"I know."

"Have you learned anything more about who has been betraying you ... who might have been working with Georg?"

"No, nothing."

"Do we know what time Heidi went to see Vera?"

"Around noon."

"Then I'll just have to cut school tomorrow and see what I can find out."

But my efforts the next day prove pointless. The problem is that a three-foot-high, thirty-eight-year-old dwarf in a winter coat looks like a child from a distance. The neighborhood shopkeepers don't recall having seen her. So the trail ends at eleven in the morning on the previous Monday, when Heidi purchased onions, beets, tomatoes, and a slice of Black Forest ham at a grocery near her home.

She turns up three days later. A fisherman spots her compact body on the muddy bank of the Rummelsburger See, beyond the eastern outskirts of the city. She is putrid from exposure to the lake water and air. A clump of her hair comes off in his hand. Blue paint smudges are faintly visible on her face.

CHAPTER FOURTEEN

When I find out about Heidi's death, I cry only a little while. Maybe I'm getting used to vultures wheeling in the sky high above my head. Germany's new national bird. Or maybe I simply can't believe she is gone.

Did the blue smudges on her face once form swastikas?

Late one evening, after Papa and Mama are snoring away, I try to draw her from memory but my likeness is pathetic and I rip my paper to shreds. Like any good Young Maiden who can't get enough air into her lungs, I ought to simply take a luminal or two, then slip under my covers and join the rest of Germany in slumberland. But I won't drug myself any longer, especially now that Isaac and I are together. So I crawl into bed behind my brother and rest my hand atop his head. I listen to the cars and other night noises of the city as if Berlin will protect me if all else fails.

I call Vera off and on for weeks, but she never answers. Isaac tells me glumly that she won't talk to him either. The police come to interview him, but they won't tell him about the circumstances of Heidi's death. Even with his red-rimmed eyes and heavy, hopeless hand gestures, he is a suspect.

Rolf soon learns that an autopsy has revealed that Heidi had been poisoned with enough tranquilizers to sedate a small army.

"Someone wanted to copy Georg's murder," Isaac tells me. "To give us a symbolic message."

"What message?"

"He's telling us that he's prepared to kill us all in the same way. And discarding the body in the lake – it means we are trash to him." Later, after I've made Isaac eat some lunch, he adds that the autopsy also revealed that Heidi's ovarian tubes had been tied. She'd been sterilized.

"But I overheard her saying that her doctor promised her fertility drugs to get pregnant, and you were giving her teas recommended by Julia."

"Rolf says he and Heidi were never told about her sterilization. Do you remember her miscarriage? Afterward, Dr Stangl told them that she was hemorrhaging and had to have an emergency operation. That must have been when a surgeon tied her tubes."

"But why didn't Dr Stangl inform them? Why give Heidi hope of having a baby?"

Isaac reaches for his pipe and starts to clean the bowl, trying to distract himself. "The Nazis hadn't yet made their sterilization laws, so what they did was illegal. Besides, even at the best of times, people like Stangl like to be cruel to dwarfs. It keeps them entertained."

Isaac tells me that the members of The Ring have had a special meeting where they voted not to even telephone one another for at least six months to avoid provoking more murders – and not to get together with one another, even in small groups, for a year. No letters either. I am not to so much as speak the names of Rolf, K-H, Roman, or Marianne. And I am not to visit Vera.

"But Vera needs us now," I insist.

"Don't worry, I'll check up on her. I'll take her back her sewing machine and give her the special orders for garments I've received, then check up on her now and again. Once she gets back to work, she'll be all right."

"How can you be sure?"

"I can't be." From the way he looks at me, unapologetic, daring me to challenge him, I understand that certainty will not be in our vocabulary for some time.

On Tonio's next weekend visit in late November, we make good use of his father's apartment – sex as my refuge, once again. And I adore his slender angularity and polished skin more than ever, maybe because of their contrast to Isaac's more masculine contours. One change: Tonio seems lonely. I suspect his soldiering isn't as fulfilling as he hoped. Or maybe his father is angry at him. He drops vague comments about both these possibilities, but I don't ask. He'll tell me what he wants to at his own pace. Or he won't. In any case, sharing his thoughts with me doesn't much matter, because his loyalty to me is in his lips and hands. If a similar devotion to me is not in his mind, well, at least I'm better prepared now.

And the best way I can help both of us, I sense, is through our physical intimacy.

Is Isaac bothered by his being relegated to the quiet corner of our triangle? When I come to his apartment on Monday afternoon, he says, "On the contrary ... You need to have sex with someone your own age."

I'd question him more about his magnanimous feelings, but he doesn't give me time. He leads me to the rug in his sitting room and tugs my skirt off. Kneeling before me, he pulls my panties down and buries his head between my legs, working at me so voraciously that I have to laugh. Twisting me around, he has a go at my behind, moistening me, then he lays me on my belly and explores me with his fingers and finally his cock as though he's searching for a treasure my other lover may have left behind in a

place where no one is ever supposed to look. Does it excite him
that he can scent another man on me? I hope so.

After our lovemaking, Isaac reads at his desk. As usual, he's
naked, with his legs crossed. It's a charming pose worthy of
Rembrandt, but I grow to feel helpless when he's hunched over
his manuscripts, puffing smoke signals toward the ceiling. It's as
if his true life is in another world – the one in his mind where an
angel named Metatron writes down the good deeds that even those
of us living by the rules of the Opposite-Compass manage still
to make on occasion. I drape a blanket over his shoulders, since
such remote lands of the mind may be even colder than Berlin in
the autumn, and I leave him with his thoughts. I refuse to be the
gravity holding him back.

We talk sometimes about Jewish mysticism when he's finished
with his studies, and when we do it's with a new urgency. I sense
that Isaac needs to hear his own theories spoken aloud. And to see
if I understand them – if he is being clear. I have become his mirror.

He performs breathing exercises now, as well, and once while
he is in a trance his naked body grows so hot that wisps of vapor
rise from his brow. He calls this process *tov*, from the Hebrew term
for light stored away for the righteous in the World to Come. "It
keeps me warm on my longer journeys," he grins. "That and your
blankets!"

He also practices what he calls letter permutation – repeating
common words aloud with their letters rearranged. When I ask
him why, he says, "Are there stars in the sky during the day?"

"Not that we normally see."

"Exactly. They're there but we can't see them because of the
blanketing light of the sun. Now, imagine nighttime does not exist,
Sophele. Daylight is all we have. We'd have to wait for an eclipse to
see the stars. And we'd be astonished by them, though we might

also be scared out of our wits! What are all those millions of tiny radiant eyes peering down at us ...? Now, imagine the stars and moon and planets are a form of deeper reality inside ourselves. Letter permutations can create an eclipse inside our mind ... can block out the overwhelming light of our thoughts so we can see galaxies of stars ... so we can see subtle patterns and constellations. And if we are blessed with grace, we might even see God somewhere inside them."

Once, I get a quick glimpse of what Isaac might mean. He's at his desk, reading, and I'm sitting on his bed, my legs crossed, my sketchbook in my lap. The glare of his wall lamp has made his hair shine like polished silver. Is that what moves me beyond myself? While watching the rise and fall of his chest, I feel a constriction of energy in my gut, a knot of sexual need tugging me toward him, but I draw instead. My hand moves fast, and I'm not thinking about what I'm creating. I am the paper giving itself to me and the zigzagging bee-movements of my hand, and even the light bouncing ecstatically off Isaac's hair and everything else around me, all pulsing, breathing with existence.

The border between inside and outside has dropped away.

When I'm done with my sketch, I see that I have not drawn Isaac at all; the face seems like a stranger's at first, but then I realize it's Hansi's – a Hansi who has grown up, as he might look fifty years into his future.

Unbeknownst to Isaac, Vera and I sometimes speak on the phone over the next few months. On a couple of occasions, we risk meeting in a foul-smelling beer hall for theatergoers and gay men just off the KuDamm. She always tells me she's doing well, and she tries to be amusing, but I can see in her eyes she's still grieving for her baby. Once, just after New Year's celebrations, I call her up and tell her to meet me at the entrance to the Berlin Cathedral in the early evening. "We'll light candles for your child," I tell her. "And for all the other babies that were murdered last year."

I'd suggest we go to visit her child's grave, but it has none, of course.

Vera thinks religion is absurd and dangerous, so she makes a counter-proposal and I meet her near the Tiergarten instead. And then we walk through the park, arm in arm, letting the bare, merciless silence of winter make us feel as if we are alone on the earth.

The patterns of my life continue largely unperturbed for the next five months, until the end of May 1935. I'll be eighteen in three-and-a-half months and am finishing my second-to-last year of school. Hansi is almost twelve. Still not a word out of him, but Dr Hassgall is teaching him sign language for the deaf, and I pick up words here and there: hungry, tired, itchy, squirrel, jigsaw puzzle. The essentials.

"How do you say, 'Peel faster or I'll drown you in your fish tank?'" I ask my brother one afternoon.

He laughs. A victory! Especially since we can have something like a normal conversation again. Not that he tells me anything about the dramas taking place in the Hansi Universe, but at least I can ask if he wants to go roller skating and he can signal, *Yes, and can we get some ice cream, too?* His new love affair is with chocolate ice cream. He'd bathe in it if he could. An inheritance from Papa, which seems promising, because if my father sees that he and his son are alike, maybe he won't continue to find the boy an embarrassment.

Hansi is more confident and secure than ever before, and he gives me a real smile when I hug him and even studies the drawings

I do of him. He is growing up. And he's five feet tall now, only an inch shorter than Mama, and four inches shorter than me. Now he can subtract, add, multiply, and divide, and he can read quite well, though he pushes away the books I suggest. When I ask him why, he tugs at imaginary whiskers on his upper lip in order to sign, "Too many cats." I don't know what that means but I figure it has to do with not wanting a meddling sister.

Our fish-tank residents Fred and Ginger have been replaced by Groucho and Harpo. My choice of names, and Papa and Mama don't forbid it. Maybe they've forgotten the Marx Brothers are Jewish. The weird thing is that Groucho always tries to munch on Harpo's fins. *Cannibalism Among Prussian Goldfish*, The title I imagine for Hansi's doctoral thesis.

Hansi at the Third Gate, age 13

Tonio has become happier with his life as a soldier – or more resigned. And he, too, is growing up. At least physically. He's five foot nine inches tall now and needs to shave every day, though sometimes I ask him not to so I can feel his stubble against my cheek when he is on top of me. He has become more generous in his lovemaking, as well, as if he has discovered – a revelation!

– that I have needs that don't always match his. One troubling sign: he has become ashamed of his mother's imperfect German and refuses to speak Russian any more. "Talk German or don't talk at all!" he once snapped at her in my presence, and the way she looked at him – as if she feared her own son – raised gooseflesh on my arms and neck.

He and I hardly go to movies anymore. Hollywood has lost most of its glamour, and I no longer even fantasize about being a star. We go skating in winter and take long hikes through the Grünewald and the Spandauer State Forest in summer. Hansi tags along.

In early June, I answer Isaac's phone while he's shaving and speak to Andre Baldwin for the first time. "I'm a friend of Isaac's," he says with a Czech accent. When I identify myself, he says eagerly, "Isaac has told me a lot about you. Don't worry, all good!"

Isaac comes to the phone and tells Mr Baldwin he can't talk now. Because one cheek is still under a mask of shaving foam or because I'm there?

"What's Mr Baldwin do for a living?" I ask when he hangs up.

"He acts as a front for my business, so non-Jews will buy from me. Which is illegal," he notes, walking back to the bathroom, "so just forget you ever heard his name."

Such a schemer Isaac is. And if I knew my films of Conrad Veidt better than I think I do, I might even guess that there's more to his schemes than he's telling me.

I also get a first photograph from Rini at this time. At least, I assume it's from her. A black-and-white still will come from someone, if not her, once every few months all the way up until the summer of 1938. Never with any accompanying note.

The first is an autographed picture of Paul Wegener, the great silent movie star. He's dressed as *The Golem*, the legendary man of clay given life by Rabbi Lowe in order to do battle for the Jews of medieval Prague. Wegener has a muddy face, a helmet of wooden-looking hair, and a puffed-out chest. And a star around his chest. He looks like he hasn't bathed in twenty years. Not very Jewish, if you ask me ...

It's reassuring to have even the distant edges of Rini's friendship back, and I begin sending her cigarette cards of stars, also without notes. I hope that – unlike me – she hasn't lost her delight in Hollywood; a young woman like her, whose every gesture is graceful, could really end up in the movies.

I still go to Young Maiden choir practice every Thursday, though I skip our meetings and athletics training on Tuesdays. How many times can a girl hurl a javelin without concluding that it's not an entirely useful skill? Maria, our group leader, has warned me recently that if I continue trying to set a record for unexcused absences, I will risk expulsion.

I have my heart set on going to university at the Lehranstalt des Kunstgewerbemuseums, the School of Applied Arts, but my parents find that unrealistic. A woman artist in Germany? "Like a goldfish writing poetry" was how I overheard Papa describing my goal to Mama, since everyone in my family has become an expert at fish analogies by now. My father wants me to get a good, solid engineering or science degree that can be of use to the *Volk*, and my mother – though she hasn't said so – wants me to marry Tonio and have at least three babies. If I looked into my crystal ball, I'd say there is great disappointment ahead for either them or me.

In mid-June, my mother wakes up feeling queasy. She vomits blood into the kitchen sink. Papa is already out and Hansi is still asleep, and she swears me to silence.

"Just tell me if you've thrown up blood before," I plead with her.

"Sophie, forget it. It's not important."

Over the next month, Mama's abdominal pain becomes so bad that she cries out in her sleep, and she's unable to keep even crackers down. The hollows deepen in her face as if she is caving in, and her hair becomes as dry as hay. One day, she calls me into her bedroom and asks me to touch the spot in her belly where the pain is centered.

Why doesn't she ask her husband to do this? That question occurs to me only days later.

Mama is so thin now that her hips jut out like shovels, and her face is skeletal and gray. It's terrifying – like seeing a demon replacing her. When I touch the spot that hurts her, a lump about the size of a plum meets my fingertip and makes me gasp. "Mama, you've got to see your doctor. It's big."

"Oh, Sophie ..." Her face peels open and, before I know it, she's weeping in my arms. Years of resentment vanish as she shakes. I learn that the magic cure for grudges is despair – not that I forget my grievances, but glimpsing a mother's gravestone on the horizon is the greatest wind in the world, and it blows all the dry, resentful leaves in my heart far away. At least for the moment.

I call Papa at work, and he phones Dr Nohel. Two days later, Mama is admitted to the hospital. She's operated the very next morning. Afterward, the surgeon tells us that her tumor has been removed, but the cancer has spread to her liver, which is misshapen. He uses the word *missgestaltet*. I'll never forget because Vera says that about her own face. Her lungs are affected, too. She must have been feeling symptoms for at least six months.

I don't know if Papa ever asks her about why she never told us, because when she comes home from the hospital they keep their door closed and talk in hushed voices. Papa orders me not to bother her in a stern voice, but that hardly seems enough reason to keep quiet.

"You were ill for a long time, weren't you?" I ask Mama the moment we have some time alone.

"How was I to know that it was something serious?" she replies as if she really means it. She's sitting up on her bed, the floral lacquer tray she loves on her lap. I've just brought her lunch – two hard-boiled eggs that I've cut very thin, and a slice of pumpernickel. Her appetite is back, and she looks almost like herself, except for her hollow eyes, which have lost their shine. Dull jade sitting inside heavy crescents of yellowish skin.

She never leaves her bedroom. I wake at six every morning to get the oven started and make her lunch, then head out to take Hansi to school. I don't mind the extra duties; I'm grateful for being exhausted and nervous all the time because it's proof that I am making up for all the time I spent disliking my mother. I also become her hairdresser, and I tape two magazine pictures of Claudette Colbert to the bathroom wall to match them to my mother's bangs from every angle. After Mama looks between Claudette and her reflection in the mirror, she smiles warmly. "I should have asked you to cut my hair all along," she confesses, kissing me on the cheek.

She calls me into her room early one morning and hands me a gold brooch studded with fourteen tiny amethysts in the shape of a rose. I count them as she talks to me, as if each one is a step down into a lightless dungeon. "This brooch was given to me by my mother," she says cautiously, as if she wants me to remember every word, "and now I want to give it to you." Which means she is going to die, so I refuse her present, screaming that it's ugly and she can throw it into the Spree for all I care. I run out.

Wandering in hopeless circles around the neighborhood, I realize that the life I had may be over. Before bed, Mama shuffles into my room, drops down beside me, and presses her lips to my brow. When she asks me why I fled from her, I reply, "Mama, don't talk, just hold me."

And she does. For a long time. Till we sense death receding and know that the present moment is only made of life. We laugh together about being so silly and emotional.

A few days later, Papa takes Hansi into his bedroom to talk to him seriously about Mama's prognosis. The boy looks eager and happy when he emerges, and he asks me in sign language if I want to feed Groucho and Harpo with him.

"What did you tell him?" I ask Papa, with Hansi tugging on my arm.

"Just that Mama will be all right, because even if the worst happens, she'll be with God."

"And what did he say?"

"Nothing, of course." For a moment, I'd forgotten that he doesn't talk. And Papa hasn't learned much sign language yet.

My father thinks the Christian God is a hoax, though he doesn't say so aloud any longer. But maybe Hansi keeps altars and incense in his universe. If so, and if the Lord really appears to us as what we find most beautiful, then my brother must pray to a giant squirrel – the red-furred, tufted-eared, long-tailed variety that we find all over the Grünewald and Tiergarten. *Sciurus Vulgaris* – a god who knows where every nut in the world is hidden.

And maybe *Sciurus Vulgaris* creates a miracle for us from up there at the top of the Hansi Tree, because Mama's health improves and she starts being able to cook, which isn't such good news, in truth, because that means we're back in boiled-potato-land. I help her every evening. We talk about dresses, my friends in the Young Maidens, and our favorite movie stars, since that makes us both feel as if we're safely in our past. I gab for hours, quick as I can, because this period of grace probably won't last much longer;

when she gets all better, she'll turn back into the narrow-minded victim of circumstance who sees only willfulness and defiance crouching in her daughter's eyes. Mama listens to me as she never did before, as though the death that was growing in her belly has taught her to treasure my run-on sentences and convoluted fantasies. When I say I don't have time for the Young Maidens any more, she replies, "Then quit." And when I tell her I intend to go to art school in a year and a half, when I finish high school, she tells me, "It's your life, Sophie. If that's what you want, then don't let anyone dissuade you."

I feel like poking my finger into her arm to make sure she's real.

Was she dissuaded from going to college herself? Maybe I'm just reading once-upon-a-time, secret ambitions into the way she says, "You'll make something of yourself, Sophie. I know it."

I almost ask her about what went wrong when she was my age, but then I think, *No, this is a fragile balance we've achieved on our seesaw, and she will either tell me or she won't*. Yet if I were to extrapolate on the advice she gave me over those weeks of relative health, I'd say she always felt rejected. Except by a high school history teacher who suggested that she become a nurse. When she speaks of Hilde van Loewen, a Dutchwoman from Rotterdam, her eyes become radiant. A golden age that's gone.

She also tells me once that her father was "a hard man". She shakes her head when she says the word *hard* as if she means *cruel*. Speaking of him, her shoulders hunch and she becomes a beaten young woman again, cowering in front of an unforgiving, hardfisted taskmaster. I also learn he never wanted her, because she tells me, "He'd have killed to have a son instead of me."

When, contrary to my expectations, she warns me about marrying Tonio too young, to wait until I am twenty-one, I get the distinct feeling that she agreed to wed Papa simply to get out of her father's house. She escaped from one jail to another. I read that in the way she warns me not to have a big wedding. "Just the people you really trust," she advises me, "because the rest won't help when you really need to change your life."

Once, she whispers to me conspiratorially, "The year you were sick with whooping cough, when Hansi was only a year old, your father didn't lift a finger to help me. He fled the house. I could never forgive him for that. I tried, but I couldn't do it." She instructs me then not to have children until I know my husband very well.

If we had enough time together, I think I'd learn all of Mama's secrets by gleaning tidbits here and there, but in late July, she gets a high fever that won't come down. So back she goes into the hospital.

Her mother arrives by train from Bavaria the next day, and both of Mama's sisters, Ilse and Angela, come in over the next week. Grandma is a quail of a woman with a bun of wavy, steel-gray hair, thin, judgmental lips and a haughty glare. If we were living in China she'd be a dowager empress, but this is Berlin and she has no servants to order around except me, which means I have to fetch her tea, iron her pillow cases, and fluff her eiderdown. Her green eyes are constantly moist, and she clears her throat noisily after each meal, which grates on Papa's nerves. She sleeps in my bed, dressed in a floor-length, pink-lace nightgown that looks like it would be just the thing for Marie Antoinette, and I take the couch. When I ask her why Grandpa didn't join her, she says he hasn't been well for years. "What's he got?" I ask, and she sticks her finger into her temple and turns.

Our aunts talk too loudly, stink of cheap lemon perfume, and fuss with Hansi as if he's a doll they've inherited. I can see why Mama dislikes them, though she never actually says that. Papa charges out of the room like a spooked stallion whenever they come over. He reads the paper and smokes cigarettes with his window open so the smell won't give him away.

Hansi isn't able to sleep soundly in the same room with our grandmother – probably because his snoring creates a dissonance with her higher-pitched honking – and when I wake during his first night with her, I find my brother seated on his heels in front of the fish tank, shivering, wearing only his pajama bottoms. I can tell from his swollen-looking eyes that he's been crying a lot. When I snuggle with him and ask what's the matter, he points to the tank. As usual, Groucho is munching on poor Harpo's fins, which look like a shredded fringe of white satin. "What should we do?" I ask.

Hansi stands up, grabs our tiny net, and scoops the bully out of the water and drops him on the floor. "No good!" he signs to me with a swift downward motion of his hand.

Groucho flails around, blood-red gills flexing madly. It's horrid to watch, so I lift him by his tail, go the bathroom, and flush him down the toilet. By now, Berlin's sewers must be a frenzied knot of discarded goldfish and guppies. Good for feeding the albino, mutant crocodiles rumored to live down there.

Hansi and I go back to watching Harpo. Will his fins grow back? "Let's buy a Ghico for him," I say, and my brother gives me a big happy nod. Such an easy boy to please.

Hospital tests reveal that Mama has an abscess in her lungs, and her doctors stick tubes into her chest to draw out the fluid. Her face becomes gray and pasty – like wax. Still, she asks me to draw her one afternoon, which stuns me. By way of explanation, she tells me, "I want one person to really see me. And it has to be you."

A desire I will always remember. Because she spoke it so desperately, as if I were her link to what might have been – and what could still be. Because there is still hope in her words.

I want one person to really see me. Who wouldn't want that?

She must have concluded that I knew nothing essential about her – and that nobody else did either, not even Papa. Which means she lived like a ghost, talking in an imposter's voice. How many of the German women I see every day in the street go through their lives like that, pecked at by bullies and giving up the struggle?

Not me, not me, not me ... That's what I vow while drawing Mama.

I was just seventeen. Now, I realize that it wasn't my responsibility to know who my mother was, or why she was misunderstood, or what happened between her and her sadistic, crazy father, but at the time her words hit me like a slap across the face.

She stares at me the whole time I sketch her. With eyes like water on the surface of a deep lake. Does she see cragged, snow-capped mountains around her? She told me that the Alps appear to her in her nightmares of late, and when I asked her why, she bit her lip, ashamed, and said, "Because I can't see over them."

She is a thirty-seven-year-old woman who wants more time and who needs to be sure her children love her. That's what her unblinking green eyes say to me. And what do mine say to her? She must know I'm terrified, but she doesn't reach out a hand to comfort me. She wants tremors to shake my hands. Is that cruel? Maybe it gratifies her to see me distraught because it signifies that we both want her to go on living. "Thank you for your tears," she once told me toward the end, squeezing my hand so tight it hurt, and I understood just what she meant.

She is a woman, not just a mother, and her life is not a dream. She has emotions she cannot explain, feelings no different from any of us.

Those are conclusions that should have been obvious to me but weren't. And this woman before me, who wanted to be a nurse and who was fettered to me when she was only twenty, will die before her time. That is what I realize, sick with guilt, as I add shading to her cheeks in my sketch and try to keep from jabbing my pencil through the paper.

I never finish my portrait. How could a drawing of a dying mother ever really be done? No, I keep that sketch in my head even now. When I show her what I've done, she studies it carefully, biting her lip again, which is something she does nearly all the time now.

"It's not very good," I say, "but I really tried. I tried hard, Mama, I promise." I don't want her to die hating me for not being a good enough artist, and every word I say really means, *Please forgive me for being born too soon* ...

"No, it *is* good. It's just that my face ... that face ... it's not the one I thought I had," she tells me.

After a few more days, we take Mama home again from the hospital. Her mother and sisters return to Bavaria the next day. Mama doesn't shed a single tear during their good-byes.

For a week all is quiet, but one evening Mama goes through her cookbooks to find the piece of paper on which her mother wrote her recipe for *Knödel*, potato dumplings. She knocks everything from our pantry onto the floor during her frantic search, shrieking, "It's gone, it's gone ...!" Her nightgown comes undone, so she's half naked, too. A shrieking skeleton with lost eyes. When I beg her to stop, she pulls at her tufts of hair over her ears and screams, "I hate you! I hate all of you!"

Papa comes in and tries to get her to calm down, but she pushes him away so hard that I know she blames him for her wrecked life.

"You'll scare Hansi!" he shouts at her. "Stop it!" He stands there with his hands on his hips like a Prussian general. All that's missing is a chest full of medals. I had no idea he could reach the end of his patience so quickly. Do no men have stamina for suffering or is it just my father?

I wrap my arms around Mama from behind and shout at him, "You're the one who's scaring people! Get out of the kitchen!"

I promise Mama I'll find the recipe, which makes her stop fighting me. After she catches her breath, she says, "Don't bother, Sophie, I must have burned it accidentally with your father's things." She speaks as though she's inside a dream. She looks drugged. Could she have found my luminal?

Once I get her back to bed, she murmurs curses at my father. She calls him a son-of-a-bitch and a thief. Maybe the cancer has spread to her brain. Maybe that's also what happened to her father.

She goes to sleep when I agree to caress her hair and not to leave her. "Thank God you're with me, Sophie," she says. She's become a little girl who wants to sit at her mother's kitchen table and scent the *Knödel* cooking on the stove.

That evening I write to Grandma and ask her to send the recipe as fast as she can.

The next day, Mama starts coughing as if barbed wire is stuck in her throat. The towel I hand her becomes flecked with blood, so she goes back to the hospital. A knot of tears forms in my throat whenever I see her there, and my legs grow tight with the need to flee. Hansi sits on Mama's bed so she can hold him. Once, he tries to pull out her tubes while she's sleeping. Maybe he wants to sneak her out. A nurse hollers at him, and from then on the hospital staff keep their distance from him as if he's got leprosy.

The smell of her hospital room ... I'll remember that rank odor for years. I'll dream of it. Black dreams that cleave to me, as though made of blood and urine.

I'm sitting in a chair in Mama's room, reading the newspaper, half-sleeping, when she dies: the 6th of August, 1935, ten days short of Hansi's twelfth birthday. She doesn't call out or gasp. She simply stops breathing. Her mouth is open and her head is leaning back. I don't know how long it takes for me to notice. Five minutes, ten ...?

The room grows dark and my legs lose all their strength when I stand, so that I have to kneel to keep from fainting. Then I rub her feet, which aren't yet dead to me, because I can bring her to life in my head, and I sit beside her, closing her eyelids and neatening the hair falling over her brow, telling myself that now she'll be able to walk over the rim of the Alps and go wherever she wants to, that she'll even be able to go back in time to her golden age, when a Dutch schoolteacher believed she could become a nurse.

The things we tell ourselves when a loved one dies, all of them made from the fringes of hope still in our hands.

Papa comes to the hospital a bit later, sits alone with her, then takes me home, his arm over my shoulder. But before we go, I snip a lock of Mama's hair – the hair I've cut – and put it in an envelope that a nurse finds for me. I want to have something from her that could only be hers.

The *Knödel* recipe arrives from Grandma a few days later. It includes nutmeg. Who would have guessed? I bury it with Mama; the last thing I want is another recipe for potatoes. And in any case it belongs to her.

Isaac is kind and patient with me during my mother's illness, even when I'm yelling at him for no reason at all, and I bless him every day for not trying to cheer me up. Sometimes, we say little more than a *How did your day go?* before we make love. He moves slow and soft when he's inside me, knowing I'm made of fragile hopes, and he stops if I ask him to, and he holds me in his warm arms, whispering in beautiful German that he will always help me. Afterward, he doesn't rush off to his desk to read. A miracle.

The week Mama dies, my tangled, fraying mind comes completely undone and, sitting in the black puddle at the bottom of my grief, I decide, sobbing, to give myself bangs. I come out looking like a lampshade, so I run to Isaac's flat and beg him to cut it short everywhere.

"Do it!" I shout when he hesitates.

As he snips, his face becomes so serious and determined that it makes me want to laugh, yet I can't, and I keep telling him to cut it even shorter, as if I were a boy, and maybe that's what I intended all along – a disguise, so I don't have to be me. Or so I can fulfill my grandfather's wish for no more girls.

"My Joan of Arc," Isaac tells me after I've finally let him put down his scissors, and he rubs a delighted hand over the bristly top of my head.

I look like an imposter in the mirror. But I don't feel bad. I don't feel anything, in fact.

A few days later, I decide to tear up the drawing I did of my mother in the hospital, since her eyes and nose are all wrong, but Isaac pleads with me to give it to him for safekeeping. "I'll keep it for you until you've come up again," he says.

"Up from where?"

"From your mother's grave."

Isaac also reads poetry to me in bed, Rilke in particular, which would make Dr Fabig happy, wherever he is. Maybe we have to watch a loved one die before we can understand anything about Rilke's work, about the sweet, subtle presence of sadness and joy between his words, as if those opposites are really just intertwined vines, and our little lives are the façades they must constantly climb. These are the verses I remember most clearly, and I always hear them in Isaac's voice:

All things are the bodies of violins, full of murmuring
    darkness; inside are dreams of the weeping of women,
    inside stirs in sleep the resentment of whole generations ...
I shall tremble silver: then everything under me shall come
    to life,
and that which errs in things shall strive towards the light ...

I buy Isaac a black Basque beret to thank him for being so gentle
with me. His eyes open wide with enchantment when I hand it to
him. He wears it even in the house, and I adore the way his silver
hair ribbons out beneath the rim. Such a handsome man, and he
doesn't believe it, which is another reason I trust him.

CHAPTER FIFTEEN

Tonio comes to the funeral in uniform. We link hands with Hansi between us, and later he speaks to my father alone. I can guess what they talk about, because when my boyfriend catches up with me, he brings up marriage for the first time, but I do not want to be tied to him or Isaac or anyone else. Still, he obliges me to talk of our future, and as we do, I decide I want black borders to grow around my life, the ones Mama should have had. I want to be a girl in a Rouault painting.

"I can't talk about anything right now and know what I'm saying," I finally tell Tonio. "We'll talk again in a couple of months."

"Maybe your hair will have grown back by then," he says, trying to cheer me up.

"I hope not," I warn him.

While the minister's sermon drags across our emotions, Hansi sits right on the lawn, his legs crossed. I can tell the boy fears rain. Papa looks at him as if he's a lost cause, his face compressed by anger. I'd like to punch him for forgetting how to love my brother at the worst possible time.

After exchanging whispers with my father, Aunt Ilse marches over to Hansi and informs him that he's a ridiculous sight. She grabs his wrists and tries to tug him to his feet, whispering that he'd better not fight her, which makes him shriek like a cornered animal, so I rush to her and say, "If you don't leave my brother alone, I'll break your neck! *Ich breche dir den Hals!*" I use those exact words, and even now I can feel the drum-tautness of righteousness in my heart. Aunt Ilse, ready to burst into tears, lets go of Hansi and orders me never to talk to her like that again, but I don't apologize. I take Hansi's hand and ask him to step back with me from the grave, which he does. Later, I overhear Ilse informing Grandma that I may already be suffering from the family madness.

What family madness? This is news to me. And good news, too, since maybe my aunts will keep away from me forever.

The life I imagined for myself slides away from me after that, as if it's a message carried out to sea. I do our food shopping and cook every night, and I quit the Young Maidens without attending a final choir practice. Fräulein Schumann never calls, which surprises me.

Now, so many years later, I'm astonished that I didn't resent having to make this sacrifice. Without being aware of it, I must have spent those months after Mama's death in a state of dissipated shock, doing my best to simply keep walking.

Papa seems to react to Mama's death much like a Rilke poem, slowly, subtly, and also in surprising ways, though he would dismiss my comparison to verse with a derisive snort. He takes a week off after the funeral and goes around the house quietly, as if walking on tiptoe. He closes his eyes all the time, and sometimes his lashes squeeze out tears, which makes me sit with him and rub the back of his hand as if I'm polishing our grief. He takes his time when he eats supper but says little to us, as though he's a condemned man living out his sentence. He's aged, too – I'm aware now that the hair on his temples and over his ears has grayed. He helps me wash the dishes, mostly so we can talk about my studies, which have not gone well since Mama's illness began. He's worried I may fail all my classes, but for better or worse, I'll do what I have to do to pass.

He's good with Hansi, too, and does jigsaw puzzles with the boy even first thing in the morning. We don't talk about Mama. I don't bring her up because I sense that whatever I might say would only make him feel worse, and he must be thinking the same about me.

Papa becomes the man he was for a time, but when he goes back to work, his sudden absence is like a second death to me. I know it's unfair, but I want him waiting for me when I get home from classes, and Hansi does too. For a time, the boy goes on strike the only way he knows how, by refusing to go to school. Papa pleads with him and, when that has no effect, yells at him so cruelly – calling him an embarrassment to his face for the first time – that Hansi bursts into tears and starts scraping at his neck with his fingernails. Is his frenzied swiping a symptom of his realization that the red-faced bully screaming at him is all he's got left? Dr Hassgall comes over the next morning. God knows what magic powder that man keeps in the pockets of his tweed coat, but Hansi goes back to school with him.

As for Tonio, he's particularly good with Hansi during our period of grief. When he's on leave, the three of us go for long walks down by the Spree. We bring stale bread along so we can feed the ducks and geese.

Over the next few months, Papa distances himself progressively from Hansi and me. When he doesn't think I'm watching, he looks at the boy as if he's an intruder, and he flees to his bedroom after supper. Our father never sits with us to read his newspaper or listen to the radio. *I want to be alone* ... Garbo's famous line, but now it could be Papa's. Could he be sobbing into one of Mama's blouses, breathing in the lost scent of her like I sometimes do?

Only now do I realize that Mama – and not my father – was the center of our family.

Then the next phase of his flight from us begins: Papa leaves for work every day before Hansi and I are awake. Maybe we're too painful a reminder of our mother. Or maybe he knows he needs to earn a living for our family and has to get on with his life despite his grief. That doesn't occur to me at the time, but it seems an obvious explanation now.

At times, he becomes affectionate again and takes us out to supper. Afterward, he buys Hansi all the chocolate ice cream he can eat. Isaac says that I need to give Papa time. "The death of a wife is a road that has no end."

True for the death of a mother, too: I cry tears enough to fill the giant hole inside me, but it never gets filled. Gurka and her milkmaid friends whisper and snicker about how boyish I look whenever I pass. Their amused stares open old wounds, but I've already left school behind in my mind. I take one or two mornings off each week after Mama dies and discover that life is much easier when I have half the day free.

When I tell Isaac I'm quitting, he takes out his wallet and replies, "I've been expecting this. I know all rational arguments will fail with you, so I'll pay you to stay in school."

"How much?" I ask, laughing.

"However much it takes." He spreads out a fan of Reichsmark.

"I don't want money, I want affection."

"Deal!" he says, opening his arms.

So it is I am bribed back into those dreadful classrooms, with curses against the Jews carved into the desks and "Heil Hitlers" in our teachers' greetings, and exams on racial characteristics. What I remember most from my second-to-last year is our German professor, Dr Hefter, informing us in a proud voice that German is superior to English and French because even Negroes can speak those other languages. It's then – for the first time in ages – that I raise my hand to speak.

"Yes, Sophie?" Dr Hefter asks, astonished that I want to participate. Such an innocent smile he has. It's almost a shame to betray his pleasure in inviting me to talk.

"Seeing as how Dr Goebbels can speak German reasonably well," I tell him, "I think we can put aside your argument that it's a language for superior men."

Hushed, pressure-filled silence fills the classroom around me and Dr Hefter jerks his head back as if I've whacked him. In his poodle-brown eyes, I can see his tiny mind racing around in circles, trying to find an explanation for this dangerous effrontery. Seizing the only one his faulty nose can sniff out, he grins. "Sophie has made a joke, but I must tell you, young lady, that ..."

"It's no joke," I interrupt. "Anyone with eyes can see that Dr Goebbels is of inferior breeding, and yet he can speak German with reasonable accuracy. Does he speak even broken English or French? I doubt it. If he did, then he wouldn't be a minister in this government because he'd be too cultured for the National Socialists."

Dr Hefter coughs to cover his discomfort, then goes to his desk, and picks up the play by Schiller we're to begin today: *William Tell*. "Please open to page one," he tells the class.

And we *do* open our books. And no one ever says another word about my blasphemy, though Dr Hildebrandt, our headmaster, gives me a stern lecture on proper behavior the next morning. He ends by slapping his metal ruler into his desk so loud that I jump. "Consider yourself just a single infraction from expulsion, young lady!"

That I manage to get through the school year without being expelled is a testament to my patience, though it is not often a quality I associate with my younger self. And it is good to have the

summer free – for my Jewish studies with Isaac and long walks in
Berlin's parks with Tonio and Hansi. But these months of graceful
ease end all too soon. Just after the start of my final year, on the
15th of September, our government passes two new laws designed
to keep the vermin off the main deck of the refurbished ship we're
sailing on. The "Reich Citizenship Law" strips Jews of their German
nationality and their right to vote, as well as to hold public office;
and my favorite, the Teutonically pompous "Law for the Protection
of German Blood and German Honor", forbids Jews from marrying
"Germans" or even having sexual relations with one.

These enactments will be remembered in years to come as
the Nuremberg Laws. But whatever their name, Isaac and I are
now outlaws. And abracadabra ... he is stateless. Our orgasms
have now become evidence proving our guilt, and we risk either
imprisonment or hard labor, according to the new law.

"I don't know about you, but I'd prefer hard labor, since I'm
already used to that," I tell Isaac, laughing. I've just raced up to
his apartment, and I'm giddy with the news that I'll be fighting
on the front lines every time we dive under his down comforter.

"It's not the least bit funny," he replies, annoyed, pouring me
a cup of coffee since he says I need sobering up. "The Nazis want
to change our instincts about what is natural."

"But no one, not even the most ignorant peasant in the Black
Forest, could really believe that you can change who is a German
from one moment to the next. Declaring that you're not a citizen
is like declaring that that an oak tree isn't a tree. My God, you've
been in the army – you're more German than my father!"

"Sophele, you want our people to behave rationally, but they
never have and never will. And this is a very bad sign." He shakes
his head morosely.

"A sign of what?"

"In 1449, the Spanish monarchy passed laws that stated that the Jews had tainted blood. As a consequence, we became defined not by our religion, but by our *impure* nature. Converting a Jew to Christianity would not take away that impurity, because our religion meant nothing. It was only our blood that counted. So the only way to prevent us from infecting those with Spanish blood was to kill us, and the Inquisition set up by the Church did just that! Then the Portuguese copied them. For hundreds of years they hunted us down. You see? The Church would have tortured and killed Berekiah Zarco and the rest of my ancestors if they hadn't escaped to Istanbul." He ends his sentence on a sharp intake of breath and doesn't continue.

"What is it?" I ask

"I think that Berekiah has been trying to tell me that the killing is about to return, and that this time it will be worse, but I didn't want to believe it." He gives me a penetrating look. "Sophele, these laws are a prerequisite to legislating murder."

I think Isaac is wrong to be so worried until the next day at school. Dr Habermann, our philosophy teacher, has written the new rules about who is a Jew on the board, from which I learn that a Jew is anyone with at least three grandparents who are Jewish, or anyone who has two Jewish grandparents if he or she was a member of the Jewish religious community when the new law was passed, or joined the community later, or was married to a Jewish person, or … I don't read to the end, because all these clauses are absurd; we are all aware that a Jew is anyone who practices Judaism, just as we know that Jews have been German citizens for as long as there has been a Germany, but all the other students copy down every convoluted word in their notebooks as if they're sleep-walking through life. And so it is that we come to accept that an oak tree is no longer a tree. And if Hitler decides tomorrow that gravity no longer exists, will we fly up into the air?

On his next weekend off, Tonio agrees with me that these laws are absurd, but he says that Hitler's genius is in knowing that a nation's dreams don't always make sense. "It's simple," he tells me in his preacherly voice when I tell him I don't have a clue what he's talking about. "Germans have always dreamed of having their own country, free of ... of impurities and foreign imperfections. And the Führer has taught us that we have every right to live out that dream."

We're lying together in bed when he declares this, and I roll over onto my belly so that I don't have to see his self-assured face asking for my agreement. And because I'm remembering Vera telling me – when I first met her – that it's better that dreams remain in their own realm. If only Tonio weren't so pleased about Hitler's malignancy, our relations would be easier. Though I'm beginning to see that he could be useful to me in terms of knowing what the *Volk* are thinking. After all, it will be important to know when it has become too dangerous for Isaac and Vera to remain in Germany.

As a result of the Nuremberg Laws, two of Isaac's oldest Christian clients refuse to do business with him any longer – or even to pay their outstanding bills. Isaac tries to meet with them, but humiliation is the result; they refuse to even let him in their offices. Is this a turning point in his way of thinking? Instead of spending extra hours drumming up new business, he buries himself in Berekiah Zarco's manuscripts more obsessively than ever. When I ask if there's anything I can do to help with his business, he replies matter-of-factly, "Don't worry, the factory is healthy enough to take care of itself," then asks me to make him some coffee so he can concentrate better.

One cold evening in late November 1935, Papa takes us out to supper at the indoor restaurant of the Köln Beer Garden, and a woman in a fur coat the size of a brown bear joins us there. She's twenty-seven. I know, because I ask. She talks sweetly to me, and she is full of sincere and sad glances at Hansi. She wears bright red lipstick and cobalt blue mascara, which makes her look like a mutant parrot. Her low-cut black dress is elegant and a bit slutty, like an outfit a gangster would choose for his girlfriend. Her earrings are gigantic pink pearls. Her name is Greta Pach, and Papa introduces her to Hansi and me as a secretary at the Health Ministry.

"Your *father's* secretary," Greta adds, staking her claim, and Papa gives her a quick-tempered glare.

That single glance from my father gives their game away before it's even started. And when I ask Greta how long she's been at the ministry, she replies in a breathy voice – proto-Marilyn Monroe – that she started nearly four years ago, which means she was on the job the day Papa arrived.

Hansi doesn't do the math, which is just as well, but I know now that she and Papa have been working together – and probably sleeping together – since the moment he joined the Health Ministry in August 1933. Two years, four months ago.

I go to the bathroom since I don't want to break down in front of Papa. Will he leave us now, so he can start making little red and blue parakeets in Greta's womb? I splash my face and neck with cold water, but I'm burning up. Sitting in a stall, I realize I have a decision to make: I can either make a scene and risk losing Papa, or I can act as sweet as possible so that he'll stay with us.

As soon as I see Hansi slurping his soup, I realize I really have no options. I'll be nice to our father for maybe the same reason Mama was. *He Who Earns the Money Holds All the Cards.* That's what I'd like to engrave now on Mama's gravestone.

"I'm glad you could join us for dinner," I tell Greta after I sit down, and I ask where she lives, doing my best to sound cheerful.

Papa, believing I'm up to no good, tells me I'm being far too inquisitive, but she waves him away and says, "No, Sophie has a right to know about me," and I can see from the cheeky, amused way she looks at me that she knows that I know what's up. She says she lives in "too large" an apartment in Charlottenburg. To my subsequent questions she tells me that she divorced her stockbroker husband four years ago. Her maiden name was Allers. She adds that she loves painting, particularly Cézanne's landscapes. Is that indicative of good taste or did Papa tell her what she'd need to say to win me over?

Papa's hand rests like an awning over his irritated eyes during our friendly exchange as if he'd like to drop through a hole in the floor. From the way he's fingering the salt shaker I can tell he's dying for a cigarette. I understand now that this dinner was Greta's idea.

"Someday when you come over, I'll be happy to draw you," I tell Greta. And I will indeed be gratified; I'll give her a beak and feathers, and I'll add a big cheetah behind her, with my own saber-toothed smile, ready to swallow her whole and spit out her goddamned pearl earrings.

"And you'll have to come to my apartment," she gushes. "You and Hansi both. You'll love my new curtains! They're blue and green brocade."

"I'm a real big fan of brocade," I reply.

She doesn't recognize my sarcasm but Papa gives me a look of warning. Though he's the one who's going to have to watch it, because I understand now why we never had enough money to buy a bigger apartment; keeping Greta warmed by a brown bear and getting her new drapes has sentenced Mama, Hansi, and me to a smaller life. Still, I compliment her dress, which makes Papa nod at me as if to say, *That's more like it!*

Does he suspect I'd like to tip over the tall white candle at the center of our table and set his pin-striped suit on fire?

After dessert, he lights Greta's cigarette and takes one for himself from her tin – Haus Bergmann, his own brand. I ask her for one, too, which she offers me with a pleased smile, but Papa is quick to add in an outraged voice, "Sophie, I didn't know you smoked. And I don't think it's a good idea."

"You don't know a lot of things," I say. "So just give me a light."

He frowns nastily, so I give *him* a look of warning, though my nervousness is like a fist around my throat, and I don't know where this crazy courage to defy him comes from, and I hope Mama won't hate me if I don't have the will to fight him for long.

When I tell Isaac about Papa's affair, he says, "You'd best be very careful with him. If he's fallen in love, he won't have much patience for anyone who tries to get in the way."

Tonio tells me much the same thing: "Just let your father and Greta get on with their lives."

Their advice infuriates me. And seems indicative of a secret world-wide conspiracy of men.

I search in vain through my father's coat and pants for his key to Greta's apartment over the next couple of weeks, and while seated bent-backed on his bed, I realize Mama also must have done a lot of searching over the last two years – for lipstick stains, hotel receipts, and God knows what else. Or maybe her torment began much earlier; she must have suspected – like I do – that this wasn't Papa's first affair. If only she'd had the courage to confide in me. Then, all our interactions – even the difficult ones – might have been based on trust, and everything I feel now might be so much less weighted with a sense of having missed out on our life together.

Maybe my mother even met some of the other women, though

I can't think of any possibilities except Maria Gorman, Papa's old friend from Communist Party headquarters. After all, Mama threw out her raspberry jam without even tasting it and never demonstrated any concern over her being arrested. Two clues to a marriage gone wrong. I suppose that's not much less than most children get, so I shouldn't feel so cheated.

Though maybe I'm all wrong about Maria's having slept with my father and the frequency of his instances of infidelity; sometimes now I think of him as a chameleon, blending into situations and events. There's so much about him I never understood.

At the time, I reason that there's little point in my speculating further about Papa's double life because the past is a puzzle whose pieces are already formed, and no amount of rearranging I might do will make those odd little shapes fit any differently. So maybe Tonio's and Isaac's advice to me was perfect. Still, couldn't my father have waited more than four months to show Hansi and me that his heart is not with us? No stamina, as I've said.

A year has passed since the members of The Ring agreed not to see or talk to one another, so to celebrate their being able to socialize again Isaac invites Vera, K-H, and Marianne to Hanukkah dinner, and on the windy, bone-chilling evening of the 20th of December, I sneak up there for an hour, leaving Hansi in front of Harpo and his new underwater ballet partner, Chico.

As we await his guests, Isaac tells me, "I only hope we've spent enough time apart from each other to convince our traitor that we're harmless."

"Are you harmless?"

"Yes and no," he says, pinching my cheek and looking at me lecherously.

He's wrapped in his favorite cardigan sweater – brown, with

holes at the elbows – and I'm wearing his floppy fur slippers and a scarf; heating an apartment is expensive and his business has been crippled by the Nazis.

Roman doesn't join us; he's with the Circus Cardinali for the winter. Rolf doesn't come over either. None of us has seen him since Heidi's funeral.

As soon as K-H and Marianne arrive, they offer me condolences and hugs for Mama's death – and rub my new short hair with appreciative laughs. Vera does too, since we're pretending we haven't seen or spoken to each other.

K-H doesn't take his probing eyes from me as we sip our wine and finally says, "I'd like to photograph you now that you've become who you were meant to be."

How does he know? When I ask, he points to his eyes. "I'm trained to see," he tells me.

When our guests ask after Hansi, I tell them about his scooping Groucho out of our tank and me flushing the murderous fish down the drain. Vera says we should have eaten him. "Goldfish are good on top of toast," she says, rubbing her belly, "especially with a little horseradish."

Despite her humor, Vera looks wan and tired, and I read in the obsessive way she smokes that she's barely hanging on, but she assures me she couldn't be better. As we sit down at the dinner table, I ask K-H and Marianne if they've spoken to Rolf.

"No, I'm afraid he blames all of us for Heidi's death," K-H tells me.

"Why does he blame you?" I ask.

"Because Vera and Isaac asked her to do some investigating."

"Heidi discovered something that ended her life," Marianne adds, "though we'll never find out what it was."

A statement I hear as a challenge ... Did she learn the identity of the person who'd helped Georg to undermine The Ring? I let the conversation pass me by and look below the glass. Maybe it wasn't something she knew but something she'd *done* that got her murdered. Could she have been the traitor who denounced Raffi and told the Gestapo where to find Vera? Someone did, so why not her? Which might mean that another member of The Ring took revenge and poisoned her.

"Oh, get this, Sophele," K-H says indignantly, drawing my attention away from my speculations, "I got kicked off the deaf swim team for being Jewish."

"And I got thrown off the bird-watching club for giants," Vera adds sarcastically.

"Vera, I'd been on the team for seven years. I love swimming. It was a disappointment."

"Oh, shut up! All we do is complain. We don't *do* anything anymore. I hate it!"

Over the next hour, Vera snaps at the others a couple more times for their abandonment of the struggle. "Working with foreign journalists isn't getting us anywhere!" she tells them. "And working separately makes no sense."

Depression settles over me because the solidarity these old friends once shared has vanished. K-H doesn't even take pictures. I hadn't realized that working together against the Nazis had given them not just a mission, but also such optimistic delight in one another, and now, disappointed in themselves, they will have to discover a new way to be together – if they can. Do they know that Isaac and I are lovers? I don't sense any drumbeats of scandal beneath our conversation. After the first Menorah candle is lit and Isaac leads us in Hanukkah prayers, it's time for me to go home. He leads me to his door. I'm already two glasses of wine more dizzy than usual, which may be why I kiss him on the lips.

He starts as if pierced by an arrow, but I want our friends to know I'm an outlaw – and to encourage them to keep battling any way they can. And maybe I even wish to live up to K-H's assessment and be seen as myself. That was Mama's goal and maybe it's also my most important inheritance from her.

The next day, after school, I let myself in to Isaac's apartment and find him in his usual sculptural position: sitting at his desk, hunched over his manuscripts. Except that this time he's holding a big ivory-handled magnifying glass, and when he turns to me, he puts it over his nose, which grows the size of a pear. His eyes twinkle from the pleasure of making me laugh, but he doesn't jump up to kiss me. Unusual. He lowers the lens as though the air has been let out of him. "Sophele, if I were ruining your life, you'd tell me, wouldn't you?" he asks in a hesitant, concerned voice, which makes me feel as if we're tiptoeing toward danger.

"Where'd that come from?" I ask.

Last night, K-H, Marianne, and Vera though I might be taking advantage of you."

I roll my eyes, then comb his tufts of wild hair with my hand. We sit together, me on his lap. On my insistence, we talk of his childhood, which makes me feel sleepy in a good way. "I'm not too heavy, am I?" I ask every few minutes, and he just scoffs as if I'm being silly.

I like hearing his stories over and over. I like being able to lean against the reassurance of knowing what's coming next; Mama's death has made me that fragile and childlike again.

After we make love, he slips his arm under my head, and we talk about his wife for the first time. "For many years, she was my shadow, and I was hers," he says. "Maybe we were even too close. Our son's death drew us together but isolated us." He shrugs sadly.

"Then one day, I woke up and I looked all around me, and there was nothing there. A terrible thing to cast no image in front of you or behind you. Like not being born. Like living as a *dybbuk* – a ghost who haunts the earth."

Knowing what he has lost makes me hold him tightly, and he doesn't resist. His generous ease with me is why jealousy doesn't poison us. Yet our intimacy makes me shiver after a time; the chill of being too naked in front of a lover. I stand up and fetch his magnifying glass. Sitting by him on the bed, I look at his lips – giant petals of a fleshy flower. I ask why he needs it.

"I want to see if Berekiah Zarco wrote any references to the Seventh Gate in the margins of his manuscripts ... in tiny letters. I hate wearing my reading glasses and my vision isn't what it used to be."

"That's because your eyes are no longer German."

"True," he replies, morosely.

"And I didn't even know you had reading glasses."

"Because they only get in the way. Sophele, Vera asked me last night to help her blow up Gestapo headquarters. We need to persuade her to emigrate before she kills somebody."

Though maybe she already has murdered someone, I think, and I picture her wrapping her giant hands around Heidi's throat and squeezing. I'd ask Isaac if he suspects her, too, but I'm pretty sure he'd lie to protect her. "Do you have Rolf's address?" I ask him instead.

"Do me a favor and don't see him," he replies. He turns away from me abruptly, stands, and goes to the window. Opening the curtains a crack, he looks out.

"Why?" I ask.

"Because ... because I'd prefer you didn't. And I think that should be enough for you."

The harsh way he talks to me makes me ask a question I didn't know I had. "Isaac, you're not involved in Heidi's murder in any way, are you?"

"Me?" He turns to face me, outraged. "Heidi was a good friend of mine!"

"Still, if she were betraying you ..."

"Do you think she was?"

"I have no idea. In any case, I promise I won't break any Nuremberg laws with Rolf," I joke, trying to ease the ill-feeling between us.

"You shouldn't always try to be amusing," he snaps.

He walks to his desk, where he's left his pipe. Are we going to have our first fight? Perhaps, since I'm in no mood to cede him an inch of my right to be whoever I am. "I never thought I'd have to apologize to you for my sense of humor," I tell him. "In any case, since you're no longer a citizen, you don't get a vote on how I behave."

"You're unstoppable."

"Because I'm an Aryan. I've got honor and character."

He gives me such a contemptuous look that I feel as if I've swallowed dirt. I get up and dress without a word. Who'd have thought our first quarrel would be so sickeningly silent? At the very least, I'd hoped for some smashed Mesopotamian crockery and Yiddish curses: *May you grow six extra feet and not have enough money for comfortable shoes ...!* This is more like a fight between two crippled hens.

He lights his pipe and goes back to reading, so self-contained that it leaves me bitter.

"So what's Rolf's address?" I say when I'm dressed.

"Kronprinzenstraße, Number 34, second floor. But if you visit him," he tells me, as if it's an order, "then go straight from school. We can't be sure we're not being watched, so I don't want anyone following you from your apartment or mine. For all I know someone has a magnifying glass trained on us right now."

Rolf lives in a dimly lit, gritty neighborhood that was built for workers at the Knorr break factory in Rummelsberg. I can't go over in the early evening without Hansi, so he's been dragging after me since we reached the Frankfurter Allee Station. My explanations about why I'm bringing him so far from home must not have landed in solid ground inside that miniature brain of his, so I have to threaten to do my imitation of King Kong subduing a dinosaur every few minutes or he might just start a sit-down strike on the slush-filled sidewalk and wind up with pneumonia, which I'll have to pay for, since who else is going to care for him? Is he aware he's slowly torturing me to death?

We've taken a circuitous route to get here in order to throw off anyone who might be on our trail. It has taken a full hour, and so we're also half-frozen – another reason for Hansi's disaffection. Rolf lives in a handsome pink and white building with ironwork balconies. He answers my knocks right away, still mostly head and legs, but his hunchback has grown and makes him lean his head down cruelly to the left, as if he's listening for squeaking in the floorboards. He's clipped his hair as severely as a prisoner, and his eyes are smaller than I remember them – peepholes surrounded by deep wrinkles. He's aged many years since I last saw him.

A glorious smile of surprise brightens his round little face, but he's unable to lift his gaze all the way up to meet mine: "Sophele!"

I kneel down and we kiss cheeks. He stinks of cigar smoke. The whole apartment does. And it's so cold that he's wearing a long frock coat, midnight blue, undoubtedly Vera's handiwork. "I think you met my brother once," I say, reaching behind me for Hansi before he wanders off.

"Yes, of course. Come in, come in ...!" He unfolds his arm graciously.

"What brings you to this side of town?" he asks with a sweet smile.

"I just wanted to see how you were."

He turns on the ceiling light, a white Chinese lantern. "I'm glad you came. Sit ..." He points to a tattered black velvet couch with lumpy orange cushions. The coffee table between us is covered with dishes crusted with leftovers, including a rim of cheese that's grown a smelly gray beard, and a nub of cigar. Seeing Hansi sniff at the offending smells, Rolf picks up all the porcelain and cradles the mess into the kitchen, saying, "My cleaning lady didn't come this week ..."

A crash makes me jump. I get the feeling Rolf is part of a club of Berlin widowers who grow towers of dishes in their sinks. Isaac is, of course, a charter member.

He questions me about my schoolwork and my parents, and he pats my leg stiffly when I talk of Mama's death. I can see from his sheepish look that he thinks I might refuse a more intimate sign of his solidarity, so I kiss his cheek, which allows him to hug me. Happy with our renewed friendship, he shuffles eagerly off for his scrapbook, which documents his two decades in the circus. He sits between Hansi and me. The elephants and tigers in the background hold Hansi's attention, but Rolf always points to Heidi. "There she is ... you see her? And here I am."

He's a man who would notice his wife first even if she were photographed behind Jean Harlow. Rolf had a full head of luscious brown hair back then. A squashed, neckless Samson. In several pictures, he's wearing gold Moroccan slippers, the kind with long curling toes.

"We had an act in which I played the servant of a clown who

thought he was a pasha," he explains. "When I think of the idiotic things I did ..." He rolls his eyes.

Heidi wears her blond hair in braids in the old pictures. "She'd have made a much better Young Maiden than me," I tell Rolf, which makes him grin.

Next, he brings in piles of napkins that he saved from the restaurants he dined in on his circus travels. My favorite is of ruby-colored lace. It glows like stained glass when I hold it up to the light. "That one's from Prague," he tells me.

Rolf as a young man, dressed for
a circus performance

He also shows us his cane collection – more than fifty. He keeps them in a beer barrel in his bedroom. His two favorites have white, ceramic monkey-heads. The devilish creatures are smiling cheekily, as if they're hiding some glorious gossip under their tongues. "I bought them in Warsaw, in a Jewish antique shop," Rolf tells us. "I was told they're magic wands." He holds one out to me and says, "Make a wish, Sophele, then blow on the monkey."

I'd wish for Heidi to return, but that's not likely to happen, so I think, *Let Isaac and me outlast the Nazis*. It's in that moment that I learn I've given up any hope of sending Hitler back to his Vienna garret anytime soon.

Hansi reaches out for the cane, and Rolf lets him have it. The boy presses his lips to the monkey head for far longer than would be considered normal by most people.

"You can keep it if you want," our host tells him sweetly, which prompts the boy to fold his lips inside his mouth and make a moaning noise. "Does he need to pee?" Rolf asks me.

"That just means 'thank you' in the Hansi Universe."

"You're welcome," Rolf tells the boy, patting his leg.

"Sophele," he suddenly gasps, "I think I see something for you, too." Reaching behind my ear, he produces the napkin from Prague. "*Voilà!*" he says, beaming.

I kiss his cheek again and spread the fabric on my lap. "I'd forgotten what a magician you are." Leaning forward to look across at my brother, I say, "Did you see what Rolf did?"

But he's courting the monkey with his enraptured eyes and says nothing.

"Sophele, why don't I teach you the trick!" Rolf exclaims. "You'll be able to keep your kids entertained."

After fifteen minutes, my hands have grasped the basic idea, and I practice so many times over the coming weeks that I learn to pull my mom's old watch from behind Hansi's ear.

Rolf and I talk for a time about the disadvantages of being three foot tall in a big city like Berlin, then about Paris, Budapest, Munich ... Hansi falls fast asleep. As Rolf gazes at the boy, his eyes turn to liquid. He whispers, "Your brother is beautiful, beautiful, beautiful." *Schön, schön, schön ...*

Only a poet of the heart would say *schön* three times, and now I understand more about why Heidi adored him. And I can speak of important matters. "Rolf, Heidi was wonderful. I won't ever forget her."

"This may sound silly to you," he replies, "but I never realized that her dying would be so very final. The lesson I've learned is that death is the only thing that never ends. You understand?" He locks his fingers, then pulls them apart. "The world has come undone ... has been emptied of meaning. Like the story I just told you about Paris ... All my stories are stones I toss out into the world in the hopes that one of them might make a dent that will prove I'm still alive. But they only prove the opposite – that I'm not really here."

He talks so eloquently, and with such an effort to be understood by me, that I'm moved to tears myself. But I feel useless, too. So little good I can do for him ...

"I'm being a terrible host," he says, regaining his enthusiasm. "I'll make us some tea, and I'll put more coals in the stove. You poor things must be frozen."

He and I go to the kitchen together, and while he busies himself with cups and saucers, I scrape the bearded cheese into the garbage and start soaking his dishes, which makes him tug me away from the sink. He's a strong little man – a tiny tractor. Our struggle – back and forth – makes me burst out laughing. "We'd make a good comedy team," I say.

After I get my way, and all the crusted porcelain is soaking nicely, he says, "Sophele, let me give you some of Heidi's silk flowers."

He leads me into his bedroom. Hansi is snoring, which makes Rolf grin as though he's the cutest thing in the world, so I whisper, "Be glad you don't have to sleep in the same room with the midnight express to Cologne. Sometimes I wish he'd derail."

Rolf's bed is only four feet square. His dresser comes up to my hip. We're in Lilliput and I'm the awkward, oversized foreigner here.

"Look at this," he says excitedly, and he turns the key in the bottom drawer, which is his hiding place for hundreds of silk blossoms. "When Heidi wasn't cooking, she was sewing flowers. Vera taught her how. Take some. She'd want you to have them."

I take a blue lily and a white rose.

"Vera says she hasn't seen you in a while," I say as he re-locks the drawer. I use a light tone so as not to upset him.

He glares up at me. "So you've spoken to her about me?" he asks, as if I've committed a crime.

"Just once. The other night, she came to Isaac's apartment."

"I've nothing to say to her. Or any of the others." He waddles out of the room angrily.

"But why?" I call from behind him. "They're worried about you."

In the kitchen again, Rolf angles his head up to meet my gaze as best he can, his tiny eyes flashing, his neck trembling from the effort to look up. "I'll never forgive Vera for not opening her door to Heidi on the day she vanished. If she had, then ..." He doesn't finish his sentence because nothing now can save his wife from being murdered.

"Vera told me she asked you and Heidi to look into who might be betraying The Ring. Do you know if she'd discovered anything that might have gotten her into trouble?"

"We didn't have much time to really ask around."

"Do you have any idea who might have been informing the Nazis of The Ring's activities?"

"No." The water for our tea has come to a boil and Rolf begins to pour it into his pot.

"Do you think that Vera might have something to do with Heidi's death?"

Rolf starts, spilling water on the oven, which hisses. "Shit!" he exclaims under his breath.

"Sorry. Did you get some on yourself?"

"No, I'm all right." He secures the wooden handle of his pan with both his hands and holds it out from his body like a sword. When he's done filling his teapot, he gazes out the window, capturing his thoughts. He looks younger in profile, and I can easily imagine him as a mop-haired little boy, dashing through his parents' legs, delighted by simple things like silk flowers and cakes. I hope his parents recognized his bright nature as a gift.

"I considered the possibility that Vera may have been involved," he tells me. "But Vera and Heidi were close. They had an understanding about women's things, about ..." He sighs at his failure to find the right word. "I can't imagine Vera discarding Heidi in some lake. If I believed that, I couldn't ... couldn't go on."

After Rolf, Hansi, and I have had our tea, it's time to go, since we have to reach home before Papa. At the door, Rolf waves me close to him and says, "Something odd has happened that I haven't told anyone about."

"What?"

"Sebastian Stangl, the doctor who fooled me and Heidi, who had her sterilized ... He vanished, too, but no body has been found."

"Did you read about him in the newspaper?"

"No, I went to his office just after I received the results of Heidi's autopsy. I wanted to confront him for betraying us, but one of his nurses told me he'd already been missing for ten days. Two policemen came to interview me shortly after that. They searched my apartment and then brought me down to the station for more questioning. Then they released me. If they had any proof, I'd be in jail now. I'm pretty sure they'd need to have a body to accuse me of murder, in any case."

"But you didn't kill Dr Stangl, did you?"

"No, but I wish I had. Not that the police believe me. They're still watching me. I can't help thinking that there's a kind of symmetry to what's happened."

"A symmetry?"

"Dr Stangl is now dead most likely, just like Heidi. I wouldn't be surprised if he were lying in the Rummelsburger See. In fact, I'd wager everything I own, even Heidi's flowers, that if the police find out what happened to him, they'll discover who killed my wife, as well!"

On reaching home, I look up Dr Stangl's number in the phone book, but I find only his office number. When I call, no one answers. I try several times the next day without any luck. It's only on the following morning that a nurse named Katja Müller finally picks up and tells me I was lucky to find her in; she's putting files into storage. She gives me Dr Stangl's home number, since I tell her I'd like to express my sympathy to his wife. Mrs Stangl doesn't answer that day, but I find her in the next afternoon. Her suspicion of my motives chills the line between us. When I explain about being a friend of Heidi's, thinking that will warm her tone, she bursts out that she's sure that Rolf has killed her husband.

After she calms down, she explains that Dr Stangl received a phone call on the day he vanished. "He left the house right away because the patient who called was in distress. Sebastian was like that ... he'd go out in the middle of the night to rescue a friend."

And then he'd sterilize them against their will, I think. "Who did your husband say the call was from?" I ask.

"Rolf."

"Did your husband actually mention his last name?"

"No, but he said it was the dwarf. And to think of how many times my husband saw him after hours! If I could count the number of visits that little bastard made to our home for help … in the morning, at night … And my husband never turned him away. Never!"

"I think someone pretending to be Rolf lured Dr Stangl out on the evening he vanished," I tell Isaac.

No answer. He talks little these days and spends nearly all his time studying Berekiah Zarco's manuscripts. If I didn't prepare him hard-boiled eggs and toast, he'd starve to death. Even so, his ribs have begun to show, and he looks a bit like a Picasso goat. Sexy in a desperate way. We've got the heat back on temporarily, though it's still a bit chilly, and at this moment he's sitting on the end of the bed in his bathrobe, scanning *The Third Gate* with his ivory-handled magnifying glass from Istanbul. I'm lying behind him on my side, propped on my elbow. My bare feet are warming against his back, because he's the best oven in the world. No coal necessary. Just sex, toast, and eggs.

"Isaac, do you have any idea who might be able to imitate Rolf's voice?" I ask loudly.

He looks back at me, annoyed that I'm disturbing him. "What makes you think Rolf didn't do it?"

"He said he didn't, and I believe him. Is that stupid of me?"

"Maybe a bit naïve." He turns the page of his text and leans forward, so low that he looks as though he's sniffing his ancestor's sixteenth century Turkish ink.

"Could Dr Stangl have been the person betraying The Ring?" I ask.

"Sophie, I'm trying to read!"

"Raffi is dead, and so is Vera's baby. And now Heidi … I want some answers!"

"I never let Stangl in on our plans. I'm not that big a *Dummkopf.*"

"But maybe someone else did. You said that your circus friends had him as their doctor."

He flaps his hand at me over his shoulder. A sign I should keep quiet, but I like testing his patience. "Did you like him?" I ask. "His wife seemed to think he was a saint."

"A saint!" he exclaims in an outraged voice as he whips around. "He was a horror. Though it's true that he was kind to us when I first met him." He shrugs. "People change ... *he* changed."

Standing, he goes to his desk to look at another manuscript. He opens his bathrobe so he can scratch his balls. Then he tugs on their hairs. Maybe Tonio will enjoy the same mild torture when he's pushing seventy.

"Isaac," I say, sitting up, and when he doesn't look at me, I make the cackling noise of a Berlin crow; I've discovered it works better than words.

"What is it?" he asks without turning around.

"Why do you think someone would kill both Heidi and Dr Stangl?"

He looks at me pleadingly. "Stop! I've told you before, I don't like you running around Berlin asking questions about murders." He gives me his fatal, squinty-eyed glare, but I've been vaccinated against his indignation by now.

"I'll stop when I get to the end of the mystery," I tell him. "That's my Araboth."

He lets his body sag. Another strategy to get his way – he wants sympathy for the frail old tailor who started working when he was ten. "I worry about you," he says.

"I promise I'll be careful."

"Sophele, if you ever get into trouble, you are to come to me. Or call me. No matter what has happened, I'll help you. Do you remember what *mesirat nefesh* means?"

"The willingness to go into the Land of the Dead to rescue a loved one." I know what's coming next, so I add, "You won't need to make any sacrifice for me."

"But if you do get into trouble ..."

"You'll be the first to know. I promise."

His eyes brighten. "I want to give you a present. I thought of waiting until your birthday, but it's too far away."

"I think I can see what you've got for me," I say, since his *putz* has begun to stir.

"Oh, you can have that old thing anytime you want it," he says, stretching out his penis to do his silly imitation of an elephant trunk, then letting it fall. "No, I've got a real present for you!" Kneeling down, he takes out a red-wrapped box from the bottom drawer of his desk and holds it out to me. "Open it."

Inside, I find a wooden case of forty-eight oil pastels, all the colors Chagall, Cézanne, and Sophie Riedesel might want, even that particularly helpless shade of gray that glazes over Isaac's eyes when I lead him away from Berekiah Zarco to our bed.

After he's spent and moaning on his back like a shipwrecked man on the Island of Insatiable Lovers – more to amuse both of us than from actual exhaustion – I take out the oil pastels and try to make a color portrait for the first time. But my hands and eyes are confounded by too many possibilities. It's as if I've been handed a deck with 200 cards, and I make such a tangle of lines and colors that Isaac ends up grimacing and hiding his eyes from his lopsided likeness. Nobody born after the age of silent movies could make such a melodramatic face. The man has talent.

I try right away to sketch him again, but I'm unable to translate the textures and emotions of his face – the soft, tender folds of his eyelids, the shell-shadows inside his ears, his tired affection for

me – into blue, red, and yellow. In fact, it takes months before I
begin to feel as if I am coming to learn how to deal with color. Isaac
says that it's no wonder; the spectrum is one of the most powerful
emanations of God, and the ability of white light to separate into
its constituent parts is a very great mystery.

He also tells me that color symbolizes the joy of creation.
"Imagine Adam when he saw the blue sky for the first time! Or
Eve, when she held that red apple!"

"Was Eve wrong to eat the apple?" A question I've wanted to
ask him for a long time.

"No, no, no. If she didn't take the apple, we'd never have left
Eden, and men and women would never know there was a world
around them, or have any sense of themselves. In any case, Eve
didn't *do* anything that we all don't do."

"No?"

"Each of us in our lives takes a bite of that same apple in the
moment before we first recognize ourselves in a mirror. We are all
Eve, just as we are all Adam. And as we chew the apple, we say to
ourselves, '*I exist, and I am separate from God.*'"

"So the snake isn't evil?"

"No, the snake is eternity – the earth-born spark of eternity that
starts the fire ... the blaze in each of us. The snake is life recognizing
itself, and knowing that we have a great deal of work to do while
we're here. Remember, the only hands and eyes God has are our own."

"So why do people regard the snake as evil?"

"Because they think the world is made of prose when it's made
of poetry."

"I don't understand."

"Because you've only just reached the Third Gate," he says,
kissing the center of my forehead. "You're just a little *pisher* who's
figuring out how to use her pastels."

"When will I reach the Fourth Gate?"

"When you marry and have children." Groaning he adds, "Though you'll see it approaching when you start to have all the headaches that come with falling in love."

CHAPTER SIXTEEN

By the end of February, I grow to love the layering I can achieve with my pastels. And just as Isaac would wish I'm astonished by how they constantly remind me of all that lies below the surface of what we see and hear and feel. I learn that a landscape of nearly invisible color lies underneath what looks like the uniform black enveloping Ribera's figure of St Sebastian in the Emperor Frederick Museum, where Isaac takes me to see the Spanish, Italian, and Dutch masters. And I learn, too, that there is so much effort we don't notice in Rembrandt's canvases unless we study them closely – so much drawing, blending, and shading needed to summon forth the images that he saw straining to be born ... And so much experience. A lifetime of sadness and hope in the eyes of the old rabbi whose portrait he has painted, and who watches me as if he knew I'd one day come to visit him. And all that work an attempt to give shape to the border between the artist and the world. That's what I grow to value in those hard little sticks that become extensions of my fingers. They speak to me in voices as quiet as the slanting yellow light in van Ruisdael's *Oak Forest* and as loud as my growing love for Isaac. And they whisper to me what each sheet of paper wishes to become. Another great mystery: how paintings determine themselves; how everything – including us – unfolds toward completion.

And I have Isaac to thank for this chance to begin again; if left alone, I'd have denied myself the world of color, I now realize.

Still, I don't inform myself over the coming months about how I'll need to proceed if I want to compete for a place at the School of Applied Arts next year. That goal just seems now like a dream that vanished while I wasn't looking.

Tonio takes me skating one clear cold day in February 1936, and as we're gliding arm-in-arm across the ice he brings up marriage again. He assures me that his mother adores me.

"But what about your father?" I ask.

"Oh, he doesn't like anyone. But he'll accept you once we tie the knot. And he'll love you once you give him a grandson."

The thought of Dr Hessel getting his big coarse hands around any son of mine sends a message of doom shooting right to the top of my head. And it doesn't help my mood to learn that Tonio's plans for us may really be about pleasing his father.

"We'll discuss it when you're free of your commitment to the army," I tell him. And I think my performance is excellent, but I see in his distant look that he doesn't believe me. And that I've hurt him. I always tend to forget how sensitive he is. "Forgive me," I say, bringing his fingertips to my lips. "Mama's death has left me so disoriented that I don't know where I am half the time."

The letter ordering my brother to appear in court for a sterilization hearing comes in early March. The date set is Monday the 16th. I rush away from Hansi to the bathroom and lock the door so that I can be alone with my terror, then leave the letter on the kitchen table to await Papa. Has the notification come now because Mama is no longer around to oppose her son's operation?

When my brother is finished changing out of his school clothes, he drops down in front of his jigsaw puzzle. I join him. I try to hold his hand, but he keeps snatching it back. I could get him in a head lock and force him to hug me but that wouldn't change anything; the Taj Mahal will always be more interesting than his sister.

Papa reads the Health Ministry's letter as soon as he gets home, then slips it into his coat pocket and stands up to flee to his bedroom. I cover my pot of chicken and say, "What are we going to do?"

His resentful look means I don't have permission to put him on the spot. "Do about what?" he asks, feigning incomprehension, undoubtedly hoping I'll turn away from him and simply add another onion to the stew.

"Do about preventing a surgeon from removing your grandchildren from Hansi's future."

"Sophie, have you looked at your brother lately?" he asks defiantly.

"I look at him more than you do!" I snap back.

"How wonderful to be so attentive! You win the goodness contest between us."

"I don't want to win anything. I'd just like you to spend more time with him. Papa, he knows that you think he's an embarrassment."

"Sophie, shut up! You don't know what he knows. Or what I feel about him. Can you honestly tell me he'd make a proper father?"

"Have you made a proper father?"

His clenched jaw means he'd like to clout me, and my glare means I'd like him to do just that, because then I could be free to despise him without being menaced by guilt all the time. He reaches into his coat pocket for a cigarette to steady his nerves. Good for Greta for convincing him to smoke openly again!

"How easy it has become for you to judge me," he says, sorrow in his voice, the cigarette dangling from his lips.

He looks and sounds almost like his past self, which means that this is where a generous screenwriter would have me apologize and melt into my father's arms, but I feel as if I'm a bitter, vengeful ghost – the role my mother ought to have but has handed over to me, since the spirits of betrayed, cancer-ridden wives are not permitted in our ever-optimistic Germany these days: too subversive, too real, and too complex. I'm surprised that Hitler hasn't banned cancer entirely. I watch Papa light his cigarette, and I can tell he enjoys my waiting for him because it means he's in control of our relationship. But I'd bet my K-H Collection that my thoughts would surprise him. *He's still a good man, despite everything, and I can't help but love him.* I come to such an unlikely conclusion because my contempt for him makes me feel my old affection that much more strongly, imbedded in the deepest, most silent part of myself, so mixed with my own blood and breath, and so much more resilient than words that nothing could ever dispel it – not even our final betrayals.

My father's tragedy is that he knows he is miles from the man he might have been. And my tragedy is that I see that distance in his eyes every time I look at him.

"Papa," I reply, "I'll stop being rude if you'll only tell me what you intend to do about the hearing." I speak with pleading and prayer in my voice because I've realized our family won't survive Hansi's sterilization. Because I will send the walls of this cramped apartment crashing down and destroy what was probably Mama's last hope – that our family might outlive her death – unless I convince this chain-smoking coward to help me.

He sits down. A concession on his part, since it means he's willing to have a long talk with me. I'm grateful. "Thank you for staying, Papa," I say.

"You don't have to thank me." He smokes greedily. "Sophie, after all the difficulties we've had with Hansi, you can't really believe that he has a right to have children."

"Papa, he's not an imbecile," I say desperately. "There's hidden life inside him."

"I didn't say he was stupid. I just think we'll never know exactly what he is or isn't. And neither would his children. Having Hansi as a parent would not be fair to them."

A good argument, but I've been saving a better one since my outburst at school. "If Germany can grant a puny, repulsive propagandist like Dr Goebbels the right to have children, then I think Hansi should have the same right."

Ein widerwärtiger Propaganda-Winzling. My description of our Propaganda Minister has a wonderfully condescending ring to it, but Papa thinks I've gone too far. He jumps up so quickly that I've no time to defend myself. He slaps me across the face, which makes me gasp and drop the wooden spoon I've been holding. Then he grabs my wrist and shakes me hard. "Don't you ever say anything like that again!" he shouts.

"Don't touch me!" I yell back, and I twist out of his grasp. I want to curse him, but humiliation has robbed me of my voice. I look down for a long time, unable to think.

"I warned you," he says.

The excuse all bullies use. But the only thing that matters is Hansi. My heartbeat, swaying me from side to side, reminds me of that. I kneel down to pick up my spoon. "If you get the notification annulled," I tell Papa, "then I won't oppose your marriage to Greta."

He laughs caustically. "Who said anything about marriage? Besides, you think it's that easy to overturn an order from the ministry? Sophie, there are laws in this country – laws all Reich citizens need to obey." As if reading from a cue card, he adds, "Obeying our Führer's laws is our freedom."

No wonder the films the Nazis make are all so stilted and artificial. Men like Papa can't even read a heroic line properly. "Is that from *Mein Kampf*?" I ask.

He shakes his head patronizingly. "Despite all your supposed sophistication, you're just like your mother."

"You talk as if she was beneath you," I say challengingly.

Something in the way he stretches his arms over his head, smokes, and says nothing ... I feel as if I've opened Pandora's box and he's taking his time to decide which monsters of our past to summon to his side to join the fight against me.

"She never understood how the world works," he finally observes, adding threateningly, "And you don't either. So let's just leave it at that before someone takes a bad fall."

Papa wants me to know that he's taking it easy on me – is being generous – but I get the feeling he has been meaning to insult Mama to my face since her death. He wants to justify his sexual escapades to me by rendering her unworthy of his love.

"Does it make you feel good about yourself to condemn a woman who is no longer around to defend herself?" I ask.

"Sophie, you don't know anything, though you sure as hell think you do. Your mother knew she didn't understand the ways of the world. She agreed with me!"

"So you convinced her she wasn't up to your standards. Good work. Are you sure Greta is up to your image of what a German woman should be?"

"Greta loves me, which your mother didn't. That's the only standard I have. So you can dislike me for finding affection at my age if you want. Greta is a bright, lively woman, even if she isn't up to *your* standards. That's what you really want to say, isn't it?"

Papa, too, can launch a dart into the center of the truth on occasion. But who would want to describe a lover as *munter*

– lively? Is Papa a dull man with mediocre desires, despite all his big talk of creating a paradise for the *Volk?* Maybe that's what he's tried to hide from the world all his life. A fourth-place gymnast and nothing more ...

"You're the last person who can judge me, in any case," he adds.

Does he know about Isaac? "What are you trying to say?" I ask.

"That I've known for years what you do with Tonio. It's a disgrace. You should marry him while he'll still have a sluttish girl like you."

He uses the ugly German word *schmutzig* for sluttish, which also implies I'm filth. I wish he'd simply have hit me again; it takes me twenty years to pull *schmutzig* out of my gut.

Now that he's really hurt me, he turns to leave, but there's one more question that will keep me up nights forever if I don't ask it. "Why did you marry Mama if she didn't love you?"

"Because *I* loved her. And I *thought* she loved me. We both mistook her gratitude for love." He gives an ironic laugh. "We were two kids with very bad eyesight."

"Did you manage to convince her before she died that she was wrong to want to save Hansi from sterilization?"

"I convinced her that there was no point in wrecking everything we'd worked for by fighting a legal battle we'd only lose."

"Everything *you've* worked for, you mean."

He sighs with exasperation. "In a German family, that amounts to the same thing."

Another cue card, but this one he has managed to read much more convincingly. Maybe he just needs more practice.

"So before she died, she knew Hansi would be sterilized?" I ask.

"Of course. And if you'll think for a minute, and stop hating me for telling you the truth, then you'll realize you had no reason to hope otherwise."

*

Tonio hugs me hard when he hears what's about to happen to Hansi, but he spoils our closeness when he informs me in a rigid, military voice that difficult sacrifices must sometimes be made for the good of the nation. I push him away, and he apologizes right away, which is why I don't get up off the bed and put my clothes back on even though I know I should.

Dr Hassgall tells me that hiring a lawyer will prove useless; parents of two of his students have tried that route and failed. Could I earn enough money in France to care for my brother and me? Isaac wakes me from my fantasies of becoming a waitress in Paris. "Hansi is a minor," he points out. "You'd have to leave him behind with his father."

"I could never leave him behind."

"But you've got to make your own life!"

That incenses me. "I've already made my own life. For better or worse, this is it!"

I end up begging my father to intercede again. But Papa tells me not to worry, that he knows what's best for his son. I can see he's about to add, *Which happens to be what's best for Germany!*, so I cut him off by saying, "I understand – there's no need to say anything more."

Maybe part of why I remain in Germany long after I know I should leave is so I can go on despising my father. Contempt can be very sustaining, as I come to learn.

I do not attend Hansi's hearing at the Heredity Court on the 16th of March, since it falls on a school day. Also, Papa prefers to go without me.

"Everything went very smoothly," he tells me as soon as they come home that afternoon, adding that the date for my brother's vasectomy has been set for two weeks away, the 30th of March. A happy Hansi comes traipsing in as we're talking, loose-limbed and gangly, as he is when he's exhausted. He hands me his coat, then shuffles off to his room to lie down, leaving a trail of muddy footprints behind him.

"Take those shoes off!" I call after him. "And if you get your sheets and blankets dirty I'm going to stuff you in the goddamned fish tank!"

"I thought it better that we get it over with fast," Papa tells me, "so I had them set the first available date."

"Good thinking," I reply. "Why wait to lose your grandchildren!"

On the 30th of March, I get up early and draw my brother with my pastels while he's snoring away. I give him fire-red hair, flaming hands, and hollow sockets for eyes. Papa comes into our room, wakes him with a kiss, and tells him he's to have a checkup this morning with a wonderful government doctor. "He's very important," Papa says enticingly. "You should be honored."

My brother buys that line; he's either too sleepy or too damn dumb, or both. When my father gazes down at my sketch, he says, "That doesn't look at all like my Hansi."

My Hansi...? "No, it looks like *my* Hansi," I reply angrily. "And *my* Hansi has the power to destroy all the people who want to hurt him." I turn to the boy. "Right?" I ask, and the flashes in my eyes mean, *Please agree with me*, but he just shrugs.

Papa looks at me as if I'm mad. Does he fear the curse of his wife's family? I hope so.

In the taxi over to the Buch State Hospital, Hansi grows excited – we hardly ever get to ride in a car. He rolls and unrolls his window while we're zooming out of town on Prenzlauer Allee, giggling, and he sticks his head out so the wind can blow back his hair. I hold onto his coat just in case he decides it would be fun to hurl himself onto the street.

Buch is a castle-like building with comforting ivy growing up the handsome brown brick. Civilized and stately. Clever architecture for a sterilization center. Even sniffing rabbit-like as we go inside and scenting all those sour hospital odors doesn't set Hansi off. Only when he sees a physician in a surgical mask at the top of the central staircase does he start jiggling his hands and moaning.

"Stay calm!" Papa orders him.

A miscalculation. Papa's gruff voice is all the proof the boy needs that he's walked into a trap with his name scripted on iron jaws, and he begins to holler as if there's a rainstorm blowing through his head. When I take his arm, he starts flailing, and he catches me on my bottom lip, so hard that I taste blood right away. I staunch the gash with my ruby-colored Prague napkin – ruined forever – while two nurses help Papa get the boy under control. One of them jabs Hansi's arm with a needle and then he's led up the stairs to the surgical theater.

I slink off to the waiting lounge, blotting blood, feeling as dull and wooden as the sound of my footsteps. A mind unsure of the present sometimes seeks assistance from the past, and I recall a time when Hansi – maybe six or seven – is running across Marienburger Straße without paying attention to the traffic. Maybe he's chasing after a bird call or has spotted a rabbit. A big black car comes from the left and swerves to keep from hitting him. I see the peril before Hansi does. The tires squeal as space contracts around my head, and the honey-slowness of the skidding automobile makes me feel as if I'm as small and powerless as a single thought. I start to yell, but it's already too late; Hansi has made it safely across the street.

The driver gets out to talk to my brother. All I remember is that the man is in short-sleeves and that he doesn't raise his voice. He must only want to warn my brother of what can happen to children in a big city, but Hansi drops down on the sidewalk and clamps his hands over his ears. The boy looks back and forth, trying to find me – 180 degrees of yearning anguish. When he doesn't spot me, he knocks his fists against his head, and at that same moment, I feel the condensation of a thousand vague impressions into a revelation I do not want to have: this boy does not experience the world like other people do.

When the car passed me, I felt a special wind in my hair, like Mama's fingers, and I heard a sound like the ocean, and now a stranger is talking to me and I don't want to hear anything he says, and I can't find the girl who always takes me outside …

That's what I imagine his thoughts are. All he later says is, "I got confused," too embarrassed to say more. He stands in front of me squirming, his legs like coiled snakes.

The moment that he sits down on the Marienburger Straße sidewalk I know for sure that he is different from other children. And that I am too. Because I am the big sister of a boy who is not quite at home on the earth.

To this day, Hansi is still dashing across a street in my mind, risking death. He turns this way and that, scared and lost, a boy barely treading water in an urban ocean that conceals in its depths all the bad things that can happen to brothers and sisters.

I wonder if he ever knew that I wanted to call out to him in time and failed, and that I was sorry.

Sitting in the waiting room, where Papa soon joins me, I tell myself that a boy who survived so many dangers will also survive a surgeon. And he will fare better than Isaac, me, and Vera over the course of this slow war. All the children who will be summoned for operations – pointy-headed kids and epileptics, girls who converse with Jesus in their heads and boys born mute ... They will bear no responsibility for the crime done to them. None of them will ever have to deny they are Jews or name the people they betrayed. Or stay up at night wondering if they could have done more.

What is good in Hansi will never be destroyed. Three times I tell that to myself before I walk home without waiting for him. And I remind myself that he is *schön*, *schön*, *schön* ...

When Hansi and Papa return from the clinic the boy is heavy from the sedation, but his eyes show no sign of distress. I run my hands over him to make sure he is still with me, just as I did when he was almost run over by a car.

"How's your lip?" Papa asks me, squinting at the crusted gash as he takes his coat off. He reaches for me, meaning to make peace, but I lean away.

"So it's all over?" I ask him in a flat voice.

Papa nods and goes to the kitchen. I hear the sink turned on. He's washing the hospital off his hands. In a minute, he'll feel he's perfectly clean. Astonishing what a little water, soap, and propaganda can do.

"Will you sit with me and watch Groucho and Chico?" I ask the boy, and he gives me one of his big nods. Then, in sign language, he signals, "There's a hole in my stomach."

"I've made onion soup." Smiling cheekily, I add, "I think that that's someone's favorite, but I can't remember who."

He leans his head into my chest and sniffs at my neck like a cat. He always loved to curl into Mama's arms. And now that's a role I'll have to take on, which petrifies me.

"We'll eat soup and then watch the goldfish," tell him. I look to my father, who has just returned to us. "And Papa will keep us company," I add.

"Yes, of course," he says.

Seeing my gratitude, he smiles. He believes I've reconsidered my anger and forgiven him. Bad eyesight, as he himself admitted.

I have a talk with Hansi that evening. I want to give him the chance to ask me about his operation. He's sitting up in bed, getting ready to go to sleep, which is always the best time to get him to signal more than a few words. I'm sitting next to him and I've handed him the pad he uses to write down what he means when I don't understand his sign language. We talk about school. He doesn't mention his visit to the hospital. He tells me he's learning to read music and play the recorder. He and another boy share an instrument.

"Who's the other boy?"

"Volker," he jots down.

"Maybe Volker could come to dinner sometime. Would you like that?"

He shrugs. The idea never even occurred to him.

"Can you get me his parents' phone number?"

"Maybe."

While I'm considering what two distant children might talk about when they're alone, he notices the gash on my lip and reaches up with a forefinger to touch it, which makes me wince, though now he's as gentle as a whisper.

"Who hurt you?" he writes down, then gives me a worried look.

Despising my father frees me to fight in the war again, and the undeniable proof of that is that I wake up one morning with the Semitic Wall gone from my head. And the first thing I do is burn my swastika armband.

To celebrate my tossing those ashes out the window, I bake Mrs Munchenberg some *Mandelschnitten* – almond cookies. She has let her hair go gray, and she combs it into a crest at the front, which makes her look dramatic – an aging opera star who's still the talk of the town. Framed photos of Raffi form a kind of altar on the wall above her couch. She asks me about my mother's illness in a hushed voice, her hand over her mouth, as if not to wake the dead. Then I offer her my plate of cookies, which she takes with an embarrassed smile. "You shouldn't have gone to all this trouble."

"No trouble. And I'm not much of a baker, so don't thank me yet."

She takes one and breaks it in half, and we munch together. "Delicious," she says.

And there we are again, soldiers from a Remarque novel, sharing a cigarette at the front, which is why I say, "I think of Raffi all the time."

She manages a fleeting smile.

"Come up anytime my father isn't home," I tell her. "We'll have tea. Don't worry about compromising me. I prefer being compromised."

Over the coming months I mail Rini a dozen photographs that I cut from movie magazines – most memorably, Robert Taylor and Greta Garbo in *Camille*, a tearjerker that made me cry buckets.

She continues to sends me stills – mostly of half-forgotten silent film stars. One spring afternoon, a big, glossy one of Pola Negri as *The Gypsy Dancer* comes in the mail, autographed in blue pen. Pola has a dozen gold leaves for earrings and arabesque eyebrows – like butterfly wings. Where does Rini get such treasures?

Hansi and I go to visit K-H, Marianne, and Werner, who's now three-and-a-half years old, and who never, seemingly, runs out of steam. K-H takes photographs of me holding Werner in my arms down by the Spree. It's a glorious day, and I'm as happy as I've been since Mama's death. My hair has grown out by now and I keep it shoulder length. Hansi converses more with K-H and Marianne than he does with me, since they're fluent in sign language, of course. Why didn't I take him to see them earlier? Is it the jealousy in the pit of my stomach?

Tonio gets into the habit of taking my brother and me out to lunch on Sunday afternoon whenever he is on leave. I'm certain that the first time he invites us out is to make up for his telling me that Hansi had to be sacrificed, but he soon discovers that he enjoys showing me off to other army men. It's flattering that he considers me pretty enough to give him cachet, and it's exciting to be kissed in public, but it's also a troubling reminder of what I cannot do with Isaac. Often, I think I must be a mad-as-a-hatter young woman to be able to give myself to two such different men.

Once, while Hansi, Tonio, and I are having dessert at a café in the Tiergarten, Tonio shocks me by asking if I see a lot of Isaac and Vera, whom he calls "that tall ugly woman."

"Hardly ever," I say. "Only when I bump into one of them in our building."

He looks at me skeptically, then at Hansi, who is too busy devouring his chocolate mousse to give anything away. A close call, I think at the time. But when I'm alone in bed that night, I realize that Tonio must have been testing how I'd react; if he really wanted the truth, all he'd have to do is ask my brother when I'm not around. Or have me followed by a friend. Which means that either he doesn't want to know or already does. Maybe he's just trying to scare me.

*

I invite Isaac out with me to the movies one Saturday in late April, mostly because it irritates me that Tonio has the advantage of being able to have a public relationship with me. Hansi comes too. Papa is spending the afternoon with Greta. God bless the day he walked into his office and found that mutant parrot waiting for him, because I can nearly always come and go as I please now.

Isaac and I have never been out as a couple before. He warns me we mustn't even brush against each other. While he's buying tickets I overhear a young woman tell her husband how nice it is that "that old man" takes his grandchildren to the movies. "Thanks, Gramps," I say when he returns to us, and I stand on my toes to give him a peck on his cheek.

I adore provoking Isaac. It's a game that means *I am loved*. And now that he knows how the game works, he makes his exaggerated silent movie faces. My very own Lon Chaney.

The movie we see is *Captain Blood*. Not my choice, but it seems that Isaac and my brother would both like to be pirates, and Errol Flynn is dashing with his shoulder-length hair, so I agree. Isaac is sure all those luscious locks are real, but Hansi disagrees. I vote with my brother because he wants me to. Isaac fakes being disgusted with us both, and I reach for his hand about the time Errol is made into a slave. We conceal our locked fingers beneath Isaac's beret. And just before the credits, I kiss him full on the lips. Not quite public lovemaking, but a good start.

Greta calls to invite me to her apartment a few weeks later, and she instructs me not to tell Papa, which makes me think I should leave a trail of breadcrumbs in case she traps me in her oven. "A secret meeting just for us girls," Greta laughs in her breathy way, as though her lungs were made out of wind. An early sign of emphysema? I can hope ...

Her sitting room has a black marble floor that's so slick that I skate over to the high-backed leather sofa where she's asked me to sit, my hands out and waving for balance. "Great floor," I tell her. "You could sell tickets."

"Your father warned me you were amusing," she replies with a wink of her bright, blue-shaded eyes, and she gives a little, sputtering laugh. Her lips shine like wet red peppers and maybe she doesn't want to spoil the glossy effect by stretching them into a full smile. Or maybe she's one of those people who talks about emotions but doesn't actually feel them. No matter, she's got on a low-cut blue gown – with tufts of black-dyed ermine at the shoulders – that makes her look slinky and glamorous, and a bit goofy, all qualities much more in demand than authenticity. It occurs to me that we could have fun together if she weren't my father's lover. We could act out entire plays and she'd never even be aware we were performing.

Two stuffed chamois-heads are staring into nowhere-land over a white-marble fireplace that looks too polished and perfect to have ever been used. Crossed swords and halberds hang on the far wall, and a polar bear rug – its toothy mouth wide open – is splayed at my feet. Are Hansi and I next in line to provide decoration? "Who's the hunter?" I ask, just in case.

"My ex-husband. He shot at anything that moved. And a few things that didn't."

"He should join the Gestapo."

"He prefers making lots of money."

She hands me my sherry. A new experience, and I associate the rest of our conversation with the syrupy sweetness coating my tongue. "There are your new brocade curtains," I say, pointing.

"Yes, you like them?"

"Who wouldn't?" That's Isaac speaking from inside me, though I refrain from adding a Yiddish accent.

Two gilded mirrors, each the size of a barn door, frame the entranceway that I've just come through. I catch a glimpse of an awkward girl who plays the clown too often and who might just prefer to be Greta than herself.

"Guess which one's the real thing," she challenges me.

"I don't understand."

"Only one of them is a real Regency antique. Guess which one."

The left mirror has a crack down the middle. To be contrary, I say, "The right one."

"Exactly! Which proves you and I both know that most people are easily fooled. I put the crack in the left one on purpose – made it myself with a hammer. Ping! You know," she says, putting her hands on hips in a defiant way, "it gives me pleasure to see how naïve people are. Does that make me evil?"

"No, I'd say that makes you just about average for Germany these days."

"You *are* clever, aren't you! Just as well then that I won't try to fool you." She sits opposite me on the arm of a big armchair, looking at me admiringly. Then she takes a silver cigarette case from the tea table beside her, leans forward and offers me one. We smoke together, like sisters in a drawing-room comedy, though I'm still no good at it.

"I bet you're wondering why I asked you here," she says. She gives her head a little shake as if she's being mischievous.

What film have I seen her in? Maybe it was *Dinner at Eight*. "I guess I have been wondering a bit," I reply.

"I just don't want you to be angry at me. And neither does your father."

"I'm not angry at anyone." I smile because how else could she possibly believe that?

"Sophie, my goodness, what a time we've all had of late," she says, sighing.

By now, I don't believe a word she says. Not that I don't find her charming. And I can see what Papa likes about her. What widower wouldn't want a slinky divorcée with a real Regency mirror to fuck him for the Fatherland after two decades of unhappy marriage?

"How can I help you?" I ask.

"It's like this," she says, and she stands up and smooths down the gossamer silk over her hips. "I'd be no good with children. I think you sense that about me, right?" She gives me a knowing look.

"I think so."

"So I invited you here to tell you that although your father would like to move in with me at some point ... not now you understand ... sometime later ... and to take in Hansi as well, I just couldn't do that. It wouldn't work. So what I wanted to know ..." She kneels down beside me and looks up at me very seriously. Good staging, at the very least. "Has your father talked to you about any of this? I mean, about him moving in with me?"

"No."

"Nothing?"

"Not a word."

She puts her hand over her heart. Almost believable. "That's a relief," she says. "I was worried that he was too eager. He can be an eager beaver. But I guess I don't need to tell you that."

"Yes, an eager beaver, that's Papa," I agree, but I don't know what she's talking about.

She sits back on her perch, her legs crossed. "So, what I wanted to know is whether you'd support me. I mean, you really don't seem to mind taking care of your brother."

She says that as if watching over Hansi is tantamount to mining sulfur. "I love my brother," I reply.

"So it wouldn't be much of a hardship if you did it for a few more years."

"No."

She pats my leg as if we're now chums. "Oh, I'm so glad," she beams, and she really does seem relieved.

"That's it?" I ask. I feel like a patient who's just had her head x-rayed, but without knowing exactly why.

"Of course, silly," she assures me, smiling demurely. "And now," she says cheerfully, "I can show you the rest of the apartment."

A tour of her palace is my reward. I suppose I should be glad she doesn't toss me dog biscuits. After I've seen the three big bedrooms, in which there are enough stuffed animals to populate all the Edgar Allen Poe nightmares I might ever have, she leads me to the front door, where she takes my shoulder. I fear she'll kiss me, but she doesn't. "I think it best if I don't invite you back," she says, smiling. "We'll be friends from afar."

We shake hands. And before I know it, I'm standing outside her closed door wondering what just happened.

Isaac says, "Do I look like I'm any good at figuring out young women?" when I ask him what Greta might have really wanted from me. But when Vera, K-H, Marianne and Werner come for Sabbath dinner I get an answer that makes good sense.

Vera is helping me by chopping onions and Hansi is looking at picture books with the others in the living room, the monkey-head cane that Rolf gave him across his lap. Papa and Greta are dining with friends at a trendy beer hall where big-shot Nazis like to be seen. More and more, I get the feeling that Greta is a key part of Papa's ambition to be seen as a winner. By now, he and I have reached an unspoken agreement: we will put no impediments in each other's way. Not that we talk about that or anything else these

days. Our relationship is built on distant grudges. Hansi provides
the only bridge between us.

I make Vera laugh by telling her everything about my visit with
Greta. Then she volunteers to decipher it all for me. "Everything
that woman said is the opposite of what it usually means," she tells
me. "Good is bad, yes is no, right is left ..."

"So what were her intentions?" I ask.

"First of all, Greta didn't want to tell you anything. She wanted
you to tell her something. But in such a way that you didn't know
you were telling it to her."

"And what did I tell her?"

"That your father hadn't yet broached the subject of his moving
in with her. If I'm right, she's the eager beaver! She wants him with
her and he's probably said no. You must have disappointed her.
And she most assuredly does *not* want to be friends from afar. As
for that mirror trick ..." She rolls her eyes and tosses me an onion,
which I catch in both hands. "That was to gain your confidence
through flattery. Whichever mirror you picked would have been
the antique."

"How can you figure all this out so easily?" I question. I toss
her back the onion.

"I behave the same way as Greta sometimes." She shows me a
pleased-with-herself face. "Don't tell me you're too stupid to have
noticed that!"

Rolf calls several days later. "Dr Stangl has been found in the
Rummelsburger See," he tells me, triumph in his voice.

"Did he have any swastikas painted in blue on his face?" I ask.

"Sophele, he had no face. He was all just rotted flesh."

"How did you find out?"

"The police called me in for more questioning. They're

convinced that Heidi's murder and Stangl's are no coincidence. And they think *I'm* the connection. But someone else killed them."

I assure Rolf that I believe him, but after I hang up I think about Mrs Stangl telling me that he would visit her husband all the time. Then I hear again the urgency in Rolf's voice, and just like that I can see what I've failed up until now to notice below the glass.

I take the stairs two at a time to Isaac's apartment, but he isn't home from work yet, so I let myself in and scribble a note. He calls an hour later, and I go right up since Papa isn't home yet.

Isaac has tossed his work shirt onto his bed and is putting on his favorite, moth-eaten pullover when I explain about Dr Stangl. Except that I lie about where he was found, saying it was in the Jungfernsee, which is west of Berlin, thirty miles from where he was actually dumped. I want to see if that location shocks Isaac. After all, if he is somehow involved in Stangl's death then he already knows where the body was left and should at least show some surprise.

"Well, I suppose it's as good a place as any to leave a body that you don't want to be found too quickly," he tells me matter-of-factly, which makes me take a deep breath of relief. He's kneeling at the time, looking through his pile of clothing in the corner – which I'm not allowed to touch. When he finally finds the fraying old pair of woolen pants he likes to wear in the evenings, he says, "There you are!" Stepping into them, leaning on my shoulder for balance, he gazes around the floor. "Have you seen my slippers?"

"They smelled like week-old *bratwurst*. I threw them out."

"You didn't!"

I squat down and take them out from under the bed, where he kicks them nearly every morning. Isaac takes them and kisses my forehead. "Thank you, Sophele."

"Someone pretending to be Rolf called Stangl," I say, "and got him to leave the house."

"You already told me that theory, but I don't think he'd go all the way to the Jungfernsee for Rolf. And if Heidi and Stangl were murdered by the same person, it doesn't make much sense that the killer would leave them so far away from each other." He stares off into his thoughts. "Unless he wanted to give the impression that there was nothing linking their deaths. I better call Vera. She'll want to know."

He starts out of the bedroom, but I cut him off. "I'll call her," I tell him.

"Why?" His furry eyebrows join together in puzzlement.

"Because *I'm* the one who heard from Rolf." He looks at me as if I require a great deal of patience, which may be true, so I take the pipe out of his mouth and press my lips to his.

Vera is surprised to hear Stangl was found in the Jungfernsee. "Who'd waste their time going all that way just to dump that son-of-a-bitch?" she tells me.

"So if you'd killed him, where would you have left him?" I ask, testing her reactions. And giving her the chance to confess she was involved in his death – if, of course, that's the truth.

"The nearest garbage. Or maybe I'd have boiled him for glue." After a pause, she adds, "I didn't do it, you know – kill Stangl, I mean."

"I didn't accuse you."

"But you've long suspected I might have killed Heidi. And for all I know, you might suspect me of Georg's murder, too. And now you're wondering about Stangl. I can hear it in your voice. But I didn't commit any of the murders."

"Why should I believe you? You've got quite a temper."

"Wouldn't you have a temper if you had my face?"

"Maybe. But is the fact that Heidi and Stangl knew each other and were killed only a short time apart, and that both of their bodies were left in lakes ... Is all that just coincidental or is Rolf lying? I can easily imagine he murdered Stangl to avenge Heidi. In fact ..."

"There are other possibilities," Vera interrupts. "Maybe Stangl was working with Georg and whoever else was betraying us. And maybe ..."

"You said *was*."

"What?"

"You said, 'whoever else *was* betraying us.' But someone must still be working against you from inside The Ring. Unless you know for sure he's dead. Is that why you said *was*?"

"All right, *is*! Christ, Sophie, what a bulldog you are! Now, if you'll let me continue ... When Heidi discovered the identity of the bastard from The Ring who was working with Stangl, the good doctor killed her and dumped her where no one would find her for quite some time. Then Stangl himself became a liability, because the police might have discovered he murdered Heidi, and he could have revealed to them who was giving him orders. Whoever was pulling his strings wouldn't like that. If you ask me, Georg and Stangl might only be the tip of the iceberg ... a lot of Nazis might have been working against us."

"Why would they be so interested in The Ring?"

"Maybe because we've been having some success with the foreign press and they hate the bad publicity. Or maybe our discussing the possibility of an embargo at the English and French embassies scared them more than we ever realized. How the hell should I know? Ask them!"

"I think that Rolf was the traitor," I tell her.

"Rolf? I don't buy it. I asked him to help me and he agreed."

"You fell into a trap. All the time you trusted him, he was betraying you ... Rolf and Heidi both. Maybe they were just like

Greta and enjoyed fooling people. Rolf might even have followed me that time I went to see Julia. Maybe he was the one who called the Gestapo to go to Tieckstraße."

Which would mean that Tonio wasn't guilty of betraying me on that occasion, I think, hoping it's true. "Anyway," I conclude, "it's my bet that Rolf and Heidi were being pressured to report on The Ring's activities."

"Who was pressuring them?"

"Dr Stangl. He must have been ordered by one of his superiors to get information on you and your friends. Mrs Stangl told me that Rolf went to visit him all the time, at all hours. And not at his office, but at home. Vera, I think he was giving Stangl damning information about you on a regular basis."

"But why would Rolf agree to tell him anything? He's been my friend for many years, and there's no one he respects more than Isaac."

"Stangl had leverage on him because Rolf desperately wanted children. He may have refused to help Heidi get pregnant unless ..."

"Unless Rolf betrayed me ... The bastard! He killed my baby!"

"Vera, it's even worse, because there was no way Heidi could get pregnant. She'd already been sterilized. Stangl was an incredibly evil man and ..."

"And Rolf played into his hands!" she shouts.

"Stangl must have been very persuasive. Rolf must have been going through hell. It must *still* be hell. Heidi is gone and he has betrayed the only people who could comfort him. His loneliness, I could feel it when ..."

"Sophie, shush! Give me a moment to think."

Isaac has been listening to my conversation and has stepped progressively closer, smoking anxiously, which is why I reach out my hand to him, and though he takes it, I can see that he wishes I wasn't so independent. Maybe all men would really prefer a colorful parrot to the likes of me.

Vera lets the silence build until I blurt out, "Stangl was also found in the Rummelsburger See. I lied before."

As I say that, I look up to see Isaac glaring at me. So predictable. Not that that makes being disapproved of any easier. He drops my hand and stalks off to his room, slamming the door.

"But why did you lie?" Vera demands in a hurt voice.

"Because I had to test you," I reply, picturing Isaac fuming in his bedroom. "I'm sorry, Vera. Please, forgive me."

"I do," she replies, hurrying to add, "Tell me the reason you think Stangl was murdered. I need to figure this out."

"One of two possibilities. Either the Nazis who were controlling Stangl began to see him as a liability, as you said, or someone in The Ring decided to kill him for forcing Rolf and Heidi to betray their friends. And maybe for sterilizing Heidi, too." Now that I've spoken Vera's theory aloud, I understand why she can't be right. "If it was one of Stangl's Nazi bosses who lured him out of the house to kill him," I say, "then he wouldn't have had to pretend he was Rolf. He'd have just ordered Stangl to meet him."

"So it's someone I know," Vera concludes.

"And someone who probably convinced Stangl that he had new and damning information on The Ring. Vera, do you know anyone who could imitate Rolf's voice?"

"No."

"Or anyone with a connection to the Rummelsburger See ... with a house out there, for instance?"

"No."

"You're sure you don't know anyone from your time in the

circus who could use his voice in a special way – who could do imitations of people?"

"No one. Sophele, there's something I don't understand. If you're right about Rolf, then why was Heidi murdered?"

"I think that Rolf must have told her what he was up to. She might have gone along with his betrayals, reluctantly or otherwise. And the killer found that out."

"I don't think that can be right."

"Why, was Heidi such a saint?"

"In a way, yes, and maybe only now I'm beginning to realize that. She and I ... we had an understanding. And there's one more thing ... Your theory doesn't explain why Rolf wasn't murdered too."

"Maybe because the killer knew that Rolf's life would be over the moment that Heidi was killed. What could be cruder than to let him live without her? Besides, now that The Ring no longer has any meetings, and everyone is working on their own, Rolf no longer poses much of a danger."

"I don't buy that either."

"Maybe ... maybe the killer isn't finished yet. The opportunity to murder Stangl presented itself before any opportunity to kill Rolf."

"Which means," Vera speculates menacingly, "that he'll be next to die."

"I lied to you for a reason," I tell Isaac as soon as I step into his room. He's got his nose buried in his manuscripts and doesn't look up. "You should be pleased – I followed your advice and looked below the glass. I discovered what we hadn't seen before."

He turns around, his eyes angry slits. "So, I should be pleased that Rolf may have betrayed us? And that I love someone who lies to me so easily?"

"It wasn't easy. And would you prefer to be kept in the dark?"

"Maybe."

"You didn't want me to visit Rolf. That was because you suspected him, too, isn't it?"

"I suspected everyone who knew of our plans. Now leave me alone."

"What have I done that's so bad?"

"Sophele, go away! I don't want to see you!"

He's speaks as if he hates me, which leaves me desolate. "I can't bear you talking to me like that," I tell him. "And if you decide ..."

"You should have thought of that before," he interrupts gruffly. "You care more about solving a crime than people's lives."

"That's not fair!" I reply, angry now – at his resemblance to my bullying father more than anything else. "I care about what happened to Dr Stangl because Raffi and Vera's baby were murdered. And Heidi, too. I'm not still the little girl who chased after tram accidents, you know. Though you may think I am."

"But you still enjoy living with danger. It makes you feel alive."

"Maybe so, but I have no choice, do I? Would you prefer a Young Maiden learning to harpoon rabbis in her spare time? And be careful what you reply, because no blond teenager with plaited hair is going to fall to her knees for a foul-tempered old Jew like you."

That gets his attention, and he jumps up.

"And what I enjoy," I add, gazing at him defiantly, "if you really want to know, is the feeling that I'm doing something meaningful ... that I'm living a life that counts. You're the one who told me we all need meaning in our lives. Why should I be different?"

"Sophie," he says, "you're too complicated for me right now. Just go away." He makes a weary, sweeping motion with his hand. "Go to your father and Tonio. Go to Hansi ..."

His air of profound exhaustion – as if I'm a burden – only

deepens my fury, so I blurt out something I wasn't going to say, having become used to keeping silent about my deepest fears. "Has it never occurred to you that I've been worried about you ... that you're a good part of what keeps me up at night? Because I've been thinking ever since Raffi was killed that you might wind up dead on some dark Berlin street corner, swastikas painted on your face. I'm worried about that even now, because if I'm wrong about Rolf being the traitor, then an unidentified someone is still out there who hates troublemaking Jews like you. Especially the kind that sleep with little troublemaking *shiksas* like me!"

Isaac's eyes open wide and he tries to put his pipe down, but misses the desk, so that it tumbles to the floor, spilling ash.

"Sophele," he says, opening his hands in an apologetic way. "I'm such an idiot."

"You live so deeply in those manuscripts of yours that you don't even see what is going on around you. Wasn't it Berekiah Zarco who said you shouldn't abandon the living for the dead? Well, that's just what you've been doing."

"I'm sorry," he says. He embraces me, his breathing warm and desperate on my neck, and he whispers, "Forgive me."

I can tell from the way he presses against me that he wants to make love, but for once in my life I'm not in the mood. When I tell him, he laughs good-naturedly and says, "I'm not in love with you because I can have sex with you anytime I like."

"Though that helps," I reply, grinning.

"In any case, I'm still not pleased about you lying to me," he says gently, and he picks up his pipe from the floor.

"I'll try not to," I assure him. "Now, during the time you headed The Ring, how many people helped you plan your activities?"

"Everyone. We voted democratically."

"But you must have had an inner group. Some people you

trusted completely, who knew what you were thinking before the others."

"Yes, but that inner group got smaller as time went on, because I began to suspect there was a secret Nazi among us."

"In April 1933, when we went to Weissman's to break the boycott, and the Nazis were ready for us ... You said that most members of The Ring didn't know where they were headed until the last minute. Who knew we were going to Weissman's beforehand?"

"Vera, Georg, Rolf, K-H, Marianne, and ... and Julia."

"Then I don't understand. K-H and Marianne couldn't have imitated Rolf on the phone because they speak with those deaf-people voices and couldn't have heard anything that Stangl replied to them. And Julia couldn't have done it because she was already in Istanbul."

"So maybe someone didn't imitate Rolf," Isaac surmises. "Maybe he was on the phone for real. We still can't be sure he didn't kill Stangl. Or whoever the murderer was could have put a gun to Rolf's head and forced him to make the call."

"So how can I prove that Rolf betrayed you?" I ask.

"I don't know. Unless you could find some incriminating document, and by now he'll have destroyed anything and everything in his possession that might implicate him."

"Should I go see him again and confront him? He wouldn't lie to me if I was there with him. Not a second time."

"Who do you think you are?! If he betrayed us, he'd lie to you as many times as he needs to." Isaac sits with me on his bed and holds my hands tight, as if to keep me from fleeing. At times, I must seem like a top spinning away from him.

While he's trying to convince me not to do anything, the phone on his night table rings. With a groan, he reaches past me to answer it. "Yes, hi ... yes ... all right," he says. After a pause, during which he listens intently, he adds, "Fine, I'll meet you at my office tomorrow, in the late morning, around eleven."

On hanging up, he faces me and rubs his hand over his eyes, looking tired again and troubled.

"What's wrong?" I ask.

"Andre Baldwin needs to talk with me."

"About what?"

"Do I know? Nobody explains anything to me anymore." He looks up to God, shakes his head, and intones: 'The hand of the Lord came upon me, and he carried me out by his spirit and put me down in a plain full of bones.' Ezekiel Thirty-Seven," he tells me.

"Why doesn't Andre come here? Would you prefer he didn't meet me?"

"Of course, not! Andre isn't Jewish, and unlike you, he hasn't lost the Semitic Wall in his head. He doesn't want to risk being seen coming to my apartment."

I speak to Vera over the next week about Rolf and how we ought to proceed, but she, too, begs me not to see him, and I end up promising her I'll do nothing for the moment.

"If you're correct about him betraying us, which I now firmly believe, then you're also right that he's been punished already," she tells me. "Heidi is dead, and that's enough. And if you're wrong, and he's innocent, then talking to him will only drive him further from us."

I don't entirely believe her, but I make *her* promise that she won't plan any vengeance against Rolf without telling me first.

One sunny Saturday in May, when Papa is picking out sofa cushions with Greta to match her brocade curtains, Isaac and I go for a long walk in Friedrichshain Park, where spring has transformed the plum trees into pink clouds. Hansi and his friend Volker – tiny and sweet-natured, with sweaty hands and a squeaky voice – are hunting for squirrels somewhere in the undergrowth behind us. At least, I think they are. I refuse to keep track of zigzagging twelve-year-olds searching for rodents.

"Andre is leaving town and wants to meet you before he goes," Isaac tells me.

"Why?" I ask.

"Why's he leaving or why does he want to meet a *nudnock* like you?"

"Both," I say, rolling my eyes.

"He's leaving because he's been fundraising for a Jewish theater company, the *Jüdische Kulturbund*, and the government is about to close them down, and he wrote a stinging letter to the Culture Ministry, which got him summoned to Gestapo headquarters the other day, and ..." Isaac finally takes a breath. "He's one of the people I'm helping to get out of Germany. And as for you, he's dying of curiosity."

"You're helping people get out?"

"I've decided that books are no longer enough."

"Who have you helped?"

"Two Jewish seamstresses who worked for me recently left for Switzerland. And five members of The Ring so far. You remember Molly and Klaus Schneider?"

"Of course, the trapeze flyers who owned Minnie."

"They're in the United States now ... in New York!" he tells me, beaming.

"That's fantastic!"

"They chose to work with American journalists on anti-Nazi articles – especially pieces about the sterilizations. So it worked out perfectly. They were able to get visas because the people at the Barnum & Bailey Circus were keen on getting them."

"If I can help, then please let me know." I tell him.

"I hope I won't need to call on you, but if I do ..." He ends his sentence by nodding and caressing my hair lightly. Our substitute for the kiss we'd prefer.

"Did you tell Andre we were lovers?" I ask.

"Yes, though I also told him you take terrible advantage of me."

"True enough," I reply, and to prove the point, I grope him, which makes him bat my hand away. "Sophele, you could get us into trouble." He gives me an ugly, silent-movie frown.

"So where's Andre going to go when he leaves Berlin?" I ask.

"Antwerp. Listen, he's proposing we have dinner this weekend. Is your father going out on Saturday or Sunday with Greta?"

"I'll check. Though we'll have to bring Hansi along."

When we pass a ring of tall rhododendron bushes, I lead him inside. He knows what's up, though he exclaims, "Where are you taking me?" like a damsel in distress. That's so he can later moan that I kidnapped him. Not that anyone would believe an old satyr with grass stains on his knees and elbows.

Andre lives across from the Wallner Theater, just around the corner from Vera. Back in September, for my eighteenth birthday, she let out the seams on my troubadour coat, so I'm wearing it for the first time in ages. I feel like a peacock with its tail spread.

Andre has short brown hair cut in a dashing, off-center way. He has strong, broad shoulders, but a bit of a paunch. I'd guess he was once athletic, but now – in his fifties – he leads a sedentary life. He's put on a stunning black-silk coat and red tie for our supper, but my favorite thing about him are his eyebrows, which are long and flaring, and make him seem part owl.

His green eyes lighten with gladness when he sees Isaac, as if the old man is a present just for him, and they kiss cheeks.

"I'm so glad to meet you," he tells me, smiling excitedly. The handsome, masculine way that wrinkles spread from his eyes makes me believe he could once entice any girl he wanted into his bed.

"Vera made your jacket?" I ask.

"Absolutely! And yours?"

"Who else!"

We smile at having Vera in common. Andre turns to Isaac. "So how was *Dr Mabuse*?"

We've just come from a clandestine revival of the Fritz Lang movie at the Jewish Old Age Home.

"Wonderful," Isaac says. "The way Mabuse controls people with his stare ... I thought it was ridiculous when I first saw it, but now I understand it was a metaphor for the period we're living through."

"But the print was awful," I add. "It looked like cats had been trying to eat it."

Andre turns to Hansi for his opinion. "Both awful and wonderful," the boy writes on his pad.

The men laugh appreciatively and I give my brother a happy kiss. Who would have thought he'd one day be able to make jokes?

Andre's sitting room is small but comfortable. A Venetian-glass chandelier plays facets of ecstatic light over us.

"My one treasure," Andre tells me. "Saved from my parents' house."

Andre's Czech accent is charming, and he has four glasses of port wine already waiting for us on a silver tray, though I let Hansi drink only a thimbleful; God knows what sort of bushy-tailed genie might come out of that boy if he ever gets drunk.

When our host hands me my drink, I notice his topaz ring. I know I've seen it before, but where?

"It was my inheritance from Georg Hirsch," Andre tells me. "He was kind enough to leave it to me in his will."

"So you were friends with him, too."

"Yes, a wonderful man. Kind, intelligent, handsome ..." He speaks with an amused twist to his lips that strikes me as odd, though maybe he's simply recollecting happy moments they had together. I could almost believe that he knew Georg was a traitor and was using his words ironically, but Isaac has already told me that Andre was never a member of The Ring and knows nothing of its history.

"Andre," Isaac pleads, "can we please not talk about Georg?"

At the time, I think that he simply doesn't want to be reminded of a man who betrayed him.

We talk about Andre's background for a time. He grew up in Prague. His father was German and a violinmaker, his mother a Czech singer. Andre studied piano, but he later chose graphic design as his profession. He's been painting scenery on a volunteer basis for the last several years, while making his living at a publishing house.

"I'd love to go to Prague," I tell him, thinking of Isaac's stories about the famous mystic, Rabbi Loew.

"We could go together. I'd show you some places no one knows about." He changes to a whisper. "Including where the Golem is buried."

"And where is that?" I ask.

"In a Christian cemetery," Isaac answers for him. "For safekeeping, because that's where our persecutors would never look!"

Andre switches off the Venetian chandelier and lights tall white candles around us. Throughout our subsequent conversation, the dancing flames give his sharp, precise hand gestures long, mysterious shadows – an expressionist film come to life, and undoubtedly his goal. He says he studied Jewish history and lore with Isaac for a time, though he was raised Catholic and is an atheist by conviction. "I'm indifferent to whether or not God exists," he tells me with a dismissive wave. "The world is wondrous enough for me as it is. But I do believe that the Jews are important. Because they are a test of the evolution of the human mind and spirit. Must we all have our own country or can we get along together within the same borders?"

Isaac tells me that he once prepared Andre to step through the Fifth Gate at the Prague Cathedral.

"Yes, we fasted, prayed, and chanted, and then I stepped through the gate, and the most glorious thing happened."

"You found yourself in the Fifth Heaven?" I ask.

"No, I was in such a nervous state that I fainted dead away ... plop!" He laughs merrily. "But lying there on the ground, bleeding from the back of my head like a stuck pig ... After I awoke, the cathedral was so beautiful and quiet. And strangers were fussing over me! A man took off his sweater and put it under my head. An old lady whispered prayers over me. I'll always remember their faces. It was as if ... as if their good wishes had brought me back from the dead. I felt I was just where I was meant to be." He pauses, collecting his thoughts. "And I thought, dying isn't so bad." He smiles sweetly at Isaac. They seem almost like father and son. "It was a moment that changed my life. Fear for myself, my physical well-being, left my life ... I'm still a different man even today, ten years later." He gives me a serious look. "Even if I were sent to Dachau, I'd be all right." Turning to Isaac, he adds, "I want you to know that."

"You are *not* going to be arrested," Isaac tells him definitively. "You will be safe where you are going. Trust me."

When dinner is nearly ready, Andre leads us to the dining room. A rug with a fringe of knotted violet cord sits below the round wooden table.

"That rug is yours!" I tell Isaac.

"*Mein Gott*, what a memory you have, Sophele! I gave it to Andre."

"Isaac took pity on me," our host tells me. "I had nothing but the clothes on my back when I moved here." He beckons us to sit at the table.

"Why did you come to Berlin?" I ask him, but he holds up his hand to have me wait and rushes off to the kitchen.

"For the ocean air," he calls back after a few seconds. He appears in the doorway and pats his chest. "I've got the lungs of a lobster."

"But we have no ocean here," I say.

He shrugs. "I was poorly informed."

He disappears back into the kitchen.

"I don't get it," I call in to him.

"Neither does Isaac," Andre calls back.

"Andre's sense of humor isn't normal," Isaac observes.

"Yes, I prefer humor that isn't funny," our host says, appearing in the doorway again.

He's a bright, curious, and unpredictable man, which is all in his favor, and he wins my eternal allegiance when he brings in a golden-brown goose drenched in berry sauce that smells like heaven. "It's gorgeous," I exclaim, and I swoon, knocking into Hansi on purpose, which makes him hit me playfully on the top of the head. Andre carries the bird to the table on a silver platter, wearing white gloves. He makes me feel I'm in the presence of a star on his day off, and when I catch his eye, he gives me a knowing smile, as if to say, *I'm overjoyed to have you in my home, so please don't mind my performing a bit.*

Our conversation over dinner becomes relaxed, and even Hansi writes us a list of all the famous places he'd like to visit, most of which come from his jigsaw puzzles – Big Ben, the Taj Mahal, the Eiffel Tower ... I've never seen him scribble so quickly. The effect of an ounce of port wine? Maybe if I got him really drunk he'd start talking again.

After dinner, the men puff on their cigars and I open the windows as wide as they'll go so Hansi and I don't cough to death. On Isaac's insistence I've brought a couple of props with me, and I extract Mama's old wristwatch from behind Hansi's ear, then take Heidi's lily out from behind Andre's elbow. The men applaud. Hansi takes a bow with me, as my lovely assistant.

Andre smiles generously at me when Isaac sits beside me on the sofa and puts his arm over my shoulder. "It makes me more happy than you can imagine to see how good you are for each other," he tells us.

I know right away I'll always remember his words because he has seen our love. And I hadn't even guessed I'd wanted anyone to serve as our witness.

Isaac, Hansi, Vera, and I help Andre put his possessions in boxes a week later, though Vera crams his crockery in so hard that she breaks an old Delft teacup and is relieved of duty, which was probably her goal all along, since now she is free to criticize our efforts from the sidelines. Andre calls her "The Queen of the Damned", which is a perfect nickname.

When we're finished, he takes us all out for cake and coffee at Karl's Cellar. He and the Queen of the Damned waltz to a scratchy *Blue Danube* on the phonograph. Vera insists on leading, her head scraping the ceiling.

Andre leaves the next day for Antwerp. Isaac sees him off at the station, and when he returns, he hugs me long and hard, declaring, "I've helped put one more beyond their reach!"

*

Eight weeks before the end of school, Greta Ullrich, a.k.a. Gurka Greulich, comes to class with crusty eyes, her lashes dabbed with a viscous ointment. The diagnosis: conjunctivitis. Delighted by this turn of events, I steal two sheets of Health Ministry stationery from my father's desk on reaching home, bound down the stairs and cross the courtyard to Isaac's apartment, and, with my heart diving gleefully into my evil plans, type a brief but well-worded note to the headmaster of our school. Isaac hasn't come home from work yet. I'm still reworking the letter when he pokes his head in to the guestroom, where he keeps his typewriter. "I'm creating a harmless hoax," I explain.

"I do not believe *harmless* is a word in your vocabulary," he replies, which gratifies me enormously.

Having been lectured in the Young Maidens on the various horrific venereal diseases we're likely to get from Jews and Gypsies if we so much as brush against them or give them a kiss – the Jew's fleshy lips and giant nose being extensions of his perverse sexual nature – I know exactly what I want to write, though I admit to having to look up how to spell gonorrheal ophthalmia. After presenting the facts of the case, I write:

I must stress that Fräulein *Greta Ullrich is to be kept away from the other students because this particular venereal disease is highly contagious and may even lead, in acute cases, to blindness. I would also highly recommend that you oblige her close friends to go for medical check-ups at the earliest possible convenience and have the girls provide full details about their sexual history over the last few months to their doctors.*

I write a slightly different letter to her parents, calling into question the morals of the Ullrich family. Maybe that will prove to them how easy it is to be regarded as trash in Germany.

As I'm about to post my letters, however, I realize that school officials might be able to trace them back to me, since I may be the only student with a parent in the Health Ministry. To be safe, I decide to simplify my fraud and send a single letter from a doctor at Wittenau State Hospital to the headmaster. I call the intake desk to find out the name of the chief pediatrician – Christian Keller – and sign his name to a letter I type on plain white stationery. I take Hansi with me to Wittenau that Saturday. Having put stamps on the letter already, I convince the nurse at the reception desk to put them in the hospital mail for us.

Two days later, Gurka is sent home early from school and four of her friends are summoned to the headmaster's office. By the next morning, all the other students are trying to guess in what unusual and disgusting ways she might have caught gonorrhea in her eyes! And yet, seeing Gurka humiliated, I do not feel the triumph I'd expected. Guilt clings to me, and I realize that no one will really benefit from my prank.

Is my hoax finally exposed? It must be, since Gurka is back at school within a week. And she clearly suspects me, since she glares at me with hate every time we cross paths.

We speak only once more. A month before the end of school, she marches up to me in the hallway and says, "I'm going to make sure you're shot one day by the Gestapo. You and Irene Bloch both. And I'll dance on your graves!"

She's a frightening girl, and she has a kind of obscene power, like a witch in a fairy tale. I sometimes wonder if she'd have carried out her threat against me if I'd remained in Germany. In Rini's case, she might have even succeeded.

At the time, however, I'm glad she speaks to me hatefully, because it gives me a chance to shed all my guilt and to have the last words between us. I suspect my sudden eloquence comes from how much I *really do* fear her. "Gurka," I say, "don't fuck with me, because I'm smarter than you, and I have no scruples, as you've just discovered. And I have a gun that I won't hesitate to use, and you can be sure that every Jew and Gypsy in Berlin will be delighted at the chance to dance with me on *your* grave! And I'll invite them all!"

My exultation doesn't last long; as graduation approaches, my failure to apply to art school becomes an acid eating through my days. I refuse to make love with Tonio one afternoon because he arrives half an hour late to our rendezvous. And I start quarrels with Isaac at every opportunity. One evening, I hurl insults at him for his refusal to let me into the bathroom while he's shaving. I'm standing in the doorway, threatening to invade the poor man's last private territory, and he warns me – his hand up, forming a shield – not to dare go any further. His cheeks and chin are sculpted with foam, and his eyes are cold gray beads.

"How can you be so mean-spirited?" I demand.

"Where do you get such *chutzpah*? I need some time to myself. Is that so difficult to understand?"

"Mean about everything, not just this."

"Look, you wanted revenge on yourself, and now you've got it. So don't blame me."

"I don't like the way you presume to know my mind."

His shrug means, *Why would I care what a little* pisher *like you thinks?* Then he starts mumbling to himself about me in Ladino, since he knows I don't understand.

"So what revenge have I gotten?" I interrupt.

"You've prevented yourself from continuing your education."

That accusation feels like a slap. "And why do you think I wanted revenge?"

Shooing me away, he replies, "Sophie, can't you see I'm busy at the moment?"

For not loving my mother enough, and for not being worthy of my father's respect. Those are the answers I give him when he emerges from the bathroom. "Is that right?"

"That sounds reasonable to me, but only you can say for sure."

He smiles in his patient way and caresses my fingers across the polished smoothness of his cheek, then presses the palm of my hand over his nose, breathing in the scent of me.

Feeling his need for me, the mantle of my anger drops off my shoulders. "So what do I do now?" I ask.

"You find a job and make some money, just like the rest of us. And next year ..." Here, he gives me his Biblical glare, "you go to university!"

A good plan, but Dr Hassgall has other ideas. He comes to lunch at Isaac's apartment that weekend, looks at the pastels I've been working on – his hands clasped gentlemanly behind his back – and says, "How would you like to teach art at my school?"

"I've never thought about it before."

In an amused voice, he says, "The pay is abominable, and the kids will tie your patience in knots, and the classrooms are cold in winter, but once you've taught my students, you will know you are capable of much more than you once believed possible. Three classes a day, eight to ten students per class, and I won't give you any pupils you'd have no hope of reaching. What do you say?"

As quickly as that, I seem to be lifting up and out of my dilemma straight toward the sun of his yellow schoolhouse. Still, it's a big decision ... "I don't know anything about Rudolf Steiner and his philosophy," I reply, pouring him and Isaac their pre-lunch schnapps.

Dr Hassgall takes his glass and thanks me. "My senior teachers know Steiner back and forth. You just use any techniques you can to help the kids climb up to the tip of their crayons." He steps his fingers up through the air, as though ascending a ladder.

"I'm afraid the Young Maidens only trained me for climbing ropes," I reply.

"Stop with the cleverness!" Isaac snarls, and since he takes the withering look I give him as an accusation, he adds, "And no, this wasn't my idea."

"Sophele, my dear," Dr Hassgall says in a tone of peacemaking, "all you'll have to do at first is keep the kids from swallowing their paints."

He and Isaac laugh like old poker buddies. Extremely irritating. "I'll think it over," I tell him, which makes Isaac roll his eyes. I can hear him thinking, *More revenge* ...

Later, over his soup, Dr Hassgall points his spoon at me and says, "I want you to name your brother's enemies."

"What?"

"What enemies do distant children have?"

"Not being understood. Not being wanted or ... or even loved. Cannibalistic fish. Jigsaw puzzles with missing pieces. And cars driving too fast on Marienburger Straße."

"Yes, *exactly*, my dear," he says, and the solidarity for me I see in his eyes seems to push away the rest of the world for a moment. While considering his next words, he takes a sip of wine and wipes his lips carefully, his little finger out at a dainty angle. At such times, he seems to be posing for a nineteenth-century canvas of an aristocratic gentleman.

"A distant boy who loves to draw or paint just might cope more effectively with not being understood by his parents," he tells me. "And he will be less lonely all his life because he will be able to count on his own resources, which is vitally important for kids who don't make friendships easily, and maybe he'll even learn how to cross the street safely and make his *own* jigsaw puzzles."

Dr Hassgall talks in run-on sentences when he's impassioned, and I'm charmed by his effusive hands gestures; it's as though he's conducting an orchestra.

"I doubt I'm a good enough artist yet," I protest.

"Sophele, I don't think you realize how unusual your dedication to Hansi is. Most of these children have been discouraged from living ... from becoming creative beings. This Nazi sterilization program is abominable, but it needs to be seen as part of the general climate of discouragement that keeps boys and girls like Hansi from realizing their potential."

"I've never thought of it that way."

"We take away their right to have children because we're afraid of their expressing their desires, their affection ... of their becoming *creative* beings. We don't want them to defy our expectations. But they deserve more than our cowardice. And with your talent for drawing, you may even help a few of the kids become more than they thought possible ... a few who can be reached only through form and color."

The moment he mentions art as a way to fight all the evil done to Hansi and the other children, I realize that this is my way forward. So that summer of 1936, while the Nazis finalize plans for a spick-and-span Olympics – taking down the anti-Semitic posters across Berlin and herding the city's Gypsies into camps in the suburbs – I plan my counter-attack in a series of forty lessons designed to get Hansi and his friends sketching their differences and desires. I work every evening on my project.

"Dr Hassgall is a poet posing as a headmaster," I tell Isaac after he leaves.

"That's why he's so good at his job. Children don't really understand prose, though we fool ourselves into thinking they do."

THE FIFTH GATE

Five are the books of Moses, the prayers of Yom Kippur, and the senses we use to contemplate the splendor of the Lower Realms. With the number five, *heh*, God created the world.

As you move through the Fifth Gate, past commitments fall away and you may either turn back toward youth – and find yourself trapped on a cliff overlooking Gehenna – or gather your courage to continue the journey. The corresponding heaven is Ma'on, where angels sing before the Lord during the night and grow silent during the day, so that even the voiceless prayers of those in the Lower Realms may be heard.

God said, 'Let the waters teem with countless living creatures, and let birds fly above the earth across the vault of heaven.' ... Evening came, and morning came, a fifth day – Genesis 1.

Berekiah Zarco, The Book of New Beginning

CHAPTER SEVENTEEN

I lug my lesson plans to school on my first teaching day in September 1936, a couple of weeks prior to my nineteenth birthday. Dr Hassgall introduces me warmly to an assembly of all thirty-seven students, but my first lesson, beginning with a brief talk about classical Greek art, leaves three of my younger pupils with their heads flat on their desks, eyes closed, drifting toward dreamland. Panic sets in when I look at Hansi and see worry ribbing his brow. I stop in mid-sentence. How did I get here? I feel as though I'm an actress who's stepped on stage only to find she's in the wrong play, and my audience – eight children from nine to fifteen – is a wall of puzzled eyes.

Several of the kids don't draw anything when I distribute paper. They don't even grab a crayon. They're confused and so am I.

And my other two classes go no better. Afterward, Else König, Hansi's main teacher, comes to sit with me on the steps down to the back garden. Her thick copper-colored hair now falls to her shoulders. She wears black woolen trousers and a simple white blouse. Her earrings are dots of red – garnets. She radiates down-to-earth optimism. I can see why the kids fight for her attention.

We share a cheese sandwich. She's bright-faced and eager to help, but I'm near tears, shipwrecked on my inexperience.

"Please tell me I don't have to come back tomorrow," I plead.

"Look, Sophie," Else replies, "you are going to make mistakes, just like I did. But teaching *will* get easier."

Else talks to me sweetly and intelligently for some time, but she fails to dispel any of my discouragement until she says, "I've discovered that children are sponges, and they do their best to clean up any mess we make, so don't worry so much."

I'm unwilling to be cheered up, however, and reply, "I don't want them to clean up my mess."

"Go home and take a hot bath," she advises me. "Everything will seem better in the morning."

The eternal promise to the disheartened ... But the prospect of teaching doesn't seem any better at dawn. I sit next to Hansi and comb my fingers through his hair to calm myself.

At five to ten, just before my first class is to begin, Else hooks her arm in mine and says, "I had an idea last night. Draw them. They'll love that, and they'll be gratified that you've taken the time to look at them closely."

"Draw my students?"

"Of course! Most of them will be happy to pose for you. And the others can watch. Start with Hansi."

Else's challenge reminds me of my mother's wish to be really seen by me. So it is that I begin my second day at the King David School with Mama's hand at the back of my neck. And God bless Else for tossing me a lifesaver.

I start with quick portraits of Hansi and his best friend Volker. The younger students crowd around me to watch, and a couple of them light up when I sketch their likenesses. Volker stares at me open-mouthed, as if he's only just realized I've got supernatural powers. He trembles when he runs his finger over the big watery eyes I've given him. Has he never realized before how stunning they are? One boy, Stefan Neuhauser, stares at his portrait with his arms blocking everyone else away, afraid he might have to share his gift.

Still, some of the kids can't imagine what a portrait might be for.

And half of them refuse to say a word to me or even show me with their eyes that they are conscious of being in the room with me.

"What ... what should I do with it?" says Monica Mueller in a fearful voice, shrinking back from my drawing of her, as if the paper might be hiding the tiny spiders that she always fears might get lost in her thick brown hair. Monica has been diagnosed with *folie circulaire*, the name physicians at the time have given to bi-polar disorder, but Dr Hassgall says she probably has some form of schizophrenia.

"You don't need to do anything with it," I tell her gently.

As I reply, a slender girl with deep-set brown eyes and her auburn hair in tight braids, Gnendl Rosencrantz, rips up my portrait of her and exclaims, "All wrong!" She has the angriest expression I've ever seen, and she tears my paper into confetti as if she has to destroy a curse against her family. When she's done, she makes fists with her tiny hands and squeezes them up by her ears. Maybe she likes to hear the grinding knuckles of her own rage.

"Does Gnendl have yellow eyes and no thumbs?" Isaac asks me when I describe her to him.

"No, why?"

"If she did, I'd make you a protective talisman because you'd be dealing with a powerful Jewish demon."

In spite of Gnendl making holes in my lesson plans, I continue to sketch portraits that day, and I get the majority of the kids to make their own hesitant drawings before the bell rings. As far as I'm concerned, they and I have passed the First Gate. I'm even optimistic about coaxing the more diffident kids over that threshold over the coming weeks. Who knows, maybe Gnendl will unmake her fists one day, though I doubt she'll ever stop breaking the crayons, which she pushes into her paper as if she needs to stub out all life on earth.

My most titanic obstacle soon becomes a blond pixie on the verge of puberty named Inge Hohenstein – the Silesian Shirley Temple, as I will call her in years to come, because she has curly cascades of blond hair and a stubborn nature. Her strategy is to keep me too busy with questions to teach.

"How long does crayon take to dry?"; "What would happen if the ceiling fell on us?"; "Why can't Monica draw a straight line?"

She reduces me to hopeless tears a few times in September and October, and I regard her as my nemesis until late into the first term, when she asks, "What color is a pink crayon in the dark?"

"A pink crayon is always pink!" comes my slingshot reply, but later that day, Isaac, imitating Einstein, reminds me that color does not exist in the dark.

"An object can only be *potentially* pink if there is no light," he tells me.

Maybe Inge was trying to tell me something about her own prospects. Is it far-fetched for me to believe that she has been waiting all her life for the sun to come up in whatever black-and-white universe she calls home and bring violet through red into her life?

I apologize to her the next day, which only makes her turn away as though I'm of no interest. It chills me today to think of so much I may have misunderstood about her and the rest of those kids.

But number one on my list of complete failures remains Gnendl, my eternal winter. When I ask Dr Hassgall for advice, he says, "She's scared of you."

"But I'm terrified of *her*!"

"She has trouble interpreting your facial expressions. You think you're communicating tenderness or pleasure, but she thinks you're furious at her – so enraged you might kill her."

"My God!" I exclaim, because it occurs to me that this may be part of Hansi's problem.

"Just try to be very clear in what you say to Gnendl and the others. Sooner or later she may figure out that you're on her side."

Number two on my failure-list is a chocolate-skinned boy named Karl Skölny, who has glowing blue eyes that make my breathing quicken. I've never known a black person before, and when I meet his mother, Helen, she talks of the night-scents of southern Africa, and the sunsets as "fire falling through a dome of blue". What must Karl make of our frigid winters? He never speaks except in indecipherable mumbles, and he never draws even a line. He hardly moves except to scratch his nose. *I itch, therefore I am.*

I teach three hours a day. It's odd having Hansi as a student, and there are times when he curls into me, eager to let his friends know he's my favorite, but Dr Hassgall says that he'll soon get used to my being his teacher and stop trying to secure favors. "You can't stop loving him in class, so don't even try," he counsels me, to my great relief.

I get through my first term on adrenalin and *chutzpah*. My paychecks help too. The first time I take Hansi and Isaac out to a restaurant with my own money, I feel as if I'm the star of my own big-budget Hollywood movie.

My important revelation that year comes in November: each lesson doesn't have to be clever or unique. Quite the opposite, in fact, since the kids thrive on knowing what's coming next. I have them draw the weepy-limbed spruce tree in our garden every Tuesday throughout the late fall and winter, whether it's glittering with sunlight or collecting snowflakes in its fingertips, and they get right to work, hunched over their papers, their hands moving as fast as bees.

But even knowing what's coming next does little for Inge ... One day during that first term, she gives me her angelic smile and says, "Fräulein Riedesel, would you mind moving the spruce tree?" To my confused expression, she signals to the right and says, "Over that way. It would be much better there."

"I'm afraid the tree will always be where it is," I say with false niceness. "But if you move your chair, the tree will *seem* to move."

A clever answer, I think, but Inge shifts her chair around so many times over the next five minutes, setting it down with a brutal clack each time, that the others grow jittery, and Volker, who is always only one unexpected bump or thud from tears, ends up sobbing.

No matter, even Inge and Gnendl can't stop me from loving how serious most of the kids get about drawing and painting, and the way they absent-mindedly bite their fingernails and tap their feet. It's as though they believe that no matter what they are sketching they are always designing bridges between themselves and the world, which maybe they are. For Volker, the bridge must be the night sky, because he puts different phases of the moon and stars in every drawing he does. He is such a quiet, reticent boy, though the few words that do come out of his mouth often fly out too fast, as if shot by a machine gun. We are always asking him to slow down.

Other kids delight in designing monsters. Veronika Vogt – or VV as I come to call her – draws red and brown gargoyles – precisely formed, snouted, pointy-eared creatures that seem to be made from blood. I ask her about them, but all she tells me is that the monsters need to be fixed to the paper, which involves covering them with a goopy layer of Henkel glue. Sometimes her hands get so sticky I have to take her to the sink and scrub them with pumice. She says her mother does that a lot, too. "I like my hands being clean," VV tells me, holding them up for me to inspect, "but I like glue more."

We laugh together over that. And I kiss the top of her head because I'm learning that distant kids appreciate physical closeness more than talk. Just like me, of course.

I like glue more … Just one of a hundred declarations from the kids that I will tell Isaac, Vera, and everyone else I know over the coming years.

On Mondays we draw portraits; on Tuesdays we go outside, weather permitting, and sketch flowers and trees; on Wednesdays the kids bring in objects from home and I arrange them into still-lifes on my desk; on Thursdays we sculpt clay figures; and on Fridays I read them a story, and they paint any scene they want.

Their love of knowing what to expect becomes the ground beneath us. I often stumble, but I can't really hurt myself because there is simply nowhere to fall.

I show them pictures of my favorite paintings and drawings, too – Dürer's sketch of his mother, Ribera's light-infused figure of St Sebastian surrounded by darkness … I even bring in Isaac's Chagall one day – a man and woman flying through a cockeyed village centered by an Orthodox church – and we sketch the other people who might live in the artist's hometown. I hang some of the reproductions around the room, including the *Portrait of a Rabbi* by Rembrandt that taught me about taking time with my work – years, if necessary, to make every line and shadow what they want to be. Gnendl grabs hold of Goya's *Saturn Devouring One of His Sons* as if it is the long-lost package she'd been expecting for years. Maybe that Titan's appetite for human flesh justifies her fists. So one spring day I bring her in some reproductions of gruesome paintings that I've cut out of magazines. She gives me a surprised look, gasping, then stares at me so penetratingly that I have to turn away. Is she pleased that I indulge her morbid preferences? She doesn't ask a single question that morning. A few days later, when she gets through an entire class without breaking a crayon, I suspect she is starting to trust me.

I also hang the students' drawings up on our walls; I want them to know I'm grateful for all they are showing me of their inner worlds. And proud of them.

My own work from this period becomes freer than it was before. I make faces blue and pink, and my lines become less intent on realism. I give people pointy, Pan-like ears and horns. I no longer want to make proper Prussian likenesses of people. I want to evoke the feel of them – their animal nature and solidity, their capacity for transformation. I even draw crescent moons around Volker, pulling him out toward the world. Other than Hansi, he is my favorite. Volker and I sit happily on a see-saw together that entire year, going up and down effortlessly, as though the school is teaching us to breathe together. When I think back to those times, I can feel my arms around him and my brother, and it is as if the world itself were giving everything back to me that I ever wanted.

Dr Hassgall and Else take photographs of all the kids just before the Christmas holidays, and I hide the results in my K-H Collection because so many of the students are Jews. Most of their parents have had their jobs taken away, in fact, so they can't afford our full fees, which is why our blue walls are flaking and the steps to the garden remain crudely cemented. Why, too, we shiver throughout the winter.

Dr Hassgall, Else, me and the other teachers are standing in the back row of the photographs. After the war, I'll look at all of us every couple of years and never fail to think, *My God, I was only nineteen years old, just a kid myself* ...

All of those beautiful children are sterilized by the end of that 1936–37 school year: the Silesian Shirley Temple, Monica, Volker, VV, Gnendl ... Which makes me wonder at the time how the surgeons and doctors of Germany can sleep at night. Later, of course, we'll all learn that they slept perfectly.

One day, Volker takes a sketch I've done of him and draws stars all over his face. I'm furious, because I worked hard to do a faithful portrait of him, and demand to know what he's doing in a nasty voice. Shuddering, he replies, "Raking leaves."

When tears gush in his eyes, I kneel next to him and apologize. He falls into my arms, and I hold him tight, begging him to forgive me. From then on, whenever one of the kids would ask me why I was doing something they found odd, I'd often reply, "Raking leaves," before giving my real explanation, which would always make Volker and me grin in unison.

Holding that gorgeous boy as he shakes is an important moment for me because I hadn't realized how much power I had over these little beings. And that I'd still been holding back a good deal of my love until then, thinking teachers shouldn't show their students their hearts.

We must be gentle, gentle, gentle with each other because we are very fragile ... That's what my kids teach me that year, and it's a lesson I badly needed to learn.

Tonio talks mostly about his army regimen when we're together now, and though he speaks proudly of the precision his superiors have inculcated in him, and with good humor about the terrible food, the way he often grows silent without any warning is new. It leads me to believe he's dissatisfied with the path he is on. Once, he volunteers the reason: "I wish I were free to lead a normal life."

"What's a normal life?" I ask him.

We're strolling arm in arm around the rose garden in the Tiergarten at the time, watching Hansi and Volker racing around, and he shrugs morosely, then changes the subject. As we're nearing home, however, he says, "I sometimes still dream of settling down with you and having children. Though I know you don't want that."

I feel terrible about not being able to give him what he dreams of, and this is clearly my cue to say something reassuring, but all I reply is, "A great many things have already happened to us that I could never have predicted. So let's not be too certain what the future will bring us."

After I begin my teaching career, I have my afternoons free to work on art projects and prepare supper for Hansi and my father. I go back to buying books for Isaac on occasion, though so many works have been burned, hidden, or already shipped to safety that it's getting difficult to find the authors he wants. Once a week he meets me after school, and we go for a long stroll by the Spree or in one of the city's parks, and have tea together. Or, if we're feeling in the mood for company, we head to the Jewish Old Age Home to bring chocolates to Mrs Kaufmann, which always makes her clasp her hands together and lick her lips. Sometimes, in a whisper, she asks after Roman, her high-wire Prince Charming.

Papa spends every weekday evening with Hansi and me, in the good cheer of a man who is moving up in the world. Apparently, Greta is bringing him into the upper echelons of the sewage company running our country.

He sleeps over at her apartment on Fridays and Saturdays, however. I don't mind – in fact, I prefer his absences, since the mistrustful tension between us has become a stretched cord that neither of us can quite get up the courage to cut or even talk about. So we struggle – forever linked – in silence. Very German, I'd say.

Papa, Hansi, and I listen to the radio while we eat supper so that we don't have to talk. I keep it on, in fact, whenever my father is in the house. Disembodied voices become our barrier against quarrels.

He takes Hansi out to the movies or lunch every Sunday. Guilt? Probably, but that doesn't matter because the boy hops up and down at the chance to spend all day with his father. Greta sometimes flaps along after them, but I always turn down their invitations; I'd only spoil their fun, and Mama's ghost prefers that I keep my distance.

I encourage Hansi to stay over at Volker's house on Friday nights so that my dream of sleeping beside Isaac until morning can come true. When this miracle finally comes to pass, he and I are as nervous as kids hunting for money in their father's pockets, which is probably why, when we try to make love, our bodies don't fit. I'm in tears from the palace of expectations crashing down around me. Isaac cuddles me and tells me stories about his childhood I haven't yet heard, and it's the gentle wind of his voice that leads me into sleep, until sunrise, when I wriggle free of his heavy arm over my waist and take his handsome penis in my mouth. It's while he's thrusting inside me one morning that I first realize I want to have his child. But I say nothing yet; I like the idea of a happiness that's all mine. And I probably ought to honor Mama's wishes and wait till I know Isaac better before I even broach the subject. And till I'm at least twenty-one years old.

Sometimes I wake up in the middle of those Friday nights with the softness of his penis pressed to my bottom, his hand on my head, and the faint scent of tobacco in the rise and fall of his chest, and I make myself stay awake so I can continue to feel the quiet touching of all that we are.

Being free of Hansi and Papa on Fridays also enables Vera, K-H, and Marianne to join Isaac and me for Sabbath dinner nearly every week. Little Werner usually follows me around the kitchen as I cook, watching me with captivated eyes. A future chef? He calls me Aunt Sophie in sign language, which I love. Roman comes to supper too, if he's in town. K-H goes back to photographing all of us.

Isaac's new project has become copying all of Berekiah Zarco's manuscripts out by hand into special silver-covered notebooks. He expects the work to take him two years, because – like Hebrew scribes in olden times – he must discard any page on which he makes even a tiny error. "Copying my ancestor's words is the only way I'm going to find the password to Araboth," he assures me. "Berekiah meant me to find it while writing. He's left clues. I'm sure of it."

When I see Tonio for our monthly weekend of erotic acrobatics in December 1936, he announces that his father has offered him a spectacular allowance if he'll make a career in the army. I haven't seen him this excited in a long time. "Sophie, if I save up for a few years, I'll be able to buy a used Bugatti," he explains to me as if he needs my approval. "Imagine ostrich leather seats and Brazilian mahogany doors."

So that's what God looks like to Tonio now – bird skin and tropical wood! Though I also believe he's settled on this youthful fantasy because he now accepts that his adult one – taking marriage vows with me – is very unlikely to happen. Or maybe I'm just flattering myself.

"Sounds absolutely perfect!" I tell him gushingly, wanting to encourage him.

We're in his father's apartment, naked. I'm lying on my back, studying the top of his head, which – because of his army haircut – seems too flat to me, and he's sitting up with his legs crossed, pictures of tanks spread between us, since he's desperate for the chance to drive a Panzer. His cheeks are shadowed with manly stubble, making his long-lashed brown eyes – lit captivatingly with future dreams at the moment – more seductive than ever. Can you be sure you'd break up with such a young man over politics?

"I have only one question," I tell him. "What will you do with the Bugatti in the army?"

"I'll quit as soon as I have it and buy my own garage, and fix fancy cars for movie stars!"

I adore the way his lips curl into a wily smile, and I realize I want him to be happy and fulfilled. Maybe breaking up with him right now and letting him find a Young Maiden who wants nothing more than three blond children and a ride in a fancy car would be the kindest thing for me to do.

Yet I don't. And I enjoy seeing him one weekend a month as much as ever. Are we joined by the gravity of a friendship that began long before we first kissed, a solidarity that is deeper than his adoration of Dr Goebbels and his wish for a normal life? Nevertheless, when I'm not inside the magic circle he makes out of his charm and enthusiasm, I get angry with myself for not finding the courage to move on. Maybe if Isaac were to grow jealous, I could tell Tonio we're finished. Yet he never once voices an objection.

Two months later, Tonio is transferred to the 1st Panzer Division. Trying to impress me, he writes that his best friend is Franz Wittelsbach von Bayern, the son of Prince Georg of Bavaria and grandson of Prince Leopold. "Franz is royalty, but he has to salute Colonel-General Schmidt just like me!!" Tonio tells me, his two exclamation points giving me the distinct impression he's been hoodwinked into believing that he and Franz are really regarded as equals in Germany.

I'm glad he has realized his goal of sitting atop a Panzer, but I wonder if he'll ever grow up. And will I?

During 1937, I have no contact with Rolf. And neither do Vera or Isaac, at least not that they'll admit. Though I'm pretty sure that he must have been the traitor working with Georg, a big crack often opens in my certainty as soon as I turn off the lights in my bedroom and think about all that could still go wrong with our lives. And it's no comfort that we know nothing about whom Rolf and Dr Stangl might have been passing on information to in the Nazi hierarchy.

I once tell Isaac about the terrors that still keep me up at night, and he assures me that I'm safe, as if my own welfare is all I'm concerned about. "But what about you?" I demand, of course. "What if Rolf still wants to hurt you? Maybe we need to do something about him."

"The pressure is off Rolf now that Heidi is dead," he replies. "Even if he was the traitor, he's finished hurting anyone. I'm sure of it."

"Have you spoken to him? Is that how you know?"

"No, but it doesn't matter. We've had no meetings of The Ring in a very long time. I'm living and working in a world the Nazis can't even glimpse." He pokes his finger into the center of his forehead in case I've failed to grasp his meaning.

"Be serious!" I plead.

He takes my hand and gives me a dark look. "I'm more serious than you could ever know."

Let him believe nothing can happen to him if that's what he wants, I think angrily, but what really infuriates me is that he'll no longer even tell me how he's faring with his Turkish journalists, or who he is helping to flee Germany. "It's far better for you not to know anything about all that," he says.

Over that winter and early spring, our life together stitches itself into secretive but regular patterns. Isaac and I are careful never to reveal our affection in public, and, having heard that the government is bugging thousands of lines, we learn to say only banalities over the phone. He and I almost never have a quarrel, and when we do it's nearly always because he works till dawn copying

Berekiah Zarco's manuscripts and is too exhausted the next day to supervise work at his factory or even eat the supper I prepare.

Isaac receives letters from Andre and Julia every few months, and though they are relieved to be Nazi-free, they even miss Berlin's red-neon dinginess and stink of hops. Vera, K-H, and Marianne still come over for Sabbath dinner nearly every Friday night. Herr Wachlenberg, the owner of the River Jordan Bakery on Prenzlauer Allee, is a friend of Isaac's and always helps me choose the *challah* bread for the ritual meal. Marianne teaches me how to make stuffed cabbage, Isaac's all-time favorite food. The recipe is Heidi's.

In late March, Vera, Marianne, and I make a huge Passover dinner, and the pièce de résistance is a gigantic goose with *Preiselbeeren*. It's not quite as good as the one Andre made, but K-H and Isaac gnaw at it down to the bone as if they've been starved for a month.

Tonio writes once every few weeks, as well, and we get to see each other for weekends in April, June, and October. I bring up politics now and again, to see if he'll give me any clues to what he and his friends have in store for the Jews and those who've been classified as genetically inferior. I know it's irrational to believe that he has been made aware of some top-secret strategy, but my worries make me inquisitive and, on his October visit, foolishly insistent. In consequence, he becomes tight-lipped with me in a way he never was before. "Sophie, stop! You should know by now that we don't set policy in the army," he snaps at me. "We just carry out the wishes of the government."

His continuing impatience with me leads me to believe he may have found another girl, which terrifies me at first, then becomes a kind of unspoken wish. To stay on neutral ground with him, I end up talking mostly about the school kids. He listens closely, gives me advice meant to ease my doubts, and laughs in all the right places. In a dictatorship there's safety in small talk, of course.

Even so, being able to discuss the weather, art lessons, and movie stars must be little consolation to Jewish accountants and dentists, who are soon prevented from practicing their professions. Or for the heartbroken parents who have their children taken away from them by our courts because they oppose National Socialism. Still, there is some good news for all these unfortunates: those who are arrested for protesting too vehemently will no longer be sent to the overcrowded *Konzentrationslager* at Dachau because a brand-new one called Buchenwald has opened for business!

Papa and Greta become glued to each other that summer and even take a cruise down the Danube in August. He spends only one or two nights a week at home now, usually on Tuesday and sometimes Wednesday, and he gives me an allowance so I can take care of the apartment and buy food. Hansi has learned to dial the phone and calls him sometimes in the evening, then hands me the receiver, clinging to me like a limpet while I invent some reason for interrupting Papa's dinner or cocktails, sputtering on about mail he's received and how the goldfish seem sick – anything but the taboo subject of how much his son misses him.

"He'll come home on Tuesday and take you for dinner," I tell Hansi every time I hang up. And I'm not lying. On his weekly visit, Papa is attentive and kind to his son. I don't want to let my anger tear up the shreds of a relationship they still have and usually flee the house.

Hansi's main teacher Else and I go out for a drink after school every Friday, and whenever she gets a little tipsy, she reveals bits and pieces of her love life. Her great passion, Bettina, was a salesgirl from Charlottenburg, but their clandestine relationship ended when the young woman went back to her husband two years ago.

Else doesn't care for movies, but she adores theater and opera. In November, she takes me to *Tristan and Isolde*. All those voices rising and falling together are like a warm ocean of sound washing over me and the entire world. I could almost forgive Wagner for being the Opposite-Compass' favorite composer.

When I look back at that year, I think of it as a peaceful island, when I was still young enough – having recently turned twenty – to believe that the distant horizon in every direction belonged to Isaac, Vera, Hansi, and me, and not our enemies.

Then 1938 arrives and I realize we've been descending into the underworld without our even knowing it. Though it begins calmly enough ...

Isaac has his seventieth birthday party on the 1st of February, 1938. Vera comes over early, and she and I prepare two ducks in orange sauce and bake a chocolate cake, though she keeps trying to make me deviate from my mother's recipe and pours two shots of kirsch into the melted cocoa while I'm fussing with the oven. Then she scrapes the leftover batter from the bowl with her finger and licks it off with wolf-like joy.

Mama's ghost watches Papa and Greta

"Why do I think you might even eat seagulls and crows on occasion?" I tell her.

"I prefer hamsters," she replies. "More light meat!"

She and I manage to cram seventy yellow candles – and one red one for good luck! – into the icing, which bears Isaac's name written in butter-cream. He is not allowed in the kitchen. When I go to the bedroom to see what he's chosen to wear – since I've forbidden him from putting on anything with holes or stains – he's naked except for the blue and yellow argyle socks I've bought him as part of his birthday present, which also includes new flannel pajamas. He's staring into his wardrobe as if it's an abyss, his pipe dangling down from his mouth.

"What are you doing still undressed?" I demand.

"I've got so little choice!"

"You have beautiful trousers and shirts you've never even worn!"

He wrinkles his nose. "They smell of mothballs."

"Is this hesitation because you're anxious about turning seventy?"

"You tell me!" He presses himself into my hip so I can feel that hesitance is hardly his problem, but I don't give myself to him because he'd end up snoozing through dinner.

Has his birthday sent extra hormones pulsing to his *putz*? He moves my hand to his impressive erection while we make quick work of the ducks, then gets tipsy and dances with me to Kurt Weill as if he's got warm coals in his belly. He even leans me back – Rudolf Valentino-style – and gives me a long kiss. The *alter kacker* as *The Sheik* ...

The next day, after work, he goes back to copying his manuscripts, and he tells me he's gratified to be getting to know his ancestor better. "I can sense him standing behind me and blessing me.

Though he doesn't look like I expected. His hair is shoulder length, a bit curly, and he has a scar on his cheek."

"So you really do see Berekiah?"

Raising his eyebrows, he asks, "Is that unusual?"

For the first time, Isaac reads the *Megillah*, the Book of Esther, to me on Purim eve, which falls that year on the 14th of February. He sings the text in his warm tenor, and though I don't understand a word of the Hebrew, I sit happily between his legs, daydreaming of the baby he will make in me. He taps my head whenever he says the villain Hainan's name, and I boo and holler, as is the tradition. After I go back home, he stays up all night praying by the light of a single candle.

The next day, just before sundown, he and I rush off to the Jewish Old People's Home, Hansi and Volker straggling behind us. We make a brief detour to the River Jordan, and Herr Wachlenberg hands him a giant box of triangular cookies – *hamantaschen* – that are special to Purim.

Hansi and Volker are fourteen years old now, and both of them are taller than me. My brother is slim and graceful – like a faun. He needs to shave his mustache twice a week, and his cheeks have an adult angularity that I find exciting. He's also become fastidious about combing his hair to the side. Have his bangs been banished by thoughts of girls? I don't ask. Volker admits that he thinks about his classmate Monica all the time but hasn't yet told her of what he calls his "admiration" for her.

Vera and Isaac have sewn masks for us to wear at the Old Age Home – another Purim tradition. We've all got different colored snouts – gold for Hansi, ruby-red for Volker, silver for me, and black for Isaac. Mrs Kaufmann and most of the old folks feign terror when they spot us, which makes Isaac howl with joy. He prances around the hallways, growling, his teeth bared.

"Happy is the man who inspires shrieks and then gets to give

everyone *hamantaschen*!" he tells us exultantly on the way home,
handing me one last cookie that he's saved just for me.

On the 7th of March, Isaac bolts his apartment door and won't
answer my pleas that he let me in.

"Go away!" he hollers once, and then says nothing more.

Panicked, I call Vera. She comes over and bangs on the door
with her fists to no avail. We go Prenzlauer Allee and call up to his
window, which makes him yank his curtains closed. Only two days
later does he open his door. His face is lined with exhaustion and
he smells like hell. Pouches sag under his eyes. He tells me he's been
praying for forty-eight hours. "The stained glass of our world has
become so fractured that it cannot sustain its own weight, and it
will soon shatter to pieces," he explains somberly. "It's unbelievable
how quickly it's happening."

He sobs in my arms. I lead him to bed, his steps labored. I try
to get him to sleep, but he's restless and inconsolable. The only
way I can get him under the covers is by promising not to leave
him. I get him to swallow half a luminal with a glass of schnapps,
and that finally does the trick.

He remains despairing over the next few days, but he refuses
to talk to me about the shattering of our world. Then, on the
12th of March, Germany annexes Austria. On the radio, we hear
that thousands of Hitler's opponents have been arrested, and the
newspapers show photographs of bearded rabbis made to sweep
the streets, onlookers laughing merrily behind them. Do Aryan
seamstresses make lampshades and purses out of the skin of the 500
Austrian Jews who commit suicide over the next month? That's a
question we can only ask in hindsight, of course, but Isaac and I do
already wonder how long will it take for the good Christian doctors
of Graz and Salzburg to take their knives to the distant children, as

well as to the deaf, blind, and deformed. Such speculations might explain Isaac's deep depression, except that he tells me, "No, we have a far bigger problem than Austria."

He's hunched over his copying work at his desk, and I'm sitting on his bed. He's wearing my beret because he claims it helps him keep his thoughts inside his head.

"So what's our bigger problem?" I ask. When he remains buried in his text, I add in a tone of warning, "Tell me right this instant or we're going to have a quarrel like you won't believe!"

He turns around with sunken, distant eyes. "The three upper *kelim* won't last much longer. They're already spilling blood on all of us."

"What are the *kelim*?"

"You remember when I told you about Isaac Luria, the kabbalist from Safed? Luria says that ten *kelim*, vessels, were originally meant to contain the Lord's light, but that they weren't strong enough. Seven of them shattered, which multiplied injustice and imbalance in our Lower Realms. The moral substance of our world came undone, and the *kelipot* came to have real power."

"What are the *kelipot*?"

"Evil beings, or if you prefer, our capacity for evil deeds and thoughts." He fills the bowl of his pipe. "But you see, Sophele, three of the vessels did not shatter, which is a good thing, because if they had, our world would have been reduced to the chaos before God spoke His initial word."

I come to him and kiss him on the lips, since he looks as if he needs my reassurance. "What are the three vessels that remained intact?" I ask.

"*Kether Elyon, Hokhmah, and Binah*. The Crown, Wisdom, and Insight. But I believe that what is happening now is that these three last vessels are coming undone. The stained glass into which we have been born will come crashing down, and our lives will end. It will be as if all this" – he sweeps his hand in a wide arc to indicate our universe – "never existed."

Is he a madman or the most clear-sighted person in Germany? We await a sign, since he's convinced the Lord will make it known to him when the upper vessels have shattered.

"And once they have, how long will it take for the world to end?" I question as he lights his pipe and draws in the calming smoke.

"There's no way to know. A second, a year, a decade ... God's time is not like ours."

"And if you journey to Araboth and ask the Lord to stop this from happening?"

"He will redeem the world."

What is the sign we await? Isaac doesn't know. Could it be the mandatory registration of all property held by Jews, which comes on the 26th of April? He's certain that isn't it. Or Hitler's order to destroy the Munich synagogue? After that grand old building comes crashing down on the 9th of June, Isaac shakes his head. "That's not it either."

Isaac after staying up all night to search for the prayer formula he will need to enter Araboth

How about the mass arrest of those Berlin Jews who have police records on the 15th of June? "After all," I tell him, "fifteen hundred Jews in concentration camps sounds like an alarm bell to me."

"No, no, no!" he replies angrily. He points his pipe at me. "And close the door on your way out. I need to work."

Among the Berlin Jews dragged out of their homes on the 15th of June is Gnendl Rosencrantz's pharmacist father. Dr Hassgall says he has been arrested because the police were called to his shop in 1934 when he got into a fistfight with a customer who called him a dirty Bolshevik Jew. Isaac tells me that's nothing; Moshe Cohen, the Walking Stock Exchange I met on the day we protested against the first Nazi boycott of Jewish shops, was taken away for having unpaid parking tickets!

The day after her father's arrest, I try to talk to Gnendl as soon as she arrives, but she squirms out of my grasp and sits at her desk, vibrating with such clenched anger that I decide to wait an hour or so before trying again. But while we're drawing a bouquet of flowers, she pushes all her crayons to the floor and rushes into the back garden. She sits on the swings. I kneel next to her.

"I only want to be nice to you," I say, because I know by now my intentions have to be absolutely clear. "May I touch you?"

She shakes her head and moans.

"Then would you let me push you on the swings?"

No answer. I stand behind her and grip the wooden chair she's sitting in. As she pendulums through the air, she closes her eyes tight, as though craving darkness. I push her for a long time, and the other kids crowd by the door, watching us and whispering nervously.

The next morning, Gnendl doesn't come to school. And not the next day either. A few days later, after Dr Hassgall makes some frantic phone calls, we discover that her mother, lacking any means of support, has had to give up their apartment. Fearing that her phone was being tapped and letters intercepted, she didn't dare tell us that she and Gnendl had left for her sister's house in the suburb of Spandau.

In July, K-H takes a record number of photographs, because the government has decided that all Jews must carry special identity cards. I clip Isaac's silver tufts back for the shot since Nazi geneticists have decided that the left ear of Jews gives away their Semitic descent and must be clearly visible in every picture.

We have special ear-inspectors now, and yet the world regards the Germans as a rational people. To my utter astonishment, it's a reputation that will even persist after the war.

I keep my hair pinned behind my left ear during classes now. A hollow gesture perhaps, since I am a Christian, but I will not let Volker, Inge, and the rest of my Jewish students be threatened without showing them clearly that I'm on their side.

Isaac and all the other Jewish men of Germany have also had *Israel* added as a middle name to their identity cards, as decreed by law, just as Jewish women have been forced to add *Sarah*. And his fingerprints need to be registered; after all, as Dr Goebbels explains, it is the responsibility of any good government to keep track of what he calls *Ungezieferr*, meaning vermin. So one sunny afternoon we wait on line at our local police station on Rykestraße, right next to the synagogue where Isaac attends services. Nearly everyone is more offended than angry. "Who would have believed proper law-abiding Germans could be treated like common criminals!" one elderly woman in a wheelchair tells me.

How could you still not understand the Nazis don't regard you as German! I want to shout at her, but Isaac reaches for my shoulder to keep me from making a scene.

His left and right index fingers are inked and pressed down to paper by a policeman. I almost quarrel with him on the way home for his not even voicing a protest, but all my energy dissipates on seeing the ink smudges that he's rubbed onto his cheeks. Beneath his dark eye pouches, they look like bruises that will never heal. On the way home, we see Gestapo officers smashing the windows of a printing house on Prenzlauer Allee. On the door, they've painted "On Vacation in Dachau!" We don't say a thing. Our silence feels like a betrayal for which we'll never be able to make amends.

That night we learn that Jewish doctors are prohibited from practicing medicine.

"When Jews are no longer allowed to use bathrooms we'll have mass protests," Vera tells me, trying to make light of the new laws, but my sense of humor is gone, having vanished when Isaac, K-H, and Marianne had a big *J* stamped on their passports. By now, K-H has warned me that Isaac better ask for a Turkish visa quite soon because that *J* is making it much harder to emigrate. "Countries are reducing their quotas," he tells me. "You've got to convince him to make plans."

I sneak up on Isaac late one Friday night after our Sabbath dinner. He's in his kitchen preparing the strong coffee that helps him continue his work into the early morning.

"Isaac, maybe you should go visit your Cousin Abraham in Istanbul for a little while," I tell him. "I'm sure he's worried about you, and all your relatives there would undoubtedly love to see you." I don't dare add that he will also then be able to further his work with Turkish journalists.

"I know what you want," he replies, glaring at me, "but I'm not fleeing. Has it never occurred to you that Germany is my home?"

"I know it's your home, but what's that got to do with anything?"

"My wife and my parents are buried in Berlin. And as much as I regret it, my son died fighting for this wretched country."

When he turns away from me, I grab his arm. "And when they knock down all the synagogues, what then?"

He marches out of the kitchen into his bedroom and shuts the door.

Over the next few days, Isaac refuses to eat more than matzo and cheese or to turn away from his manuscripts. Despite what he once confessed to me about my gravity keeping him tied to me, I am helpless against his withdrawal.

He never hugs or kisses me now. I miss our tenderness. And the caresses of his whispering voice. And the sense that we are in this fight together.

This is a time of cold distance – the winter of my heart.

Vera tries to help, as do K-H, Marianne, and Roman, but nothing they say to Isaac can make him return to us. He no longer sets foot in his factory, and Vera tells me that his workers are petrified that Zarco Industries will soon go bankrupt, leaving seventeen tailors and seamstresses unemployed, six of whom are Jews who'll probably be unable to find other jobs. I set off for the factory to try to help with the accounts, but the files are a complete jumble, so I phone Dr Hassgall, who once again saves the day. He calls our work together *forensic accounting*, since it's more archaeology than arithmetic.

The little hope that enters my life at this time comes from Mr Mannheim, who plays *Jesu Joy of Man's Desiring* every evening now, as if he knows that Bach is what we need in this wilderness. The melody – a dance up to the sun – seems to come from a simpler world that's long gone, however.

One evening, Hansi announces to me that he won't get undressed with me in the room. I don't need to look long into his challenging eyes to know that he needs – and deserves – his privacy, so he and I move my bed into the sitting room, between the fish tank and the radio. I leave the music on sometimes to help me fall asleep and wonder why I didn't think of this before.

In September, K-H sells his studio to a Christian friend because a lawyer has advised him that the Nazis may soon start confiscating Jewish property. He and Marianne have applied for visas for both England and the United States. Marianne has a cousin in London who can sponsor her.

Later that month, we get a big scare: Isaac is arrested by the Gestapo on the evening of Wednesday, the 28th of September. He'd previously given me instructions to contact his one remaining Christian client – Wolfgang Lange of Munich – if he were ever in trouble with the government. On the phone that night, Herr Lange is patient with my tearful explanation, and he assures me in a calm, avuncular voice that he'll have Isaac out in a day or two. He somehow makes good on that promise and Isaac comes home the next evening, his walk a fragile balancing act, his eyes puffy and bloodshot. I sense the horror he's been through in the desperate way he grips me when we embrace, and in the solemn, moist-eyed way he gazes around his apartment. While he's shaving in the bathtub, he tells me he was taken to the police station in Alexanderplatz and interrogated through the night. "Which wasn't so bad," he shrugs, dipping his razor in the bathwater, "because the mattress on my cot was so lumpy that I couldn't sleep anyway."

He wants me to laugh but I can't. And he won't tell me if he was beaten, though there's a red welt on his cheek where he must have been slapped or punched. I sit on the edge of the tub and shampoo his hair. "How did Herr Lange get you out?" I ask.

"He knows some important Nazis, and he told them that my factory is indispensable to him – that he couldn't stock his women's clothing shops without me."

"And what information did the Nazis want to get from you?"

"Who knows? They kept pressing me to tell them how I was trying to undermine the government. I assured them I wasn't working against Hitler or anyone else, and that I was simply journeying as far as I could in my prayers. After a while, I got the feeling they thought I wasn't right in the head." He smiles up at me boyishly and places some shampoo foam on my nose with the tip of his finger. "Which was, of course, exactly what I wanted them to think."

Isaac's arrest is a very bad sign, of course, and Vera and a committee of seamstresses from his factory meet with him to beg him to sell his business and apartment to a Christian before the Nazis seize all his property. Despite my protests, he puts his flat and boathouse in my name, and sells Zarco Industries for one Reichsmark to Dr Hassgall, who enlists me to go around to former clients to drum up more business for the company, since Herr Lange and Isaac's two remaining Jewish clients are hardly enough to pay salaries and bills.

So it is that I again learn the humiliation of dressing like a Young Maiden. Vera does my lipstick and mascara, and I show a Greta-like, red-pepper smile to the Aryan businessmen I entertain. I drink the champagne they slip into my hand, and to my eternal shame I once even let a jowled Prussian stinking of cheap cigars run his fat hand along my thigh. "Now that the management is Jew-free," he says, making a gangsterish clicking noise with his tongue, "I think we can work something out."

This from a man who invited Isaac to his daughter's wedding nine years earlier.

I have to scrub myself in the bath to get the stink of his fat fingers off me. But the contract is all that counts, Vera assures me. Maybe that's just her self-interest talking, but who among us can judge her? And who can say where she gets a gun ...?

*

In mid-October, Tonio's Panzer Division rolls past Dresden into Sudetenland to "free" that province from its Czechoslovakian rulers. In his first letter, he writes that the German army has been met with open arms, and he even had red roses tossed to him by two girls standing on the balcony of a house in the town of Teplice v Čechách. "To keep you from getting jealous," he writes, "I enclose a gift from one of the shops there. I hope you like it!"

Enclosed is a pale-blue scarf. Very handsome, but I can easily imagine a terrified Jewish shopkeeper on his knees, handing it to Tonio as part of a bribe to spare his life. I never even try it on.

A couple of weeks later, 17,000 Polish Jews, some of whom have been residing in Germany for a decade or more, are rounded up and sent in boxcars to the Polish border town of Zbozyn, where they languish in no-man's land – camping on the train or on the streets – since the government of Poland refuses to accept them. Vera joins a small protest in the Neukölln neighborhood of Berlin, a workers' stronghold. I hear the story told breathlessly by Isaac only that evening, but apparently the Gestapo started shooting, and so did Vera. She told him she put a bullet into the shoulder of a storm-trooper. When he collapsed, she stepped on his face.

She's exultant when she sneaks over later that night to Isaac's apartment. "I should have started stepping on those little men five years ago!" she tells me. Leaning close to me, she adds, "When I heard his nose cracking under my heel ... It was the most wonderful sound I ever heard!"

"Except that you've put yourself in danger!" Isaac bellows. "And you may be needed here with me."

He has a Biblical way of talking and gesturing now, as if every word he says might be the stone that fells Goliath. His stern power terrifies me, and at times the playful man I fell in love with seems to have vanished entirely.

Vera must be the easiest woman in Berlin to identify, and the Gestapo are sure to search Isaac's apartment, factory, and warehouse for her. So where should she hide?

We set out for Emdener Straße right away, but the city does not seem to be on our side. I'll never forget the dim, miserable glare of the streetlamps, and the black, coal-like hardness of the Spree, as if it were about to blaze into flame, and the gawking of a group of Nazi Youth standing in front of Heiland Church. We take turns carrying her suitcase, which contains her sewing machine. "It's all that stands between me and ruin," she tells me. "I'd never go anywhere without it."

That makes me feel a strange sense of disquiet, and I soon remember a time when she didn't take it with her. But for now I say nothing. I take out the key to the King David School, let us in, and turn on the lights. We walk to Dr Hassgall's office, whispering in shameful voices, because we're endangering the school.

Vera drops down on the couch. "I promise I'll leave before classes start in the morning," she assures me. Weariness having finally overcome her exultation, she closes her eyes and leans back.

"But how will you get out of the city?" I ask her.

"I'll take care of that," Isaac tells us. "Vera, I'll pick you up here at six in the morning. I'll ask K-H for his car."

"Where will you take her?" I ask him.

"We'll go to Cologne," she replies. "I have cousins and an uncle there. And from there I'll make my way to Andre." She looks up at Isaac. "Then, Istanbul."

Isaac nods, and I can see from the way they look at each other that they agreed on this plan long ago. Andre must have gone to Antwerp to help Jews and others fleeing Germany. How did I fail to understand that they'd developed an ongoing strategy?

"How many people have you helped get out by now?" I ask Isaac.

"Nine. Not including Julia and Martin. But there'll be more."

Turing to Vera, I say, "So you knew that you'd need to leave one day."

"Once the Opposite-Compass started pointing us toward our graves, how could I make my future in Germany?"

"And your gun, what did you do with it?"

"I tossed it in the Spree."

"Where'd you get it?"

"I inherited it from Andre."

"Vera, when you fled Isaac's apartment after your unborn baby was murdered ... you left without your sewing machine."

"I don't remember."

"Still, that's what happened."

"So what's the difference?" she snarls.

"You said before that your sewing machine is all that stands between you and ruin. Why would you leave it behind unless you had to?"

"Listen, Sophele, I'll solve all the mysteries for you one day soon, but there's no time right now," she says enigmatically, and she shushes me with an angry gesture when I insist on answers.

Saying good-bye to her makes me ache with hopelessness. When we hug, she presses her lips to the top of my head for a long time, as though to make sure she will remain in my memory forever. When we separate, I feel as if I'm standing in the presence of a timeless being, because not even a day seems to have passed since we met in the courtyard of our building. The knowledge that my world will be much smaller when she leaves chokes my voice.

"Why did you choose me?" I ask in a whisper. A question I didn't know I had.

She wipes away her tears. "Choose you? What do you mean?" She fumbles around in her bag for her cigarettes.

"You befriended me. Why?"

"Sophele, who the hell ever knows why two people are attracted to each other? Besides, it was Isaac who brought you into our circle." She lights her cigarette.

"Sophele, I've always thought you were beautiful," Isaac tells me, his hands on my shoulders, and his eyes are full of affection for me for the first time in months. I fall into his arms.

Vera smiles at me as I'm encircled by his protective embrace and says, "Maybe it's because I'm not envious of your good looks. Because you're one of the *Erbkranke* – hereditarily diseased. Just like me."

"What's my disease?" I ask.

"It's always been Hansi, of course. And happily, you'll never be cured."

CHAPTER EIGHTEEN

"What did Vera mean when she said that she'd solve all the mysteries for me?" I ask Isaac as he and I head home. "Do you think she knows for sure who murdered Heidi and Dr Stangl?"

"I have no idea," he says.

"Was she involved in their deaths?"

"I only know what she promised me – that she didn't kill them."

At dawn the next morning, Isaac picks Vera up and they drive across Germany to Cologne. After a quick supper together in a beer hall she's always liked near the main train station, he drops her at her cousins' apartment, then speeds back to Berlin. He manages to make it home by eight in the morning. He's been up for twenty-eight straight hours when I visit him. He's washing dishes in the pajamas I bought for his seventieth birthday, barefoot. His eyes are red and his back is bent, but he claims he's drunk too much coffee to sleep. I make him sit down and heat up some milk, then pour it into a glass with a healthy shot of schnapps. Leaving Berlin seems to have been good for our intimacy, if not his body; as I put him to bed, he talks about his concern for Vera and, pressing my hand to his stubbly cheek, begs me to stay with him. So I call the school and leave a message for Else saying I'll be late to work, then lie down next to him, caressing his beautiful hair. Once he's snoring, I sit at his desk and watch him. He's part of my breathing now. That's what I realize while he sleeps.

Will either of us ever see Vera again?

K-H and Marianne visit Isaac a few nights later, distraught. Her cousin in London has written that he will be unable to sponsor them because he is opening a second creamery in Manchester. She shows us the letter, which is written in German: "Once the new creamery starts turning a profit, I assure you we'll apply for your visas, though we've been told that your deafness may complicate matters."

Shanghai is said to be accepting Jews, and she and K-H have applied for visas there in case the United States also fails them.

On the radio that evening, Monday, the 7th of November, Hansi and I hear a news bulletin about the attempted assassination of Ernst vom Rath, the Third Secretary at the German Embassy in Paris. His assailant is reported to be a seventeen-year-old German Jew named Herschel Grynszpan. He apparently walked into the embassy and asked to speak to Ambassador von Welczek. Vom Rath was sent out to meet with the boy, who promptly shot him twice in the abdomen.

Vom Rath teeters between life and death for two days. Isaac prays he falls on the side of life, fearing reprisals, since the newspapers are full of grotesque threats against the Jews and the need for a final resolution to what they call the "Jewish question."

Rumors I hear at school explain away Grynszpan's act as the result of vom Rath having broken off their secret love affair. Only after the war do we learn that the boy's parents, sister, and brother had been shoved on boxcars and shipped to Poland in late October.

On Wednesday the 9th, vom Rath dies, and his assassination is described as a moral outrage by the Nazi leadership. Later that day, two Gestapo men arrive at Isaac's warehouse and factory, searching for weapons, but all they find is an old saber stored in a backroom. "My army sword," Isaac explains. "Stupid of me to forget it. I could have sold it and used the funds to help get more people out of Germany."

That night, near midnight, I awake to the sound of shouting. I rush into my old bedroom, worried about Hansi. He's standing bare-chested at the window, which he's thrown open.

"Are you all right?" I ask him.

He nods, then makes a breaking motion with his hands and designs the sign for glass. He points down Marienburger Straße. I slip in beside him and lean out. The sidewalk outside Frau Koslowski's grocery is covered with shards from her shattered window.

"Burglars," I whisper. "I better call the police."

He shakes his head and crosses his index finger and thumb – his shorthand for *swastika*.

"Nazis broke her windows?" I ask.

"Yes," he signs, so I go back to the sitting room and slip on my clothes. Papa is home tonight and comes to me, scratching his head, also bare-chested.

"Where are you going?" he asks me in a drowsy voice.

"Someone's robbed Frau Koslowski," I lie. "I'll just check she's all right."

"Sophie, let the police handle it!" he orders.

I go to the door. "Watch Hansi," I tell him.

Outside, I smell smoke from the west mixing with the odor of hops. And I hear shouting voices, which must mean a crowd has assembled wherever the fire is, but I go instead to Frau Koslowski's grocery. I walk slowly, tense, ready to run, because I realize that my neighborhood – the east, west, north, and south of my mind – is no longer safe. A puddle of milk has spilled through Frau Koslowski's smashed doorway; several of the shelves have been knocked to the floor.

I find the old woman sitting in her beige nightgown at the back of the shop, in front of the doorway to her flat, pressing a bloody towel to her cheek with her bony hand.

Another woman is sitting next to her, young, in a rumpled floral dress. I've seen her in the neighborhood before. She looks up at me, startled.

"I'm a friend," I say. "I live just down the street."

"I'm her upstairs neighbor," the woman tells me.

"It's me, Sophie, Frau Koslowski," I say, waving.

She looks up at me with pink, squinting eyes. She doesn't recognize me. She's terrified.

"They mistook her for a goddamned Jew," the upstairs neighbor says bitterly.

I walk west, across Prenzlauer Allee, then begin to run ahead. Just as I'd guessed, flames are curling out the windows of the Rykestraße synagogue, releasing a thick black smoke. Firemen have arrived and are blasting water inside. A police captain from the station next door has taken charge and his officers are holding back a crowd of about a hundred.

"Let the damn thing burn down!" shouts a Nazi Youth. Around him are at least a dozen of his colleagues and four storm-troopers. One with a thick mustache still carries a can of gasoline, and he makes no effort to hide it. All of them are in a back-patting, good-humored mood.

"Let it turn to ash!" another of the boys shouts.

An old man with pajama bottoms showing under his overcoat grabs his arm. "I live two houses away. You want my home to go up in flames too?"

Fuck off!" the Nazi Youth replies, wriggling free.

Turning to the woman next to me, I ask, "Is anyone trapped inside?"

"I don't know," she tells me.

Her husband looks at me angrily, so I walk away and look for Isaac, Rini, and the Munchenbergs, but the only Jewish person I recognize is Herr Wachlenberg, the baker at the River Jordan. At the corner of Tresckow Straße, he's been forced down to all fours by Gestapo officers. I'm only twenty paces away. I should run to him, but terror has gripped my gut and I dare not move. A Gestapo officer orders him to crawl on his hands and knees. A small group laughs caustically.

A big man in an overcoat, his hands in his pockets and an unlit cigarette dangling from his lip, steps forward and kicks Herr Wachlenberg in his belly. With a grunt, the baker falls on his side, moaning. He brings his knees up by his head protectively.

It's the assailant's hands in his pockets I'll never forget – as if breaking a Jew's ribs is a casual thing. As easy as lighting his cigarette, which he does while standing over the wounded man.

Herr Wachlenberg spots me as I stride toward him. Giving me a panicked look, his eyes black with dread, he shakes his head. I can hear his thoughts easily enough: *Don't risk it!*

I'll sketch and even paint my feelings dozens of times in subsequent years, though I never get them right. Maybe only Hieronymus Bosch could do justice to that burning atmosphere of hate and cruelty.

Trembling with rage, I reach for Herr Wachlenberg's shoulder to try to tug him to his feet.

"Get away from the dog!" I hear a man shout.

I'll never be certain what happens next. As if God Himself takes hold of me – with no time passing, in between the ticks of a clock – I find myself thrown back onto the cobbles, the air ripped from my chest. Has a Gestapo officer struck me in the gut? Or was it the man with his hands in his pockets?

I've skinned both my hands badly and am fighting for air. An old woman with a tangle of gray hair is leaning down toward me. Behind her I can see the night sky. When did the sun go down? Maybe that's why I'm so cold. And where is Hansi?

"You'll be all right," she tells me.

From behind, I feel pressure on my shoulders, and soon I'm sitting up again. Then I see Isaac's worried face.

"What happened?" I ask him.

"I'm not sure. I just got here. I was hoping you'd stayed at home. You'll never learn, will you?" He kisses the top of my head, then tries to lift me up, but I'm too dizzy.

"Just let me sit here for a minute."

After I catch my breath, he manages to get me to my feet. My legs are cold and numb, so I lean on him. He notices that my right palm is bleeding and pulls out a splinter of glass. Taking out his handkerchief, he ties it around my hand.

The smell of smoke brings me back to myself. "Herr Wachlenberg ... where is he?" I ask, and I look around without spotting him.

"Sophie, we're going home," he replies sternly.

"Take me to his bakery first."

Isaac keeps his arm behind my waist to prop me up. Onlookers curse us. A bit of luck under the circumstances, because if they knew what we do in bed, they'd murder us instead. I recognize some of the shouting people – a butcher named Mueller from whom Mama used to buy sausages, a blond woman who'd always sit in one of the front pews at church, a bearded businessman who walks his white whippet on Marienburger Straße ... How could I ever have thought that everyone in my neighborhood was a good person at heart? What illusions children carry!

The River Jordan is all broken glass and splintered wood, but that makes no difference now; dangling out the first-floor window, just above the bakery – stripped naked, his head in a noose and a piece of bread stuffed in his mouth – is Herr Wachlenberg.

Another image I will try to sketch and fail. Part of my collection of half-finished pictures.

Professor Munchenberg answers our knocks and tells us that he and his wife are fine, and that she's trying to fall back to sleep. The radio is on at a low volume. "Nothing will ever be the same now," he tells me in a resigned voice. "Though maybe that's a good thing."

When we reach the landing outside Isaac's apartment, a man, thin and pale, with short, unkempt gray hair, is sitting on his heels in the corner. He's wearing a long white nightshirt but is naked from the waist down. He holds his own left arm, which is bleeding near the elbow, and his head jerks, as though in spasms. One of his eyes stares at nothing, the other darts around, seemingly in search of a fluttering butterfly. I recognize him as the man I've seen walking on the arm of an elegant young woman in the garden at the center of Wörther Platz. They have a bouncy, brown-and-white Shetland sheepdog who smells like an old pillow and whose name is Ringelblume, German for Marigold. I know, because Hansi insists on petting her whenever we spot them.

"Who's there?" he whispers.

"It's me, Isaac." He offers his hand, slowly, tenderly, as if this foundling might run off.

"I hear other breathing," the man says suspiciously.

"A friend. A young woman named Sophie."

He shudders, so Isaac takes another step forward and touches his cheek, which makes the man seize Isaac's hand. He gently steps the old tailor's fingertips over his closed eyes and lips. "That is you, isn't it?"

"Beethoven is even beautiful in Braille," Isaac replies, as if it's a sentence in code.

The man laughs in a relieved burst. "How many years ago did I tell you that?" he questions.

"Too long." Isaac helps him to his feet.

"There was no time to dress," the man says, crossing his hands over his private parts. "I'm sorry."

"Don't be silly. I helped your mother change your diapers when you were a baby. I'll get you some clothes as soon as we get inside." Isaac nods for me to open the door and leads the poor man forward, but then, suddenly pale, he asks in a fearful voice, "Where's your cello?"

"Back at the apartment, smashed."

"Damn those bastards! I'll go for it as soon as I make you comfortable."

"No, leave it for now."

"And Ringelblume?"

"In my wardrobe hiding. I locked her in there as soon as the Nazis started shouting for me. She'll be fine. I gave her a bowl of water."

I reach for Isaac's shoulder, hopefulness in my expression. Smiling as though presenting me with a treasure, he says, "Yes, Sophele, this is Benjamin Mannheim."

And that's when the tears I've been holding back flood me.

After Isaac bolts the door and brings out a bottle of schnapps, we sit together in his living room, our guest in a pullover and pair of trousers that I've fetched for him, both far too big. He doesn't want slippers. "I want to be able to wiggle my toes," he says, laughing as he demonstrates. "They're proof that I'm still alive. I thought I was a dead man."

Mr Mannheim is a bit giddy, and as if to prove it, his one real eye keeps dancing around.

It's chilly in the apartment, so I've draped a crocheted throw rug over my shoulders and given a blanket to Mr Mannheim in case he needs it. I'm sitting cross-legged on a cushion in front of our guest, staring up at him. He and Isaac sit close together on the sofa.

"I can't believe you're here," I tell him excitedly. "I've wanted to meet you for years. I've seen you many times in Wörther Platz, but I didn't know you were you."

"I hope I'm not a disappointment," he replies with amused lips.

"Of course, not."

I study his slender face. Another Jewish man who doesn't eat enough. Berlin must have 20,000. A long, painful-looking scar leads from his right eyebrow across his forehead, then down to his left ear. "You play beautifully," I tell him.

He bows his head gracefully. "Thank you."

"So, don't keep me in suspense, what happened to you?" Isaac asks him.

"I counted four voices. They smashed the cello, and some crockery, and then they led me out to the street and spun me around so that I lost track of direction. They told me to find my way home, and that when I did, they'd have a gift waiting for me. I suspected their present might be a bullet, so I sat down on the sidewalk until I could get my balance back. They didn't like that, and one of them whacked me hard on my left arm with what must have been a plank of wood." He holds his hand up and grimaces. "It might be broken."

"I'll call a doctor," Isaac tells him.

"Is he Jewish?" Mr Mannheim asks anxiously.

"Yes."

"Examining my arm could get him into trouble."

"Listen, Benni, I won't tell the Gestapo if you don't."

Our guest laughs, and Isaac telephones Dr Löwenstein, but his wife says he was arrested a few hours earlier. She doesn't know where he's been taken.

"I'm afraid things are worse than I feared," he tells us. "Mrs Löwenstein says that Jews are being beaten up and hauled off by mobs and brownshirts in some other areas of the city."

Mr Mannheim closes his eyes and leans back as though into memories. And for the first time, I wonder if Jews carry a genetic vestige of 2,000 years of persecution in their very bodies.

"Sophele, would you be kind enough to make us some tea?" Isaac asks me, and when I nod, he adds, "And bring in some matzo. I'm famished all of a sudden."

"Because you don't eat anything during the day!"

"Do you have a Gentile doctor?" Isaac asks Mr Mannheim as I leave the room.

"Almost," our guest replies, bending over and folding cuffs on his trousers to keep them from hitting the floor. "He's three-quarters Christian, which means he can still practice medicine with two hands and one leg."

"He must do a lot of hopping."

Two Jewish men laughing gleefully in the middle of a pogrom. I don't know how they do it.

"I'll call him in the morning," Mr Mannheim says.

"For now, the schnapps will help take away some of the pain," Isaac says. "Drink up."

Isaac and he talk while I boil water and brew our tea. I also fetch some aspirin. Mr Mannheim takes the pills out of my hand with delicate but quick movements, his hand like a pecking bird. Then he reaches up to my cheek. "May I feel your face?"

I sit next to him on the sofa and close my eyes as he sculpts me into his memory. His purposeful touch carries me back to the day I met Vera.

"What happened next, Benni?" Isaac asks.

Mr Mannheim takes a greedy gulp of his tea. "The men ran off and I stumbled over here. You know, Isaac, I thought I'd managed to avoid this sort of ... of attack. An old colleague of mine from the conservatory is at Gestapo headquarters now. He's still a reasonable violinist. On occasion we play duets at his apartment. He's protected me against the denunciations until now."

"What denunciations?" I ask.

"Neighbors have been complaining about my playing." He holds up his bad arm again. "They'll be overjoyed I'm out of commission. And my poor cello..." He grimaces.

"I'll go get it," Isaac declares, standing up.

"No, don't!" Mr Mannheim orders, thrusting up his hands. "You can go in the morning. Whoever is there waiting for me will get bored and leave by then."

"All right, if you think it best." Isaac squats by our guest. "I'm glad you had the good sense to come to me," he says, and he leans his head against the cellist's. Glancing at me, smiling to keep tears away, he adds, "Benni was a very good friend of my son's."

"Isaac, I need to call my children," Mr Mannheim tells him. "May I use the phone?"

I walk him to the bedroom, so he can have some privacy. Having him on my arm makes me tingle. He walks daintily and slowly, like a mantis. I realize with a start that he may not be blind by birth. While he's speaking with his children, Isaac tells me, "No, he was in a car accident. He lost his right eye and most of his vision in his left one. The poor boy was a pile of broken bones!"

Mr Mannheim's son and daughter are both safe. It's my turn to make calls next. After all our years of separation, I still know

Rini's phone number by heart, but no one answers. We can't call Marianne and K-H because they're deaf, and we can't risk going to their apartment at the moment. Roman is safe because he has recently left for Italy. As for Dr Hassgall, his teenaged daughter answers his phone and tells me he's gone to the King David School to stand guard, so I call his office, but there's no answer. Else is safe at home. She answers my call in a drowsy voice; she was unaware that Berlin was in the middle of a pogrom and was sound asleep. But she's thankful I called so that she can try to reach her Jewish students. I tell her I'll call Volker. He answers in a terrified voice, speaking gibberish at his usual breakneck speed. As best I can decipher, both his parents were taken away near midnight.

"Listen, Volker, talk slowly. Do you have an aunt or uncle in the neighborhood?"

"No." He repeats to me how the Gestapo came for his parents. Apparently, one of the men punched his father. It's all a bit hard to decipher, since he can't stop weeping.

"Don't get off the line," I tell him, and I explain to Isaac that I have to go fetch Volker.

"You are not leaving this apartment!" he orders, jumping up and glaring at me.

"Well, someone is going to have to get him! I'm not leaving him alone."

"I'll go," he assures me.

"No! One look at your identity card and they'll know you're a Jew."

"We'll send a taxi," Benni interjects.

"What do you mean?" I ask, thinking, *This man is an idiot!*

"I have a taxi owner who takes me wherever I want to go. Where does Volker live?"

"In Gesundbrunnen, near St George's Hospital."

"Good, not too far. Tell the boy to get ready. And have him leave a note for his parents."

A taxi in the middle of a pogrom? Such are the contradictions of Berlin these days.

Rainer Kallmeyer – I'll write down the taxi driver's name in my diary that night, and also note how he brought us a boiled chicken, sent by his wife. Within half an hour, he's knocking on our door; he's walked the trembling boy up to Isaac's apartment. Volker rushes into my arms, nearly knocking me over.

Isaac then gives me the number of the Jewish Old Age Home; we fear it's been set on fire. But the night nurse who answers is as calm as can be. "Storm-troopers came and went without doing too much damage," she assures me.

A chicken never tasted so good. Handing Volker a wing, I say, "Let's rake some leaves," which makes him try to smile. Mostly he gazes down into his fear, so I keep kicking his foot; I don't want him vanishing into himself. Near three in the morning, the boy steers Benni into the guestroom so the two of them can get some sleep. I go back home to tell my father I'm fine, but he's fast asleep in his armchair. Hansi is up, so I tell him where I'll be and that Volker is safe, then tuck him in and return to Isaac. We talk until dawn, sitting under the covers, holding hands. His words of outrage spill between us. When we speak of Benni, he tells me that after the accident, he stopped seeing people. "He likes his privacy, but maybe now that his hands have memorized your face, we can visit him from time to time."

The next day, Isaac frees Benni's exuberant Shetland sheepdog, Ringelblume, from his wardrobe, and retrieves his cello. Its neck has been snapped off, then broken in half. "I can have another one made, and the sound will be perfect," Benni tells us, scoffing at the difficulty, which relieves us all.

What he doesn't say is that he has no money to pay for the repair, and none of us will ever hear him play another note. He hides his despair well. I suppose he feels that we hardly need more bad news, which is true enough. Or maybe he already understands that the time for men like him in Germany has come to an end.

The *Morgenpost* describes the pogrom as a "spontaneous day of vengeance" for the death of vom Rath. Every Jewish shop in Berlin has been ransacked and destroyed, and all the synagogues have been damaged or burned to the ground, including the New Synagogue on Oranienburger Straße, the largest in the world. Thousands of Berlin Jews have been arrested and reportedly taken to a new concentration camp called Sachsenhausen, though the rumor is that dozens have already been shot or hanged.

After the war, we'll learn that 7,500 Jewish shops were smashed to pieces in Germany on what comes to be known as *Kristallnacht*, the Night of Shattered Glass. Nazis and their supporters turn 1,600 synagogues to ruins of splinters, shards, and ash. Walking through Berlin over the next days, seeing the Jewish shopkeepers and children sweeping up piles of broken glass and shattered wood, I believe that we've survived the worst the government can do. Yes, I am still *that* naïve.

A melted streetlamp on Kantstraße, curling toward the ground like a weeping tree in a surrealist nightmare, is the strangest sight I see that week. But it's the brown bloodstains I spot all over Berlin – and that can never now come off our sidewalks – that seep hot into my dreams.

Even so, the pogrom is not the sign Isaac has been waiting for. How can he be certain? "I would sense the sky descending and the waters beginning to rise," he tells me.

"Please, Isaac, I'm too exhausted for poetry," I plead.

"That's all I have," he says, and as he turns his pockets out, he says, "Prose is powerless now, and, in any case, I've none left."

Benni's daughter, Deborah, comes over the next morning, full of thanks, and she leads her father home. Isaac heads out to check on K-H, Marianne, and countless other friends.

On the way to school that morning, I take Volker and Hansi to the Rykestraße Synagogue to show them the wasteland the Nazis want to create out of what was once our culture. The boys and I don't speak. Silent outrage is not enough, but it is all we have.

When we stop by Rini's apartment, a man I've never seen before answers my knocks and tells me that the Bloch family moved out last July. None of the neighbors knows where they've gone.

I'm too late for Rini by four months. Each day I let fall between us is a weight on my heart.

Only a third of the students come to school that day. Having stood guard all night, Dr Hassgall naps in his office after giving his morning classes. I call Volker's aunt in Frankfurt that afternoon, but she won't be able to fetch him until the weekend, so I bring him home. My father has unglued himself from Greta because of the pogrom and returns from work while Volker and Hansi are concentrating on a jigsaw puzzle of a muscular athlete by Arno Breker, Hitler's favorite sculptor. It was a present from Papa.

"What's that Jewish boy doing here?" my father whisper-screams at me in the kitchen.

Having predicted his disapproval, I have my reply ready: "Trying to find some fragments of Breker's balls, I'd guess."

"That's not funny, Sophie. Get rid of him."

"You get rid of him," I say, calling his bluff.

"Volker!" my father hollers, and the boy comes into the kitchen, all eagerness. "Listen, son," Papa tells him. "You've got to go."

That's proof enough that there's no bottom to his evil, as far as I'm concerned. Volker gazes down, petrified. "What my father means," I tell him softly, "is that we've had a small change of plans. I'll be going over to Mr Mannheim's apartment later this evening to make certain he's all right. Could you stay there until Saturday when your aunt can come and get you?"

"Yes, that's all right," he replies, his face brightening.

"We'll leave in an hour – after supper."

As soon as the boy is back at his puzzle, Papa says, "You think I'm a monster, but I'm only protecting our family. You'll realize that someday."

If I were a man, I'd probably deck him with a punch as my reply, but I limit myself to the essential, "That beautiful boy's parents have been arrested by your friends. If it weren't for Hansi, I'd leave you."

He opens his arms wide. "Be my guest – go whenever you want." And he grins so as to stick the knife in deep enough to hit bone.

Mr Mannheim is surprised that I've brought Volker to him, but his guestroom is free and Ringelblume gives her approval, licking the boy as if he were made of marzipan. If only all our problems were solved so easily.

On Saturday, Isaac shows me a new government threat in the newspaper, "Jews, abandon all hope. Our net is so fine that there is no hole through which you can slip."

The threat's reference to the inscription on the gates of Hell in Dante's *Inferno* – *abandon all hope* – makes me wonder where all our good Christians have been hiding. Shouldn't at least thirty million of them have come out in the streets by now to protest against the pogrom against their savior's people? Except for the preachings of Bernard Lichtenberg, the provost of St Hedwig's Cathedral, we haven't heard more than an occasional squeak from our priests and ministers since Reverend Niemöller's march in

Dahlem nearly a year before, when 115 demonstrators were arrested. Apparently 115 is just the right number to tie a gag on the next 29,999,885. Or maybe the pious prayers of German Christians have always been lies.

So it is that I lose hope that any organized group will fight for the Jews. And now that the Nazis have destroyed synagogues and shops, only Jewish homes can be next. That is the meaning of *Kristallnacht* to me, and I tell Isaac he'll have to get out as soon as possible.

"Where would you like me to go?" he asks, turning away from the radio to challenge me.

"Istanbul."

Giving me one of his Biblical frowns, he leans forward and raises the volume.

The frigidity of his reactions makes me curse him at times. Weeks go by without our conversing as friends or making love. Even little annoyances now seem like acute forms of torture. For instance, he leaves trails of ash and pipe tobacco everywhere, even in his pajamas and slippers. I see in his eyes that he still loves me, but the *me* he cherishes has to make no demands or risk being locked out. I feel cornered by him, my father, and my country, backed up to the imprisoned center of my own powerlessness. I crave Vera's rudeness, which I can see now was an effective barrier against complacency. I fantasize about leaving for Antwerp all the time.

At school now, I often pause in the middle of a lesson and wonder why I'm discussing how to draw the slope of a neck or the limbs of a tree. At times, I simply can't fathom the importance of teaching. A stale taste is in my mouth nearly all the time. Maybe that's what's left of my sense of humor. Or a symptom of my continuing lack of sleep. Once, while I'm preparing supper for Hansi, I find my old pillbox and discover six luminals left. They're tempting, but Hansi is watching me with worried eyes, so I dump them down the toilet for the mutant albino crocodiles, who are also probably suffering sleeplessness these days. I let him do the honors of flushing.

After the war, dozens of Americans will tell me in their ever-so-earnest way that they'll never understand how Jews and their supporters could have failed to flee in time. *We had people depending on us*, I always want to shout. *Is that so hard to understand?*

And then there are reasons that are harder to put into words ...

We were waiting for a whole country to wake up. We were offended and wanted an apology. We thought we could outlast them. We didn't want to drop the novel in the middle.

Those replies sound either pitiful or laughable after watching newsreels of rag-doll corpses being tossed into ditches inside the death camps, so I keep my lips sealed tight.

Rioters destroy K-H's studio and steal his cameras during *Kristallnacht.* The next day, two Gestapo officers come to his apartment and interrogate Marianne. He has gone to the Fasanenstraße synagogue to photograph its smoldering shell, but she tells her guests that he has gone hiking in the Tegeler Forest and won't be back for several days. After they leave, Marianne grabs Werner and leads him on a circuitous route to Fasanenstraße in case they're being followed. She finds K-H taking portraits of the rabbi, who is holding a melted brass *Exit* sign that looks as if it slipped off a canvas by Salvador Dali. K-H picks up Werner, and as a family they head to the Savigny Platz Station. They sleep at K-H's cousin's apartment that night and come to Isaac's home the next morning to get the key to his converted boathouse on the Havel River. Unfortunately, they have meager savings and almost nothing valuable to sell.

Isaac gives them all the cash he keeps hidden in a pair of moldy old Moroccan slippers, and I fetch the amethyst brooch I inherited from my mother, but Marianne refuses to take it.

"Cantor Kretschmer told us we were sisters that time we ducked into the Kaiserstraße synagogue," I remind her. "And sisters protect each other. Besides, it's only jewelry."

Beautiful words, but my mother whispers to me disapprovingly as I hand it to her.

I manage to reach Rolf over the weekend. "Sophie, thank God, you and Isaac are safe," he tells me. "And thank God, too, that Heidi wasn't here to see what's become of her beloved Berlin."

He doesn't ask after Vera, and I don't tell him anything.

As if to re-earn our nickname for him, Hitler soon fines the German Jewish communities one billion marks for the destruction of their own shops and temples, estimated at a fifth of the combined wealth of the 200,000 Jews still living in Germany. Over the next months, they're also forbidden from going to museums, concert halls, and parks, and their businesses are given to Aryans. The government section of the city south of Unter den Linden becomes off-limits. Their driver's licenses are taken away, too.

"*Rotz* – snot – doesn't drive, so why should Roth!" The punchline to a joke circulating around Berlin at the time. No, the Nazis will never be funny, but they try on occasion ...

Juden verboten. Almost all the shops along Prenzlauer Allee now have such signs in the windows, though a popular variation is, *No Jews or Dogs.* But the winning sign is at Lehmann's Florist Shop: *Dead Jews Accepted As Fertilizer.*

My father goes back to spending nearly all his time with Greta. Once, Hansi writes on his pad, "Is Papa married to her?"

It's then that I realize they may very well have had a wedding without telling us. "Maybe," I reply. "Would it bother you if he was?"

"Not much," he writes. "But I think it would upset Mama."

So he still considers what she would think. Just like me.

Tonio's letters to me from that autumn and winter speak of his pride in being able to help Hitler create an empire of German culture in Europe. He does not mention *Kristallnacht*; maybe he's certain I'd never see him again if he voiced his opinion.

One day in early February 1939, K-H and Marianne disappear. At the boathouse, Isaac finds no evidence of a break-in or a struggle, and the hurried note they leave says only, "It is time for us to go. We'll try to contact you soon. Thank you for everything." Over the next weeks, we get no call or letter. Isaac is sure they don't send news because our mail is probably being read and our phones tapped.

Later that month, when Jews are ordered to turn in all their valuables, Isaac begins selling his artwork, though in this buyer's market he receives almost nothing for them, even the Chagall. He holds on to my favorite, Otto Dix's portrait of Iwar von Lücken, but he also sells three early Grosz drawings. In all, he earns enough for four months of groceries if he eats at his usual mouse-like pace.

By that time, most of the 30,000 Jews sent to concentration camps on *Kristallnacht* have been returned to their homes on the condition that they emigrate. Volker's father and mother are among them, so the boy can return from his aunt and uncle's house in Frankfurt.

Soon after that, Dr Hassgall tells me that Zarco Industries is sinking fast, so he has ordered a pay cut for all the workers, including Isaac, who has received a modest monthly stipend since the sale of his business. I also suffer a twenty percent reduction of my school salary. Happily, Papa keeps getting raises, and he's up for a big promotion. I ask him for more household money than I need and spend what's left over on Isaac.

Jewish schools start to be shut down on the 1st of April, which is a lopsided piece of good news for Dr Hassgall, since seven new students enroll with us. Then, the father of one of our old students writes a protest letter to him. The man – Lothar Strauss – claims that there are too many Jewish pupils and that we are no longer able to provide a "healthy, German atmosphere."

Dr Hassgall invites Herr Strauss and all the other parents – Jews and Gentile alike – to a meeting in order to talk over school policy, but the disgruntled man proves himself a coward and refuses to show up to face the people he is most injuring. Only when the Jews are excluded does he come, along with seven other fathers and twelve mothers. He gives a showy, stiff-armed "Heil Hitler" to the other parents.

Papa is not there; fearing that he'd remove Hansi from school, I tossed his invitation into the garbage.

Dr Hassgall conducts the tense session with his dignified, nineteenth-century demeanor until Mr Strauss says that our headmaster has been threatening the education of his Aryan majority simply to please some rich Bolshevik Jews.

"Give me the names of these rich Bolsheviks!" Dr Hassgall challenges him.

The first parent Mr Strauss names is Volker's father, who has lost his job as a supervisor at a candy-making factory and is living on handouts from relatives and what he can make at contract bridge tournaments. The lout goes on to name all the other Jewish parents. When he's finished, Dr Hassgall replies, "I'll give you this – you have a fine memory for names." His admiring and amused tone takes us off-guard, which is why several fathers and mothers gasp when he adds, "Now, Herr Strauss, if you don't leave my school immediately, I'm going to fetch my old army pistol and put a bullet in what's left of your brain."

Else, shaken by a tremor of emotion, grips my arm. If I were still the wayward danger-seeker I'd been as a girl, I'd be thrilled that we seem to have entered a German Western just prior to the big shootout, but my nerves are always one raised voice from panic these days and it's all I can do to keep from running out of the room. For better or worse, Herr Strauss refuses to write himself into the gunfight, and he stomps out after telling Dr Hassgall he's pulling his son out of the school. Five sets of parents decide to do the same.

After the meeting, Dr Hassgall apologizes to the teachers for his outburst. His shirt collar is soaked and he can't get enough breath. I fetch him his bottle of Russian vodka from his office and hand it to him with a kiss on the cheek. "I know it cost you to get angry, but it was worth it!"

Vera writes every two weeks. As could be predicted, she hates Antwerp. She has made no friends and tells us that Andre is sick of sharing his apartment with her, and the only thing more wretched than the Flemish sense of humor is the cuisine. "Everything tastes like old cat food," she alleges.

When I read Hansi her letter, he writes on his pad, "How does she know what old cat food tastes like?"

We laugh and laugh; hysteria, too, accompanies my long slide into depression.

Vera has found employment making men's suits for a Jewish tailor who pays her a decent wage and lets her work at home. Andre is designing ads for a toothpaste manufacturer. He scribbles brief greetings on the final page of her letters and always tries to be humorous.

Tonio writes once a month. He is still in Sudetenland, though he gives me hints that he might soon be leaving for Prague. I fear that he will end up murdering Jews. In my first letter to him, I beg him to make sure the Czech Jews are treated respectfully in his presence. "If not for me, then for all our fond memories of Raffi."

In mid-June 1939, Isaac becomes disoriented. My first clue is that he gets the pages of Berekiah Zarco's manuscripts badly mixed up and pleads for my help in ordering them.

"I can't read Hebrew letters," I remind him.

"My memory must be going," he replies, knocking himself in the forehead.

He works alone at reassembling the manuscripts, his hands shaking from the strain. His crinkled brow and constant smoking mean he's worried that he'll never locate the incantation he needs inside the jumble. Forensic accounting is one thing; forensic kabbalah, quite another.

In his search, he's now employing a medieval system called *gematria*, which takes advantage of the numerical values of Hebrew letters, all of which are also numbers. He calculates the sums of key words, then looks for words or expressions of equal, double, or half their value and tries to interpret what these correspondences mean. On a hunch, he's also translating Berekiah's references to the Sixth and Seventh Gates into Aramaic to analyze hidden possibilities.

Toward the end of that month, he asks me if I want to meet his son.

"Your son?" I sense us both caught in a trap that's been waiting for months. "Where ... where is he?" I ask hesitantly.

"At school, of course. We'll meet him when classes let out."

I decide to see how far afield his mind has wandered. As we near the Jewish high school on Große Hamburger Straße, he finally realizes he's made a mistake. "My son's dead, isn't he?" he asks me, his face blanching.

"Yes, he died in the war."

"Oh, Sophele, I don't know what's happening to me." He reaches out a straining hand.

The poor man is so scared that he falls to his knees onto the Auguststraße sidewalk. On reaching home, I call Dr Löwenstein, who has recently been released from the Sachsenhausen concentration camp. He comes over that evening, and he's gotten so thin that his tweed coat hangs around him like a clown suit.

He takes Isaac's pulse, listens to his heart, and asks him a series of questions: What year is it? How old are you? If it was four o'clock three hours ago, what time is it now?

Isaac gives the correct replies. "And what would you like to happen to the Chancellor of Germany?" Dr Löwenstein finally asks.

Dryly, Isaac replies, "His eyeballs should drop out, and his ears fall off, and pack horses should eat them."

The doctor turns to me with a grin. "The good news is he's got his mind back. The bad news is he curses like a Yid."

Dr Löwenstein has a long talk with Isaac about his need to take things easier. "And you've got to get out of this apartment more often!" he orders him. "Your bedroom smells like old socks. I bet you don't even stick your head out the window more than once a week."

Isaac agrees, but he still never leaves the apartment. Until, that is, I begin secretly putting half a luminal in his supper, which stops the occasional tremors in his hands. He even enjoys the taste of food again and puts on a few pounds, which means, among other things, that his cock gets hard when I touch it. He starts going back to work two mornings a week. On my absolute insistence, he studies his manuscripts at a more measured pace.

In July, the rhetoric in our newspapers against England and France turns virulent. We hear frequent radio bulletins about supposed attacks on Germans living in Poland. My favorite is of a German baker's widow allegedly raped by a rabbi and a gang of Warsaw Jews. It says a great deal about the *Volk* that they believe this sort of fiction. *Germany As the Victim* – that's the way Dr Goebbels has decided to sell the coming all-out war, and judging by public opinion, he's having good success.

Tonio reaches Prague in early August. From the way he describes the friendliness he meets everywhere, you would think his tank is made of chrysanthemums. He never mentions abuses against Czech Jews, but in stiff, formal language, he refers to "enemies of the Reich who are being made to pay for spreading vicious lies about the Fatherland and its goals".

On the 21st of August, Benni Mannheim's daughter, Deborah, comes over to inform us that her father has committed suicide. Isaac reaches behind him to steady himself and, finding nothing but air, crashes backward against the wall.

Deborah says that Benni took a kitchen knife to his wrists while lying in the bathtub. She sits in front of us, her hands clutched in her lap, and she explains in a lost voice about the cost of repairing his cello being beyond their means, and of his visit to the British Embassy, where he was told that it was unlikely, given his blindness, that he'd get a visa for England, Palestine, or anywhere else.

After she's gone, and after I've cried over all the Bach, Mozart, and Telemann we'll never hear again, and over Benni's talent about to be buried under the earth forever, and over all the nights I spent listening to him and wondering who this miracle-man was, I ask Isaac, "Why didn't he come to ask us for help?"

He hangs his head. "I don't have any answers any more."

"And why in a bathtub?"

"No stains. The blood ... it goes down the drain with the water. Since his accident, he feared being a burden."

"I understand now," Isaac says, putting down his newspaper.

Three days have passed since Benni's suicide and Hitler and Stalin have reached a pact of non-aggression.

"What do you understand?" I ask.

Isaac is in his pajamas; he hasn't dressed or shaved since Benni's funeral. Our mirrors are covered with black cloth.

"Saul was from the tribe of Benjamin," he states definitively.

"I don't get it."

"In the First Book of Samuel, Saul kills himself with his own sword. But in the Second Book of Samuel, Saul tries to take his own life and fails, so he is given a death-blow by an enemy of Israel, by an Amalekite." He gives me a hard look. "Benni took his own life, but he was also murdered by the Nazis. His death is a sign from Samuel and Saul that the waters have risen. And this pact between Hitler and Stalin ... it is the sky descending. Hitler will be free to make war on England and France and America. First *Binah* will shatter, then *Hokhmah*, and finally *Kether Elyon*. Wisdom and insight will disappear from our world. The Crown of God will lose all meaning. Both inside and outside are collapsing. God is about to recoil into Himself."

"But Benni's suicide can't have such important consequences. He was just one man."

"Sophele, you once told me that whether Benni knew it or not, his message was that the world has chords whose sound and structure obey physical laws, and scales that cannot be altered no matter what Hitler might say or do. You remember? You had reached a great truth that day, but Benni's death ... Silence will descend over all our voices now. The physical laws are coming undone."

"Isaac, I think you need to stay calm," I say, fearing he'll become disoriented again. "You're finding symbolism that simply isn't there."

I expect him to shout, or to rush to Berekiah Zarco's manuscripts, but he walks to me with a warm radiance in his eyes that I haven't seen in months. "Sophele, I am going to leave you now. I will not be able to love you the way you deserve, but I want you to know I am aware that I'm failing you. And that I'm sorry." He takes my hands and shakes them playfully. "I also want you to know that I haven't lost my marbles." He grins. "At least, not any more than a few."

"You're worrying me," I tell him.

He presses his lips gently to my eyes and then my lips. "I'll be gone from you for as long as it takes, but don't be concerned. I feel strong now that I've seen the sign. I have been washed seven times in the River Jordan, and I have seen the desert blossom, and I am clean again." He caresses my cheek. "Bless you for leading me back to myself. But there is one thing I *do* want from you."

"What?"

"You have to leave Germany. The breaking of the vessels ... If you stay here, you'll be killed. I want you to go to Istanbul. Berekiah, in his last manuscript ... Wait, I want you to hear what he says." Isaac fetches Berekiah's seventh manuscript, an account of the Lisbon massacre of 1506, and translates part of the last page for me into German: "'The European kings and their hateful bishops will never stop dreaming of the Jews. They will never allow you and your children to live. Never! Sooner or later, in this century or five centuries hence, they will come for you or your descendants. So face Constantinople and Jerusalem and start walking. Cast out Christian Europe from your heart and never look back!'" He gives me a resolute look meant to enforce his meaning, then carries the manuscript back to his desk.

"But Berekiah wrote that in the sixteenth century," I protest.

"It doesn't matter," he replies, exasperated. "His words are still valid. You must go to my cousins in Istanbul. You must leave Christian Europe. Take Vera and Andre with you. Will you do that for me?"

"Only if you come with us."

"I can't. I must stay here in Berlin. I need to be here to do any good."

"Then I won't leave. You'll need me to look after you and ..."

"I can live on next to nothing for longer than you think – for years if I need to. How is an old Jewish man like a camel?" he asks.

"No jokes!" I warn him. "And I can't go. I have to consider Hansi."

"He's doing much better now. He gets around the city all by himself, and he has friends. If all goes well, you can come back here after a year or two. And if the worst happens, I'll send him to you. I promise."

"I'll need time to prepare Hansi for my going. I'll need to stay at least a year." That's a lie; what I really believe is that Isaac will either be too exhausted to fight me or completely mad by then.

"A year is out of the question!" he declares. He clamps his pipe in his mouth to certify that decision.

"It's now the end of August. Give me nine months, till May. We'll celebrate Purim and Carnival. We'll have Passover together and then I'll flee for your Promised Land."

"No. Three months maximum."

"That's too soon for all I'll need to do. Give me six."

"Only if you agree to be ready to leave at a moment's notice if I sense the worst is happening."

"All right."

"And you promise not to back out at the last minute?"

"I swear. But I want something from you in return."

"What?" His eyes open wide with amused curiosity. Maybe he thinks I'll make him promise to have sex with me as often as I want.

"I want your child," I tell him, which makes his jaw drop and his pipe fall. As I retrieve it, I add, "I'll leave Germany only if I am carrying your baby."

He raises a hand to his cheek in horror. "A child ...? But I'm ... I'm seventy years old!"

"Abraham had Isaac when he was a hundred."

"I'm no Abraham."

He flaps his hands at me, but I catch them and grip them tight. "I won't go otherwise. Those are my terms. Take it or leave it."

My secret belief is that he'll never send me away if I'm pregnant with his child. He sits on the bed and opens his arms to me. I lay my head on his lap, and he kisses me on the top of my head. I expect him to say *no* as gently as possible, but he never does.

"All right," he finally agrees, "we'll make a baby right away. And you'll leave after you've missed one cycle of the moon." Eyeing me purposefully and speaking as if it's an order, he adds, "Even if six months aren't up yet."

"Two cycles," I bargain. "To make sure I'm really pregnant."

We shake on our agreement like gentlemen, and that afternoon Isaac writes a long letter in Ladino to his family in Istanbul. Isaac's aunts and uncles are long dead, but he has several cousins and is particularly close to his Aunt Luna's eldest son, Abraham. Only after he's sent it does he warn me that he's told his relatives I'm Jewish. "It'll make life easier for you and the baby."

On the 27th of August, our neighborhood superintendent distributes food-ration cards. Five days later, on the 1st of September, Germany invades Poland. Air-raid sirens go off across the city because France and Britain are rumored to have sent bombers to attack Berlin. Hansi and I take our emergency supplies into the shelter. These include his jigsaw puzzle of Michelangelo's *David* and the cane that Rolf gave him. Isaac, the Munchenbergs, and our other Jewish neighbors are forced to sit in the corner, and most of them dare not even look at those of us in the Aryan section. When the all-clear sounds, the gray-uniformed warden instructs them to wait without talking for the Aryans to leave before they stand up.

We have our first blackout that night, and I rush out onto Prenzlauer Allee to see what Berlin looks like. No streetlamps, no neon signs, no car headlights. We are living now in a dark forest, and the moon above us is an eye. Prenzlauerberg and the Mitte, Schöneberg, Neukölln and Wedding, the KuDamm and Unter den Linden ... Berlin has become the setting of a fairy tale, but is the story being told by the Opposite-Compass or by Isaac and me?

CHAPTER NINETEEN

England and France declare war on Germany on the 3rd of September. Tonio comes home on a one-day leave three weeks later, just after a conquered Poland is partitioned by Germany and Russia. I've had my period, so I'm feeling disappointed in myself. I'm nervous, too, because I don't want to sleep with him now that I'm trying to have Isaac's baby. We meet at his father's apartment, but when I rush up to embrace him, he pushes me away.

"We need to talk," he says in a grave voice. Almost the first line I was going to use.

I drop down on the bed. He takes the armchair. He crosses his legs and sits up straight. *The German Soldier On Leave.* The title of a sketch I'll try to make of him several days later.

I am expecting a heroic speech, imagining that Tonio will tell me – in a voice choking back tears – that I must make a life for myself if he should die, because he is being sent to do battle in France. And I already know that if that's the news he has, I'll make love with him one last time in the hopes that our union will magically keep him safe.

"Tell me what's wrong?" I ask, leaning forward and smiling so as to show him I plan to listen closely – to play the part he expects of me.

"I just found out what you've been doing while I've been fighting for our country," he begins in a coarse tone.

"And what's that?" I ask. I'm expecting him to say I've been teaching Jews at a school for genetically unfit children.

"My father told me you've been having an unnatural relationship with Mr Zarco."

He uses those exact words: *unnatural relationship. Ein widernatürliches Verhältnis*. A strange phrase, but adequate in its way. And a tonic for me, too, because I feel *unnaturally* revitalized by the truth finally coming out.

"What we do together is certainly illegal," I tell him, "and perhaps by your standards even sinister and odd, *unheimlich*, but I assure you that nothing we do is unnatural. Or, at the very least, no more unnatural than what you and I do together."

"But he's in his seventies!" he shouts.

It's a relief that his false calm is gone. We will be honest with each other now.

"That's true, and I do wish sometimes he were a bit younger." I almost add, *So we could make love for hours on end*, but I decide not to hurt him unnecessarily. As I've said, Volker, Hansi, and my other students have taught me to be gentle.

"Stop trying to be clever!" he snarls.

"I'm sorry. Cleverness is a personality defect of mine. I realize that it can be irritating. But I would think you could overlook it after so many years together. After all, I haven't complained about a single one of your flaws since you joined the army."

He stands up and joins his fingertips together. He looks like his father when the old Prussian tyrant is preparing to give him a lecture. This is usually where Dr Hessel would ask me to leave his apartment so he can talk to Tonio alone. No such luck now.

"If you don't mind my saying so, Jews will always be your downfall," he tells me, and he begins to pace. "So that if ..."

Who would have thought that Tonio would ever become pompous? "I do mind," I interrupt. "In fact, I mind very much."

He gives me a startled look; I've broken the rules of discourse by interrupting before he's found his rhythm. He coughs purposefully, then continues: "It's a kind of disease in you, this fondness for Jews. I thought you might be cured in time, by my friendship and love, by the influence of the Führer. That's why I gave you *Mein Kampf* all those years ago. I really did think that Hitler's fine words could Aryanize you. I still may think so, but I can no longer be a part of that project. That's what I've come to tell you."

"So you regard me as a project?"

"Don't look so horrified! I regard you as part of the Führer's project for us *all*."

I haven't a clue who this man pacing in front of me is. I hadn't realized till now how I'd left so much of my intuition and sense outside the door of this apartment over the years. "So I was to be part of the victory over what we once were," I observe.

"In a way." He glares at me. "But if you could sleep with a swine three times your age, then I've failed!"

"Who told you about Isaac and me?"

"My father."

"How did he find out?"

"He says it has become obvious over the past two years. Apparently, you and the old Jew have become less careful. Everyone knows."

Even Papa? Maybe he's waiting for the right moment to have me arrested, and maybe this is the real reason he called me a slut. "So you've forgotten your Jewish friends ... forgotten Raffi?" I ask.

"He was never my friend!"

"He was! You used to play poker every other Friday evening. I remember, even if you don't."

"But we were never friends! You should know that – I proved it when I informed on him to the Gestapo."

I jump up, tense with horror. "You did what?"

"I thought you guessed. I told the Gestapo about his hieroglyphic messages, and when he came back from Egypt, I went to them again."

"You son-of-a-bitch!" I shout. "You fucking bastard!"

"It was my obligation to turn him in. Otherwise, I couldn't have lived with myself."

"Then ... then it must have been you who followed me when I went to Julia's shop."

"Who's Julia?"

"I went to her shop that day I told you Hansi had pinworms. But you followed me and called the Gestapo."

He shrugs as if it no longer matters. "I did what I had to."

"You were in their car ... waiting outside when they came here. You betrayed me! You've betrayed me every step of the way, and I didn't want to see it!"

"I was trying to keep you out of trouble. Someday you'll realize I've been kinder to you than you had any right to expect."

It was in the moment that Tonio told me my fondness for Isaac was a disease that I began to believe that the physical laws of the world had indeed been inverted: up was down, cruelty kindness, and love hate. Yet I also realized he'd been telling me the kind of person he was all along. He'd made no secret of his allegiances; he had even said that Hansi had no place in the new Germany. I'd refused to believe he'd ever act on his beliefs. And I'd convinced myself that he was hiding kinder sentiments.

A lesson learned too late: when people tell us who they are, we should listen closely and believe them.

When I tell Isaac about my break-up with Tonio and how he informed on Raffi, he grows silent, then flees his bedroom for the kitchen. When I chase him down, he proposes that we stop seeing each other for at least a couple of months.

"But if people already know about us, what's the point?" I ask.

He has no answer to that. We end up agreeing that I should go up to his apartment only after dark. And never meet in public or talk on the phone.

Probably because of our rushed, irregular lovemaking over the next months, pregnancy eludes me. What I dread most is being told I'm barren, so I will not visit a physician. At least not yet.

Papa says nothing to me about my relationship with Isaac; maybe he doesn't know about us, after all. Or more likely he's still waiting for the perfect moment to up his assessment of me from slut to whore.

I question Hansi about whether he'd be all right if I left Germany for a while.

"Could I come?" he asks by pointing to himself.

"Later. I'd go first, and then you'd join me."

He writes hurriedly on his pad. "Could Volker come, too?"

"If he wants to. Listen, would you get frightened if you didn't see me everyday?"

"No," he signals.

"And you'd go to school?"

"Where else would I go?" he writes.

When he turns back to his studies, I knock him on the head with my fist, hard enough to earn an irritated look. "What's that for?" my brother's puzzled eyes ask.

"I just felt like it. You can hit me back if you want," I say invitingly.

But he doesn't. He squeezes my hand instead. He's definitely growing up.

Isaac says that we need more propitious circumstances – biological and mystical – to make a baby. So he writes to Julia for help and receives a package of dried herbs in the post. Following her instructions, he boils her mixture into a sour concoction that I drink on waking and again on going to bed. I have my doubts that her witch's brew is doing anything but making my stomach churn and my tongue furry, but he assures me that it is turning the liquids in my body more fluid and giving his "ancient Mesopotamian sperm" a better chance to swim upstream to my egg.

Despite our best efforts, I menstruate normally in October and November.

"You're a tough case, but sooner or later the baby will come," he assures me.

"Maybe I can't conceive," I moan.

"You're just anxious all the time. I don't think I've seen you completely relaxed since that day I discovered you potting pelargoniums in the courtyard."

I don't realize the truth of Isaac's words until the 1st of December, when Papa and Greta go off to Rome for two weeks; she's a Catholic and has always wanted to visit the Vatican. His parting words to me are, "Try not to do anything too scandalous while I'm gone."

"For you, anything," I tell him sarcastically.

After he and Greta are safely on a train zooming south, I can finally sit in a quiet house where hostile footsteps never approach, and where a man who despises me can't criticize what I've made for supper or how I wear my hair. Heaven is drawing Hansi while he feeds the goldfish and in knowing that Isaac is the only man who will walk through the door. We spend all night together in his apartment, since Hansi and Volker have been invited to another classmate's house, and I sleep through the night – without waking even once – for the first time in years.

Hanukkah is the Festival of Lights and therefore ideal for bringing a new spark of life into the world, according to Isaac. "And even if it weren't," he adds cagily, "your father being gone means we can take our time and do things right."

On the first evening of the celebration, the 6th of December, he leads me into his bedroom, walking on tiptoe. He carries his menorah ahead of us like a shield, and its single candle sends our thick shadows wobbling over the walls. Twelve days have passed since my last period, so the timing is almost perfect.

"Are we allowed to make love by the light of a menorah?" I ask Isaac softly as he sets it down on his night table.

"As long as you don't read while we're at it. Reading is strictly prohibited."

"Then I better not bring any novels to bed."

After he helps me undress, he takes my head in his hands and asks, "Are you sure this is what you want?"

"How can you even ask that?" Looking up into his apologetic eyes, I realize more of how his mind works. "You thought my doubts might have been preventing me from getting pregnant."

"Maybe."

"Silly man, I never wanted anything so much in my life," I tell him, kissing his lips while standing on my toes. I adore the way my body stretches to him. It's a kind of ballet that I will dream of many times in years to come.

I jump onto the bed like a little girl, and as we kiss, I feel as if life has already begun in my womb – just from touching the man I want to father my child and wishing it so. And I feel as if my body is truly mine for the first time in years. "If only Papa would move permanently out of Berlin," I tell him.

As Isaac enters me, he recites a verse from Isaiah: "'Never again shall your sun set, nor your moon withdraw your light.'"

I try not to laugh, but I do. That prophetic voice he uses ... it's like being fucked by Moses. "I'm sorry," I tell him.

He grins, then kisses my eyes. "To laugh when making a baby is a kind of *mitzvah* – a good deed."

We whisper as we make love because our voices make me feel protected. Soon, I catch up to his rhythm, and we are children digging up buried treasure, and I would like us to dig so far down that no one else could ever find us.

We make love once more that night, and this second time it seems as if Tonio is being purged from me. The baby will consign him to a past that cannot wound me.

Over the next seven nights of the holiday, Isaac leads me to bed behind our menorah, and the last time we make love in his bedroom it is under the protection of all seven candle flames. Just as he asks, I recite the verse from Isaiah when he enters me for the eighth time: *Never again shall your sun set, nor your moon withdraw your light.*

Papa comes home on the 15th of December, looking rested and happy. And with his hair parted on the side. This new style is clearly designed to make him look youthful enough to be dating

Greta, and maybe it works. His smile is boyish and bright when he greets me. He's brought me a gift, too, an old recording of Enrico Caruso. As we listen together, sharing astonishment at the singer's vocal acrobatics, I sense that his voice is leading us toward a delicately balanced truce. If I manage to become pregnant, maybe Papa will even welcome the news. A complete fantasy, I know, but can I really be blamed for still wanting my old father back?

A few days before Christmas, I'm summoned to the Turkish Embassy and given my visa by the ambassador himself, a bullish man with a waxed mustache, who insists on offering me a sumptuous lunch, which is when I taste my first *manti*, meat-stuffed ravioli topped with yoghurt. Have I met my culinary future? He says Istanbul is a small city compared to Berlin, and chaotic, and that the packs of wild dogs are a nuisance, but that it's lovely when blanketed with snow. "The needle-towers of the minarets against all that white ..." he says, taking a big breath of ecstasy.

"Any moussaka?" I ask.

"Everywhere. We have a huge Greek community."

The next day, the 23rd of December, I have my period, which sets me weeping. When I tell Isaac, he hugs me hard, then runs me a bath. The feel of his big kind hands washing every inch of me only makes my melancholy even worse, however, since this is a man who should have children and I'm helpless to make that happen. "I'm a failure," I tell him. "And everything has gone wrong."

"Shush ... Besides, it's probably me. My Mesopotamian sperm may be defunct."

By the time we're done Isaac is soaked with water, his rolled-up shirtsleeves dripping, just like Raffi and me when we used to bathe Hansi. At first that makes me laugh, but then I start sobbing again. I can't recall ever feeling so hollow.

"Get dressed and I'll take you out for tea and cake," he says, holding out a big white towel for me.

"Cake isn't going to help," I tell him.

"I know. But what can I do?"

He holds open his arms for me to come to him, but I don't. Two helpless people at an impasse in their very bodies, and neither of us knows the password.

On Friday the 29th, Monica Mueller comes down with scarlet fever and enters St George's Hospital with a high fever. Then, on the 3rd of January, she becomes delirious and begins hearing voices. Else and I try to visit her, but we're turned away by a doctor who tells us that her condition is too precarious for visitors.

Monica must have given her scarlet fever to her friends before she started showing symptoms, and Hansi breaks out with a red rash all over his face on the 9th of January. He is running a fever of 39.2 by the next afternoon. I put cold compresses on his forehead and give him aspirin. At the same time, Monica's mental state deteriorates further, at least according to a supervising physician who speaks to her great-aunt on the phone.

"The poor thing must be terrified," I write in my diary that evening. "Call parents tomorrow!"

Monica lives with her diabetic, eighty-two-year-old great-aunt, and the fragile old woman gives me their phone number. They live in Dortmund and tell me they'll be unable to visit Monica before the weekend. From her father's sour tone, I have a feeling that they will not come, which means that the girl is on her own.

On the 11th, Papa insists that my brother be taken to the hospital because he's read in the newspaper of several recent deaths caused by scarlet fever and Hansi's temperature is up to 39.8. Having seen all my students sterilized and Vera's baby murdered by German doctors, I tell him it's a bad idea. "I'll stay home and look after him," I promise.

"You can't – you'll lose your job. And he needs professional care."

"Then let's send him to the Jewish Hospital."

"Sophie, are you mad?" he questions, and his sneer is so disdainful that it marks the end to our truce.

"You and I both know that we can trust Hansi only with Jewish doctors," I tell him.

"I don't know anything of the sort. The boy is an Aryan!"

Papa calls Dr Nohel, who telephones for an ambulance. After he hangs up, I plead with my father again. "You know what the doctors are going to think of Hansi once they find out he's been sterilized for feeblemindedness. He won't get proper treatment. You've got to send him to Jewish physicians!"

"Don't you tell me what to do! A girl like you ... Don't forget I could have you put away for how you lead your life."

"I'm twenty-two. You can't touch me!"

"What you do is illegal. And immoral. I could have you arrested. You and that filthy Jew! If your mother knew ... You know what I'll do? I won't have you imprisoned, but I'll have you put in an institution for the insane for the rest of your life. That happens to girls who display sexual misconduct, you know."

Now that Tonio has taught me the value of believing what I'm told, I realize that Papa is letting me know precisely what he intends to do if I continue to fight him. His honesty is a form of generosity in the upside-down world we've entered; he's giving me fair warning.

I stand by the fish tank, my hand gripping its glass, wondering if I should quarrel more violently now, but I decide to wait. A fatal error? Dr Nohel comes over and does his best to reassure me. I find him so physically repulsive that the hairs on my neck stand on end. When the ambulance arrives, I realize I've been outdueled.

My brother has been in his pajamas for a week, so I ask everyone to leave his bedroom and dress him in woolen pants and his winter coat. I also want a chance to talk to him alone.

"I don't feel well," he signals for at least the twentieth time in the last few days.

"You can get better more quickly at the hospital."

He signals for me to hand him his pad. His brow crinkled with worry, he writes, "You'll tell Volker where I am?"

"Of course." I'm not supposed to kiss him because he's contagious, but I do anyway, right between his eyes, just as I once saw him kiss Minnie the dachshund. A silly gesture given the risk, but my heart is pounding too hard to abide by boundaries.

The ambulance races away with Hansi to the Herzberge State Hospital, and Papa and I follow behind in a taxi. Everything goes smoothly there, especially since Dr Nohel clears a path through the bureaucracy. The room my brother is given has a window looking out on oak trees. I try to divert his attention by saying that I saw a squirrel, but he's scratching his behind nervously. I let Papa talk to him alone to calm him. After our father leaves for home, I read to Hansi until he falls asleep. Then I draw him until early evening. The familiar movements of my hand ease my mind. When the nurse tells me it's time to go, he's still snoozing, so I leave my sketch on his chest. I write on top, "Be back tomorrow. Love, Me."

When I get to Isaac's apartment, he says, "My God, you look like you've been run over."

"I have." I explain to him what has happened and he orders me into the bath again. That's his new solution for all the ills of Germany, at least as they affect me. He scrubs me down and dries me in a big luxurious towel, then helps me dress and orders me to go straight home to sleep, which is exactly what I do.

The next morning, Else tells me that she spoke to Monica's great-aunt. The girl has been sent home. Her mind is still in a manic tangle, but her rash and fever are gone. I burst into tears of relief, especially because this is such a good omen for Hansi.

Two of our other students – transferees from a closed Jewish school – are in the Jewish Hospital and doing well. This is the only occasion I can remember in the past six years when I think, *We'd be much better off if we were Jews.*

When I visit Hansi on the afternoon of Sunday the 14th, he sits up for the first time in days. His back is sore, so I rub it, then we play poker. He doesn't grasp all the rules, but I let him win, so he's happy. And he has his sense of humor back: when I ask him if the hospital cuisine is all right, he writes, "It tastes like old cat food."

The next day Hansi's rash is almost gone. I beg his physician, Dr Schmidt, to send him home with me.

"I don't like the sound of his chest," he replies. "He's wheezing. I want to keep him here for observation for two more days. After that, he's all yours."

Dr Schmidt smiles warmly and is very reassuring. I consider that Papa may have had better judgment than I did. I admit that to him that night, but he simply walks past me out of the kitchen and turns up the radio. I escape to Isaac and return home only after midnight.

When I arrive the next afternoon at the hospital, a floor nurse informs me that Hansi has been transferred. Dr Schmidt tells me that an x-ray of the boy's chest revealed tuberculosis. "It went undetected for some time, I'm afraid. He's been transferred to the Buch Waldhaus, a sanitarium that specializes in cases like Hansi's."

"Without my permission?" I ask, outraged.

"Your father agreed to the transfer. We called him at his office yesterday."

The sanitarium is an imposing three-story building in the shape of an E, topped by a red-tile roof and fronted by a lawn and pleasant garden. The receptionist and staff are friendly, and Hansi is in a light-filled triple room on the third floor, but there's a problem: his two roommates seem to be either catatonic or schizophrenic. One of them looks like a waterbug, with bony elbows and big hollow eyes. He doesn't move or speak. The other has a shaved head and crust on his hands. He's tied to his bed with a belt. He mumbles to himself about horses.

A nurse explains to me that the sanitarium is filled to the limit and Hansi had to be put in the psychiatric wing.

"I want him out of here now!" I shout.

"You'll have to talk to the director."

"But these men in here could hurt my brother."

"They're on tranquilizers, and Herr Feldman is also belted. Nothing is going to happen."

I wait for an hour to speak with the director, Dr Hans-Jürgen Dannecker. From behind a giant vase of red tulips – his shield – he repeats what the nurse told me, but also adds in a calming tone, "I'll see what I can do to have your brother moved. I realize how upsetting it must be for you to see him there. We'll take care of it. I promise. Give us a day or two."

From his window, Hansi can see a small pond, so when I go up again, I try to cheer him up by summoning him to the window but he won't come. He is as silent and impenetrable as the high walls guarding his universe, and I know from experience he's terrified. For one thing, he's sitting up with his legs pulled in to his chest.

His fortress position. And his rapid blinking means he's got his finger in a dyke of tears. Offering a quick prayer to his squirrel god, I take my secret weapon out of my book bag. "Drum roll, please ..." I announce, and then I put down my new jigsaw puzzle between us. "The great pyramid of Giza!"

Not a single stone in the Hansi Fortress even loosens, though we might have a chance if roommate number 2 would end his private monologue. "I found it in this crowded little shop on Hutten Straße," I tell my brother, and since he's always been fond of geographic details, I add, "right near the power plant. I'll take you there when we get better. It's full of amazing junk."

I speak in a cheerful voice and keep the sentences short, just as he prefers, but he knocks the puzzle box off the bed with his foot and it falls with a dry thud.

Before I leave, he writes, "You didn't tell them to let me go home." That's just to make sure I understand I'm being punished.

I visit him every day, but he won't write another word. Papa is staying at home this week, so I don't even have the benefit of being able to spend nights with Isaac. Three more days go by and not only hasn't Hansi been moved to a better room, but Dr Dannecker will no longer admit me to his office. His secretary tells me to have my father come in the next day.

I accompany Papa to the sanitarium on the 20th. Hansi's eyes have grown as dull as pewter. I'm in a clinging, sweaty panic, which may be why I don't consider that the physicians are drugging him. I try kissing my brother on the lips and holding him in my arms while whispering my apologies, but he fails to turn back into a prince.

Papa returns from his meeting with Dr Dannecker and tells me, smiling, "Hansi will be moved tomorrow."

"Thank God, Papa. You're wonderful." I press my lips to his cheek.

This is the first time I have felt Papa and I are on the same side since my mother's death, but he doesn't even kiss me back.

As promised, my brother is moved the next day, into a pleasant double room. His roommate looks to be in his twenties and also has tuberculosis. His name is Karl. He talks in a calm, educated voice and is friendly to me. Still, Hansi won't say a word to either of us. All the silence between us ... It seems like a metaphor for how helpless we are to really help our loved ones at their most difficult moments. And every time I leave the sanitarium, I feel as if I've been spun around like Benni Mannheim, with a lethal gift – Papa – waiting for me back at home.

By the 23rd of January, I should have had my period, because I'm usually quite regular. I don't say anything to Isaac yet, though when I see Hansi on the 24th, I whisper, "I'm trying to make a baby with Isaac Zarco. And just maybe I've succeeded. Will you give me your blessing?"

But he's still punishing me and won't even look up at me. I move the palm of his hand over my cheek so he can feel my words, and I say: "Nothing and no one could ever make me abandon you. I will be with you every step of the way." Trying for a little humor at this terrible moment, I add, "You'll never get rid of me."

When I let his hand go, he tugs it back into his lap as if I've burned him. And his eyes close.

By the 26th, I allow myself to believe I might be pregnant. When I tell Isaac, he dances me around his bedroom, then listens to my belly. "Strange – all I hear is gas," he tells me, giggling.

Since I don't want to get too excited over a false alarm, we agree that we'll consider ourselves successful only if I don't have a period by the 1st of February.

I've brought Isaac real coffee – a luxury – that I purchased on the black market, and we drink it while eating matzo smeared with butter and honey, his favorite snack. Then we listen to a Bach violin concerto on the phonograph. I sit between his legs and he massages my shoulders. Unfortunately, the happiness of knowing I'm just where I want to be only makes me feel my little brother's terror all the more deeply.

When I tell Isaac about how Hansi is not coming out of his desolate state, he offers to come with me to meet with Dr Dannecker. "Somehow, we've got to either get Hansi home or have him moved to a smaller, more cheerful place," Isaac tells me, as if he's reading my thoughts.

I call for an appointment, but Dr Dannecker has no free time until after the weekend. On the morning of Monday the 29th, he listens to us patiently, but tells us that he can't release Hansi without Papa's agreement. "The boy is a minor. My hands are tied."

Papa has moved back in with Greta and when I go to her apartment to plead with him to sign Hansi's release papers, he doesn't invite me in. Sighing mightily, he says, "Sophie, I'm getting awfully tired of your theatrics. As soon as he's cured completely, I'll bring him home."

I call Papa every other day to see if Dr Dannecker has given him any good news, but there's none. I stay away from Greta's apartment, which means I never see him. And neither does Hansi, who sits in bed with his eyelids shut tight. When he does open them, all I see is a despair so deep that it terrifies me.

The 1st of February comes and goes without any traces of blood, which means I must be pregnant. Isaac kisses me all over and thanks me, tears so thick in his eyes that he complains he can't see me, and I'll never forget our long, grateful embrace. I'll allow us only a small celebration until Hansi is allowed to come home, and since we no longer go to local restaurants together, we take the tram to a vegetarian restaurant on Friedrichstraße named Behnke that I've been to with Else and where no one who could get me in trouble would ever go.

"I think my father wants a few weeks to see how it feels to be free of both his kids," I tell Isaac over our soup.

"My fear," he replies, taking my chin to fix my attention, "is that Greta will pressure him to leave Hansi in the sanitarium so she and your father can live together permanently. It's quite common for parents to want to put difficult children in institutions."

So maybe Greta is the person I should be talking to. That never happens because Hansi's room is empty when I arrive at the sanitarium on the 2nd of February. I rush into Dr Dannecker's office, ready to squeeze the life out of him, but he assures me that everything is fine; Hansi was simply transferred the previous afternoon to a specialized institution in Brandenburg in order to determine the best course of treatment. "They want to know if he is a good candidate for a chest operation called a thoracoplasty," he adds.

Tears are already flooding my eyes. "I'll need the address of the hospital," I tell him.

"I'm sorry, that's impossible. They don't allow visitors. But your brother should be back here within a week – two weeks at the most. I'll let you know as soon as he gets here."

"At least give me the phone number," I plead, but Dr Dannecker tells me that's also strictly forbidden.

I phone him twice that week, but each time his secretary tells me he's received no news about Hansi. I don't see Papa over this period. Whenever I call Greta's apartment she tells me he's not there, and he comes home to pick up his mail while I'm teaching.

Then, ten days after Hansi's transfer, on the 12th of February, Papa receives a letter from Brandenberg's Trostbriefabteilung, the Department of Condolence Letters:

We are sorry to inform you that your son, Hans Riedesel, who was transferred to our institution on the 1st of February, 1940, suddenly and unexpectedly died here on the 9th of February due to complications caused by his tuberculosis, most particularly acute cardiac insufficiency. In spite of all medical efforts, we were unable to save him.

We offer our most sincere condolences for your loss, and we hope you will be able to find comfort in the thought that your son did not suffer. He died quietly and without pain. Police ordered an immediate cremation of your son's body because of the legal requirement to combat epidemics.

The letter continues with bureaucratic details and informs Papa that he will be able to obtain Hansi's ashes once we send a certificate from a licensed cemetery indicating that proper burial arrangements have been made. Two copies of Hansi's death certificate are enclosed. I fold these papers in my hands over and over while I sit on the cold floor in front of my bed. My next memory is of knocking on Isaac's door.

"Hansi is dead," I tell him.

I remember the reassuring firmness of his arms around me and my sense of complete helplessness, of needing to enclose myself in his apartment forever and never venture outside, because the hardest part of my life will now begin: the long walk alone into a future I don't want.

I'd have taken on Hansi's tuberculosis and silence to save him. I'm certain of it. *Mesirat nefesh* – I now know what that means. But my realization is useless; I will never know how his life was meant to turn out. I will never meet the girl who captures his heart. I will never help him find a job or choose an apartment. He will never again pose for me and look over my shoulder at his likeness, his breathing warm on my neck. And I will never press my hand to his hair when he is sleeping and feel the rise and fall of him, the soft and delicate presence of the person who taught me what it meant to give to the world without demanding anything in return. And I'll never again receive a love so quiet that it could be poetry spoken by Isaac or the sound of wind through the linden trees on Marienburger Straße.

Isaac and I talk in his apartment but I don't recall what we say. I think I tell him that I know better now what Vera felt when she learned that her unborn child had been murdered, and maybe, too, what Benjamin Mannheim felt when he learned that he'd never play his cello again.

Perhaps, too, I am beginning to understand why Isaac doesn't talk about his son. What is there to say except that there is a hole in him that will never be filled up, not by confessing his emotions to me, not by lovemaking, not by weeping, not by the passage of time, not by whispering prayers all night to the Lord of Abraham and Moses.

"Not even love can do much to ease the way you are feeling," Isaac whispers to me during my first week of grief. "And I'm not sure we would even want it to. After all, my son and your brother deserve a pain as big as all that we are. And they deserve for it not to ever entirely disappear."

The Hebrew language understands this, he tells me. "The word *chalal* means both an empty space and a person who has been murdered or killed in battle."

Is it worth saying that I weep for Hansi and myself for years, even when I make no sound at all? Until the end of the war, I will spend a portion of every day trying to figure out what I should have done differently and how he could have been saved. And for decades I will wonder what he might have become. My favorite fantasy – Hansi as an animal trainer at the Berlin Zoo. Silly, but that's what my mind arranges for him.

I'm eighty-nine years old now, but Hansi will forever be sixteen. That's too young to end up in a jar of ashes underneath a gray-marble headstone in a Prenzlauer-Berg cemetery.

I'd like to inscribe *Too beautiful, beautiful, beautiful for this ugly country* on the stone but I don't dare tell Papa. He chooses: *Beloved son and brother.*

Papa cries real tears when he tells me what he has asked the stone carver to write. A surprise.

Yet a girl like me knows by now that tears are easy. Even Hitler and Goebbels must cry on occasion. And I'm fairly certain that Werner Catel, Max de Crinis, Julius Hallervorden, Hans Heinze, Werner Heyde, and all the other Nazi physicians who murdered boys like Hansi weep when they learn of a loved one's death.

Not that I know anything about any of these fine Germans yet ...

Was Hansi really a beloved son? If I try to be fair, which I don't often want to be, then I have to admit that human beings are contradictory creatures. Our minds are made of darkness and light, and our hands are dexterous enough to juggle affection and resentment for sixteen years with no difficulty at all.

I dream of Jacob's Ladder awaiting Hansi

I take a break from teaching over the next two days and wear Hansi's shirts around the apartment because I don't want to lose the smell of him. When I can't sleep out of the need to touch him, I bury my face in his pillow and breathe in as deep as I can. I break out into the sweat of a condemned prisoner whenever I picture the pit where he will lie forever. I don't dare take out my last drawings of him.

Isaac asks me if he can go to the funeral, and I say yes. Some Jewish friends of Hansi's from school also agree to come. I've called Else and Dr Hassgall, and they will be there.

Papa overhears me talking to Else on the phone and forbids her and my other friends from coming. "If my superiors from the Health Ministry see any Jews, we can say goodbye to my promotion – maybe even my job." He shakes his head at me as if I'm a witless fool.

"At least let Dr Hassgall come."

"No. I took heat for leaving Hansi in that school of his, and I can't risk his being there."

"Then I won't go."

"Don't be absurd. Everyone will expect you there." Seeing I'm about to say no again, he plays his trump card. "Hansi would want you there."

"Yes, he would," I agree, "but he's dead now and has no say in the matter."

"You make it very hard for a father to love you, you know."

"Should loving a daughter always be easy?"

"And there you go again … always too clever! You'll go to the funeral, or I will do something I don't want to do."

You and Greta got what you wanted when Hansi died, and now you want me to be sent away too! I want to shout that at him but I eat all my words of rage these days. I live on them and nothing else, which means I grieve for Hansi while starving. As it should be.

THE SIXTH GATE

Six is the inward direction, the silver hook joining the Upper and Lower Realms, the days of the week leading to and from the Sabbath, the points of the Star of David, and the sections of the Talmud (the seeds, seasons, couplings, ethics, holy things and purities).

The Sixth Gate holds the mirror of memory, in which we are enjoined to watch the reflections of the journey past and consider their consequences as we prepare to venture forth into one last palace of mystery. The Sixth Heaven, Zebul, is presided over by Moses, and its radiant angels stand guard over the Upper Realms.

Behold, six men came from the direction of the higher gate, which lieth toward the north, and every man carried a battle-axe in his hand – Ezekiel 9.

Berekiah Zarco, The Book of Memory

CHAPTER TWENTY

It's not until after the war that I find out that Brandenburg became a killing center for handicapped children and adults at the end of 1939, one of six such institutions that would soon be established by the Health Ministry. Tuberculosis was one of the fraudulent reasons for death commonly given to concerned families.

I did a great deal of reading into the killing centers when books started appearing on the subject in the 1960s. I learned that Hansi must have been transferred to Brandenburg in a gray bus belonging to the Gemein-nüzige Kranken-Transport, the Charitable Foundation for the Transport of Patients – a government company that was hardly in the charity business. He and any other sanitarium patients on his bus were undoubtedly met by a nurse or technician and led to a reception room, where they were told to undress because they would later be bathed, though it's possible the showerheads had not yet been installed by February 1940. In that case, the patients would have been told they were to inhale a special therapeutic vapor. Hansi's clothing was sorted, labeled and numbered, and he was weighed and measured. He was five-foot eight inches tall, and the scale would have shown a little less than 139 pounds; that was the last weight for him we'd recorded at our school. Then he'd have been questioned and examined by a physician – wearing a reassuring white coat – who would have tried to determine which fraudulent cause of death might best meet the boy's appearance. Perhaps Hansi tended to present a wasted, tubercular look to physicians because he was so slender.

My brother's gaze would not have met the doctor's eyes when he was questioned. By then, he'd have been hiding deep down inside the Hansi Universe. I pray he was untouchable, beyond pain and humiliation.

The physician would have marked Hansi with a cross on his back to indicate that he had gold fillings to be robbed before cremation.

Hansi would then have had a number stamped onto him or attached to him with adhesive tape. He'd have been photographed sitting and standing. Maybe he was filmed, too, for propaganda purposes – as evidence of the danger posed to Germany by the feebleminded.

He was then assembled together with other patients, some from different transports, perhaps, and they'd have been led to the shower room.

Hansi would have stepped on tiptoe over the tile floor, because he always hated his feet being cold. Maybe he sat on one of the wooden benches along the wall after he entered the low-ceilinged room. I bet he remained standing, however, with his hands over his penis and testicles. When I draw him in that position, I feel certain that's how he'd have looked. He would have glanced down, too, to keep from having to see any panicked faces. Maybe he didn't notice the showerheads, if they were there, or the holes in the ceiling where they would soon be installed. The idea of being sprayed with water would have terrified him. Too much like rain. Which means, of course, that it's possible he started shrieking. A doctor, most likely the supervisor, Christian Wirth, would have given him a sedative in that case.

What did my brother think when he heard the hollow thud

of the steel door closing behind him? Were some of the patients around him already shouting or sobbing?

The hard metallic sound of the door being locked scares me the most. That's the moment when Hansi would have guessed that the rusted iron teeth of this trap would soon be biting into his leg.

I try not to put myself in Hansi's place too often because the feeling of dread that enters me is like a nighttime ocean – endless, with no lights from land in sight. And now that I am old I can no longer find the courage to live inside my brother for more than a few minutes at a time.

A technician in an adjoining room would have been given a signal that the patients were ready. He'd have had his hand on the valve of a compressed canister of carbon monoxide. Maybe the canister had the name IG Farben printed on its top, and *made in Ludwigshafen*.

The technician would have started to turn the valve and, using a pressure gauge, would have measured the amount of gas released. His name would be Franz or Werner or Karl. He'd be a careful man, obedient and loyal. He'd have two or three beautiful children. He probably always opened doors for women and stopped for red lights. He occasionally went to the opera to please his wife, but he'd be a fan of dance tunes or jazz or maybe even Lotte Lenya.

Frans or Werner or Karl would have kept the valve open for ten minutes.

I'm told carbon monoxide gas is odorless, but Hansi would have heard the hissing sound coming from the ceiling and then he'd have felt terror gripping his chest. With his heart caving in, he'd have reached out a hand to steady himself. Maybe he began scratching at the wall because he couldn't get enough air and there must be a way out …

Does he see Dr Wirth's face pressed in the window, eager to

learn how long it will take for this particular batch to expire? Some of Hansi's neighbors must see a curious face in the glass – either Wirth's or someone else's – and they'd be banging on the window with their fists, calling out for help. Others fall to their knees, grimacing in agony, their chests heaving, their bladders emptying ...

Though perhaps they felt only a dizzying mist swirling around them and lost their balance, falling helpless – panting and confused – to the ground. I've been told by American physicians that carbon monoxide is painless, though since it causes asphyxiation I'm not certain what that means.

What do I hope that Hansi was thinking as the gas rushed into his nose and eyes, pushing all the life out of him? That life was worth living even if this was the end? No, that's not it. That life was beautiful? Hardly.

I hope he had no thoughts at all, because any thought he had would have only made him more terrified and desperate. I hope his mind was empty. And I hope that spreading inside that emptiness was another emptiness so deep and wide that it cannot be named or labeled. Or murdered.

After the gas chamber was ventilated with fans, Dr Wirth and several other physicians would have checked that this latest group was dead, which they were, because not even Harry Houdini could survive ten minutes of carbon monoxide. Not even God, very likely.

Hansi would have probably been dead after two or three minutes. Five minutes at the most. Though my chemist father might know better.

His body would have been dragged to the autopsy room, by technicians whose job it was to burn the bodies. It was hard work, not just because the corpses had to be disentangled from one another and piled, but also because idiots, epileptics, and deaf-mutes are heavier than one would guess. So much life they had. As much as normal people. Surprising.

Prior to cremation, the staff would have hunted in Hansi's mouth for his gold fillings and knocked them out. With hammers? There are some details I don't allow myself to know. Maybe he'd have been autopsied, too, so that the young physicians on staff could earn academic credits toward their specializations. If so, then his heart and liver would likely have been stolen. And his brain. Professor Julius Hallevorden of the Kaiser Wilhelm Institute for Neurology collected more than 600 of them from Brandenburg and kept them in jars in his office. Science must goose-step forward, after all.

"Where they came from and how they came to me was really none of my business," Professor Hallevorden would later testify. A good German answer!

The thick smoke from the crematorium carried all the way to Werder, some twelve miles away, when the wind was blowing from the west. I know, because I questioned people in Werder when I returned to Berlin years later. And I went to Brandenburg itself. So I know the city's 55,000 residents grew to recognize the smell of burning human flesh, but what did they tell the tourists visiting the fourteenth-century St Catherine's Church? "We just said it was from the slaughterhouse," an old man told me. Accurate enough.

Hansi's gold-filled molars would have been sent by courier, along with hundreds of other rattling teeth recently collected, to a villa at 4 Tiergartenstraße in Berlin – code named T4. This handsome three-story manor house served as the headquarters for a program that would end up murdering more than 200,000 people.

Did the killing centers turn a profit from the sale of gold and organs? Did T4 medical director Paul Nitsche and business manager Gerhard Bohne become wealthy? Questions that no true German need ask, of course, because saving the race is its own reward.

Hansi in Brandenburg

CHAPTER TWENTY·ONE

Before Hansi's death, Isaac and I had agreed that I would leave for Antwerp shortly after Purim, in late February. As that date approaches, however, we both realize I'm in no condition to travel. For one thing, morning sickness has weakened me, in large part because I can't keep anything down but a little matzo, cheese, and onion soup. And the truth is, I do not want to leave Germany. I want to be left alone to sit by Hansi's grave, and I want to have my baby at home. Is that too much to ask? Evidently it is, because Isaac is so gruff and insistent that I end up begging him, sitting on the edge of his bed with my head in my hands, to leave me be. "We'll put the date back," he finally gives in. "But just by a few weeks."

When I resume teaching, he accompanies me every day to the school, and he waits for me when classes end. He carries my book bag. At times, it seems he doesn't want to let me out of his sight. What I don't realize is that he already suspects that my brother has been murdered, and he fears that the same will happen to me.

"Vera will meet you just across the border," he tells me whenever I lose my nerve about leaving.

"And you'll come to me as soon as you do what needs to be done?" I ask him.

"Yes, I promise."

He kisses my hands these days. And steps my fingers over his face. Having more experience than me at farewells, he is already preparing himself for my departure.

I agree to leave on Friday, the 22nd of March. I can see now that it's the sense that I am about to hurl myself off a cliff into absolute darkness that makes me provoke one last quarrel with my father. After all, my contempt for him will strengthen my resolve to leave. Still, if Papa had not revealed his plans, maybe I'd have simply turned away from him and walked quietly into the sunset.

He comes home on Friday, the 15th of March sparkling with eagerness because he has a dinner with high officials of the sewage company and decided to pick up his best brown suit. Greta will not be accompanying him; this is men-only.

Just before he leaves, he says, "Greta and I are engaged. But it's a secret at the moment, so I'd prefer you not tell anyone."

"Have you set a date?" I ask, sensing the complete dissolution of our family as an invisible hand pressing at the back of my neck.

"Sometime toward the end of the year," he replies. "Maybe in November."

"I suppose I should offer you congratulations."

My ambivalence makes him laugh. "I suppose you should," he says.

Grudging admiration for me makes him continue to smile. He's still a handsome man, and he cultivates the firm stance and confidence of an athlete even now. I can sense the love I used to feel for him prompting me to confess I'm leaving. I want to tell him in order to bring to life a fantasy in which he begs me to stay. It's a scene that has been playing in my head for the past two weeks: Papa, on his knees before me, holding my hand, saying, "Forgive me for having betrayed you so disgracefully." Yes, I've borrowed John Gilbert from one of Garbo's finest movies, *Queen Christina*, and added some dialogue of my own. In fact, in my version, Papa confesses, "I feel terrible guilt over what happened to Hansi. I acted very badly."

These are the only words that would ever permit me to forgive my father, and I want to give him a last chance to say them. I'm being ingenuous again, of course, and I'm taking a risk, but the force of feeling between a daughter and father evidently cannot be underestimated.

"Papa, Hansi died because we didn't get him proper treatment at the hospital," I tell him. "You see that now, don't you?" I say *we* as a bridge over which my father can walk toward me.

"Hansi died of tuberculosis," he replies, tugging on his jacket sleeves to bring them perfectly even with his cuffs. As a Health Ministry official, maybe he already knew the diagnosis was a ruse. Perhaps he'd been toying with Hansi and me ever since the boy's sterilization.

"Have you ever admitted you're wrong about anything?" I question in a frustrated tone, since it now occurs to me that I never heard him once apologize to Mama.

"Only about you," he tells me.

A cruelly clever reply, delivered with perfect timing, and it catches me off guard. If only he'd gone on to soften his words by saying, *I thought you loved me once*, but instead, he says, "I once believed you'd turn into a fine young woman, a credit to the Fatherland, but you're an embarrassment. And you were an embarrassment to your mother, too."

As soon as he leaves, I sit on Hansi's bed and go as deep down within myself as I can, as far from the pain as my mind can travel. I make a slice in my forearm with a paring knife to see my blood and to test how Benni Mannheim must have felt. But I don't feel anything. Then I bandage my wound and take down my framed photograph of Garbo from the wall, removing from its backing my K-H Collection. Papa and Comrade Ludwig Renn look like old friends.

I head to Isaac's apartment. I let him kiss my hands. Then, while he resumes his work, I remove the cover from his typewriter. The photograph slips right into the carriage. I know what to type because Mr Renn has written Isaac at least one letter since fleeing Germany.

Dearest Comrade Friedrich Riedesel,

I am glad to hear that you are once again working with us, and I assure you that your position as a trusted National Socialist will serve us well. All goes as well as can be expected in Spain, and fighting with the Republicans has given me back a bit of my youth. I shall contact you when I am next in Germany. Keep up the good work and keep sending news!

Isaac gives me a suspicious look when I go into his bedroom and ask for his letter from Mr Renn, so I say, "It's just another small hoax I'm planning." On receiving the full blast of his disapproving stare, I add, "My last, I promise. After this, I renounce my criminal past."

With Mr Renn's letter to Isaac in my hands, I practice his signature, then sign the photograph. With ink, I blacken out the date that K-H typed on the back and substitute the 14th of July, 1937. Bastille Day seems an amusing touch from where I am, though, of course, destroying a parent is hardly funny.

I call Greta that evening. We can't meet on Friday because she'll be dining with Papa, so we agree to get together at her apartment on Thursday the 21st. That means I'll have to leave one day early for Antwerp, because I won't be able to come home again after I give Snow White my poisoned apple. We decide not to tell Vera about this change in plans in case the government is listening to our calls. Isaac and I will spend a night in a hotel in Cologne, and I'll cross the border on the 22nd as originally planned.

I use that week to pack. I will take with me only my favorite drawings, some art supplies, my K-H Collection, and a suitcase of clothing. I'll also take Berekiah Zarco's original manuscripts with me – all seven. Isaac will do his work using the copies he's made, and he'll ship me the rest of what I need when I get to Istanbul. He gives me a talisman for the journey, which I wear around my neck. It's a piece of vellum depicting three Jewish angels, Sanoi, Sansanoi, and Samnaglof. Isaac's renderings are little more than stick figures. "I never claimed to be the artist in the family," he says, smiling cheekily, "but the angels know who they are and that's all that's important."

I also take the lock of hair I snipped from Mama just after she died.

On Thursday afternoon, I put on a rumpled blouse and do my mascara haphazardly, which is why, as soon as Greta lets me into her apartment, she asks with breathy urgency, "What's happened – is your father all right?"

"Oh, Greta, everything has gone wrong. I didn't know who to turn to except you."

"Sit yourself down," she tells me, leading me to her sofa, and she brings me a drink – sherry again. She's in a dressing gown – mauve silk with a white ermine collar.

"Now tell me what's happened ... calmly," she says, and she eases down beside me. Her fingernails are the same shade as her dressing gown. Why does that detail remain in my mind for more than sixty years?

I take a big sip. "I ... I don't know where to start. I'm so ... so confused." I don't want to overdo my stammering, but I'm too pleased with my performance to stop.

"Tell me why you're so upset," she says.

"It's Papa ... oh, Greta, I feel ... I feel terrible! You see, last week, I was looking in his dresser to see what keepsakes of my mother he might have held onto, and ..." Here, I lift my book bag onto my lap and take out my photograph. "I found this. You may have seen it already." With my hands trembling, I *accidentally* drop the picture onto the floor so she can pick it up and discover the damning evidence herself. A nice touch, if I don't say so myself.

"Who's this man with your father?" she asks.

"Ludwig Renn, the Communist journalist. He was famous for a few years. He was arrested in 1932 and later released. I think he was in Spain fighting with the Reds for a while."

"Your father knew him?"

"Then he hasn't told you either about his activities?" I ask, sounding astonished.

"No."

I moan. "I thought that maybe you could explain this to ..."

"Sophie," she interrupts roughly, because Greta is a quick woman who needs quick answers, "are you saying your father was friends with a famous enemy of Hitler's?"

"They were more like acquaintances. Though I thought Papa had renounced his past with the Communists. I was sure of it, but now ... I have to admit, Papa had me fooled."

Greta finishes reading the typed inscription, then jumps up, realizing she could be implicated in Papa's treachery. "Tell me again where you found this?" she demands.

"In one of his drawers, hidden under his shirts. I shouldn't have been looking but ..."

She stares at the phone – does she mean to call the Gestapo?

Then she goes to the window and gazes down purposefully at the street below.

"I wasn't followed," I assure her. "I was very careful."

"Thank God," she tells me. She rubs a tense hand back through her hair.

"Greta," I say hesitantly, as if this is painful for me, "if Papa is involved in some sort of conspiracy, then what do you think we ought to do?"

"Shush!" she says harshly. "I need to think." She takes a cigarette and taps it on the coffee table, then lights it and smokes with an absent gaze, envisaging her strategy.

"He's going to hate me for finding this," I tell her. "And now I'm going to worry all the time about the Gestapo coming for him ... and me." *Gestapo* is my cue to start crying, but I've suddenly lost my nerve. I bring trembling hands up to my cheeks and close my eyes instead.

"Sophie," she declares, "I need to keep this photograph. Now I want you to go home. Don't say a word to anyone. You understand?"

Will Greta keep the photograph a secret, to use as evidence against Papa should the need ever arise, or will she turn it in to the police immediately? I'm betting she's already slipping into something slinky in order to impress the Gestapo, but either way is fine with me.

Isaac has waited for me in our getaway car, a Berlin taxi. He throws his coat over our joined hands as we ride to the Potsdam Station.

Most of what I remember about the train to Cologne is the feeling that I am outside my own body. Floating free of all I've been. Distanced from everyone except Isaac and Hansi.

We spend the night in a dingy pension next to the main station, since the fancier hotels refuse to admit Jews. I lie on the sunken mattress in Isaac's arms and try to forget the urine odor in the carpeting and my previous life. We stay up most of the night talking. In the early morning, we find sleep. We make love on awakening at dawn. I weep in his arms afterward because he says no when I plead to be able to stay with him.

"I'll join you as soon as I can," he assures me. "I promise."

"I'd like to hide inside you until the Nazis disappear."

"Alas, human bodies aren't made like that."

"Mine is. I've got our baby."

"Yes, women have that advantage," he observes, caressing my arm.

"Our son or daughter will need a healthy father, so please be careful."

"I hope that you'll need me, too," he whispers, since he's now lost his voice.

He rests his head on my belly and I comb his soft silver hair with my fingers. I'd give all the drawings I've ever done – even my whole future – to stay in this room forever.

As we walk to the train station, I confess what I've done to my father. Isaac already knows that my rash behavior will complicate his life, but he doesn't want to hurt my feelings or make our farewell any worse. "You did what you had to do," he tells me. "And it's not for me to judge you."

Once we're standing beside the train, he says, "When you're in Belgium, try not to get too angry at me for not coming along."

"I'll try, but no promises," I reply, doing my best to smile.

"I've got a tiny going-away present to help you appreciate what Vera will tell you when you reach her."

"What's she going to tell me?"

"You like mysteries, so have a little patience."

"So what's the present you have?"

He hands me a piece of paper on which he's written a riddle: *I cross the German-Belgian border and rise on the Mount of Olives. Who am I?*

"But the Mount of Olives is in Jerusalem?" I say.

"Yes, and it's where we shall all be reborn when the Messiah comes."

"I don't get it."

"Because it's a riddle!" he exclaims, throwing up his hands.

We laugh at his comic exasperation, and I put the square of paper in my card case, next to the photograph of Raffi that Mrs Munchenberg gave me when I said good-bye to her. I kiss Isaac, and I tell him I love him. And in that one word live so many other emotions that I cannot express, so I simply hold him tight. He kisses me back, taps his finger at the center of my forehead, and recites my favorite poem:

Last night while I lay sleeping,
I dreamt – oh blessed illusion
that a beehive I was keeping
inside my heart;
And from my bitter, rotting
failures, golden bees
were making
a pure white comb with the sweetest honey.

"Remember those magic words as long as you live," he says. "And let the bees do their work!"

The conductor strides past us, about to signal the train to depart. Each step up the staircase into my wagon feels hard and brittle, as though I'm breaking a pact between us. I turn to him from the landing. We both look at who we're about to leave. The whistle sounds, making me start. I wave good-bye, the weight of my tenderness for him heavy on my shoulders. He waves, as well, then puts his pipe in his mouth and stares at me, his eyes moist and shoulders hunched, as though he's a little boy.

I don't know what he sees in me at that moment, but I see everything that's ever made me feel my life was important – Hansi kissing Minnie as she lay dying, Dürer's portrait of his mother, Vera handing me my troubadour coat ... I see Berlin in a fairy-tale darkness and a girl who sits between her beloved papa's legs while listening to American crooners, and a mother hunting for a dumpling recipe, and all the past that will never be repeated even if I am reborn a thousand times.

When will Isaac and I meet again?

Andre and Vera are waiting for me at the station in Liège.

"I'm so sorry about Hansi," Vera tells me, bending down to kiss my cheek. She holds me away and studies me. "Was the journey all right?"

"I survived."

"And the baby?"

"Fine, I hope. So Isaac told you I'm pregnant?"

She gives me an evil squint. "He knew better than to try to keep important news from Aunt Vera!"

When I reach out to shake Andre's hand, he grins like a trickster. "I'd prefer it if you use my real name," he tells me, and he no longer has a Czech accent.

CHAPTER TWENTY-TWO

"I don't understand," I tell Andre. "What's your real name?" We're threading through the crowds at the end of the platform. People gape at Vera and speak in hurried French about her height. *Je n'ai jamais vu une femme si grande ...*

"I'll give you a hint," Vera says. "Isaac's Carnival party, 1932. We almost went to the Botanical Gardens together." Seeing me stumped, she adds, "*The Cabinet of Dr Caligari.*"

"Georg Hirsch?"

"That's right." He takes my shoulder. "I'm sorry we had to fool you."

"But Georg Hirsch is dead," I tell him, thinking that it would be just like Vera to welcome me with a practical joke. "Isaac was in tears when he told me ..."

"Isaac is no romantic lead, but he gives a fine performance when he has to."

"But I saw the photos that K-H took of Georg at the morgue!" I exclaim.

She grins at my confusion, patting my head as if I'm a little girl. "Wait till we get in the car."

Andre summons me over toward an old, battered Mercedes parked on a side street. He unlocks the doors. I sit in the back seat but lean over the front to talk to them. Though Vera slouches, her head still scrapes the ceiling.

"We faked my death," Georg tells me, starting up the car, gazing at me in the rear-view mirror. "I became Georg again here. I'll put on my Cesare make-up later and you'll see."

So this is the answer to Isaac's riddle. "You were the one who crossed the border and rose on the Mount of Olives," I tell him.

"In a way of speaking."

"And all these years you've been lying to me!" I tell Vera, punching her shoulder.

"I had to." She gives me a stiff-armed salute. "General Zarco's orders, Private Riedesel."

"And he lied to me too!"

"What makes you think you always have a right to the truth?" she tells me, sighing as though I'm a cross to bear. "As a matter of fact, lying to you was very important. Though we tried to keep it to a minimum. You'll have to hear more about Georg before the reason will make sense to you."

"All that you told me about Prague ... that was all made up?" I ask him.

"No, I lived there for four years. That's why I chose the name Andre Baldwin. He's the main character in Paul Wegener's *The Student from Prague*."

I pound my seat because I should have guessed. "I knew I'd heard the name somewhere!"

In *The Student from Prague*, Andre Baldwin makes a deal with a sorcerer. He gets wealth and a wonderful marriage, but the sorcerer is permitted to makes use of the student's reflection, which he coaxes out of a looking glass and brings to life.

"I was being targeted by the Nazis," Georg continues. "They shot at me once in Savigny Platz. They might have got me next time. So we faked my death and summoned out a new identity for me from the looking glass."

"So that was why you once told me the safest place to be was already dead," I tell Vera.

"Bull's-eye!"

"And that's why," I say, speaking to Georg, "when you had Isaac and me over for supper you got such amusement about saying nice things about your alter ego."

"I couldn't help being a little silly."

By now we're driving west out of Liège. "Then who was in the photographs I saw?"

"What *was* his name?" Georg asks Vera. "I can't recall."

"Helmut something." Vera turns to me. "K-H must have told you he was a police photographer before he started working at the deaf newspaper. Well, he knew everyone at the coroner's office. That proved useful when we needed a body."

"Though we had to wait a month to get a man of my age and build," Georg tells me.

Their hoax now seems a fitting opening to my life beyond Germany, though I still don't guess just how clever Isaac, Georg, and Vera have been.

"And Helmut was a good match?" I ask excitedly.

"Actually, he wasn't so hot," Vera replies, "but we couldn't risk waiting any longer. We bribed one of the vampires at the morgue to give us Helmut's body and made him up to look like Georg." She offers me a cigarette, but I pass. "We even dyed Helmut's hair," she says in an exhale of smoke.

To Georg, I say, "And you cut your hair short to match his. One of your neighbors, Mrs Brill, told me about your haircut."

"Yes, as it turns out, she's got a pretty good memory."

"Guess who got stuck with clipping Helmut's yellow, dead-man's fingernails?" Vera asks me, and her snarling tone makes the answer obvious. "Because this old hen here refused to do it!" She pushes Georg's shoulder. "As for your brave friend Isaac, leader of the Hebrew tribe of *shvuntzes* – cowards – he wouldn't look at the cadaver's face." She hides her eyes behind her hands, then peeks out girlishly. "After Helmut's transformation, we took him to Georg's apartment. I was ..."

"Wait, how did you get him there?" I interrupt.

"At first we wanted to put him in Benjamin Mannheim's cello case," Georg says.

"Isaac's idea," Vera adds, snorting, which makes me laugh out loud for the first time in weeks. I seem to have entered a Chaplinesque comedy; outwitting the Nazis – and being across the border – has revived my humor.

"The case was too small, of course," Georg tells me. As he tilts his head, he makes a cracking noise. "We nearly broke the poor man's neck trying to stuff him in. So we took Isaac's rug to the morgue in a delivery truck that Julia had access to, and we rolled Helmut inside – just like a *bratwurst*."

"So *that's* why neighbors saw you moving things just before your death. And that's why you had Isaac's rug when you turned into Andre!"

"We were too exhausted to bring it back," Georg tells me. "And besides, we didn't want to be seen coming and going from Isaac's place."

"And the police believed Helmut was you?"

"They must have. Isaac, as my only local relative, identified the body, and we know they were investigating my murder thoroughly because they questioned Vera and Isaac so roughly."

"We diverted the attention of the authorities with my excellent make-up job," Vera says. She bats her eyelids. "My idea, and a very good one, especially those blue swastikas, which matched Helmut's skin discoloration so nicely. I didn't want anything to clash, of course."

"You used Georg's make-up kit," I speculate. "And then removed it from his apartment."

"Exactly."

Georg says, "The idea was to confuse the police with small mysteries – the blue swastikas, the missing make-up kit, the precise cause of death ... That way, they wouldn't notice the identity switch. And we wanted to confuse you, as well."

"Why me?"

"Patience," Vera says seductively.

"All right, but tell me if Helmut was really poisoned, like I thought?"

"Yes. We were told his wife did it. Antimony, I believe."

"Which is why his face turned blue."

Vera shrugs. "I suppose that's what caused it. I don't really know."

"Do you know why she killed him?"

"Not a clue," Georg replies.

"But she strangled him after she poisoned him, didn't she?"

"Yes, and she was so forceful that she broke his windpipe," Vera tells me. "I bet she was petrified he'd wake up. She probably hit him over the head, too. There was a bruise on his forehead that didn't show up in the photographs."

"Sophie, there was another reason why I had to vanish," Georg tells me in a grave voice.

"We'd decided to kill the traitor in The Ring," Vera tells me. "And Georg could do that now with little risk of being caught. Because he was dead!"

"Except that it wasn't easy finding the traitor," Georg confesses.

"But in the end, you learned it was Rolf?" I ask. "I mean, was I right about that?"

"Yes and no. Just before I received the notice about my sterilization hearing, we'd narrowed down the list of possible traitors to Rolf, Heidi, K-H, and Marianne. Then, when I went into hiding to avoid appearing in court, I decided to tell Rolf and Heidi that I was going to be at Isaac's factory, but I told K-H and Marianne I'd be at the warehouse across the street. And I made them swear not to tell anyone else ... not even members of The Ring."

"So all you had to do was wait to see which of the two places the Gestapo searched," I say, admiring their strategy.

"They went to the factory," Vera reminds me.

"So you knew Heidi and Rolf were the traitors," I observe.

She nods. "But were both of them betraying us or only one? And which one? We had to know for sure. Do you remember that going-away party for me you came to – when you made a wicked face at me because you overheard me telling Heidi that the get-together was a last-minute decision, and you knew that wasn't true."

"I remember. I thought you were acting very suspicious."

"I'd decided to invite Heidi and Rolf over to see if I could trick one of them into slipping up, but their performances were line-perfect. I took such a stupid risk!"

"Though none of us thought so at the time," Georg reassures her. "We had Isaac tell Heidi and Rolf about Vera's party at the last minute, at their apartment, and he escorted them straight over to his place. That was so they wouldn't have time to alert Dr Stangl or any other Nazi who might be working with them."

"And after the party, K-H took Heidi and Rolf home. We told him to drive slowly and not let them out of his sight for at least half an hour – to give me time to get away."

"But the Gestapo still came for you," I say.

"They must have been watching Rolf and Heidi's every move. They followed them to Isaac's apartment and then dragged me away."

"It's possible that Rolf and Heidi didn't know that Nazis were watching them so closely," Georg observes. "That's what Heidi told Vera, and maybe it's true."

"You spoke to Heidi about all this?" I ask, stunned.

"After I'd lost the baby, I confronted her. I didn't want to face Rolf and her together. I felt I could get the truth out of Heidi alone. She agreed to come to my apartment. I think there were some things she wanted to tell me, too. I ... I was planning to kill her."

She shakes her head at the difficult memory and takes a long puff on her cigarette, then tosses it out her window. The passing houses seem so small and quiet, and the sky hangs low over the red-tile rooftops and darkened fields. The deep, steady beating inside my chest is Berlin disappearing behind me, and my fear that I will never live there again.

"Sophele, I was three minutes from escaping," Vera continues in a desperate voice. "Three minutes from saving my baby, and Heidi took that future away from me!"

Georg asks Vera to check we're headed the right away. As she compares town signs with the indications on her map, he and I share a look of concern for her in the rear-view mirror.

Certain now that we're headed away from the Fatherland, Vera turns around to face me. "Heidi explained to me about Dr Stangl giving her expensive fertility drugs in exchange for information about The Ring. The poor little thing was weeping. She said she never once thought my baby would be killed. I ended up believing her."

"And all that time she'd had her tubes tied, just like Vera," Georg reminds me.

"Heidi told me that Rolf hadn't betrayed me," Vera continues. "She said she always went alone to Stangl to report on our activities."

"And that's why," I speculate, "when I told you that Dr Stangl's wife had complained about all the visits from Rolf, you got so upset. You realized she'd lied to you. And fooled you."

"Yes, but things get complicated here. You see, I didn't believe her *entirely* – I thought she might be lying to protect Rolf. She asked me to come to her apartment the following afternoon, while Rolf was at work. She'd prove that only she was responsible. 'Why should I trust you?' I asked her, and she said, 'Because I hate what I did to you. And because even after all that's happened, you must feel we're still friends or you'd have killed me by now.' She was right, so I went to see her."

"With me," Georg adds. "Because *I* didn't trust Heidi at all. And I took my gun. But Heidi wasn't at home ..."

"Was your gun the same one you had before you changed your identity?"

"Yes. Why do you ask?"

"Because when I asked Vera what happened to your gun after you were supposedly murdered, she hesitated, which made me suspicious. Then she said she gave it to the police."

"You're right, Sophele, I almost slipped up. I didn't realize you'd ask that question. I wasn't prepared for everything." She smiles cagily. "Though mostly I gave a pretty good performance, don't you think?"

"*Too* good."

"Anyway, Heidi wasn't home when we got to her apartment," Georg continues. "We waited to see if she'd show up, and when she didn't, we returned to Isaac's place. In the kitchen, we found her body, lying on the floor."

"She'd left a note for me," Vera says. "She wrote that ending her life was the only way she had to try to make up for my dead baby. She begged me not to tell Rolf she'd killed herself, because he'd feel responsible. She repeated that he had nothing to do with betraying us."

"How did she commit suicide?"

"I found an empty bottle of tranquilizers next to the sink," Vera replies.

"So Heidi gave up her life to save Rolf," I say.

"Yes, and to even out our destinies," Vera replies. "You see, without intending to, I gave her a way to make her death have some purpose ... some meaning. Knowing Heidi, she'd have wanted that, especially after being duped by Stangl."

"And how did she get into Isaac's apartment?" I ask.

"She left his key on top of her note. She'd borrowed a spare one years before, and she must have still had it."

"And you discarded her body in the Rummelsburger See," I say.

"We panicked," Georg tells me. "After all, this was a surprise, and we were amateurs."

"I painted swastikas on her face so the police would think the same person had murdered her who had killed Georg," Vera says. "And so Rolf would think that too. Then I put her in my big suitcase."

"So that's why you left your beloved sewing machine behind! You had nothing to carry it in!"

"It was partly that, but I'd also forgotten about it for the first time in my adult life. Maybe I even wanted to leave it behind – to punish myself for putting my baby at risk. I don't know."

"So I carried Heidi to my car in the suitcase," Georg adds, "and drove out to a wood I knew near the Rummelsburger See, to a place where Isaac and I used to go birdwatching when I was a kid. I left the suitcase there. I expected whoever found it to report the body to the police, but they apparently dumped her in the lake instead. Whoever found it must have been terrified they'd be implicated in the murder."

"And meanwhile, you went back to your apartment," I tell Vera.

"Yes, I didn't go with Georg because I'm so noticeable. But I also didn't want to stay at Isaac's place. I couldn't face him. The guilt ... and my continuing grief over my baby ... I needed to be alone. So I went home."

"And you didn't come out of your apartment for days."

"I was overwhelmed by what had happened. And I couldn't risk revealing my part in Heidi's death to you. You had to figure that out yourself."

"Why? You know I wouldn't ever have put you in any danger."

"We'll tell you that, but first I need to tell you about Stangl," Georg says. "You see ..."

"Wait, first tell me about Rolf," I interrupt. "Why didn't you kill him when you found out that Heidi had lied to you in order to protect him?"

"As you told me at the time, he was living in hell without Heidi, and he was being punished enough. I ended up agreeing with you. And Georg and Isaac did too. Besides, the Nazis had lost their leverage on him. He wouldn't do anything more to hurt us."

"Rolf will never know how close he was to being murdered," I observe.

"And now for Dr Stangl!" Georg announces. "I called him on the phone after I learned about how he'd used Heidi, and I told him I had important information for him. And that his life was in danger. He'd believed that Nazis had murdered me, so he was shocked to hear my voice. I told him I'd gone underground because Isaac and Vera suspected that I was a traitor to their cause and had tried to kill me. I said that the Gestapo had faked my death so I'd be free to continue to help the Nazi Party in secret."

"But he told his wife that Rolf called," I point out.

"He couldn't very well tell her I was on the phone because she must have heard I'd been murdered and would have asked too many questions. He must have chosen Rolf's name because they'd spoken so often in the past."

"I had him meet me out by the Rummelsburger See because we wanted to follow the same pattern. And I shot him."

"Just like that?" I ask.

Georg raises his furry eyebrows and gives me a curious look in the rear-view mirror. "Does that shock you?"

"A bit."

"I gave Stangl a chance to tell me why he'd betrayed us, but he sneered and said that he didn't need to justify his actions to me. So I replied, 'In that case, I don't need to justify what I do either,' and I aimed the gun at his chest. I was dizzy with nervousness, and I wasn't sure I could do it until I pulled the trigger. But I couldn't let him go on hurting good people."

"This ... this must be the first time a dead Jew ever killed a Nazi," I say, thinking that Isaac must have appreciated that irony.

"And let's hope it's not the last," Vera replies. "We could use all the Jews who are going to die in this war to keep fighting for those of us who manage to stay alive."

"So why was keeping me in the dark so important?" I ask.

"You, *meine Liebe*, were our safeguard," Vera tells me mysteriously.

"Given your personality," Georg says, "we reasoned that you'd probably keep trying to get to the bottom of all the mysteries – just like the police. We figured that you'd do at least as well as their detectives, since you had the advantage of knowing us. And you demonstrated that you'd keep sniffing around when you tried to prove that Julia was responsible for my death. Then, when you figured out that Rolf was the traitor, we reasoned you'd start suspecting Vera of having killed Heidi and Dr Stangl. And you did."

"As I recall, you once accused me of murdering Heidi," Vera tells me.

"I'm sorry."

"Don't be! You were right to – that's the whole point."

"Sooner or later, you might have started checking up on Vera and following her," Georg says. "And who knows, maybe you'd even figure out that I wasn't dead."

"But I didn't."

"No, life got in the way," Vera says. "You got busy with your teaching and Isaac, and with protecting your brother. And I'm glad you did, though we couldn't afford the luxury of assuming the police would also be too busy with their home lives to forget about us."

"Isaac was especially relieved that life got in the way of your detective work, of course," Georg tells me. "He was not in favor of our using you to gauge our safety. He didn't want you doing any investigating, though he also knew only too well he couldn't stop you. In any case, Vera and I had agreed years ago that when we felt you might start getting too close to the truth we'd leave Germany – first me, because I'd killed Stangl and had disposed of Heidi's body, then her."

My tiny bedroom in Antwerp is a converted larder off the kitchen, with a sad little window looking out on the backs of apartments. I hang my framed photo of Garbo above my cot and tape a small sketch of Isaac hunched over a manuscript to the back of my door. Still, I feel trapped, hemmed in by all the choices I've had to make, and – paradoxically – as though Berlin is the only place I'll ever be free. Sensing my daydreams are leading me toward despair, Georg takes me aside and says, "We'll soon have you feeling at home here." He holds my shoulders and looks at me hard – as though to show me that his strength is on my side. He wants to help, but all I can think of is that he isn't Isaac.

Georg takes Vera and me out to dinner at a Jewish restaurant that night. We gorge on matzo ball soup, stuffed cabbage, and kasha. "This doesn't taste at all like cat food," I tell Vera.

"My God, you still haven't figured that I'm a world-class *nudnock*?" she replies, laughing from her belly.

The next day, I go to museums and walk through the elegant old streets with their ornate Dutch houses, listening to the harsh, scraping sound of the Flemish language, picking out words with cognates in German, pressing my forehead to shop windows to see the intricate, colorful displays, researching the prices of art supplies. No swastika flags or anti-Jewish signs hang on the streets. It's a miracle. And it's a relief to be alone with my thoughts. Once again, I'm reminded that I need a few hours to myself each day or I'm no good to anyone.

I also phone Zarco Industries and leave a coded message with Arnold Muller, the German-American typist, that all is well. Isaac calls back that evening from the house of Frau Hagen, who takes care of his converted boathouse. "I got tipped off that I might be arrested," he explains, "so I grabbed my manuscripts and some clothes, and some paintings to sell, and I fled."

"Who tipped you off?"

"Now, don't be upset, but you did."

"Me?"

"When you told me you'd framed your father, I realized he was going to come after me, that he'd think I was involved in your little hoax. So when I returned from Cologne, I got my things and left. As it turns out, your father and two Gestapo officers showed up at my factory two days after I got back. He was in a wild rage, and he threatened to have all the workers arrested unless they told him where you and I were hiding. He'd assumed we'd fled together."

It seems impossible that I didn't foresee this. "I'm so sorry, Isaac. I've been very careless."

"It's all right. You were angry and upset. In fact, I'm better off here. You made me realize that they'd probably come for me one day soon. You might have got me out just in time."

"And you're all right?"

"I'm happy as a kid on summer vacation. It's beautiful here. And no one knows where I am except Frau Hagen. She's an angel."

We have a long talk, but the phone lines are too thin to carry the weight of our emotions. When I fall into silence, he says, "Sophele, picture me with you every night upon going to sleep, because I will be there, right by your side. And do whatever you need to do to live well." I fear he is about to tell me that if I need to have a relationship with another man, he will understand, but he doesn't add that, thank God.

The mind has its own strange and silly ways of showing loss; right after I hang up, I think, *Who's going to water the poor pelargoniums?*

Is Papa fired from the Health Ministry because of how I've framed him or is he able to clear his name? Are he and Greta married? I learn nothing more about him while I'm in Antwerp.

The Belgians expect a German invasion within a few months, so, in mid-April, just after the Fatherland crushes Denmark in a single day, we book passage to Genoa on a Dutch ship leaving on the 2nd of May. From there, we'll take an Italian freighter to Istanbul. Isaac calls a few days before we go to wish us well. He's in a state of electric excitement. "All those years I was looking for the incantation in the wrong place, but now I know where it is!"

"And where's that?" I ask, hopeful that this means he will soon be joining us.

"It's not in any of the mystical treatises. It's in the seventh text, in *The Bleeding Mirror*."

"I thought that was just the story of how Berekiah survived the Lisbon Massacre of 1506."

"I thought so too, but it's much more than that. He used the pogrom symbolically." Isaac tells me that Berekiah intended *The Bleeding Mirror* to serve as preparation for those seeking to enter the Seventh Heaven. The six mystical treatises were hidden together with it because they serve as complementary texts. "The most important clue to the higher purpose of *The Bleeding Mirror* comes at the very end," he says, "where Berekiah prophesies the shattering of the last vessels."

"Does that mean he'd entered Araboth and viewed the future?"

"Yes, I think so. Now listen ..." Isaac translates various prophetic sections of *The Bleeding Mirror* into German for me. He finishes with a paragraph he showed me once before, when he was trying to convince me to leave Germany. In it, Berekiah writes that the European kings will always persecute the Jews. "'Sooner or later, in this century or five centuries hence, they will come for you or your descendants,'" Isaac reminds me, quoting from the text. "'*No village, no matter how remote, will be safe when the final reckoning comes*.'" Isaac speaks these last words as if seizing them with his fists. Could Berekiah Zarco, writing in the sixteenth century, have foreseen all that was now happening in Germany? "Of course, he did – that's part of what I've just realized!" Isaac assures me. "And do you remember that riddle I once read you ... the one Berekiah wrote?"

"Vaguely."

"'The Seventh Gate opens like wings as we begin our conversation. It speaks with a million bleeding voices and yet just one. Only he who hears the voices with the eyes of Moses may

enter Araboth.' The answer to the riddle is *The Bleeding Mirror*!
Its pages open like wings, and the million voices are the words
of the book, which speak to each reader in his or her own voice.
'The eyes of Moses' is a reference to mirrors, to their backwards
images ... to reading Hebrew from right to left. In other words,
Sophele, Berekiah was giving us a clue that *The Bleeding Mirror*
had a sacred aspect to it."

"It's all too complicated for me," I tell him, more dismissively
than I intend, probably because Isaac hasn't yet asked after our
travel plans. How silly we can be at times!

"Sophele, what's wrong?" he asks, his voice suddenly fearful.

"Nothing. It's just that we've booked passage to Istanbul. We
leave on the 2nd of May."

"Thank God!" he exults. "And bless you for taking our baby to
safety. I'm so very grateful to you for making this *mesirat nefesh*."

The solemn way he speaks ... Ever since leaving Germany, my
tears flow without resistance, as if the river I'd been holding back
for years has broken through my defenses, and now is no different.
I'd had no idea of how thick and high the cold stone walls were
inside me. Insight often comes only years after we need it most.

"What is it, my dear?" he asks softly. "Tell me ..."

"I'm just happy. And my emotions seem to be out of control
of late."

"That would be the baby. All unborn children turn their mothers
upside down because they're under the domain of Metatron."

"What is that supposed to mean?"

"Metatron is the angel who is the bridge between the Lower and
Upper Realms, and the guardian of the unborn. He is as dazzling
as the sun, and you are simply feeling his heat."

"You're completely *meshugene*," I say affectionately.

"Very possibly. So how are you feeling?"

"Bloated. And I'm starting to show."

Laughing, he says, "Take photographs. I'll want to see them later."

"I'll try. Any news of K-H and Marianne?"

"Nothing yet."

"Now tell me how Berekiah used the Lisbon Massacre symbolically," I say, since he won't be satisfied until he's revealed much more of the intricate workings of his mind to me. And I want to listen to his voice for as long as he will talk to me.

"It's like this, Sophele ... Berekiah wrote *The Bleeding Mirror* as a guidebook to the dangers the mystic would encounter on the way toward the territory of prophesy. The difficulties faced by the Jews of Lisbon – the constant peril they experienced during the massacre – are symbolic of what the mystic will encounter along his journey."

"And what does that mean for your work?"

"It means I am re-reading *The Bleeding Mirror* with infinite care, and taking notes. I think the key is Aramaic, which, not coincidentally, was the language spoken in the Promised Land at the time of the destruction of the Hebrew Temple."

"Not coincidentally ...?"

"The destruction of the temple is the perfect symbol for the shattering of our world. It left the Jewish mind in ruins. The center of the world became not a place, but a time – the Sabbath." Isaac goes on to provide me with more kabbalistic explanations, most of which I don't understand or now remember, but I've been able to reconstruct at least some of what he said from a letter he later wrote me about his revelations. I *do* know that he told me that day, "Berekiah uses the Aramaic phrase *Elah Skemaiya*, the God of Heaven, to refer to the Lord. He doesn't use Hebrew. That's because *Elah Shemaiya* is also the God of Prophesy. Which means that the incantation I'm looking for will be in Aramaic – or in Hebrew *disguised* as Aramaic."

"Does this mean you'll be able to join me in Istanbul soon?" I ask hopefully.

"I think it may."

"Do me a favor and ask Berekiah for a specific date."

I expect Isaac to laugh, but instead he says, "When I next see him, I'll ask."

Eight days after we set sail, we learn that Germany has invaded Belgium, France, and Holland. As we cruise down the rocky, sunlit coast of Portugal, a group of us listen to the BBC every night on a little red bakelite radio belonging to a Flemish journalist, and by the time we dock in Istanbul on the 28th of May, we're all gripped by pessimism, having heard that King Leopold of Belgium has declared his country's surrender. France and Holland are expected to fall soon.

Istanbul from the sea ... If I close my eyes, I can see the city's profile silhouetted in the sunset of our arrival, like a grand sculpture made by children whose secret fantasies have been given form. The tall, slender minarets are the white-white of falling snow, just as the Turkish Ambassador once implied to me, and the domes of the mosques have been glazed bronze by the melting sun. Luminescent gulls wheel and caw overhead, and the Galata Bridge – spanning the Golden Horn – sags under the weight of a thousand donkey-wagons, wooden pushcarts, and hooting automobiles. Hundreds of bedraggled fishermen lean over the railings, their lapels upturned against the biting wind, smoking and chatting, their lines also forming a kind of bridge, between the mysteries underwater and the land. The Galata Tower crowns the hill just ahead of us, rising 200 feet above its neighbors. "Built in 1348," one of the Turks we've befriended tells us. He also says that he's always thought of it as an arrow of stone pointing to heaven – a summons for protection from Allah. *And from* Elah Shemaiya, *too*, I think, *because they are one and the same.*

After a few years of life in Istanbul I realize that none of the city's monuments has a universal meaning, however. Everyone in Istanbul guards his own version of the city, his own tiny silver globe – just as I always kept my own map of Berlin in my heart, and still do. Yet for me the Galata Tower will always signify freedom – ours from Germany, of course, but also of being able to rise above the decay of the chaotic world and emerge into sunlight. Sand-colored stone against the deep medieval blue of a Giotto fresco. The cry of a muezzin to prayer. Wild dogs barking. A little mop-haired boy in bare feet playing with a ball, and his mother – me – kicking it back to him. That is the Istanbul of my dreams even today. And in truth, it is my son who forever links me to the city, because he was born there.

Isaac's cousin Abraham and his wife, Graça, meet us with effusive hugs and kisses at the dock on that cool May evening in 1940. They are wary of Vera, but we don't take offense, because we know from experience that meeting a goddess is daunting. Abraham holds my hand lightly, like a dance partner, and steers me around the debris on the street, which is a good thing, since my belly is fairly big now and my balance has become faulty. Do they wonder at my youth? *My God, how did Isaac seduce so young a lover? She must be crazy!*

Abraham's driver steers his dusty black Ford through the crowded streets to the family home in Ortaköy. Georg and Graça follow behind in a taxi; Abraham was sure that Isaac's description of Vera was an exaggeration and failed to bring a second car.

They live in a balconied, Ottoman-style wooden house that

is painted a brilliant canary yellow, with scarlet trim around the windows. It could be the grand manor house in a Turkish fairy tale, assuming that such stories exist, but it seems a bit ominous to me on that first, moonlit evening. Haunted, I'm sure, but that doesn't bother me; I fear only ghosts who speak German.

"Our house is golden yellow and red because they are the colors of God's strength," Abraham says to me in French, making a fist, and Georg translates. Our host uses charming hand gestures when he talks to me. It reminds me of how I'd give Hansi visual aids when he was a boy.

Except for Abraham's eldest son David, a dermatologist who studied at the German School, none of the relatives waiting for us at the house speaks any German. They speak Ladino with Vera, who is fluent in Spanish, of course, and French with Georg. As for me, I'm pretty much lost.

We settle in to the three bedrooms on the second floor that once belonged to David, his sister Luna, and brother Mordecai. Out my window, I have a view of the Mecidiye Cami'i Mosque, standing guard over the Bosphorus with its lance-like minaret. In the distance is Asia, a second Milky Way of lights below a moon as friendly and soft as the ones Volker used to draw.

Though we are only a few miles from Istanbul's business district, the next morning I discover Ortaköy to be a quiet fishing village, with a row of ramshackle taverns near the water, children running around barefoot, and a local troubadour named Üstat who sings droning ballads while accompanying himself on a lute-like instrument called a *saz*. Many years later, the neighborhood's weekend market will become popular with tourists, and the bridge between Europe and Asia will be built only a mile to the north, but for now Ortaköy looks like a sepia postcard of an insular world that few northern Europeans would ever be able to penetrate.

Abraham has Isaac's thin, sensitive lips, and his same look of diligent concentration when he reads. He smokes a curving meerschaum pipe. He is seventy-one, a year younger than Isaac. I find myself staring at him on occasion, wondering what he makes of us. He shows me pictures of himself and Isaac when they were boys: two amused, eager-eyed devils sitting in a rowboat in the Golden Horn, clowning for the camera.

A first letter from Isaac is already waiting for me, along with a new set of oil pastels and two sketchbooks. My heart jumps a thousand miles back to Berlin as I open the envelope. He speaks of the stunning sunrise over his scruffy boathouse garden. "The Nazis have no power over trees and birds and light," he writes. "All of nature is on our side in this battle. Please remember that when you are feeling down."

Isaac's goodness is even in his small, elegant handwriting. I sleep with the letter under my pillow for months.

We try to speak to Frau Hagen that first evening, but getting a call through to Berlin proves impossible even for David, the technology expert in the family. Finally, two days later, we manage to get her, and we leave a message for Isaac. He takes a risk and calls back that afternoon from the Turkish Embassy, where they have a better chance of getting a connection. With all the static, he sounds as if he is calling during a hailstorm, and since he warns me that the line could "disappear into *Gehenna*" – the Jewish hell – at any moment, I don't say much more than I am well. He tells me he loves me and will write long letters.

The letters come once a week, and I answer them with equal frequency. He only rarely describes his progress in his work. He speaks of big-eared rabbits who peer in his windows, an owl that hoots every night, and how he slipped over a moss-slickened stone only to find himself face to face with an angry-looking yellow and black salamander. "I'm sorry we never came out here, but we'll rectify that when our beloved Berlin is healed."

Georg, Vera, and I spend our first two weeks visiting the Grand Bazaar, the Hagia Sophia, and other attractions. Unfortunately for us, the Turks, Kurds, Greeks, Armenians, Jews, Albanians, Circassians, Georgians, Assyrians, Azeris, Tatars, and others who call the city home stare even more satanically than Germans. Do we look like Hollywood has-beens? Visitors from another planet? Their gazes give nothing away. Poor Vera. Children follow her in the streets, laughing, shouting things we don't understand. "It's all part of my job," she tells me, smiling, but I can see in her eyes she's suffering.

I write my father a two-line letter: "I am well, but I won't be coming back to Berlin until your sewage company is destroyed." Abraham posts it when he goes to Salonika on business; I want Papa to know I'm alive, but I don't want him tracking me to Istanbul.

We have a giddy, laughing reunion with Julia and Martin at our home. Julia is working in a herb shop in Beyoğlu, one of the main shopping districts. Martin makes deliveries for her. When I apologize for forcing them to leave Berlin, she embraces me tenderly and says, "Don't think about it any more. I always knew the risks I was taking, and I prefer being here at the moment."

We also visit the different branches of Isaac's extended family, and we spend a week at Abraham's summer home on the island of Büyükada, twenty miles from Istanbul in the Marmara Sea. No cars are allowed on the island, so we ride like Hungarian aristocrats in horse carriages. The floors in the wooden Ottoman houses all creak and moan, as though they come alive when we enter. I fall in love with the resplendent sunlight, the sea breezes, and the night-quiet. On a glorious June afternoon when we have a picnic, David helps me count Isaac's cousins and other relatives: twenty-four. "Enough for a football match plus two substitutes," Georg points out. He, Vera, and I appreciate all the attention, but we sometimes talk in hushed voices about needing to spend more time by ourselves.

I'm intimidated by Abraham's gentlemanly reserve with me until a little over a month after our arrival, when he leads me out to the back patio, kneels before me as if he's a medieval knight, and says in halting, childlike German, "Isaac is a dearest brother to me, so the people he loves are my friends, too. You must not fear me. I mean only good things for you."

I burst into tears, especially because by then, early July, I'm six months pregnant and plagued by all the fears of an expectant mother. Later, David tells me that he wrote out his father's speech phonetically in Ladino. "Papa memorized it," he says, such admiration for the old gentleman in his eyes that I'm won to him and Abraham forever.

I plan to learn Turkish or die trying, and Georg, Vera, and I soon have a tutor. His name is Manuel Levi, and he has a doctorate from the University of Vienna in Near Eastern History. He wears wire-rimmed spectacles and suspenders, and he combs his thick black hair straight back, so that he looks like a Chicago gangster. The "Turkish Jimmy Cagney", Vera calls him. She's taken to giving nicknames to all our new acquaintances. Manuel desperately wants to be American, and he has a crush on Judy Garland. He teaches history at the German School. He is the first friend I make in Istanbul.

David helps me by correcting my Turkish pronunciation. He is slender and soft-spoken, but with an undercurrent of eccentricity. He usually wears a flower in his lapel – carnations most often – and he often sings to himself. He and his wife, Gül, a Moslem convert to Judaism, go for long bicycle rides in the country with their two teenage children, Samuel and Naomi. He likes working with his hands and repairs the bicycles of neighborhood children for free. If he hadn't become a dermatologist, he'd have opened a bike shop, he assures me.

Graça is always perfectly dressed and coiffed, and she thrives on doing tasks around the house, whether it's making fig jam, supervising roofers, or weeding the back garden. In her spare time, she campaigns for aid to the Allies. She is also a woman of odd contradictions; one evening, for instance, I walk in on her embroidering traditional Ottoman patterns on a towel while listening to Benny Goodman on her gramophone. Vera calls her the "Lady with the Talking Earring" because she can spend hours on the phone, the receiver pressed to her ear. She has dozens, if not hundreds, of lady friends she meets for tea. She's been to Paris, London, and Berlin, which she found a boisterous, exciting city. "But that was before Hitler," she says darkly. She thinks Istanbul is quaint and often lovely, but also dirty and cruel. *Pittoresque et souvent belle, mais aussi sale et cruelle.* Georg likes to translate her French for me because she uses surprising word combinations. He believes that in order to appreciate Sephardic Jews and their culture one must realize that they far prefer poetry to prose. "German and Eastern European Jews are prose storytellers; Portuguese and Spanish Jews are poets."

The second time I enter Ortaköy's Mecidiye Cami'i Mosque to admire its colorful tile patterns, a gray dove flies in after me. The bird lands on one of the red-toned Persian carpets and starts cooing and prancing. *I've got to find Hansi!* I think gleefully. *He'd love this.*

How can one forget that a little brother is dead? The realization that he's buried in Berlin falls like a hood over my mind, because my second pair of eyes is gone forever.

What am I going to do with myself in Istanbul? As always, I

worry my way into a maze of insomnia. Georg and Vera share my preoccupation. Do the Zarcos intend for us to stay in their home forever? Georg thinks so. "After you give birth," he tells me, "the Lady with the Talking Earring will never leave your side. We're going to have to find our own place before that happens." More and more, he takes on the role of my protector. I suspect Isaac asked him to intervene on my behalf whenever he felt it necessary. I'm grateful to them both.

Pregnant in Istanbul and imagining my parents

Georg and David conspire together to find us lodging, and in early July we move in to an apartment below Taksim Square, a block from David's house. Abraham and Graça take the news graciously. What I don't know yet is that for the next two years she'll visit me twice a week for afternoon tea and bring along her own servant and samovar!

Vera starts work that same week in Abraham's factory. She is creating patterns for men's suits and fancy waistcoats for export to England. She's overjoyed by the challenge. Abraham secures work for Georg as a designer at a small advertising agency that has contracts with French and Dutch companies.

We decide not to try to find me work during the last three months of my pregnancy, so every morning I go to one or another of the cafés on the Istiklal Caddesi, drink pomegranate juice, and sketch the astonishing variety of faces around me. I try my hand at landscapes for the first time, as well, but terrors I do not want to admit make my hands shake when I'm alone: what will I do if my baby is born dead? How will I cope if he is a distant child like Hansi?

Georg reads about the war every day, and each German victory lowers our heads a little more and makes us speak more quietly in public. On the 15th of June, the *Wehrmacht* rides victorious down the Champs Elysées in Paris, and I can easily picture Tonio, grinning, sitting triumphantly atop his Panzer. A week later, all of France surrenders. Then, on the 7th of August, Frau Hagen telephones, frantic. She tells me that the Gestapo came to the boathouse the day before, forcing Isaac to hide in the attic. "After the Nazis left," she says, "I went to check on him. He was scared, and a bit dusty, but fine. We came back here to my home."

"Can I speak to him?" I ask.

"I'm sorry, he left this morning. We tried calling you but we couldn't get a line. He said to assure you he was fine and will try to write soon. Sophie, I'm worried. He took off with only one change of clothing and he didn't know where he was going."

Frau Hagen would never have turned Isaac in. I fear that Rolf may have played one last terrible trick on us. Vera and Georg regret letting him live.

Though it's possible that Isaac is finally on his way to us in Istanbul. That is the hope that keeps me from returning to Germany to search for him. A long letter arrives later that month, containing writings over a two-day period. It begins – on the 17th of July – much like Isaac's previous correspondence, with grateful observations of life in the country. But then he moves into verse – prophetic poetry from the Torah, most of it seemingly about what is now taking place in Germany and a good deal of it in his own translation from Hebrew: "A fourth kingdom shall appear upon the earth. It shall differ from the other kingdoms and shall devour the Lower Realms ..."

Years later, I will do some research and find out that Isaac took all his verses from Ezra and Daniel. Why only those two books? A researcher at the Sorbonne will inform me that they are the only two Biblical books in which the Lord is referred to as *Elah Shemaiya*, the God of Prophesy.

Isaac adds that he's been thinking of Rolf and his betrayals of late. "I feel that he represents unfinished business for me, and before I can make reparations to our world, I'll need to speak to him. Perhaps, too, I could ask him for a favor, an important one, and that would be good for us both – a kind of reconciliation."

The next day, Isaac's handwriting becomes wild and erratic, as though he can't write fast enough. "Last night, as I prayed, facing the Mount of Olives, a vision descended upon me, so powerful that it pulled me to my feet. I saw myself as an ibis stepping across the cover of *The Bleeding Mirror*. First my bird's feet, then all of me, entered the manuscript itself. The beating of wings passed over me, creating a warm wind, as though I were in the desert of the Promised Land, and as my own pages opened, I looked up to see the shadow of that angel who can never be glimpsed in all his glory, and the darkness covered me and the entire world. Metatron had passed over me. The sky, turning red from the angel's heat, was melting around me, and I was melting too, but I wasn't scared, because as the garment of form slipped away from me, the Seventh Gate appeared before me. On its archway, scripted in silver in my own handwriting, was an inscription – an incantation. After I read it, I awoke. And I knew just where to look in my manuscripts for what had been written in silver – and what needed to be done. Sophele, the inscription turned out to be the last line of *The Bleeding Mirror*: '*Beruchim kol deemuyei Eloha*,' which means, 'Blessed are all of God's self-portraits.' It was one of Berekiah's favorite expressions because he believed it was essential for us to remember that every man, woman, and child, and even all animals, are all self-portraits of the Lord.

"I was right about needing to know Aramaic, because when I joined the first letter of each word in Berekiah's blessing together – *bet khaf dalet aleph* – the word *bekada* was spelled out. *Bekada* means 'Inside a vessel'. In other words, he who has passed through the first Six Gates and who has prepared for the Seventh, upon speaking the words *Beruchim kol deemuyei Eloha*, will find himself at the very center of God's Realm. He will enter the vessels, and he *himself* will effect the needed reparations from the inside, as it should be. I ought to have guessed! We are, after all, God's hands and eyes!

"I also know now why the destroyed Seventh Gate of Europe was never re-consecrated. Because he who would enter the vessels must consecrate the gate himself, at the central point around which the world is shattering. That was what Berekiah intended for me, so if you do not hear from me for some months, do not fear. I shall try with all my heart to come back to you, but I'm on a journey now whose end I do not know. Yet this I *do* know: the Opposite-Compass and all the forces of the Fourth Kingdom shall not turn me around. I shall hold tight to the silver winds of *mesirat nefesh*, and the music I hear will be the souls speaking in Araboth, readying to meet me. You shall be with me on the journey, as well as Hansi, Benni, Raffi, Vera, and Georg. And my wife and son. And we shall not fear the shadows that come to pursue us, because the secret of those shadows is that they are light! We shall not fear being cast into the earth, because that fall into our Mother is also the ascent into our Father. We shall not tremble as the fire burns away our bodies because that fire means everlasting life for us for those who come after us.

"Sophele, stay strong! You need fear nothing over the coming months and years, because your courage is much greater than you imagine. I thank you for helping me, and I bless you. I kiss your eyes every night before you sleep. And I kiss our baby. Isaac."

Despairingly, I realize this is a letter of farewell. Vera and Georg sit with me as I sob. Then Vera grips my hand. "Look at me!" she orders. "Now listen closely," she tells me, her eyes flashing. "I may make fun of Isaac and his beliefs, but that doesn't mean I'm not aware that he's the most powerful man any of us have ever met. So if there's any way to make it back to us ... to *you*, then I assure you, he will."

She means well, and I know what she says is true, but her words only seem to freeze my mind. Soon, I grow furious with Isaac for sending me away. I want a father for my baby and a warm man in my bed, not a mystic riding on prayer to imaginary worlds. It takes me weeks before I can listen to any encouragement without wanting to run and hide. I sit by the front door as I await our postman every afternoon, hoping for another letter. I try to sketch Hansi and Isaac from memory, but it's hopeless.

It's the kicking and flexing of my child that saves me. Life has entered into me and is growing. And if that miracle can happen, then maybe Isaac and I will be granted another chance.

On occasion, I take a taxi to Abraham's house in Ortaköy and sit quietly with Graça, whom I like more and more, and sometimes we go listen to Üstat, who has taken over Benni Mannheim's work on behalf of the physical laws of our universe. The old musician smiles on seeing me now. He has leathery skin, wild black eyes, and deep creases in his cheeks. He looks like a desert warrior, but Graça tells me that Üstat is an *ashik*, a person so consumed by love that he can express himself only in song. Ashiks can sing for hours from memory – "Of the pain and joy of love, of ancient heroes, of death, cruelty, and friendship." I know enough French to understand what Graça tells me. Squeezing my hand, she adds, "And of loneliness."

I give birth to Hans Berekiah Riedesel Zarco on the 14th of September, 1940, only five days shy of my twenty-third birthday. He's fragile, compact, and as deeply creased as Üstat. The good news: he weighs six pounds, eleven ounces, and has all his fingers, toes, and private parts. Graça says he's small but perfect – *petit mais parfait*. The bad news: Vera says he looks like a hungry Tiergarten squirrel.

Everyone in Isaac's family comes to see Hans over the next weeks: Magi bearing gifts. The women admit me to the international club of mothers with their warnings about colic, worms, head colds, and a hundred other ailments harder to name. What a time I have trying to decipher their Ladino, Turkish, and French! Graça informs me that by Jewish law I'm not permitted to leave the house for forty days after Hans' birth.

"Did the SS write that law?" Vera asks, which makes the delicate old lady laugh out loud.

When Graça visits our apartment, we stay inside, so Lilith and other demons cannot carry off either Hans or myself, I'm not sure who. Otherwise, on warm days, I risk dangers both mundane and otherworldly and venture outside. I often walk down to the Bosphorus to watch the ships from all over the world. I wish my mother could see my Hans. Our quarrels have ended, even in my head.

I miss Isaac on waking more than at any other time. The shock of finding myself alone – with no idea of where he might be or what he might be suffering – leaves me frenzied. At times, I picture him a prisoner in Dachau, just like Raffi. Or working in a munitions factory or mine. I write him long letters in my mind.

A month of waiting becomes two and then four ... By now, German troops have taken control of Romania and Hungary, and both puppet governments have passed anti-Jewish legislation. In Poland, Jews are being confined in ghettos. Georg reads in a Zurich newspaper in November that a Warsaw neighborhood has been sealed with half a million Jews inside, and that a similar fenced-in area of Lodz holds 230,000. But I have trouble understanding how these ghettos work. "If they're sealed," I ask him, "then how do the people inside get food deliveries or medicines?"

"I don't think they do," he replies ominously.

Given my lifelong battle with sleeplessness, who could have predicted that Hans would slumber so peacefully at night? Vera and I take turns walking him around on those occasions when he does cry or fuss, and she helps me change his diapers. Each gigantic, bread-dough hand of hers is as big as he is, and it amuses me to see the two of them together. "The Amazon and the Tiergarten Squirrel", Georg calls them, which I think would please my brother.

Sometimes Vera entertains the baby by singing lieder in her gravel-toned baritone. What does Hans make of the giant with the cavewoman forehead and German melodies?

Vera's delicacy with my son – treating him if he's made of whispers – allows me to steal some tranquil moments for myself and even take a nap now and again. Once, I awake to find tears rolling down her cheeks and Hans cradled in her arms. When I ask what's wrong, she replies, "Being ugly makes no difference for the first time in my life. I feel as if my heart has been ransomed."

The birth of Hans is my excuse to write letters to Else, Dr Hassgall, the Munchenbergs, and Roman. I even send a card to Frau Mittelmann at her mill. Are my letters arriving? It seems doubtful because no replies arrive. Though maybe my friends don't write back because they're sure their letters will be confiscated or read by the police.

Finally, a long, congratulatory letter comes from Roman in December; he'd been traveling with the circus and couldn't write until now. "I am in love!" he tells me, underlining that sentence. His friend – who has written the letter for him – is a twenty-eight-year-old acrobat named Francesco, and when they're not on the road performing, they live with Francesco's parents in the family home in Frascati, an ancient town in the hills high above Rome. "Francesco and his mother both cook like angels!" Roman adds. "I have learned how to eat well."

God bless Roman for proving that happiness is still possible!

We soon learn that in each new territory claimed by Germany the Jews are rounded up and massacred, often by local troops only too pleased to delight their new rulers with ever more horrific atrocities. Only after the war will I learn the extent of this genocide, and that disabled people are being shot and gassed as well. For now, the distant children of Poland and German-occupied Russia fall even below Jews and Gypsies on the list of priorities held by European diplomats and journalists. *Garbage*, as Isaac once said.

Georg devours everything he can find about the concentration camps during 1941 because he's certain that Isaac must be a prisoner.

He reads excerpts of articles to me about men and women forced to dig in quarries with their hands, typhus outbreaks in the barracks, children freezing to death ...

A Romanian Jewish refugee named Lucian whom Georg befriends soon tells us the kind of stories that will become so well known after the war – of Jewish children tossed into pits and buried alive; of thousands dragged into forests and shot, their bodies left to rot. "It's the same story all over Europe," he tells us in his broken, urgent German, desperate to shake us awake. Lucian is painfully thin, with the thoughtful black eyes of a Picasso harlequin. In his presence, I often think of how important geography is: here we are, safe in Istanbul, while a few hundred miles to the north and west Jews are being slaughtered.

One story Georg reads to me – and that becomes symbolic of evil for me – dates from late June 1941: after the German army takes Biolystok, troops set the Jewish quarter on fire and hunt down all its residents. Some 800 of them are locked inside the Great Synagogue and the building is set ablaze. All of the trapped Jews are burned alive.

"No more stories," I plead with Georg after that, and he abides by my wishes. But over the next months, not even begging stops Lucian. I rush out of the room whenever he visits and eavesdrop only on the parts of his stories I can bear. But Lucian does me a service; it's thanks to him that I come to believe that Hitler is deadly serious when he tells an enraptured audience at the Sports Palace in Berlin: "The war will end with the complete annihilation of the Jews."

Lucian has tugged me below the glass to get a good look at what has been waiting for us to see since 1933.

*

The not knowing is the hardest part – harder even to bear than my regret at leaving Isaac. Would learning he was dead be preferable to the still-born futility in my gut? That's a question I do my best to subdue by telling myself over and over that Hans ought to be enough for me, but the truth I admit to no one is that he isn't. Even when we're most joyful together – when I'm feeding him from my breast or watching him as he reaches for a fire-colored tulip that Vera's holding – real happiness, of the kind we don't need to think about, still walks a dozen paces ahead of me.

Am I burdening him with a legacy of sorrow?

In November of 1942 racist legislation comes to Turkey: Jews, Armenians, Greeks, and other minorities will have to pay a special wealth tax called *Varkik*, which is assessed not only on a person's salary but also on savings and equity. Officials proud of being "pure Turks," our local equivalent of "pure Aryans," demand up to half of a person's holdings. Moslems, however, are taxed at a maximum of only 12.5 percent. The penalty for those who fail to pay is forced labor in eastern Turkey and confiscation of all property.

At our Hanukkah dinner in early December, Abraham tells us that he and Graça will be moving out of the family home in Ortaköy. They will rent it out in order to earn enough extra income to maintain their textile business. David is selling his home in Beyoğlu and will move with Gül and their two teenagers to a small house in Balat, the old Jewish quarter. He'd bought two dilapidated properties there two years before and is nearly finished fixing up one of them. Abraham and Graça have been loaned a small flat near the Galata Tower by Moslem friends.

The entire Zarco family is in a state of shock, and greatly offended, since their ancestors have lived in Turkey for 450 years. Graça falls into a deep, silent despondency because she'll have to dismiss their cook, Safak, driver, Konstantin, and housekeeper, Solmaz. These three servants have been working for her for more than thirty years and, given their advanced ages and the country's faltering economy, are unlikely find work elsewhere. "My children have always called Safak *abla*, big sister, and now I'm sentencing her and the others to an old age of poverty," Graça explains to me while gazing forlornly out the window at the Asian shoreline.

When the day comes for the servants to leave, she gives the two women gold earrings and Konstantin a magnificent silver pocket watch. Graça is dry-eyed and regal until they leave, then runs to her room. Shortly after that, Abraham gives Vera, Georg, and me the additional bad news that – as foreigners – we, too, are to be taxed at fifty percent. After discussing our options, we decide to take David's offer and move into the house in Balat that he has not yet fixed up.

Hans is two years old when we move. It's October 1942. Our house is squat and damp, with a foul white fungus splotched on the furniture, and ceilings so low that I can jump up to touch them. We have no shower or bath, and a pencil-thin stream of rusty water comes out of each of the two sinks. On the first floor, where I have my room, the soot-covered windows are so tiny that, even when I wipe them clean, they hardly let in enough light to read. When I gaze out, I see a grimy little street of tilting houses, most of which look as though they're sure to fall over in the next stiff wind. Mouse-droppings are all over the floor, and the drawers of the dresser in my room are fly cemeteries. Vera calls our house the Mushroom Cave. Our first purchases are buckets, mops, and soap. Gül and her kindhearted kids help us scrub everything.

Living on the ground floor are Graça's brother and sister-in-law, Solomon and Lisa Lugo, as well as their twenty-one-year-old son, Ayaz. Ayaz was studying architecture at Istanbul University until a month ago; now, he is apprenticed to a carpenter so that he can help with the family's finances.

Next door, David's house has been completely remodeled. He has two new bathrooms with white marble floors and walls. All of us make use of them: eight adults, two teenagers, and one infant. On good days we are a Marx Brothers comedy. On bad days, Hans and I pee into milk bottles.

My son has colds all winter from the Mushroom Cave, and he gives me most of them. Heat, light, and health – my three wishes for him and me. But how am I supposed to earn money to afford better lodgings with a two-year-old in my arms running a fever? Georg rides to my rescue, once again. He takes some old pastel portraits of mine to his office and secures a commission from one of his clients, a wealthy olive oil baron. Haydar Zeki has a thick mustache and jowls, and a saber scar across his cheek. He poses at his office in a matching white shirt and bow tie, black jacket, and derby hat. "It's in fashion to look like Ataturk," David explains. On his advice, I slim Mr Zeki's face, erase his scar, and add a mysterious glint to his eyes. Overjoyed with the results, he has his wife and children pose for me.

Mr Zeki and Georg spread the word about my shamelessly flattering portraits. After my first six pastels are paid in Turkish lira, I buy coal heaters for our bedrooms; although spring has brought out the yellow daffodils and violet crocuses in the city's gardens, the nights are still chilly.

In June, I continue my work on the island of Büyükada, where Abraham has kept his summer home. Leaving our dank lodgings for that sunlit island of pine, catching a horse-buggy up the hill from the port to his magnificent house, I feel as if I've leapt off the gloom of van Gogh's *Potato Eaters* into the awe-struck ecstasy of

Starry Night. The moment I see Hans sitting on the beach, putting stones in his pail as if he's found his spot on earth, I know I'll never leave the island again until Berlin is free.

Vera and I live on Büyükada for the rest of 1943 and all of 1944. I sketch portraits of wealthy Turks; she designs and sews. Hans learns to walk and talk. He tells me what he wants in German, Ladino, and Turkish. His laughter is like rays of light to me, and he rarely fails to giggle when I pull magic eggs from behind his ears or out of his elbows. He has Isaac's radiant blue-gray eyes, which is both good and bad, since they are as deep and beautiful as the Marmara Sea but also a constant reminder of the affection that lies far beyond my reach. Georg visits us on weekends, and he has lost his war-induced gloom; in fact, he has fallen in love with a Greek waitress named Nitsa and spends most of his time in her flat in Fener, near the Golden Horn. Such is his delight in her that when they're together he sings and dances as if life has turned into a musical.

On collecting all my possessions from our home in Balat and moving them to Büyükada, I hand Berekiah Zarco's manuscripts to David, telling him, "The pages are still in a bit of a jumble, but we don't have time to straighten them out. We need to hide them right away in case the government starts burning books." He thinks I've left part of my mind back in Berlin – which is true enough – but cedes to my wishes. We seal *The Bleeding Mirror* and its complementary mystical texts in a silver *tik* – Torah case – that's been in his family for hundreds of years, and David buries it in the cellar, behind a false wall.

*

By the middle of 1944, the newspapers report that Germany will soon lose the war, and Vera, Georg, and I share a bottle of champagne to celebrate. As we get a little tipsy, we begin to discuss our return to Berlin, but I fear for Hans' safety; after all, he's half-Jewish, and the massacres may continue long after the armistice. "When I get there, my first purchase will be a gun," I tell Vera, but she thinks I'm joking.

By now we've heard stories about the death camps, and I'm convinced that all of Jewish Europe – the people, theaters, cafes, bakeries, synagogues, and old-age homes – has turned to ash. The distant children and adults, as well. I see their faces below the glass when I close my eyes – Hansi and Raffi most clearly. But I don't tell anyone, because successfully destroying the Jews may mean that Hitler has achieved his real goal – and won the war – even if he loses.

Germany signs an unconditional surrender on the 8th of May, 1945. We celebrate on Büyükada with a Zarco family picnic, complete with a whirling dervish performance by Sufi friends. Hans makes himself sick by eating an entire plate of baklava. In the bathroom, cleaning his face and hands, I take a good look at myself. I'm amazed I don't find gray hair, and that I'm still a young woman. I am twenty-eight. Isaac is seventy-seven if he is still alive.

Georg has heard that Berlin is without electricity and food, so he, Vera, and I wait until early July to go home. We convert our savings to American dollars on the black market and board a train to Budapest. From there, we'll go on to Germany. I can't speak for the others, but I know already that I will not stay there unless I can find Isaac. I won't raise Hans in a country that murdered his father.

We bribe officials along the way when they say our papers aren't in order. At stations in Romania and Hungary, Georg asks passengers boarding our train if any Jews are left in their towns. Shrugs are what he gets from most of them, their puzzled faces saying, "Jews? What Jews?" Then one tattered-looking Romanian border guard with a pencil behind his ear, either misunderstanding the intent of Georg's question or mistaking him for an official of the Reich, says in an eager voice – and in quite good German: "No, sir, by the grace of God we are Jew-free now!" *Nein, mein Herr, durch Gottes Gnade sind wir jetzt judenfrei.*

THE SEVENTH GATE

Seven are the heavens, palaces, and pairs of archons; the gates to the soul and the Holy Temple; the days of the week; the notes of the scale; the seas and the continents; the ages of the body and spirit. And seven are the rulers of the material world.

Beyond the threshold of Seventh Gate lies Araboth, the inner landscape of prophesy, resplendent with light from the Throne of Glory.

Prepare well all who seek to enter Araboth before death lest you drown in your own ignorance or be burnt by the guardians for speaking one false word.

At the Seventh Gate your story ceases to be told and listened to, though every word is destined to be reborn.

Six years you may sow your field and six years you may prune your vineyard and gather in the yield, but in the seventh year the land shall have a Sabbath of complete rest – Leviticus 25.

Berekiah Zarco, The Six Books of Preparation

CHAPTER TWENTY·THREE

We arrive in Berlin in the late afternoon of the 10th of July. The train stations and ministry buildings seem to have been hit particularly badly by Allied bombings. As we walk through the government district to Unter den Linden, past all those jagged piles of brick and stone, past the ruined columns and the doorways leading nowhere, past a way of life that will never be repaired, I have the sensation I've returned to a damned city that will have to be razed before it can hope to rise again. The façades of many buildings have been blown off, so we have x-ray vision now, too. It is with the eyes of an astonished thief that we gaze into an office at the shattered desks and chairs, or into a bedroom at a ruined mattress and what's left of a wardrobe. We say nothing as we walk by the carcass of the State Library on Unter den Linden; those angels given earthly form as books that were fortunate enough to survive the Nazi burnings must have been turned to ash by foreign bombers. In front of the main entrance is an old man in a derby hat sitting on a bench reading the shreds of a colorful magazine. Beside him looms a wrecked and twisted German tank. Looking far west, we see that the Brandenburg Gate seems to have survived reasonably well, but to the east the cathedral has had its dome and spires shattered. As we cross over to Museum Island, we confirm that the Spree has not changed its course. Nature, as Isaac told me, is on our side – the side of life. And yet the water seems so still, so indifferent. Though maybe that's a good thing.

Hans senses our mood and talks little. He's exhausted from the trip, so I carry him for a time. In front of the makeshift cafés, scantily clad, blond prostitutes stand chatting with Russian soldiers, who call out well-meaning greetings to my son. Everyone – even the enemy – likes little children after a war, I discover. Proof that the cycle of human life will go on. But would the prostitutes and their Russians ask if he wants a piece of cake or sip of beer if they knew he was Jewish? And have I raised a reticent son without meaning to? When the men offer him candy, he looks back at me with supplicating eyes to see if he can accept their gifts. I suppose it's for the best that he's wary, but I can't help wishing his spirit were freer. I've instructed him not to reply if anyone asks if he is Jewish. Despite what Vera thinks, I will indeed buy a gun. Anyone who tries to hurt him will carry a bullet with him to his grave.

My heart feels like a ticking grenade when Prenzlauer Allee opens before us. And the smell of a beer factory – can one be up and running already? – makes me dizzy. Home is straight ahead, and an electric jolt of anguish halts my thoughts. My feet lead me onward but my head is now inside a glass jar made of disbelief.

Passing the Immanuel Church, I picture Isaac's face, and I see him open the door to my knocks, his pipe clamped in his mouth. Overjoyed, smiling with relief, he says, *Welcome home!* In his embrace, I release five years of grief and cede to him all the resilience I've kept coiled in my body. I can be the person I want to be because he is holding me. I'll hand him Hans. "Our son," I'll say, and a glow of gratitude will burn in Isaac's eyes, as in a Renaissance painting of grace and sainthood, and he will cry the tears that fathers since Adam have shed, then dance the boy, laughing, around the apartment.

I have fantasized about making love with Isaac a thousand times, and now he will enter me again. And I will enter him. The sea and the mountain shall meet in a damned city.

Seeing our building, I give Hans to Vera and start to run. My eyes, clouded by emotion, do not yet notice the ruined roof or the gouged windows. I rush through the courtyard and take the back steps two at a time. *Please, please, please*, I am thinking, *let my life begin again ...*

I knock on Isaac's door, and I keep knocking, and I call out his name from a place so deep inside me that my voice is a stranger's. A short man I've never seen before finally opens the door. Wiping away my tears, I say, "I'm looking for Isaac Zarco. He used to live here."

The man shakes his head. "I don't know him."

"When did you move in?"

"Who are you?" he asks suspiciously.

"A good friend of his. I've just returned to Berlin. Please tell me how long you've been living here?"

"Nearly two years."

My mind is caught on the thorns of simple subtraction. Two years ...1943, 1942 ...? Georg comes up the stairs carrying Hans, who reaches out to me with both arms.

"Isaac isn't here," I tell Georg, taking the boy from him.

"Do you have any idea where he might be?" Georg asks the man, who again shakes his head.

"Are any of his things still here?" I ask.

"Nothing."

"A portrait I did of him was hanging in the main bedroom. Maybe you found it?"

"There was nothing here when we moved in."

The miserly wretch won't even open his door more than a crack to let us look in. I'm convinced he's lying, and I'm about to argue with him, but Georg takes my shoulder and says, "Let's go to the Munchenbergs' apartment."

A last question: "And the Riedesel family? They were living in the front building."

"I never met them."

Vera meets us in the courtyard. I can tell from the stony way she looks into the distance that she is trying to accept that Isaac is dead.

A boy of fifteen or so answers our knocks at the Munchenbergs' door. He calls for his mother when we explain why we've come. Georg talks for us. He's got on a handsome linen suit and looks like a professor, which is probably why she invites us in. Georg and I stand in the sitting room, and Vera waits outside with Hans.

None of the old furniture is here, and the photos of Raffi are gone from the walls.

"When we moved in," the woman tells us, "a neighbor mentioned that the previous tenants had been sent away on one of the transports. I don't know anything else."

She claims never to have heard of Isaac or my father. These are my first experiences of a city in which no one will ever admit to knowing anything about the Jews except that they were sent away and never came back.

I had hoped to avoid talking to Tonio's parents, but the awkwardness I feel no longer matters. Mrs Hessel answers the door. Gasping, she raises both hands to her mouth. Her eyes open wide with panic. Maybe she thinks I've come for vengeance, so I kiss her tenderly on both cheeks.

Her hair is gray now, and fraying, and her hands tremble in her lap when we sit together. She's aged miserably. She tells Georg and me that she hasn't seen Isaac in years. She doesn't recall when he vanished. And she knows nothing about my father. She thinks she saw him for the last time in 1943. "But maybe early 1944," she adds. Tonio is doing well, however. He was held in a Russian prison camp for six months but is now staying with her husband's brother in Vienna. "His Russian improved while he was a prisoner and he is working as an interpreter."

"So the Russians have hired Nazis?" I ask her.

It's not my intention to wound her, but she gives me a startled, then affronted look. "Tonio was never a Nazi!" she declares.

All my tender feelings for her are pushed aside by a surge of contempt, and in that doom-soaked way that understandings about injustice spread through us, I realize that all the National Socialists in Germany are rewriting their pasts at this very moment, burning all evidence against themselves. How many millions of copies of *Mein Kampf* have already been thrown in ovens? I've no doubt that Papa's copy is already just smoke. Unless he has been imprisoned because of my betrayal ...

No one answers my knocks at our old apartment. I try my key but the lock has been changed. When I think that Hansi's puzzles and clothing might still be there, I don't know how I'll ever be able to turn away, but I do.

The restaurants have little food, and rationing is tight. We eat dumplings and turnips at what's left of the Köln Beer Garden. A cheap rooming house on Straßburger Straße has two rooms available, so Vera and Georg take one, Hans and I the other. The electricity isn't reliable, so we buy candles. At two in the morning, Hans starts crying and says his back and neck are sore. I hold up a candle to him; bedbugs have made red welts on his tender skin, so I wipe him down with a wet towel, dress him, and carry him to the garden in Wörther Platz. We sleep in our clothes on the grass, my arm under his head. It's a warm night, and the stars above the city accompany us toward sleep. The lindens and oaks have all been cut down, which means we can also see the bombed-out apartment houses embracing the square. They seem to stand guard over us, and I recognize them all despite the damage. After all, we grew up together.

And here in the only place on earth where I could never be lost, I will find Isaac.

What does my son think of sleeping in a park in a strange city? He doesn't say. He has elemental needs and right now he craves only slumber. He wakes me just after dawn to pee. In the slanting light, I take him behind an exuberant pink azalea bush. He leans his little belly out and sprays some yellow-flowered weeds. Like boys everywhere, he is pleased to use his pee-pee to hit a target. "Good work!" I tell him.

We meet Vera and Georg for breakfast. Vera says she squashed ten bedbugs. "And then I ate them!" she announces, earning a horrified face from Hans, which gratifies her.

When they go off to hunt for old friends, my son and I walk to Else König's apartment. I talk to him about why the city was bombed. He doesn't understand my explanations, but he hates for me to think he's thick-headed and keeps nodding.

Else comes to the door in her bathrobe, half-asleep. "Sophie?"

Before I can speak, she's already thrown her arms around me. We kiss and laugh. "And who's this?" she asks, kneeling down.

"Hans, my son."

Her eyes are so bright with joy that Hans shrinks back from her when she offers her hand.

"She's an old friend," I tell him. "We used to teach at the same school."

"You taught in Berlin?" Hans asks her, his mind trying to embrace my past.

"Yes," she answers.

"Are we in Berlin?"

"You most certainly are!"

Else hasn't heard anything about Isaac. We tell her about Istanbul as we sip our linden tea. After five years of Turkish coffee, it tastes like hot water. Hans sits on a puffy old armchair by the window and watches the passersby in Potsdamer Platz.

Else's face has thinned and she has let her copper hair grow out. Only now do I realize she could have been a cover girl for *Worm-Eaten German* magazine. I tell her she was courageous to give all that up.

"It wasn't a conscious decision," she replies. "Just looking at those perfect Young Maidens made the hair on the back of my neck stand up."

Hans asks me if we can go now to the Berlin Zoo. I've told him about it as a bribe.

"What a good idea!" Else exults, plainly trying to please my son. "We'll walk through the Tiergarten. I think the zoo might still be closed, but we can look at ducks in the ponds on the way. A few have come back."

"They left?" I ask.

"We were starving. We ate ducks, rabbits ... anything we could catch or raise."

Hans turns up his nose.

"Yes, it wasn't pretty," she tells the boy. Whispering to me, she says, "The zoo animals were slaughtered too," then adds in her regular voice, "We raised rabbits ... my mom and me. But even half-starving, we couldn't bear to eat them, so we exchanged them for chickens. My mom lived here with me during the bombings."

She leans toward me and whispers, "People ate squirrels, too. Hansi would be heartbroken." She squeezes my hand when she says his name.

"She means your uncle," I tell Hans, because he's got excellent hearing and thinks Else is talking about him.

"Where is Uncle Hansi?" he asks. I've told him but he doesn't understand death yet.

"We'll go lay flowers at his grave one day soon," I reply.

Else slips away to her bedroom to dress.

"Any news from Volker?" I call out to her. She's left her door open a crack.

"Nothing, I'm afraid."

"And the school?"

"Shut down. It became impossible to keep it going. No revenues."

Hans climbs down from his armchair and looks at the photographs on Else's coffee table. One of them, framed in silver, is of our students and teachers, but I don't dare take a good look at it.

"And Dr Hassgall?"

"Wait till we go out. I'll tell you everything."

"There you are, Mama!" Hans says, pointing to me in the photograph.

Is that youthful, smiling girl really me? "Yup, that was me – in another life, before you came along," I tell him.

Else has put on men's trousers and a short-sleeved white blouse. She looks like a long-distance runner, which may be an accurate description, given that she's survived. We sit on a bench in the Tiergarten, by Rousseau Lake. Such a despairing and empty place it is now; only a few scraggly trees have survived people's need for firewood. I've encouraged Hans to look for goldfish in the pond because I don't want him to hear what we'll discuss. He turns around now and again to make sure I'm close by, and I give him a big wave. Mama the lighthouse ...

"Four Gestapo officers came to take away the Jewish kids," Else tells me. "It was January 1943. We still had six with us. David and Ruthie, Saul, Werner, Volker, and ... and Veronika. I think you'll remember Veronika Vogt."

"How could I forget VV? 'I like glue more than clean hands!'"

Else laughs freely. It's good to hear. "I didn't know she was Jewish," I say.

"Her mother was. The Gestapo made her and the other Jewish kids line up at the front of the classroom. They did what they were told and the young ones started crying. Even the students still in their seats were terrified. I started to go stand by the Jewish children, where I could reassure them, but a Gestapo officer ordered me not to move. Everyone in the room was looking at me, and I felt as though this was the central moment in my life. I had been born only for this. And either I did what was right or I'd never be able to go on living. You know, Sophie, in years since, I've thought that maybe we're all born for only one moment."

"So what did you do?"

"I went to the door. One of the men shouted for me to stop, but I kept walking. When I got to the hallway, I ran to Dr Hassgall's office. I figured I'd hear a shot and then I'd fall to the floor, dead. But all that mattered was doing what was required of me in that one moment." She gives me a confused look. "Sophie, I don't know why they didn't kill me. And I don't know why I'm alive when so many good people died."

Looking into the distance, as though unwilling to listen to my reassurance, she's quiet for a time, then lifts my hand and presses it urgently into her cheek. "Thank you for trying to help," she says. "So when I got to Dr Hassgall's office, I knocked. Can you believe

I knocked on his door at such a moment? But you remember how formal he was." We smile together. "I rushed in and told him what was happening. He ran past me to the classroom. I'd never seen him move so fast. When he got there, he told the Gestapo officers that there had been a mistake. He named a high official he'd been bribing to keep the school open. The man in charge told him to shut up or he'd shoot all the Jewish kids on the spot, though he called them swine. Dr Hassgall and I knew that if these men took the students away, most would probably die, though one or two might survive. Sophie, we didn't know about the mass killings yet, but we had no illusions about the labor camps. The kids who couldn't work as expected would be shot or starved. Others would die of cold or dysentery. I thought there must be something I could say to the men to make them change their minds. But my courage had vanished by then." She swirls her hand in the air. "I failed to speak from absolute terror."

"Was Dr Hassgall afraid?"

"I've asked myself that a thousand times. He looked calm, but inside ... I don't know. He was hard to read. All I know is that in that wonderful clear voice of his he told the men, 'I will never let my children leave without me.' Calling across the room to me, he said, 'Else, you're in charge now.' He must have seen the state I was in because he smiled gently and added, 'I'm counting on you.' Then he took Volker by the hand, because he was already in tears, and he instructed all the kids to link hands. He led them out of that classroom and out of the front door of the school and into the police van waiting on the street."

"Did you ever learn what happened to him and the kids?"

"I tried, but I couldn't find out anything. They must have been gassed. It's odd, but I keep expecting to see Dr Hassgall at a café, in the metro, strolling down Unter den Linden ..."

She looks into the distance at Hans, who's petting a big shaggy dog. "Or to see Volker sitting by a pond in the Tiergarten. But in here," she says, tapping her chest, "I know that they're long dead. The thing is, Sophie," she adds, "Dr Hassgall refused to let the kids go off to die alone. I can't stop thinking about his doing that. He didn't have to go, but he did. It means everything to me now. It means he must have known this was the moment he was born for. And he didn't fail." She gives me a frightened look. "But maybe I did. I can't help thinking that I should have gone with them and that everything I do now, for the rest of my life, will be wrong."

So Volker is gone. Else and I cry together, but I keep waving to Hans when he looks back for me. Then he comes running over to us – panting and squirming – to describe the marvels of the sheepdog he's befriended. But his breathless excitement turns to concern when he notices my red eyes. "What's wrong, Mama?" he asks.

"I'm all right, Hans. I just found out we won't be able to see an old friend of mine."

"How come?"

"He's no longer living in Berlin."

As we walk to the zoo, Else and I reminisce about how the kids made us laugh – the conversation of women who've escaped the Angel of Death. Hans gives Else his hand, then walks between us, which he loves because it means he is at the center of the world. Else tells me that after the school closed she worked as a nanny for the two small daughters of a banker living in Grünewald. The man fled for Argentina at the beginning of 1945.

"I stole as many valuables as I could from him before he left," she grins. "I still have some of his silverware. Good for the black market."

"And since then?"

"Odd jobs," she replies. "But now that the Russians are here, life is looking up."

The zoo is still closed, so to cheer up Hans we buy an old loaf of bread and feed some ducks in the Tiergarten's Neuer Lake.

I've told Else of our encounter with bedbugs, and before we go our separate ways, she invites us to stay in her guestroom. I'm hesitant to agree, but she puts a spare key in my hand and says, "Doing what's right is the only thing that will keep me alive now."

Greta's building has escaped bombing, which means that although the city may look like Pompeii, her windows overlooking Pfalzburger Straße are still framed by blue and green brocade curtains! But she isn't home. I knock at her neighbors' doors, and an old lady on the floor below confirms to me that Greta still lives upstairs. I leave a note under her door, asking her to get in touch with me through Else.

Hans and I eat lunch in Savigny Platz, but he decides he doesn't like German food. He pushes away a perfectly reasonable sausage like it's a dead snake and eats only his boiled potatoes. Obviously, he did not get his taste buds from me.

"How can you not like it? I've made you German food all your life!" I tell him, feigning outrage, because he likes me pretending to be angry. *That* he did inherit from me.

He exclaims, "But not this crap!"

He uses the word *tref* for crap, though it really means unkosher food, an idiosyncratic usage picked up from Georg and Vera. I admit it's both slightly rude and Yiddish, but an elderly vamp smoking a cigarette in a silver holder, a white silk scarf hiding her turkey-skin neck, gives him a look that could set the poor boy's underwear on fire. Is she irritated because she has heard that a few thousand of Berlin's big-nosed, thick-lipped Jews have escaped the purifying ovens of the Reich and this boy might be one of them? She continues to stare at us, so I say, "Can I help you, madam?"

"I just think you ought to teach your son some manners," she tells me.

Should I laugh or cry? The Nazis have murdered half a million German Jews and God knows how many distant children, and she wants proper Prussian etiquette. *This woman is why I need a gun*, I think, but all I tell her is, "Your complaint is noted so now you can go back to your crappy German food!"

On the way out, I promise to make Hans his favorite meal, *manti*, if I can find yoghurt. When he continues to moan I beg him to stop being such a *nudnock*, which makes him snort with laughter. Our similar sense of humor remains our bridge even at bad times.

In the afternoon, we take a bus to Rolf's apartment. Hans lays his head on my lap and takes a nap. The ease of his breathing calms me, and passengers look at him sweetly. "He's handsome," one young woman whispers to me. I'd never have expected so many smiles around me. I suppose it's the sense that we've all survived a shipwreck. A lie, of course, because some of us were in the luxury cabins and others were tossed overboard. But I smile back.

"Oh, Sophie, thank God you're here!" Rolf says, and he tugs me inside. His spine is so bowed now – and his hunchback so bulky – that he's unable to lift his eyes to see me.

Hans is terrified, though I've warned him what to expect. I feel his shivering through my hand, which is resting on top of his silken, auburn hair.

"Come in, come in ..." our host says excitedly. "Is this your son?" he asks, smiling.

"Yes, and Isaac's. His name is Hans."

Rolf, overjoyed, asks my son what he'd like to drink but the boy can't form an answer.

I'm gripping his hand tight and we're standing by the sofa. Rolf's asks us to sit and we do. To calm Hans, I say, "Rolf is the man who taught me my magic tricks. He's a wizard!"

The frightened boy leans into me and won't look at him. So I ask Rolf to just make us some tea or coffee, whichever is easier. I mouth for him to give me a minute alone with my son.

"Do you want us to leave?" I ask Hans as soon as Rolf is in the kitchen. "I can come back alone later."

He shakes his head.

"If you want, you can go into Rolf's bedroom and play there by yourself. I'm sure he won't mind, and maybe you can find some picture books."

He nods, so I take him down the hall. Hans' mouth falls open at seeing the tiny furniture. Clothes and books are everywhere. Plenty to keep him amused.

"Don't get lost," I tell him, which is what I say whenever I leave him alone, but he's already lifting up a red shirt and showing it to me. "Can I put on some of Rolf's things?" he asks in Ladino. He tends to speak Ladino whenever he's nervous or excited. The clothes are just about the right size for him, so his question makes sense.

I translate for Rolf, who gives his permission.

"Yes," I reply to Hans in German, "but don't make a mess."

"Mama, it's already a mess," he points out solemnly. I love it that he doesn't even know he's funny.

As Rolf hands me my cup of tea, he says, "I know what you think, but it wasn't me. I didn't turn Isaac in." He goes on to say that after Isaac fled the Nazis hunting for him at his boathouse, he went straight to Rolf's apartment. "It was the 7th of August, 1940," Rolf tells me, and I can tell from the momentous way he says that date that it has been branded in his memory. "He came here to hide, in part, out of kindness to me. He gave me a chance to make up for the evil I'd done. He stayed here for a few days, looking over those manuscripts of his. Then he said he was going to have himself arrested. I tried to reason with him, but he told me, 'It is not my decision to make.'"

"Did he say whose decision it was?" I rush to ask.

"Maybe he meant the Nazis. Or that ancestor of his who wrote the manuscripts he was studying. I don't know. He prayed all that first night. In fact, for the next two days and nights he did nothing but chant and pray, facing Jerusalem. At times, he'd breathe in a special way and shout out syllables in Hebrew. It was odd, and a bit scary. He fasted, too. He would drink only warm milk and honey. Then, on the third morning after his arrival, he began talking to me again. He took a bath and shaved, and we ate together. He was very playful. You know how he could be. And he laughed a lot. He was in a kind of vibrant, ecstatic state. And he ate all I could feed him, as if he was storing up for a long journey. When he got dressed to go out, he put on a nice coat, very stylish in an antiquated way. It may have been his father's, or maybe Vera made it for him. And he put on a beret that he said you'd bought for him, though it was August and it was really too warm to wear. I gave him one of Heidi's red silk roses for his lapel, which made him happy. When he hugged me to thank me, he was vibrating, like ... like a kind of tuning fork. And his eyes, they were water, clear water ..." Rolf shakes his head. "I can't describe his appearance well, but I'd say that in his head he was flying ... flying very high. Then he asked me for two more favors. The first was to accompany him to the Reichstag. He said that he needed to make his way to the center of Hitler's power, that the Reichstag was a first level. He used the

word *Stock*, as if it was a floor in a building. And from there he said
he'd descend ever closer to the center until finally he would enter
what he called the vessels. He said that would make sense to you."

"It does – more or less."

"I begged him not to go, but he told me he had no choice. And
then he asked me his second favor, which was to tell you what I'm
telling you now. There was no time to write to you. And anyway, there
was too much to explain, and he didn't feel he could control himself
enough to write the long letter you deserved." Rolf holds out his hands
and makes them shake. "He was too volatile. Though he *did* hand me
an envelope with a few lines he'd written for you. I will give them to
you in a moment, but he told me to talk to you first and describe what
happened to him." Rolf takes two quick gulps of his tea. "So then Isaac
took a copy of the Torah from his suitcase, and we left together. We
walked west toward the center of the city, talking of old times. He was
happy, like a man off to meet an old friend. I pleaded with him again
not to go to the Reichstag. He just shook his head and smiled. And
he told me that this was why his father had moved back to Europe,
for this chance to keep the world from ending. As we got closer to
our destination, while we were crossing the Friedrich Bridge, he put
his hand on my shoulder and said he wouldn't be able to talk to me
any longer, that he needed to prepare himself. I didn't know what he
had planned, so I still had some hope that nothing bad would happen.
Then, as we were walking down Unter den Linden, his lips began to
move. He was praying in Hebrew and breathing in his funny way.
He began walking so fast that it was hard for me to keep up. It was as
if he were being tugged forward by a cord ... or by a power beyond
him. I had to run to stay even with him. He strode straight through
the Brandenburg Gate, and just after we emerged on the other side,
he turned back for me and said, 'Rolf, this next gate is for me alone.
It would be dangerous for you because you haven't prepared. Wait in

the Tiergarten. And thank you for your help.' Those were his exact words. I wrote them down because I knew I'd tell them to you one day." Rolf takes a big breath and straightens up as best he can, so he can look me in the eye. "Isaac then squatted down next to me and he ... he kissed me on the lips." Rolf looks down to compose himself. At length, he says in a quivering voice, "You'll think it strange, but I remembered that scene in *The Kid*, where Chaplin kisses the tiny boy he's just rescued. After that, Isaac said, 'That kiss was for both you and Sophele.' You can imagine how stunned I was. It was like I might never breathe again. It was as if my heart ... as if my heart were beating outside of my chest. And when he walked on without me, I could feel that force that was tugging him forward, because my legs and arms ... they were tense with the need to go after him. But I stayed where I was, as he had instructed me. He walked to the Reichstag, which was guarded by soldiers, and turned west, then continued on until he reached the center of Königsplatz. There, he turned around to face the Reichstag and put on the beret you'd given him. He opened his Torah and began to chant. I rushed to the edge of the Tiergarten to watch him."

"Do you know what he was chanting?"

"No, I wasn't close enough to hear. I was standing at the edge of the park. And anyway, it must have been in Hebrew. Two soldiers approached him and talked to him, but he wouldn't look up from the Torah, so one of the men knocked it out of his hands. The other pulled off his beret and threw it down. Isaac raised his head and looked up into the sky, and he began to chant louder. And he wouldn't stop. So the men grabbed him and rushed him away, past the north side of the Reichstag. He didn't resist. And I never saw him again."

*

Barren winter branches and frozen lakes, and welcoming words never to be spoken – these are my surroundings in the world that descends over me. Hans races into the room to show me several hats he's found, including a floppy yellow one with bells that I remember well. I put that one on him and say he looks handsome, but I am miles and years away from the here and now. And I don't fully return while I'm in Berlin.

Rolf brings me Isaac's last note and the beret I'd given him. "I retrieved it after the soldiers took him away," he explains. "I couldn't let it just lie there."

Inside the sealed envelope are two gold wedding bands. "Sophele, one of the rings is for you and the other is for our son or daughter," Isaac tells me, his usual neat handwriting wobbly and erratic. "I've been wearing both of them since you left. Know that I am happy and well, and that I am on the road that Berekiah has asked me to follow. Enclosed is a second note for our child. Give it to him or her when you feel the right time has come. I have begun to hear the winds of Araboth in the sky around me and must go now. You're *schön, schön, schön*, and I love you. Isaac."

The note for Hans reads: "Your mother will tell you about me, and maybe you will hear about me from other friends of ours. I hope so. Know that you were made in love. And inside that love may you always remain. I want you to know that I would be with you if I could. And I will come to you if I can. Wear my ring. I have placed my love in its band, because it is a circle, and as you know a circle has no end and no beginning. Your father, Isaac Zarco."

Hans and I walk home. Rolf has let the boy keep the yellow hat – the same one he wore when I met him thirteen years before. Hans wears it proudly, like the king of the elves. When I tell him Vera made it for Rolf, he dances around. Then he starts skipping and jumping down the street. So much energy he has! Passersby point and smile.

We meet Vera and Georg back at our rooming house, as we'd agreed. I explain about Isaac while Hans naps in Georg's lap.

"That's it, then," Georg whispers, as though it means Isaac is dead, and he begins to cry.

But I grew up on Hollywood plots, and I keep thinking, *there is still a chance …*

We sleep at Else's place over the next week. Hans sleeps clutching his hat. Vera and Georg stay with an old friend of his in Wilmersdorf. How am I to find out where Isaac was taken by the Gestapo? Surely a concentration camp, but which one?

When I tell Else I want to buy a gun, she suggests the black market behind the Friedrichstraße Station. There, we find the scrap metal seller who's renowned for his stash of weapons. Else returns from the man's "office" in the shell of a nearby building with a PO8 Parabellum pistol and two bullets. Its wooden handle fits perfectly in my hand.

We discover the Jewish Old Age Home has been shut down. Neighbors tell us that Nazis used the building as a collection point for Jews being transported to the camps. Thousands passed through there. Maybe Rini and her parents, Mrs Kauffmann, and the Munchenbergs. Maybe Isaac.

The River Jordan bakery is boarded up. Weissman's Fabrics, where we tried to break the Nazi boycott of Jewish shops, is now a small beer hall catering to boisterous Russian soldiers. The King David School was damaged by Allied bombs in 1944 and has been bulldozed down as a public hazard. Greta does not phone.

*

Georg helps me ask French, American, and British soldiers how I can find lists of Jews transported to the camps, but they've been informed that the Nazis destroyed most of their records. Some of the Americans speak Yiddish. They tease me merrily and sometimes suggestively, but they could be my younger brothers. And in any case, I am as dry as a desert inside.

Hans is bored and restless, as well he should be. He wants to play in the rubble of burned-out buildings, like the German street children he watches, but I don't let him. He asks if we can see if the zoo is open yet, and when I tell him that I've been informed that it won't be ready for visitors for months, maybe even years, he punishes me with silence. He could be his Uncle Hansi. If only he liked jigsaw puzzles, but he thinks they're stupid.

Else leaves her apartment every evening after supper to work on Unter den Linden. I've never seen her in make-up before. She wears bright pink lipstick. "I know, I look like a neon sign," she tells me, laughing.

"You're beautiful," Hans tells her in Ladino – *És fermosa*.

She kisses him for that, then explains to us that Russian soldiers don't appreciate subtlety. Using a kind of coded German, so Hans won't understand, she tells me that she works with an old high-school friend because the soldiers will pay a week's salary for two women at once. She also sells them watches that she buys on the black market. "As best I can tell, Russian boys think only about sex and showing off their German timepieces," she says.

I make no judgments of her and she knows it. Still, she tells me, "I'm saving up so I can leave Germany and never come back."

"You could join us in Istanbul," I tell her, and Hans and I take turns describing the wonders of Büyükada.

But she has her heart set on Palestine. "I read about a kibbutz near the Dead Sea with so much sun that even the shadows there are a lesser form of light. That's where I'll go."

Isaac's factory is unoccupied, but the sewing machines and furniture are gone. A dozen handwritten notes are taped to the walls, along with two photographs. Hans runs right to the pictures, points to one and turns to me excitedly, exclaiming, "*Tia* Vera!" – Aunt Vera. But another photo has already captured my attention: it's from the series K-H took of Isaac in which I had to pin back his silver hair in order to show his "Semitic" left ear. Between the two photos is a note from K-H himself: "I'm looking for information on Isaac Zarco and Vera Moeckel." I jot down the address of the factory in Charlottenburg where he's staying. Hans has been standing on his tiptoes and pleading with me for a closer look at the photos, so I lift him up, but I point to Isaac instead of *Tia* Vera: "Your father," I say in Ladino. *Tu papá*. And I repeat my words in German and Turkish when Hans gives me a puzzled look.

"The Day We Lost Our Sight" and "Portraits of Men Who Have Sold Their Minds" are two of the exhibits K-H wanted to create before the war. Banners hand-painted with those titles are hanging over the entranceway to an empty factory in Charlottenburg. Was beer produced here or is the scent of hops a part of me now? Photographs are taped to the walls. Mr Weissman is the subject of the first picture. He's gazing down, his shoulders hunched as if he'd like to recoil into himself, and the sign around his neck reads: *Kauft nicht bei Juden, kauft in deutschen Geschäften!* Don't buy from Jews, shop in German businesses. Next is the burly storm-trooper who grabbed my arm when I tried to break the boycott. He is shouting, his mouth open, teeth ready to bite, like a flesh-eating demon in a medieval fresco. Then comes an angry young Nazi, frowning at Arnold Muller, who is passing by in his wheelchair. The fourth photo is Hansi reaching down for Minnie as the rose of blood blossoms on her belly, his face torn open by misery.

"Look, it's you, Mama!" my son yells.

The boy is already ten paces ahead of me, pointing up. This must be an astonishing day for him; photos of his mother and her friends are appearing all over the city ...

I can't answer him. I'm sitting on the ground because I wasn't prepared to see Hansi. My son climbs onto my lap because he's scared. "Too many memories," I explain to him.

He leans into me, catlike, and I take off his hat and scratch his head. He loves that. After a while, he puts his arms around me. God only knows what he sees when he closes his eyes, but I picture the Büyükada beach he loves. Nothing can harm us. Not even German-speaking ghosts.

"Sophele?"

My name has been spoken as a question, and when I look up K-H is smiling down at me, tears in his eyes. He's still hollow-cheeked and handsome, and he's wearing bright red suspenders.

Hugging him is like discovering that this nightmare will one day end. After a while, he wants to look at my face, but I press my head to his shoulder until Hans starts tugging at my skirt.

"This is Karl-Heinz," I tell the boy. "The photographer."

When I introduce Hans, K-H says, "Wait here, I'll get my camera!" And he dashes off.

We pose beside a photo of Isaac lifting Hansi into his arms. "To show that there is an after-time," K-H explains to me.

"You talk funny," Hans tells him.

"Because I'm deaf," K-H replies.

"Then how do you hear me?"

"I read your lips."

Hans looks up at me suspiciously, as if K-H might be lying, so I say, "It's the absolute truth. Just like his photos."

I tell K-H about my brother, Vera, and Georg – and that I'm still hunting for Isaac. He says that Marianne and Werner are in Lisbon. He didn't want them to return to Berlin until he could be sure it was safe. Lisbon? Over glasses of cheap red wine at a nearby café, K-H tells me that a French friend of theirs managed to sneak them over the border. From there they made their way to Paris. "We didn't dare write to Isaac. We figured all his mail was being read."

On the 12th of June, just before the Germans took Paris, they made their way south, hoping to catch a boat from Marseille to North Africa or Istanbul. "But on the way, we heard of a Portuguese Consul in Bordeaux who was issuing transit visas for Jews and other refugees. We reached Bordeaux on the 16th and waited outside his apartment. Hundreds of Jews and others were there. We formed a line and kept filing inside. He was issuing visas for everyone who came to him. It was a miracle." K-H's eyes moisten. "His name was Sousa Mendes. He was signing visas as fast as he could. I took pictures of him. I'd like to make an exhibition of people who saved Jews someday."

"So you've been living in Lisbon all this time?"

"Yes, we thought of going to Brazil, but Marianne had this idea ... Isaac's family was originally Portuguese, so we looked up the name Zarco in the phone book and found five in Lisbon alone. We visited them with a German refugee friend who'd been in Portugal since '33 and who could speak the language. We explained that an Isaac Zarco from Berlin was a good friend of ours. The first three Zarcos didn't want anything to do with us. But the fourth one, Samuel, said he'd help. Marianne started cooking at a small restaurant he owns. I take photographs of tourists at the city's sights. Werner goes to a Portuguese public school."

Before we go to meet Georg and Vera, I ask if K-H shouldn't lock the door to the factory housing his exhibit. "No," he says, "if visitors want to steal the pictures for their own use, so much the better. I have the negatives. I'll make as many copies as people want."

CHAPTER TWENTY·FOUR

Hans adores posing for K-H in his yellow hat. We're seated around a big round table at Karl's Cellar. The peroxide-blond waitress – Bettina – still works there. We kiss cheeks, and she takes Hans back to the kitchen so he can choose what he wants to eat, since he's being fussy. Most of the customers these days are Russian soldiers and their escorts. She tells us that the gay men have gone the way of the Jews, though a few survivors have trickled back in of late.

The train ride to Isaac's boathouse will only bore Hans, so the next morning I leave him with Vera, who has decided to try to bribe Russian soldiers into letting them visit the Neue Museum. She's hopeful she can take the boy to see the sculptures of the Pharaoh Akenhaten, whose face resembles hers and whom she has always regarded as her royal ancestor.

I go to Frau Hagen's house first, and her daughter Maria gives me the sad news that she died a year and a half ago. Maria hands me a folder with three drawings by Otto Dix and four by Georg Grosz. My favorite – Dix's portrait of the poet I war von Lücken – is amongst them. "Isaac told my mother that you should sell them only when the prices go back up," Maria informs me. "You're to auction them in London or Paris, where they'll fetch good prices."

Maria tells me I'm far too thin and insists on feeding me soup made of turnip greens from her vegetable patch. She's charming and gentle. *The Good German's Daughter Showing Me Her Garden.* The sketch I make of her that day, on my way back to the city.

This is my first visit to Isaac's converted boathouse. It has a pier extending into the lake and a large balcony. Birds have stolen all but a few of the fruit from the cherry trees in the garden. It's peaceful and lovely, but my spending an hour there is enough to condemn me to years of useless fantasies about the life we never got the chance to make.

A few days later, a lawyer in Berlin will tell me that my deeds for Isaac's apartment and boathouse are still valid. I may never get to use the flat, however, since it has been occupied for years and it would take a lawsuit to evict the tenants, but the boathouse is firmly mine and I will save it for Hans. Until then, Maria will rent it out to vacationers for its upkeep.

I go back to Greta's apartment a week later. She comes to the door and gushes – kissing my cheek – that she is absolutely delighted to see me. "But I can't invite you in because I have a guest," she adds apologetically.

Is he Russian, American, British, or French? I want to ask, astonished that after all these years I'm still that angry.

We stand in her doorway. She's wearing a black, low-cut gown and impressive pearl earrings – the same ones she had on when I first met her, I'm pretty sure. In her hand is a white silk handkerchief. Fifty million dead in the war and she still wants to look like Jean Harlow.

I've left Hans with Vera. Of late, she's able to entertain him better than I can; he adored the Egyptian wing of the New Museum and has decided he wants to live on a boat in the Nile. Could he be the reincarnation of Raffi?

I don't question Greta about why she hasn't called me. Instead, I ask, "My father ... do you know what's happened to him?"

"Not entirely. We broke up after you left."

"Did that have to do with the photograph I gave you?"

"Oh, that!" She gives a little laugh. "Don't be silly! I knew it was a forgery. I was well aware of your ... your sense of humor by then."

She gives me a knowing smile. What a sensational actress she is, and how foolish I was to believe I was any match for her!

"Still, I was angry at your father for not telling me about his past," she continues. "One thing led to another ... We began to quarrel all the time, about all sorts of boring things." She heaves a sigh. "Your father was frustrated that he wasn't rising through the Ministry as he had hoped. And his disappointment made him disagreeable. So we broke up. I could no longer be his secretary, of course. I stopped working. And then the world collapsed around him ... around all of us. Your father, along with others at the Ministry, ended his life before he could be taken prisoner and reveal any secrets. It was very courageous of him."

"He's dead?"

"Cyanide tablets."

Papa's death is like a trap-door opening beneath my feet. "Do you ... do you know where he's buried?" I stammer, reaching out for the wall to steady myself.

"No, I have no idea."

And then, as I'm trying to assemble my next question out of my thoughts of disbelief, Greta tells me it was lovely to see me and ushers me out into the hallway, locking the door securely behind me.

I get all the way to Savigny Platz before thinking, *Greta has given another stellar performance!* So I dash back to her place and stand down the street. And sure enough, after an hour or so, my father holds the front door for her as they come out. He's a middle-aged gentleman in a beige felt hat and handsome matching jacket. The little I can see of his hair is gray, and he looks lean and healthy. And happy. Thankfully, he and Greta walk the opposite way on Pfalzburger Straße. I feel the tension of the rope that will always be stretched between Papa and me, but I let him go. Not even today, six decades later, can I describe my emotions about him in any precise way. It's as if the man he was simply cannot fit inside my head. A square peg in a round hole, as Ben would one day tell me.

A few days later, a U.S. lieutenant steers Georg and me to a representative of the American Jewish Joint Distribution Committee, a relief organization. The young man's name is Henry Lefkowitz. Having spoken Yiddish throughout his childhood and studied German literature at Brooklyn College, he's fluent in German. "Call me Hank," he tells me, in that cheerful New York way, holding out his big, baseball-player's hand to me. He starts a new page in his little notebook with my name and addresses in Berlin and Istanbul, then takes down all I can tell him about Isaac, Rini and her parents, the Munchenbergs, Mrs Kauffmann, Volker, and Veronika Vogt. Georg tells him about friends of his that are missing, as well. Hank tells us that it may take months, if not years, to track down where they were taken.

Is it worth my staying in Berlin to wait for Isaac? When I ask Hank that, he pats my hand and replies, "You can't really think someone else can answer that for you, Sophie."

Hans and I live with Else until the end of August, then leave for Büyükada. Georg and Vera return with us. Rolf sees us off at the station. Vera and Georg won't talk to him. She refers to him as the Toxic Tree Stump, which she finds amusing. I hug Rolf, however, knowing that Isaac had trusted him. Karl-Heinz will remain for a few more weeks, then head to Lisbon. We have agreed to try to visit him as soon as we put our finances in order. Hans wears his yellow hat and carries an old KaDeWe shopping bag saved by Else. In it are a dozen photographs of himself and our friends. His own K-H Collection.

The day before, alone, I sat by Hansi's grave. I thought of him peeling potatoes and racing after squirrels. I spoke to him of his nephew.

Isaac once told me that the dead can sometimes be more generous than the living. If so, then maybe my brother has already forgiven me for not saving him and Volker.

Over the next six years, I receive letters from Hank Lefkowitz every Passover, saying that he and others from his organization are still working on my cases. Then, in 1951, he writes to say that he discovered Professor and Mrs Munchenberg on a list of Jews transported from the Grünewald Station in Berlin to Lodz, along with 1,250 other Jews, on the 18th of October, 1941. If they survived the miserable conditions of the Lodz ghetto, he suspects they were sent on to Auschwitz. A year later, he writes that Rini and her mother were on the transport to the Theresienstadt concentration camp on the 24th of August, 1942. As for Rini's father, there's no indication. Hank believes he might have been on an earlier transport. "Families were often separated by circumstance or by the Nazis themselves," he writes.

Nothing yet on Isaac, Mrs Kauffmann, Volker and his family, or Veronika.

Then, in April 1953, Hank locates a survivor of Buchenwald who knew Isaac in the camp: Gabe Sonnenberg. Hank's letter includes his phone number in London.

By then, I've spent eight years reading about the camps and the trials against Nazi war criminals, particularly the Soviet proceedings of October 1947 against the commanders of the Sachsenhausen camp. So I know all that I want to know about Buchenwald, especially about the "medical" experiments on prisoners. And I've heard enough about Ilse Koch for two or three lifetimes: wife of the Buchenwald camp commandant, she had prisoners killed for their body parts – skin, thumbs, and bones – which she then had fashioned into household objects such as lamps.

Gabe tells me that he'd been at Buchenwald for only a month when Isaac arrived. They were both newcomers and became fast friends. This was in December 1942. Isaac had come from Theresienstadt, and he was painfully thin and riddled with lice, though his eyes were clear and lucid. "He hadn't lost his mind – no, not at all," Gabe assures me.

He says that the sleeves of Isaac's striped uniform were too short, which irritated him. He could be kind and witty, but like everyone else, he was often exhausted, short-tempered, and disconsolate. He missed his pipe terribly and sometimes traded his morning bread for half a cigarette. Gabe and Isaac shared a bunk and a single blanket with three other prisoners. Isaac faced Jerusalem and prayed every morning before leaving for the quarry where he and Gabe labored all day, and again in the evening after supper. During their moments of rest, they spoke in whispers about their lives, and Isaac told him about me. He said he often sensed me sitting on his cot with him and drawing his face. It made him feel protected. "He tried to guess the name of your child," Gabe tells me. "He figured that if you'd had a boy, you named him Hans, after your brother. If it was a girl, he figured it would be Greta or Marlene. After Garbo and Dietrich, of course. He said you were nuts about those two."

"His name is Hans," I tell Gabe.

"So he got it right!"

"Sometime in early January 1943, Isaac developed typhus," Gabe continues. "One evening, Isaac told me, 'The time has come,' because he didn't think he had the strength to work in the quarry and would be executed. He wanted to stand, so I helped him up, and he etched something in Hebrew on our bunk with a nail he'd hidden. I walked him to the end of the barracks and he etched the same sentence by the door, where we'd have affixed a *mezuzah* if we'd had one. What he wrote was in Hebrew, so I didn't know what it meant. When I asked him, he smiled and said it was his calling card."

"*Beruchim kol deemuyei Eloha,*" I say in my wretched Hebrew.

"How did you know?" Gabe asks, shocked.

"He needed to speak those words before the Seventh Gate of God in order to be admitted."

"I was told by a rabbi that it means 'Blessed are all the images of the Lord.'"

"Yes, or 'Blessed are all of God's self-portraits.'"

"I then helped Isaac shuffle back to our bunk and he prayed sitting up, with his eyes open, which I'd never seen him do," Gabe continues. "They were very reflective, even in the winter darkness. I've never seen anything like them before or since. Maybe because he was so skeletal, they seemed like dark jewels embedded in ... forgive me, now for saying so ... embedded in death. It was a cold night, but he was sweating because he was producing an enormous amount of heat. It was astonishing. I'd never have believed it possible. I was worried about him. Another prisoner and I, Marko ... we stayed up with him an hour or so, but then he broke his trance to tell us that it was all right for us to sleep. He kissed me and Marko and said, 'Everything is going to be all right. I am with

God now and He has agreed to help.' I can't say I thought he was crazy, because I'd already seen far stranger things in the camps. Marko and I were still worried about him, but we soon fell asleep again. We were always exhausted, you understand. When I woke for breakfast, I found Isaac still seated next to me, leaning against the wall, and his eyes open. But the light was gone from them, and he was cold ... so very cold. The nail with which he'd etched his calling card was poking out of his fist. I took it and buried it at the camp, and after we were liberated, the first thing I did was have a soldier dig it up for me. I hadn't the strength." Gabe, overcome by the memory, loses his voice for a time, then goes on. "I have it with me still. It means a lot to me. You know, Sophie, I sometimes think that knowing Isaac saved me. Marko and I still talk about him every time we speak on the phone. The thing is, I didn't realize it then, but he was someone blessed. Not that I even know what that really means. But there was something about him ... a resilience, a grace, as though he had a compass needle inside him to show him where Jerusalem always was, a mechanism, in any case, that most people don't have. And I don't mean he had it because of the camps. He was as broken as any of us – as diseased and desperate. It was something from before the camps, something that not even typhus and lice and starvation could touch."

So it is that I learn that Isaac descended from the Reichstag into a tangled machinery of death that fed on men and women and children – and from there he prayed his way into the center of the last three vessels.

As I thank Gabe in the best voice I can assemble, I think, *Why am I alive when Isaac is dead?* The question that has been at my throat for the rest of my life.

CHAPTER TWENTY-FIVE

One Friday morning during the spring of 1954, Vera takes the boat from Büyükada to Istanbul so she can meet with Abraham to discuss her new designs for men's suits. She arrives back in the afternoon and collapses just after she steps off the ferry.

"She just fell over," Mr Hasan, one of our neighbors, will tell me later. He was coming back with her and was a few paces behind her. Vera always exited the boat like a rocket.

Mr Hasan and Mrs Ahmet, the baker's wife, run to help her. They'd known her for more than a decade by then. All the islanders had.

A buggy driver jumps down from his perch and dashes up the hill to get me. Hans isn't home from school yet, so I'm alone. I find Vera lying with her head in Mr Hasan's lap. Her eyes are dull and glassy.

I already know she's gone, but I kneel next to her and reach for a pulse. Dr Levi comes running out of nowhere. He listens to Vera's chest with a stethoscope. On his orders, five men, including Mr Hasan, carry her to his medical office. But it is too late.

"Her heart simply gave out," Dr Levi tells me.

"Yes, she knew it would, sooner or later."

Vera was fifty-three years old.

We bury her on the island. At the funeral, I drape the troubadour coat she made for me over my shoulders and Hans carries his beloved yellow hat with bells.

Charismatic people like Vera help us define ourselves. *I know who I am because I am Vera's friend* ... Without knowing it, that's what I told myself for twenty-two years, and for a long time afterward, I'm forced to wonder who I am. Isaac and Vera – two continents gone.

My consolation: her last years were good ones. She walked everywhere on Büyükada during the day, without any covering and without any shame. The sun and the sky became welcome companions for the first time in her life. And the islanders, once they got used to her, invited her over for apple tea and baklava. They praised the way she'd learned Turkish so well. They marveled at how much she could eat and how directly she talked.

Hans adored walking beside her, just like me. "Tia Vera is bigger than Ataturk," he used to say.

Even the local children stopped making fun of her after the first year. Once, I witnessed a fight between two boys because one of them, an outsider, had dared to shout that she was a monster. Mario, who grew up down the hill from us, punched the offending visitor right in the face. But just before he did, he shouted, "She's no monster, she's ours!"

Which is why we put on her headstone: *Courageous, Loved, and Ours.*

In 1955, Istanbul has its own *Kristallnacht*. Fomented by nationalist politicians with claims over Cyprus, thugs destroy more than 4,000 Greek shops on the 6th and 7th of September. Nitsa's restaurant goes up in flames. Rather than start over in a city that no longer wants them, she and Georg decide to move to Venice, where Nitsa has relatives and where Georg decides to open a guesthouse. To help with his down-payment, I give him one of the drawings by Otto Dix to sell, and he is able to get a very good price for it from a dealer in Milan.

Georg and Nitsa live out their lives as managers of the Canaletto Hotel. We speak on the phone at least once a month, and I visit them every few years. They always insist I stay in their executive suite, which is lit by the sinuous Venetian chandelier I first saw in Berlin when Georg was posing as Andre Baldwin.

Georg dies in 1964, Nitsa three years later. Their niece, Antonia, inherits their hotel.

I also visit K-H and Marianne in Lisbon, and she hands me back my mother's amethyst brooch. "I couldn't sell it," she tells me. "It was too beautiful."

Touching my finger to its violet radiance is like taking my mother's hand. I hope she was able to forgive me for not understanding her before she died.

K-H and Marianne are buried now in Portugal. Werner has moved back to Germany and lives in Düsseldorf. He teaches sign language at a deaf school.

I never learn anything more about Mrs Kauffmann, Rini and her parents, Volker and VV. I've had young Turkish friends do searches on the Internet, but they can't find a trace. Maybe one or two of them survived and are living quiet lives in Melbourne, San Diego, or Vancouver. Or maybe Rini made it to Hollywood and changed her name. Perhaps I've even seen her as a German-accented extra in a movie. I hope so every day of my life.

Else moved to her kibbutz in 1947. She met her partner, Solène, in the early 1950s and they moved together to Tel Aviv, where Else began teaching again. I went to Israel in 1978 to visit her, and she, Solène, and I traveled around the beautiful desert together in their old Ford. Until she died in 1994, she practiced *tai chi* every morning on the beach. We'd speak on the phone all the time.

Roman retired from the circus in 1969, and he and Francesco

lived in Frascati for the rest of their lives. I met them twice in Istanbul, for the last time in 1970. During that stay, Roman gave a heart-stopping benefit performance in Ortaköy for the Jewish cultural center where David was then serving on the board of directors. Gazing up at that sixty-one-year-old Antinous prancing like an elf across the high wire, his white-gray hair falling to his shoulders, I thought, *God bless Roman for defying gravity and so much else.*

Before the Berlin Wall went up, Tonio opened a language school in Charlottenburg. Else found that out for me. He must be a rickety old man these days. Or maybe he's dead. I'm not tempted to find out.

My father and Greta married just after the war. I don't know any more than that.

In the summer of 1957, I'm dining at a restaurant near Taksim Square with David and Gül, when a man with gray hair like porcupine-bristles and clear blue eyes walks in. He looks lost and is squinting like a mole facing a long, dangerous tunnel, since the restaurant is dimly lit. He puts on his tortoiseshell-rim glasses and takes a deep, calming breath. I do too, because for the first time in seventeen years I feel a dry thud inside my heart that seems to mean I have a second chance. The mole-man studies the menu, then hands it back to the maitre d' and leaves. I tell my dinner companions I have to pee, but instead rush out to the street and call after him. I don't know much more English than "Wait!" but that's enough to get him to turn around. God knows where I find the courage.

He recognizes my accent when I apologize for bothering him, and we talk for a time in a mixture of Yiddish and German. His name is Benjamin Arons. A specialist in ancient Middle Eastern Languages, he is in Turkey to do research at the Royal Hittite

Archive at Boazköy. He accepts my invitation to join us for dinner, thank goodness. It's while David is quizzing him about how he first became interested in Anatolian history that I have the daring to reach for his hand under the table. His is warm, reassuring and strong.

The next day, we meet for coffee and profiteroles at my favorite café on the Istiklal Caddesi. He spends the night with me in Büyükada. It was love at first sight for me. Ben will tell me later, "It took me a few weeks to fall in love with you. I'm a bit slow."

He's playful, kind, and witty. And American, which means that he's sure that the world will clear a place for him if he works hard enough. I like that philosophy, though I think it's an illusion. It's a particular relief that he doesn't ever sulk. He gets on with things. And he goes to the movies with me anytime I want.

Vera would have liked him. Isaac too. Maybe that shouldn't be important, but it is.

The only problem becomes Hans. He is seventeen and an architecture student at Istanbul University. Büyükada is too inconvenient for attending classes, so he has recently moved in with David and Gül, who have returned to Ortaköy. David's parents, Abraham and Graça, both passed away two years earlier, within four months of each other.

After he meets Ben, my son shrieks at me for the first time in our lives. He tells me I've fallen in love with someone "inappropriate." Maybe he is under the mistaken impression that Ben will want to be a surrogate parent, but my son refuses to talk to me about his feelings.

How hard was it growing up with a father who died in a concentration camp and a mother who still wonders all the time why she survived? It will be another seven years before Hans discusses with me how deep what he calls his "sense of precariousness" has been, though I am only too aware that he has always felt as if he had to look over his shoulder, both to get my approval and to make sure that no one was after him.

It's during our Long Winter, as I come to call our silent frigid war, that Hans decides he doesn't want any of Ben's relatives to know about him. To honor his wishes, we tell my new in-laws that he's my nephew.

Ben and I are married in July 1959, in a small ceremony on Büyükada. Unfortunately, we spend months apart at a time, because I'm not yet ready to leave my son. I move definitively to America only in 1962.

The Long Winter finally comes to an end when Hans finishes his degree and marries his college girlfriend. It's 1964 and he's a twenty-four-year-old with Isaac's intelligent and radiant eyes, and his Uncle Hansi's slender build. He works as an assistant to a Swiss architect whose specialty is urban planning. I attend his wedding, of course, but without Ben. Right after his honeymoon in early May, he flies to New York to see me. He says he has wanted to talk with me for a long time and that he regrets having been so distant in recent years. Fine, except that he doesn't explain further. Ben tells me to be patient with him and takes him to a New York Mets baseball game and the Museum of Modern Art. We go to the Bronx Zoo together. Hans discovers he likes both hummingbirds and his step-father. He and I stay up late together on his second-to-last night in New York. He lays his head on my lap, just as he did on a Berlin bus when he was five years old, and he tells me that he wants to know everything I can tell him about his father. I've been waiting his whole lifetime for that request, wondering, in fact, if it would ever come, and we spend the whole night talking. I hold nothing back. We dive into the river of memory that has been wide and deep enough to hold all my conflicted, half-understood emotions. And then Hans invites me into his waters, as well ...

There was so much I didn't know about him, though I'd had inklings: how he didn't like to speak German as a boy because it made him feel as if he couldn't be his own person; how he felt as if my past was too important and his own life could never have nearly as much meaning; how he felt torn in half by the tug-of-war between my Berliner friends and our Turkish relatives. These things are hard for me to hear, but his voice has lost the anger that once made me fear him. "Mama, you don't need to defend yourself or Papa or Tia Vera or anyone else," he tells me at one point. "I just need you to listen."

As we sit together in Ben's study, surrounded by the reassuring landscape of manuscripts translated from ancient languages, I realize that Hans is far more than my son now, or even Isaac's – that he is a man. And that he will make his way in the world regardless of what I do or don't do. It took me too long to understand that. Maybe my lack of faith in him – or, more likely, the fragile, stained-glass world he was born into – was a big part of our problem.

By dawn, I'm exhausted, but in a kind of tingling, ecstatic state – as if all my senses have been tuned to a higher frequency by the sound of my son's voice, which is very much like his father's. And as if my acceptance of his manhood, of his being separate from all my thoughts and memories of him – has tugged me through one of Berekiah Zarco's gates.

Maybe this pleasant and fulfilled weariness is what Isaac felt when he would stay up all night praying and chanting – at least, in the days before the Nazis made his dialogue with God so urgent that he could find no peace.

When, just after dawn, our conversation reaches a place of well-deserved rest, Hans kisses me on the lips for the first time since he was seven or eight. And we head off to our bedrooms.

Our Long Winter is over. And now we are free to set off on the rest of our life, whatever it may bring us.

Late that afternoon, while we're watching a baseball game in Central Park – with Ben trying to explain the *meshugene* rules to him one last time, I realize I've missed the sound of my son's laughter most of all. And the way he creeps up on me and presses his lips to my cheek when I least expect it, hoping I'll gasp and then give him a swat. He can be very silly, which means he is his father's son. How lucky for us all!

My heart has been ransomed, as Vera once said to me.

At the airport, after we hug, he holds up his hand to show me he's put on his father's ring for the first time. "It fits perfectly, Mama," he assures me, smiling through his tears. Having now heard my stories about Isaac's mystical beliefs and powers, he adds, "Though I'm beginning to believe that Papa always knew it would."

How I wish they could have known each other! Every memory of Isaac – and even every dream of him – is, in a small way, a protest against the injustice of their never meeting.

It's Ben who reminds me that many historians consider the Battle of Stalingrad the turning point in the Second World War. Some 750,000 Axis troops and 850,000 Russians were killed during the German siege. It remains the bloodiest battle in recorded history. "And it ended on the 2nd of February, 1943," he tells me pointedly.

He mentions this after I speak to him about the Seven Gates of Europe and Isaac's theories.

"I don't understand the connection," I tell him.

"Isaac died in early January 1943," he tells me. "A month before the Germans lost the Battle of Stalingrad. It was then that the war turned around."

"Oh, I see. Isaac dropping dead on a bunk in Buchenwald won the war for the Allies!"

I'm in a righteous fury because if six million Jewish dead doesn't mean that God is as deaf as the lowest layer of hell, then what does?

He kisses my brow. "I'm not saying there's a connection. I just think it's interesting."

But I can't give up my anger just yet. "A thousand Jews must have died on the 2nd of February itself. Probably hundreds of Communists, Gypsies, and distant children too. Do you think they saved the world by being gassed?"

"Look," Ben says, spreading his hands to ask for patience, "going through the Seventh Gate meant a great deal to Isaac. It gave his life significance. And since I am quite certain from all you've told me that he knew far more than you or I about any of this, I'm willing to give him the benefit of the doubt. Why can't you?"

I don't know what I believe today. I *am* glad that Isaac died thinking he had reached God and stopped the vessels from shattering. If his journey had to come to an end, I'm relieved that it had meaning for him.

And I am certain that he saved me and Hans by making me leave Berlin. And Georg, Vera, Julia, Martin, and a good many other people I probably don't even know about. The Torah teaches us that in saving a single life one saves a universe, and Isaac saved quite a few.

We are the only eyes and hands God has on earth, he used to tell me. I try to live up to that truth every day. It's my inheritance from him.

Sometimes when I can't sleep, I think of Isaac and Hansi sitting beside me at the Errol Flynn pirate movie we saw together, *Captain Blood*. Nothing stupendous happened that day, and it was a silly film, but we were together inside that magical, flickering darkness

– and defying the Nazis at the same time. Now, nearing my end, I realize I had a great many wonderful days with Isaac and Hansi. I try not to be greedy and to want more.

In recent years, I can feel Isaac grasping my hand just before sleep, sometimes even kissing me on the lips when I awaken in the morning. As I am moving away from life, toward either another world or nothing at all, he and I are coming closer together, and I have begun to think that it may very well be possible that the mountain and the sea shall meet again in the moment I pass through the Seventh Gate.

I suppose I have finally learned to put my trust in him as well as our son.

CHAPTER TWENTY·SIX

A final revelation takes nearly thirty years to thread its way through the cramped shadows of my life and make itself known to me in a single burst ...

After Vera and I return to Berlin in the summer of 1945, she tells me it's unfortunate that Hansi was cremated, because it would have been important for me to see his body, so I could be absolutely sure that he was dead. She sits me down on a bench on the KuDamm so we can look at the ruins of the Kaiser-Wilhelm Church, and she explains to me that she never saw her mother's body, because her father didn't allow her to come to the funeral. "After that, I'd see Mama on the street all the time," she tells me. "Or on a bench in the Tiergarten, a bus ... It was terrible. Then, when I'd rush up to her, I'd see it was only a woman who looked like her." In disgust, she adds, "Sometimes not even that. All that misery, all those ghosts, because I never saw my mother dead."

"I didn't have to see Hansi dead," I tell her. "People are different. You needed to, I didn't."

"Still, it would have been better if you had," she says threateningly. "I know about these things. And now that we're home in Berlin, you're bound to mistake some other boy for him."

"It's enough I went to the funeral," I assure her.

She scoffs. "The funeral was nothing. It was just the beginning."

*

During our stay in Berlin, and even back in Istanbul, I never once mistake anyone on the street for Hansi. Instead of being content about it, as Vera thought I'd be, I'm disappointed.

'Hansi, the Angel of Marienburger Straße'

She is right, however, about the funeral being just the beginning. For many years after my brother's death, I'm plunged into nightmares of him running away from me at the zoo, being hit by a car on Marienburger Straße, disappearing into the counterfeit Milky Way of the Zeiss Planetarium ... I suppose my mind creates these images because I am powerless to keep from rushing forward into the future. And I wish to remain with him in the past. Probably because it's only there that I can have a second chance to protect him.

In 1953, I go back to Berlin for a second visit, and I stay with Rolf. By then, I've read extensively about the Brandenburg killing center where Hansi was gassed. I take the train to Brandenburg one afternoon. I find that almost all the residents have worked hard to forget where the Nazi factory of death was, but one gnarled old grandfather leads me there while walking his Alsatian. We amble together down a street shaded by plane trees, and I'm fine until I see a dark smokestack looming ahead of me, tilting, as if about to collapse. I kneel down, because I suddenly can't get enough air into my lungs. And when I realize that some of the soot on that tall, sinister tower of brick was left by Hansi, I sit right on the sidewalk, dizzy and sick. The old man tries to help me up but I push him away. When I feel strong enough, I get to my feet and hurry back to the station.

I spend most of my stay in Berlin visiting places I used to go with my brother. In particular, I feel the gravity of memory taking me back to where the King David School once stood. I suppose it's because so much hope once walked the hallways there.

One bit of good news: the owls, camels, and elephants – even the squirrels – have returned to the Berlin Zoo. Hansi would be relieved.

In the evenings, I sometimes lie back and stare at the ceiling of Rolf's guestroom and wonder how a government could gas a boy who was just starting to learn who he was. And what it means about us as human beings that we can be trained to murder the quietest among our children and knock the gold fillings out of their mouths? He was only sixteen – far too young to pass through the last gate.

Standing in front of our apartment house one warm afternoon, I half expect my brother to come dashing out the front door and run into my arms.

"Believe me, it's for the best that you didn't see him," Vera assures me after I return to Istanbul. "So stop torturing yourself waiting."

"Sometimes I can't remember what he looked like," I reply. When she fixes her eyes skeptically on me, I say, "I can't. Not really. He's disappeared."

"You have photographs and drawings," she tells me.

I let the silence accumulate between us because we both knew that I'm talking about an internal image that has somehow dissipated.

She takes my hands and says, "It's scary coming face to face with a dead person."

"I accept that, but just a glimpse would be nice."

Another two decades pass.

One spring day in 1974, I try to sketch Hansi for the first time in years, but my hands can no longer find the shape and substance of him. He has slipped away from me forever, and even worse, I feel as though I've invented our childhood together, as if all the people who gave my life its form – Isaac and Vera most of all – never existed.

That night, however, I get up to go to the bathroom at three in the morning. I flip on the light. And there he is staring back at me from the mirror above the sink. "Hansi," I say, as if it is the most natural thing in the world to greet him.

Then I grow frightened; I remember that he's dead. Yet there he is: his thin face, his silken hair, his questioning eyes. I can feel our neighborhood in Berlin pulsing around us both, waiting for us to grab our coats and dash outside. I can even smell the hops from the Schultheis Brewery and hear a cello playing softly in the distance. After all my searching, I know now that he has been hiding in the most obvious place all along. And helping the bees do their work inside me.

AUTHOR'S NOTE

The narrator of the preface to *The Seventh Gate* is based on a reader who was kind enough to speak to me at great length about the destiny of a German branch of the Zarco family, whom I first wrote about in *The Last Kabbalist of Lisbon*.

ACKNOWLEDGMENTS

I am extremely grateful to Alexandre Quintanilha and Jupp Korsten for reading the manuscript of this book and giving me their invaluable comments. Thanks, too, to Jacob Staub for his help with Hebrew and Aramaic, and an especially big hug for Jupp for his quick – and ever-cheerful – replies to all my questions about German. I'm also thankful to have had the encouragement of several German friends, especially Martina Hildebrandt, Wilhelm Schlenker, and Caroline Benzel. Special thanks to Richard Davies, Robert Harries and everyone at Parthian Books.

PARTHIAN Also by Richard Zimler

HUNTING MIDNIGHT

SEPHARDIC CYCLE

BOOK 2

978-1-913640-65-1 • £10

Paperback

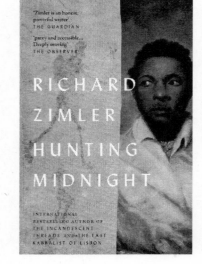

At the dawn of the nineteenth century, John Stewart Zarco lives out an inquisitive, naive childhood in his idyllic Porto community. But societal prejudices against his family's Jewish faith shatter his innocence and even come to threaten his life.

Following the tragic death of his dearest friend, it is only his unlikely bond with Midnight, an African healer and freed slave, that restores a sense of safety. But this fragile, fleeting peace is destroyed when Napoleon's armies invade Portugal and John suffers another devastating loss – one rooted in unspeakable betrayal and authored by those closest to him. The revelation sets John on course for antebellum America, in what might ultimately prove to be a doomed quest for hope amid unspeakable cruelty and sin.

Rich in historical detail and mysticism, *Hunting Midnight* is Richard Zimler's mesmerising tale of deception, guilt, forgiveness and devotion, played out against a backdrop of war, slavery and religious oppression.

'pacey and accessible . . . Deeply moving.' *The Observer*

'Wonderful . . . a big, bold-hearted love story that will sweep you up and take you, uncomplaining, on a journey full of heartbreak and light.' Nicholas Shakespeare

'A gripping adventure story' *The Independent*

PARTHIAN Also by Richard Zimler

GUARDIAN OF THE DAWN
SEPHARDIC CYCLE
BOOK 3
978-1-913640-66-8 • £10
Paperback

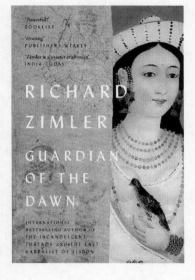

After his Jewish family fled the Catholic
Inquisition in Portugal, Tiago Zarco lives
a tranquil existence in colonial India,
enjoying secret sojourns with his sister into
the heady festivities of the local Hindu
culture while evading the ruling Portuguese
authorities.

But as he comes of age in sixteenth-century
Goa, Ti struggles to keep the far-reaching
influence of the Inquisition from destroying
his family and pulling him apart from the Hindu girl he loves. And when an act of betrayal
sees his father imprisoned, he is forced to hunt down the traitor and make an unimaginable
choice, triggering a harrowing journey that will show him the depths of human depravity
and the poisonous salvation of revenge.

At once passionate, furious and hopeful, *Guardian of the Dawn* is both a saga of horrifying
religious persecution and a riveting, tender multicultural love story.

'Zimler is a master craftsman, and this book is Art . . . a riveting murder
mystery.' *India Today*

'limpid and encompassing' *The Guardian*

'deeply absorbing' *Kirkus Reviews*

PARTHIAN Also by Richard Zimler

THE SEARCH FOR SANA

978-1-913640-68-2 • £10
Paperback

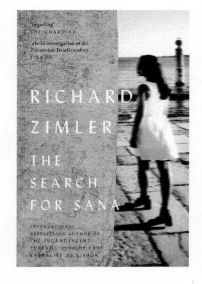

In February 2000, the writer Richard Zimler met a mysterious dancer at an Australian literary festival, only to witness her tragic suicide the next day. This shocking act was to trigger an investigation into her past that would alter the course of his life forever.

His search initially leads him to the tranquillity and tolerance of 1950s Israel, where he learns of the powerful sisterhood forged between two girls – one Palestinian, one Israeli. But as Zimler is drawn deeper into their story, he uncovers illusion, deceit and – most shocking of all – a connection to the most horrifying atrocity of the twenty-first century.

At once a memoir and a thriller, *The Search for Sana* sees the internationally bestselling author of the *Sephardic Cycle* create an unflinching exploration of lifelong friendship, loyalty, cruelty and dispossession.

'A bold investigation of the Palestinian-Israeli conflict . . . [Zimler] writes in calm, clear prose adorned by the occasional glistening image like a jewel in a fast-flowing stream.' *Tikkun*

'beguiling' *The Guardian*

PARTHIAN Also by Richard Zimler

THE INCANDESCENT THREADS
SEPHARDIC CYCLE
BOOK 5
978-1-914595-33-2 • £10
Paperback

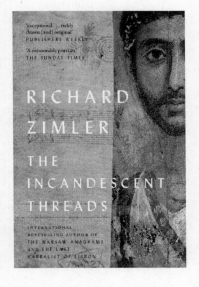

Maybe none of us is ever aware of our true significance.

Benjamin Zarco and his cousin Shelly are the only two members of their family to survive the Holocaust. In the decades since, each man has learned, in his own unique way, to carry the burden of having outlived all the others, while ever wondering why he was spared.

Saved by a kindly piano teacher who hid him as a child, Benni suppresses the past entirely and becomes obsessed with studying kabbalah in search of the 'Incandescent Threads' – nearly invisible fibres that he believes link everything in the universe across space and time. But his mystical beliefs are tested when the birth of his son brings the ghosts of the past to his doorstep.

Meanwhile, Shelly – devastatingly handsome, charming and exuberantly bisexual – comes to believe that pleasures of the flesh are his only escape, and takes every opportunity to indulge his desires. That is, until he begins a relationship with a profoundly traumatised Canadian soldier and artist who helped to liberate Bergen-Belsen – and might just be connected to one of the cousins' departed kin.

Across six non-linear mosaic pieces, we move from a Poland decimated by World War II to modern-day New York and Boston, hearing friends and relatives of Benni and Shelly tell of the deep influence of the beloved cousins on their lives. For within these intimate testimonies may lie the key to why they were saved and the unique bond that unites them.

A *SUNDAY TIMES* BEST HISTORICAL FICTION BOOK OF 2022

'exceptional... richly drawn' *Publishers Weekly* (starred review)

'A thoughtful and affecting novel about generational trauma.' *Kirkus Reviews*

PARTHIAN

A Carnival of Voices

'For almost thirty years, [Parthian] have been one of the most consistently agile imprints in Wales.' – Mike Parker, *Planet Magazine*

'From the selection of its authors and topics covered through to the editing and production of the books, Parthian exudes quality. It puts out a dazzling, stimulating, thought-provoking selection of books on par with (if not better and more interesting than) the bigger publishing houses.' – Jenny White, journalist

'a vital part of our publishing scene in Wales and great ambassador for the best of Welsh writing.' – Rebecca Gould, Head of Arts at British Council Wales

We have always published first-time fiction and aim to give new writers as much development support as we can. Our recent success includes writers such as Richard Owain Roberts (Not the Booker Prize winner 2020), Alys Conran (Wales Book of the Year winner 2017), Tristan Hughes (Edward Stanford Travel Writing Award – Fiction with a Sense of Place winner 2018), Lloyd Markham (Betty Trask Award winner 2018) and Glen James Brown (Orwell and Portico Prize shortlistee 2019).

We have an ongoing engagement with the literary culture of Wales through our Library of Wales series, which has reached fifty titles of classic writing. The Library of Wales as a publishing project, with support from the Welsh Government and the Books Council of Wales, has been a significant investment in the literary and educational culture of Wales, with over 100,000 copies sold. The series includes books such as *Border Country* by Raymond Williams and Dannie Abse's *Ash on a Young Man's Sleeve*. Recent books include *Dat's Love and Other Stories* by Leonora Brito, *In and Out of the Goldfish Bowl* by Rachel Trezise and *Sugar and Slate* by Charlotte Williams. It has changed the perception of Welsh writing in English, with *Poetry 1900–2000*, a title commissioned by Parthian for the series, being adopted onto the Welsh Joint Education GCSE syllabus, while many of the books are now studied at university level in Wales.

The Modern Wales series, a collaboration with The Rhys Davies Trust, engages with the recent history and culture of Wales. The series includes the publication of major works of biography: *Rocking the Boat: Welsh Women who Championed Equality 1840–1990* by Angela V. John and *Labour Country: Political Radicalism and Social Democracy in South Wales 1831 to 1985* by Daryl Leeworthy.

We aim to produce attractive and readable books in our areas of interest: new writing, the heart of Welsh culture, and fiction of the wider world through the Parthian Carnival.

The Parthian Carnival includes a growing list of fiction and poetry in translation from many European languages. It includes novels and poerty translated from Basque, Latvian, Estonian, Greek, Macedonian, Catalan, Czech, Lithuanian, German, Irish, Welsh, Danish, Spanish, French, Slovakian and Turkish. Most recently, we published a series of books with support from Creative Europe, with a programme of publication over three years and collaboration with the literature councils of many European countries.